Work Experience

Christopher G. Nuttall

Twilight Times Books
Kingsport Tennessee

Work Experience

This is a work of fiction. All concepts, characters and events portrayed in this book are used fictitiously and any resemblance to real people or events is purely coincidental.

Paladin Timeless Books, an imprint of
Twilight Times Books
P O Box 3340
Kingsport TN 37664
http://twilighttimesbooks.com/

First Edition, December 2014

Library of Congress Control Number: 2014957678

ISBN: 978-1-60619-304-4

Cover art by Brad Fraunfelter

Printed in the United States of America.

Prologue

THE FIRST THING OLD MOTHER HOLLY KNEW, WHEN SHE SNAPPED AWAKE, WAS THAT SHE was no longer alone.

The second thing she knew was that the intruder had cast a complex spell on her. She couldn't move a muscle, apart from her mouth. Even her eyes refused to open.

But she refused to panic. At fifty years of age, most of them spent living in her shack, Holly had little fear of death. It was just a part of life. Besides, the intruder had to be a powerful magician—he'd walked through her wards and protections without triggering any alarms—but it was unlikely that he meant her any real harm. If he had, he could have cut her throat before she ever woke up.

"Good morning," a cultured voice said. It was male, but otherwise unfamiliar. A spell was probably being used to disguise the speaker. "I apologize for casting a spell on you, but I would prefer to remain unknown."

"I am sure of it," Holly said, dryly. "And why, exactly, have you invaded my home?"

"I came to make you an offer," the voice said. There was a *clink* as something was dumped onto the rickety table. "An offer of power."

Holly snorted. She'd heard such offers before. Hedge Witches lived closer to the untamed wild magic than any of the snooty graduates of Whitehall, Mountaintop or the other magical academies. She'd seen her first demon before she even had her first blood.

And she knew what *demons* wanted. "And all you want in exchange is my soul?"

"Not at all," the voice assured her. "I merely wish you to use what I bring you."

Holly didn't believe him. In her experience, nothing was ever given for nothing. There was always something desired in exchange, no matter how many pretty words might be used to hide it. And power always came with a price.

The voice became seductive. "Have you never wished for more power?"

Holly would have nodded, if she had been able to move. She'd been born to a poor family in a poor village. Only a talent for magic had saved her from being sold or married off as soon as she first passed blood. But she had never been powerful enough to go to one of the academies. Instead, she had learned from the local Hedge Witch and, when the elderly woman had died, Holly had taken her place.

But it was a frustrating job. People relied on her and were terrified of her in equal measure. They begged for her help and whispered about her behind her back. And no matter what she did, she knew she couldn't help all of them. She had dedicated her life to the folk of the mountains, yet it was never enough. And the demons knew how she felt. It was why they kept coming to her, tempting her with dreams of power.

"Yes," she said aloud.

"These are the tools of a magician who garnered power," the voice said. He tapped something that sounded like wood. "A skull of ˌmemories. A book of spells. And a knife of power."

"I can't read," Holly confessed.

There was a chuckle from the darkness. "The New Learning hasn't spread this far yet, has it?"

He cleared his throat, then pressed on before Holly could ask him what he meant. "Don't worry," he assured her. There was an easy confidence in his voice that both puzzled and alarmed her. How long had he been spying on her to have such an accurate idea of her capabilities? "The skull will provide all the guidance you need. All I ask in return is that you help the folk of the mountains."

Holly clenched her teeth, pressing against the spell. It refused to break. "Why... why are you doing this?"

"Because someone has to," the voice said. It was a delightfully uninformative answer. "And because the people need help. You know how powerless they are."

He was right, Holly knew. The mountainfolk scrabbled to make a living from the soil. What little they had was taxed, often heavily, by the lords of the high castles. Their sons were pressed into armies, their daughters often forced into effective prostitution; entire families had been broken up because their masters decided that it was necessary. Hedge witch or no, Holly had never been in a position to stop the aristocrats from bullying the common folk. If she'd tried, she knew the aristocrats would have called for a magician from the academies to deal with her. All she could do was watch.

But if she were offered the power to change it, would she?

She had to admit that she probably *would*. The only reason the aristocrats held power was that they were powerful, not because they had any intrinsic right to rule. If she had more power, she could make them bend to her will. And then she could ensure that the mountainfolk had a chance to live free.

"Good luck," the voice said.

The spell unraveled moments later. Holly's eyes jerked open, but all she saw was the cramped interior of her shack. Her tutor had told her that a hedge witch shouldn't crave luxury; the shack was barren, apart from a pile of blankets, a table, a handful of shelves and a small fireplace. The shelves were crammed with potion ingredients Holly had collected herself. She stumbled to her feet and looked around, sharply. Her vast family of cats seemed to have vanished.

Carefully, she tested the wards. As far as she could tell, they were intact. But the intruder had walked right through them.

She looked down at the table and scowled. As the voice had promised, there was a skull, a book...and a knife. The skull glittered with magic of a kind Holly had never seen before—she resolved to be careful when trying to use it—and the book seemed impenetrable. But it was the knife that caught her attention. It was a long dagger, with odd runes carved into the blade...

...And it was made of stone.

Chapter One

THE ROOM LOOKED PERFECTLY SAFE. EMILY WAS SUSPICIOUS AT ONCE.
She stepped into the room, hand raised in a defensive posture. Magic crackled over her fingertips as she glanced around, looking for unexpected surprises. Blackhall was *crammed* with traps, some magical, some mundane; the merest touch could trigger something that would explode in her face. And, with Emily the only student in the building, the traps could be keyed to her personally.

The room was empty, save for a slender tree that grew out of a pot and climbed up through a hole in the ceiling. Emily eyed it doubtfully, then cast a series of magic-detection spells. The tree was completely out of place, so out of place that she suspected it was part of a trap. And yet it just seemed to be a perfectly normal tree...

Puzzled, she inched over towards the door on the far side of the room and cast another detection spell. The door itself seemed safe, but there was a powerful spell on the doorknob, one keyed to touch. The moment she touched it, she would unleash...what? So far, Blackhall's defenses had included everything from stunning spells to immediate eviction from the building. Emily couldn't count the number of times she'd touched the wrong thing and triggered something.

She glanced behind her and swore under her breath. The door through which she had entered was gone. The only way out was through the sealed door. Absently, she tested the walls—she'd escaped once by blasting through the walls—and discovered that they were held firmly in place by magic. Clearly, Sergeant Miles wasn't about to allow her to use the same trick twice.

There was no time for further reflection. Kneeling down beside the door, she started to work on the spell guarding the doorknob. She expected it to be tricky—the sergeants were brilliant at inventing complex puzzles—but the spell unraveled almost as soon as she touched it with her magic. Emily blinked in surprise; that had really been *too* easy. And then she sensed the second spell coming to life. A second spell had been hidden behind the first, waiting for the first spell to be removed. Emily threw up her hands as a wave of magic surged out at her. But it was too late.

She felt the spell strike her, warping her body. The experience wasn't painful, but it was thoroughly uncomfortable—and interfered with her own magic. She saw hairs sprouting on her bare arms a moment before her head started to swim, her perspective changing rapidly. Her vision faded, then recovered. The room suddenly seemed a *great* deal larger...

Dear God, she thought, as she looked down at herself. *I'm a cat!*

Feline instincts crashed into her mind a moment later. Prank spells provided their victim with protections against losing their minds, but the sergeants had obviously gone for something nastier. Emily found herself leaping across the room before her mind quite caught up with what she was doing. The tree she'd dismissed as unimportant suddenly looked great fun to climb. She looked up, remembering that the tree led out of the room. If Sergeant Miles hadn't come to get her, she might not have failed...yet.

She climbed up the tree, marveling inwardly at how nimble the cat-form was, then slipped into the crack in the roof. Inside, there was a long low passageway, smelling of something that alarmed her feline side. Emily concentrated–it would be far too easy to lose herself inside the cat's mind–and forced her way onwards, hoping and praying that the spell wouldn't wear off while she was in the passageway. If she was lucky, she would end up trapped; if she was unlucky, her human body wouldn't be able to fit into the passageway...

There was a faint hissing sound–her fur stood on end–and then the snake came into view, sliding towards her with deadly intent. She was probably imagining it, she told herself, but the snake seemed to look *malicious.* Beady eyes fixed on her as it advanced. Her cat-form shuddered, then went still. Emily remembered *The Jungle Book* and felt a flash of alarm, realizing just how the snake had caught its dinner. It had hypnotized the animals into walking right into its open mouth. Despite her human mind, she too had almost been hypnotized into waiting patiently to be devoured.

She braced herself–and jumped as soon as the snake lunged at her. There was a dull thud as its head struck the stone floor, followed by an angry hiss. Emily felt the feline side of her mind panic as she ran forward, past the writhing tail and out through another crack. The snake's hisses seemed to grow louder, but it didn't follow her out into the room. Emily wondered, absently, if the snake was actually part of the tests, before deciding that it probably was. The wards would have kept it out if the sergeants hadn't wanted it there.

The cat instincts seemed to grow stronger as she looked around the room, threatening to overwhelm her human mind. Emily mentally gritted her teeth as she struggled to cast the counter-spell; her mind was starting to merge into the cat's, which meant that she no longer thought that being a cat was odd. Panic howled at the back of her mind as she fought the spell, but it refused to break. Was she doomed to spend the rest of her life as a cat?

"That's a nasty spell," a masculine voice said.

Emily jumped, then skittered towards the far side of the room. She'd been so caught up in the mental struggle that she hadn't realized that she was no longer alone.

"Let me help," the voice added.

There was a snapping sound, as if someone had snapped his fingers. Emily closed her eyes hastily as her body *twisted,* then slowly returned to human form. When she opened them, she found herself kneeling on all-fours. And, standing in the center of the room, was the sorcerer Void.

He looked older than he had the last time Emily had met him, something that bothered her. For a man who claimed to be over a hundred years old, he had a streak of vanity in his character that kept him using rejuvenation spells to appear young. Now, his brown hair was shading to grey and his skin was lined and pitted with wrinkles. He wore a simple black robe, loose enough to cover everything. Emily had the odd impression that he was actually weaker than he looked.

She straightened up, embarrassed. "Void," she said, feeling an odd mixture of emotions. He was her Guardian—and the closest thing she had to a father. And yet he hadn't visited Whitehall since the Mimic had been destroyed. The other students had been visited by their parents, who had descended on Whitehall *en masse*, but Emily had been left alone. Part of her resented it. "It's good to see you again."

"And you," Void said. "I was...gratified to receive your exam results."

Emily found herself blushing. Back on Earth, no one would have given a damn about her grades. Knowing that Void cared pleased and worried her in equal measure. It was strange to have someone looking out for her welfare, yet it made her feel unsteady. The person who *should* have looked out for her welfare had climbed into a bottle and never come out.

"Thank you," she said. She knew she'd done well. Thanks to Mistress Sun and Lady Barb, her charms were head and shoulders above her classmates. The only class she'd actually failed was Martial Magic, where she simply hadn't been able to keep up with the more experienced students. She would have to repeat most of the class in Third Year. "Were you pleased?"

"Of course," Void said. "I'm very proud of you."

Emily's blush deepened. "Do you...do you want to go back to Whitehall?"

"I'd prefer not to speak with the Grandmaster," Void said. He looked around the room, contemplatively. "Besides, this place brings back old memories. I ran through the maze myself too, once upon a time."

When dinosaurs ruled the Earth, Emily thought, snidely. She didn't say it out loud.

"Besides, I came to talk to you personally," Void added. "There have been interesting developments. A necromancer is dead."

Emily blinked. Necromancers were immensely powerful magicians, feeding on the life and magic of their victims to power their spells. Channeling such power through their minds always drove them insane, eventually. Shadye, who had brought Emily into her new world and then been killed by her, had been utterly barking mad when he'd died. Emily still had nightmares about facing him. She suspected she wasn't the only one.

She forced her mind to work properly. "Poison?"

"Apparently the necromancer's throat was slit," Void said. "Necromancer Harrow lived on the far side of the Desert of Death, ruling the remnants of a small kingdom. I...kept an eye on him, worrying about the day he would decide to cross the desert and attack the Allied Lands. And then his wards shivered and collapsed. When I investigated, I discovered he was dead."

Emily considered it. Necromancers did not die easily—and, from what she'd heard, their deaths brought on massive explosions as their stolen magic erupted from their bodies. The only exception to that rule had been Shadye, whom Emily had trapped in a pocket dimension which had then been snapped out of existence. Harrow's body should have been utterly destroyed, along with a large part of his enslaved kingdom.

"That's not bad news," she said, slowly. "Is it?"

"We do not know how the necromancer was killed," Void pointed out. "Fingers were pointed in your direction." He quirked an eyebrow at Emily. "Was it your work?"

Emily shook her head, hastily. Her method for killing necromancers required a nexus and enough time to set up the trap. She certainly hadn't left Whitehall to go hunting.

"The Desert of Death," she said, slowly. She'd taken an interest in the geography of the Allied Lands, but map-reading had never been her forte. "Isn't that near where I'm going?"

"Yes," Void said, tonelessly. "You should be very careful. We do not know what happened to Harrow, which leaves us with a worrying mystery. Whoever killed him may have powers about which we know nothing."

Emily nodded in understanding. The Allied Lands didn't know what she'd done to kill Shadye, thanks to the Sorcerer's Rule. It had given her a reputation that made her feared and admired in equal measure. No one had ever taken on a necromancer in single combat and lived to tell the tale—apart from Emily. Some claimed she was naturally powerful, others that she'd cheated in some way...and still others that she must be a necromancer herself. Rumors and innuendos would follow her for the rest of her life, she supposed. If someone else had beaten a necromancer, one on one...

"You think we might encounter the killer?"

"It's a possibility," Void said.

"Maybe it was another necromancer," Emily pointed out. "They're not exactly *friendly*..."

"We don't know," Void admitted. "Few necromancers would willingly lower their guard when another necromancer was close by. But it is a possibility."

He cleared his throat. "I want you to be very careful when you're on your roving patrol," he added. "Keep a sharp eye out for trouble. Hell, keep a sharp eye out for trouble *anyway*. I hear that the mountain lords have been plotting trouble for each other ever since the Empire fell. You might wind up in the midst of another coup."

Emily shook her head. "I very much hope not," she said, primly. The last attempted coup had been nightmarish, with one of her best friends a prisoner and the other very much at risk. "Lady Barb intends for us to stay out of danger."

Void smirked. "Danger will find you," he assured her. "It always does."

Emily nodded, reluctantly.

"I meant to ask," she said. She'd actually written several letters, none of which had been returned. That had hurt, but if Void had been spying on a necromancer, he wouldn't have had time to reply. "What are you planning to do about Lin and Mountaintop?"

"The Grandmaster has requested that he be allowed to handle it," Void said. His face twisted into a thin smile. "I have agreed to respect his wishes."

Emily lifted her eyebrows. If there was one thing she had learned about Void, who had saved her life and sent her to Whitehall, it was that he had a habit of riding roughshod over everyone else if he felt it was the right thing to do. Lady Barb disliked him, with reason; the Grandmaster seemed to be wary of him. And non-magicians found the thought of Emily being his bastard daughter worrying. Void had *quite* a reputation.

"And I understand that you have been corresponding with young Jade again," Void said, hastily changing the subject. "Have you made up your mind about him?"

Emily blushed bright red. Jade had proposed to her at the end of her first year at Whitehall–and, by his lights, he'd done her a favor. But Emily had been reluctant to commit herself, not after watching how badly her mother had screwed up her life by marrying the wrong man. And then Emily had been ennobled and Jade's letters had dried up for months. Now they were talking again, but there was a barrier between them that hadn't been there before. It wasn't considered socially acceptable for a commoner, even a combat sorcerer in training, to court a baroness.

"We're going to meet soon," she said. Jade's letters had talked endlessly about the Great Faire, which was apparently going to be held near Lady Barb's home. "I think we'll talk about it."

"Good luck," Void said. He smirked. "Would you care to know how many requests for your hand I have received?"

"*No*," Emily said, quickly.

Void laughed. "I'll see you again soon," he said. He gave her a small wave. "Goodbye."

There was a surge of magic and a flash of light. When it faded, he was gone. Emily felt a flicker of envy–she planned to learn to teleport as soon as possible–and then scowled as the door opened. Ahead of her, she saw a passageway leading out of the building. Sergeant Miles clearly felt that having Void's help to return to human form was cheating. Gritting her teeth–if the sergeant decided she'd done it deliberately, she wouldn't be sitting comfortably for a few days–Emily walked through the doors and out into the grounds. Bright sunlight struck her and she lifted a hand to cover her eyes.

"Careful," Sergeant Miles said. "You never know what you might miss."

Emily turned to face him. He was a short, friendly-looking man, the sort of man anyone could trust on sight. And he *was* trustworthy, Emily knew. He took very good care of his students, including Emily, giving them good advice and encouragement when they needed it. But woe betide the person who tried to take advantage of his good nature.

"That was Void," he said, shortly. "I thought it was him."

"Yes," Emily said. "I didn't call him..."

"I didn't say you did," Sergeant Miles pointed out, dryly. "Is it just me or are you being too defensive these days?"

Emily shrugged. Term had ended a week ago; Alassa and Imaiqah had gone home to Zangaria, leaving Emily to wait for Lady Barb. She'd been...*encouraged* to spend her days practicing with Sergeant Miles, who didn't seem to have anywhere else to go. But the tests had gotten harder and harder, constantly pushing her to the limit.

"Lady Barb wishes you to meet her in the library," the sergeant added. "Good luck on your patrol."

"Thank you," Emily said. "And thank you for keeping me busy."

It was hard work, she knew, but she didn't want to *think* about the tiredness in her mind, or the growing exhaustion with life. Shadye, the Iron Duchess, the Mimic—and exams, of course—had all taken their toll. There had been too many days, as the term came to an end, when she'd seriously considered just trying to stay in bed. If it hadn't been for her friends, she had a feeling she might well have plunged into complete depression.

As it was, she had failed one subject in the exams—and come far too close to working herself to death

"You're welcome," Sergeant Miles said.

Emily dropped him a curtsey, then turned and walked through the forest, back towards Whitehall. For once, there wasn't even a cloud in the sky. It was pleasantly warm; she smiled as she caught sight of butterflies flitting about in the air, and bees moving in peaceful purpose from flower to flower. Just breathing the peaceful air made her feel better, for a long moment, despite the tiredness in her limbs.

When Whitehall came into view, she stopped and stared at the castle before resuming her walk. The white walls of the massive building, topped with towers reaching up towards the sky, still had the power to take her breath away. It was a wondrous sight, even after two years. There was nothing like it on Earth.

Inside, she blinked in surprise as she saw two boys cleaning the Grand Hall, an eagle familiar hovering over their heads. Both of them had been held back after a prank had gone wrong—Emily didn't know the full details, although the rumors had ranged from possible to the completely absurd—and had been set to cleaning the castle. Given Whitehall's multidimensional nature, Emily rather doubted they would be finished before the holidays were over and schooling resumed. There were literally *miles* of corridor in the building.

She walked past them and headed up the stairs to the library. Whitehall felt strange to her without most of its students, although at least there wouldn't be a crowd in the library. Lady Aylia was sitting behind her desk, carefully marking and tagging the new books from various printers. Emily couldn't help a flicker of pride at seeing books produced by her printing presses. Given a few years, they were likely to revolutionize education in the Allied Lands.

"She said to take a seat and wait," Lady Aylia said. She barely looked up from her work. "I believe the Grandmaster wished to speak with her."

Emily nodded, unsurprised. They had planned to leave two days ago, but something had popped up and Emily had been told to stay at Whitehall. The Allied Lands didn't believe in precise schedules, something that amused and irked her in equal measure. Sitting down at one of the desks, she pulled her notebook out of her pocket and started to write down ideas and thoughts she'd devised in her spare time. There were spells she wanted to develop, spells that might help the Allied Lands when the necromancers finally came over the mountains...

She'd faced Shadye and won—by cheating. The next necromancer she faced might be far harder to defeat.

And she knew precisely what they would do to the world she had come to love.

Chapter Two

"**A** HEM," A QUIET VOICE SAID.

Emily jumped. She'd been so wrapped up in her work that she hadn't heard Lady Barb come into the library and walk up behind her. She glanced at her watch and discovered that she'd been sitting at the table for over an hour, scribbling down possible ways to make the spell she'd invented work properly. But, no matter how she worked the variables, there didn't seem to be any way to use the spell safely.

She turned and looked up at Lady Barb. The older woman smiled, although there was something in her expression that suggested she was deeply worried. As always, Lady Barb looked *formidable*. Her long blonde hair cascaded down over stout shoulders and a muscular body. She might not have the porcelain-doll features Alassa enjoyed, but she had attracted the attention of dozens of male students. Emily rather suspected that the students were the ones who didn't take her class. Lady Barb was a hard taskmaster.

"You have to be more careful," Lady Barb warned, dryly. "You never know who might be sneaking up on you."

Emily smiled. "In the library?"

"Most of the spells used to keep students quiet have been deactivated for the summer," Lady Barb pointed out. "If there were more students here..."

Emily shrugged, her mind filling in the blanks. Students were allowed—even encouraged—to prank one another, in the belief that it taught them how to react to unexpected situations and learn how to defend themselves. But, right now, there were only a handful of students left in Whitehall. Even the Gorgon, who was one of the most studious students in Second Year, had gone home. Emily was the only student of her age to remain in Whitehall.

Lady Barb nodded towards Emily's notebook. "Are you keeping up with your security spells?"

Emily gritted her teeth, then nodded. After Lin had stolen her notes and vanished from Whitehall, Lady Barb had given her a crash course in security spells that were normally untaught until the student took on an apprenticeship. Making them work was difficult, but no one apart from Emily herself should be able to read her notes. Lady Barb had warned her that she *would* be testing the notebook on a regular basis and Emily would regret it if she managed to crack the protections hiding her work. Part of Emily resented it, but she understood just how dangerous it would be if her notes fell into the wrong hands.

More of my notes, she told herself, as she closed the notebook and felt the spells slide into place. They were based on her blood, rather than anything else; Lady Barb had told her that her unique blood—she had no relatives in the new world—would be the strongest protection she could hope to provide. She didn't have to worry about a brother or sister accidentally cracking her protections. But there was no such thing as a completely unbreakable spell...

She passed the notebook to Lady Barb and settled back to watch, hoping and praying that the spells remained unbreakable. Some of the spells she'd designed were harmless—or at least not particularly innovative—but some of them were revolutionary. She'd used memory charms to write down as much of the Mimic's spell-structure as she could, knowing that whoever had created the mobile spells was a genius as well as a monster...and she dreaded to think what use an evil magician would make of them. The Mimic had been based on necromancy...somehow, the creator had managed to make necromancy *practical*. There was just too much room for abuse.

But it wasn't the worst of the spells.

She caught her breath as Lady Barb broke the first ward. Shadye had died through luck, she had to admit, and there were other necromancers out there. One day, Emily knew, they would come over the mountains and attack the Allied Lands in force... and, on that day, they might prove unstoppable. She'd devised the nuclear spell to repel that offensive, but it refused to work properly. If triggered, it would detonate within seconds...taking out the caster as well as its target. And splitting atoms didn't seem to require a very powerful magician. There were times when Emily suspected that this world's industrial revolution would lead to complete and total disaster.

Good thing it wasn't a computer wizard who came here, she thought. *He'd be a God-Mode Sue by now.*

Lady Barb muttered an oath as her hands jerked back, shocked. "Not bad," she said, drawing Emily's mind out of her thoughts. "And the first ward was well-placed to distract attention."

Emily smiled, feeling a flicker of pride. Lady Barb rarely gave praise, but when it was given it was always deserved. The heavy security wards she'd wrapped around the notebook would almost certainly attract attention, so she'd crafted the first ward to resemble a normal privacy ward and the second one to conceal the others. Anyone who had seen the wards without that cover would have *known* that there was something inside worth concealing. No one, with the possible exception of Alassa, would conceal their personal journal with so much determination.

She took the notebook back and dropped it into her bag. "Are we ready to go?"

"More or less," Lady Barb agreed. She gave Emily a reproving look. "Do you have your bag packed?"

"It's in my room," Emily confirmed. "Most of my stuff is going to be stored at Whitehall."

"It should be safe enough," Lady Barb agreed.

Emily had her doubts. Whitehall was supposed to be invulnerable, but Shadye had broken into the school in her first year and the Mimic had killed dozens of students in her second year. There were times when she wondered if the Grandmaster blamed her for the series of disasters, even though he'd shown no sign of it. Her arrival at the school had triggered off the series of events that led to Shadye's invasion.

She stood up. "Where should I meet you?"

"In the Entrance Hall," Lady Barb said. "I hope you have packed everything I told you to pack...?"

Emily nodded. Lady Barb had told her that she would have to carry everything herself, without benefit of magic. She was stronger than she'd ever been on Earth, but she knew there were still limits to how much she could carry. During Martial Magic, it had taken her months to build up the muscles the boys had taken for granted.

"Go on then," Lady Barb ordered with a smile. "But there's no real hurry."

Emily waved goodbye to Lady Aylia, then walked out of the library and down towards the dorms. The school was quiet, too quiet. She found herself looking around warily as she passed a line of statues–famous magicians through the ages–and stopped in front of a painting one of the older students had produced. Every time she looked at it, she couldn't help feeling embarrassed. It purported to show her battle with Shadye, but she knew all-too-well that the battle had been very different. She'd certainly not been a match for the maddened necromancer in raw power.

She'd protested to Lady Barb when the painting had first been hung on the walls, but the older woman had pointed out that the painting helped reassure the younger students and their parents that Whitehall was safe. Emily hadn't been convinced– magic could be very dangerous, even without a necromancer or a dangerous monster running loose in the school–yet further argument seemed futile. She looked up at her figure in the painting and shook her head, running her hands through her long brown hair. Painting-Emily stood tall, practically glowing with light, her long hair spinning around her as she cast a spell. She'd never been so beautiful in her entire life. Hardly anyone could recognize her from the painting.

Snorting, she pressed her hand against the stone and watched as the door slid open, revealing a darkened corridor leading towards Madame Razz's office. The stout housemother was nowhere to be seen, thankfully. Most of the First Years had gone home, but the handful who hadn't were driving the housemother slowly insane. Emily smiled as she walked down the corridor and stepped through the door leading to her room. She rather liked Madam Razz, but the older woman could be quite strict.

Inside, Emily couldn't help wincing at how bare the room seemed. Emily and the Gorgon had shared it for the rest of the year, after Lin had made her escape, but the Gorgon was gone and there would be another room next year. The Gorgon's bed had been stripped down to the mattress, leaving her side of the room looking mournful. Emily felt an odd lump in her throat as she walked over to the mirror and looked at her reflection. Once, she'd had problems growing used to the idea of sharing her room with anyone. Now...she found she missed the Gorgon. And the rest of her friends.

The Emily she saw in the mirror was no longer the girl she expected to see. Her once-underfed face was filled out and healthy, the outdoor exercise giving her pale face at least a little healthy color. Her brown hair was thicker and with a little shine, an effect of better food. She had muscles she had never dreamed possible, even if she was still worryingly thin, and other developments she hadn't expected either. It was chilling to realize she would never have developed into a grown woman on Earth.

Shaking her head, she glanced into her bag. There was one set of dress robes, carefully tailored for her at Dragon's Den, one standard student set of robes and four walking outfits. She'd also been warned not to bring more than a handful of books, something that bothered her more than the prospect of wearing dress robes. Her collection of books was small, but growing rapidly. Being separated from them bothered her, even though she knew it wasn't logical.

Emily picked up the white envelope from the cabinet and opened it, pulling out the single sheet of creamy white parchment inside. She'd never really cared about her grades on Earth, not when they were meaningless to her. No matter how well she did at school, it wouldn't help her get out of poverty. But in Whitehall, grades were important. The exams she'd taken a month ago would help to shape her future, at least the part of it she would spend at Whitehall. She skimmed through the parchment, noting—again—that she'd done very well. Martial Magic was the only course she'd failed outright, and then only because the other students had had four extra years of schooling.

I would have had to retake parts of it anyway, Emily consoled herself. *Sergeant Miles wouldn't let me waste time.*

Shaking her head, Emily undressed, removing the uniform she'd worn in Blackhall, and jumped into the shower for a quick wash, then dried herself with a spell and pulled on the first walking outfit. Lady Barb hadn't told her what she should wear for the trip, but Emily was already dreading the passage through the portal. If nothing else, she could clean one of the walking outfits easily. The garments were already charmed to keep dust and mud from sticking permanently.

Once she was dressed, she took one last look at her trunk, feeling oddly upset at the thought of leaving it behind. The first trunk was long gone, but it had been the first thing she'd bought with money she'd earned at Whitehall, while the second was actually an improvement. Yodel had done very good work, she had to admit, even if he'd helped Emily get into real trouble. But it hadn't really been his fault...she picked up the trunk, marveling at the charm that made it almost weightless for its rightful owner, and carried it out of her room. Down the corridor, she could hear Madame Razz telling off one of the first years. Emily rolled her eyes as she walked into the storeroom and carefully placed the trunk in a sealed compartment. It should be safe for three months.

"Your parents paid for you to stay for extra tuition," Madame Razz's voice proclaimed, as Emily stepped back into the corridor. "I don't *think* they meant for you to try to rig the beds with itching spells. Or were they just trying to get rid of you for a few more weeks?"

Emily winced as the two came into view, Madame Razz dragging the unruly First Year by her ear. Parents of magical children who weren't magical themselves were often unsure of the way to treat their gifted children. Emily had heard horror stories about children—teenagers, really—using their magic to lord it over their parents, relatives and childhood friends. Imaiqah had been lucky, she knew. Other parents tended to allow their children to fade away into the magical community.

She wondered absently if the First Year knew how lucky she was to have decent parents. Emily's father had left his family when his daughter had been very young, her mother had been steadily drinking herself to death and her stepfather...Emily shuddered as the memory rose up to torment her, before she forced it back into the darkness of her mind. She was no longer on Earth and she would never see him again. Stepping back into her room, she glanced around to make sure that she hadn't left anything behind. The dirty uniform would be picked up by the servants and washed; there was nothing else in the room that belonged to her. It looked almost as if she'd never lived there at all.

Emily picked up her bag, slung it over her shoulder and walked out of the room, refusing to look back. There was no sign of Madame Razz now. Emily hesitated, wondering if she should find her to say goodbye, then decided against it and walked out of the compartment and down towards the Entrance Hall. The two pranksters were still cleaning the Great Hall thoroughly, supervised by a grim-faced Master Tor. Emily scowled at his back—Master Tor had made his intention of leaving Whitehall quite clear, but he had yet to actually *leave*—and walked around the Great Hall. She didn't really want to talk to a teacher who'd disliked her long before he'd actually *met* her.

Lady Barb was waiting in the Entrance Hall, a small bag slung around her shoulder. Emily caught the look in her eye and wordlessly handed over her own bag for the older woman to search. It was irritating not to be trusted to pack her own bag, but Lady Barb had made it clear that it would be hard to replace anything she'd missed once they were on their way.

"Good," Lady Barb said, finally. "But you probably shouldn't carry so many books. You *will* be busy."

Emily nodded, but made no move to remove the books.

Lady Barb smiled and passed the bag back to her. "Just remember you have to carry them," she warned, as Emily took the bag. She'd said the same thing time and time again. "I won't be carrying them for you."

"I know," Emily said quietly.

She looked up as the Grandmaster stepped into the hall. He looked older, somehow, the lines on his face clearer than ever. His eyes, hidden behind a cloth, seemed to twitch in Emily's direction. Lady Barb dropped him a long sweeping bow, which Emily followed a moment later. The Grandmaster bowed in return, then smiled tiredly.

"You should take great care," the Grandmaster said. He looked directly at Emily. "I do not believe that your guardian came on a whim."

Emily blinked—she hadn't told anyone what Void had said—and then recalled that Blackhall was as closely monitored as Whitehall. The Grandmaster had probably known Void was there the moment he'd passed through the outer protective wards.

"We'll talk about it soon enough," Lady Barb promised. There was a hint of irritation in her voice. "And I thank you for your patience with me."

"You're welcome," the Grandmaster said. Emily glanced from one to the other in bemusement. What were they talking about? "And I wish you a safe and educational trip, Lady Emily."

"Thank you, sir," Emily said.

"And I will expect regular reports," the Grandmaster added. "In triplicate."

Lady Barb snorted. "Only if you write them yourself," she said. "I don't think either of us will have the time."

Emily nodded, quickly.

Lady Barb caught her arm and pulled her towards the door. Outside, the sun was high in the sky, casting rays of light towards the ground. Emily looked behind her as they walked down towards the edge of the wards surrounding the castle, catching sight of the two pranksters as they were marched into the Entrance Hall. Neither of them looked even remotely happy.

The woebegone look on their faces piqued her curiosity. "What," she asked, "did they do?"

"They came up with an ingenious scheme for sneaking into the girls changing room," Lady Barb told her. Unlike most of the other teachers, she never withheld anything from her charges. "It really was quite clever...but they were caught. The Grandmaster assigned them to clean the school in hopes of deterring others from trying the same trick."

Emily shuddered. She had enough problems undressing in front of her fellow girls, let alone boys. The thought of someone spying on her as she undressed...she shuddered again, remembering just how many spells there were protecting the changing rooms. If one of the boys had managed to bypass them...

She opened her mouth to ask how they did it, but Lady Barb caught hold of her arm before Emily could say a word. "Close your eyes," Lady Barb instructed. "And don't open them until I say so."

Emily blinked in surprise. "We're not going to the portal?"

"No," Lady Barb said. She wrapped her arms around Emily in a gentle, but firm hug. "Close your eyes."

Emily obeyed.

A moment later, she felt a surge of magic surround her.

Chapter Three

EMILY FORCED HER EYES TO STAY CLOSED AS THE WORLD SHUDDERED AROUND HER, THEN the magic faded to nothingness. There was a long moment of complete disorientation—Emily realized, suddenly, that they were teleporting—and then Lady Barb slowly let her go.

"Open your eyes," she ordered.

Emily did so and immediately looked around. It was twilight, the last traces of sunlight falling behind the mountains in the distance. High overhead, the stars were coming out, twinkling madly in the darkness. They had to have teleported over half the continent, she deduced, because it had been early afternoon at Whitehall. Her head spun, but she managed to keep her footing.

At least, she thought wryly, *teleporting isn't anything like as bad as stepping through a portal without proper precautions.*

"This is my family's land," Lady Barb informed her. "And that's my home, over there."

Emily followed her gaze. A wall, almost two meters high, was broken by a pair of wrought-iron gates, allowing her to see the garden and the manor house beyond. It looked like an Edwardian building, Emily decided, with at least three floors. She followed Lady Barb towards the house, feeling the outer edges of the wards as they brushed lightly against her magic. The building looked indefensible, but as long as Lady Barb had magic it wouldn't be a problem. It was simple to construct wards to keep non-magical thieves out.

The gates creaked open as they approached, allowing them to walk up the path towards the house. Emily couldn't help admiring the garden, even though it looked like someone had scattered seeds at random just to see what would happen. The bushes and trees looked natural, while—in the undergrowth—small animals scuttled for cover. Lady Barb stopped in front of the heavy wooden front door, then pressed her hand against a stone set in the wood. There was a flare of magic before the wards protecting the door unlocked, piece by piece. Emily stepped backwards as the magic flared again, looking up at the house. Up close, it had a vaguely sinister appearance that bothered her.

The door opened, allowing Lady Barb to step inside. "Come," she ordered, as Emily hesitated. "I bid you welcome to my home."

Emily had to think to remember her etiquette. "I thank you for welcoming me," she said, after a moment. "I pledge to hold my hand in your house."

Lady Barb clicked her fingers. The corridor flared with light, bright enough to make Emily cover her eyes before it dimmed to a more manageable level. She looked around, fascinated, but only saw bare wooden walls...no, the walls were carved into elaborate patterns and runes. There were no paintings or other decorations, but there wouldn't be. The runes were almost certainly part of the house's defenses against intruders.

"You need to practice your etiquette," Lady Barb warned. "The last place you want to accidentally insult another magician is his own house."

Emily swallowed. She hadn't yet started to study wards, but she did know that a magician who owned a house and crafted the wards himself was almost impossible to defeat on his home territory. Etiquette was important for magicians, if only to prevent accidental insults, but she had to study aristocratic etiquette as well as magical etiquette. Something that would insult Alassa's father would be ignored by a magician. But this was the first time she'd set foot in a magician's house, at least since entering Whitehall.

She looked up at Lady Barb. "What did I do wrong?"

"Nothing," Lady Barb said. "But you have to pledge to respect your host quicker, in future."

Lady Barb led her into a large kitchen. Emily couldn't help admiring the structure, although she had no idea how the two of them could cook anything by themselves. It looked as though at least four cooks were required, but they were alone. The house felt empty. Lady Barb grinned, then motioned for Emily to put her bag down on the table.

"Take a seat," she ordered, as she used a spell to light the fire. "I'll make some chocolate for us both."

Emily nodded. Hot chocolate—or something that passed for it—would help her to sleep, particularly if she combined it with a small dose of a sleeping potion. Jet lag wasn't a problem in the new world, but teleport lag might well be…her body insisted that it was early afternoon, even though it was dark and cold outside. She sat down on a wooden stool and watched as the older woman moved around her kitchen with easy competence. It was barely five minutes before they both had a steaming cup of chocolate in front of them.

"There are some matters we need to discuss," Lady Barb said, once she had taken a sip of her drink. "For a start, you do realize that you are both famous and notorious?"

"I might just have noticed," Emily said, sardonically. "It's hard to avoid being aware of it."

They shared a smile. Most of the ballads about the Necromancer's Bane bore little resemblance to reality, but that didn't stop the bards from singing and spreading her fame everywhere. Some were so outrageous that Emily had actually considered trying to sue for libel, only to discover that she would have to invent the legal framework first before doing so.

It wasn't something she found comfortable—and not just because people were judging her by the ballads, rather than anything she'd actually done. Fame had never really been one of her ambitions, particularly not when it brought worse enemies than depraved stalkers. The innovations she'd introduced to the new world, starting in Zangaria, were slowly turning it upside down. Her long list of enemies might have started with the necromancers, but it didn't end there.

Lady Barb reached into her bag and produced a small pendant. "This is a glamorstone," she said, dropping it on the table. "It will disguise you from anyone who doesn't actually know you personally. The fact you're wearing it will be obvious, but no one will be so gauche as to try to take it from you. And you won't have to expend any energy to maintain the glamor."

Emily nodded. Almost all of the girls at Whitehall—and quite a few of the boys—used glamors to hide tiny imperfections in their bodies. The only girl she knew who didn't use glamors was Alassa—and she had been engineered to be stunningly beautiful. Even Emily herself had been tempted, although in the end she had chosen to stick with her natural appearance. If nothing else, she didn't have to expend energy maintaining it.

"Emily is also not a common name," Lady Barb added, as Emily picked up the stone and examined it carefully. She'd been warned, more than once, to be careful with anything someone else provided for her, no matter who it was. Sergeant Miles had demonstrated several of the simplest traps for his students, leaving them all more than a little paranoid about their fellows. "I'm going to call you Millie when we're in public. Make sure you cast a privacy ward if you want to talk to someone who knows your identity."

"I understand," Emily said. It seemed embarrassing to have to hide her identity, but she knew Lady Barb was right. "Will I have to talk to others?"

"I thought you wanted to talk to your young friend," Lady Barb said. "But he would recognize you at once, naturally. A glamor won't fool someone who actually *knows* you."

Emily felt her cheeks heat up. It would be the first time she'd seen Jade in over a year, a year of somewhat strained correspondence...she pushed the thought aside, firmly. She couldn't hide behind email—or letters—at Whitehall, not indefinitely. Hell, she couldn't use email at all. She had only a faint idea of how to start generating electricity.

If it works in this universe, she told herself. She was fairly sure it would—there were electrical currents in human brains, after all—but she didn't know for sure.

"We are going to be here for three days," Lady Barb said. "Your mornings will be spent brewing specific potions, which you should have no problems with"—she ignored Emily's groan of dismay - "and doing some private studies. You may spend the afternoon at the Faire, if you wish. As my apprentice, at least for the summer, you will not be expected to mingle with the great and the good. They won't know who you are."

Emily nodded, relieved. She knew enough about the politics of the magical families to want to avoid them as long as possible. The deluge of messages asking for her hand in marriage had taught her that she would have to be careful. They knew her as someone who could give her children powerful magic, not as a person in her own right. In some ways, it was just as bad as the arranged marriage Alassa had been raised to accept.

"Thank you," she said, and meant it. "I don't like crowds."

Lady Barb shrugged. "Most magicians tend to become unsociable as they grow older," she said, softly. "I...forced myself to overcome it."

She finished her chocolate and stood up, forcing Emily to take her last sip. At least it was sweeter than the chocolate served in Whitehall, she told herself. Normally, she had to add at least a spoonful of sugar to drink it properly. Lady Barb waved a hand, banishing both cups to the sink, and then led Emily out of the kitchen and up a flight of stairs. There was a musty atmosphere in the upper levels that suggested that no one had entered the house for a very long time.

"This is the library," Lady Barb said, as she opened a door. Inside, the walls were lined with books, old books. It was tiny compared to a library on Earth, but Emily knew that she was staring at thousands of gold coins worth of books. Before she'd introduced the printing press, books had been written and bound manually. The various Scribes Guilds had made fortunes copying rare and important books for their clients. "Do you like it?"

Emily nodded. She'd always loved libraries.

"You can read anything, apart from the books on the top shelf," Lady Barb said. She gave Emily a warning look. "Some of them are too advanced for you, as of yet, while some of them are specific to my family. Reading them would be very dangerous for your health, Emily. *Don't* try to open them."

Emily felt a flicker of resentment. She'd always hated being told that something was too advanced—or too adult—for her to read. The librarians back on Earth had sometimes questioned her when she'd taken adult books out of the library, demanding to know if her mother knew she was reading them. But her mother had been too drunk to care.

She shook her head. These books weren't adult fiction, but books of magic, keyed to a specific family line. Lady Barb was right. Reading them could be *very* bad for her health.

"I won't," she promised. She hesitated, then asked the question that had come to mind. "Could your brother's wife read them?"

Lady Barb shook her head. "Only someone who shared the family's bloodline could open the books safely," she said. "A wife wouldn't count, no matter how close she was to her husband."

Emily shivered, remembering the offers of marriage. They'd been made to Imaiqah, too...and, before she'd been ennobled herself, Imaiqah might well have been tempted. A place in a magical family, adding her wild magic to the family's bloodline...it was a better match than she could have hoped for as a merchant's daughter. But she would never truly be one of the family. She would never be able to read their books.

Lady Barb placed a hand on Emily's shoulder. "I know how you feel," she said, quietly. "But you have to understand the dangers. *Don't* touch the books."

"I won't," Emily repeated.

Lady Barb strode over to the bookshelves and pulled a book off the shelf, followed by three more. "These are for you to study, when you're not brewing potions," she said. "Be warned; I shall expect you to be *perfect* with the potions. The people we will be visiting will have no other sources, but us. A mistake could have lethal consequences."

Emily gritted her teeth. Alchemy—which included potions—was not her best subject, despite a handful of private lessons with Professor Thande. She knew she could brew most of the First Year potions in controlled conditions, but she'd come alarmingly close to flunking the exam completely. If Lady Barb hadn't forced her to take advantage of being a Second Year to use one of the private rooms to practice, she suspected she wouldn't be able to make the potions she wanted now.

Lady Barb smiled at her expression. "I think you'll do fine," she said, placing the books on the table. "Consider this your reward."

Emily glanced down at the covers. One of them was a guide to the Cairngorm Mountains, where they would be travelling, but the others...all three of them were on enchantment. She recognized one of the titles and winced, remembering the book she'd borrowed from Yodel that Master Tor had confiscated. But why did Lady Barb have a copy?

"You can read these books," Lady Barb said, "but *no* experimenting without my agreement and supervision. I expect you to study them carefully, write out whatever you have in mind and then discuss it with me *thoroughly* before we actually try any experiments. Do you understand me?"

"Yes," Emily said, flinching under Lady Barb's gaze. The last time she had tried an unauthorized experiment, it had nearly got her expelled from Whitehall. If the Mimic hadn't started its murder spree at the same time, she knew it would have been a great deal worse. "I won't try anything without your presence."

"Good," Lady Barb said. She tapped the table. "You can take the books to your room, if you like, but don't try to remove them from the house. The wards will take exception to it."

She turned and marched out of the library. "There are three floors to this house," she said, as Emily hurried after. "Don't try to enter any locked doors; they're rooms belonging to other members of my family and I can't vouch for any wards or other unpleasant surprises they might have left behind. Your room is safe, but feel free to erect wards of your own—just remember to dismantle them before we leave the house for good."

Emily followed her into a smaller room. "This is the guestroom," Lady Barb said, by way of explanation. She dismantled a set of stasis wards surrounding the bed, which was larger than Whitehall's standardized beds but smaller than the beds Emily had enjoyed in Zangaria. "There's a bathtub in the next room, beside the toilet. You'll have to use magic to heat the water, I'm afraid."

"Ouch," Emily said. Sergeant Miles had taught her a whole series of spells that would be useful on camping trips, starting with a simple spell to boil water, but he'd also warned her of the dangers. Making the spell too powerful was a good way to get burned. "No hot running water?"

Lady Barb snorted. "This isn't Whitehall, you know," she said. "And everyone who lives here has magic."

Emily nodded. Running water was rare outside Whitehall and various aristocratic castles—and hot running water was even rarer. Imaiqah had told her once that she had fallen in love with Whitehall's showers, even though they were weaker than showers on Earth. But, in many ways, Emily was the only student at Whitehall whose living conditions had actually worsened since coming to the school. Hot and cold running water was one of the things taken for granted on Earth.

"Get a good night's sleep," Lady Barb said, as she turned and headed towards the door. "My room's at the bottom of the corridor, but don't disturb me unless it is truly urgent. I don't like being disturbed at night."

"Me neither," Emily said. She'd had to disturb Madame Razz more than once, when she'd had nightmares after the Mimic had been destroyed. The housemother had not been pleased at all. "And thank you."

Lady Barb smiled, rather coldly. "This is the easy part," she said. "It will get harder—much harder—once we're on our way."

She was right—again. Emily had done enough forced marches with the sergeants to know just how difficult it could be to walk from place to place carrying a bag. There were no cars in this world, no helicopters or airplanes. There was nothing more advanced than a horse and cart for the average non-magical citizen. And she still hadn't learned how to teleport.

Pity no one flies broomsticks here, she thought, ruefully. *But it would be way too easy to knock them out of the sky.*

Emily watched Lady Barb go, closing the door behind her, before she turned to look around the room. It was bare, no more decorated than any of the other rooms, but there was a simplicity about it that appealed to her. She opened the door and walked down to the kitchen to pick up her bag, then walked back to the room, feeling the wards pressing in around her as she moved. The house felt far less friendly than Whitehall, no matter how much its mistress liked her guest. But the effect faded as soon as she was back in the guestroom.

She undressed rapidly, then opened her bag and produced the nightgown. She'd never been able to sleep naked in her life, certainly not since her mother had remarried. The house was empty, apart from Lady Barb, but Emily still couldn't relax. She pulled the gown over her head, used a simple spell to clean her teeth and then reached back into the bag for a phial of sleeping potion. Placing it by the bedside, she climbed into bed and took a sip. As always, it tasted unpleasant. But it did its job.

And then the nightmares started.

Chapter Four

...The Mimic advances towards her, a glowing mist of eerie blue-white light. Emily raises her hands to cast the counter-spell, but the Mimic doesn't even flinch. It just keeps coming. She feels her mind start to shiver under the pressure of its magic, her thoughts scattering in preparation for being absorbed. The Grandmaster should be here, but he is gone...Emily stumbles, then falls to her knees. Her body starts to break up into dust...

Emily snapped awake, screaming.

For a long moment, she fought for control. Her entire body was drenched with sweat, soaking her gown. It took minutes to remember where she was and what she was doing, lying in an unfamiliar bedroom. Somehow, she managed to sit upright and push the blankets aside, then swing her legs over the side of the bed and stand. Her legs felt wobbly and unstable.

A dream, she told herself, firmly. It had all been a dream.

But her mind refused to believe it, not really. She'd had nightmares for the first month or two after the Mimic had been destroyed, but then they'd faded away. Now, however, with the change to a new bedroom...she gritted her teeth and walked towards the bathroom, hoping that the water wasn't *too* cold. She needed to wash the sweat from her body and hope it helped her recover from the nightmare.

The bathroom was larger than she'd expected, with a large bathtub in one corner. Emily turned on the tap and splashed water on her face. The shock woke her up, allowing her to concentrate on casting a heating spell for the water. It bubbled rapidly and started to steam, but she kept pouring cold water into the tub until it was warm rather than boiling hot. As soon as she could, she removed her gown and climbed into the bathtub, washing the sweat from her body. The water, thankfully, helped her relax.

She winced at the half-remembered dream as she allowed the water to work on her tense muscles. There was much to admire in Whitehall and the surrounding world, but one thing she couldn't admire was the complete absence of psychologists. She couldn't talk to anyone about PTSD, not when any hint of mental instability was sure to cause a panic. Mental instability was associated with one particular kind of magician -- necromancers. If she'd gone to someone—anyone—and confessed to any form of mental disorder, she suspected she wouldn't like the consequences.

In some ways, it made sense. No one wanted the necromancers to discover a way to come to terms with their own madness. Shadye had been dangerously irrational, lashing out with a staggering amount of power...and completely fixated on the so-called Child of Destiny he'd kidnapped from Earth. If he'd been less focused on Emily, he might well have destroyed Whitehall completely and killed Emily herself. But it was no reassurance when she wanted someone to talk to.

Naked, she stepped out of the tub and dried herself with a spell, then glanced in the mirror. Her eyes looked tired, her face pale; she scowled in annoyance before she walked into the bedroom. Lady Barb hadn't issued any instructions for what she should wear, so she reached for the standard student robes. Alassa might bemoan their shapelessness, but Emily had always found them reassuring. Besides, there was no need to wear anything underneath them apart from a set of equally shapeless panties and one of her makeshift bras.

Carefully, she opened the door and smiled as she smelled something cooking down below. It smelled faintly of bacon and eggs, although there was something else in the mix she didn't recognize. She walked down and into the kitchen, where Lady Barb was frying something on the grill. The older woman looked up and frowned when she saw Emily.

"Rough night?"

Emily flushed. "You could hear me?"

"Your face tells it all," Lady Barb said. She ladled eggs, bacon and fried bread onto a plate, then passed it to Emily. "What did you dream about?"

"The Mimic," Emily confessed. The food smelt heavenly. "Is there no potion for barring nightmares?"

"You soon wouldn't be able to sleep at all without it, if you took it more than once," Lady Barb pointed out, dryly. She placed a plate of her own on the table, then sat down facing Emily. "The best cure for nightmares is to work hard, sadly."

Emily nodded as she started to eat. The bacon tasted lovely, the eggs were nice... but there was something odd about the bread. It struck her, a moment later, that she wasn't entirely sure it *was* bread. Or, if it was, it was a very strange kind of bread.

"We're going to leave after eating breakfast," Lady Barb said. "I suggest you wear your dress robes, unless you have a very strong objection."

She smiled at Emily's expression. "And saying you don't like the style doesn't count," she added. "I expect you to wear them today, then perhaps you can leave them behind."

Emily made a face. Her normal robes were brown, but the dress robes were golden and made her look faintly ridiculous. Only the fact that everyone else in Second Year and above was expected to wear them too made them even remotely bearable. Alassa looked good in them, but Alassa looked good in everything. Emily, on the other hand, had no real sense of vanity, yet she still felt absurd in the robes.

"You'll be fine," Lady Barb assured her. She finished her food and banished the dishes to the sink. "Go get dressed. I'll meet you downstairs in twenty minutes."

Sighing, Emily obeyed. The dress robes weren't comfortable, no matter how many charms she used to try to make them tolerable. She looked at herself in the mirror, then strode downstairs, unable to escape the feeling that she looked a giant target and nothing else. Lady Barb met her at the bottom of the stairs, wearing a long black set of robes that marked her as a sorceress. Emily felt a flicker of envy which she rapidly suppressed. Lady Barb had worked hard to become a combat sorceress.

"Two words of warning," Lady Barb said, as she opened the door. "This is neutral ground, so be polite to everyone you meet. You don't want or need more enemies. And, if you have to come back to the house, just remember what I said about the locked doors. The house is always more aggressive about guests when none of its family are home."

Emily swallowed, then nodded.

Outside, the air was fresh and clean, smelling faintly of honeysuckle. Emily saw tiny insects buzzing through the garden, while birds flew high overhead, calling out to their fellows. The garden looked even less tidy in daylight, but she had to admit that it was all the more attractive. She'd seen organized gardens in Zangaria, where not a leaf was out of place, but they seemed unnatural compared to the wilderness.

"My grandmother used to grow her own herbs in the garden," Lady Barb said, as they walked out the gate and started down a long road. "I didn't inherit her talent, so I merely left the plants to grow as they saw fit. Whenever I wanted something from the garden, I'd just take it; sometimes, I'd let my cousins explore the garden for something they wanted for themselves."

The road led downwards into a large valley. Emily sucked in her breath as she saw the tents coming into view, crammed together around a handful of larger houses. There were hundreds of people milling around, chatting and looking at stalls. Emily fought down the urge to run as she realized just how many people had gathered, instead forcing herself to follow Lady Barb down towards the gates. A ward brushed against her mind and she shuddered, before the magic parted to let her through.

"The only people allowed to enter are magicians," Lady Barb said, softly. "But not all magicians. One of your friends would not be welcome here. Can you guess who?"

Emily remembered Lady Barb's warnings about the books and nodded. "Imaiqah."

"Wrong," Lady Barb said. "It's Alassa. She would not be welcome here."

Emily blinked in surprise. "Why?"

Lady Barb shrugged. "She lucked into her position, purely through choosing the right parents," she said. "The Patriarchs and Matriarchs of the Great Houses fight for their positions, testing magical skill against magical skill. They make certain to breed their children with new magicians, just to strengthen their talents. Alassa's father... will breed her with someone who suits his kingdom, not her magic. She wouldn't be welcome here."

"It sounds absurd," Emily said.

"It's the way they are," Lady Barb said, without seeming to take offense. She smiled at Emily. "Welcome to the Annual Faire."

Emily followed Lady Barb through the maze of stalls and performance artists, unable to believe the sheer variety. There were stalls overloaded with potion bottles, wands, magical tools and books. Behind them, hundreds of sellers chatted rapidly to prospective customers, their words blurring together into an omnipresent buzzing that threatened to overwhelm Emily's senses. She couldn't help pausing in front of one of the bookstalls and looking at the titles, although there didn't seem to be anything too interesting. Most of the texts on offer were textbooks she'd seen at Whitehall.

"Most of the...more sensitive titles are kept hidden," Lady Barb explained, as Emily followed her away from the stall. "If you happened to want a copy, you'd have to give the Bookseller's Guild a request—and they'd find it for you, if they could. Some books you can't have for love or money."

She paused, nodding to another bookstall. "But you might have changed all that, Millie."

Emily followed her gaze. The bookstall was crammed with books produced by a newfangled printing press, one of the later designs out of Zangaria. Unlike the previous stall, there were several copies of each title on display, just waiting for someone to pick them up. None of the titles looked particularly interesting, save two. One discussed famous magicians of the last century, the other claimed to be a history book. She picked the latter up and saw another book underneath. This one was a reprint of a textbook she recalled from First Year, one so rare that the only copies in Whitehall were in the library.

"Traditionalists say that the printing press takes something out of us," the seller said, as she examined the book. "But for us, business is booming."

Emily had to smile. The printing press had revolutionized the world already—and the pace of change was only going to increase. There were already dozens of newspapers in Zangaria and the rest of the Allied Lands, while producing copies of older books would help knowledge to spread quickly from place to place. In ten years, perhaps less, every student at Whitehall would be able to have their own copies of each and every textbook required for their studies. Emily almost envied them. As exams grew nearer, competition for rare copies of books only grew more and more fierce.

"You can look for books later," Lady Barb said, firmly. "There are quite a few other people you should see."

She pointed towards a group of women sitting behind a long table. Somewhat to Emily's surprise, they were wearing face veils that concealed almost everything. Their robes were even more shapeless than Whitehall's standard robes. Behind them, a second set of women wore chainmail bikinis and carried long swords as well as staffs. They glared at anyone who paid too much attention to the first set of women. Emily's eyes narrowed in puzzlement. The table was almost completely empty, despite its size.

"They're the Virgin Sisterhood," Lady Barb explained. "There are certain rites that can only be performed by a maiden, a virgin girl. The women in veils are the virgins, the ones who can and will do the work. Their sisters, the ones behind them, are their guardians and protectors. If someone wanted to harm a maiden, their sisters would die in their defense."

Emily found herself giving the women a second look. It was hard to take a chainmail bikini seriously, no matter how dramatic it looked. But perhaps wearing them was a statement, reminding everyone of their femininity, rather than an attempt at protection. "They're combat sorceresses?"

"Some of them are," Lady Barb said. "Others...are mere fighters, which doesn't stop them being dangerous."

She led Emily further into the tightly-packed mass of stalls, pointing out isolated items of interest along the way. "That storekeeper is selling love potions," she said.

"It's barely legal; it's charmed to ensure that only two people, who drink it willingly, are affected by the magic. The magical families tend to use them to ensure that a young couple remains in love long enough to produce children."

Emily shuddered at the thought. Love potions were banned at Whitehall, considered effectively akin to rape. *Did it make a difference*, she thought, *if two people took a potion to bind them together? Or did it merely mean that they were raping themselves?*

"Those charms are fidelity charms," Lady Barb continued, jabbing a finger at another stall. "It makes it impossible to sleep with anyone other than your wife or partner. That potion is a conceptive potion. If you take it before sex, you will almost certainly become pregnant. Behind it, there's a contraceptive potion. It's stronger than anything you will be allowed to use at Whitehall."

"Oh," Emily said.

Lady Barb turned to look at her. "A little overwhelmed?"

"Just a little," Emily confessed. The stalls seemed to be crowding in on her. She wanted to run and escape. "Is there somewhere we can go?"

Lady Barb nodded and led her through the crowd of people, heading towards a large tent on the edge of the Faire. Outside, a young girl—Emily estimated her age at thirteen, although it was impossible to be sure—was singing sweetly to the crowd. Emily hesitated, studying the girl's face. She looked vaguely Chinese, mixed with European. If she had magic, it was impossible to tell.

Inside, there were tables, chairs and a handful of serving maids carrying trays of drink everywhere. Lady Barb motioned for Emily to sit down, then ordered two mugs of Kava from the maids, who nodded and leapt to obey. Emily found herself taking deep breaths as she focused her mind, remembering what the sergeants had taught her. Magic was always safer when used by a focused magician.

"Don't worry about it," Lady Barb said, as she sat down beside Emily. "The magic in the air gets to everyone, at first. You'll grow used to it."

Emily rubbed her forehead, feeling something throbbing under her skull. "Do you really?"

"It's a sign of strong magic to react to magical fields," Lady Barb reminded her. "You shouldn't have forgotten that so quickly."

She nodded towards the entrance. "See anyone you recognize?"

Emily looked, but it took her several moments to spot a familiar face. Melissa was standing in the open air, speaking to a woman who looked old enough to be her great-grandmother. Unlike Emily, she wasn't wearing golden dress robes, but a white dress that showed off her long red hair and the shape of her body. It didn't look as though Melissa was enjoying her discussion with the older woman.

"Melissa comes from a magical family," Lady Barb said, quietly. "By now, she will be expected to enter into a marriage contract with someone approved by her family. Quite a few such contracts are made at the Faire."

Emily felt a flicker of sympathy for Melissa, despite knowing just how badly Melissa could act, on occasion. She'd hated Alassa—at least the royal brat she'd been before encountering Emily—and that hatred had been transferred to Emily, when

Emily had actually helped Alassa get through her basic classes. Since then, they'd sniped at each other constantly at Whitehall.

She looked up at Lady Barb. "What if Melissa says no?"

"Her family might disown her," Lady Barb said, softly. "If they did, she would be obliged to make her own way in the world. Which she probably could—her tuition fees are paid, so she could certainly stay at Whitehall until Sixth Year if she tried hard. But I don't know if she would do such a thing. Most people raised in magical families understand that they have a duty to help the family expand."

Emily looked over at her. "Like you?"

Lady Barb gave her a sharp look. "Like me," she said, after a moment. "But I never married."

She nodded towards the door before Emily could question her further. "You may recognize someone else here," she added, changing the subject. "Who do you see?"

Emily felt her heart leap into her mouth as she recognized the youth making his way towards the tent, following an older man with a grim expression on his face. He was older, his hair had been cropped to his skull and he walked with a confidence that outshone the young man Emily remembered, but there was no mistaking Jade. Emily found herself rising to her feet as they entered the tent, a silly smile spreading across her face. Whatever their relationship actually was—and she honestly didn't know—it was genuinely good to see Jade again.

Jade cast a privacy ward in the air, then smiled back at her. "Emily," he said. She couldn't help noticing that his face had acquired a couple of new scars. "How are you?"

The man beside him cleared his throat, loudly.

"This is Master Grey, my master," Jade said, introducing the man. "Master, this is Emily of Cockatrice."

Master Grey met Emily's eyes as she curtseyed, then introduced Lady Barb. She couldn't help thinking of a monk; bald, muscular and grimly determined to trample over whatever opposition barred his way to his destination. His eyes were dark and cold, studying her as though she was something he'd scraped off his shoe.

"A pleasure to meet you," he said.

Somehow, Emily found it hard to believe him.

Chapter Five

"WELL," LADY BARB SAID, AFTER THE MAIDS HAD SERVED THEM ALL KAVA, "HOW HAVE you been coping with your new apprentice?"

Master Grey gave her a long considering look. "Well enough," he said, heavily. "And yourself?"

Emily exchanged a glance of mutual embarrassment with Jade. She'd heard that some children found their parents permanently embarrassing, particularly when their friends had met them, but it was never a sensation she had experienced–until now. Hearing Master Grey and Lady Barb exchange careful compliments–as if Jade and Emily weren't even there–was definitely embarrassing. And then there was the way Master Grey looked at her while drinking his Kava.

"We are currently undergoing a temporary arrangement," Lady Barb said, stiffly. "She cannot enter a full apprenticeship until she leaves school."

Master Grey lifted his eyebrows. "Tell me," he said, addressing Emily directly, "how did you defeat the Mimic?"

"The Grandmaster starved it of magic," Emily said. It was the official cover story; the Grandmaster had flatly forbidden anyone who knew the truth to share it. "And then it died."

Master Grey didn't look as though he believed her. "And how did you kill Shadye?"

Emily felt sweat prickling on her forehead. "Through magic," she said, finally. "And..."

Lady Barb cleared her throat. "The Sorcerer's Rule protects her," she said. "And such knowledge should not be shared widely."

She looked over at Jade. "Why don't you young folk chat over there while we... discuss matters?"

Emily stood up before Jade could say a word. Jade blinked in surprise, but followed her over to a table on the far side of the tent. The maids gave them an enquiring glance, then left them alone as Jade cast a privacy ward. Emily looked down at the table as she sat down, feeling utterly unsure of herself. What did Master Grey think of her? Nothing good, she was sure.

"I'm sorry about him," Jade said, awkwardly. "He's obsessed with defeating the necromancers."

Emily had to smile. They *did* sound like a pair of children commiserating about their incredibly embarrassing parents. But then, apprentices were bound to their masters until the apprenticeship came to an end. In one sense, Master Grey was Jade's father–or at least someone standing in his father's place.

"He seems to have agreed with you," Emily said, frantically casting around for something to say. "Have you enjoyed yourself?"

Jade brightened, slightly. "I've had a very good time, but a very hard time," he said. "Master Grey thinks that Sergeant Harkin was too soft."

Emily winced in sympathy. Sergeant Harkin had pushed his trainees relentlessly, teaching them never to surrender or simply give up. No one would have called him soft, certainly no one who had seen how he treated his trainees. But then, with more than a handful of students, he hadn't had time to give everyone his personal attention. An apprentice was assured of the personal attention of his master.

She listened with genuine interest as Jade outlined a handful of stories. Master Grey believed in plunging his apprentices into the deep end, apparently; they'd started out near the Desert of Death, then explored the mountain range near Whitehall in hopes of finding Shadye's tunnel before another necromancer could discover it. Emily had a private suspicion that the tunnel had collapsed when Shadye had died, but she knew the Allied Lands couldn't take it for granted. It was only a matter of time before Shadye's lands were absorbed by another necromancer.

"The rumors say you beat the Mimic in single combat," Jade explained, when he'd finished. "No one knows quite what happened."

Emily rolled her eyes. Compared to some of the stories about her, including the ones that implied the use of forbidden sex magic, that story was almost reasonable. But it still wasn't true.

"I just helped to locate it," she said. That much, at least, was common knowledge within Whitehall. "And I passed all of my exams, save one."

Jade quirked an eyebrow. "Martial Magic?"

Emily nodded, embarrassed.

Jade reached over and patted her hand. "You've already had a year I never had," he pointed out, dryly. "By the time you leave Whitehall, you will have a far better grounding than I did. Master Grey had to teach me so much."

Emily looked down at her hand, feeling her emotions spin around until she was unsure of what she felt. She disliked being touched, at least without invitation, but Jade made her feel...nothing. Was that even remotely normal?

Jade looked up. Emily followed his gaze. Master Grey was standing, but still speaking to Lady Barb.

"Emily," he said, quickly, "will you walk out with me this evening?"

Emily hesitated. Was he asking her out on a date?

Of course he is, idiot, she told herself.

Dating wasn't something she'd done on Earth, not when she was considered weird by just about everyone...and hadn't dared expose herself in any case. And, at Whitehall, her obscure social status made it harder for people to ask her out...if, of course, they managed to look past her defeat of Shadye. Jade was the first person who had expressed interest in Emily herself, rather than her genes. But her personal feelings were incredibly conflicted. Part of her wanted to accept—she trusted Jade—and part of her wanted to run to Lady Barb and hide.

"I will," she said, forcing the words out. "And thank you for coming..."

Jade smiled. "My master is one of the guards here," he said. "I wasn't really given a choice."

Master Grey dispelled the privacy wards, then nodded for Jade to follow him out of the tent. Emily watched him go, then looked up at Lady Barb. The older woman had a pinched, disapproving expression on her face that made her look older, somehow. Emily hesitated, then told her about Jade asking her out.

"Go tomorrow," Lady Barb said, firmly. "Not tonight."

Emily opened her mouth to argue—the longer she delayed, the easier it would be to have second thoughts—but she saw the glint in Lady Barb's eye and nodded in submission. She would have to send Jade a message, she knew, or call after him...but she didn't know where to find either Jade or Master Grey. Lady Barb caught her shoulder and steered her towards the open air, then out past the tents. Emily realized, as they made their way around the edge of the Faire, that they were heading back towards Lady Barb's house.

"There are things I need to show you," Lady Barb said, shortly. "And you may not be in any fit state for anything tonight."

Emily swallowed. What did Lady Barb have in mind? She had warned Emily that they would be keeping up with her lessons in unarmed combat, training her to fight without magic or blades, but she didn't mean to do it today, surely? Or had Master Grey annoyed her to the point where she wanted to work it out somehow? But Emily knew, without false modesty, that she was no match for the older woman.

Lady Barb said nothing else until they were back inside her house. She led the way into a living room, which looked oddly informal. The chairs scattered around in front of the fire were old, but comfortable. Emily liked the room on sight. It might not be anywhere near as elegant as the aristocratic chambers she'd seen, but it seemed more suited to Lady Barb somehow.

"Take a seat," Lady Barb ordered. She perched on a cushion, folding her hands in her lap. "Do you want something to drink?"

Emily shook her head as she sat down facing her tutor. Lady Barb seemed tense, unsure—for once—of what to do. It bothered Emily more than she cared to admit. The Mimic might have left them all a little unsure of what was happening, but Lady Barb had recovered from that experience quicker than anyone else. But now she was unsure again...

"My father was the youngest son of the family patriarch," Lady Barb said. "He wasn't a powerful sorcerer, so he tended to spend most of his time in the library. Not that he was incompetent, of course. Given time, he could still beat his older brothers."

Emily nodded. Stupid and incompetent magicians didn't tend to last very long—and a magician lacking in raw power wasn't necessarily a pushover. Someone with enough knowledge and skill could make up for a shortage in power, particularly if he or she had time to prepare the battleground in advance. Sergeant Miles had taught her more than a few tricks she could use against a stronger opponent, if she was forced to fight against her will.

But she had no idea why Lady Barb was telling her this, *now*.

"One day, he met a Traveller witch in the woods," Lady Barb added. "They became lovers—and she became pregnant. Nine months later, she left me on the doorstep and ran off."

Emily stared at her. "Why?"

"There are different...traditions in magic, as you know," Lady Barb said. "My mother believed that I should be raised by my father, which I was. His family weren't too pleased at first, but when they discovered I was quite powerful they changed their tune." She rolled her eyes. "I grew up here until I was twelve, when my mother returned and asked to take custody of me for a few years. My father exploded with rage."

"I'm not surprised," Emily said. She could imagine exactly how Lady Barb's father had felt. He'd raised his daughter, taught her everything from magic to letters and numbers, and then her mother had come back into his life and demanded custody, if only for a short while. It was utterly outrageous. "What happened?"

"There was a big shouting match," Lady Barb said. Her lips twitched. "I overheard most of it, particularly when my grandfather joined in. In the end, I was allowed to go stay with my mother for the summer months."

She shrugged. "The Travellers have a very light existence, but it isn't an unpleasant one," she added. "I rather enjoyed it, once I got used to living in a wagon and moving from place to place. My mother wasn't a powerful witch, but she knew how to brew potions and use small magic. I learned a great deal from her."

Emily remembered all the times she'd fantasized about her father–her biological father–coming back to take her away and shivered. Lady Barb hadn't been unhappy, growing up with her father; if Christopher had been a real custody battle it might easily have torn the family apart. But things were different for magical families...who knew? Perhaps they would just have booted Barb's mother out of the house and told her never to come back.

"When I was sixteen, they offered me the chance to choose between Whitehall, Mountaintop or homeschooling," Lady Barb continued. "I chose Whitehall. Most of my relatives were homeschooled, but I didn't want to go straight into the family. Mountaintop seemed more ominous to me, for some reason. Most magical families send their children there."

She snorted. "It turned out that I had a natural talent for healing," she admitted. "Or so they said. My mother forced me to learn how to take care of patients while I was studying with her. It was simple to add magic to the mix once my powers developed properly. I don't think it was a real talent. And I had to fight tooth and nail to convince them that I could become a combat sorceress. They didn't want to risk a skilled healer."

Emily heard the cold ice in Lady Barb's voice and shivered. She'd been told, more than once, that careers in magic were often determined by a person's talents...and if Lady Barb had looked like a skilled healer, Whitehall wouldn't have wanted to steer her away from healing.

She looked up at the older woman. "Why did you want to become a Combat Sorceress?"

Lady Barb looked at her for a long chilling moment. "I grew up here," she said, waving her hand around to indicate the house. "It was safe and warm, particularly for children. The worst danger was accidentally picking up something magical and we were taught, almost as soon as we could walk, to be careful what we touched. And my father was a decent man.

"Spending time with my mother was an eye-opener. I learned that people outside weren't safe, that they were preyed on by those stronger than themselves...I had the idea that I could protect the weak and powerless, if I learned how to fight. And I was good at it."

Emily nodded. "Why didn't you apply to replace Sergeant Bane?"

Lady Barb scowled. "It's untraditional for training officers to be women," she said, darkly. "Young men tend to need more thumping before they learn to respect women as warriors—and most trainees are young men. Most of them are idiotic enough to convince themselves that they must've held back when they faced a woman on the training field, no matter how convincingly they were thrashed. But I may well return for Third or Fourth Year to give you additional training."

Emily considered it. She hadn't noticed any of the male students at Whitehall giving the female teachers grief, but most of the teachers—even Master Tor—knew their subjects well enough to convince their students not to mess with them. But Martial Magic, which was half physical exercise, might be a harder class for a woman to teach. There were only a handful of girls in the class and all of them were worked to the bone. The sergeants didn't hold back for them.

"Stupid," she said, finally.

"Very stupid," Lady Barb agreed. "After I graduated from Whitehall, I was apprenticed to a sorcerer, learned the ropes and gained my mastery. And then I met Void."

Emily nodded, remembering what she'd been told.

"Master Grey doesn't seem to like me," she said, changing the subject hastily. "What did I do to him?"

"Distracted Jade, I imagine," Lady Barb said. "It isn't customary for apprentices to maintain relationships outside of the apprenticeship. Most apprentices cut themselves off from everyone else during their training. Master Grey is enough of a traditionalist to be irked at you distracting his student."

Emily flushed. "I didn't mean to distract his student!"

Lady Barb laughed, not unkindly. "I wouldn't worry about it," she advised. "Here, in the Faire, there will be time for you and Jade to talk properly, without interruption."

"Thank you," Emily said. "Can I ask a question?"

"You just did," Lady Barb pointed out. She smirked, then grinned at Emily. "Go ahead."

Emily braced herself. "Are you married?"

Lady Barb lifted her eyebrows. "Tell me," she said, "do you see a husband around here?"

Emily felt her cheeks heat, but she pressed on. "It's just...you're...your family will want you to get married, won't it?"

"I never found the right person," Lady Barb said, taking pity on her. "There was a Combat Sorcerer I met once, but he died in battle against the necromancers. Since then, no one has really managed to impress me. And my family knows better than to try to push me into anything."

"That's good," Emily said. "Where are they?"

"My father died a long time ago," Lady Barb admitted. There was a bitterness in her tone that made Emily sit up and take notice. "My mother...I haven't seen her in years. She might well be dead by now too. I inherited the house and little else. My uncles sometimes try to talk me into spending more time with the family, but I don't listen to them very often. They weren't always kind to my father."

She shrugged. "We may meet some of them over the coming week," she added. "It would probably be best to make sure they don't know who you are, Millie."

Emily nodded. She couldn't help wondering if Lady Barb had an ulterior motive for chatting about her past, although Emily *had* been curious. Lady Barb was an intensely private person in many ways, rarely telling anyone much about herself. For her to open up so much...either she wanted Emily to know or she had something else in mind.

"I have something to teach you," Lady Barb said, standing up. "But I think we should eat lunch first. You will need energy for this."

Emily stood and followed her into the kitchen. Lady Barb opened a set of cabinets, canceled a series of stasis spells and produced bread, cheese and ham, which she placed on the table. Emily started to carve up the bread to make sandwiches, while Lady Barb boiled soup. It was a simple meal, certainly compared to the aristocratic feasts, but Emily didn't mind. Besides, the aristocracy often seemed to be competing to win a prize for worst table manners in the world.

"Good work," Lady Barb said, as she placed a bowl of chicken soup in front of Emily. "The last person I brought here didn't know how to help at all."

Emily felt an odd flicker of jealousy. "Who was he?"

"He suffered a nasty accident and I found myself detailed to look after him for a few months," Lady Barb said. "If you're cooped up with someone, you either get very close or you wind up hating each other. I definitely ended up hating him, even though it wasn't entirely fair."

She shrugged. "Eat up," she ordered. "You are going to need your strength."

Emily nodded and tucked into the food. The prospect of learning new magic always gave her an appetite. Besides, she'd learned from the sergeants that she should always eat when she had the chance. She might not have the chance again.

Chapter Six

"**W**HAT I'M ABOUT TO SHOW YOU," LADY BARB SAID, AS THEY WALKED BACK TO THE library, "is rarely shown to anyone beneath Fifth Year. In fact, the senior tutors can decide that a certain pupil should *never* be told about this kind of magic, let alone taught how to do it safely. You must not discuss it with your friends, ever."

Emily gave her a sharp look. "So why are you teaching it to me?"

"Because you will probably wind up rediscovering it for yourself," Lady Barb said, as she stopped in front of a bookshelf. "And because it has been decided to push your education forward as fast as possible. And because you should be able to handle it now."

Emily hesitated. "Will you get in trouble for teaching me?"

"I'd prefer not to discuss it with anyone," Lady Barb admitted. "The Grandmaster is the only other person who knows and he gave his approval."

She pressed her hand against the bookshelf. There was a dull rumbling sound and the entire bookshelf retreated backwards and to the side, revealing a darkened stairwell leading down into the bowels of the earth. Lady Barb cast a light-spell, illuminating the stone stairs, then started to walk down into the darkness. Emily hesitated again, then followed her, pressing one hand against the stone wall. It reminded her uncomfortably of Shadye's fortress in the Blighted Land, but now she could sense the magic running through the stone. Something—or someone—was constrained down below.

"You are free to back out at any time," Lady Barb called back, as she reached the bottom of the stairs. "There are magicians, including some quite powerful ones, who cannot commit themselves to any form of ritual. Their own doubts and fears make it impossible. If you want to back out, just say so. I won't be upset."

Emily swallowed as she stepped into the stone chamber. It was dark, so dark that the darkness seemed to absorb the light from the spell. A moment later, the spell flickered out completely and Emily froze, trapped in the darkness. It took her several seconds to realize that there was a faint blue glow from the floor...and several seconds more to realize that the glow emanated from runes carved into the stone. Some of them she recognized, others were completely unfamiliar. They surrounded a glowing blue circle in the center of the room.

She found her voice. "What is this place?"

"A modified spellchamber," Lady Barb said. There was a grim note to her voice that suggested that she, too, had doubts. "My great-grandfather built it, back before he was shipped off to an isolated island to carry out his research in private. It's been tested extensively since then, but I haven't used it very often."

Emily nodded. A spellchamber was nothing more than a safe place to practice spells...looking around, she could see that most of the runes were designed to channel magic away from the circle, allowing the spell to be cast without interference. But this chamber was far stronger than the chambers she'd used at Whitehall. The closer she stepped to the circle, the harder it was to sense any ambient magic in the air at all.

Lady Barb stepped over the glowing blue line and turned to face her. "This should not be dangerous," she said, "but it can be. Do you want to back out now?"

Emily shook her head. She didn't even know what was going on.

"Then step into the circle," Lady Barb ordered. "But don't put your foot down on the blue light."

Emily obeyed. A shiver ran down her spine as she sensed the sudden absence of the remaining ambient magic. The runes, she realized, had to be absorbing and directing the *mana* out of the circle, creating a space that was completely empty of undirected magic. Her own magic suddenly seemed to blossom within her, making her very aware of its presence.

"Sit down," Lady Barb ordered. She produced a knife from her robes and examined it, carefully. Emily stared at it in horror until she realized that the blade was silver, rather than stone. "We are going to explore the simplest form of ritual."

Emily nodded, her throat suddenly dry. The books she'd read in the library had talked about how magicians could use rituals to cast formidable spells, but they hadn't gone into details, beyond a handful of warnings about how immensely dangerous such spells could be. Given some of the stories, Emily could well believe it. One story talked about a group of magicians who had destroyed an entire city.

"Sit down," Lady Barb repeated. Emily obeyed, hastily. "And give me your hands."

Emily hesitated, then held out her hands. Lady Barb took them and held her, gently.

"Now," Lady Barb said. "I want you to close your eyes and focus on your magic. It should be easy here."

It was, Emily already knew. She closed her eyes...and the sensation of her magic, pulsing in tune with her heartbeat, grew stronger and stronger. The magic seemed to swell within her, then fade away, then swell again in an endless tide. Lady Barb rubbed her palms gently as the sensation overwhelmed her. The touch was all that was keeping her from being completely absorbed in her own mind.

"Visualize the magic moving through your bloodstream," Lady Barb instructed quietly. "Imagine it moving from place to place, carrying power through your body."

Emily nodded, keeping her eyes closed. The more she focused her mind, the more she was aware of magic moving through her bloodstream...and concentrating in her mind, her heart and her womb. It reminded her of the moment Shadye had forced her to stab Sergeant Harkin with a necromantic knife, right in the heart. Shadye had intended to force her to drain the Sergeant's magic, unaware that Harkin had no magic. Now...

"Be aware of your skin, holding in the magic," Lady Barb said. Her words made it real, somehow. "Concentrate your mind on visualizing the skin."

There was a long pause. "I'm going to cut your palm," she added. "When I do, try to direct some of your magic up and out of your body. Don't channel it through your mind, channel it through the cut. Do you understand me?"

Emily nodded, nervously. There was a faint stabbing sensation from her palm, then nothing. But she could *see* her magic reacting to the cut, flickering around as if it wasn't quite sure what to do. Emily hesitated, then attempted to guide some of her magic out of her body. But it refused to do more than spin around the cut. And then the cut closed up completely.

"You healed yourself," Lady Barb observed. She sounded more amused than annoyed. "I'm going to cut you again."

There was another stabbing sensation. This time, Emily managed to guide a little magic up and out of her body. It seemed to fade away into the chamber, directed by the runes. Emily felt a sudden dizzy sensation, then the cut healed again. Lady Barb's grip tightened, just slightly, then relaxed.

"Using your mind's eye," Lady Barb ordered, "look upwards. Sense the magic."

Emily forced herself to concentrate, despite the sudden weakness in her limbs. Above her, magic was slowly seeping into the runes. It was *her* magic, she realized, now as familiar as her own face. And it was fading away...

"Open your eyes," Lady Barb said.

Emily opened her eyes and looked around. The entire chamber was glowing with light, banishing the shadows. Her magic, she realized, was powering the runes, which had directed the magic into harmless light. Lady Barb let go of her hands, then stood. But when Emily tried to stand, her legs betrayed her. She couldn't stand upright at all.

"It always leaves a magician weak, the first time," Lady Barb said. "How are you feeling?"

"Spent," Emily said. She tried to analyze her own feelings, but they were in such a conflicted mess that it was impossible to sort them out. Giving up magic like that made her feel uncomfortable, yet there was a strange tingling in her hand that was almost pleasurable. "What...what happened to it?"

"Here, the runes redirect the magic," Lady Barb said. "When a ritual is used in the field, one of the magicians is placed in charge of shaping the magic and directing it towards its target, leaving the others vulnerable. Does it remind you of anything?"

Emily shivered. "Necromancy."

Lady Barb nodded. "There are two differences," she said. "First, the magicians involved in a ritual are giving up magic willingly–and a controlled amount of magic, rather than everything they have. Second, the magic gathered is not channeled through the prime magician's mind, but through the spell-structure and runes he has created. Insanity is not a serious risk."

"I see," Emily said. It was still almost impossible to even think about moving. "Can't this be used to match a necromancer?"

"Once or twice, if you happen to get lucky," Lady Barb said. "But setting up a ritual can take time and effort. Necromancers don't have to worry about it."

Emily nodded.

Lady Barb squatted down until she was facing Emily, looking into her eyes. "Can you think of another danger?"

The basic necromantic rite wasn't complicated, Emily knew; Shadye might have taught her, but she could have figured it out from what she'd learned in books and private sessions with Mistress Sun. But it was all-or-nothing; the necromancer took everything his victim had, drawing it through his mind and driving himself insane. And yet...it wasn't just magic they took...

She shuddered. "Life force," she said. "A ritual can be used to share life force."

"It can," Lady Barb agreed. "And only necromancy is considered so vile."

Emily blinked in surprise. "Why?"

Lady Barb gave her a reproving look. "Oh, Emily," she said, in a voice more suited to an aged grandmother than a middle-aged woman, "you have so *many* years left and I have so *few*. Why don't you give me some of your years?"

She continued in a more normal voice. "There are rejuvenation spells that drain life force from their victim and give it to the caster," she added. "If enough life force is drained, the victim will die of old age."

Emily shuddered at the implications. "A magician could have a child, then drain that child," she said, remembering how her magic had concentrated around her womb. "Or they could kidnap a newborn and drain her. Or..."

"It's been known to happen," Lady Barb said, shortly. "And while rituals require a degree of consent, you know how easy it is to just strip magic and life force from an unwilling victim."

She helped Emily back to her feet. "We need to leave the chamber to finish draining away the magic," she said, as she picked Emily up in a fireman's carry. "It will take some time for it to be clean again."

Emily nodded, still feeling exhausted. Lady Barb carried her out of the chamber and back up the stairs, then placed her down gently on a chair in the library. Emily sat there and watched as Lady Barb resealed the bookshelf, then walked away and left her alone. She couldn't muster the strength to move until Lady Barb returned, carrying a mug of hot Kava in her hands. Emily took it and sipped gratefully.

"Be very careful with the drink," Lady Barb warned her. "If you spill it on a book, my father will come back to murder you personally."

"I understand," Emily said, quickly. She'd always hated people who damaged books—and that had started on Earth, where truly irreplaceable books were rare outside academic libraries. Here, where only a relative handful of books were printed on her printing presses, a damaged book might be impossible to replace. "I won't spill a drop."

"See that you don't," Lady Barb said. She looked around, her gaze moving from shelf to shelf. "My father loved this room. He designed it personally."

Emily nodded, sipping her drink.

"You did very well, for a beginner," Lady Barb added. She looked up, meeting Emily's eyes. "I would suggest that you don't try again for several days, though. And *don't* discuss this with anyone else. If Jade asks you what you were doing, tell him that I was forcing you to brew."

"I won't," Emily promised. The Kava made her feel better, although her magic felt weak and wan inside her. She couldn't help wondering just how long it would take to regenerate. Her palm itched and she glanced at it, seeing two faint scars where Lady Barb had cut her. "What happened to the blood?"

Lady Barb smiled and passed her the knife. Emily tried to cast a cleansing spell, but it refused to work properly. Lady Barb shook her head, then offered Emily a cloth. Emily cleaned the knife carefully, admiring the way the light glimmered off the silver blade, then put the cloth in her pocket. She knew better than to leave samples of her blood lying around, particularly after Shadye had used one to control her.

"Sit here until you feel better," Lady Barb urged. "I can find you a book, if you like, or we can chat..."

"Batteries," Emily said, as something *clicked* in her mind. "That's why you showed me the ritual."

Storing magic wasn't easy, if only because it tended to leech out into the surrounding atmosphere. The only way to lock it in for longer than a few hours was to use wards or dedicated spell-structures, which had to be carefully configured...and still tended to lose magical energy over a long period of time. Building semi-permanent wards was Fifth and Six Year level at Whitehall. But even wards weren't raw magic.

Emily had reasoned that the magic wouldn't flow away if the magic had nowhere to go. If a pocket dimension was used as a storage space, the magic would be trapped. But her first experiments had been halted and while she'd done some theoretical work, she'd never been able to create a pocket dimension of her own. And she hadn't worked out how to insert magic into the dimension.

But the ritual might work, she saw now. All she would have to do was concentrate, cut her own palm and emit magic into the pocket dimension. It would be stored there...

"Very good," Lady Barb agreed. "And how do you plan to use it?"

Emily hesitated, realizing Lady Barb was right. Necromancers went insane because they channeled vast amounts of power through their minds. If she drew on a battery, she would be running the risk of being driven insane by her own power. Coming to think of it, could she draw on someone *else's* power from another battery? What if it was that, rather than contact with their own magic, that drove necromancers insane?

But it was something she didn't dare try to test.

"You could probably use it like a modified ritual," Lady Barb said, after a moment. She stood up, pulled a book from the shelves and opened it, looking for a particular chapter. "You'd have to set up the spell-structure, rather like using a wand, then open the hatch and let the power flow. But if it failed...well, you might end up with an explosion. Or a wave of wild magic."

Emily frowned. The whole concept sounded obvious to her. "No one ever tried this before?"

"Not as far as I know," Lady Barb admitted. "But you know how easy it is to hide something in this world—and how many sorcerers keep secrets."

The Mimic, Emily thought. Everyone had believed that they were living creatures—and why not, in a world that included dragons, demons and gorgons. But they were actually spells, the most elaborate and complex spells Emily had ever seen. Someone had created them, built them up piece by piece, then sent them out to wreak havoc. And no one had had the slightest idea what their creator had done until Emily had uncovered the truth.

"We will be practicing creating pocket dimensions while we're walking from village to village," Lady Barb said. She pointed a long finger at Emily. "And you will be *very* careful what you do. There isn't anyone who can help out there, apart from me."

Emily nodded, ruefully.

"I learned my lesson," she said, tartly. "I..."

"Really?" Lady Barb asked. "Remind me; which students were faking library passes when they should have been in New Learning?"

Emily flushed. New Learning was her least favorite class, if only because most of what it taught was derived from innovations Emily herself had introduced. She wasn't even sure why the Grandmaster and Mistress Irene had inserted her into the class. But Alassa had talked her into skipping once, then they'd faked library passes for the next two classes. Eventually, inevitably, they'd been caught. They hadn't been able to sit comfortably for several days afterwards, to say nothing of having to redo several essays and other assignments. It hadn't been a pleasant week.

She yawned, suddenly.

"You can have a nap," Lady Barb said. She gave Emily a smile as Emily blushed furiously at her sudden loss of control. "I'll send Jade a note explaining that I've worked you halfway to death and you'll see him tomorrow. Speaking of which, I will have to leave the house early tomorrow morning. When you wake up, make sure to eat breakfast, then start practicing your potions. I want them all perfect by the time I return."

She helped Emily to her feet, showed her the brewing chamber, then escorted her into her bedroom. Emily closed her eyes as soon as her head hit the pillow, and fell asleep.

This time, there were no dreams to torment her.

Chapter Seven

THE FOLLOWING MORNING, THE HOUSE FELT ODDLY EMPTY—EMPTIER THAN YESTERDAY. Emily awoke, feeling much better, washed herself and walked down to the kitchen. A note on the table reminded her about her potions work, ending with a dire threat to forbid her from seeing Jade if she hadn't produced a series of perfect potions by the time Lady Barb returned home. Emily rolled her eyes, then took the bowl of porridge off the stove and ate it slowly, savouring every bite. It wasn't something she'd expected to like, after having to subsist on her own homemade gruel, but she enjoyed eating it at Whitehall.

Once she'd finished eating, she walked into the brewing chamber and examined the piles of ingredients. There was nothing too dangerous, according to two years of Alchemy; she wasn't expected to brew anything really complex. But it was still not one of her skills, even though she rather liked Professor Thande. The man's willingness to constantly push the limits—and encourage his students to do the same—made her feel much better about her poor lab work.

The first potion was a standard pain relief draught, one she knew how to make from memory. It was commonly used for headaches, she'd been taught, although—like all potions—it had a tendency to become addictive if overused. The one time Professor Thande had been genuinely angry with an experimenting student had been when the student had made a potion actually taste nice. Thande had pointed out, sharply, that anything that *encouraged* people to take potions was asking for trouble.

Emily sorted out the piles of ingredients, one by one. Imaiqah had worked with her for hours, helping to improve her technique. One of the simplest tricks was to lay everything out beforehand, then start brewing. She lit the fire under the cauldron with a simple spell, then poured in water and waited for it to boil. Once it was ready, she added the herbs and then a handful of less pleasant ingredients. There were times when she suspected she would have preferred not to know what went into the potion.

She kept stirring it until it boiled again, then settled down into an unpleasant green color. Once it was done, she removed the cauldron from the fire and poured the liquid into a bottle, then left it there to cool down. Lady Barb wouldn't be able to find anything wrong with it, she told herself, as she cleaned the cauldron and set it up again. The next potion was taught to both male and female students, but female students had a strong motive to learn. It helped prevent cramps and bleeding during their time of the month.

The first potion went wrong, somehow. Emily swore, poured the mess into a container for disposal and started again. Frustration was a problem when making potions, Professor Thande had told them more than once; their magic could accidentally interact with the magical transformation taking place inside the cauldron. Disasters—cauldrons were known to explode on a regular basis - occurred when someone was irritated or frustrated. But the second version came out fine.

Emily sat down to rest for half an hour while it cooled down, reading through one of the books on transfiguration Lady Barb had picked out for her, then returned to the brewing chamber. The third potion was designed to handle poison, flushing out any toxins within the victim's body. It wasn't even remotely clean, she knew, but it worked. She brewed it perfectly, then went on to the fourth potion. It took her four tries to get the contraceptive potion to come out properly.

She looked up as she felt the wards shiver around her, then heard the sound of Lady Barb making her way down the corridor and into the chamber. She looked tired, but happy; Emily smiled at her, then waved a hand at the prepared potions. Lady Barb nodded to her and checked them, one by one. They all passed muster.

Emily relaxed, slightly, as she finished the final potion. "I finished them all," she said, as Lady Barb moved over to stand beside her. "They're perfect."

"Good enough," Lady Barb agreed, after a careful inspection. "You used a little too much rabbit blood for the contraceptive potion. It won't last more than a week outside a charmed bottle."

"Sorry," Emily said, tiredly. She still didn't understand what kind of mind would devise tests to explore the magical potency of rabbit blood. Professor Thande and the other alchemists had to be out of their minds. "Do you want me to redo it?"

"Not now," Lady Barb said. She turned and headed back towards the door. "Bottle up the potions you've made, clean up the room and then wash yourself, thoroughly. There aren't so many wards here."

Emily nodded and started to clean the cauldron. Professor Thande had taught his students not to use magic anywhere near their tools, pointing out that it could produce unexpected results the next time they started to brew. She wiped it clean with boiling water, then placed it and the rest of the tools on a shelf to drip dry. Once she'd bottled the potions, she left the room, washed herself and walked back down to the kitchen. Lady Barb was busy laying out food and drink for lunch.

"I spoke to Jade," Lady Barb said, when Emily sat down. "He's going to pick you up at sixteen bells so you can both watch the dueling."

Emily blinked. She knew that magicians used duels to settle disputes, at least when one side refused to back down or apologize after a long argument, but dueling wasn't taught at Whitehall unless the student wanted to become a champion dueler. Sergeant Miles, when asked, had pointed out that duels followed rules and war tended to have none—and teaching his students to respect rules wasn't doing them any favors. Emily tended to agree with the sergeant, although she knew that some of the boys had objected.

She looked up at Lady Barb. "Why does Jade want to watch?"

Lady Barb's lips twitched. "Master Grey is going to be competing," she said. "I believe that Jade wishes to support his master."

"Oh," Emily said. She had never cared for sporting events—she'd done her best to support Alassa in playing *Ken*, but it wasn't one of her pleasures—but she had to admit that she was curious. Besides, it would give her a chance to evaluate Master Grey. "I see."

Lady Barb nodded. "You can read in the library until he arrives," she said. "I'd suggest wearing your student robes, rather than the golden ones. You don't want to be mistaken for a qualified magician."

Emily lifted an eyebrow. "Magicians tend to jostle each other," Lady Barb elaborated. "If one of them thinks you're a qualified magician, he might try to put you down in hopes of boosting his own status. But it's considered unwise to try any games with a student. The Grandmaster would not be amused."

"I see," Emily said.

She ate her food, then went back to the library and started to reread Yodel's book on pocket dimensions. As before, it was complex, often taking entire pages to explain something that could have been covered in a paragraph or two. She finished it, scribbled a series of notes, then opened one of Lady Barb's books. Much to her irritation, it was simpler and far easier to understand. She was so engrossed in it that she didn't hear Lady Barb behind her until a hand fell on her shoulder.

"You need to pay more attention to your surroundings," Lady Barb reproved her. "It's nearly time for Jade to arrive."

Emily glanced at her clockwork watch, then jumped up and ran to her room. Lady Barb's laughter followed her as she undressed, washed again and pulled on her student robes. It seemed impossible to do anything with her hair, apart from tying it into a long ponytail...but she hadn't done anything more complex when she'd first met Jade. She glanced at herself in the mirror, decided she looked as good as she was going to get, then walked downstairs as she felt the wards shiver, announcing his presence.

"Welcome," Lady Barb said, opening the door and calling out to Jade. "She's just coming."

She winked at Emily, turning her head so Jade couldn't see. "I want you back home before midnight," she warned. "Or there will be consequences."

Emily felt herself flush, although part of her was a little relieved. Her impulses were confusing; part of her wanted to spend time with Jade, part of her wanted to leave him and remain alone. Shaking her head, she nodded to Lady Barb and walked out of the door. Jade smiled at her as the door closed, then turned to lead her back towards the Faire. In the distance, she could hear the sound of cheering crowds.

"It's been a long time," Jade said, as they walked. "I've missed you."

"I've missed you too," Emily said, although she wasn't sure if that was true. "Martial Magic just hasn't been the same."

Why didn't I notice he liked me? She asked herself. She'd enjoyed Jade's company... but that had been before he'd come out and proposed to her. Everyone had noticed that he liked her, apart from Emily herself. Having him propose to her had been a shock. *Because the thought of someone liking me seemed so absurd.*

Jade smiled. "You would have done well, with or without me," he said. "You have talent."

"But I still failed," Emily said. "I don't know what I will be doing next year."

"Most students tend to take Martial Magic in Fifth or Sixth Year," Jade pointed out. "I think they won't have a problem with you repeating the class in Third Year."

Emily nodded, silently. As embarrassing as it was to repeat a class, she did need the practice...and she wasn't sure what she would do after completing the second year of Martial Magic in any case. Normally, students went straight into apprenticeships with qualified sorcerers, like Jade, but she had four more years of schooling ahead of her first. She looked up at Jade, wondering what had happened to get his face scarred—and why he hadn't healed the scars completely.

"I made the mistake of asserting that I was ready to face a master swordsman," Jade admitted, when she asked. "He cut my face—and Master Grey told me to keep the scars."

They stopped outside a hollow in the ground, surrounded by watching magicians. In the center, a set of wards had been drawn up to protect the spectators and prevent outside interference. They reminded Emily of the wards Sergeant Miles erected to protect his pupils, although they felt as if several different magicians had created them together. Perhaps they had, she decided. One person working alone could always decide to cheat.

"These are the newcomers," Jade told her, nodding towards the two magicians inside the wards. One of them was holding a staff, Emily noted, while the other was carrying a pair of wands, one in each hand. "The serious fights don't start until later."

Emily nodded, remembering a piece of advice from Alassa. "So," she said, "what happens?"

Jade smiled, apparently glad to be able to explain. "Level One dueling means the fighters will duel until one of them is unable to continue," he told her. "Level Two is fought out until someone is seriously injured and the referee calls a halt. Level Three is a fight to the death, with no quarter asked or received. Most of the duels here are Level Two, but sometimes there's a grudge match where one participant is killed."

"Oh," Emily said. In the hollow, the two fighters were throwing spells at each other with icy determination. It was hard to tell which one of them was more advanced; they seemed evenly matched. "Why are they using wands?"

"They're allowed to use wands and staffs by prior arrangement," Jade explained. "The challenged party is allowed to set the terms for the duel, but there are limits. You cannot use something you don't bring into the arena with you, for example, and you can't take help from outside the arena. That would count as cheating and the mediators"—he pointed a hand towards a pair of men dressed in white—"would intervene."

Emily looked back towards the arena, just in time to see the wand-holding magician thrown back against the wards. He crumpled to the ground and lay still. His opponent eyed him carefully for a long moment, then turned and bowed to the crowd. There were a handful of scattered cheers, but not much enthusiasm. The winner didn't seem amused and stalked out of the arena as soon as the wards were lowered.

When she asked why, Jade told her. "That was a very basic duel. It isn't what these bloodthirsty bastards came to see."

The next two magicians looked flamboyant, both wearing robes that suggested they were color-blind. Emily had to fight down the urge to snicker when they bowed to each other, then stared in awe as they threw waves of raw magic without bothering to wait for a countdown. The wards flashed blue time and time again as streaks of magic slammed against them, suggesting that both magicians were unleashing vast amounts of power. Emily found herself wondering what would happen if the wards collapsed, then pushed the thought aside as the two magicians converged. It was growing harder to see them in between flashes of magic.

"A grudge match, if not one to the death," Jade explained. Emily barely heard him over the roar of the crowd. "Those two are brothers—and rivals."

There was a final multicolored flash of light...and one magician collapsed to the ground, his hand severed. Emily saw blood and shuddered. She knew that a healer could reattach the hand within moments but it was still hard to imagine such pain. The winner picked up his opponent's staff, ritually broke it—there was a sound like a thunderclap as it snapped—and tossed the pieces to one side. Emily had to cover her ears as the crowd went wild. The winner waited until the wards dropped, then marched outside, waving to his fans.

The next three duels were less violent, but considerably more interesting. There must have been some careful negotiation prior to the match, Emily decided, for the participants seemed more interested in placing their spells carefully than actually winning. The crowd didn't seem too amused either, but the competitors ignored them. By the time the matches came to an end, the crowd seemed relieved. Emily tended to agree.

"They probably agreed to hobble themselves," Jade told her, as the final pair of duelists limped off the field. The duel had ended in a draw. "There are several schools that limit the type of spells you can use in a formal duel."

He winked at her as someone new stalked onto the field. Master Grey stood in the center of the arena, holding his staff above his head. Emily watched with sudden interest as the mediators announced him as the undefeated champion, three years running. The crowd went wild, shouting and screaming for their hero. To his credit, Emily decided, Master Grey didn't look impressed. Indeed, he almost seemed bored.

"He insisted that anyone who wanted to challenge him had to declare a Level Three," Jade said, as the first competitor stepped into the arena. He was a tall bulky man, stripped to the waist, with runes carved into his bare flesh. The crowd gave him a good-natured cheer as he bowed to Master Grey, then lifted his staff. "He thought it would cut down on challengers."

Emily stared at him. "This duel is to the death?"

"Yes," Jade said.

Emily opened her mouth to ask what would happen if Master Grey lost, but the Mediator blew his whistle before she could speak. Master Grey lowered his staff and waited; his opponent gazed at him, seemingly unmoving. Emily watched, puzzled, as the two magicians stared at each other, neither one making a move. They both seemed to be biding their time.

The newcomer snapped first, hurling a powerful curse at Master Grey. Master Grey blocked it with seemingly effortless ease, then dodged two more before launching his own curse back at the challenger. The challenger caught it on his staff—brilliant green-blue balefire flared around it for a long moment—then threw another curse back at Master Grey.

Emily found herself staring as the two competitors exchanged spells. Master Grey was *good*, she had to admit, good enough to be intimidating. Some of his spells actually worked on the surrounding arena, rather than on his target; one of them even turned part of the ground to quicksand, just long enough to snare his competitor. Emily felt her heartbeat starting to race as Master Grey unleashed a cutting charm, then a transfiguration spell that turned the quicksand to solid rock. His competitor held up his staff, blocking the cutting charm, but he was hopelessly trapped. A moment later, it was all over.

The crowd went wild. Emily felt sick. She'd seen death—and sudden brutal injury—but she was never comfortable with it. Master Grey held up his staff, then looked towards the wards as the next competitor was shown into the arena. Emily looked at Jade and shivered as she realized just how excited he was. His tutor had probably taught him how to duel.

"Disgusting," she said, quietly.

"It can be," Jade admitted.

Emily flushed. She hadn't realized he could hear her.

"But it can also be exciting," Jade added, seriously. "Facing someone in single combat, *beating* someone in single combat...knowing that you're alive and a victor and he isn't. It's addictive."

It must be a guy thing, Emily thought. She'd faced Shadye in single combat—and cheated. Even so, she knew how close she had come to losing everything. The entire world had been at risk.

"Come on," Jade said, holding out a hand. "We'll go get something to eat."

Emily gave him a surprised look. "You want to leave your master?"

"I think you're more important right now," Jade said. "And besides, he'll never notice."

Chapter Eight

THE NOISE OF THE CROWD FADED AWAY AS JADE LED EMILY TOWARDS A LONG LOW BUILD-ing, illuminated by magic lights hanging in the air. Inside, she could hear the sound of people talking, but garbled by a basic privacy ward that prevented her from actually understanding any of the words. A man wearing a butler's uniform met them as they entered the door and escorted them to a small room, where a candlelit table was waiting. Emily blinked in surprised as she saw it, then looked up at Jade, who smiled back at her. She was touched, despite herself. It was very romantic.

"Order whatever you like," Jade said, nodding towards the menu. "I'm buying."

Emily had to admit she was impressed as she looked down at the menu. The Empire might have spread cooking and traditions all over the world, but it was rare for a restaurant or eatery to serve more than one style of food. Here, though, there was food from all over the world, probably prepared in advance and stored in stasis compartments. Magic made preserving food so much easier than freezers and microwaves. And it tasted better too. She picked a dish of chicken cooked in cream, and lime juice. Jade picked roast beef and non-alcoholic wine.

"Master Grey is good at dueling," Jade said, when the waiter had been and gone. "What did you think?"

"He's killing his fellow magicians," Emily said, shaking her head in disbelief. "Is he mad?"

Jade looked surprised, then cast a privacy ward. "He isn't the one issuing the challenges," he pointed out, mildly. "He only set the terms of the duels."

Emily rolled her eyes. "But either he dies or his challenger dies," she countered. "Either way, the Allied Lands lose a magician."

"He can't back out or deliberately allow someone to win," Jade said. "If he did, someone would call him a coward."

Men, Emily thought. Did dueling win someone the post of most powerful magician in the world? It couldn't, she decided; she hadn't seen Void or the Grandmaster dueling with their rivals. Or Lady Barb, for that matter. It clearly wasn't necessary to duel to earn accolades.

"If someone challenged me," she said, "could I avoid having to fight?"

"Depends," Jade said, thoughtfully. "If you were a duelist, you couldn't really avoid the challenge without conceding your position without a fight. If you'd insulted someone so badly they felt the urge to wipe the smile off your face, you couldn't avoid the duel without sacrificing all the respect you'd earned. Otherwise...you could simply decline the duel without consequences."

He smiled. "But most people are too scared of you to pick a fight."

Emily shivered. Her status as the Necromancer's Bane—and now the person who had defeated a Mimic—had given her a formidable reputation, but it was largely undeserved. There was no easy way to duplicate the trick that had killed Shadye, while the Mimic had been overwhelmed by the combined power of several magicians. If Master Grey or someone on the same level challenged her to a duel, she would lose.

"Let's hope it stays that way," she muttered. She looked up, meeting Jade's eyes. "Why doesn't he like me?"

"I think he thinks you upset the natural order," Jade confessed. "He wasn't too happy over me writing to you, I can tell you."

Emily flushed. Master Tor had been the same, judging her by her reputation before he'd even met her. And Master Tor had tried hard to get her blamed for the Mimic's first attack and then expelled from Whitehall. He'd had political motives... if she'd realized just how many problems King Randor making her a baroness would cause, she might have refused the honor, even if she had to speak up in front of a giant crowd. Emily might have hoped to fly under the radar, but *Baroness* Emily was a political figure.

"I didn't mean to make life difficult for you," she mumbled. She clutched Lady Barb's pendant, silently grateful for the protective glamor. "I'm sorry."

"Don't be," Jade said. "It wasn't your fault."

"It might well have been," Emily said. "I..."

She was interrupted by the arrival of the waiter, two trays of food floating in the air behind him. Emily smiled at the display, then watched as the trays were unloaded and spells removed, allowing the aroma of the food to reach her nostrils. The smell was good, although not quite as good as some of the places she'd tried in Dragon's Den. She waited for the waiter to withdraw, then tasted the chicken. It tasted more than a little dry.

"Someone made you a political pawn," Jade said, once the waiter had vanished again. "I don't think that was your fault, no matter what Master Grey says."

Emily rubbed her forehead, feeling a headache coming on. She knew, intellectually, that people talked about her, but she was still unprepared for the reality. It hadn't been something she'd had to worry about on Earth, not when she was so utterly unimportant. Here, someone could make a decision concerning her in the White City or Alexis and she would never hear of it until it was too late.

"Still, you might want to be careful," Jade added. "King Randor might not have expected you to be more than a baroness in name only."

"I know," Emily said. The handful of lessons she'd had in estate management had only underlined just how little she actually *knew*. Aristocratic children, even Alassa, were taught the basics at their parents' knees, but Emily had only recently been ennobled. How could she hope to learn enough to keep her from depending on subordinates? "But I couldn't say no."

"He might have thought he was doing you a favor," Jade pointed out. "You saved his throne; he *had* to reward you in a manner consummate with your deeds. Most people would be delighted to be ennobled, even if they didn't have lands added as part of the deal."

Emily shuddered. *Baroness* was no empty title. She was, to all intents and purposes, the owner of hundreds of square miles of land—and thousands of people, some of whom were effectively bound to her family line. The sheer weight of responsibility had fallen on her like a hammer from above, forcing her to hire managers to handle the task. And she'd hidden from it afterwards, she knew. She didn't really comprehend what she'd been given, not at an emotional level.

"He should have given me a smaller title," she admitted. Even the smallest title brought a stipend from the Crown, one that could only be canceled in the event of outright treason. "I might have been able to handle it."

She shook her head. Stipends were one of Zangaria's major problems, although the coup attempt against King Randor had allowed him a chance to take aim at some of the useless aristocrats infesting his court. Their ancestors had done something useful and had been rewarded, but the current crop merely drew on the King's money and protested loudly when he hinted they might want to find proper jobs. But then, there weren't enough positions suitable for all of them in Zangaria.

Or at least positions consummate with their titles, she thought. *Muckraker sounds about right for most of them.*

"But then he wouldn't have given you a suitable reward," Jade said. He smiled, then changed the subject. "I understand that Lady Barb is a hard taskmaster...?"

Emily blinked, then realized that Lady Barb had told him that Emily would be busy on the first day. "She is," she confirmed. "Healing was the hardest class at Whitehall."

"Cat told me that she gave no quarter," Jade said. "And now you have her all to yourself."

Emily snorted and turned the question back on him. "What sort of person is Master Grey?"

"Tough, very tough, but fair," Jade said. "He's taught me more than I ever learned from the sergeants."

"You should have gone into Martial Magic in Fifth Year," Emily said, rather tartly. She *liked* the sergeants. Men less like her stepfather were hard to imagine. "We spent the year learning how to crack defenses and pick our path carefully through Blackhall."

"So I heard," Jade said. "And Alassa started her own *Ken* team?"

"She did," Emily said. "And she's definitely having fun."

She felt an odd flicker of envy. She'd never liked team sports on Earth, yet part of her had always envied those who could throw themselves into the game. Alassa and Imaiqah had done just that, but Emily hadn't been able to follow them. She couldn't even play for fun.

"Good for her," Jade said. "Cat had quite a lot to tell me."

Emily groaned. "What did he say?"

She listened to a somewhat warped recounting of last year at Whitehall as she finished her meal, pointing out the problems from time to time. The Allied Lands didn't have the Internet, but somehow rumors still moved at the speed of light, mutating very quickly into something utterly unrecognizable. No wonder Master Grey viewed her with dire suspicion, she decided, as she heard that she'd somehow forced Master Tor to hand in his resignation. The tutor's decision to leave the school hadn't been *her* fault.

"The only true story in all of that," she said, when Jade had finished, "was the one about us sneaking out of class to go to the library."

Jade snorted. "What were you thinking?"

Emily shook her head. Once, she'd watched a movie where the hero and his girlfriend had skipped off school and gone to an art gallery. She hadn't been unable to avoid wondering if there would be fewer complaints from the teachers if all skipping pupils had spent their day off so productively. But then, she had never felt as if she'd learned much in school on Earth.

"They were trying to teach me what I already knew," Emily admitted, finally. "And I'd taught Alassa and Imaiqah myself."

"Your class," Jade said. He laughed, quietly. "I don't even know why they made you take it."

Emily wondered, absently, just how many people knew that *she* was responsible for the New Learning. English letters and Arabic numerals had already worked a colossal transformation in the Allied Lands and there was much more to come. Merely having the ability to write and sound out words phonically made it much easier for people to learn to read and write. There might be no agreed system of spelling yet, but someone who could read could work out what a word was, even if the spelling was different. The Scribes Guilds had had a bumpy introduction to the new system, yet they'd adapted fairly well. Others hadn't been so lucky.

If the Accountants Guild knew that I'd destroyed them, she asked herself, *what would they do?*

She had a terrible feeling she knew the answer. The accountants had worked with numerals that made Latin numbers look simple, a system that took years to master. They'd taken ruthless advantage of their position too, charging their clients vast sums of money just to do their accounts. But Arabic numerals, double-entry bookkeeping, algebra and a handful of other tricks had revolutionized the world. The guild had never recovered.

"I don't know either," she admitted. But she had a very good idea. "Maybe they didn't want to call attention to what I'd done."

Jade nodded as the waiter returned, took away the dishes and offered the desert menu. Emily shook her head and, after a moment, Jade shook his head too. The waiter bowed and retreated, leaving them alone again. Emily watched him go, then looked up at Jade. She knew him well enough to know that he was nervous, even though he was trying to hide it. The sight made her feel nervous too.

"Last year," Jade said, slowly, "I...I proposed to you."

Emily nodded, without speaking. It had been no surprise to anyone, apart from her, that Jade had been interested, but he hadn't said anything until the very last day of term. But then, there were rules governing relationships within Whitehall's walls. Jade would have ended up in hot water if he'd spoken to her earlier.

She hadn't been quite sure what to make of it at the time. Part of her had to admit that she liked Jade, part of her thought she only liked him as a friend. He'd kissed her—and she'd enjoyed it—but the thought of going further bothered her deeply. In the end, she hadn't really given him an answer at all...

And that, she knew, had done him no favors. Jade wasn't...well, *her*, but he would have his own set of marriage offers from magical families. If he picked one of them, particularly after concluding his apprenticeship, he would be well-placed for the future. Marrying Emily as she'd been at the end of First Year—a stranger in a strange land, feared more than loved—wouldn't have been as good for him. It was easy to believe that he had genuine feelings for her. She hadn't had much to offer him then.

But now...? She was a baroness.

She cringed, mentally. Earth's modern-day love stories said that love could appear anywhere, among people of any class. But the past said otherwise and the Allied Lands agreed. Alassa wouldn't have had so many problems finding a husband—she still hadn't found a husband—if she hadn't been heir to the throne of Zangaria. Back then, Jade's proposal had almost been a *favor*. Now, it was socially laughable.

He'd meant well; she *knew* he'd meant well. But she wasn't even sure she wanted it.

Jade cleared his throat. Emily realized she'd retreated into her thoughts.

"I...know that it must be awkward for you now," he said. "But I gave my word."

He hadn't, Emily recalled. He'd made her no promises. She hadn't asked for them.

But her feelings were a tangled mess. Did she want him? Had he found someone else? The thought stung, even though logically she knew it shouldn't. She hadn't promised him anything either; they certainly hadn't agreed not to look elsewhere. And it had to have been hard for him, studying under a man who disliked Emily herself.

"No, you didn't," she said, very quietly.

Jade didn't disagree.

Emily winced, inwardly. She knew she should cut through the tangled mess and talk bluntly, but she couldn't bring herself to do it. The fear of hurting him was too strong. She would sooner have faced the Warden with nothing more solid than a feeble excuse. And she wasn't even sure what she felt herself.

"I liked you—I still like you," Jade said. He stared down at the table, unwilling or unable to meet her eyes. "But things have changed. You're a...noblewoman now."

"I can be a noblewoman and a magician," Emily pointed out. She was hardly the only noblewoman with magic; Alassa had been *born* noble, as well as magical. "But I know what you mean."

She wished she'd sorted out her own feelings beforehand, but she'd shied away from the thought. If she'd known—she *had* known. But she hadn't done anything about it.

He doesn't want me anymore, she thought. She could understand his feelings—in the cold-blooded calculus that governed aristocratic marriages, she was well above his station—but it still hurt. If he married her now, he would be little more than her consort, forever tied to her apron strings. No one would take him seriously.

And Jade was ambitious. He wanted to make a name for himself.

"Look at me," she said, quietly. Jade looked up, meeting her eyes. "Did you find someone else?"

Jade shook his head, wordlessly. Emily wondered, absently, if that was actually true. One advantage of being in Martial Magic was spending time with older boys, boys who sometimes forgot that Emily was young and female. They'd talked, unaware that she could hear them, about a brothel in Dragon's Den. It was quite possible that Jade had indulged too...

"I understand," she said, softly. It hurt–and yet it was also a relief. "Can we just be friends?"

Jade looked relieved, just for a moment. Emily felt a sudden sharp desire to hurt him, to lash out verbally or physically, a desire she forced back into the back of her mind. At least he'd tried to talk to her, openly. She mentally gave him credit for that. Boys found it hard to talk about their emotions, almost as hard as she found it herself. She'd never talked openly to anyone until she'd met Alassa and Imaiqah.

"Friends," he agreed. He held out a hand. Emily shook it firmly. "Do you want to go to a play tomorrow?"

Emily found herself torn between laughing and crying. "A play?"

"There are some actors here," Jade said. "They're putting on a performance tomorrow–I think it's *The Folly of The Heart.*"

Emily gave him a sharp look, then nodded. "I'd be glad to go," she said. It wasn't entirely untrue. She hadn't seen any plays in the Allied Lands–or on Earth, for that matter. The closest had been an amateur performance of *Romeo and Juliet* at school, which hadn't gone very well. Too many people had giggled when Romeo kissed Juliet. "And thank you."

She stood, feeling the urge to get back to her bedroom and think about what had happened.

"I'll pay for half the dinner," she said, as Jade followed her. "It isn't fair for you to pay all of it."

"It isn't a problem," Jade assured her. The waiter reappeared, holding out a piece of elaborately-decorated parchment. Jade took it, passed him a pair of gold coins, then shoved the bill into his pocket. "Really."

Emily frowned. The value of coins–even gold coins–was variable, but she'd never eaten a meal that cost so much in Dragon's Den. Clearly, the cooks had a captive audience.

"I'll walk you home," Jade said. "Coming?"

Shaking her head, Emily followed him out the door and into the darkness.

Chapter Nine

"WELL," LADY BARB SAID, THE FOLLOWING MORNING. "DO YOU WANT TO TALK ABOUT it?"

Emily shook her head as she sat down at the table, rubbing at her eyes. She hadn't slept at all, if only because she had replayed her conversation with Jade over and over in her head. Part of her regretted agreeing to be just friends, part of her was relieved. And yet she still felt...*snubbed*, for want of a better word. Her feelings were a mess.

"No, thank you," she said, finally. "I just need some sleep."

"I noticed you didn't sleep," Lady Barb said. "Why didn't you take something to make you sleep?"

Emily's eyes narrowed, then she realized that the wards monitored her condition as long as she was in the house. Parents tended to use them to keep an eye on their children; Whitehall's wards alerted the staff if someone was seriously hurt or bullied by someone in a higher year. It wasn't something she liked, she had to admit. She'd spent most of her life hiding from her stepfather's gaze.

"I didn't feel like it," she said, regretfully.

"You should have two more potions to brew," Lady Barb said. She placed a plate of bacon and eggs in front of Emily, then reached out and touched her forehead. "I would suggest reading books, though. You're bleeding magic."

Emily looked down at her palm, then realized what Lady Barb meant. Magic responded to emotion and, the more she used her magic, the easier it was for her power to slip out of control and produce unpredictable effects. Most new magicians, she'd been told, were discovered after they produced their first spark of magic when hurt or upset. Emily herself was something of an exception to that rule, but only because she'd grown up on Earth.

"I'm sorry," she said, slowly. "I..."

"Just go to the library after breakfast or take a sleeping potion," Lady Barb told her. She sat down facing Emily and opened a parchment letter. "We have our official orders."

Emily lifted an eyebrow, so Lady Barb held out the parchment for her to read. It was written in the old language, forcing her to struggle to decipher it. Not for the first time, she wondered just how Whitehall had managed to get so far without phonetic letters. If it hadn't been for translation spells, she doubted half of the students could even read. She'd certainly needed one for her first year at the school.

The orders seemed simple enough, but the writer had padded them out. Lady Barb and her apprentice—Emily wasn't mentioned by name—were ordered to walk through the Cairngorm Mountains, helping the locals and searching for traces of magic. If they found anyone with new magic, they were to provide basic instruction and then invite the new magician to Whitehall or one of the other magical schools. There wasn't anything more specific, much to Emily's surprise, apart from a note about wages and discretionary funds. Emily was barely being paid enough to stay alive. Somehow, she wasn't surprised. Her experience on Earth had taught her that student workers were often grossly underpaid.

"Interesting," Lady Barb said. "Here."

She passed Emily a second note. Emily read it, quickly. It warned that a handful of children had been reported missing in the Cairngorms, all too young to have developed magic. Emily looked up, worried. Missing children were never a good sign.

"Could be werewolves," Lady Barb said. "There's a werewolf pack on the other side of the mountains. Or vampires. Or plain old human unpleasantness. We'll see what we see when we get there."

Emily nodded. "There's a letter for you," Lady Barb added. "The Grandmaster forwarded it here. No one else knows where you are."

Jade does, Emily thought as she took the letter. *And so does Master Grey.*

The letter was enfolded in creamy white paper, sealed with a spell that ensured that only the recipient could read it. Emily frowned down at it for a long moment, then opened it with her bare hands. She knew from experience that using anything else, even a paper knife, might convince the spell that someone unauthorized was trying to read it, destroying the paper and erasing the message. Inside, there was another sheet of expensive paper. She pulled it out and read it, carefully.

"They're asking me to host the next Faire in Zangaria?"

Lady Barb looked up, surprised. "Interesting," she said. "I wonder how many deals were made behind the curtains."

Emily hesitated, rereading the letter. It was simple and quite uninformative, as if the writer had assumed that she would know what he was talking about. He wanted the next magical gathering to be held in Zangaria, in Cockatrice. Emily read it a third time, then looked up at Lady Barb. The older woman seemed more amused than puzzled.

"Well," Emily said. "Should I agree?"

Lady Barb considered it. "The Faire is traditionally neutral," she said. "It won't reflect badly on you to host it, if you wish to do so."

"And I should show off some of the other innovations in Zangaria," Emily said, thoughtfully. "Let word spread far and wide."

She gritted her teeth. Some innovations had spread far already, others were moving slower than she would have preferred...and some she would prefer to keep under wraps. But she wasn't entirely sure just how many innovations Lin had managed to steal before she'd vanished from Whitehall. It was quite possible that whoever was backing her knew about gunpowder, cannons and steam engines. Emily hadn't expected to keep the latter a secret–they'd shown off a very basic locomotive in Zangaria–but the others would really upset the balance of power.

"It would," Lady Barb agreed, tonelessly. "Still, it's your choice. No one will think any more or less of you if you say yes or no."

Emily looked down at the letter one final time, then made up her mind. "I'll write to Bryon," she said. "He can have permission to arrange everything and I'll leave it in his hands."

Lady Barb shrugged. "Go to the library after you finish breakfast," she said, again. "Or go back to bed."

Emily nodded. Once the breakfast was finished, she walked back into the library and settled down in front of the books Lady Barb had found for her. The final book on enchantment talked about anchoring a pocket dimension to an object, outlining the basic spells to create a trunk that was bigger on the inside than on the outside. Emily had seen the spells before, but these were actually simpler. Yodel's book had skipped quite a few stages in creating pocket dimensions. She worked her way through the book, feeling exhaustion slipping up on her...

The next thing she knew, someone was poking her in the arm. She started awake, embarrassed. Lady Aylia had told her that sometimes students had to be awakened in the library, before their snores grew loud enough to trigger the security spells. Lady Barb laughed at her confusion, then helped her sit upright. Emily's arms ached from lying on the books.

"You're lucky my father didn't see you doing that," Lady Barb said, dryly. "He would have been furious."

Emily nodded, blearily. "I didn't mean to fall asleep..."

"You've been asleep for nearly six hours," Lady Barb told her. "I think you probably needed it."

She looked down at Emily's notes. "What are you planning *this* time?"

Emily had to smile at the resigned note in the older woman's voice. "A protective shelter," she said, seriously. "A pocket dimension capable of hiding someone from pursuit."

Lady Barb frowned. "You do realize that such a dimension might not be safe?"

"I know," Emily said.

The books hadn't been too clear, but she'd reasoned out that time did funny things inside pocket dimensions. It didn't flow at all within her trunk, keeping whatever she'd locked inside in stasis, while other pocket dimensions sped up time or slowed it down. Whitehall didn't seem to have those problems, but Whitehall had a nexus for power. There was no way a single magician could produce anything akin to the school.

"You'd also have problems getting out," Lady Barb added. "I don't think you could open a gateway back to the normal world."

Emily scowled. She had a feeling that the energy levels required to get into the pocket dimension were much smaller than the energy levels required to get out. There was no way to be sure, though. Whitehall's best researchers hadn't come up with a way of measuring magic like electricity.

"I could program the dimension to open up automatically after a set period of time," Emily said. "If the dimension was still anchored to this world..."

"It might work," Lady Barb said, after a moment of silent contemplation. "However, I would advise you to be very careful. Being trapped in a pocket dimension might be fatal."

Emily nodded.

"Tell me," Lady Barb said, changing the subject. "Did you make any plans with Jade?"

"We're going to see a play tonight," Emily said. "I..."

Lady Barb studied her for a long moment. Emily scowled, inwardly. She wasn't quite used to the idea of someone looking after her, even Lady Barb. God knew Emily's mother had been more interested in drinking herself to death than paying attention to her daughter. Emily could have worn the skimpiest of clothes and stayed out all night; her mother would never have noticed. But Lady Barb definitely would.

Emily wasn't sure how she felt about that either. It felt nice to have someone looking out for her, but at the same time she didn't like having someone looking over her shoulder. Her mother had betrayed her and she didn't really want another mother, no matter how nice it felt to have someone caring. Maybe she should compromise at big sister.

"Make sure you have a proper nap tonight," Lady Barb ordered, finally. If she had doubts about Emily meeting Jade again, she kept them to herself. "I'll expect you to catch up with your potions tomorrow, or you won't be going out again."

Yes, mother, Emily thought, even though she knew it was immature. She also knew why Lady Barb wanted her to master the potions. In the mountains, there were no alchemists or apothecaries. She would have to make the potions the locals needed or they would have to go without. Lady Barb would be too busy discussing other matters with them.

"I will," she promised.

"Good," Lady Barb said. She made a show of checking her watch. "The play is at nineteen bells, so I suggest you have a wash and then dress in a different set of robes."

Emily looked down at her matted robes and scowled. They were designed to survive everything from alchemical accidents to pranks played by the students on each other, but they couldn't disguise the fact she'd fallen asleep in them. Standing up, she nodded to Lady Barb and walked out of the library, leaving the books behind. A moment later, she heard Lady Barb clearing her throat loudly.

"Watch your notes," she warned, picking up the pieces of paper and shoving them at Emily. "You never know who might be watching."

Flushing, Emily took the notes and returned to her bedroom, where she buried them under a handful of security wards. She would have to copy them down into her notebooks later, she knew; there was no point in erecting solid wards over the pieces of paper and parchment she'd used in the library. Cursing, she removed the pendant and looked at herself in the mirror. Her face was pale and there were dark shadows under her eyes. The sight bothered her more than she cared to admit. Walking into the bathroom, she undressed and washed quickly, allowing the cold water to shock her awake. She was barely dressed again when she felt the wards quiver in welcome.

"That's Jade," Lady Barb called, as Emily hurriedly pulled the pendant over her head. "Be careful, all right?"

Emily nodded, although she knew Lady Barb couldn't see her. Just how much had the older woman guessed? She had far more experience than Emily; she'd probably read the full story off Emily's face in the morning. And then a sleepless night wasn't a good sign...shaking her head, she walked downstairs and nodded to Jade. He'd clearly exchanged a few words with Lady Barb.

"Thank you for coming," Emily said, as they walked through the gates. "I had no idea where to meet you."

Jade looked at her, surprised. "What did you say to her?" He asked. "She was quite insistent that I should behave myself."

"Nothing," Emily said, wondering just what conclusions Lady Barb had drawn. Did she think Jade had molested her in some way? But Jade wasn't that sort of person. Besides, molesting a student would draw the wrath of the Grandmaster...and Lady Barb herself. And Void, in Emily's case. "I just didn't sleep very well."

Jade said nothing, leaving Emily wondering just how easy it would be to maintain a friendship after a semi-relationship. They walked down the hill and into a larger tent, the largest Emily had yet seen. Inside, it had been set up like a theatre, with a large stage at one end of the room and uncomfortable-looking benches lined up and crammed with people. Emily smiled at the sight of a handful of comfy chairs, clearly reserved for the elderly or important people, then sat down on one of the benches. Jade sat next to her and cast a silencing ward as the tent slowly filled to the limits.

"This play dates back to the days of the Empire," Jade explained, as the magical lights started to dim, focusing attention on the stage. "The basic plot hasn't changed at all."

Emily had her doubts about that, but she kept them to herself as the actors appeared on stage and the performance began. Most of the special effects were literal magic, she saw, more interesting and exciting than any play performed on Earth. The plot itself seemed a little confusing at first, until around thirty minutes into the performance. It clicked in Emily's mind.

"But love is mine to take and hold," the male lead proclaimed. "Love to be found where I choose."

"And yet, love blinds one to the truth," the secondary female lead warned. "You cannot hope to gift the gifted."

Emily couldn't help thinking of *Doctor Faustus*. The male lead had fallen in love with a mundane woman, a woman possessing no magic at all. It wasn't a choice his family approved, unsurprisingly, and they were very unpleasant to the poor girl. The actress playing the mundane woman was turned into a pig, a goat and a donkey in the first act alone, despite the best efforts of her lover. And then her lover had made a bargain with a demon to grant her magic powers. But the price turned out to be more than they could pay.

"You ordained that power would be granted in spite of the gods," an actor proclaimed, calling out the male lead. "Did you always assume it came without a price?"

"I loved her, I know, and yet I love her still," the male lead countered. "But I no longer know why."

Emily shivered. The demon's price for granting the woman magic powers had been their love for one another, all that held them together. They might still be physical lovers, but the sensation of true love was gone. How could the relationship last when they were little more than friends with benefits? In the end, the couple parted, no longer truly lovers.

"The play is popular," Jade explained, when the actors finally took their leave. "But I don't know why."

"I think I do," Emily said. Perhaps it was her studies on Earth, but she thought she understood. "It's a warning."

She scowled. It was a warning to children of magical families, warning them not to marry powerless mundanes. The power imbalance in the relationship could destroy it, completely. But really...what was the difference between a man being strong enough to beat his wife when she disobeyed him and a woman having the power to turn her man into a frog for being a bastard? Power wasn't just counted in magic.

But a wife could fight back against her husband, she thought. *A mundane couldn't fight a magician.*

She allowed Jade to lead her to a smaller eatery, then sat down beside him for dinner. It was easier talking to him now, she decided, even though he seemed to want to spend most of the time talking about his apprenticeship. Emily listened, filing everything he told her away in her mind. One day, she knew, she might well have a full apprenticeship herself. But she didn't want it with someone so determined to kill anyone who challenged him.

"It's not common for a male sorcerer to take a female apprentice," Jade cautioned her. "I think the only exceptions were when the sorcerer was more interested in men than women."

Emily smiled. Homosexuality wasn't taboo, but it was hedged around by customs and traditions that seemed to change depending on wealth or social class. A magician wouldn't draw any raised eyebrows if he was doing the penetrating, yet he would be sneered at if he allowed himself to be penetrated. Emily suspected the taboo said more about men than anyone would care to admit. There was nothing comparable for lesbians.

"We're due to leave tomorrow," Jade said, softly. "Will you write to me?"

"I will," Emily promised. Hadn't she been doing that all term? "Where are you going?"

"I'm not sure," Jade confessed.

He led her back to the house, then stopped outside and gave her a tight hug. Emily returned it, but she felt nothing, no sense that she wanted it to go further. She'd felt more the first time he'd kissed her, almost a year ago. Was there something wrong with her?

"I will write," she said, pushing her thoughts aside. There would be time to think about them later. "And you take care of yourself."

"You too," Jade said. "I'll see you soon."

Emily watched him walk away into the darkness, then turned and stepped through the gate into the house.

Chapter Ten

T HE NEXT FEW DAYS PASSED SURPRISINGLY QUICKLY. EMILY SPENT HER MORNINGS BREWING potions and her afternoons reading her way through Lady Barb's library or writing letters to her friends. Lady Barb took her around the Faire one day and introduced her to a handful of people, but most of them weren't particularly interested in just another apprentice. Emily rather preferred their indifference to the interest they would show if they knew who she actually was.

On the final day, Lady Barb took her into a different chamber and produced a small pencil-sized stick from her bag. Emily stared down at it, unable to escape a nagging sense of familiarity. It was tiny, yet somehow she knew she already knew what it was; she just couldn't place it. Lady Barb snorted and removed the miniaturization spell. The staff snapped back to its normal size in her hand.

"Your staff," Lady Barb said. She held it out for Emily to take. "I trust you recall how to use it—and the dangers of using it?"

Emily nodded. Sergeant Miles had taught her how to shape spells and embed them within the wood, but he'd also warned her of the dangers of excessive use. It was far too easy to lose the ability to cast spells without a staff or a wand...and, if she did, she would be dependent on someone else to prepare the wand for her. Alassa, thankfully, had mastered the art after spending years using a wand, but Emily wasn't sure she could match it. Only sheer determination had kept Alassa trying until she'd gained the skill.

She took the staff in her hand, feeling it quivering against her bare palm. It felt... seductive, the magic in her responding to the handful of spells lodged within the wood. She had to smile, wondering what a psychologist would make of men using staffs, then carefully let go of it. As always, it stood on its end without falling over.

"You are to carry it with you, but you are not to use it without permission," Lady Barb told her. "Shrink it down and keep it hidden."

Emily nodded. She was seventeen—at least she was fairly *sure* she was seventeen—and it was rare for anyone to start working with staffs until they were at least twenty. Using it in public would suggest either vast power or little skill, both of which would attract unwanted attention. She cast the shrinking spell, then stuck the staff up her sleeve. If nothing else, she could use it to fight physically, rather than using magic. Sergeant Miles had taught her how to use a staff for that too.

"Good," Lady Barb said, once the staff was safely concealed. "Have you packed everything?"

Emily nodded. She'd spent half of the previous day washing her robes without using magic, then hanging them on the line to dry. Lady Barb hadn't been very understanding when Emily had asked why they couldn't use magic, pointing out that they had to learn not to use magic for everything. Emily couldn't help wondering what Whitehall would make of a washing machine or an iron. It was astonishing just how easy life was, in many ways, on Earth.

"Splendid," Lady Barb said. "Come with me. I have something to show you."

Emily followed her back into the library, then stopped in front of a bookcase. For a moment, she thought they were returning to the spellchamber, but it was very definitely a different bookcase. Behind it, there was another staircase leading down into the darkness. Lady Barb cast a light spell, then started to walk down the stairs. Emily followed her, nervously. The last time hadn't been fun at all.

She swallowed. "How many secret passages are there like this?"

Lady Barb turned and grinned at her. "That's a secret," she said. "But there are quite a few."

Emily smiled, trying to calm her nerves. Secret passages seemed to be common in Whitehall, Zangaria's castles and now magical houses. But it did make a certain kind of sense, she knew. The Grandmaster, King Randor and the others would want a way of moving around without being seen—and besides, looking for the passages in Whitehall was one of the great student traditions. Emily knew where a handful of them were, but there were dozens of others.

They reached the bottom and stopped, on the edge of a patch of earth. Emily watched as the light spell grew brighter, revealing patches of earth intermingled with stone, as if it were a giant chess board. No, she realized suddenly, as she saw the runes carved into the stone; it was a graveyard, a crypt. None of the names below the runes were familiar.

"My family members have been buried here for centuries," Lady Barb said, very softly. In the distance, Emily was sure she could hear dripping water. "One day, I'll be buried here too."

Emily looked up, peering into the darkness. It was impossible to tell how far the chamber stretched, but it had to be colossal. Hundreds of people could be buried here, deep below the ground. She looked back at Lady Barb and saw that she was pale, suddenly much older.

"When I was a child," Lady Barb said softly, "we were told that the dead held parties here while the living slept. I always envied them, because my father wasn't inclined to hold many parties in his hall. One night, I slipped down into the crypt and saw...nothing."

She shook her head. "My mother's people taught that the dead are reborn as part of the world surrounding us," she added. "I like to believe that's true."

Emily felt a moment of sympathy. As a child, she'd known that Santa Claus wasn't real; he'd never visited her house. She'd never really understood until she was older why so many other children had believed in him. They hadn't lost the illusions that came with being a child, the belief that their parents could fix anything and the Tooth Fairy was real. Emily had never been allowed such illusions.

Lady Barb turned. Emily hesitated, then called out to her. "Why did you bring me here?"

"I wanted you to see it," Lady Barb said. She walked up the stairs, but her voice floated back. "Don't linger, Emily. There are dangers down here."

Emily took one final look at the nondescript patches of earth, then followed her up the stairs and into the light. Lady Barb's expression was tightly controlled, suggesting that she was upset about something. The last time she'd looked like that, she'd been scolding Emily, Alassa and Imaiqah for skiving off their classes. This time, however, she didn't look unhappy with Emily, but someone else.

"Grab your bag, then make sure you have everything," Lady Barb said. "I'm going to be sealing the house and I will be very upset if I have to unseal it before the end of the summer."

"Understood," Emily said. She looked at Lady Barb for a long moment. "Are you all right?"

"Go," Lady Barb snapped.

Emily fled. She'd never been very good at noticing when someone was hurting, or when someone was feeling anything at all. It had surprised her when she'd realized just how badly depressed Alassa had become, or that Jade was interested in her...she pushed the thought aside as she walked into her room and picked up her bag, then checked around for anything she might have left behind. The notes she'd written had been copied into her notebooks and then reduced to dust in the fire. Taking the bag, she walked back downstairs. Lady Barb was waiting at the door, a pinched expression on her face and a wand in her hand.

"I'll meet you outside the gates," Lady Barb said. "Just wait for me there."

It took ten minutes before Lady Barb joined her, putting the wand into her bag as she closed the gates behind them. The wards shivered back into place, sealing the house. Emily wondered, absently, just how long they would last before they collapsed into nothingness without a magician to sustain them, but there was no way to ask. There were questions it was unwise to ask out loud.

"Come on," Lady Barb said. "Our transport is waiting at the other side of the Faire."

Half of the visitors had already departed, Emily discovered, as they walked through the area where the Faire had been. The others were busy shutting up their stalls and loading their remaining goods onto carts, protected by magicians or armed mercenaries. Emily reminded herself, sharply, of her plans to set up a proper bank. It was something she intended to do, either in Cockatrice or somewhere else, once she had enough money to make it work. But she hadn't worked out all the details yet.

"They normally sell some books cheaply after the Faire officially ends," Lady Barb commented. "Would you like to stop and see what they have?"

Emily hesitated, tempted, then shook her head. "I'd have to carry them all, wouldn't I?"

"Yep," Lady Barb said. She smiled, brightly. "But I wouldn't have minded."

"Of course not," Emily agreed. "I'd be carrying them."

Lady Barb laughed as they walked past the half-dismantled stalls and headed towards a number of gipsy-like wagons. They looked almost too small to be real, she saw, as if they were expensive toys rather than real wagons. A handful of young children, some of them wearing ragged clothes, were running around them, playing a game of chase. Behind them, their older relatives were slowly loading some of the wagons with supplies and the remains of their stalls.

A dark-skinned girl who looked no older than Emily herself stood and walked over to meet them. "Karman," Lady Barb said, formally, "I would like to introduce Millie, my apprentice. Millie, this is Karman of the Diddakoi Travellers."

"Pleased to meet you," Karman said. Her voice was oddly accented in a manner Emily didn't recognize. "You are welcome among us, if you come in peace."

"I do," Emily said, formally. She couldn't help a flicker of envy as she studied Karman. The girl was naturally beautiful, without the inhuman perfection of Alassa. Her long dark hair reached all the way down to her thighs. There was a suppleness to her body that suggested she spent most of her time in the open air. "I thank you for accepting us."

"We will leave in an hour, we hope," Karman said, addressing Lady Barb. "You will ride in the guest wagon."

Emily couldn't help being charmed as they walked past the family wagons. They were decorated with carved wood, tiny icons and runes, almost imperceptible behind a concealing glamor. The guest wagon was larger, but the bunk beds were tiny and there was no room to swing a mouse, let alone a cat. And there was someone inside already. Emily blinked in surprise as she recognized the singer from the first day of the Faire. The girl looked back at her shyly.

"We don't bite," Lady Barb assured the girl, dryly. "Don't worry about us."

The girl would have no problems in the bunk beds, Emily saw, but both she and Lady Barb would have real problems. Even Imaiqah, who was shorter than Emily, couldn't have fitted into one of the bunks safely. There were certainly no charms expanding the space inside the wagon. Lady Barb saw her face and grinned, mischievously.

"We'd normally sleep under the stars," Lady Barb told her. "Unless it was raining, of course."

She motioned for Emily to climb into the wagon, then left her and the singer alone. Emily exchanged glances with the young girl—at a guess, she couldn't be more than thirteen—then opened her bag and found a book. She was engrossed in it when Lady Barb returned, leading a large horse by the reins. The horse looked larger than any of the riding horses Emily had seen, but definitely tamer. Emily smiled in relief as Lady Barb hooked the horse to the wagon, piece by piece. Alassa might like riding over the countryside at breakneck pace, jumping hedges and ditches with abandon, but Emily had never liked riding. She always had the impression that the horse was just biding its time before throwing her off and bolting.

"Most people sit on the edge of the wagon and watch the countryside go by," Lady Barb pointed out, as the first wagon started to move. The guest wagon, it seemed, would be at the very rear of the small convoy. "Don't you want to see where we're going?"

Emily sighed, put the book aside and peered into the distance. A handful of mountains could be seen, rising up until their peaks were hidden in the clouds. Mapping wasn't one of her skills, even after months spent working with the sergeants on following map-based directions, but she was fairly sure that the mountains were the Cairngorms.

"Right," Lady Barb said, when Emily asked. "The Travellers won't be going up the mountains themselves, but they'll let us off when we finally reach the bottom of the mountainside. There's a road there we can follow until the first village."

Emily nodded, feeling nervous. The first village was where their mission would truly begin and, despite all the preparation, she felt unready.

It was a bitter thought. *I have risked my life, for my friends*, she thought, *but why would anyone put other lives in my hands?*

She shuddered. There were no shortage of ways to make mistakes that would risk lives, if she were trying to heal, or poison someone, if she made a potion that went bad...she swallowed at the thought, shivering. What if she made a mistake and someone died?

She wanted to crawl back into the wagon and hide, but instead she found herself looking at the countryside as the convoy moved onwards. The disorganized woodland slowly gave way to fields, with peasants working the farms and a small castle in the distance. She guessed that Lady Barb's extended family owned the land where the Faire had been held, while the territory outside it was owned by the local nobility.

"I should have read more about this area," she muttered.

"Yes, you should," Lady Barb agreed. "Did you read the material I gave you on the Cairngorms?"

Emily nodded. It hadn't sounded very welcoming. The region had been ruled by a king for the first fifty years after the Empire had collapsed, but then something had happened to the monarchy and the Mountain Lords had ruled the territory ever since. Reading between the lines, Emily suspected that the lords had actually assassinated their monarch. Relations between them and the Allied Lands were fragile at the best of times, with only the distant threat of the necromancers to keep them working together.

"You'll need to keep it in mind at all times," Lady Barb warned. "We don't need to get entangled in local politics."

"I understand," Emily said, silently reminding herself to reread the material. Lady Barb had told her she could keep that particular set of notes in mind. "But what happens if we do?"

"We try to get out of it," Lady Barb said.

The farmland gave way to a river running down towards the sea, too deep and rapid for them to dare to cross. Instead, the wagons turned and headed northwards until they found a bridge and crossed over. Emily felt an odd shiver of magic as they passed over the running water, but couldn't attach a name to the sensation. Lady Barb didn't seem surprised when she pointed it out.

"There's often traces of magic in water," Lady Barb explained. "Didn't you learn that from Professor Thande?"

Emily nodded, embarrassed. Alchemy was all about releasing the natural magic in raw materials. Water was normally neutral, but it could pick up magic and transfer it elsewhere, under the right conditions. She couldn't help wondering what such magic would do to someone who drank the water. Perhaps, she decided, it accounted for the appearance of magic talents. She'd read a fantasy story where a magic fountain had gifted its first drinkers with magic powers.

"I did," she confessed.

"My parents wanted me to go to school," the singer said, piping up suddenly. "But my uncles said no."

"That's not uncommon among Travellers," Lady Barb said. "They're not counted as new magicians, so their fees are rarely paid by the Allied Lands. Most of them have to learn from their parents and never really qualify as trained magicians. My mother might not have let me go, if I'd stayed with her."

Emily looked at the singer, feeling an odd hint of pity. She was a good singer, one who could charm anyone who heard her...and she would never have a chance to develop her magical talent. Her family considered it more important to let her sing for money than pay for her to go to Whitehall. But there were other sources of cash...

I could fund her, Emily thought, wondering if Lady Barb would read her face. *I have the money.*

She looked down at the girl, silently resolving to discuss the matter with Lady Barb as soon as they were alone. Whitehall wasn't *that* expensive compared to her income from Cockatrice; she could easily fund one student. Hell, she could fund a dozen students and never notice the loss. But she had no idea of the practicalities of the situation.

Lady Barb gave her a sharp look, as if she had understood what Emily was thinking. "Do you want to take the reins for a while?"

Emily shook her head. She didn't trust horses, even horses that acted docile.

"I'll take them," the singer said. "Horses like me...except when I tried to clean them as a kid."

"If you like," Lady Barb said. "What's your name?"

"Jasmine," the singer told her. There was a hint of pain in her voice. "Just plain Jasmine. My parents died years ago."

Poor girl, Emily thought, bitterly. *She loved her parents before they left her.*

Chapter Eleven

THE SUN WAS SETTING AS THE CONVOY PULLED INTO A CLEARING IN THE MIDDLE OF A FOR-est. Emily jumped down from the wagon, her body aching from sitting too long, and stretched until she had worked some of the kinks out of her muscles. Lady Barb stepped down with more dignity, then released the horse and led the beast over to a place he could pick at the grass. Emily watched as the Travellers organized their wagons and started to prepare dinner. She wanted to help, but she wasn't sure what to do.

"Set up the cauldron," Lady Barb ordered, when she returned. "I agreed to provide them with pain-relief potions, ones using Whitehall's specific recipe."

Emily blinked in surprise. She'd never heard of a specific recipe from Whitehall. As far as she knew, the potions were fairly commonplace—and even if they'd started out unique, someone would have analyzed and duplicated them by now. But she pushed the thought aside and dutifully unloaded the small cauldron from Lady Barb's bag, followed by a small handful of ingredients. Painkiller potion was fairly easy to brew.

She lit a small fire, carefully placed the cauldron over the heat and filled it with water. Jasmine sat down next to her and watched, saying nothing, as the water slowly started to bubble. A handful of young boys came up too, but walked away disappointed when they discovered that Emily wasn't using toad's eyes, fish eggs or anything else equally gross. Emily had to smile at their reactions; normally, she passionately disliked cutting up small animals and insects. No wonder, she decided, most alchemists were male.

Once the potion was cooling, she sat back and studied the Traveller family, trying to work out who was who. In Zangaria, it would be blindingly obvious who was in charge—and their sons and daughters would wear their colors. Here, with everyone wearing simple ragged clothing and little in the way of jewelry, it was hard to tell. Everyone adult either looked young, not much older than Emily herself, or old enough to pass for her grandparents. She wasn't even sure who were the mothers and fathers of the dozens of kids running around the encampment.

"They don't take blood relations as being all-important," Lady Barb explained, when she returned from speaking with the older Travellers. "A child born to a Traveller family will have at least five or six mothers and fathers, no matter who actually sired the child or gave birth to him. It's a loving environment, but it can be a little stifling at times."

Emily wasn't so sure about that. The children were running wild, despite shouts from an older girl who seemed to be their designated nursemaid. There was a look on her face of quiet desperation, reminding Emily of Imaiqah as she'd been on the first day she and Emily had met. The older girl eventually dragged two of the boys back to the fire and plunked them down in front of a stern-looking elder man. Emily couldn't help noticing that the man winked at the boys as soon as the girl's back was turned.

The Traveller adults seemed surprisingly varied. Half of the adults looked as though they'd grown up in Germany, complete with blond hair and blue eyes that would have made Hitler proud, the remainder being a strange mixture of ethnic groups. She saw a young woman who looked Chinese, a man with black skin and an older woman who might have been Indian, although her skin was so wrinkled it was hard to be sure. The children seemed to be mixed race, like many of the magical families. Emily reminded herself that racism—at least among normal humans—was largely unknown among the families. They found it more useful to combine genetic heritages from all over the globe.

And then they take it out on werewolves and gorgons, she thought, cynically. *What's the point of discriminating against humans when there are non-humans about?*

"You must have found it hard to adapt," Emily said, looking up at Lady Barb. "How did they treat you?"

"I did," Lady Barb said. Her lips quirked with hidden amusement. "My father wasn't quite as bad as King Randor when it came to spoiling his daughter, but I was the apple of his eye. I was not always a very well behaved child. My mother...was not amused."

She leaned over and checked the potion, carefully. "Good work," she said, finally. "Let it finish cooling, then they can drain it into bottles for themselves."

Emily felt a flush of pride. She'd never really been praised by her mother, and her stepfather would sooner have joined his wife in a bottle than offer an encouraging word. And there was no point to praise at school, not on Earth. She'd known all too well that it was utterly pointless to work hard. But Lady Barb's praise meant something to her. She wasn't someone who gave praise easily.

"Thank you," she said. "What are we going to do now?"

"It doesn't look like rain," Lady Barb said, looking up at the darkening sky. High overhead, the stars were starting to glimmer into existence. "Fetch the blankets from the wagon and we'll sleep under the stars."

Emily nodded, just as a young boy ran up to them, carrying two bowls of stew and a pair of spoons. Lady Barb took them, smiled at the boy and passed one of the bowls to Emily. Emily sniffed it, decided it smelled good, and took one of the spoons. She was careful not to ask what went into the stew, knowing that it might put her off eating it. She'd watched the sergeants make food from ingredients they'd scrounged from the surrounding countryside more than once and it never failed to bother her. But she was the only person at Whitehall who *would* be bothered.

Jasmine walked off, back towards the fire. Moments later, Emily heard her voice drifting back as she started to sing. She felt a shiver of envy—on Earth, Jasmine would probably have had the talent to escape being born in poverty—before realizing that she was being silly. Talent and fame didn't always go together. But then, she'd never shared the music tastes of the other girls on Earth. She'd never really had an opportunity to develop tastes at all.

She looked over at Lady Barb. "Jasmine should go to Whitehall," she said, seriously. "Can I sponsor her?"

Lady Barb frowned. "You'd need to speak with her uncles," she said, after a moment's thought. She smiled, but it didn't quite touch her eyes. "Do you even know the girl well enough to make such an offer?"

Emily scowled. Lady Barb was right. She barely knew Jasmine...and she was considering making a fairly sizable financial commitment to the young girl's education. But there was something about Jasmine that reminded Emily of herself, a girl caught in a family situation she couldn't escape on her own. *Emily* hadn't escaped on her own. Shadye had kidnapped her, stealing her from Earth. If he hadn't tried to kill her immediately afterwards, Emily suspected that he wouldn't have had any problems turning her to the darkness.

"But it isn't uncommon," Lady Barb added, softly. "You do realize that you'd be creating a permanent tie between you and her?"

"I think so," Emily said. The richer magical families often sponsored new magicians—or magicians from poorer magical bloodlines—in exchange for later favors. Imaiqah's fees had been paid by Whitehall's fund for new magicians, but several others she knew were committed to their sponsors. Some of them would probably wind up marrying into the magical families, adding their wild magic to the family's genetics. "But I wouldn't want much from her."

"I'm glad to hear it," Lady Barb said, dryly. There was a long pause as she looked up at the stars, then over at the gathering Travellers. "If you wish, I will speak with her current guardians on your behalf. Maybe, in fact, I will not mention that *you* wish to do it. But they may well say no. The Travellers dislike obligation to anyone outside their families."

Emily understood. One of the traditions at Whitehall that puzzled her, then alarmed her, was that obligations had to be repaid, somehow. Outside very close friends, there was no such thing as holiday presents. Every gift had to be repaid in kind with something of equal value. The dresses Alassa's mother kept sending Emily, Alassa had explained, created a tie between Emily and Queen Marlena, even though Emily hadn't wanted to create the tie herself. Or, for that matter, wear the dresses. But it was hard to refuse without permanently damaging their relationship.

It was easy, she knew, for someone to be pushed into a subordinate position. A richer or better-connected student could create an obligation to a poorer student, simply by giving him or her expensive gifts. Whitehall's rules on relationships made sense in that light, she knew; an older student could easily take advantage of a younger student. But the rules only seemed to push the practice underground. If Emily hadn't been close friends with Alassa, she suspected she would have been drowned in expensive gifts.

"I repaid my own fees," Emily said, finally. "I'm sure Jasmine could do the same."

Lady Barb snorted. "I rather doubt it," she said. "You were very lucky."

Emily nodded. She wasn't quite sure who had actually paid her fees—Mistress Irene hadn't been very clear on the matter when Emily had asked—but she'd returned the money anyway, once she was sure she could support herself. Neither the Grandmaster nor Void had commented on it. She suspected—she hoped—that meant they approved.

"I will speak to her guardians," Lady Barb said, again. "It will be a year or two before she can go to Whitehall in any case. She isn't that old and her powers have yet to develop properly."

She smiled, suddenly. "The Travellers hold the record for the greatest number of child magicians," she added. "They're so frequently exposed to wild magic that their powers often develop earlier than their parents might wish."

Emily shuddered. Students at Whitehall could be cruel—but children could be crueler. The thought of a young boy or girl armed with magic was horrifying, particularly as they wouldn't be in an environment where their use of magic could be monitored and supervised. And she'd read horror stories about what happened to such magicians when they finally went through puberty. Quite a few of them didn't survive the experience.

"I'll go speak to them once the entertainment is over," Lady Barb added, sitting up. "Go fetch the blankets, then you can get some sleep."

Emily obeyed, scrambling back into the wagon and finding the blankets on the cramped bunks. She couldn't help feeling a little wistful as she jumped back down, watching the Travellers gather around the fire. An older man played a violin, several of the young couples danced...they were a family, no matter how strange, and had an easy companionship that she'd never known. Their children grew up knowing there were people looking out for them at all times. Even if they chafed sometimes under the restrictions, they also knew they were safe.

She felt a tinge of envy as she laid out the blankets, one by one. It would be nice to share such companionship, but she wasn't even sure where to begin. She liked her handful of friends, yet she wasn't always sure how to handle being friends with anyone. There were times she just wanted to be alone, in the company of her own thoughts...she shook her head, bitterly. She'd never really had friends—or respected mentors—until she'd come to Whitehall.

It was far too dark to read—she half-wished for a Kindle, although she had no idea if it would even work—so she lay back on the blankets and stared up at the stars. She'd never paid much attention to them on Earth, not when she knew she would never be able to reach orbit, let alone the moon or Mars. Now, she knew how to use them to find her way, thanks to the sergeants, but she had no idea if they were the same stars as those visible on Earth. If they were different, she asked herself, what were the implications of *that*?

She tensed as she felt someone moving next to her, then relaxed slightly as she realized it was only Jasmine. The younger girl lay down on the blankets and closed her eyes, seemingly unaware of just how badly she'd alarmed Emily. Emily sighed, waiting for her heart to stop pounding in her chest. It had taken months for her to get used to the concept of having roommates, people who slept in the same room. And now, Jasmine had casually disturbed her...

The entertainment had come to an end, she realized. She looked around and saw Lady Barb, her long blonde hair glistening in the firelight, talking to an older man. It was hard to believe that he was related to Jasmine; where Jasmine was pale, he was dark. But there were so many ethnic groups mixed in the community that it was quite possible he was related to Jasmine's father. Emily watched for a long moment and then settled back on her blankets and closed her eyes.

"I liked watching you brew," Jasmine confided. "What were you making?"

Emily smiled. "Green," she said, without opening her eyes. "A nugget of the purest green."

The next thing she knew was a shock as cold water splashed over her face. She jerked awake as water cascaded down her shirt, looking around in shock. No one at Whitehall would have disturbed her sleep, certainly not during the run-up to exams. They needed their sleep just as much. But now...she sat up, choking, and saw two boys running away. The sun was inching its way into the sky, casting brilliant rays of light over the land.

"Little brats," Lady Barb swore. She lifted her hand and cast a spell after the boys, just as they dodged behind a wagon. Emily sensed a flare of magic and knew that the spell had reached its targets, even though they were out of eyeshot. If she'd had any doubts about Lady Barb being a powerful magician, that would have erased them. She smiled to herself at the sound of outraged croaking. "I'm sorry about that, Millie."

It took Emily a moment to remember that *she* was Millie. "It's okay," she said, although it wasn't. Her clothes were not only drenched, they were clinging to her skin in a manner she found uncomfortably revealing. "Let me dry myself."

It took three tries before she managed the spell properly. Her hair still felt damp afterwards, but at least she no longer had water dripping down her body. Lady Barb stood up, dried herself and stalked off towards where the boys had tried to hide. Emily wondered what she'd done to them, hoping it was something truly unpleasant. Beating someone halfway to death didn't seem like enough, somehow. She helped Jasmine to her feet, then cast another drying spell for the younger girl. Jasmine didn't seem too upset by the whole experience.

"They're always like that," she said, as Emily ran her fingers through her hair. "You get used to it."

Lady Barb reappeared, dragging both boys by their ears. They both looked rather shell-shocked, neither of them fighting or trying to escape. Lady Barb dragged them over to the adults, then had a terse conversation. Emily checked on the potion and discovered to her relief that it was unharmed, then started to move it into the bottles for storage. She'd had to clean the cauldron before they packed up for the day.

"I'm sorry about that," Lady Barb repeated, as she walked back to the wagon. "They're going to be punished."

"Thank you," Emily said, feeling an odd surge of vindictiveness. There had been times when she'd wished she had siblings, but she wouldn't have wanted to expose anyone else to her stepfather. Besides, she liked being alone and it was hard to be alone when surrounded by family. "When are we leaving?"

Lady Barb nodded towards the mountains. "We'll be there in a couple of hours, once we depart," she said. "And then we'll be on our own."

Emily allowed herself to look forward to it as they ate breakfast, then packed up the campsite and buried their waste. Neither of the boys reappeared from their wagon, perhaps fortunately. Emily couldn't help feeling murderous towards them, even though they probably hadn't meant to scare her. But it wouldn't be easy for her to sleep again in the campsite.

"Set up wards," Lady Barb advised, when Emily asked for advice. "You can hold one in place long enough to get some sleep, can't you?"

Emily scowled, irritated at herself. She didn't use protective wards at Whitehall, nor had she used them in Zangaria or at Lady Barb's home. But she could have used them at the campsite to ensure that her sleep was undisturbed, at least by children. Lady Barb wouldn't have any difficulty waking her if necessary.

"I can," she agreed, sourly. She dried the blankets, then returned them to the wagon. "What did…"

She nodded towards Jasmine. "They said we could provide the money, provided the obligations were all on her," Lady Barb said. "It sounds cold, but it isn't uncommon."

Emily hesitated, looking at the younger girl.

"I'll talk to her," Lady Barb said, as the Travellers started to hitch the wagons to the horses. "If she accepts…you can talk to her later."

"I understand," Emily said, reluctantly. She knew Lady Barb knew more about the whole system than her, but it still annoyed her. "I'll let you handle it."

Lady Barb gave her a long look, then nodded.

Chapter Twelve

EMILY HAD NEVER SEEN MOUNTAINS IN PERSON UNTIL SHE'D BEEN KIDNAPPED BY SHADYE. Since then, she'd seen the mountains that surrounded Whitehall and explored them with Jade, but the Cairngorms were different. She couldn't help staring as the mountains grew closer, reaching up towards the sky, their peaks lost in dark clouds that flickered with lightning—and perhaps magic. The countryside changed too; trees clung closer and closer to the road, casting dark shadows over the wagons. Emily shivered as she peered into the forest, wondering what might be lurking inside. She'd read enough to know that *anything* could be waiting for them in the darkness.

The convoy lurched to a halt. "Here we are," Lady Barb said, as she passed the reins to Jasmine. "That's where we're going."

Emily followed her pointing finger. The trees parted, just enough to reveal a rocky path leading up into the mountains. Emily shivered when she saw the shadows moving ahead of them, then pushed the thought aside and picked up her bag. Lady Barb exchanged a few brief words with Jasmine before she jumped down and headed to the lead wagon. Emily said goodbye, biting her tongue to keep from asking Jasmine what she'd said to Lady Barb, then jumped down herself. Up close, the path didn't look any more inviting.

A cold wind blew through the trees as Lady Barb came to join her, the horses neighing in farewell as the convoy started to move out. Emily waved to Jasmine as the last wagon moved past, then drove down the road and vanished in the distance. She couldn't help missing the convoy, now they were alone. It seemed impossible to believe that there were any other humans nearby. She would almost sooner be somewhere—anywhere—else.

"No time to waste," Lady Barb said, briskly. If she thought the surroundings were ominous too, she kept it to herself. "Come along."

She turned and started to walk up the path. Emily followed, silently grateful for the long marches in rough terrain the sergeants had forced upon her. Without them, she knew she would have had real trouble walking up the path. The footing was unstable and there were nasty-looking jagged rocks everywhere, as if whoever had made the pathway had deliberately set out to make it all but impassable. She heard the sound of water tinkling in the forest, but saw nothing within the shadows. There didn't even seem to be any animals anywhere nearby.

"Jasmine was very interested in your offer," Lady Barb said. She didn't sound winded by the march. "I gave her a signed paper to show to the recruiting officers, when she comes into her magic. Her fees will be paid at that time, if she still wants to go."

Emily nodded. "Will she actually go?"

"It depends," Lady Barb said. "She may not develop enough magic to fit in at Whitehall—or she may never develop magic at all. If so..."

Her voice trailed off, but Emily understood. There were a handful of people who had magic, but were never able to actually access and use it. For an ordinary person from an ordinary family, it was no hardship; they might never even know what they had. But for someone from a magical bloodline, being unable to use magic would be disastrous. There were only a handful of courses at Whitehall that didn't include magic.

She shivered. It hadn't taken her more than a few days before she'd learned enough spells to make her really dangerous, at least to someone without magic. That, she'd been told, was the real reason why Whitehall and the other magical schools recruited from non-magical bloodlines, quite apart from any genetic requirements. It simply wasn't safe for magical children to be taught alongside non-magical children.

"We shall see," she said, out loud. "That was an impressive spell you used on the brats."

Lady Barb smiled. "Keep concentrating and you might be able to do it yourself," she said, dryly. "But it isn't particularly easy."

They walked in companionable silence for nearly thirty minutes before they came to a bridge. Emily felt a chill running down her spine as she looked at the bridge—and at the rushing water underneath, racing towards an unknown destination. There were enough jagged rocks half-hidden by the water to make crossing without a bridge a dangerous prospect. But there was something about the bridge that bothered her, even though she couldn't place her fingers on it.

"Look at the logs," Lady Barb said. She pointed a finger towards the pieces of wood. "They weren't cut with axes or saws."

Emily frowned. They looked almost like someone had *chewed* them. Something very big. The teeth marks looked several times the size of her mouth, yet there was something disturbingly human about them. Lady Barb looked around, studying the water, then smiled and pointed towards a large rock on the far side of the river. Emily followed her gaze, but frowned in puzzlement. The rock was large enough to stand on, easily. But there was nothing else odd about it.

"Watch," Lady Barb said. She picked up a stone and tossed it towards the rock, striking it easily. "Watch and learn."

Emily jumped as the stone started to move, standing upright and revealing a humanoid form. For a moment, she thought it was *made* of stone, before she realized that it was actually very good at blending into its surroundings. Emily couldn't help thinking of a giant misshapen baby, made of grey flesh. It had to be a troll, a wild troll. The creature stood, dark eyes searching for the person who had dared to set foot on his bridge.

"Don't worry," Lady Barb said, before Emily could say a word. "Just don't show any fear and it will be fine."

Emily swallowed nervously. Trolls were slow, she knew from lessons, but they never gave up their prey without a fight. And their thick skins protected them from all kinds of magic.

Lady Barb stepped forward, holding her staff in one hand. The troll stopped moving its head and glared at her, never taking its eyes off the staff. It recognized it, Emily realized.

"Follow me," Lady Barb hissed. She knelt down and started to crawl across the bridge. The troll made a hissing sound, like a kettle that had been left on too long, but made no attempt to grab her. "Hurry!"

Emily hesitated, then crawled after the older woman. The bridge felt terrifyingly unstable, as if one false move would toss her off into the troll's waiting jaws. It hissed again as she passed over its position, then fell back into hiding. Emily sighed in relief as she reached the far side of the bridge and looked back. The troll was almost completely concealed within the rushing water.

"They're not very smart," Lady Barb commented, as they walked away from the bridge, "but they have a natural talent for building bridges that appear safe until it's too late. Most people who live here know to look for signs a troll built the bridge."

Emily frowned. "Why don't the locals try to kill it?"

"They're not fond of visitors in these parts," Lady Barb admitted. "They wouldn't care too much if the troll ate someone, particularly a taxman."

She smirked. "But those particular people are probably inedible," she added. "They couldn't be eaten at all."

Emily had to smile, feeling some of the tension draining away. "What about the children?"

"They generally learn better from a very early age," Lady Barb said. "Although they have to be careful. Some of the creatures that lurk in the innermost reaches of the forest are quite cunning and very dangerous."

She launched into a story that reminded Emily of *The Boy Who Cried Wolf*, except the boy actually *did* see a dangerous creature, which vanished the moment he called for his father and uncles. His relatives didn't believe him, beat him and left him alone with the sheep. But the creature reappeared and kept reappearing until the boy no longer cried for help. And then it ate him up, followed by the sheep.

Emily had no trouble that the story was factual, at least in some ways, even if it did raise the question of just who had managed to tell anyone what had happened. There were all kinds of monsters running loose in the world, from centaurs to goblins and orcs. Even dumb animals could develop a kind of intelligence if they were exposed to wild magic—or to the experiments of magicians with more power than ethical boundaries. Hell, there were even magicians trying to breed intelligent horses, claiming they would be useful in war. But there were so many variables in magical breeding that Emily suspected the whole idea was asking for something to go badly wrong.

They were trying to breed royals, she thought. Alassa's beauty wasn't natural; it was the result of decades of magical experimentation. *But it comes at a cost of near-sterility.*

She mulled it over as she kept walking, wondering just where the troll had come from. It might have looked humanoid, but there was no hint of humanity around its eyes, suggesting that it wasn't a descendent of a human who'd been touched by the Faerie. Maybe it had just evolved through contact with wild magic, like the dragons and the other completely non-human creatures that hid from human eyes. She shook her head, dismissing the thought. It was unlikely she would ever know.

They reached a clearing and stopped long enough to catch their breath. Emily looked up towards the higher mountains and saw a dark castle perched on a peak, towering ominously over the land. It didn't look any bigger than her castle in Cockatrice, although it was difficult to be sure.

"It belongs to the local lord," Lady Barb said. She shrugged, expressively. "You can imagine how hard it was to build, even with magic."

Emily rolled her eyes. If there was one constant between this world and Earth, it was that the rich and the powerful demanded accommodation in line with their status. The aristocrats built towering castles and manor houses for themselves, while the commoners had to struggle in tiny hovels, fighting to survive another day. This was something she knew her innovations would eventually challenge, but it wasn't going to be an easy transition. There were times when she wondered if she shouldn't have kept her mouth shut instead of introducing new ideas to the Allied Lands.

But gunpowder might make it easier for them to fight the necromancers and their armies, she thought. Orcs were tough and bred like rabbits—and the necromancers could intimidate them into unquestioning obedience. And each of them was tougher than the average human. *And English letters will allow millions to learn to read.*

Lady Barb smiled at her before leading her back to the path. This time, it snaked into a long, tree-covered valley. Emily was suddenly very aware of birds flying through the trees, while a handful of small animals could be heard in the undergrowth. It was almost as if someone had flipped a switch, turning on the sound. She shook her head in puzzlement as she heard something ahead of her, then caught sight of a handful of sheep—and a pale-skinned boy watching them. He started, lifting a heavy wooden stick, but relaxed when Lady Barb held up her hands.

"We're almost there," Lady Barb commented. "Not long to go now."

Emily nodded at the boy, who smiled shyly. She had to look strange to him, she realized slowly, almost like someone from a different planet. Even though she was wearing a basic walking outfit rather than robes, she still looked different. She wondered, absently, what sort of life the boy led among the mountains, but she didn't dare pause long enough to ask. Lady Barb was walking faster now that the end of the walk was in sight.

"A word of warning," Lady Barb said, once they were out of earshot. "You've grown used to magic at Whitehall."

Emily hesitated. She'd been at Whitehall for two years and there were times when magic—and the customs of the Allied Lands—could still surprise and horrify her. There was so much she had to learn, more—she suspected—than she would ever be *able* to learn, no matter how much time she spent in the library. And then there was the strange and confusing history of the Allied Lands. The more she looked at it, remembering what she knew from Earth's history, the more she suspected that history had been ineptly rewritten.

"Yes," she said, finally.

"You use magic as naturally as breathing, now," Lady Barb continued. "When you are injured, you can be healed within a day. You turn your friends and rivals into small animals or objects and think it's nothing more than a great joke."

Emily shook her head. Magical transformation—voluntary or involuntary—might be a regular part of life at Whitehall, but it wasn't something she suspected she would ever grow used to. And then there were the transformed beasts she'd seen hunted in Zangaria...

Lady Barb looked into her eyes. "That isn't true for the people here," she warned. "Magic is strange, powerful and unpredictable...for them. They've seen people warped and twisted by wild magic, to the point where they're often glad to give up their children who happen to have developed magical powers. Quite a few of your fellows at Whitehall will never go home once they graduate. Some of them may not even wait that long to break all contact with their families."

Emily swallowed, her mouth suddenly dry. She had never really wanted to go back home, but surely someone who had a loving family would feel differently. But if the locals were so scared of magic...

"Don't use magic directly, unless you have no other choice," Lady Barb said, gently. "We don't want to scare them if it can be avoided."

She turned and led the way down the path. Emily followed after a moment, remembering how much magic she'd seen in Whitehall—and how little she'd seen in Zangaria. But even there, among the aristocracy, there was power enough to allow them to stand as equals to magicians. Here...she swallowed again, realizing just how powerless the locals actually were, compared to her friends. Magic would terrify them.

"They used to kill very young children who showed signs of magic," Lady Barb called back to her, without turning around. "We think it still goes on, in places."

The path broadened as it led down into the village. Emily wrinkled her nose as the smell hit her, a combination of dirty animals and filthy humans that reminded her of some of the smaller hamlets she'd seen on the trip to Zangaria. Basic sanitation, it seemed, had never reached this village. The handful of locals she saw looked filthy, wearing clothes that wouldn't even have been used as rags in Whitehall. A handful of children, too young to be put to any proper work, were gathered outside one of the houses, listening to a lecture from a man who looked old enough to be Emily's great-grandfather.

The houses looked strange to her eyes. Most of them were built out of wood—there was no shortage of wood in the mountains—a handful were built using stone. She guessed they belonged to the handful of important men in the village; if they followed the same pattern as villages in Zangaria, there would be a headman who served as the village boss. But there would also be some degree of discussion among the older villagers, she suspected. The headman wasn't powerful enough to keep *everyone* in line if they decided they wanted to get rid of him.

Lady Barb strode directly into the village, heading straight for a large stone house. A door opened and a man strode out, followed by a teenage boy. Emily found herself disliking both of them on sight; the older man had a greedy fleshy face, half-concealed behind a short reddish beard, while the boy made no attempt to hide the fact he was staring at her chest, even though her shirt was largely shapeless. She fought the urge to hide behind Lady Barb as the older man came to a halt in front of her and bowed, politely. Lady Barb nodded in return.

"My Lady Sorceress," the older man said. "I bid you welcome to my village."

Emily studied him thoughtfully. His clothes were obviously homemade, but they were slightly better than the clothes worn by the other villagers—they looked almost new, lacking the patched holes the other villagers showed on their clothes. He wore a thin gold chain around his neck, an oddly girlish decoration that—she suspected—marked him out as the headman.

"We thank you," Lady Barb said. She indicated Emily with a nod. "This is my apprentice, Millie."

"Charmed," the younger man said.

His father gave him an indulgent smile. "My son, Hodge," he said. "A fine young man."

Emily kept her face expressionless, somehow. Hodge was a younger version of his father, save for not having a beard. She didn't like the look in his eyes at all, or the way his gaze kept dropping to her chest and below. When he looked up again, she looked away, unwilling to meet his stare. It was a relief when the headman turned and led the way towards another stone building right in the center of the village.

"I will have food and drink sent to you," the headman assured Lady Barb. "How long will you be staying?"

"Two to three days," Lady Barb said. "We will start seeing people tomorrow." Her voice hardened. "And I trust there will be no delays this time?"

Emily gave her an enquiring look, but Lady Barb said nothing.

The guesthouse was larger than Emily had expected, yet it was all one room. There were two beds placed against one wall, a large pail of water and an empty bucket. It took her a moment to realize, with a shudder, that it was intended to serve as a chamberpot. At least they weren't expected to go outside to do their business, she told herself. It wasn't very reassuring.

"Set up the cauldron, then start brewing all of the potions, one by one," Lady Barb ordered, as she erected wards around the guesthouse. "There should be ingredients in the cupboard. Make a list of everything you take and use. Someone will have to replace them, sooner or later."

Emily nodded. "I will," she said. "What was the delay?"

"Some people didn't want their relatives to seek treatment," Lady Barb told her. "The mountainfolk can be very secretive at times. And they often have things they want to hide."

Chapter Thirteen

THE BED WAS UNCOMFORTABLE AND ITCHY. EMILY TOSSED AND TURNED FRANTICALLY FOR a couple of hours, despite her exhaustion, before giving up and taking a swig of sleeping potion. She still felt tired when Lady Barb poked her in the ribs, snapping her awake. Muttering curses under her breath, Emily rolled out of bed and glared down at her body. There were tiny insect bites covering her legs.

"Next time, set wards against them," Lady Barb reminded her.

Emily groaned. She knew how to cast an insect-repelling ward, but she'd forgotten to set one before she went to bed.

"Rub a potion on them," Lady Barb suggested. Her voice lightened. "There's an anti-itching potion in my bag. Then get into your working robes."

Emily nodded and did as she was told. Lady Barb didn't seem fazed by their living conditions, but as a combat sorceress she'd seen much worse. The sergeants hadn't insisted on camping in the middle of an insect nest, no matter how hard they'd made her march from Whitehall to a camping site and then back again. She wiped her body with cold water, then pulled on her robes. Thankfully, the charms on the robe would help keep other insects away.

"There's food on the table," Lady Barb added. "I let you sleep in a little. You needed it."

The food turned out to be bread, milk and cheese. All three tasted stronger than anything she'd eaten at Whitehall, the cheese powerful enough to make her breathe through her mouth while she ate it. She guessed that they were all produced locally, rather than obtained from a larger town. The villagers would have to support themselves.

"They do," Lady Barb confirmed, when Emily asked. "They have cows and sheep, as well as whatever they can hunt and kill in the forest. The real problems come in wintertime."

Emily shivered. Snow hadn't been a problem for Whitehall, but it would be murderous for isolated villages on mountainsides. She could imagine the snow pressing down until the villages were completely buried, their inhabitants frozen to death. They'd have to store enough food to keep themselves alive over the winter. And if they didn't have enough, they would starve even if they didn't freeze. Or have their hovels collapse in on them when the snow piled high on the roofs.

"Ouch," she said, as she finished her meal. "Do the lords let them keep enough to live?"

Lady Barb smirked. "The villagers are very good at hiding food," she said. "But if you should happen to notice a cache, keep your mouth shut."

"Understood," Emily said. If the local lords were anything like the Barons of Zangaria, the question wasn't how much they took, but how much they let their peasants *keep*. "I won't say a word."

She cleaned up the table, then watched as Lady Barb filled the cauldron with water and boiled it with a simple spell. "We'll be seeing people as soon as we open until dusk," Lady Barb predicted. "I know you haven't taken the oaths, but I suggest that you keep your mouth shut about anything you see here. If someone asks, point them to me."

Emily nodded. Students who became healers took complex oaths, some binding them to secrecy and others preventing them from claiming obligations from their work. She wasn't sure she wanted to be a healer, even though she'd mastered most of the basic healing spells, and no one had asked her to take the oaths. But she promised herself she'd keep her mouth shut anyway. No one would talk to a doctor if they thought the doctor would broadcast the news to the entire world.

There was already a small queue of people outside when Lady Barb opened the door. Emily watched as the first one, an elderly woman, was shown into the room and the door firmly shut behind her. The woman gave Emily a droll smile, then removed her skirt and sat down on the table without being asked. Her legs were marred with dark marks, as if she was bleeding under the skin.

"Old age," Lady Barb said, very quietly to Emily. To the patient, she remarked; "It's a wonder you're still alive."

"Too stubborn to die," the old woman said. Her voice was cracked and broken, but Emily could hear grim determination in her tone. "I've outlived four lords and I would like to outlive a fifth."

Emily watched as Lady Barb cast a healing spell, doing what she could. "Your body is slowly breaking down," she said. "I don't think it can stay active for much longer."

The woman shrugged, stood upright and pulled her skirt back on. Emily felt an odd sense of queasy fascination as the woman nodded to her and hobbled towards the door. Lady Barb opened it, allowed her to leave and then invited the next person inside. He was a young boy, holding his arm as though it pained him.

"See what you make of it," Lady Barb said, addressing Emily. She looked at the boy and smiled at him. "Don't worry. My assistant will take care of it."

Emily gulped. Healing was complex; she might not be *bad* at it, but she wasn't sure she wanted to test her skills on a young boy. He couldn't be older than ten, she decided, as she placed her fingertips on his arm—he gasped in pain—and cast the first spell. Sensations flooded through her mind, telling her that he'd broken his arm and then had it badly set by a mundane doctor. He'd been incredibly lucky not to wind up a cripple, which would have ensured an early death. The villagers wouldn't be able to provide for a cripple.

"Good work," Lady Barb said, when Emily explained what she'd found. "Now... fix it."

Emily braced herself and cast the second spell. Most healing spells tended to deal with the immediate problem, but in this case there were other problems that might only be made worse if she sealed the bone back into place. The body *wanted* to heal, she'd been told, yet if the damage remained untended long enough the body might come to believe that was the natural state of affairs. Emily slowly returned the bone to where it should be before carefully repairing the rest of the damage.

She settled backwards with a sigh, feeling tired and exhausted. And to think that was only her first patient!

"Stay still," Lady Barb said. She checked Emily's work, and nodded in approval. "Good work."

Emily flushed in relief.

"Take this potion for now," Lady Barb directed the boy, "then come back this evening if you are still sore."

The boy nodded, sat upright and scurried towards the door. Emily watched him go, silently praying she hadn't missed anything.

Lady Barb reached out and squeezed her hand gently, then called for the next patient. An alarmingly thin woman, obviously pregnant, crept in as if she expected to be attacked at any moment. Lady Barb stood, helped her to sit down, and checked on the baby with practiced ease.

"I think he'll be coming out in a few more days," she said. The woman relaxed with obvious relief. "But you need to eat more and avoid heavy activity."

The woman snorted. Emily saw her point. The villagers might make some allowances for a pregnant woman, but they couldn't afford to have anyone just doing nothing. For all she knew, the woman was expected to go straight back to housework and the other endless chores village women did. They were expected to do everything from cook to sewing new clothes for their families. No peasant woman could afford to laze around like a lady aristocrat.

"It could easily be worse," Lady Barb said, as the woman left the room, closing the door behind her. "I've seen children strangled in the womb when the umbilical cord wraps around their neck, suffocating them. They're often still in the womb until delivery, but when they are delivered they're dead. Even magic can't bring them back to life."

Emily shuddered. Pregnancy wasn't something she'd thought much about, even though she knew it was her duty to deliver an heir for Cockatrice. On Earth, there were midwives to help with the birth and technology that could tell a baby was in trouble before it was too late. But here...death in childbirth was far from uncommon.

If the woman had needed emergency help, could they have helped her? She'd never practiced helping someone to give birth.

The next few patients were simpler, thankfully. Lady Barb inspected them, used some magic to heal their damage and then lectured her patients on being more careful next time. Some of the damage reminded Emily of battered students after Martial Magic, although Sergeant Miles had normally healed any damage as soon as the class had finished. Here...if there was fighting, there would be no one to help the injured. One man had even lost an eye.

"I can't repair your damaged eye," Lady Barb told him, tartly. "What *happened* to it?"

The man shrugged. He'd been in the pub, he explained, and a fight had broken out. He didn't remember what the fight had actually been about, only that he'd enjoyed himself and wanted to do it again. Emily looked at him and shook her head. What was the point of battering one's fellow villagers to a pulp, then doing it again and again?

"They don't have much else to do with their lives," Lady Barb told her, once the patient had departed. "They work with the animals, grow their small crops, sing and dance...and drink alcohol they produce themselves. None of them can read or write and they'd be suspicious of anyone who could, even us. Readers and writers work for the lords."

Emily nodded. Zangaria might have avoided the stifling bureaucracies of Earth, but it *did* have a network of educated men who kept careful tabs on what the peasants *should* be able to produce each year. They were intensely hated, if only because their predictions didn't always jibe with reality—and, naturally, their predictions were never wrong. Banishing them from Cockatrice had been one of Emily's first decisions, when she'd finally worked out just how baleful an influence they were. It had made her very popular with her subjects.

They paused for lunch, then handled the next set of patients. Most of them had minor injuries—she guessed that the headman had done some organizing—but a couple seemed reluctant to talk to either of the magicians. Lady Barb had to point out, sardonically, that they could hardly heal someone if they didn't know what was wrong before the men confessed to having problems with their private parts. Emily looked away, embarrassed, as Lady Barb inspected the damage, then promised to brew potions to handle the problem. She washed her hands thoroughly as soon as the men went out the door.

"They should have been more careful where they put it," Lady Barb said, angrily. "I've yet to see a whore in an inn who didn't have something nasty waiting for anyone foolish enough to touch her."

Emily winced. "But what about their wives?"

"What indeed?" Lady Barb asked. "I can brew a potion to deal with the wasting rot, but if their wives don't drink it too, the disease will just re-infect them."

She glanced out of the door. "There's only two more people waiting to see us," she said. "I want you to handle them while I make a start on brewing the potion. Don't worry; if you find something you can't handle, don't hesitate to call for me."

Emily nodded. The first patient turned out to be an older man who had a nasty cough. Emily ran a check, discovered an infection in his lungs and removed it, then told him to be more careful what he smoked. He was still laughing as he walked back out the door. Emily sighed, and called for the final patient. He was a young boy, short with dark hair and blue eyes; Emily quietly estimated him to be no more than ten years old. The way he looked around, peering into the darkest corners, suggested he was jumpy. But there was nothing obviously wrong.

"You're safe here," Emily said, feeling her heart go out to him. She couldn't help feeling a sense of kinship with the young boy. There was something about him that reminded her of herself. "Sit down on the table, please."

The boy walked over to the table and stopped, unmoving. Emily frowned; he wasn't sitting down or undressing...or trying to speak. Was he mute? Or...she hesitated, then motioned for him to undress. His entire body trembled as he pulled his shirt over his head and dropped it on the ground. Emily took one look at his back, then looked away, horrified. Her gorge rose within and she had to swallow hard to prevent herself from being sick.

She'd seen horror. She'd seen Shadye and the Mimic. But this was different, all too human—and somehow all the worse for it. The boy's back was covered in dark scars, several ending in very nasty bruises. Emily had seen marks on her own buttocks when she'd been caned by the warden, but this was worse. The skin had broken under the blows and become infected in several places. It was clear, she realized, as she forced herself to concentrate, that the boy hadn't been caned. The bruises at the end of the scars were where the belt buckle had hit and broken his skin.

Be clinical, she told herself. But it was so hard to look and not feel the desire to tear the person who'd beaten the boy into hundreds of tiny pieces. She could turn them into slugs and stamp on them, turn them into rabbits and set the dogs after them...there were so many options, but none of them would help him now. The infection was spreading so rapidly that she was honestly unsure how he'd stayed alive, let alone reasonably mobile.

"Finish undressing," she told him, even though she didn't really want to know. She raised her voice, hoping that Lady Barb wasn't in one of the stages where the potion couldn't be left untended for more than a few seconds. "I think you should take a look at this."

She looked back at the boy, then turned away and threw up, violently. The bruises covered his buttocks and the back of his thighs, marching down his skin with almost military precision. Emily had had problems sitting comfortably for hours after the Warden had caned her, but this...she cursed herself for ever moaning about the Warden's punishments. This was far worse than anything she'd ever endured, even in the moments everyone had wanted to blame her for the Mimic's trail of bodies.

Lady Barb looked pale as she ran her fingers over the bruises, then pushed the boy into bending over the table. Emily looked away, sickened. Lady Barb's voice was cold and clinical, but Emily knew her well enough to hear the outrage she couldn't quite hide.

"No sign of rectal damage," she said. "But, under the circumstances, it's a small mercy."

Emily shook her head when Lady Barb motioned for her to take a look. She'd always disliked examining private parts in class, even though the parts were mounted on a homunculus. Here, she didn't want to strip the boy of what little privacy he had left...no, that wasn't entirely true. She didn't want to see any signs of whatever else had happened to him. It was selfish, but she couldn't help herself.

"No physical reason for inability to talk," Lady Barb noted. "Muteness probably comes from fear. Mental damage is a very strong possibility."

No, Emily thought. The Allied Lands stigmatized any signs of mental trauma or illness, fearing that it was a sign of necromancy. There were no psychologists to help coax the boy out of his trauma, no one who might be willing to help...she closed her eyes, wondering if there was something she could do to help. But she couldn't take in everyone, could she?

"Pass me the painkilling potion," Lady Barb ordered. Her voice was still clinical, almost completely dispassionate. "And then stand ready to help me if necessary."

Emily hated her at that moment, hated her cold clinical approach to the problem. Cold logic told her that rage and fire wouldn't help, but cold logic was no comfort. Lady Barb took the potion, helped the boy to drink enough of it to numb his entire body, then started casting spells over his back and buttocks. The infection would have to be removed before the skin could be healed.

It hadn't been once, Emily told herself, as she watched, fighting to avoid retching again and again. The boy had been beaten to within an inch of his life, not once, but many times. Each of the scars lay on an older scar...she wasn't even sure how the boy had remained alive for so long. How often had he been beaten that he'd managed to keep going despite the pain?

She watched the scars heal up, remembering one of the lectures Lady Barb had given her class when they'd talked about working as healers. It was quite possible for someone to be tortured, healed and then tortured again, prolonging his torment indefinitely. Lady Barb had told them that it wasn't *quite* a violation of Healer Oaths, but they might have to be prepared to decide if they wanted to cooperate or not. And, if they decided poorly, they might be blamed for the whole affair.

"We can't send him back," she said, as the boy slipped into an enchanted sleep. Lady Barb helped him down to the floor and placed him on a rug, but even so he didn't look comfortable. Emily wondered what nightmares would torment his sleep, then decided she didn't want to know. "What are we going to do with him?"

Lady Barb shook her head. "I'll have to talk to the headman," she said. "He will have to make the final decision."

She turned and headed for the door. "Stay with him," she added, as she picked up her staff. "He shouldn't wake up for a few hours, but just in case...keep an eye on him."

Emily watched her go, then turned back to the boy, picked up a blanket and draped it over his body. He looked small, too small. He'd been deprived of food as well as love and care.

Poor bastard, she thought. *But we can help him, can't we?*

Chapter Fourteen

IT WAS NEARLY TWO HOURS BEFORE LADY BARB RETURNED, TWO HOURS THAT EMILY SPENT alternately reading a book and keeping an eye on the boy. He twitched and moaned in his sleep, but not enough to break the spell. Emily watched him, wondering if there was something she could do to help, yet nothing came to mind. All she could do was watch.

She shuddered as she looked down at the pale skin covering his back. It would be days, if she recalled correctly, before the skin had tanned enough to blend in with the rest of his body, but at least it wasn't scarred. Emily couldn't escape the memory of looking down at the scars and wondering just what sort of person would do such a thing to a defenseless boy. It wasn't punishment, she told herself firmly, it was *abuse*. No child deserved to be beaten within an inch of his life.

How long would he have lasted without their help? His scars had already been infected. It wouldn't have been long before the infection killed him. Even a necromantic rite would have been kinder.

She tried to concentrate on her book, but her thoughts kept mocking her, pointing out that her stepfather hadn't been so bad. He'd never laid a finger on her. But the thought made her sick.

She looked up as the door opened and a grim-faced Lady Barb stepped inside. Emily watched as she walked over to the child and cast a handful of spells, then swore out loud and rolled the child over. His chest looked unmarked, but he was so thin that Emily could see his bones clearly. He looked like a famine victim from a third world country.

"I spoke with the headman," Lady Barb said. "His...aunt and uncle believe that he was possessed."

Emily stared at her in disbelief. Possessed?

"Or so they claim," Lady Barb added. "There are odd traces of magic on him, but nothing demonic."

"Oh," Emily said.

She struggled to remember what little she knew of demons and demon magic, but there was almost nothing in the open section of Whitehall's library beyond a single word: *don't*. Shadye had wanted to sacrifice her to a demon-like creature, she knew that much, yet it was one of the few issues the Grandmaster seemed reluctant to talk about. The one time she'd asked, he'd told her to leave it alone.

"It's not uncommon for someone to be touched by wild magic to the point where their behavior becomes erratic," Lady Barb said. "You know just how many spells there are that influence behavior."

Emily nodded. Even First Years knew a handful of mind control spells, as well as simpler tricks to influence and manipulate their rivals and enemies. It was yet another reminder of why Whitehall was so important. Someone on the outside, practicing on defenseless mundanes, could do a hell of a lot of damage before he or she was stopped. But this boy didn't seem to have any magic of his own.

"It doesn't help that his parents died years ago," Lady Barb added. "I suspect his aunt and uncle were reluctant to take him into their home."

Emily shivered, remembering her stepfather ranting about how much she cost him. It was almost nothing, she knew, because she practically brought herself up, yet cold logic was no defense against his words. He'd told her, time and time again, that he only put a roof over her head out of the goodness of his heart. Part of her had believed him—and part of her knew that he had resented her presence.

It would be worse, she suspected, for peasants in the mountainside. There was no social security network, apart from what the other villagers could provide...and they weren't wealthy enough to provide much, even if they wanted to. An extra mouth could make the difference between surviving the winter and starving to death. And a young boy, barely on the edge of his teens, would be little help on the farm.

"I don't think it matters," she said, pushing her thoughts aside. "We can't send him back to them."

Lady Barb looked down at the sleeping child. "I don't think we have a choice," she admitted. "We have no legal authority to take the boy from his guardians."

Emily felt her mouth drop open. No words emerged.

"We could take a magician—I have taken magicians, in the past," Lady Barb continued, softly. "But this boy isn't a magician."

Emily found her voice. "You can't mean to say you'll leave him here?"

She pressed on before Lady Barb could answer. "This boy came very close to death," she added. Her voice rose until she was almost shouting at the older woman. "If he goes back there, they'll undo all the work we did and finish the job. We cannot send him back."

Lady Barb held up one hand, but Emily hadn't finished. "We can find him somewhere else to go," she continued. "Or we can even take him with us."

"And then...what?" Lady Barb said. She looked up at Emily, meeting her eyes. "Do you intend to keep picking up strays?"

Emily remembered Jasmine and flushed. "Yes," she said, bluntly. "If someone has to do it, I will."

She gritted her teeth, preparing to argue. It would be simple enough to have the boy sent to Cockatrice and given work in her castle. Or Imaiqah's father might like an apprentice. Or...

"I understand how you feel," Lady Barb said. "And I understand your feelings, but we don't have any legal power to intervene."

"To hell with legalities," Emily snarled. Magic billowed around her, feeding on her anger. "We can just *take* him from them. Or we could buy him from them. Or we could just fake his death and say we destroyed the body. We..."

Her entire body froze, solid.

"I understand how you feel," Lady Barb repeated. There was a cold edge to her voice that made Emily shiver, inwardly. "Do you think this is the worst I've seen up here?"

Emily tried to break the hex holding her in place, but failed.

"People who become cripples rarely last very long," Lady Barb reminded her. "Old men and women are lucky to be allowed to remain in the houses over the winter months, no matter how much they did for their children. I've seen girls and boys forced to marry each other, no matter what they think about it. I've seen husbands beat their wives and wives beat their husbands; parents beating children and children turning on parents when they're old enough to claim their inheritance. It's a savage life up here, Emily, and you can't help them by fixing one tiny piece of the problem."

She caught her breath. "The law—such as it is up here—raises no objection to beating one's children or relatives. Even if you took this boy, you wouldn't be able to help others...and the peasants would start to hide from us. They don't mind us taking magical children away, but they do object to losing mundane children. And we *need* to be able to work with them."

So we compromise, Emily thought, struggling to free herself. She wanted to shout and scream at Lady Barb for allowing this to happen, then rage at herself for not realizing that she would see worse than natural injuries on the trip. She'd known—she knew enough about the past to know that peasant life was no bed of roses—and yet she hadn't actually comprehended what it was really like. She recalled a handful of bucolic images she'd seen at school, during what had laughingly passed for history lessons, and shuddered. Life in the fields had never been fun for people who had no alternative.

Lady Barb sighed. "I do understand how you feel," she said, "and we will do something to try and make it better, but we cannot take the boy."

Emily cursed, mentally. The story about the boy being possessed was just an excuse, just something to give them justification for beating the tiny child to within an inch of his life. And yet, here, it might be believed...Lady Barb had even said that there were traces of strange magic on him. She silently promised herself that there would be laws in Cockatrice against child abuse as soon as she had a chance to write them. And those laws would be damn well enforced.

But childhood isn't the same here, she reminded herself. Earth decided that a person moved from childhood to adulthood at eighteen—or thereabouts—while Zangaria tended to have a far more flexible definition of adulthood. Some children were counted as adults from the moment they took up adult responsibilities, while girls were considered adults the moment they started their first periods. Imaiqah had effectively been an adult before she'd gone to Whitehall, while Alassa had remained an immature brat. No wonder Imaiqah had always been the most mature of the three of them.

"The aristocrats are far more genteel, but they can be just as bad," Lady Barb said. "I wish I could show King Randor and his barons what it is like to live as a peasant, but they would never understand. They might as well come from different countries."

Emily understood. The aristocracy in Zangaria believed—genuinely believed—that it was superior to the commoners, almost a different race. It was absurd, if only because Imaiqah's father had been ennobled after the attempted coup in Zangaria, yet they believed that nobility was something separate. But then, there had been cultures on Earth that believed that knighting someone automatically gave them knightly characteristics. And yet they should have known better.

She staggered as Lady Barb released the hex. "I..."

"Just sit down," Lady Barb advised, tartly. "Are you going to shout at me again?"

Emily gritted her teeth. Lady Barb was her mistress, at least for the summer months. She'd read enough about the role of an apprentice to know that she'd broken several rules, starting with always being polite to one's master. If Lady Barb decided to punish her...

"No," she bit out. "What are you going to do with him?"

"Have a few words with his guardians," Lady Barb said. "And then see what we can do to make it better."

Emily watched as she turned and started to dress the young boy with practiced ease. "Can you threaten their lives?"

"I can do worse than that," Lady Barb said, quietly. "But there are limits to what we can do."

Emily nodded, feeling helpless. She'd understood, intellectually, just how brutal life could be in the countryside and the mountains, but she'd never really understood what it meant. And she *hated* feeling helpless...

"This isn't going to be allowed to happen in Cockatrice," she said. "I won't *let* it happen."

"Good luck," Lady Barb said. She sounded perfectly serious. "But it won't be easy. How do you tell the difference between justified punishment and excessive punishment?"

"I'll know it when I see it," Emily said.

Lady Barb snorted. "And how do you plan to write that into law?"

Emily flushed. If excessive punishment depended on the eye of the beholder, she would either have to write laws in great detail, describing precisely what was acceptable and what wasn't, or rely on the common sense of her underlings. But common sense was rare; besides, her underlings might well take bribes to interpret the law in a particular direction. The former baron had been deeply corrupt and so had his underlings, ensuring that no one with any sense placed trust in the law.

"Something else," Lady Barb added. "Was there ever a time at Whitehall when you were punished unjustly?"

"Master Tor's werewolf essay," Emily said, after a moment's thought. "He didn't like me asking too many questions."

"Which betrayed your ignorance," Lady Barb pointed out. "I'm sure the essay taught you something useful."

She picked up the boy and looked down at him for a long moment. Emily saw a hint of wistfulness in her gaze, as if the older woman was feeling maternal. Did Lady Barb have any children? Or a lover? Sorceresses enjoyed a freedom unknown to mundanes—she knew that some of her classmates were in relationships, which she assumed were sexual—but she knew almost nothing about Lady Barb's private life. It wasn't something she wanted to ask about.

"He's too thin," Lady Barb said, softly. She looked over at Emily. "So were you, when you came to Whitehall."

Emily nodded, not trusting herself to speak. She'd had to fend for herself from a very early age, buying her own food and cooking her own meals. And she'd been an indifferent cook at best. If it hadn't been for meals at school, she suspected that she would have been far thinner—or dead—by the time Shadye kidnapped her. She'd filled out considerably since coming to Whitehall.

"You weren't there," she said, suddenly. "How do you know...?"

"Your records," Lady Barb said, dryly. "I read them very carefully when you selected me as your Advisor."

Emily mentally kicked herself. *That* was obvious. "What did they say?"

"I believe you were given a full medical scan after your escapade in Dragon's Den," Lady Barb said. "Underfed, underweight and potentially at risk was the general opinion. The healer was rather puzzled by some issues with your body, but the Grandmaster vetoed asking you any questions. Instead, they just gave the sergeants potions and told them to make sure you took them."

"I never realized," Emily said. The thought that Whitehall's staff had cared enough to take care of her health was staggering, even though rationally it shouldn't have been a surprise. She wasn't unwanted at Whitehall. "I thought those potions were for Martial Magic."

"Some of them were," Lady Barb said. "A handful to help build muscle, a potion to help limit your menstrual cycle, a couple more. Others...were specifically brewed for you."

She turned and walked towards the door, carrying the boy in her arms. "Stay here," she added. "If someone comes, tell them to wait for me unless it's a real emergency. In that case, summon me at once."

Emily watched her go, still trying to process the revelation. She'd honestly never realized that anyone cared enough to help her, even at Whitehall. No one on Earth had noticed her second-hand clothes, her isolationist habits, the showers she took at school...and anything else that might have suggested that her home life was less than ideal. God knew her mother had never visited the school, even to discuss Emily's progress. No one seemed to have cared about the children who weren't either brilliant or bullies.

But Whitehall had cared. An unaccustomed sense of warmth spread through her body as she realized just how much they'd cared. Even if the Grandmaster had vetoed the healers speaking directly to Emily—she wondered, absently, just what the scan had found—they'd still tried to help. She pulled back her sleeve and looked down at her arm, watching as her muscles flexed. Thanks to them, she was stronger and healthier than she'd ever been on Earth.

And yet there was nothing she could do for the boy.

She walked back over to where she'd left her bag and produced a sheet of parchment, then started to scribble out a letter to Imaiqah. Alassa, for all of her intelligence, wouldn't really comprehend Emily's feelings...but then, she'd grown up feeling superior to anyone apart from her parents. No, it went beyond feelings; she'd *known* she was superior. Even Emily hadn't managed to convince her to question her fundamental worldview.

There was a knock at the door. Emily stood, walked over to the door and opened it–and scowled inwardly when she saw Hodge. The young man smiled at her, rather unpleasantly, and then looked past her, searching for Lady Barb. Emily felt an odd twinge of irritation as he looked back at her. What was he looking for?

"My father wishes to invite you both to the dance," Hodge said. His smile seemed to widen, as if he were thinking of the punchline to a joke. "Will you come?"

It was the last thing Emily wanted to do, but she suspected that Lady Barb would insist they went. "I will ask my Mistress," she said, trying hard to convey the impression that she couldn't tie her own shoelaces without instructions. "She will decide for us both."

Hodge nodded, then stood on the doorstep and waited. Emily wondered, absurdly, what the etiquette for this situation actually *was*. Should she invite him in? She took another look at him and decided that would be a bad idea. Instead, she promised to inform Lady Barb as soon as she returned and closed the door in his face. It was rude, she knew, but she just didn't want to talk to anyone. Walking back to the table, she resumed work on her letter.

"I talked them into swearing an oath," Lady Barb said, when she returned. "They won't punish him excessively in the future."

Emily's eyes narrowed. "I thought mundanes couldn't swear oaths," she said. "How...?"

"I used a compulsion curse," Lady Barb said, shortly. "The results of hurting him will not be pleasant."

"Good," Emily said.

But she wasn't sure if it *was* good. Oaths couldn't be broken deliberately, but there were loopholes that could be used to avoid punishment if the oath wasn't written carefully. A curse might just be easier to wriggle around, if the person hadn't chosen to have the curse imposed on him.

And just what was defined as *excessive* punishment?

"Anything they do to him will hurt them too," Lady Barb explained. "Beating him to death will take them with him."

Emily nodded. It might work, she told herself.

"We've been invited to the dance," she said. "Do we have to go?"

"I'm afraid so," Lady Barb said. "It's part of the job. But you can bow out early, if you wish. Just remember to take an anti-alcohol potion before we go."

Chapter Fifteen

Emily heard the music echoing over the village as she followed Lady Barb towards the barn, trying hard to look like a determined and untouchable magician. Lady Barb walked with a steady confidence that suggested she wouldn't give way to anyone, but Emily had to fight to keep from slouching. Nothing, not even Alassa's patient lessons in proper comportment, had managed to have her walking upright in the same stiff posture without effort. It just wasn't something that she'd mastered.

She blinked in surprise as she saw a haystack shivering, although there was no wind. Lady Barb looked back, smirked and motioned for Emily to hurry along behind her. Emily took one last look and obeyed, wondering just what was happening inside. Was there an animal caught in the hay?

"The beast with two backs," Lady Barb whispered, when Emily asked. "There will be a young couple in there, enjoying themselves."

Emily flushed, then stared at the nearby barn. "Don't they *know*?"

"Of course they know," Lady Barb said. She shrugged. "But as long as the happy couple remains out of sight, their elders will pretend not to notice."

Just like Zangaria, Emily thought. Aristocrats seemed to care more for appearance than reality. The rules could be broken as long as they weren't broken too often, while the formalities were often nothing more than shadow plays. But maybe they were also part of the social glue holding society together. Politeness did help prevent outright conflict between lords and ladies.

The music grew louder as they reached the open barn and looked inside. A makeshift band, composed of a pair of accordions, a guitar-like instrument and a set of drums was playing a merry tune, although it seemed somewhat unfocused. Behind them, several couples were moving in the center of the barn, dancing. Emily frowned as she studied their movements. Unlike the dances at Whitehall and Zangaria, the dancers seemed to be making it up as they went along. There was no formal structure at all.

She scowled, inwardly. It had taken her months to get used to the elegant formal dances of Whitehall, which had prepared her for Zangaria. But this was different... she looked at a middle-aged woman with a pleasant smile, whirling her husband around the dance floor, and knew she couldn't join them. The handful of younger girls seemed to be talking to the younger boys, watched by a gimlet-eyed lady who seemed to be in charge of making sure they behaved. Beyond them, a handful of children were tossing a ball around in one corner of the room.

"Welcome," the headman called. "Come and join us."

Emily fought to keep her expression blank. The headman and a number of other men were sitting next to several barrels, drinking heavily. Two of them looked to be well on the way to drunkenness already, but they were still drinking from wooden mugs. Emily grimaced as Hodge pushed a mug into her hand, then took a sniff. It smelled worse than the cheap wine and beer her mother used to drink.

It wasn't just the men who were drinking, she realized, looking around the massive barn. A number of women were drinking too, gathered on the other side of the room. Even some of the children were drinking alcohol...

"One mug only," Lady Barb said, warningly.

Emily nodded as she checked the drink for poison. They'd make fun of her for drinking too little, she'd been warned, but they wouldn't say a word if she was ordered not to drink too much. She shuddered inwardly and took a sip. She might have taken a potion to ensure she couldn't get drunk, but it still tasted thoroughly unpleasant.

She held the mug in her hand and listened as Lady Barb chatted to the headman, collecting rumors. There were some odd stories about missing children, passed from village to village, and concerns that a pack of slavers were hunting for victims. Then the headman was interrupted by another man, who sneered at the whole suggestion of slavers. It was more likely, he insisted, that the children had been eaten by werewolves.

"There are no werewolves around here," a third man snorted. He was clearly too drunk to mind his words. "We would kill them if they dared show their snouts anywhere near the village."

He gave Lady Barb a nasty look. "I believe the children were stolen by dark sorcerers."

"You'd better pray that they weren't," Lady Barb said, evenly. "A single child's life could be used to raise hell."

Probably literally, Emily thought. She'd come across references to spells that demanded a human life in payment, but none of the books had been too clear on what the spells actually *did*. Shadye had presumably expected *something* from the Harrowing in exchange for Emily's life. She wondered, absently, what a powerful and none-too-stable necromancer might have wanted. Hadn't it been the Joker who had traded his soul for cigars?

Hodge pulled at her arm. "Come onto the dance floor?"

Emily shook her head. Even if she'd liked him—and she didn't—she wouldn't have wanted to join the dancers. They seemed to be cavorting around the dance floor, making up their own steps as they went along. She couldn't endure it, she knew, not when some of the couples were practically making out in public. No wonder the kids were hiding in the rear of the room, even though they probably knew more about the practicalities than Emily had at their age. She doubted the parents had kept their children ignorant of sex.

"Taxes are being raised again," another man said. "The lord wants his tribute"—he spat—"in rare animals."

Emily frowned. Taxes weren't only collected in money, not when the peasants rarely *had* any money. The lords took food, meat and service, little else. But rare animals? What sort of animal was rare?

"Last week, he even sent his huntsmen out after a centaur," the man continued. "I think he wanted the beast for entertainment."

"And he wanted us to serve in his army," the headman added. "His recruiters took five boys only two weeks ago."

That was odd, Emily knew. The mountain lords didn't have large armies, they just didn't have the manpower base to support them. Besides, the terrain made it harder for them to fight their fellows. The book she'd read had suggested that each lord kept a small army of retainers and little else. Why would they want more soldiers? The only major threat were the necromancers, and soldiers wouldn't be much help if one of them came calling.

Unless one of the nearby Allied Lands is considering an invasion, she thought. But it seemed unlikely. Even without the looming threat of the necromancers, there was nothing in the mountains worth taking. The only thing the mountains had, as far as she could tell, was timber, and the lords made a tidy profit selling it down the river to shipbuilders. They didn't need to launch an invasion to take it...

The night wore on, leaving her feeling tired and worn. Lady Barb drank enough to keep up with the men, but showed no signs of drunkenness. The men, on the other hand, started to act badly; one started to thrash his wife, in public. Not, Emily had to admit, that the men were the only ones behaving badly. One thick-set woman knocked her husband down and started to pound heavily on his chest. Another threw a mug at her husband, then fled out the door. The dancers scattered as several men rolled onto the dance floor and started to wrestle, their fellows cheering loudly and placing bets. Emily couldn't help overhearing some of the bets; they were unspeakably rude.

"They don't have much else to do with their time," Lady Barb pointed out, as Emily slipped closer to her. The headman was watching the fight with a gleam in his eye. "Fighting is one of their pastimes."

Emily shuddered. The sergeants had introduced her to the concept of controlled violence, but this was different. They weren't really trying to *win*, she realized, merely beat on each other. It seemed pointlessly sadistic to her—and it would be hellish for anyone who wasn't strong enough to fight. But then, the more intellectually-minded children would probably have had it beaten out of them. Or they would escape down the mountain to find somewhere they actually fit in.

"I want to go home," she said, miserably.

"You can go back to the guesthouse," Lady Barb said, shortly. "You remember the way?"

"Yes," Emily said. The village wasn't very big, nothing more than a handful of houses and shacks gathered together. It would have looked idyllic, if it wasn't for the people. "I won't get lost."

"We're leaving tomorrow morning," Lady Barb told her. "Go straight to sleep—take a potion if you want. We have a long walk ahead of us."

Emily nodded, put the mug of beer on the table and walked out of the barn. Outside, it was pitch black. There was no trace of light anywhere, even in the larger houses. But then, most peasants didn't have the option of making magic lights or even simple lanterns. They went to bed when the sun went down and awoke when it returned to the sky. She hesitated, waiting for her eyes to adjust to the darkness, then cursed her own hesitation. Sergeant Miles might have warned her of the dangers of using light globes in the countryside, but they weren't a danger here.

She cast the spell, then followed the globe back towards the guesthouse. It was strange—almost eerie—just how quickly silence had fallen over the village. The sound of music from the barn faded away into nothingness. She couldn't hear anything, not even the tiny river on the far side of the village. It seemed as cold and silent as the grave.

They must all be in the barn, she thought. It hadn't seemed large enough for everyone, but perhaps it was. *The rest of the village is empty.*

She paused as she passed the headman's house, then walked towards the guesthouse, looking at the smaller houses in between. There was a social structure within the village, even if she didn't fully understand it. But she suspected she didn't really *want* to understand it. She caught sight of the moon, rising slowly above the horizon, casting rays of silver light towards the village. It was far brighter than she'd ever seen it on Earth.

Was it the same moon? She had no way of knowing. The arrangement of the continents were different, but what did that prove? Maybe, just maybe, the continents had taken on a different form in this world. Or perhaps she was on another planet as well as another dimension. There was no way to know.

She heard something behind her and spun around. Hodge appeared, staring at the light globe as if he were hypnotized. Emily started, feeling alarm flashing through her mind. Had he followed her? What did he want? She hadn't heard him before, but that meant nothing. The sergeants had tracked her through the forest at Whitehall effortlessly, never betraying their presence until they were ready to show themselves. A boy who'd grown up in the countryside would know how to move with stealth.

Hodge shook himself and looked directly at Emily. Up close, it was clear that he was more than a little drunk. The look in his face, lecherous and predatory, reminded her far too much of the boys at her old school...she took a step backwards, feeling a very old fear crawling up her spine. She wanted to run, yet could barely move. It felt like a very bad dream.

"Come with me," Hodge said. He was far too drunk to realize just how stupid he was being, she realized in horror. "There's a nearby haystack..."

"No," Emily said, fighting to remain calm. The memories of her stepfather held her firmly in place. She felt terrifyingly helpless, as if there was nothing she could do to ward off her inevitable fate. "You don't want to do this..."

He reached for her and caught her shoulder. Emily shuddered, snapping out of her trance, and batted his hand away. He growled, pulled back his fist and threw a punch at her face. Emily blocked it automatically...

Hodge stared at her in numb surprise. Emily felt equally surprised.

But she shouldn't have been, she realized, as the pain from the impact jerked her awake. She'd had Sergeant Miles and Lady Barb teaching her how to fight, battering lessons into her through pain and hardship...and none of the boys in Martial Magic had gone easy on her, just because she was a girl. Hodge had no formal training at all. He looked almost as if he didn't quite grasp what had happened.

"The average man is stronger than the average woman," Lady Barb had told her. "If you try to grapple with one, chances are he will beat you. You have to be sneaky, determined and, above all, you have to keep your wits about you."

Hodge growled and threw himself at her. Emily stepped to the side, then threw a punch at the back of his neck. She hit him, but he was tough enough to shake it off.

Even so, a strange glow of pleasure ran through her mind as she realized she could *win*. She didn't have to be helpless...and the memories of her stepfather didn't have to hurt her.

Hodge pulled himself around, then glared at her. "Bitch," he growled. "They say magical sluts can do anything."

Emily felt cold hatred raging through her soul. He thought he could just...*take* her? He thought that his position as the headman's son gave him the right to have any girl he wanted? He thought that she would agree to it just because she was magical? Outrage blazed through her mind, pushing away fear and hatred. She wasn't frozen by her own fears any longer. How dare he? How *dare* he?

She shaped a spell in her mind, just as he threw himself at her again. This time, he crashed right into her and sent her falling backwards to the muddy ground, pressing down hard on her body. His hand clawed at her breast. Emily gasped in pain, then unleashed the spell. There was a blinding flash of light and Hodge's weight shifted, then fell off her altogether. Emily looked to the side, dazed. A pig sat there, staring in incomprehension. Its eyes were disturbingly human.

Hodge, she thought. She sat upright, then pulled herself to her feet. The pig emitted a sound, almost as if it was trying to talk. Emily knew it wouldn't work. Even if Hodge had been used to regular transformations, the pig's snout wasn't really designed for human speech. It was quite possible that he wasn't even sure what had happened. The spell would ease the transition from human to pig. A nasty thought occurred to her and she cast a reflective spell before she could think better of it. Hodge saw himself, turned and fled.

Emily stared after him, feeling a strange mixture of emotions. Pride, delight, triumph...and a strange kind of bitter regret. What would this do, she asked herself, to relationships between magicians and villagers? She'd turned the headman's son into a pig! But her breast still hurt...he'd deserved it, she knew. Whatever his father said, whatever *Lady Barb* said, he'd deserved it. She hadn't asked him to attempt to rape her.

And he would have raped her, she knew. She had no doubt of it.

She swallowed hard, then opened the door to the guesthouse and stepped inside. As soon as she had closed the door, she started to cast new protective wards. None of them would last very long, but the only person in the village who could dismantle them was Lady Barb. She would know that something was wrong...Emily hesitated, wondering if she should summon her teacher, then shook her head. She needed time to sort herself out. Casting another light spell, she started to undress. Her tunic was muddy from where she'd fallen, but otherwise unmarked. Her body, on the other hand, was bruised.

Gritting her teeth, she touched her breast lightly. It felt...dirty, unclean...and yet she knew it could be much worse. How many girls had Hodge forced into bed? But if there was so little privacy in the village, surely his father and their parents knew? Didn't they care? Or was there some reason Hodge was allowed to roam free? Did he have enough sense not to pick on his fellow villagers?

She reached for the cloth and washed herself, thoroughly, then pulled on her spare set of walking clothes. The nightgown wouldn't be enough for the night, she knew; she wanted to wear something more covering. Lady Barb wouldn't care; Emily had seen her sleeping in a full suit of armor before, back at Whitehall. She finished pulling on her clothes and walked over to the bed, picking up the potions bottle on the way. Before she could take a swig, she felt Lady Barb starting to dismantle the wards.

Emily hesitated. She could drink the potion and fall asleep, evading the older woman's questions that way, but it wouldn't last. And it would be cowardly. Part of her didn't want to talk, part of her knew she had no choice. If nothing else, Lady Barb would have to say *something* to the headman. Emily knew what *she* wanted to say to him.

The door opened. Lady Barb stood there, staff in hand. Her face was pinched and worried.

"Emily," she said, as she closed the door. "What happened?"

Emily hesitated. She'd won...but part of her felt as though she had lost. It would have been easy to end the fight almost before it had begun, yet she'd been too startled to try. Lady Barb would have understood, she knew that now. But her fears ran deeper than the older woman's anger...

Or they had. Somehow, she wasn't afraid any more.

Slowly, leaving nothing out, she started to explain.

Chapter Sixteen

THEY LEFT THE VILLAGE THE FOLLOWING MORNING, AFTER LADY BARB HAD A BRIEF TALK with the headman. Emily didn't know what she said to him, but no one turned out to wave goodbye as they walked out of the village and headed down a track that ran beside the river towards their next destination. Lady Barb walked in silence for nearly an hour, which was fine with Emily. She wanted time to think for herself.

"Emily," Lady Barb said, finally. "Do you want to talk about it?"

Emily hesitated, then shook her head.

"I think you should, this time," Lady Barb said. "What happened...could easily have been a great deal worse."

Emily nodded, mutely. Hodge could have knocked her out before she even knew he was there...or she might have hesitated long enough for him to do real harm. Or... her imagination provided too many possibilities. She didn't want to think about any of them.

"He thought he could just...take me," she said, softly. "I didn't do anything to suggest I might be interested."

"That isn't uncommon," Lady Barb said. "You'd think he'd know better than to try it on a sorceress."

Emily looked up, surprised. Hodge *had* been an idiot; Emily could have done a lot worse than turn him into a pig. If she'd panicked, she might have accidentally blown him into atoms—and no magic could bring someone back from the dead. What had made him think he could succeed? And he hadn't even been smart enough to knock her out when he had the opportunity.

"You...do not present the appearance of being able to defend yourself," Lady Barb added, warningly. "I've watched you ever since I first knew you; you flinch from men. I think Jade was the only boy near your own age you even talked to, if it could be avoided. Every other man in your life is much older than you."

Emily knew that Lady Barb was right. The Grandmaster and Void were ancient— Void was over a hundred years old—while Sergeant Miles, Professor Thande and even Master Tor were all in their forties, at the very least. It had been impossible to estimate Sergeant Harkin's age, before he'd died, but he'd probably been in his late thirties at the very youngest. And even Jade was several years older than her.

Which didn't stop him proposing to me, she thought. It had honestly never occurred to her that he might be interested. There was at least five or six years between them. *But just how serious was he at the time?*

And yet, why had she been scared of boys her own age?

She looked down at the ground, then at the running river. Memories rose up in her mind, memories of her growth into a young woman...and how her stepfather had watched her, almost constantly. And of what he'd said to her...She didn't want to face those memories again, yet she suspected she no longer had a choice. Lady Barb wouldn't let her avoid them any longer.

"I don't know," she burst out. "Is there something wrong with me?"

Lady Barb lifted her eyebrows. "*Is* there something wrong with you?"

Emily found her hands twisting together and angrily told them to stay still. "I don't know," she said. "I...don't even know what I felt for Jade. If I felt *anything* for Jade."

She hesitated, then pushed on. "He kissed me, last year," she admitted. "I liked it. And yet I didn't like it. And now...he feels like my brother, rather than anything else. Is that wrong?"

"Probably a good thing you didn't agree to his proposal," Lady Barb said. "It might have ruined both of your lives."

Emily swallowed, feeling tears prickling at the corner of her eye. She'd never looked at any boy with interest. Part of her felt that no boy would be interested in her, even though Jade had clearly wanted her. But she also wondered if his proposal had been made out of misplaced pity rather than anything else. Emily had been isolated at the end of First Year, feared by many of the other students. She had had no reason to expect anything better than Jade's proposal.

Lady Barb reached out and placed a hand on her shoulder, steadying her. "Are you interested in girls instead?"

"I don't think so," Emily said, after a moment's thought. She'd been careful to try to undress when no one else was around, but her roommates hadn't been so careful. She'd seen almost all of them naked. But she hadn't felt anything beyond abstract admiration for the sheer perfection of Alassa's body. "I'm not interested in anyone."

"It isn't uncommon for it to take time before someone develops an interest in the other sex," Lady Barb said, dryly. "What happened to you on...where you came from?"

Emily swallowed. "Do we have to talk about it now?"

"This is the best place for it," Lady Barb said. She gave Emily an encouraging smile. "Or would you like to sit down?"

Emily looked down at the muddy path, then shook her head. "No, thank you," she said. "Will you keep it to yourself?"

"As long as you wish me to," Lady Barb said. Her smile grew wider. "You still have to listen to my advice."

Emily hesitated, organizing her thoughts. The hell of it was that her stepfather's treatment of her had been nothing like as overt as the treatment of the poor boy in the village. There had been days when she was sure that he meant her nothing but harm and days when she had been able to convince herself that she was imagining it. It might have been easier if he had beaten her, she reflected. She could have taken that to her teachers and asked for help.

"My father left us when I was very young," she said. Her memories of him were faded and worn, leaving her wondering if they were just the product of her imagination. "I don't know why. My mother never talked about him."

Lady Barb nodded, inviting her to continue.

"She married again, soon afterwards," Emily said. "My stepfather ignored me as much as possible. I don't know what he was thinking. My mum crawled into a bottle soon afterwards and never really emerged long enough to look after me. I had to cook my own food and sort out my own clothes."

The memories mocked her. Cooking hadn't been easy, not when she was still a child. She'd lost count of the number of near-disasters she'd had trying to cook with an oversized pan, learning the hard way. And then she'd had to buy clothes on her own...and manage what little money her stepfather had given her. Most of her clothes had come from charity shops and second-hand stores. She simply hadn't been able to afford anything else. She had never understood why so many other poor children could afford expensive cell phones and fancy clothes.

Lady Barb said nothing, merely listened.

"I could never bring other children to the house," Emily confessed. "They started to mock me because of my clothing, so I retreated into myself once I learned to read. Books were my friends; most people simply ignored me as much as possible. When I grew older..."

She swallowed, feeling her throat constrict. "I started to grow breasts," she admitted. "And I grew up, despite the food."

Lady Barb tilted her head. "And people started to take an interest in you?"

"It took me a long time to notice," Emily said. "My stepfather was *looking* at me. He would watch me from time to time...and he'd never showed any interest in me before. I used to think he didn't even know that I existed."

"You could have been tapping into your magic, without knowing it," Lady Barb said. "Some very young magicians do it. Remaining hidden isn't difficult if you're not trying to hide from a magician."

Emily shook her head. Outside rumors, Earth had no magic...at least as far as she knew. It was vaguely possible, she supposed, that Hogwarts really existed and Harry Potter was a genuine person, but it seemed unlikely. The existence of cell phones with video cameras and orbital satellites would inevitably lead to the end of the masquerade. Besides, she'd never managed to cast a spell until she'd reached Whitehall. But then, she'd never even tried.

"I don't think so," she said, finally. "I think he just didn't care."

She looked down at the ground. "He kept staring at me...and I kept trying to avoid him," she explained. "Sometimes he would say things, disturbing things. I wore shapeless clothes, showered at school and spent as much time as I could away from home. He...just kept looking at me."

"And you were afraid that, one day, he would rape you," Lady Barb said. There was no condemnation in her voice, only quiet understanding. "Did you not have anyone else?"

Emily shook her head. Her mother had been an only child, as far as she knew, and she had no idea what had happened to her father. She wouldn't have asked her stepfather's family for water if she was dying from thirst. And she'd never trusted her teachers enough to ask for help.

"Then Shadye kidnapped me," Emily added. "I've never looked back."

"Nor should you," Lady Barb said, simply. She hesitated, then pushed on. "It's no consolation, Emily, but I have seen worse."

"I know," Emily said, quietly. *She'd* seen worse now, too. "But I still felt vulnerable."

"Which is why you froze in Zangaria," Lady Barb said, thoughtfully. "It isn't everyone who can take lessons learned during training and apply them to the real world."

Emily nodded. Once, she'd looked up military training, thinking that it might provide a way out of her dead end existence. Soldiers on Earth were pushed to the limits during boot camp, trained extensively by men who'd been there and done that, but even they sometimes froze when faced with real combat. Training was made as realistic as possible to hammer it out of them, but it wasn't perfect. It couldn't be perfect.

"So tell me," Lady Barb added. "How do you feel now?"

Emily hesitated, trying to parse out her own feelings. The sense of fear had faded, somehow, after watching Hodge run for his piggy life. She knew she could have taken him even without magic, after spending two years practicing with the sergeants and boys who were bigger and stronger than Hodge—and better trained too. But she still wasn't sure how she felt about men.

"Strange," she said. "I don't feel so scared anymore."

Lady Barb smiled. "He's the one who's scared," she said. "You taught him a lesson."

Emily looked up. "You're not mad at me?"

"Should I be?"

"I don't know," Emily said. Lady Barb *had* told her to try to avoid using magic where possible, but she hadn't told Emily not to defend herself. "Did I do the right thing?"

"Tell me something," Lady Barb said. She placed a hand on Emily's shoulder, making it impossible for Emily to look away. "How many girls do you think he's forced into opening their legs for him?"

"Too many," Emily said. It was the only possible answer. "Even if it wasn't the girls in the village..."

"The headman was appointed by the local lord," Lady Barb told her. "I doubt the morals of his son were considered when the man was given the job. All that mattered was squeezing as many taxes from the village as possible—and the headman is very good at that. As long as he keeps the taxes and tithes coming, the lord wouldn't care if every girl in the village was attacked by Hodge. I'd bet good money that he forced himself on most of them."

Emily shuddered. If she'd grown up in such a place...

"Not just him," Lady Barb added. "There are places where it is traditional for the husband's father to have...access to his daughter-in-law, if he feels like it. Or where a widow can be pushed into marrying a man who already has a wife, if she wants someone to help take care of the kids. Or...there are countless horrors hidden here."

"So you said," Emily said, feeling sick. She didn't want to know, but she thought she should ask. "What happened to him?"

"Hodge?" Lady Barb smiled. "I turned him back, told him that the curse would snap back if he ever tried to force himself on someone else, then gave his father a stern warning. If nothing else, the lord wouldn't have objected if I'd killed him—and he knew it. But I think he's a changed man."

Emily shook her head, doubtfully.

"Oh, he is," Lady Barb assured her. "He spent several hours as a pig, without any mental defenses or prior experience. What do you think that did to his mind?"

"I used a prank spell," Emily said. "Didn't I?"

"You didn't cast it perfectly," Lady Barb said, reprovingly. "Let's just say that parts of him are still convinced he's a pig."

Emily snickered. She knew it was wrong, yet she couldn't help it. The thought of Hodge eating at the trough instead of at the table, convinced it was where he belonged, was darkly amusing. She recalled the struggle to recall who and what she was when she'd turned herself into a rat and snickered again. Hodge would have absolutely no preparation for the transformation at all. Somehow, it was hard to feel any pity for him.

"You need practice," Lady Barb added. "We're going to work on that once we get back to Whitehall."

She shrugged. "I also told him that he was lucky that I hadn't turned him into dinner," she said. "I think the lesson will have sunk in—and if it hasn't, the next time he transforms will leave him stuck that way."

Emily nodded, wondering if a girl in the village would be brave enough to manipulate Hodge into trying something. The thought of leaving someone—anyone—stuck as a pig forever was nightmarish, but it would be worse in Zangaria. She still shuddered when she thought about the wild boar Alassa and her suitors had hunted, wild boar that had actually been transformed humans. It had horrified her at the time—executions would have been kinder—and she'd banned the practice in Cockatrice.

Lady Barb clapped a hand on her shoulder. "You made a good stride forward today," she said, as she turned to lead the way further down the path. "All you have to do is build on that success."

Emily hesitated, then asked the question that had nagged at her mind earlier. "Did you...did you take a lover?"

"I was a little older than you when I fell in love for the first time," Lady Barb said. She didn't seem offended by the question. "It didn't last. He was a little too much like my father and wasn't too keen on the idea of marrying a combat sorceress. We parted reasonably, kindly."

She looked back at Emily. "Is there a reason you asked?"

Emily looked down at the ground. "Is it normal to be so conflicted?"

Lady Barb laughed. "Welcome to the wonderful world of adulthood," she said. "People mature at different speeds, Emily. You may be physically seventeen, old enough to be a mother, but you may not be mentally ready to have a relationship with anyone. And, unlike most of the boys and girls in the Allied Lands, you will have all the time you need to make your choice."

"I don't," Emily said, miserably. "I have to provide an heir for Cockatrice."

"True enough," Lady Barb agreed. "And it *would* have to be your child. You couldn't simply adopt someone and declare him your heir."

She looked back along the path. "What sort of man do you *want?*"

Emily shook her head. Once, she'd dreamed of Prince Charming...but that had been part of her childhood. After she'd started to mature, she'd become too unsure of herself to dream of a prince—or even a princess—coming to take her away. It struck her suddenly that she *could* get a prince now and she giggled, despite herself. But if the princes who had courted Alassa were any indication, she wouldn't want any of them.

But what did she want?

She mulled it over as she walked behind Lady Barb. A gentle man, she decided, someone clever enough to hold a conversation, yet also willing to give her time to herself. Jade wouldn't be that kind of husband, she had to admit, not if the way he'd courted her was any indication. He would always want to be doing things with her; riding, swimming, exploring...and everything else. She would never be alone.

"This looks a good place to stop," Lady Barb said, as they reached a large clearing. It didn't look particularly natural. Someone had carved it out of the trees and then done something to ensure that nothing grew to replace them. "Set up the cauldron and make us some Kava."

Emily realized, to her surprise, that her legs ached. How far had they walked? She nodded and set to work, while Lady Barb paced the clearing and set up a handful of wards, then strode back to her and watched as the Kava boiled. Emily poured it into a pair of mugs, blowing on the liquid to cool it down. Using magic to cool drinks never seemed to work quite right.

"So," she said, as she took a sip. It always tasted better in the open air. "Why are we here?"

"Miles from anyone else," Lady Barb said. The smile on her face took the sting from her words. "Good a place as any to practice some magic that cannot be performed in Whitehall."

Chapter Seventeen

Emily couldn't help feeling a flush of excitement as Lady Barb started to draw runes on the ground.

"The first time you tried to create a pocket dimension," she lectured, "you tried to do it inside another pocket dimension. You were very lucky not to be expelled for gross stupidity."

Emily winced, remembering Master Tor's anger—and the dead Warden. Most students were given a list of things they shouldn't try to do in Whitehall, but Emily had accidentally fallen through the cracks in the system. Void had assumed that the Grandmaster would teach her, she suspected, and the Grandmaster had overlooked the fact *Void* hadn't taught her. And, as Master Tor had believed Void was her father, he had assumed that she was deliberately breaking the rules.

"This time, you shouldn't have any external problems affecting your magic," Lady Bar continued. "However, you should still be very careful. Pocket dimensions can be tricky things to create and maintain."

She finished drawing runes, then reached into her bag and produced a handful of sticks, which she fitted together to make a square. Emily looked down at it in puzzlement, then realized that they were going to focus on the most basic pocket dimension design of all. There was no point in trying to run, she knew, before she could walk. The book Yodel had loaned her had skipped quite a few steps.

"The simplest form of pocket dimension is a bubble attached to an object," Lady Barb continued. "They can be moved with the object, but not separated from it. Nor can they be easily accessed without the object. Should it be destroyed, the pocket dimension will collapse, blasting its contents outwards. Most dimensions have safety spells woven into their structures to prevent that from happening."

Emily nodded. There were pocket dimensions that could be accessed from anywhere, or not bound to a particular object, but they were far more complex. Even the most powerful sorcerers, she'd been told, preferred to avoid them, if only because anyone with the right coordinates could get into the dimension. It was easier to carry a bag that was larger on the inside than risk losing one's property.

"Sit down," Lady Barb directed. She passed Emily the square, motioning for her to hold it up so she was looking through it. "Are you ready?"

Emily nodded.

"I want you to close your eyes and imagine that the interior of the square is solid," Lady Barb said. "I want you to try to visualize the fabric of reality itself."

Emily concentrated. It was easy to *imagine* a shimmering layer inside the square, like a soap bubble, but harder to convince herself that it was real. The pocket dimension would expand outside reality, just like a far smaller version of the TARDIS...or was she actually expanding the space inside the square? Not entirely to her surprise, the books hadn't been too clear on what she was actually doing. There were entire fields of study that were unknown at Whitehall.

"Now," Lady Barb said. "I want you to imagine the fabric expanding, becoming a bubble."

Just like blowing bubbles, Emily thought. She felt her magic shift in response, then fade again as her imagination faltered. The pocket dimension didn't seem to be manageable without her constant attention and she couldn't concentrate on anything for that long. She opened her eyes, just in time to see the light bending around the magic...and then the pocket dimension collapsed.

"Not too bad, for a first attempt," Lady Barb said. She didn't sound angry, merely calm and thoughtful. "Try again?"

Emily nodded and closed her eyes again. This time, the magic seemed to flow easier and, when she opened her eyes, she had the strange impression she was looking through a reversed telescope. It took her a moment to realize that light itself was actually bending around the dimension, distorting her perceptions. A moment later, the dimension snapped back out of existence. Emily rubbed her forehead and felt sweat prickling there. It might not feel like a huge effort, but it was definitely draining.

"Close enough, for the moment," Lady Barb said. "The real trick is stabilizing it, then binding it in place."

She rested a hand on Emily's shoulder. "Ready to try?"

Emily swallowed. Two years at Whitehall had helped her get casting basic spells down to a fine art. Where she'd once had to build the spells up piece by piece, she could now cast many of them with a thought. But now she would have to go back to first principles and start building the spell-structure up from scratch. And she would have to do it while maintaining the pocket dimension in place.

"Yes," she said. She took out her notes and stared down at them, then closed her eyes. "I'm ready."

It was, she decided, rather like building something that had to be anchored to the seabed. An open tube could be lowered to the bottom of the water, then the water could be pumped out and concrete poured into the tube. This time, the spells that held the pocket dimension together had to be placed, one by one, inside the dimension, each one forming part of a chain that was greater than the sum of its parts. Each spell was simple by itself, but the real trick was getting them to work together.

Her first attempt at splitting her attention failed miserably. One of her teachers on Earth had assured her, with a particularly nasty smile, that girls could do two things at once, but she couldn't hold the dimension in place and assemble the spells at the same time. The second time, she managed to get two spells inserted before the dimension collapsed, striking her with a backlash from her own magic. Her hands tingled, forcing her to slap them against her thighs,

Crossly, she tried for the third time...and discovered that she could only get a handful of spells inserted before her concentration slipped. She honestly didn't understand how Yodel had made something as complex as her trunk.

"Drink this," Lady Barb said. "And then try to relax."

Emily took the mug of water and sipped gratefully. She hadn't realized how parched her throat had become until she drank. Lady Barb passed her a bar of sour chocolate and she ate it, wondering bitterly how Yodel managed to make a living. It was terrifyingly easy to manipulate dimensions with a nexus point—Emily knew that, better than anyone—but without one at her disposal she was just playing with sticks and stones. There had to be something she was missing.

"Figure it out," Lady Barb said, mischievously. "You should *know* the answer."

"I don't," Emily said, casting her mind back to recall what had been written in the books. None of them had suggested anything other than what she was doing...but she knew, from bitter experience, that some textbooks left out steps to force readers to actually comprehend what they were doing. She had to admit that they were quite effective at *that*, far better than anything she'd read on Earth. "The spells just don't form..."

She swore under her breath as she made the connection. Mistress Sun had taught her how to prepare spells ahead of time, nestling them within her wards. There was no reason why she couldn't do the same with the spells for the pocket dimension, apart from the fact that she would have to push them away from her wards and into the dimension rather than simply triggering them. She explained her breakthrough to Lady Barb and was rewarded with a brilliant smile.

"Good thinking," Lady Barb said. "Try it."

Emily picked up the square again, then put it on her lap as she built up the dimensional spells, one by one. They were actually simpler than most of the spells she'd lodged within her wards before, something that actually worked in their favor. The more complex a spell, the more likely it was to degrade rapidly over time. Once she was ready, she picked up the square, concentrated on the dimension and thrust her spells forward, into the growing bubble. There was a flare of magic as the bubble tried to collapse, but found itself firmly anchored in place. And yet it still wasn't right...

"The spells aren't chained together perfectly," Lady Barb said. She held up a hand before Emily could banish the dimension and start again. "But you should be able to modify them without collapsing the dimension."

Emily reached out with her magic...and realized, once again, just how skilled Yodel actually was. She'd tampered with her trunk on the road to Zangaria, damaging the spells that held it together, yet it hadn't collapsed or exploded. *Her* dimension was nothing more than a bubble of space and yet she was nervous about touching anything. The slightest movement could collapse the entire dimension into nothingness. It took her several minutes to lock each of the spells in place...

"Good enough," Lady Barb said. "The walls of the dimension are anchored firmly in place."

Emily opened her eyes and looked. Inside the square, she could see a thin grey space, oddly disconcerting to her eyes. She'd never really seen the raw material of her own trunk, even when she'd been trying to work out a way to safely retrieve her books without releasing the Cockatrice. And the dimension she'd tried to craft at Whitehall had been neutralized by the wards before she'd had a chance to see inside it.

Her eyes hurt suddenly as she stepped backwards, one eye seeing the trees at the edge of the clearing while the other looked into the dimension. She understood, suddenly, just how confused the Doctor's companions had been when they'd opened the TARDIS doors for the first time. The police box was tiny, but inside was an entire universe...it was difficult, somehow, to reconcile the two. Human understanding found it hard to grasp that an object could be bigger on the inside than the outside.

Perhaps it's easier for the people here, she thought. *They're used to magic.*

"This dimension won't last *that* long," Lady Barb warned. "You'd probably need to carry it with you or make sure it could draw a trickle of power from the ambient magic in the air."

Emily nodded. She'd have to draw runes around the square...how the hell had Yodel done it? She hadn't seen runes on her trunk.

"Part of the stasis charm holds the trunk secure," Lady Barb told her once Emily had asked. "As long as that's in place, the decay is minimized."

Emily took one last look into her dimension, before she put the square down on the ground. Someone could fall right *inside*, she told herself a moment later. A hidden pitfall...she'd seen something like it when Shadye's forces were besieging Whitehall. But she couldn't leave it indefinitely.

"No," Lady Barb said, when she asked. "You'll have to dispose of it, then start again."

The next two hours were spent creating, dissolving and recreating the pocket dimension. Like all magic, it grew easier the more she practiced, although there were hitches every time she tried to make the spells holding the dimension together more complicated. Emily remembered her notes for a dimensional shelter and realized it might be months before she could perfect the technique, if she could perfect it at all. She wasn't even sure what it would be like to hide in a pocket dimension. Technically, she'd done just that at Whitehall, but Whitehall was special. The entire castle rested inside a pocket dimension.

"That's what they do for certain prisoners," Lady Barb said. "They craft a pocket dimension and toss the prisoner inside. No one, not even the most powerful magician, could break out without help from the outside. Inside, there's nothing to mark the passage of time and so they lose track of how long they've been imprisoned."

Emily felt her blood run cold. That was close—alarmingly close—to what she'd done to Shadye. A normal pocket dimension couldn't be snapped out of existence, along with its contents, but she'd used the nexus to erase Shadye from existence. Under the circumstances, she was surprised that no one had ever guessed the truth—or tried it for themselves.

She pushed the thought aside. They *knew* that a collapsing pocket dimension would expel its contents back into the world. It was quite possible that they wouldn't accept that could be changed. Besides, without the nexus, it would be impossible to repeat the feat.

A thought struck her. "How do they eat and drink in such a place?"

"They don't," Lady Barb said. "The spells keep them alive, no matter how hungry they become. It's torment."

Emily shuddered. There were spells that kept someone awake and reasonably active, but they came with a cost. She'd used one once, during a cramming session before the exams, and started to hallucinate after a few short hours. It hadn't been a pleasant experience. The lecture she'd received from Mistress Irene had been even worse.

"I need to see what it's like to be inside," Emily said, pushing the thought aside. She wasn't sure why, she just wanted to know. "Can you hold it open for me?"

Lady Barb gave her a long considering look. "Not this one, I think," she said. "You couldn't fit through the entrance."

Emily flushed. The square wasn't large enough to allow anyone bigger than a baby to climb inside. In hindsight, she really had been lucky when she'd bagged the Cockatrice. Lady Barb smirked at her expression before drawing up another pocket dimension of her own. Emily watched as it took on shape and form, attached to a specific location rather than an object, and then yawned open in front of her. Somehow, looking into the drab greyness, stepping inside no longer seemed a good idea.

She braced herself and stepped inside. The icy cold hit her as she crossed the threshold, forcing her to hug herself as she turned, just in time to see the entrance vanish. She was surrounded by greyness, a pulsing mass of...*something* that pressed against her mind. It was easy to imagine something watching her, even though she wasn't sure why. She reached out and touched...nothing. The pocket dimension, she realized slowly, was like a giant hamster ball. No matter how hard she ran, she would never escape. It felt like a prison. Hell, it *was* a prison.

There was a sudden shiver as the entrance reopened. Emily cringed from the light, then stepped back out into the normal world. It was so *colorful* compared to the greyness of the pocket dimension.

Lady Barb collapsed the dimension behind her, then gave her a rather droll look. "Satisfied?"

Emily nodded.

Lady Barb rolled her eyes and put her back to work.

Emily crafted two more basic dimensions, then started to experiment with some of the spells. Half of them collapsed as soon as she altered the spells too far, but the remainder held together remarkably well. A little fiddling, Emily decided, and the dimension could be programmed to collapse at a preset time. Combined with the nuke-spell...the possibilities were endless. What would happen, she asked herself, if a nuclear-level blast had nowhere to go?

"You have to be very careful," Lady Barb said, as she collapsed the final dimension. "It's quite easy to drain yourself trying out new spells."

Emily nodded. She felt tired...not completely exhausted, but tired enough not to want to continue. It felt like experimenting with some of the more complex spells Mistress Sun had taught her, including a handful that had forced her to lie down right after casting them. But it had all been worthwhile...

"One last experiment, then," Lady Barb said. She picked up the square and broke it down into its component sections. "I want you to try to anchor the dimension to this clearing, rather than to an object."

"I'll try," Emily said.

She concentrated, but it was far harder to envisage the opening into the pocket dimension without something to serve as a guide. Every time she tried, the dimension refused to work properly or drained her too far to hold it together. She ground her teeth in frustration, then looked up at Lady Barb pleadingly.

The older woman took pity on her. "I'd be astonished if you managed to master it so quickly," she said. "It took me weeks before I could even shape a basic dimension without an anchor."

Emily was too tired to be angry. "Then why did you ask me to try?"

"Because some students leapfrog ahead if they don't know the limits," Lady Barb told her, sardonically. "You've already shown a definite talent for charms and spell improvisation. I thought...why not let you try to build a proper dimension?"

She shook her head. "But it will take time for you to master it, I think," she added. "I think you can do a little practice each day."

Emily nodded wearily.

"But you will not experiment with pocket dimensions without supervision," Lady Barb warned her. There was a grim note in her voice that left Emily with no doubt that disobedience would be a very bad idea. "If you do, you will not enjoy the consequences—if you survive."

"Understood," Emily said, looking down at the ground. She'd learned that lesson, even if part of her sometimes resented being held back. But then, she wasn't really being held back at all, was she? "I won't experiment without you."

Lady Barb passed her a vial of nutrient potion, waited for her to drink it and then stood. "It's another hour or two to the town," she said, "and it looks like rain. We don't want to be caught out here if we can avoid it."

Emily glanced up. Dark clouds were forming, high overhead, and the temperature was dropping rapidly. The weather here wasn't as variable as the weather surrounding Whitehall, owing to the high concentration of magic in the air, but it was still capable of changing at remarkable speed. She stood, packed the mug away in her bag and followed the older woman as she turned and led the way out of the clearing.

"How long will it be," she asked, as they walked, "until I can make a dimension within seconds?"

"You have the power," Lady Barb said. "All you need is the skill...and that will come, in time. Practice makes perfect."

"Thank you," Emily said. "I won't let you down."

Chapter Eighteen

T HE RAIN STRUCK THEM THIRTY MINUTES LATER. LADY BARB ERECTED A WARD TO KEEP IT from falling directly on them, but water still splashed around their feet as they continued down the path. Emily was grateful for the charmed boots she'd purchased at Dragon's Den; no matter how wet it was, they wouldn't allow water to soak her feet. But it was still a relief when the rainstorm came to an end and they looked down into another valley.

Emily sucked in her breath once she saw the town. It was larger than the village they'd left in the morning, with another castle on the nearby peak looming over the valley. She'd learned more than she wanted to know about good locations for castles, thanks to Alassa, and she had to admit that whoever had designed this particular castle had done an excellent job. It would be extremely difficult to get an army up the hill without being seen.

Magic could probably even the odds, she thought, *but if the defenders had magic too...*

She broke off that thought as Lady Barb led her down into the village. The houses looked better-made than the ones in the previous village. Here, they were almost all made of stone and looked remarkably sturdy, even to her untrained eyes.

But why do they have grass on their roofs? She wondered. *On a stone house?*

Her thoughts sharpened as she realized that almost no one seemed to be out in the open, even though it was still raining heavily. A chill ran down her spine as she recalled countless horror movies, then grew worse as they walked into the center of town and saw the soldiers.

Emily had never met a soldier before traveling to Whitehall, but she'd learned a great deal since then, thanks to the sergeants. These soldiers looked professional, wearing leather armor and colors that marked them out as household troops. They all wore the same outfits too, which suggested they weren't mercenaries. And they didn't seem to be harassing the townspeople too much...but that they were there at all was worrying.

She shook her head, mentally. The sergeants had told their classes that many soldiers couldn't be trusted not to harass the local civilians, no matter where they were based or what their orders were. Looting, rapes, and even fights weren't uncommon, even when the soldiers were at home. When they were on the march, invading another kingdom, it was even worse. Still, Emily wasn't too surprised. The aristocrats, even enemy aristocrats, were off-limits, but civilians were fair game. Europe had seen the same pattern until the First World War.

Lady Barb stopped as one of the soldiers marched over to confront them. Emily suspected, looking at the slightly finer cut of his clothes, that he was an officer, although it was difficult to be sure. The Allied Lands had hundreds of different military units and they all had different ways of signifying an officer. But his outfit was clean, suggesting that he wasn't used to actually being out and about with his men.

Or maybe she'd been imbued with more of Sergeant Harkin's feelings about officers than she'd realized.

"Lady Sorceress," the officer said, addressing Lady Barb. He didn't look at Emily, for which she was grateful. Most of his men seemed to be carefully looking elsewhere. "We are looking for the missing heir."

Lady Barb's back seemed to stiffen, just slightly. "The missing heir?"

"Rudolf, the son of our lord," the officer informed her. "He has gone missing. We have searched the town, but he is nowhere to be found."

There's an entire mountain range to search, Emily thought, sardonically. She kept the thought to herself, preferring to stay unnoticed as long as possible. Maybe the town could be searched rapidly, but it was right underneath the castle. If Rudolf had wanted to hide, he could have left his father's lands completely. It wasn't as if it had taken more than a few hours for them to leave one lord's territory and move into the next.

"He may well have hidden elsewhere," Lady Barb said. Perhaps she'd had the same thought. "Do you have any objection to us moving into the magician's house?"

The officer shook his head. "The building remains sealed," he said. "I don't think he's hiding there."

"We will be sure to check," Lady Barb assured him. Emily could hear a hint of mockery in her tone. "And if you'll excuse us…"

She walked past the officer and headed down the street. Emily followed, wishing the soldiers would keep their eyes to themselves as she strode past their positions. All of them were staring, even though some of them surely should've known better—the older ones looked just as old and scarred as Sergeant Harkin. Their stares left her feel exposed, almost naked…and yet she felt more confident than she ever had before, when dealing with male stares. Hodge had taught her, quite by accident, that she actually could defend herself.

Emily calmed herself. She could handle it. And she could follow Lady Barb's lead.

And then she remembered what she'd overheard at the dance.

"The other lord was building up his army," she muttered, as soon as they were out of earshot. "Is this lord doing the same?"

"Probably," Lady Barb said. "That isn't a good sign."

She said nothing else as they walked down the street. Emily looked around, catching sight of a temple built out of stone, resembling a Greco-Roman building from the classical age on Earth. It didn't look to be dedicated to a particular god, she decided; there were no statues outside, indicating who or what was worshipped within its walls. That wasn't too surprising; the locals simply didn't have the resources to build many temples. Their gods would have to share.

The thought made her smile. Religion was odd in the Allied Lands, at least compared to Earth. There were hundreds of gods, but a person might worship only one or two in his or her lifetime, making the choice when they reached adulthood. Parents didn't seem to expect children to follow in their footsteps; instead, they taught the children that all the gods were real and let them choose their own to worship. In some ways, she had to admit that it worked better than the system on Earth, where parents were known to disown or kill children for changing their religion.

She straightened up as she heard a clap of thunder in the distance. The rainstorm seemed to be moving back towards the town. Lady Barb stopped outside a long low building, pressing her hand against the door while casting a series of charms. The door unlocked itself, allowing them to step into the building. Inside, it was dark and cold.

Emily watched as Lady Barb cast a light-spell, covering her eyes until they became accustomed to the glare. The main room was dusty, while the next two rooms looked disordered, as if the people who'd last been in the building hadn't bothered to clean up before they'd departed. Lady Barb muttered a vile curse, just loud enough for Emily to hear, as she peeked into the kitchen. Emily sniffed and almost gagged. There was a foul smell in the air.

She followed Lady Barb into the kitchen, wondering if something had been left out to decay. "Are these places supposed to be so ill-kept?"

"No. I shall be filing official complaints," Lady Barb said, tartly. "They should have cleaned the damn place before they left."

Emily looked back into the main room. It wasn't even remotely clean—and they were meant to be seeing patients. The magicians knew the importance of basic sanitation, but not all of them seemed to care. They could cure almost anything that didn't kill them outright. She glanced into the next room and scowled. The potions table—she recognized its purpose because of the burn marks—was dangerously unstable.

Lady Barb climbed up a ladder into the loft. Moments later, her voice drifted back. "They cleaned the beds, at least," she said. "We'll have to hire some people to help clean the building before we start seeing patients."

Emily followed her up the ladder. The loft was smaller than she'd expected—she had to duck her head to avoid the ceiling—but there was something about it that charmed her. Two glass windows—rare outside the big cities—allowed her to look down into the street, while four beds, pressed close together, provided sleeping accommodation. Lady Barb pointed to a cupboard and ordered Emily to make the beds, then clambered back down the ladder and vanished. Sighing, Emily did as she was told.

It still amused her just how few of her classmates at Whitehall had known how to make their own beds when they'd come to the school. Even some of the poorest students hadn't known, while Alassa and her fellow aristocrats had always had servants to do the work for them. Emily had been making her own bed since she was a child, as well as washing her own sheets, something they *didn't* have to worry about at Whitehall. Everything was washed by the servants and then returned to the student bedrooms.

She made up two of the beds, then scrambled back down the ladder in time to see Lady Barb re-enter the building. "I've had a word with a couple of people," Lady Barb said, as she closed the door. "The entire room will have to be cleaned thoroughly, so they'll be coming in the morning. There's no point in you expending effort outside the potions lab, so you can concentrate on that tomorrow."

Emily wasn't sure if she should be angry or relieved. Cleaning was something else she'd done as a child, but she'd never liked doing it. And, at Whitehall, she'd once been forced to clean an entire suite of rooms by hand as a punishment. She'd found a way to cheat, slightly, but it still hadn't been a very pleasant experience.

"They shouldn't have left it in such a mess," she said, tiredly. "Why...?"

"The runes seem to have been degraded slightly," Lady Barb said. "Several of them have been destroyed completely. I think someone tried to break in at one point."

"And disabled the runes that should have kept the building safe," Emily concluded. She felt oddly better to hear that it might not have been their predecessor's fault. "Who would dare break into a magician's residence?"

"I don't know," Lady Barb confessed. "A mundane couldn't have entered the building without permission, while a magician shouldn't have had any problems breaking and entering. The wards weren't designed to keep out anyone with magic."

She stroked her chin. "An odd puzzle. Maybe we'll stay long enough to figure out the answer."

Emily frowned. "The missing heir?"

"It's a possibility," Lady Barb agreed. She turned and started to pace the room. "I don't recall if there was any magic in the lord's bloodline, but it is definitely a distinct possibility."

She paused, then turned away from Emily. "But local politics aren't one of our concerns, not now," she said. "Our task remains the same."

Emily wasn't so sure—the heir could easily have been kidnapped by the unknown magician, if there *was* a magician—but she held her peace. Their task was to use magic to help people while searching for new magicians, not get caught up in petty politics.

"The town is effectively occupied," Lady Barb told her. "I'd advise you to stay inside unless you're with me. Or are you feeling confident enough to stand up for yourself?"

"I am," Emily said. After what she'd done to Hodge, she felt more confident than she'd ever been in her life. "I can go out."

"Make sure you wear your robes," Lady Barb told her. She paused. "There's no point in trying to cook here. We'll go out to eat. Get changed."

Emily nodded and scrambled back up the ladder, carrying her bag with her. It would be so much easier to carry a bag that was linked to a pocket dimension, but Lady Barb had forbidden it. Instead, she opened her bag, removed her robes and then looked around for the sink. It turned out that the only place to wash was in the main room. Grateful that there were no boys around, Emily carried her robe back down the ladder, then washed and dressed quickly and silently while Lady Barb merely pulled a robe over her outfit.

Something clicked in Emily's mind. "How did he know you were a sorceress?"

"Few women would move from place to place unescorted, not here," Lady Barb told her. "The ones who do have protections...magic, for instance."

She opened the door and led the way outside. Night was falling, the final rays of sunlight cascading off the darkened castle. Emily shivered at the sight–the castle looked spooky in the semi-darkness - before following Lady Barb through a twisting network of streets and into a small inn. Inside, it was warm, but there were only a handful of visitors. The innkeeper looked up at them with interest, then pointed to a nearby wooden table. Emily sat down gratefully as Lady Barb pointed to a chalk-board. It listed only three different kinds of food.

"There are only a few people here," Emily muttered. "Is that a bad sign?"

"There are soldiers in the town," Lady Barb muttered back. "Most visitors will have moved on, even if they were planning to stay a few days."

The innkeeper marched over to stand by the table. Emily had to smile when she saw him clearly; he was a fat balding man with a pleasant smile and a tunic that clung to the wrong places. But he was definitely a decent person. Compared to the people she'd met in the last village, it was something of a relief.

"Lady Sorceress," he said, addressing Lady Barb. "What can I get for you?"

"The meat pie would be fine," Lady Barb said. "Millie?"

Emily started, then remembered what she was being called. "The meat pie for me, too," she said, quickly. "And drinks?"

"Two beers," Lady Barb said. Emily gave her a sharp look. "Your finest, if you please."

Lady Barb waited until the innkeeper had retreated, then explained. "You can use spells or potions to remove the alcohol," she reminded Emily. "But you shouldn't drink water in the towns up here, not unless there's no alternative. There's no way to know what might have gone into it."

Emily shuddered, remembering her reading. Alcohol was often safer to drink than water, certainly in eras before they'd understood the value of using boiling water to kill germs. It made sense for the villagers—even the children—to drink alcohol all the time, but it did nothing for their behavior.

The innkeeper returned, carrying two foaming mugs of beer, and a large sheet of paper. Emily looked at it and had to fight down a laugh.

"The latest broadsheet," the innkeeper assured them. "It came all the way from Garn, it did."

Emily took the paper and examined it, carefully. It was shoddy material, com-pared to anything from Earth, and there were only a handful of pages, but it was far superior to anything they'd had before she'd arrived. The words used English let-ters—she parsed them out, one by one—and talked about news from across the Allied Lands. There was even an article on the Mimic attack on Whitehall!

"Your influence," Lady Barb said, once the innkeeper had departed. "You should be proud."

"Maybe," Emily said. "At least they're not printing nude pictures yet."

She read through the article—noting just how many inaccuracies there were—and then passed the paper to Lady Barb. Investigative journalism clearly had a long way to go. But then, the writer had probably only heard garbled rumors.

She shook her head. Somehow, an entire market for romantic stories had appeared in Zangaria, competing with regular news and informational bulletins. King Randor had encouraged the spread of such bulletins, hoping to ride the winds of change. Emily had a private suspicion that he'd come to regret it, even though it did have some advantages. The population of Zangaria seemed to have an instinctive respect for the written word, perhaps because so few of them had been able to write in the old system. That was probably about to change.

The meat pie smelled good when it was placed in front of her, but Emily found it hard to eat. Much of the meat was gristle, rather than actual meat, and the potatoes that came with it were either too hard or too soft. It was a far cry from the food at Whitehall or Zangaria's castles, a reminder that anyone who went to Whitehall might well be seduced away from their homes and families.

"There's only ever one inn in the major towns," Lady Barb explained, once she'd erected a privacy ward. "The innkeeper has a captive audience. But if you were born here, you wouldn't be rejecting the meat."

Emily flushed, ashamed of herself for being picky. She wouldn't have rejected the meat on Earth, either. But Whitehall's food was perfect.

"I see," she said. There were several inns in Dragon's Den, encouraging competition. But here, one innkeeper could charge whatever he wanted. "What happens if there's no inn?"

"Travelers tend to offer money to locals in exchange for a place to sleep," Lady Barb said. "But accommodation can be uncomfortable."

Emily envisaged sleeping on the floor in a cramped room and shuddered. It was bad enough sharing a room at Whitehall, even though there was some privacy. The peasants and their guests would have a far harder time getting any privacy. And there might not be enough food or drink, no matter how much money the guests offered. What good was money to the peasants if there was nothing to buy?

They finished their dinner, paid the innkeeper and walked back to the building. Darkness had fallen completely, a faint glow over the horizon showing that the moon had yet to rise. Emily followed Lady Barb, who seemed to have no difficulty in navigating in the dark, and carefully avoided a handful of soldiers on patrol. The soldiers gave them a wide berth.

"Don't forget the insect ward this time," Lady Barb reminded her, as they climbed up the ladder and into bed. "You don't want to be bitten again."

Emily nodded, cast the wards, and lay down on the bed without bothering to undress. She was asleep almost before her head hit the pillow.

Chapter Nineteen

T HE SOUND OF A COCKEREL JERKED EMILY OUT OF A DREAMLESS SLEEP, LEAVING HER STAR-
ing blankly for a long moment. It was an unfamiliar room—another unfamiliar
room—and there was no sign of Lady Barb. After a moment, Emily rolled over and
stood up, silently cursing her decision to sleep in her clothes. They felt icky and
uncomfortable after a night in a hot bed.

"Better get up and washed," Lady Barb called, from the lower floor. "They'll be
here soon enough."

Emily scowled and headed for the trapdoor. Once she was downstairs, she washed
up quickly, then donned her working clothes. Lady Barb passed her a plate of bread
and cheese, telling her not to dawdle over her food. They had plenty of work to do.

"I think you're giving me all the boring jobs," Emily said, as she tucked into the
plate of food. "Is that what always happens in an apprenticeship?"

"Of course," Lady Barb said. There was no rebuke in her tone, merely a hint of
droll amusement. "The apprentice trades her services in exchange for training."

Emily nodded, finished her plate of food and walked into the potions lab. It was a
mess, worse than she'd realized; several bottles of potions and ingredients had been
left unsealed, their contents decaying and leaking into the air. She cursed under her
breath, trying to imagine Professor Thande's reaction to such carelessness in the
alchemy classroom, then started to sort out the damaged bottles. She knew better
than to risk using any of the decaying ingredients. *Anything* could happen if she did.

"We're short on a dozen ingredients," she said, once she'd separated out the use-
able ingredients from the unusable ones. "I don't know if I can brew all the potions."

Lady Barb stepped inside and examined the damaged bottles, then nodded. "It
looks as though our mystery burglar actually *did* manage to get inside," she said.
"Such carelessness would be rare for a trained magician."

Emily couldn't disagree. One lesson that had been hammered into her head, time
and time again, was that stupid magicians tended to kill themselves before too long.
Magicians who pushed the limits, in the meantime, were often exiled to deserted
mountaintops or deserts where they could carry out their experiments with no risk
to anyone else. There were very definite limits to just how far an untrained magician
could go before risking madness—or death.

"Put the spoiled ingredients out for disposal, then clean up the rest of the lab,"
Lady Barb ordered. "Once that's done, brew pain-relief and quick-heal potions first;
we'll see what you have left afterwards."

Emily nodded and started to work. There were spells to clean tables and instruments, but Professor Thande had told her that alchemical tools should never be
cleaned by magic. He'd told his class enough horror stories to convince even the
laziest that there were worse things that could happen than spending a few minutes
washing their tools manually. But, after scrubbing the table until her hands were aching and sore, Emily found herself wishing she could use magic. The table had been
used for years, and it showed.

Muttering under her breath, she gathered herself, then found a handful of cauldrons in one cupboard. Three of them looked clean, but one had clearly been used and put away because it was still coated with the remains of the last potion someone had brewed. Emily swallowed a curse before washing the cauldron thoroughly and placing it out to dry. It struck her, a moment too late, that she should have tried to study the residue to determine what the last brewer had actually tried to create.

Lady Barb will have checked, she told herself. *But how could she get any answers out of this mess?*

She heard the sound of voices, male and female, outside as she set out the clean cauldrons and filled them with water, lighting non-magical fires under them. Once the water was heating up, she glanced out the door and saw a handful of young men and women enthusiastically scrubbing the floor and table in the main room. Lady Barb was nowhere to be seen, but Emily heard her voice drifting back from the kitchen. Emily had to smile—Lady Barb could pay the teenagers more than they would earn elsewhere—and turned back to the cauldrons. Brewing more than one potion at a time required careful concentration and was generally discouraged unless there was no alternative. She dropped in the first set of ingredients and watched, carefully, as the potions slowly brewed.

Lady Barb stepped into the room and nodded, approvingly. "Keep a sharp eye on that one," she instructed, pointing at the last cauldron. "It smells funny."

Emily flushed, embarrassed. Alchemy was definitely not one of her skills. Professor Thande seemed to have a sixth sense for alchemical combinations that were about to go disastrously wrong, but Emily didn't share it. There were times she suspected that she wouldn't be allowed to take Alchemy past Fourth Year, no matter how well she did in other subjects. No matter how she tried, she had no idea that something was going wrong until it was too late to fix.

"I will," she promised. She glared down at the shimmering green liquid, trying to tease out whatever it was Lady Barb had sensed. But nothing came to mind. "What can you smell?"

Lady Barb shrugged. Emily gritted her teeth in frustration. Some magic senses could be described easily, but not alchemy. Either she understood it instinctively, she suspected, or she would never understand it at all. She shook her head, then lowered the temperature for four of the cauldrons. The potion needed to cool down before it became drinkable.

"We're short of bottles," she said, as Lady Barb inspected the potions and pronounced them satisfactory. "Can we buy more here?"

"Perhaps," Lady Barb said. "Bottle up what you can, then put a preservation spell on the remaining potions. I'll use them first."

She left, leaving Emily to finish the job. The final potion suddenly emitted a shower of sparks, then died. Emily swore under her breath, and carefully disposed of the wasted materials. Lady Barb had been right. Something had definitely gone wrong during the brewing process.

One of the ingredients must have decayed, she told herself. She'd been careful to make sure that the right proportion of ingredients had been dropped into each of the cauldrons. Professor Thande had taught them to make sure they used properly-prepared ingredients, but there was no alchemical supplier in the town as far as she knew. Whoever had raided the store hadn't bothered to make sure they didn't damage any of the remaining supplies.

She bottled as much as she could, checking the preservation spells carefully, then carried one of the cauldrons into the main room. The floor shone, having been scrubbed vigorously, while the tables looked perfectly clean. Emily caught the eye of a handful of youngsters eating at the table, no older than herself, before they looked away. She felt an odd sense of loss, knowing that she was from a different world in more ways than one. They couldn't be friendly with Apprentice Millie, let alone Baroness Emily.

"Good work," Lady Barb said, as Emily placed the cauldron on the table nearest to the wall and attached a handful of spells to ensure it wouldn't spill. She pointed into the kitchen, warningly. "Get some lunch."

Emily was surprised at the brusqueness of her tone, but supposed Lady Barb didn't want to appear too familiar with others around. She nodded and stepped into the kitchen, finding more bread and cheese under a preservation spell. Beside it, there was a large bowl of green and red apples. There was nothing meaty at all, as far as she could tell. Regretfully, she started to chew the bread without going back into the main room. She didn't want the others staring at her while they ate their lunch.

There was a loud knock at the door. Emily stood, hastily replaced the preservation spells, and walked back out into the main room as Lady Barb opened the door. A heavily-pregnant woman stood on the other side, sweat pouring down her face. She started to gasp an explanation, but Emily already understood. The woman's contractions had begun and she was about to give birth. A moment later, she staggered and fell to the ground.

"Help me get her onto the table," Lady Barb snapped. She waved her hand, banishing the food and drink to another table. The visitors started backwards in shock, even though they'd *known* that Lady Barb was a sorceress. Magic wasn't really part of their lives. "Hurry!"

The two boys ran forward and helped the woman to her feet, half-carrying her towards the table. Emily picked up a bottle of relaxant and brought it to Lady Barb. Something nagged at the corner of her mind as the woman was placed on the table, an odd sense that something wasn't entirely right. But she couldn't place it.

Lady Barb looked at the two girls. "Do you know who she is?"

"Jeanette," the older of the two girls said. Or at least Emily assumed she was the oldest. It was hard to tell in the countryside, when a young girl could look at least a decade older. "She's married to my cousin."

"Go tell him that she's here," Lady Barb said. She passed her hand over Jeanette's chest, casting a diagnostic spell. "She's going to give birth in a few hours."

The girl nodded and fled out the door. Lady Barb carefully poured the potion into Jeanette's mouth, holding her upright so she could swallow safely.

At least there wouldn't be much pain, Emily told herself. Theory lessons on attending a birth had noted that relaxant potion could prevent pain from overwhelming the mother, without harming the child. Emily could only hope they were right.

She frowned as the two boys stepped closer, eager to see. Something was wrong with them, something that kept nagging at her. It didn't feel dangerous...

"Go," Lady Barb ordered them, shortly. "There may be more work later."

Emily saw it, suddenly. One of the boys had calloused hands, the legacy of hard work since he was old enough to walk on his own two feet, the other...had soft hands, the hands of someone who had never lifted anything heavier than a sword. He reminded her of some of Alassa's suitors...she looked up into his face and knew, beyond a shadow of a doubt, that she was looking at the missing heir. He'd hidden out in the town right below his father's castle!

He looked back at her and knew she'd made the connection. Before she could say a word, he turned and bolted from the house, fleeing into the countryside as if devils were after him. Emily hesitated and looked at Lady Barb. The older woman seemed to have made the same connection.

"Go after him," she snapped, as Jeanette let out a moan. "Find out what he was doing here."

Emily turned and ran out the door. The missing heir—Rudolf, she reminded herself—had vanished into the countryside, jumping across the stream that marked the edge of the town and losing himself among the trees. Emily cursed and gave chase, remembering all-too-well just how easily she'd been outrun by the boys during Martial Magic. She had to hope that Rudolf didn't have any magical assistance or she'd never find him at all.

The trees thickened rapidly as she followed him, hearing the sounds of a body crashing through the undergrowth ahead of her. She gritted her teeth as branches seemed to lash out at her, holding her hands up to protect her face as she ran. The sound of his footsteps seemed to fade as she ran faster, although she couldn't tell if he was outrunning her or if he'd decided to go to ground somewhere. It would be far too easy, she reflected sourly, for him to hide. She hadn't had time to even *think* of attaching a tracking hex to his back.

She paused as the sound of footsteps faded away, breathing hard as she stared into the shadows. Sergeant Harkin had followed his students through the forest without breaking a sweat, without the use of any magic at all. It hadn't been so surprising, somehow, at the time, but in hindsight...He'd been a remarkable man. A twinge of the old guilt rose up within her—Sergeant Harkin had been one of her few father-figures—but she pushed it away ruthlessly. There was no time to let her mind wander.

What did Rudolf want? The question nagged at her mind. Why had he run from his father? And why hadn't he run *further*? Emily knew she was observant—it was one of the things she'd been taught in martial magic—but surely someone who actually *knew* him might have spotted his disguise earlier. Hell, why hadn't the other teenagers betrayed him? The town wasn't large enough for a stranger to remain unnoticed?

And was it any of their business?

Emily listened, carefully, but apart from the chirping of birds she heard nothing. Rudolf had either outpaced her completely or he was hiding, trying to sneak away as quietly as possible. The question nagged at her mind. *Was* it any of their business? Lady Barb had told her, time and time again, that they had to stay out of local politics. But Emily couldn't help feeling sorry for someone fleeing an abusive parent—if, of course, the lord *was* abusive. Was that why Rudolf had fled?

She shook her head, dismissing the thought, then slipped forward as quietly as possible. The undergrowth was even murkier than it was at Whitehall; it was quite possible that she would walk very close to Rudolf and miss him completely. If he'd been running through the forest as a child, he'd be able to hide...she glanced around, looking for signs of his path, but saw nothing. No doubt he knew how best to hide himself.

Should she call out to him? Emily considered it, then dismissed the thought. Anyone could hear her shouting, including the soldiers. If they'd noticed Rudolf as he fled...no one seemed to have followed Emily, but that didn't prove anything. She continued creeping forward, listening carefully. Something moved, far too close to her, and she jumped, then stared at a shape crouching on the ground.

She found her voice. "Rudolf?"

The shape moved, rolling over and standing up. Up close, even wearing peasant clothes, Rudolf was a handsome youth. His dark hair fell over an elegantly-shaped face, with no trace of any of the blemishes she'd seen on the other town children. In some ways, he reminded her of Jade, but there was a harder edge to his smile. He watched her with the deepest of suspicion.

Emily readied a spell, in case he attacked her, but held up her hands. "Why are you running?"

Rudolf stared at her. "It's none of your business," he snapped. "Get out of my life."

"You're the one who walked into our building," Emily pointed out. It wasn't very mature, but she couldn't help it. "I need to know what you were doing there."

"Hiding," Rudolf said, after a long moment. "I wanted to be safe."

Emily lifted her eyebrows. "In the middle of a small army of soldiers?"

"Those dunces never see anything," Rudolf growled. The disdain in his voice made her wince. Sergeant Miles had taught her that even an untrained opponent could be dangerous. "Father has been pulling in more recruits than he can train."

Emily shrugged. Clearly, Rudolf knew his father's men better than she did. And she had to admit that he'd been right. It had been an outsider who had finally spotted him. "Why are you on the run?"

Rudolf met her eyes. "Can I have your word you won't betray me?"

"I don't know," Emily countered. Oaths were dangerous things and she'd already sworn one, which might come back to haunt her sooner or later. "Can I have your word that it's none of our concern?"

"My father wants me to marry someone," he said. "I don't want to marry her."

Emily winced. She understood the impulse, all right. God knew she'd had enough marriage proposals from people she didn't even know to be grateful that Void wasn't trying to sell her to the highest bidder. Some of the girls and boys she knew at Whitehall had precisely that problem. Their families saw them as breeding stock first and individuals second. It was even worse among the aristocracy.

"Don't come after me," Rudolf said. There was a pleading note in his voice. He was begging her, she realized. Whoever his father wanted him to marry had to be horrible. "Please!"

He turned and fled at blinding speed. Emily gave chase, but this time Rudolf had a advantage. She reached for a spell, shaping it in her mind, but dismissed the magic before it had properly formed. Rudolf had done her no harm. Instead, she followed him through a tangled mass of trees...and ducked, too late, as something lashed out at her head. The world seemed to explode into darkness...

...She hit the ground, hard enough to hurt. Her head spun madly; she'd hit a branch, she realized, through the haze covering her thoughts. She felt sick; she rolled over, swallowing desperately. The world seemed to fade in and out of her awareness...she wondered, in a moment of clarity, if this was how she was going to die. After everything she'd done, it was a little anticlimactic. Her body seemed too weak to move.

There was a hiss, right in front of her. Emily opened her eyes, unaware of exactly when she'd closed them, and looked. Her entire body froze with fear.

She was staring into the golden eyes of a Death Viper.

Chapter Twenty

EMILY CAUGHT HER BREATH, TOO SCARED TO MOVE.
The snake was sitting on her chest, its eyes fixed on her face with unblinking malice. It wasn't very large, barely longer than her hand, with blue-gold scales, but she knew it was absolutely lethal. Even *touching* it with her bare skin risked losing her hand; a single bite would kill her within seconds. Its head slowly rose, moving from side to side hypnotically. She couldn't escape the sensation that it was biding its time before striking.

She tried frantically to think of a plan. A movement, any movement, might cause the snake to strike; there was no way she could get it off her by herself. She could try to use magic, but if she alarmed the snake she might be bitten faster. And her body had to be warmer than the surrounding environment, considering the chill. It was unlikely the snake would want to move elsewhere until it got hungry, and it might bite her before then anyway.

The snake hissed. Emily felt a shiver running through her body as she stared at it, wondering if she dared try to jump to her feet. If she did it fast enough, maybe she could throw the snake somehow before it could bite her.

But her mind refused to believe it; fear kept her still, as motionless as possible. She knew it was only a matter of time until the snake bit her. She wanted to use magic to call Lady Barb, but her concentration was so badly shot she wasn't sure she could cast the spell without alarming the creature. Lady Barb might find her dead and rotting body after the snake had eaten its fill.

She met the golden eyes again and shuddered, despite her best efforts. The snake seemed to reach out and invade her mind, although she wasn't sure if it was real or if it was just her imagination, aided and abetted by fear. There was something about it that held her frozen, something more than the threat of being bitten or merely touched. She felt a sudden warmth against her chest and realized, in horror, that the snake's venom was slowly oozing through her shirt. It wouldn't be long before the poison sank into her body and killed her outright.

A thought occurred to her as she stared at the snake. She knew the spells for taking a familiar, an animal companion, but she'd never been able to bond with anything. It wasn't common—only a handful of magicians ever bonded with an animal—but the spells had been hammered into her head in Second Year. Did she dare try to take the snake as a familiar? She tried desperately to recall what she'd been told about such creatures; they couldn't harm their humans, if she recalled correctly, and they aided with certain types of magic. But there was a price in return...

The warmth against her chest grew stronger. There wasn't much time left.

Emily braced herself and cast the spell despite the risk of provoking an immediate attack. The Death Viper hissed angrily as the magic reached out to touch it, then there was a sudden blur of sensation that threatened to overwhelm Emily's mind. It felt like she'd been transfigured into a snake herself in some ways, but different, too...

as if she was both human and snake at the same time. She had a sudden vision of her body, her pale face staring in fear, before the magic faded away.

The Death Viper hissed—somehow, the sound was no longer so threatening—and slid off her chest. Emily let out a sigh of relief and, despite her exhaustion, stood upright. The Death Viper looked up at her with a curiously biddable expression, insofar as it could *have* an expression. It took her a moment to realize that she was reading its emotions through the familiar bond.

It felt...strange. Every work of fiction she'd read concerning familiars suggested that they could talk to their pet humans. Instead, all she received from the creature were impressions, half of which didn't even make any sense. The ground was warm, she was warm, the rest of the world was not...she shook her head, unsure what to do. Most familiar bonds were forged under controlled conditions. But she'd never heard of anyone trying to bond with a Death Viper, ever.

She looked down at her shirt and gasped. There was a dark mark on her chest where the snake had sat, its poison slowly oozing through the material. Emily gritted her teeth, then carefully—very carefully—pushed the shirt away from her body and disintegrated it into dust, acidic poison and all. There was an odd resonance in her magic—it was linked to the snake now, she realized—which faded away almost as quickly as she noticed it. Her undershirt felt thin and revealing against her chest, but there was no alternative. Rudolf had hardly given her time to snatch up her bag before she'd run after him.

Shaking her head, she looked down at the snake, which looked back at her. The waves of snakelike sensations grew stronger as she met the golden eyes. It loved her, she realized dimly, even though part of it realized that the feeling wasn't natural. But then, what sort of idiot would try to domesticate a Death Viper? The snakes were so lethal that nature hadn't even bothered to provide them with any form of camouflage.

"So tell me," she said, out loud. "What should I call you?"

There was no response. Emily rolled her eyes at herself; of *course* there wouldn't be any response. The snake wasn't human, and it wasn't even intelligent in its own right. She suspected it hadn't even been touched by wild magic or deliberately altered to be intelligent. It was just a snake, even though it was now bonded to a human. It didn't make it automatically intelligent enough to hold a conversation.

"Maybe I should call you Voldemort," she said. The thought made her snicker. A snake called Voldemort. It sounded like a piece of fan fiction. "Or maybe Scales."

The snake didn't seem to like either of those names. It moved, curling up and uncurling with astonishing speed. Emily couldn't fear it any longer, but she still felt a cold shiver as she realized just how quickly Death Vipers could move. She'd never had the impression snakes could actually chase humans down, yet now...there was an odd sense from the Death Viper, an impression that there were dead humans nearby. Emily hesitated, then followed the snake as it plunged into the undergrowth. It seemed to want to show her what it had seen.

She half-expected to see Rudolf. She had no idea how Death Vipers mated and bred, but she was sure that where there was one, there would be others. Maybe Rudolf had run into a Death Viper, too, and been killed. Surely, someone who lived near such creatures would know better than to be caught by one, but the snakes were lethal.

She had a vision of a snake dropping down from the trees to land on its target and realized, a moment later, that it came from her new familiar. Reluctantly, she looked up and saw...nothing.

The bodies came into view a moment later, lying in a hollow off the beaten track. Emily gagged at the smell...and gagged again when she realized just how many animals had taken bites out of the corpses. Several of them had been so badly gnawed that it was hard to tell just how many of them there actually were, but there were at least three reasonably-intact bodies. All three were children—and all three had died from multiple knife wounds to the chest.

It's trying to show me what it thinks I want to see, she thought. The snake was interpreting her desires in ways that made sense to it. *I wanted to find a human; it took me to human bodies.*

She felt her senses shiver in response to magic as she stepped closer, fighting to keep herself from throwing up. The bodies were coated in magic, magic that reminded her of the feeling that had surrounded Shadye. It had to be the residue of a necromantic rite. She looked closer, feeling an odd sense that something wasn't entirely right. Two of the three children had been stabbed in the wrong place. Their *mana*, if they had *mana*, couldn't have been drained properly.

Odd, Emily thought. It looked as if the necromancer—and she had no doubt there *was* a necromancer—had wanted life energy, rather than magic. Would *that* be enough to drive him mad? She wondered just how long the bodies had been lying there and received a handful of impressions from the snake, but none of them made any sense to her. The Death Viper didn't keep track of days or weeks, not like a human. All it could tell her was that the bodies hadn't been there for longer than a season.

The snake hissed. There was another bizarre sense of impressions, followed by a sudden terrifyingly fast movement. Emily turned, just in time to see a rat-like creature swallowed whole by the Death Viper. She stared at the sudden bulge, wondering just how long it would take the snake to digest its meal. The impressions she was receiving suggested that it wanted to sleep now. She yawned in sympathy, and shook her head. Who knew what *else* was lurking in the dark forest?

"Come on," she said, taking a look up at the sky. She'd been away for hours. Lady Barb would have to be getting worried. "Let's go back to town."

She cast a glamor over herself, hiding her undershirt, and started to walk. There was a reluctant hiss as the snake started to move, sliding along behind her as if it were perfectly natural. Oddly, Emily felt reluctant—no, unable—to leave the snake behind. It was *hers* now, no matter what it had been in the forest. Besides, it could navigate the interior quicker than she could. It would have been hard to get back to the town without it.

"Don't do anything to alarm anyone," Emily instructed the snake. She wondered if she could pick it up safely, then decided not to take the risk. Familiars couldn't harm their owners, not directly, but the rotting touch could be unintentionally lethal. There were plenty of cautionary tales of magicians who'd bonded with horses and then fallen off at a gallop. "I don't want you dead."

She slowed as she reached the outskirts of the town, then walked towards the guesthouse. A handful of soldiers stood outside, surrounding a large carriage that reminded Emily of the carriages she'd seen in Zangaria, only less elegant. The soldier looked at her before staring in horror as they saw the Death Viper slithering after her. Emily had never seen grown men panic before, not outside a handful of group exercises in Martial Magic. They seemed torn between running and finding something to throw at the snake, hoping to drive it off.

Emily held up her hands in supplication. "It's perfectly fine," she said. They looked at her as though they thought her insane. "Really."

She walked past them, the snake following her like a tiny dog, and pushed open the door to the main room. Inside, the woman lay on a mattress, a baby lying next to her, while a grim-faced man was speaking quietly to Lady Barb. She'd erected a privacy ward, Emily saw, as she closed the door behind her. All she could hear from her mentor was gibberish.

"Millie," Lady Barb said, cancelling the ward. "I..."

Emily had to smile once Lady Barb saw the snake. Her mouth dropped open, and she lifted her hand, preparing to cast a spell that would reduce the snake to raw materials.

Emily stepped between her and the snake. "It's my familiar," she said, hastily. She knew it would hurt badly if something happened to the snake, now they were bonded. "I had to bond with it to save my life!"

"We shall discuss this later," Lady Barb said, finally. The snake hissed at her tone, then crawled over to the fire and curled up in front of it. "What happened to Rudolf?"

The man looked over at Emily. "What happened to *my son*?"

Emily looked at him. He was older than Rudolf, with more lines on his face, but otherwise very like him. There was something about him that bothered her; he reminded her, she realized slowly, far too much of her stepfather. His hands twitched, as if he were restraining himself from jumping up and beating answers out of her physically. She wasn't sure what she wanted to say.

She knew that aristocrats weren't often given a choice in who they married. Even Alassa had been expected to make her choice from a shortlist her father had composed, all princes and all second sons. Somehow, it was worse to hear about a girl being forced into marriage than a boy, although she had to admit that there was little real difference. But perhaps there was; a man could go out and enjoy himself, even start an affair, while a woman wouldn't have the same license. She had to carry the legitimate heir, after all.

But there are spells to ensure fidelity, she reminded herself. *Was Rudolf threatened with one?*

"He vanished into the countryside," she said, carefully. It was true enough, although she suspected that Lady Barb would see that she was leaving part of the story out. "I couldn't follow him."

"You could have used magic to stop him," Rudolf's father snapped. He rose to his feet. "My son has to be found."

"Sit down," Lady Barb ordered. "Lord Gorham..."

"I will not permit him to be hidden from me," Lord Gorham said. He glared at Emily, fists flexing violently, then he turned on Lady Barb. "I want her to talk."

"She *has* talked," Lady Barb said. There was a cold note running through her voice, one that would have made Emily think better of whatever she was doing, if it had been aimed at her. "She was certainly not ordered to bring back your son."

They stared at each other for a long moment. "She should have known better," Lord Gorham insisted, finally. "I will not have her..."

"But you don't have to have her," Lady Barb snapped, cutting him off. "I will deal with my apprentice, if necessary."

"It *is* necessary," Lord Gorham said, subsiding slightly. "She let my son escape."

He looked over at Emily, then back at Lady Barb. "I expect you to handle it."

"I will do so," Lady Barb said.

Emily swallowed. She knew from Zangaria that innocence wasn't always a defense, if the local aristocrat took a dislike to someone. Her predecessor as baron had been a very nasty man.

"And you're both invited to dinner tonight," Lord Gorham added. "It would be my pleasure to host you. You can tell me much about the Allied Lands."

The sudden change left Emily feeling oddly disconcerted. Lady Barb's face showed no reaction.

"We will be...occupied this evening," Lady Barb said, throwing an unreadable glance at Emily. "But we will be happy to join you tomorrow."

Emily lifted an eyebrow. She might not be as versed in aristocratic etiquette as Alassa, but she did know that turning down a dinner invitation was insulting. The aristocrats of Zangaria carefully kept each other informed of their plans, making sure that there was no opportunity to deliver an accidental insult. They might cut each other dead in public, but even the worst of enemies were prepared to cooperate long enough to prevent social disasters.

Lord Gorham stood, bowed to Lady Barb, then turned and strode out of the door without looking back. Lady Barb watched him go, then walked over to Jeanette and checked on her and the baby. Emily followed, marveling at just how tiny and fragile the baby seemed to be. It was impossible to believe that he would grow up into a large man...

"Don't worry," Lady Barb said, softly. She picked up the baby and cradled him for a long moment, then put him back down beside his mother. "Your child will be fine."

There was a knock on the door. Emily opened it, bracing herself for more surprises, but it was merely Jeanette's father, husband and sister. The men assisted the tired girl to her feet, then helped her out the door, while her sister took the tiny baby and carefully carried him after them. Emily wondered, absently, what happened to mothers who had just given birth. Aristocratic women were expected to go into seclusion, but could a peasant woman afford to take so much time away from work?

"The birth went well," Lady Barb said, once the door was closed again. "Mother and son are both doing fine, though I had to give her a little extra potion midway through the birth. The additional excitement didn't do her any good."

Emily winced. Most townsfolk, she suspected, wouldn't want to draw the attention of their lord. Jeanette had been giving birth when Lord Gorham had stormed into the building. If he blamed her, no matter how irrational it was...

"Someone must have told him his son was here," Lady Barb continued. "He came here barely twenty minutes after you left, demanding answers. You may have made yourself an enemy today."

Emily sighed. There were at least twenty necromancers in the Blighted Lands who hated and feared her, thousands of guildsmen whose livelihoods had been upset by her innovations and half the remaining aristocrats of Zangaria, who resented her sudden elevation over their heads. Enemies were the one thing she wasn't short of. It was part of the reason she'd agreed to be Millie for the summer. No one would connect a shy apprentice with the Necromancer's Bane.

Lady Barb looked over at the snake. "I think it's time you explained yourself," she added, sharply. "What happened to you and where did you get...*that?*"

Emily swallowed and started to explain.

Chapter Twenty-One

"ONLY YOU, EMILY," LADY BARB SAID, WHEN EMILY HAD FINISHED. "ONLY YOU." THE older woman shook her head in disbelief. "A Death Viper as a familiar. I don't know if you'll be allowed to keep it at Whitehall."

Emily winced. Somehow, the thought of being separated from the snake was unbearable. She knew, logically, that it was part of the bond she'd formed with the creature, but it didn't matter. There was no way she wanted to leave the snake behind when they left the mountains.

"There are students with other dangerous pets," she said. First Years were rarely allowed animals, but she'd seen older students with large dogs or other familiars. "Why not a Death Viper?"

"Because," Lady Barb pointed out sarcastically, "none of the other pets are lethal to the touch."

She shrugged. "*You* are immune to the snake's poison. You *may* be immune to the rotting touch. But, for anyone else, your pet is a deadly menace. And you do know how the bonds work? If you get angry at someone, the snake might attack them."

"The snake was going to kill me," she said. "I didn't have a choice. And I *like* him..."

She stopped. She hadn't had any sense of the snake's gender before. It had honestly never occurred to her that it *had* a gender.

"That's the familiar bond talking," Lady Barb said.

Emily shuddered. She could understand why Lady Barb was concerned, but at the same time she honestly couldn't get rid of the snake. There were ways to break the bond, she knew, yet she'd never heard of them being applied willingly. The snake was effectively part of her now.

"I will have to give the matter some thought," Lady Barb said. She motioned for Emily to sit down at the table, then produced yet more bread and cheese from the kitchen. "What happened between you and Rudolf? I hope it wasn't *he* who took your shirt."

Emily flushed. Lady Barb had seen right through the glamor. "It was damaged," she said, shortly. If she went into details, Lady Barb might destroy the snake at once. In hindsight, she'd come far too close to death. "It wasn't his fault."

"Glad to hear it," Lady Barb said. She put a piece of cheese on bread and nibbled it slowly. "And what actually *did* happen between you?"

"He told me that he was running away from an arranged marriage," Emily said, softly. "Is that actually true?"

"It isn't uncommon," Lady Barb said, thoughtfully. "Why *didn't* you stop him?"

Emily hesitated, then pushed forward. "I thought we weren't meant to get involved in local politics."

Lady Barb gave her a sharp look. "And the answer?"

"I felt sorry for him," Emily confessed.

"His father was unhappy," Lady Barb said. "But there was something odd about him, something that bothered me."

She looked down at the table, then back up at Emily. "What were your impressions of him?"

"The father?" Emily asked. "I think he is the sort of person who will ignore his son's feelings when he stands to benefit."

"Something most aristocrats have in common," Lady Barb said, dryly. "I believe he was under the impression that you were going to bring him back."

Emily met her eyes. "Should I have brought him back?"

"Perhaps not," Lady Barb said. "We aren't meant to get involved in local politics."

"We may not have a choice," Emily said. "I found several bodies, too."

Lady Barb stared at her, alarm in her eyes. "That is the sort of thing that should be mentioned *first*," she snapped, as soon as Emily had finished. "Why didn't you tell me at once?"

Emily stared down at her hand, unsure. Lady Barb was right. She should have mentioned the bodies at once, even dragged Lady Barb out to see them. But they'd slipped her mind...

Lady Barb stood up and touched Emily's forehead, casting a light spell. "Someone used magic to hide the bodies," she said, grimly. "Quite a subtle spell; if you hadn't been banged on the head, you might have forgotten the bodies altogether."

"I didn't notice," Emily confessed. She cursed under her breath. Lin had used subtle magic to avoid detection, but this was far worse. "I..."

"That is something of the point," Lady Barb pointed out, dryly. "But it's odd."

Emily looked up at her. "How so?"

"Necromancers are rarely subtle," Lady Barb said. "Why would one of them take a handful of children and use them for power, then *hide* the bodies?"

"I...I don't know," Emily confessed. Necromancers went insane; the first touch of necromancy started them on the path to madness. It was a law of nature. But it did take time for them to collapse completely. "It could be a newborn necromancer."

"Perhaps," Lady Barb said. She looked over at the snake. "Can your friend tell us anything useful?"

Emily shook her head. "The bodies weren't there last season," she said. "But I don't know what it means by a season."

Lady Barb nodded. "I think I should take a look at the bodies," she said. "If there is a necromancer running around, we have to deal with him."

Emily shuddered. The spell had left her feeling violated, even though she knew she had been lucky. If she'd forgotten the bodies completely, the necromancer would have hidden his victims successfully. It was quite possible that the parents of the missing children had forgotten they'd even existed...

No, she told herself firmly. *A mother wouldn't lose track of her children. Just because mine probably hasn't even noticed I'm gone...*

"Someone broke into this building," she said. "Could it be the necromancer?"

"It's a possibility," Lady Barb agreed. "But there's too much about this case that doesn't make sense."

She cleared her throat. "Lord Gorham expects you to be punished for not bringing his son back to the castle," she said. "You can stay here while I go hunting for the bodies. Don't go outside, but help someone if they come here and ask for it."

"And pretend I've been thrashed," Emily said, crossly. "Can you find the bodies without me?"

"I can follow your tracks, I think," Lady Barb said. Emily wasn't sure that it would be easy, but held her tongue. "In the meantime, I want you to write out a full report for the Grandmaster. We can put it in the postal coach before we leave town."

Emily nodded, reluctantly.

"Then sew up some basic runes," Lady Barb added. "We can provide ourselves with some basic protections, now we know to be alert."

"Understood," Emily said. She hated sewing—unlike most of the female students, it wasn't a skill she'd been taught as a child—but there was no alternative. "If someone is using subtle magic, is it possible that Lord Gorham might be affected?"

"It is," Lady Barb said. "It's also possible that he or Rudolf might be the mystery magician. That's why we're going to his castle tomorrow."

She picked up her staff and walked out of the building, theatrically slamming the door behind her. Emily looked over at the snake, then stood and retrieved parchment and a pair of quill pens from Lady Barb's bag. Carefully, she wrote out an account of everything that had happened, grateful for the essays Sergeant Miles had made her write. He'd taught her how to be observant—and to make sure she wrote down everything, no matter how seemingly inconsequential. The smallest clue, he'd said, could lead to the most significant piece of information.

Emily felt her fingers ache as she finished the letter, but she retrieved another piece of parchment and carefully started to draft a letter to Jade. The words flowed easier, she was relieved to discover, now that they'd sorted out their relationship. Perhaps they could be good friends, after all. She smiled as she reread it, wondering what he would make of her observations of village life. The only detail she'd glossed over was Hodge's attempt to rape her. Jade didn't have to know about it. Or, for that matter, about the snake.

The sun was setting in the sky when Lady Barb returned. Emily took one look at her drawn, white face and hurriedly boiled water as Lady Barb sat down, seemingly too exhausted to move another step. She made a mug of Kava, passed it to the older woman, then sat down facing her. Lady Barb gulped the liquid down, despite the heat. Emily watched, worried. She'd never seen Lady Barb so tired before, even when they'd walked all day.

"The bodies were *very* well hidden," Lady Barb said, once she'd finished drinking. "A handful of glamors, a handful of runes...and a spell of forgetfulness, intended to prevent anyone from walking away with any memory of what they saw. But it's a little harder to fool animals. Your snake clearly knew they were there."

Emily nodded.

"Whoever did it isn't a classically-trained magician," Lady Barb continued. "It would be simple to destroy the bodies beyond recognition, but they settled for abandoning and concealing them. There were hints of vast power, combined with absolute ignorance. I think I might have noticed them even if I hadn't been looking. There's little as conspicuous as someone trying to hide."

Lady Barb took a breath. "And the rite was strange too," she added. "Necromancy isn't *that* difficult."

"I think he was going for life force, rather than magic," Emily said, quietly. "The wounds were in the wrong place for magic."

"It looked that way," Lady Barb agreed. "But it doesn't quite make sense." She shook her head. "Let me see the letter to the Grandmaster."

Emily passed her the scroll of parchment. Lady Barb skimmed it before adding a note of her own at the bottom and sealing it up, casting a handful of spells to ensure that the Grandmaster was the only one who could read it. Emily took it and placed it by the door, intending to give it to the post office before they left.

"I'll have to write another one," Lady Barb said. "If there is a necromancer on this side of the Blighted Lands, we may have a real problem on our hands."

She looked over at the snake for a long moment. "I had an idea," she added, changing the subject. "You can transfigure the snake into something less harmful."

Emily narrowed her eyes. "A dog or a cat?"

"I was thinking a bracelet," Lady Barb said. "You wear it, all the time. No one thinks anything of it. But when you need a secret weapon..."

"The snake comes back to life," Emily said. She hesitated, wondering if it *was* a good solution to her problem. The part of her that was linked to the snake seemed divided on the issue. She wasn't sure how the snake felt about it. "I'd have to keep the spell in place permanently."

"You wouldn't be the only person to carry a secret weapon," Lady Barb pointed out. "And you are in far more danger than most of your classmates."

Emily nodded, remembering the knife Alassa had strapped to her leg. It had saved both of their lives in Zangaria. A hidden snake—a hidden, absolutely lethal snake—would make a very useful weapon. If another necromancer came after her, she could order the snake to bite him...if a necromancer could be killed by snakebite. But poison had been used to kill necromancers in the past, hadn't it?

And there was a necromancer roaming the mountains right now...

"There's little hope of replacing the supplies we used in this town," Lady Barb said. "I want you to write up a list of everything we used, and we'll send it in a letter down to the nearest city. They'd have supplies to send back up here."

Emily nodded and left the table. The guesthouses were meant to be kept fully stocked, but the mystery thief had taken too much to be easily replaced. Someone would have to see to it before any further help could be offered to the townsfolk. She wondered, absently, if she could work out what the thief had wanted from the stolen ingredients, before deciding that it was probably pointless. There hadn't been anything unique to one or two potions in the storehouse, not when such ingredients were too expensive to waste. Everything that had been taken had a multitude of uses.

She wrote out a list anyway, careful to separate the ingredients she'd used from the ingredients that had been stolen, then walked back into the main room. Lady Barb had fallen asleep, resting her head on her arms as students had been known to do in the library. Emily smiled, placed the sheet of parchment on the far table, and looked at her snake. It was still lying beside the fire, asleep. Emily crept around Lady Barb and clambered up the ladder into the bedroom. It was dangerous to disturb sleeping magicians.

Despite her own tiredness, she didn't really feel like sleep. Instead, she wrote out another letter, this one to Imaiqah. She was a little more honest with her oldest friend, but again kept the details about Hodge to herself. It wasn't something she wanted to talk about, even to the only one of her friends who might have understood. Alassa would have wanted to know why she hadn't killed the young man.

Finishing that letter, she wrote out another one to the Gorgon. She wasn't actually sure if it would reach her—the Gorgon lands weren't on the formal postal routes, which meant the letter would have to be delivered specially—but it was the thought that counted. Besides, the Gorgon had even fewer close friends than Emily herself. She finished the letter, undressed as fast as possible and walked over to the window. Outside, the moon was rising, casting its eerie light over the town. No one, even soldiers, could be seen in the streets below.

Emily had always liked the darkness, but this was different. The shadows could have hidden anything, from a vampire to a merely human enemy. And it *did* hide a necromancer. She peered into the darkness, wondering if the faint hints of light marked where someone had built a fire for the night...or if it was something more sinister, waiting for them. A shape fluttered across the window and she jumped, catching her breath, before she realized that it was nothing more harmful than a bat. Shaking her head, she turned and walked back to bed.

There were no marks on her skin, she discovered, not from where the snake had rested on her chest. She didn't know if she was unharmed because of the bond or because the snake's skin hadn't had time to reach her bare flesh. Even now, with the snake downstairs, she could still feel it at the back of her mind, something that wasn't quite *there*, but still present. There were some stories about mental links between humans and animals that had chilled her to the bone, but she didn't seem to have picked up any of the bad effects. Or so she hoped.

She closed her eyes and tried to sleep. But it was a long time before she dropped into a dark, dreamless sleep.

Lady Barb woke her the following morning as she undressed and changed into a new set of clothes. Emily found herself staring at the scars covering the older woman's back, including a handful that looked as if she'd been flogged months ago. Outside, the sun was barely rising in the sky, but Emily didn't feel like going back to sleep. She pulled herself out of bed and looked over at her mentor. The scars went all the way down to Lady Barb's buttocks.

She found her voice. "What...what happened to you?"

"You don't want to know," Lady Barb said, darkly. She was clearly in a vile temper. "Get dressed, then brew up the remaining potions. We will have more visitors this morning."

She kept Emily busy all day, moving between brewing potions to helping patients who needed some additional treatment. Emily tried to speak to her a couple of times, but after she was snapped at she decided to leave the older woman alone until she was ready to talk properly. She paused long enough to offer the snake something for lunch–it didn't seem hungry, which puzzled her until she remembered that snakes could go weeks between meals - then returned to work. Lady Barb wanted to get through the patients as soon as possible.

"You know how to make your own protections," Lady Barb said, when the last patient had departed and the door was firmly closed. "Have you tried applying the same principle to a transfiguration spell?"

Emily shook her head. Transfiguration spells eventually wore off–or at least the prank spells did. Hodge would have turned back eventually, unless someone turned him into pork roast without realizing what they'd done. But protections drew on her power permanently...

"You'll need to keep the bracelet on or near you at all times," Lady Barb instructed, as she showed Emily the spell. "Once it is too far from you, the snake will revert to normal. I suggest you add anti-theft jinxes to the snake, once it's a bracelet."

Emily shuddered. Someone might steal the bracelet...and find out they were clutching a lethal snake. She cast the spell carefully, keeping her eyes on the target, and sighed in relief when the snake became a simple, gold bangle. There was a faint scaly pattern on the outside, she realized as she picked it up, but nothing else to indicate that it was anything other than a piece of jewellery. She closed her eyes, concentrating. The spell had frozen the snake's mind–and it felt almost as if the snake was asleep.

She added the two protective spells, then pulled it over her left arm. She'd never been one for jewelery–she'd never had the money for anything special–but she had to admit it suited her.

There was a sharp rap at the door. "That will be the carriage," Lady Barb said. She sounded calmer now that the snake was harmless. Had it rattled her in the morning? "Go get into your dress robes. I'll delay them."

She reached out and caught Emily's arm before she could reach the ladder. "And make sure you pack your staff," she added. "You might need it."

Chapter Twenty-Two

WHOEVER HAD DESIGNED THE CASTLE, EMILY DECIDED AS THE CARRIAGE WOUND ITS WAY up towards the grim forbidding mass, had read too many gothic horror stories. The towering battlements loomed over the countryside, giving it a distinctly sinister appearance. She didn't even want to look at the road as it wound its way up towards the castle, steep cliffs on both sides. A single strong gust of wind would blow the carriage over the side, sending them plunging to the jagged rocks below. Without magic, the castle would be almost impossible to take by force.

It didn't look so forbidding yesterday, she thought. *But that was before the bodies...*

It was smaller than her castle in Cockatrice, she saw as they passed over the bridge–there was no moat, merely another plunging cliff–and into the courtyard. A handful of soldiers strode about, several clearly being trained by men who resembled Sergeant Harkin. They didn't look very happy, although she shuddered to think about how she must have looked after her first class. A man dressed in red swept past them and down towards the carriage. Emily couldn't help noticing that several of the soldiers made rude faces at his back.

"Lady Sorceress," he said, addressing Lady Barb. "I welcome you to my lord's castle."

"Thank you," Lady Barb said. "We are honored to be here."

Emily remained behind Lady Barb, like a good little apprentice. The man ignored her, concentrating on trying to impress Lady Barb. Emily rather doubted he was succeeding; the man reminded her far too much of one of Alassa's servants from Zangaria, a little creep whose power depended on pleasing the king. But she followed the two of them down a series of stone corridors and into a large dining room, far larger than it needed to be. There was one table, with one chair placed at the end and two more midway down the side. Emily guessed that Lord Gorham would take the chair at the end, being the master of the castle, and she and Lady Barb were expected to take the other two chairs.

"I welcome you to my castle," Lord Gorham said, emerging from a side chamber. He sounded...kinder than he'd sounded the previous day. "It is always an honor to play host to a sorceress."

"I thank you," Lady Barb said, as Emily hastily curtseyed. Her tone was surprisingly warm. "It is always an honor to visit a lord."

"Please, be seated," Lord Gorham said. "We have much to talk about, I'm afraid."

Emily took her seat, wondering why the aristocracy either went for sinfully comfortable chairs or chairs so hard that they hurt the posterior. Lord Gorham seemed to believe that the latter was ideal; his chair might be larger than theirs, but it had the same solid wooden seating. Emily watched as Lady Barb sat down, sensing magic flickering around her mentor as she looked for trouble.

"My son will return in time, I am sure," Lord Gorham said, as the servants brought in the first dishes. Emily hadn't seen so much food for so few people since she'd last been in Zangaria. It looked as though they'd slaughtered the fatted calf. "He will take his place in my plans for the future."

Lady Barb looked over at Emily. Lord Gorham didn't sound angry or upset, merely... unconcerned about Rudolf's disobedience. It didn't make sense. Emily recalled just how angry he'd been when he'd heard that Emily hadn't retrieved his son. Had he thought better of snapping at a pair of magicians, or was something else going on?

"You may have another problem," Lady Barb said, as Lord Gorham began to slice the meat, piece by piece. "We found a handful of dead bodies in the forest. A handful of dead bodies concealed by very powerful spells."

Emily watched Lord Gorham carefully, but he showed no reaction at all. Instead, he finished carving the meat and distributed it. That was *not* a normal reaction, she told herself; even if the aristocracy didn't care about the peasants, they had to care about a magician who was preying on their population. And then there was the proof of necromancy...

"My son will marry Lady Easter's daughter," Lord Gorham continued, as if Lady Barb hadn't spoken. "Together, they will unite our lands into one."

"The bodies were clearly used to power a necromantic rite," Lady Barb said, sharply. "You have a rogue necromancer running around in your territory."

Lord Gorham still seemed unaware of her words. "Please, eat," he told them. "My cooks are the best in the mountains."

Emily took a look at the meat. It seemed undercooked, as though they'd merely waved the pig in front of a fire and then declared it done. The bread looked more appetizing, she had to admit, but the gravy smelled unpleasant. Cooking in Zangaria wasn't very elegant, not compared to cooking in Dragon's Den, yet it was usually better than this!

I won't complain about bread and cheese again, she thought.

She took a nervous bite, then winced. It tasted unpleasantly fatty, as if the cook had carefully removed the good meat before starting to roast it. Even the half-burnt rabbits and birds they'd cooked during camping trips for Martial Magic had tasted better. She nibbled her bread, wondering just what atrocities the cook had performed to make the gravy. It looked as though the cook had merely melted some fat, then added a hint of flavor. She'd seen more appetizing food in the inn she'd visited with Lady Barb.

Maybe I can turn it into something more edible, she thought, desperately. *But that would be rude.*

"Tell me," Lady Barb said carefully, "why do you want your son to marry Lady Easter's daughter?"

"Because it will unite our lands," Lord Gorham repeated. "Lady Easter only holds the lands in trust for a male heir. My son will automatically become her lord, once he marries her daughter. And then he will succeed me and our lands will be joined."

He beamed, as if he expected them to bow down in wonder at his sheer brilliance. Emily had her doubts; Rudolf clearly hadn't wanted to marry the daughter and, for all she knew, the daughter felt the same way. And if Lady Easter was giving up political power when her daughter wed, she had a good reason to make sure that her daughter *never* married. Emily couldn't recall if anything like it had happened on Earth, but she was fairly sure it must have at one point.

Lady Barb's eyes narrowed. "How do you know that Lady Easter will allow your son to marry her daughter?"

An odd look flickered across Lord Gorham's eyes. "She will," he said. There was nothing, but absolute confidence in his tone. "She will love to have my son married to her daughter."

"Why?" Lady Barb asked. "Why do you think she would give up power so readily?"

Lord Gorham stopped, suddenly. "I..."

"And this marriage will upset the balance of power between the mountain lords," Lady Barb added. Her eyes never left Lord Gorham's face. "It could spark a war. Why do you feel it is necessary?"

Subtle magic, Emily realized. Lord Gorham had been *programmed*, to all intents and purposes, programmed to encourage his son to marry and ignore all traces of necromancy. A necromancer could dance in front of him, stark naked, and even that might remain unnoticed. But what necromancer could make subtle magic *work*? The stronger the magician, Emily knew, the harder it was for them to make subtle magic work well. It tended to be either blatantly noticeable or useless.

She stood up and checked under her seat. It was a breach of etiquette to rise before the lord, but Lord Gorham barely noticed. The human mind didn't *like* being controlled, certainly not so subtly that it was impossible to notice without someone pointing it out. There were no runes scratched under her chair, but there was a thin trace of magic glittering across the floor.

"I...I don't know," Lord Gorham said. "I..."

Emily threw caution to the winds and looked under Lord Gorham's chair. There were four runes carved into the underside, one concealing the other three. She had no idea what they did–they weren't ones she had been taught at Whitehall–but they were clearly having an effect on Lord Gorham.

"You're not in your right mind," Lady Barb said, quietly. "What happened to you?"

Lord Gorham rose to his feet, then staggered and collapsed. Lady Barb bit back an oath, then drew her staff from her pocket and enlarged it to normal size, just as a handful of guards charged into the room. Emily groped for her own staff and raised a ward, while Lady Barb cast a spell that knocked the guards over. The staff twisted in Emily's hands, reminding her of the dangers of using one. She gritted her teeth and put the staff down. As always, it was difficult to let go. It seemed to ensnare her mind.

"Your master has been attacked," Lady Barb said. "If we'd wanted to kill him, we could have done it by now."

She ignored the guards and concentrated on helping Lord Gorham to his feet. Once he was away from the chair, she snapped her fingers and the chair collapsed into broken splinters, destroying all trace of the runes. Emily felt the magic flicker out of existence, but she knew there would be more runes in other parts of the castle. Like Lin, Lord Gorham's mystery opponent had probably hidden some in his bedchamber.

"There were three runes I didn't recognize under the chair," Emily said, as Lady Barb carried Lord Gorham over to the fire and placed him on the ground beside it. "Do you want me to draw them out?"

"Better not, at least not now," Lady Barb said. "You stay with him while I go search the castle. If he starts to wake up, summon me at once, but don't let anyone else near him."

Emily nodded. Lord Gorham had been under the influence of hidden runes for months, perhaps years. They'd worked on his mind like post-hypnotic suggestions, working their way into his innermost thoughts. A simple compulsion spell would be simple enough to break, but this was worse. Even with the runes destroyed, it could take years for him to return to normal. He never know what was truly him—and what had been urged on him by the runes.

She looked around after Lady Barb stepped through one of the doors and closed it behind her. A handful of swords and shields hung from one of the walls, while the others were just bare stone. She couldn't see anything to suggest why they were there, unless they were intended as concealed weapons. Sergeant Miles had told her that every aristocrat had a handful of concealed weapons in his home—and seemingly decorative swords might surprise someone. A chambermaid poked her head into the room, then fled when Emily looked up at her.

Lord Gorham moaned, then subsided again. Emily heard a sound and looked up, just in time to see Lady Barb stepping into the room again. "There were runes everywhere," she said, grimly. "Under his bed, in the bathroom...quite a few more in Rudolf's room. But they don't seem to have had any effect on him."

Emily blinked. "Is he a magician?"

"Subtle magic works on magicians too," Lady Barb reminded her, rather sarcastically. "You ought to know that, Mille."

Emily felt her face heat.

Lady Barb's face hardened. "As far as I can tell, they should have worked. Perhaps the runes affecting Lord Gorham pushed him into trying to force his son into compliance, which made it harder for the runes targeted on Rudolf to work."

It sounded plausible, Emily decided. Subtle magic worked best when it was unnoticed and unquestioned. If someone didn't ask the right questions, they wouldn't even get a sniff of the framework the magic had made for them, let alone manage to break out. If Lady Barb was right, Rudolf had reacted badly enough to his father's orders to override the runes.

"There were quite a few different ones too," Lady Barb continued. "One of them was designed to hide all traces of magic—I think it was partly to ensure that the mystery magician's activities went unnoticed. Another was designed to make him listen to his advisor. I had a look around, but the man seems to have vanished. The guards said he left the castle as soon as the lord collapsed."

A Wormtongue, Emily thought. It had been years since she'd read *The Lord of the Rings*, but the principle of an evil advisor manipulating his monarch was far from uncommon. *But is he the necromancer?*

"I couldn't find anything magical in his rooms, not even a trace of magic," Lady Barb said, when Emily asked. "But that means he might well have been working for someone else."

"Shadye had at least one ally in Dragon's Den," Emily said, remembering the Dark Wizard who'd helped to steal some of her blood. "Why can't another necromancer have an ally?"

Lady Barb shrugged. "Call the servants and get them to bring in some blankets," she ordered, instead of trying to answer the question. "We may as well make him comfortable."

Emily nodded and obeyed. When she returned, she saw Lady Barb holding one hand against Lord Gorham's forehead, as if she were feeling his temperature. The man's eyes were open, staring up at the sorceress. His face was twisted in a confused grimace, as if he didn't quite know where he was. Emily rubbed her own forehead in sympathy. The bruise from where she'd hit her head had yet to fade, even if it wasn't sore.

"My son," he said, between gasps. "Call him."

"I don't know where he is," Lady Barb said. She shot Emily a questioning glance, but Emily shook her head. "He could be anywhere by now."

Emily nodded. It hadn't occurred to her until too late that Rudolf probably knew the forest like the back of his hand. If he'd wanted to hurt her, he could easily have led her into a trap or circled around and attacked her from behind. Or he might just have lit out for the next little kingdom and hidden until his father's madness faded away. Now the runes were gone, it would start to abate.

But Rudolf won't know that, she reminded herself. *How will he know to come home?*

"The runes won't be pushing on his mind anymore," Lady Barb said after Emily asked her. "But I find myself caught between two problems. Do we stay here and look after him, or do we start looking for the necromancer?"

Emily shrugged. She'd faced one necromancer and she didn't want to face another one, certainly not away from Whitehall. They might well not want to *find* the necromancer, if they searched for him. But their best chance of removing the threat was to find him before he started the transformation into an eldritch abomination. She felt the metal bracelet at her wrist and smiled, inwardly. Perhaps she could just let the necromancer take the bracelet and find that he was holding a poisonous snake.

Lady Barb cleared her throat. "Well?"

"We wait for a day or two," Emily said, realizing that Lady Barb expected her to try to answer the question. No doubt it was a Secret Test of Character or something like it. "If he recovers, or if Rudolf returns, we can move onwards and try to find the necromancer."

She scowled. Aristocrats had very firm ideas about who should be in charge. Even if there was a trusted subordinate around, he couldn't be left in charge for very long.

Emily privately thought the whole concept absurd, but it was Tradition. If something happened to her, she had no idea what would happen to her Barony. It wasn't as if she had a child to take over in her place.

"Good thinking," Lady Barb said. She gave Emily a tight smile. "Go organize the servants into making up some new rooms, but check the beds first–carefully. I will be very annoyed with you if you miss a single rune."

Emily nodded. "This is what you meant, isn't it?"

Lady Barb lifted her eyebrows.

"About magic being feared out here," Emily explained. "Someone was working magic, and no one even noticed until we arrived."

Lady Barb nodded. "Too many odd things have happened," she said. "Lords building up their armies, preparing for war. A necromancer who doesn't seem to have gone completely insane, one capable of using subtle magic. An aristocrat trying to make a match that would shatter the balance of power and unite his enemies against him; a son who seems immune to the runes pressing his father on towards disaster. Missing children...and no one seems to have noticed."

"There were rumors," Emily reminded her. "We heard them during the Faire."

"True," Lady Barb agreed. "But if the children vanished from the town, someone would have noticed. Wouldn't they?"

Emily nodded, mutely. Maybe her stepfather and mother hadn't noticed her disappearance, but not all parents were so careless. King Randor might have raised Alassa as a spoilt brat, yet he clearly loved her. And Imaiqah's father loved her, too. They would have noticed if either of their children had gone missing.

But she remembered the abused boy, and grimaced. Perhaps, if the children had been unloved, they would have been taken and no one would have cared.

But she had a hard time imagining that *no one* had noticed.

"It would be hard for even subtle magic to make them forget," Lady Barb added. "A child is terrifyingly important to the parents."

"I forgot the bodies," Emily said. In hindsight, it was easy to tell that magic had worked its will on her mind. If she hadn't been asked for a full explanation, the bodies might have vanished from her memory completely. "Could magic have made them forget their children *anyway*?"

"I very much hope not," Lady Barb said. "Go organize the servants. I'll stay with Lord Gorham."

Emily nodded and obeyed.

Chapter Twenty-Three

Being an apprentice, Jade had told Emily in one of his infrequent letters, meant taking on some of the mistress's power and position. She hadn't really understood what that *meant* until she'd found herself issuing orders–and being obeyed. A sorceress was, to all intents and purposes, an aristocrat, and the social equal of almost any mundane aristocrat. "Millie" might not be an entitled aristocrat, but she could issue orders and everyone assumed she spoke with Lady Barb's voice.

"I want you to sew these patterns," she told the maids, once they had assembled in a large meeting room. Unlike Emily herself, the serving girls knew how to sew properly. "Sew them into cloth, then make sure everyone in the castle is carrying at least one."

She watched the maids go to work, sewing protective runes into pieces of cloth. If she recalled correctly, it didn't take much effort to counteract the dangerous runes, once they were actually detected. Subtle Magic runes were only dangerous when they were unseen; once they were noticed, their influence could be easily countered. Lord Gorham and his men would question everything they'd done for weeks, exposing the less sensible and logical decisions for what they were.

Lady Barb took care of Lord Gorham, leaving Emily to roam the castle looking for additional runes. They were scattered everywhere, blindingly obvious once people knew to look for them, as if the advisor had carved them into every last room. Emily was unwillingly impressed. Even a Runecarver might have been unable to achieve such thorough saturation of a castle. But then, he would have been carving defensive runes.

"My Lady," one of the guards said, breaking into her thoughts. "We found a body at the bottom of the abyss. The Advisor is dead."

Emily winced. One thing she hoped she would never get used to was how cheap life was in the countryside–and everywhere else in this world. The guard didn't seem concerned by the body, no matter who it was. No doubt the mystery necromancer had killed the Advisor when he had outlived his usefulness–or included a suicide command in whatever instructions he'd been given, if he hadn't acted of his own free will. There was no way to know.

"Thank you," she said, carefully. "Were there any wounds on the body?"

"Merely a broken neck," the guard informed her. "What do you wish to be done with the body?"

Lady Barb would want to take a look, Emily knew. "Put the body in storage for the moment," she ordered. *She* didn't want to look herself. "Once my mistress has looked, it can be cremated."

She watched the guard go before resuming her wanderings through the castle. They eventually led her into the tiny library. There were only a couple of dozen books in the room, stacked on one shelf. Emily couldn't help thinking that her quarters in Whitehall deserved the title of library far more than the castle's library, at least if one went by sheer volume of books. She'd bought more books than she cared to think about over the last year, storing them in her trunk. Clearly, the Cairngorm Lords were not great readers.

One of the books was a genealogical table, tracking the bloodlines of the different aristocratic families in the area. Emily had seen something like it in Zangaria, owned by the Royal Family, but this one was different. It took her several moments to work out that while King Randor and his family had never acknowledged anyone as their equals, the mountainside lords accepted their fellows as being on the same level as themselves. The wider the range of potential mates, the greater the chance of healthy children. She couldn't help wondering if it gave them a greater chance of breeding strong sons and daughters, especially considering the problems Zangaria had had with their own Royal Bloodline.

According to the tables, Lord Gorham only had one son and no daughters. That made him unique among the mountainside lords; the second smallest brood consisted of three children, all sons. She wondered, absently, why Lord Gorham had never married again. It wasn't as if there would be any question over who would succeed him to the lordship.

Or was there? What would happen to the younger sons and daughters once their father died?

Earth's history provided several examples, none of them good. The Ottoman Sultans had butchered all other possible heirs, preventing civil war at the cost of mass slaughter. Europe had tried to find uses for younger sons, marrying them off to the right girls or sending them into the army. But how many of those were possibilities here? She traced the lines of descent and swore, inwardly. Lord Gorham's plan to marry his son to Lady Easter's daughter would definitely spark off a war. A daughter couldn't inherit power, so it would fall naturally to her husband.

He needed a second son, Emily thought, morbidly. King Randor had tried hard to produce more children, but Lord Gorham, it seemed, had just abandoned the thought after producing Rudolf. *He would have been a safer choice...*

A thought struck her *Or was that deliberate? Was he urged to have only one son?*

It was impossible to tell. There were risks, after all, in having too many heirs.

She put the book to one side and looked through the other titles. None of them seemed interesting, apart from a couple of dusty history books. Emily pulled one of them off the shelf, marveling at just how old it was, and placed it carefully on the table. There were ancient books at Whitehall, but they were touched with preservation spells. *These* books were steadily decaying into dust. She briefly considered taking them with her before resolving to ask Lord Gorham to take better care of his books. Reading would only become more and more important as the New Learning spread through the Allied Lands.

Deciphering the book's text was difficult. Emily had learned to speak the common tongue shared by the Allied Lands, but reading it was another matter. She had to cast a translation spell to make any headway at all, yet half of the words still didn't quite make sense. Gritting her teeth, she started to read what she could, only to wind up more and more puzzled. The author didn't seem to be aware of the difference between writing history and historical fiction. It was difficult to tell when any of the events had actually taken place—and almost all of the credit for gallant deeds went to a single family. Emily guessed that the writer had been paid by them to rewrite history in their favor.

Even so, it was an interesting read. The writer talked about the wars with the Faerie, of the days when monsters roamed the lands and hordes of dragons flew through the skies, breathing fire on all who dared to oppose them. Emily smiled as she read an account of a young boy taking on a giant and beating him through trickery, as it sounded like David and Goliath. Other accounts talked about fighting strange monsters that remained unnamed and unrecognized.

Sometimes, the writing became completely illegible, no matter what spells she used. Perhaps the writer might not have dared write everything down, or had thought better of it afterward?

She toyed with the snake-bracelet as she returned the book to the shelf, then walked out of the library, through a series of dark stone corridors. The castle didn't have mounted torches, let alone lanterns, to light its interior. Emily wondered, as she used a light-spell to find her way back to the bedroom, if it was intended as a defensive measure or if servants were simply expected to carry lights everywhere they went. Either one made sense.

Lady Barb looked up as Emily slipped into the master bedroom. Lord Gorham lay on the mattress, sweating heavily. Emily didn't recall feeling such effects when she'd realized just how badly she'd been influenced by Lin's runes, but then she'd been trapped as a stone statue for much of the time. It still chilled her to realize just how close she'd come to being petrified forever.

"He's recovering, but very slowly," Lady Barb said. "It may take some time before he's completely healed."

Emily nodded. She'd been shocked when she'd first discovered how easy it was to use magic to manipulate a person's mind, but she'd been at Whitehall, where help had been on hand if necessary. Here, there was no one to help Lord Gorham...and he wouldn't want to admit, even to himself, just how easily he'd been manipulated. His pride wouldn't let him. It reminded her of a lecture from her professor, months ago.

"The mind exists within a framework—and if that framework is warped by subtle magic, it is impossible to tell from the inside that it has been warped," the Professor had said. "A person on the outside might notice odd behavior, but a person on the inside will accept it as completely normal. Given time, they will betray everything they hold dear, still convinced they are doing the right thing."

She shivered. Or, as a philosopher on Earth had put it, if the universe was shrinking, and all the tools one used to measure it were shrinking as well, how would anyone know the universe was shrinking?

"Get some sleep, then go down to the town and speak to the headman," Lady Barb added. Emily glanced at her watch and realized, to her shock, that it was three bells in the morning; she'd quite lost track of time. "Ask him if the dead children came from his town—and if Rudolf is still around. *Someone* must have known he was there."

She smiled. "And post the letters at the same time," she ordered. "We need to alert the White Council."

Emily yawned as she walked into the next room. The maids had set up a small bed for her and a larger one for Lady Barb, but considering the castle, she cast wards and checked for runes before climbing into bed. If nothing else, she told herself, she could have a proper wash in the morning.

When she awoke, she discovered that the maids had to carry in a large bathtub, followed by buckets of water, just to make sure she could have a bath. Guiltily, she cursed her own oversight, tipping the maids with coins from her pouch. Of *course* they didn't have hot running water in the castle.

She washed herself thoroughly and wrapped one of the cloths around her wrist. The rune the maids had sewn into it looked to be firmly in place, but she checked it anyway, just to be sure. She'd been told that a sewn rune would start to unpick itself if it was on the verge of being overwhelmed, yet there had been so many runes in the castle that she wasn't sure if that would still hold true. Perhaps there had been so many runes in this place that the runes intended for Rudolf had been drained of power by the ones affecting his father. But, as far as she knew, there was no limit on how many runes a magician could use.

Lady Barb was still sitting next to Lord Gorham, asleep in a solid wooden chair. A protective ward spat sparks at her as she approached, so she left Lady Barb alone and walked into the main hall. The maids had already set out breakfast, which—thankfully—looked more appetizing than the meat from the previous night. Emily ate quickly, thanked the maids—they seemed astonished to be thanked for anything—and walked to the castle gates.

"I can escort you down to the town, Lady Sorceress," the Captain of the Guard said, bowing low. "It isn't safe down there."

"No, thank you," Emily said. "I want a chance to clear my head."

And Rudolf won't show himself, she added in the privacy of her own thoughts, *if he sees me surrounded by guards.*

She regretted her decision almost as soon as she started to walk. The road was narrower than she'd realized, with plunging cliffs on both sides. It was easy to imagine accidentally walking over the edge in the darkness—or being thrown off the road, if she was trying to attack the castle. She couldn't help thinking of some of the pictures she'd seen of homes built by mighty sorcerers, sorcerers with more power than sense. They'd balanced castles on tiny threads of land or sculpted them out of clouds. But it didn't take much magic to disrupt the spells holding them together, allowing gravity to reassert itself. Void's tower was far simpler, she remembered, and safer for him.

It was a relief when the road finally reached bottom and headed down into the town. Someone had pulled the soldiers back to the castle, and crowds of people were bustling around, their faces torn between worry and relief. She wondered just how much they knew about what had happened in the castle, but decided it probably didn't matter. The rumors would be much—much—worse. Several people cast odd glances at her, then looked away hastily. Emily forced herself to stand upright as she strode towards the headman's house, trying to project a display of confidence. She wasn't sure it worked.

The town was definitely better organized than the first village they'd visited. Behind the home of the local blacksmith, there was a fishmonger, calling for people to come and eat his fresh fish. The blacksmith himself—one of the beefiest men Emily had ever seen—didn't seem impressed, either with the shouting or with the stench drifting through the air.

"Get your fresh fish here," the fishmonger called, as the stench of fish drifted through the town. "Fresh fish! It's lovely!"

"Your fish stinks," the blacksmith shouted. "It's rotten!"

Emily wrinkled her nose, then walked on to the headman's house. Behind her, she heard the sounds of a fight breaking out. She didn't look back.

There were two men outside the headman's house as she approached. Emily forced herself to keep projecting confidence as she walked up to the door. One of them opened it for her and called inside, while the other bowed deeply but kept one hand on his sword. Emily wondered, absently, just why they were guarding their headman, before deciding it didn't matter. She stepped inside and blinked in surprise as she saw the headman, sitting on a chair that seemed to balance on top of a ladder. It had to be his version of a throne.

She concealed her amusement as he stepped down and bowed to her. "Lady Sorceress," he said. Up close, he was shorter than she'd realized—and fat enough to roll downhill. She couldn't help wondering how he managed to eat so well, particularly when she hadn't seen any other fat men since leaving the Faire. But he certainly looked kinder than Hodge's father. "What can I do for you?"

Emily reminded herself, firmly, that she wasn't a supplicant. "There are two matters that need to be discussed," she said, trying to channel Lady Barb. "Have any children gone missing from your town?"

The headman looked surprised. "Of course not," he said. "We haven't lost *anyone.*"

But you gained one, Emily thought. Somehow, Rudolf had managed to pose as a townsperson for several days. She kept that thought to herself.

"No one," she said. Surely, even the most powerful runes couldn't hide a missing child from her parents? "The next issue, then: where is Rudolf?"

The headman started. Clearly, he'd been anticipating some uncomfortable questions from his lord after Rudolf had been discovered in his town. Emily wondered just what Lord Gorham would do, then decided that it was likely to be horrific. Or perhaps he would just invite Lady Barb to use magic to interrogate the headman.

"I don't know," the headman said, finally. "He ran into the countryside and vanished."

Emily studied him for a long moment, deciding he seemed to be telling the truth. "Tell him that the matter has been solved and he is welcome to return home, should you see him again," she said. She suspected that Rudolf had friends in the town, insofar as he *could* have friends. The social gulf between him and the townsfolk was staggering. "But the countryside isn't safe."

The headman's eyes narrowed. "Why not?"

Emily hesitated. She could tell them about the necromancer...but what good would that do? It wasn't as if they could do anything about it—all they could do was flee. But if they did, where would they go? She doubted that any of the other tiny kingdoms in the mountains could handle a horde of refugees. And yet, if they stayed where they were, they would be nothing more than fodder for the necromancer.

"I met up with a poisonous snake on the road yesterday," she reminded him, finally. The entire village would have heard about the snake by now. "I was able to... deal with the snake, but I don't think Rudolf would be so lucky."

The headman paled. "I will pass on your message, if I see him. But he may have fled by now."

Emily hoped not. She dreaded to imagine what one of the other mountain lords would do with Rudolf, let alone the necromancer. Lord Gorham would have to make whatever concessions they wanted, just to have his son returned.

"Please tell him, if you see him," she said, "Spread the word."

"Of course, My Lady," the headman said.

Emily flushed, half-convinced she was being mocked. Sergeant Miles used the exact same tone when he was pointing out one of her mistakes, and she'd never liked it.

"Thank you," she said, tartly.

She turned and walked out of the house, heading towards the post office. The postal service in the Allied Lands was run by the White Council rather than any of the independent kingdoms or city-states; in some ways, it reminded Emily of the Pony Express. But compared to email it was slow, cumbersome and unreliable. Magic could be used to move messages faster, but that required careful spellwork. She suspected she would have to look into it when she reached Fifth Year. Linking two crystal balls together was more complex, apparently, than it seemed.

The officer on duty—a part-time worker—took the letters, checked the seals and then stowed them away in a box. If he noticed Emily's subtle check for magic or magical influences, he said nothing. Emily thanked him and left, picking up a copy of the latest broadsheet on the way out. She snorted in amusement as she read the front page story, as it was focused on the antics of Princess Lucinda, who lived on the other side of the Allied Lands. Why would anyone in the mountains really want to know about her?

She was still smiling at the thought as she returned to the castle.

Chapter Twenty-Four

"HE DOESN'T REMEMBER MUCH," LADY BARB SAID, TWO DAYS LATER. "I WISH I COULD SAY I'm surprised."

Emily nodded. Lord Gorham seemed to have blocked the whole experience out of his mind, leaving them without any leads to follow. None of his servants had any idea when the runes had first started to appear, either.

The more Emily looked at it, the more it seemed like the mystery necromancer had covered his tracks well. But why would a necromancer bother to hide?

Lady Barb smiled at her. "You did well with the sewn runes, by the way," she added. "I think it will be a long time before anyone tries the same trick again."

Emily let out a breath she hadn't realized she'd been holding. There were rules on sharing magical knowledge with mundanes, even though telling the maids how to sew protective runes had seemed the only answer. If Lady Barb had chosen to be annoyed...but Lady Barb was practical, certainly more practical than whoever had dreamed up the rules. Spreading *that* sort of knowledge far and wide would certainly make it harder for the mystery necromancer to spread his influence.

"We can't stay here any longer," Lady Barb continued. "I think we need to head onwards to Easter."

"Where Lady Easter rules," Emily said. She tried to recall the map she'd seen of the mountain states. "Isn't that two days away?"

"More like four," Lady Barb admitted. She grinned at Emily's expression. "The direct route leads far too close to old ruins, so I'd prefer to avoid it."

Emily shivered. Old ruins could only mean one thing, buildings constructed during the days of the Faerie. She'd seen one of them up close in the mountains near Whitehall and still had nightmares, sometimes. There were too many dangers in such ruins for anyone to be complacent about approaching them. Even a necromancer would have second thoughts about trying to enter such a place.

"Go pack your bag," Lady Barb added. "And make sure you pack extra cloths with sewn runes. We might need them."

Emily hastened to obey. When she returned, she found Lady Barb deep in conversation with Lord Gorham. He looked pale and wan, but at least he was moving around. Emily waited at the door for them to finish, wondering just where Rudolf was now. He'd never returned to the castle. Maybe he was just waiting for the two magicians to leave.

"Come on," Lady Barb said, finally. "Let's go."

The walk down the mountain path was no better this time. Emily kept her eyes firmly on the road until they reached the valley, then followed Lady Barb through the town and onto a path leading through the forests. This path was harder to follow than the last, she decided after spending thirty minutes scrambling over rocks and streams that were deceptively small, but treacherously fast. By the time they passed the river that marked the edge of Lord Gorham's territory, she was exhausted, sweaty and desperate for a break.

"Not too much further to go," Lady Barb said, encouragingly. For once, she looked exhausted, too. "You can do it."

Emily scowled. The older woman had never shown a trace of being tired before, so why was she tired now? God knew Lady Barb had joined route marches with Martial Magic before...she hadn't shown any real tiredness then either, any more than Sergeant Miles. She couldn't help a flicker of concern. Was something wrong...or had her lack of sleep finally caught up with her? She doubted Lady Barb had had more than a few hours of sleep while they'd stayed at the castle.

She expended a great deal of magic there, she thought. *She might be exhausted...*

Lady Barb pressed onwards, somehow, until they reached another clearing. This one looked wilder than the last, as if someone had cut down the trees without bothering to do anything else to prevent them from growing back. Emily puzzled over how they'd removed the logs, then looked at the river and knew the answer. They'd simply floated the logs down to the town below, one by one. It was simpler than trying to drag them down overland.

"They prefer not to cut trees too close to the town," Lady Barb explained, as she shrugged off her pack and placed it on a rock. "There's an old tradition about what happens to towns that aren't surrounded by trees."

Emily removed her own bag and placed it next to Lady Barb's. "What is it?"

"They believe that the trees provide some manner of protection," Lady Barb said. "If they're cut down, the town itself will die soon afterwards."

It didn't seem anything more than a superstition, Emily decided. The forest might make it hard for an invading army to reach the town, but it was far from impossible. A small band of raiders might manage to destroy the town before help could arrive from the castle, if Lord Gorham cared to try to save his people. He would, wouldn't he? Lord Gorham had seemed more concerned about his people—and his son—after the runes had been removed. But she understood just how strongly people could cling to tradition.

Lady Barb held out a hand. "Pass me your staff," she ordered. "Now."

Emily hesitated, then removed the shrunken staff from her sleeve and passed it to Lady Barb, feeling the same odd reluctance to let go of it as always. Lady Barb enlarged it to cast a spell that removed the others embedded within the wood. Emily felt an odd vibration in the local magic field, which faded away rapidly into nothingness.

"You remember the rules, I assume," Lady Barb said. "Or do I have to repeat them?"

"I remember," Emily said. Sergeant Miles had gone through the rules every time he'd allowed Emily to use her staff, reminding her that she didn't dare become dependent on it. She found it humiliating to be warned, time and time again, but she understood the dangers well enough to be careful. Alassa would never have progressed beyond First Year if she hadn't rid herself of the wand. "I know the dangers."

Lady Barb returned the staff. Emily took it, feeling an odd mixture of relief and revulsion. It was strange to realize that she was considered too young to use a staff, but there was no choice. Dozens of necromancers wanted her head, with or without it being attached to her body at the time. And then there were her other enemies. Even so...Sergeant Miles had once knocked her out, just to get her to let go of the staff. He'd had no other options.

"You know how to create a fireball," Lady Barb said. "This time, I want you to create the spell, then embed it within the wood."

Emily closed her eyes, caressing the staff with her fingers. It was strange, she realized, just how close the embedding process was to the power-sharing ritual. Sergeant Miles had never mentioned the latter, but they were definitely linked. One shared raw power, the other shared the spellwork that directed the power. She shaped the spell in her mind, envisioning it moving into the wood. There was a quiver of magic, then it was done.

"Good enough," Lady Barb said. "It won't last, of course."

"I know," Emily said. "But it will last long enough."

She sighed. Even the hardest wood couldn't hold spellwork indefinitely. Most magicians had to constantly renew the spells they kept in readiness. Alassa's former cronies had done it for her, back when she'd been dependent on the wand. Some magicians, she'd been told, were never taught how to cast spells without a wand. Somehow, they were kept from realizing that they didn't need one.

Lady Barb nodded and pointed to a tree. "That will do as a target," she said. "Blast it."

Emily held up the staff to channel her magic into the embedded spell. There was a flash of light as the fireball streaked across the clearing and struck the tree, blasting it out of the ground and sending it falling against another tree. Emily stared in astonishment as the tree slowly crashed to the ground, smashing itself into splinters.

It was so much easier to use magic with a staff.

Which is the trap, she reminded herself. *It's too easy to forget how to cast spells in your mind.*

The staff seemed to glow with power as Lady Barb directed her to embed another two spells within the wood, then trigger them one after the other. Emily concentrated, feeling her power sucked into the wood as she triggered the spells. Two more trees were destroyed, one turned to ice and shattered, the other yanked out of the soil and dashed to the ground.

It was suddenly very hard to let go of the staff. No matter how she tried to tell her fingers to let go, they refused to move...

She yelped in pain as Lady Barb slapped her rear. Her fingers unclenched, allowing the staff to fall to the ground. Lady Barb picked it up, then shrank it back down to pencil-size and shoved it into her pocket. Emily glowered at her resentfully, rubbing her behind, but she knew better than to object. She'd come too close to dependency.

"No more experiments with the staff for a week," Lady Barb ordered. There was no give in her voice at all. "And if you touch it, you'll regret it."

Emily nodded, shamefaced. There were older boys at Whitehall who'd tried to sneak into the sealed section of the armory and recover their staffs, despite the Sergeant's strict orders. Holding the staff was addictive; the temptation to use it almost overpowering. Even the threat of dire punishment wasn't enough to prevent an addict from striving for his fix. One boy had been forbidden to touch his staff ever again.

She blushed, remembering. Aloha had made a crude joke and the rest of the girls had started giggling. And then Emily had taught them the words to *A Wizard's Staff has a Knob on the End*. The boys hadn't seen the humor at all.

Lady Barb snorted, rudely. Emily realized she was waiting for an answer.

"I won't," she promised. How could she when Lady Barb was keeping it in her pockets? But then, an addict might be stupid enough to try to steal it anyway. "Why does that keep happening?"

"You're not mature enough to handle it," Lady Barb said, tartly. "If the Grandmaster hadn't insisted..."

She shook her head, long strands of blonde hair coming loose and falling down around her skull. "I told him that it wasn't a good idea. You keep dancing on the edge of addiction."

Emily blanched. Addicting her to the staff would be the easiest way to render her powerless once the staff was taken away. She trusted the Grandmaster...but what if she was wrong to trust him? Might he be hoping that she would destroy her own ability to cast spells...or would he merely be relieved if that happened? But why would he want to cripple her?

"If that's true," she said, wondering how she dared ask, "why does he want me to learn?"

"You have enemies," Lady Barb said. "The more weapons in your arsenal, the better."

Emily relaxed. It was nothing more than paranoia, driven by her feelings of loss whenever she let go of the staff. The Grandmaster controlled Whitehall and the nexus under the school. If he'd wanted to kill her, he could have done it at any moment and made it look like an accident. Besides, he wasn't an evil man. He didn't have to take her into the school and teach her how to handle her magic.

"Start carving out the runes," Lady Barb ordered. "You can make another few pocket dimensions."

Emily nodded and started to work, unable to avoid noticing how the older woman sat down to watch rather than peering over Emily's shoulder. Normally, she would be grateful to avoid such close supervision, but now it bothered her. Lady Barb seemed to be weaker than normal, far weaker...and there was a necromancer running loose. Emily watched her out of the corner of her eye as she set up the square, then started to craft out the pocket dimension, piece by piece. This time, the magic flowed easier than before.

"Good work," Lady Barb said. "Now, dismantle it and start a new one."

Emily glanced at her in concern, then went back to work. Lady Barb said nothing as she completed the next dimension, so she dismantled it and built up a third. This time, she tried adding some modifications to the programming, trying to program it to reopen and collapse at a specific time. The spells didn't seem to work quite right;

it took her a moment to realize that she was actually putting the timing spells in stasis, along with whatever was in the dimension itself. It seemed that wrapping two layers of spells inside the dimension wasn't possible, at least not for a single magician. Building something the size of Whitehall would be impossible without a dedicated team and a colossal power source.

The dimension collapsed and she swore aloud, then glanced nervously towards Lady Barb. The older woman was looking into the distance, a dreamy expression on her face. Emily blinked at her, then turned and ran to grab the woman's arm. There was a flash of light and the world spun around her, then seemed to grow much larger. Emily had only a moment to realize that she'd been turned into a mouse—or something smaller—before Lady Barb waved her hand and her body snapped back to normal.

"I'm sorry," Lady Barb said, softly. She sounded *very* tired and worn. "You surprised me."

"You should be looking at me," Emily said, in a sharp tone she would never have dared use on anyone at Whitehall - except in an emergency. "I was building dimensions and..."

Lady Barb had told her never to try experimenting without supervision. But she'd been the one to lose interest in what Emily was doing. Emily stared at her drawn, white face, deeply worried for the woman she had come to think of as a mother—or a big sister. Lady Barb looked too weak to care.

"You're not well," she said, quietly. "What happened?"

"None of your business," Lady Barb said. Her voice was too weak to hold any real sting, despite her irritation. Emily would almost have welcomed a scolding if it meant Lady Barb was feeling better. "And *don't* try any diagnostic spells."

She rose to her feet, wiping the sweat from her brow. "Come on," she said, tiredly. "I want to get further than this before we set up camp for the night."

Emily hesitated. They weren't *that* far from the town. She could use a levitation spell and carry Lady Barb back there, where they could find a bed in the inn if not in the guesthouse. And she could brew potions that might help...

Lady Barb strode off without looking back. Emily hastily grabbed up the square and their bags and followed after her, silently wondering what Lady Barb had packed in her bag to make it so heavy. Lady Barb seemed determined to force her way onwards, despite the sweat and tiredness. Emily found herself wondering if she should stun her, before dismissing the thought. Lady Barb would be absolutely furious when she woke up—if she woke up. They'd been warned that elderly or weak humans could be killed by stunning spells. What if she accidentally killed her teacher?

The march rapidly became hellish. Emily struggled under the weight of both bags, only deterred from complaining by the simple fact that Lady Barb was clearly unwell. The older woman stumbled from side to side, as if she were drunk...Emily had to fight down the urge to cast the diagnostic spells anyway, no matter what Lady Barb said. She told herself that it wouldn't matter what Lady Barb did, as long as she knew what was wrong. But then, Lady Barb clearly knew that *something* was wrong...

They reached another clearing and Lady Barb came to a halt, then half-stumbled, half-collapsed to the ground. Emily tried to catch her, but the weight of the bags made it impossible. She shrugged them off as quickly as possible and peered down at her mentor. Lady Barb was sweating profusely.

"I'm going to cast the spells," Emily said, finally. "I..."

Lady Barb reached up like lightning and caught her arm. "No," she hissed. "Put out the blankets, then cast protective wards. This isn't a good time to use magic on me."

"Why not?" Emily asked. "What's *wrong* with you?"

Lady's Barb's grip tightened. Emily winced in pain. "Put out the blankets, then cast protective wards," Lady Barb repeated. "Do *not* try to use magic on me."

Emily hesitated, then did as she was told. They hadn't been able to pack a tent, but magic could provide a shelter against the elements...unless it rained so heavily that the clearing turned to mud. As soon as she had one of the blankets in place, she helped Lady Barb to lie down and sat next to her, staring at the older woman. She seemed to be worsening by the second.

"Give me some water," Lady Barb ordered, between breaths. Emily passed her the bottle of water, wondering just where she would be able to find more. There didn't look to be a convenient stream anywhere in sight. "Whatever you do, don't use any magic on me."

"Understood," Emily said. She hated the pleading note she heard in her voice. "But what's wrong?"

"Lord Gorham needed a boost," Lady Barb admitted. "I pushed him as far as I could, at an immense cost. It's finally caught up with me."

Emily stared at her in horror. "Are you going to die?"

"I may wind up wishing I had," Lady Barb said. She chuckled, harshly. "Let me sleep for a few hours. I should be better soon enough."

Chapter Twenty-Five

EMILY HAD CAMPED OUT BEFORE, WITH THE MARTIAL MAGIC CLASS, BUT SHE'D NEVER HAD to spend time camping on her own. Or effectively on her own, she corrected herself, as she gathered firewood and turned it into a small fire. It took several minutes of careful searching to locate a spring, much to her relief. There were spells to draw water out of the ground, but they could be very tricky and never had worked properly for her. She filled the bottle and put the cauldron over the fire to boil the water. It wouldn't be safe to drink without boiling it thoroughly.

She glanced down at Lady Barb, worriedly. The older woman looked surprisingly vulnerable asleep, her skin pale and wan. Emily wanted to sit beside her and hold her hand, but there was no time. Instead, she walked back into the forest and set a magical trap. When she checked back, twenty minutes later, she discovered that she'd caught a fat rabbit and a handful of rodent-like creatures. Grimacing in disgust—she'd never liked hunting, even with the Sergeants—she broke the rabbit's neck, wishing she'd paid closer attention when the sergeants had explained how to make the trap lethal. She knew she needed to kill in order to eat, but she still disliked it.

Carrying the rabbit back to the campsite, she braced herself and started to cut it up, removing the meat and placing it under a preservation spell. The remainder of the rabbit's body was effectively useless, so she dug a hole at a corner of the clearing and buried the rest of it under the soil. She suspected a fox or something nastier would dig it up, sooner or later, but it couldn't be helped. Once it was buried, she found the mugs and made herself a cup of Kava. Lady Barb twitched in her sleep, but didn't awaken. Emily hesitated before starting to cook the rabbit over the fire.

The smell must have woken Lady Barb, for she opened her eyes just as the sun was starting to set. Emily, more relieved than she cared to admit, found one of the metal plates, dropped a piece of rabbit onto it and passed the whole thing to Lady Barb. The older woman smiled gratefully, then blew on the meat and started to chew. Emily watched in concern as Lady Barb ate her food and drank some Kava. She still looked tired.

"It's very good," Lady Barb said. "Thank you."

Emily suspected flattery. She'd never been very good at cooking, even on Earth. But then, she'd never had any proper lessons. She nodded in thanks anyway, then ate her own rabbit, which was rather overdone. Better overcooked than undercooked, she reminded herself. There were no modern preservatives in anything from the Allied Lands.

"You're welcome," she said. "How are you feeling?"

"Weak, but better," Lady Barb admitted. She changed the subject before Emily could press her for details. "Check the wards before you go to sleep. There are wild animals out here that could be dangerous."

Emily nodded. Darkness was falling steadily now, deterring her from venturing back under the forest canopy. She silently thanked the sergeants for lessons in camping, particularly the suggestion to pile up firewood while the sun was high. They shouldn't need to leave the clearing until morning. If Lady Barb *could* leave...she gritted her teeth at the thought, praying that Lady Barb would recover. Emily didn't know what she would do if Lady Barb died.

Probably walk back to town and ask for help, she thought. If she *could* find her way back to town. She pushed the thought aside and checked on the wards, one by one. If someone wanted to disturb them, he would have to break through, which would alert her to the threat.

"My father rarely left his house," Lady Barb commented. "But my mother's people always slept out under the stars. They believed it brought them closer to the world around them."

Emily shrugged. The sergeants had talked about the wonders of the great out-doors—and told horror stories about places they'd slept during wartime—but she hadn't been too impressed, even though some of the camping trips had been enjoy-able. She preferred civilization, libraries and hot running water to sleeping out in the wilds. But if someone knew no better...why would they not want the countryside?

"They used to tell stories too, around the campfire," Lady Barb added. "I wonder if I can recall..."

She launched into a story, speaking in a sing-song voice that made her sound years younger.

"There was a forest once, near the heart of the world," she said. "No mortal dared visit because it was inhabited by ghosts, demons and all manner of fell creatures. And then, one day, the monsters fell on one another in a frenzy of supernatural bloodlet-ting. By the time the fighting came to an end. Emily, they'd wiped themselves out."

Emily shivered. "Is the story true?"

Lady Barb shrugged, tiredly. "No one knows."

Emily couldn't help wondering just how much of the story was rooted in real-ity. Most stories *did* have some basis in history, even if the grain of truth had been surrounded by hundreds of lies and exaggerations, until the whole story became unbelievable. Was it something to do with the Faerie? Or was the story completely unrelated to them?

There was no point in asking. Instead, Emily listened as Lady Barb told a second story, one about a young man who had walked into an ogre's cave, only to discover two children—two ogre children—crying for food. He'd fed them, then fallen asleep—only to be discovered by the ogress. She'd thanked him for feeding her children, then given him magic gifts he'd used to found a kingdom of his own. Compared to some of the stories written to explain why the Kings of the Allied Lands held power, it was almost reasonable. Emily rather doubted it was true, though. It wasn't like anyone in the Allied Lands to leave ogres alive, no matter how young they were.

She felt a sudden surge of affection for the older woman as the tale came to an end. Was this what it was like, she asked herself again, to have a mother? Somehow, she couldn't imagine her biological mother going camping with anyone. But she knew so little about her mother's past. It wasn't as if they'd ever sat down and talked about it. There had been times when she'd wondered if her father would come back for her...

...And instead she'd fallen through the looking glass.

Lady Barb looked over at her. "Do you want to tell a story?"

Emily was struck dumb. Public speaking wasn't something she enjoyed, even though it wasn't really *public* if it was just her and Lady Barb. She thought hard, wondering what sort of stories she could tell. Most of the fantasy books she'd read were long and wordy, too long for a single night, while few of the others would have any meaning for Lady Barb. She wondered absently how one would explain *Star Trek* to someone who had no referents for the concept of a starship, then decided it was probably impossible. Instead, she told a story about a good witch who'd gone to a school for wicked witches.

"I don't understand why she didn't become evil," Lady Barb said when she'd finished. "Or why they didn't just kill her outright."

"It's a...story," Emily said. Mentioning that it was a *fairy* story would probably be a bad idea. "I don't think it was meant as anything else."

She paused, remembering Lin. "Is Mountaintop a school for wicked witches?"

"It tends to cater to magical families and new magicians," Lady Barb said. There was something in her tone that bothered Emily. "But it doesn't produce evil sorcerers or wicked witches."

Emily nodded, relieved. "How many other magical schools are there?"

Lady Barb smiled. "Six or seven, in the Allied Lands," she said. "Whitehall is the best, naturally, with Mountaintop a close second. Then there's Laughter Academy, which only caters for girls; they're very traditionalist, but still honor the shared curriculum. Stronghold is an oddity; it takes only boys, but combines magical and non-magical children in most classes. Quite a few royal brats are sent there for education."

Emily looked up, surprised. "They put boys with magic together with boys without magic?"

"I believe so, in most classes," Lady Barb said. "Most of their students are trained in combat; they're either snatched up by various armies or become Mediators. And, to answer your next question, their tutors come down hard on bullying, of either kind."

She shook her head. "The remaining schools are quite small, with only a handful of pupils and teachers," she concluded. "More like homeschooling, but with several families sharing their resources to teach their children. There used to be two more, but both of them were destroyed by the necromancers."

Emily nodded. "I meant to ask," she said, hoping that talking would make Lady Barb feel better. "How are exams arranged?"

"The White Council assigns examiners for graduating students at the end of their terms," Lady Barb said. "In Whitehall's case, there are external examiners in Fourth Year and Sixth Year. If you pass the exams, you get a degree recognized all over the Allied Lands and you can look for a master for an apprenticeship. Not every student bothers to take the exams, though."

"I didn't realize that was a choice," Emily said, surprised. "Can I evade my exams...?"

"Not unless you want me very angry with you," Lady Barb said, dryly. "And I dare say Void won't be pleased, either."

Emily swallowed. Everyone, even the Grandmaster, seemed to be more than a little nervous when they spoke about the enigmatic sorcerer. But then, she'd seen him jump into a necromancer's fortress, knock Shadye down for a few seconds and teleport out, taking Emily with him. No one else in her experience had shown so much power merged with skill. Few sorcerers would dare consider facing a necromancer alone.

"Alassa might be wise to evade hers," Lady Barb added. "She can't really be an apprentice, so exams won't give her any support and a great many problems, if someone uses them to deduce her abilities. I wonder if the Grandmaster will arrange matters so she's expelled just before taking the exams."

"He can't," Emily said, shocked. "She's worked hard...it would disgrace her."

"It would also conceal her true capabilities," Lady Barb said. She snorted. "Believe me, she would hardly be the first aristocratic brat to be expelled from Whitehall."

Emily rolled her eyes. Alassa's behavior in First Year had been awful, even though she knew—now—that it had more to do with her insecurities and badly-chosen friends than genuine malice. If *that* hadn't been enough to get her expelled, what *was*? Even voyeurism hadn't been enough to earn more than a month of detentions. And the destruction of whatever plans the boys had had for the summer, she reminded herself.

"It doesn't seem right," she mumbled.

She knew that, barring unexpected events, Alassa would leave Whitehall at the end of her Fourth Year. Alassa was a royal princess, the confirmed heir to the throne; it would be time for her to return and start acting like a crown princess. King Randor would start passing some of the burden of governance on to his daughter, preparing her for the day she would assume the throne. But Emily knew that she would miss Alassa terribly.

It was still two years away, she reminded herself. And they would still be friends. But it still felt immediate. She'd gone through so much of her life without friends that having some now made it hard to face the prospect of losing them.

"I don't think it would blight her future," Lady Barb said. "She *is* the crown princess, after all, and the barons have been thoroughly cowed."

Emily had to admit she was right. King Randor had taken advantage of the chaos caused by the attempted coup to remove a handful of ambitious noblemen who hadn't been directly implicated in the conspiracy. Between the purge and the ennoblement of others the king wanted to reward—including Emily herself—the remaining noblemen weren't sure quite what the new rules were. By the time they figured it out, Alassa would be solidly in place.

"She still needs a husband," Emily said, mournfully. "Is she going to find one?"

"Let us hope so," Lady Barb said. "She'd be better off with someone who isn't aristocratic, someone who can introduce new blood into the royal family. But he would have problems being accepted."

Emily nodded, ruefully. Alassa was smart—but she was also the product of her culture, a culture that looked down on people without aristocratic blood. It was odd to realize that they would sooner accept a bastard child than someone who was perfectly legitimate, at least as long as the child had aristocratic blood. And, if the father was high enough, they could even overlook the mother being a commoner, no matter what she did for a living. But they didn't extend such license to the aristocratic women.

Would Alassa accept a commoner? It didn't seem likely, somehow. And would King Randor accept it if his daughter brought a commoner back to Zangaria? Perhaps Alassa should find someone at Whitehall, a powerful magician who would be on a social level of his own. But, as far as Emily knew, she'd never shown any interest in dating anyone at Whitehall. Only Imaiqah had shown any real interest in the opposite sex.

The thought reminded her of her own predicament. "I was a fool to accept the Barony, wasn't I?"

Lady Barb looked over at her, her face unreadable. "Most of your loyal subjects think otherwise," she pointed out. "You could hardly do worse than your predecessor."

Emily cringed, mentally. She'd looked at the laws the previous Baron had written—and enforced, when he felt like it—and banished all of them to the fiery depths of legal hell. It didn't take a lawyer to realize that the laws contradicted one another in several places, or that the peasants barely had enough food to survive the winter. In the end, she'd designed a handful of laws and left Bryon to ensure that they were not perverted. It hadn't taken long for the peasants to start reaping the benefits of some of her changes.

But she wasn't sure if she *wanted* to remain Baroness Cockatrice.

"That wouldn't be difficult," she said, tartly. "If I only molested ten girls a month I'd still be a net improvement."

She shook her head, pushing the previous baron out of her mind. How was *she* supposed to act? A sorceress had sexual freedom, but an aristocratic girl did not. And *she* fell into both categories. She shook her head again, a moment later. It was hard enough to imagine being touched, let alone going further. Even the memory of Jade kissing her felt like it had happened to someone else. But eventually she would need to give Cockatrice an heir.

"I could adopt someone," she said. It had worked well enough for the Roman Emperors, at least until Marcus Aurelius had been succeeded by Commodus, his biological son. The more she thought about it, the more she thought she saw advantages. Her adopted son would be an adult by the time she chose him, allowing her to judge his character for herself. If Marcus Aurelius had been able to do that, perhaps Commodus would have been quietly strangled one night and dumped in the river. "Can't I?"

"The bloodlines would be disrupted," Lady Barb pointed out. "Unless you used an adoption rite and they can go wrong, if you picked badly."

Emily rolled her eyes. What *was* the obsession with aristocratic blood? *She* was no aristocrat. Maybe, just maybe, it was vaguely possible she was related to an aristocratic family on Earth, but she had to admit it was unlikely. Even if she was, the aristocracy on Earth was hardly acknowledged by the Allied Lands. Or would they recognize an aristocrat from Earth?

"Magic runs in the blood," Lady Barb reminded her, when she asked. "So do any little...quirks someone might have engineered into their line."

"I have none," Emily pointed out, tartly.

"You might have, sooner or later," Lady Barb added. "Besides, there would be no questioning of a legitimate child—or even one born out of wedlock, as long as you were the mother."

Emily shook her head. "I don't think I want to do it," she said, unsure precisely what she meant. "It's a terrible mess."

"If you want to remain baroness, you have to learn to come to terms with its obligations as well as its rewards," Lady Barb said. She shifted slightly, then lay back on her blanket. "I should say, though, that there are worse things in life than raising children."

"How would you know?" Emily asked, before she could stop herself. "I..."

It said something about how tired and ill Lady Barb was, she realized mutely, that she didn't get her head bitten off for cheek. "My father always said I was the best thing in his life," Lady Barb said, instead. "Even though he would be happier digging through dusty archives than bringing up a child, he still didn't abandon me to the tender mercies of the servants. He was always there for me."

Emily felt a flicker of envy. Void might be the closest thing she had to a father in this world, but he showed himself only rarely—and always on his own terms. She didn't even know how to contact him, short of writing letters. Lady Barb, on the other hand, had been very lucky.

"I need to sleep," Lady Barb added. "Make sure you keep the fire from burning out. We might need the warmth."

Emily nodded, banked the fire, and settled down on her own blanket. But it was a long time before she fell asleep.

Chapter Twenty-Six

S HE AWOKE, UNSURE OF WHAT HAD STARTLED HER.

For a moment, she lay still, remembering the day a maid had tried to kill her in Alassa's bedroom back on the road to Zangaria. An alarm bell yammered in her mind, but it took her a long moment to realize that something was pressing against the wards. She heard the sound of breathing as her eyes snapped open. The moon was descending in the distance and the clearing was wrapped in shadow. But there was no sign of anything outside the wards.

Bracing herself, Emily sat up, one hand reaching for her staff before remembering that it was hidden in Lady Barb's pockets. The wards shivered again and her head snapped round, but she still saw nothing unusual. Carefully, she cast a night vision spell over her eyes, casting the clearing into eerie light, but still saw nothing, apart from a faint disturbance in the ground. It looked as though a giant invisible creature was prowling the edge of the wards.

Emily hastily tested the wards, just as they shivered for the third time. They didn't look as if they were going to break. Even so...she stood upright, staring towards where she knew the creature had to be. Faint clouds of dirt rose up from where it placed its feet, suggesting that it was the size of a lion, perhaps bigger. The sound of deep, heavy breathing grew louder as Emily carefully added a pair of extra wards. If the first set collapsed, they wouldn't be left defenseless.

An invisible creature...she'd never heard of anything like it from the factual stories reported in class. But there were quite a few stories of people encountering monsters and never managing to report back, although she hadn't been able to avoid asking how they knew that monsters were involved, if no one had escaped to report. What if their missing explorers had run into an invisible monster, too? But the creature didn't seem *that* dangerous, not compared to a Mimic or a Werewolf.

Could it *be* a Werewolf? Werewolves could use magic—could one of them have cast an invisibility spell on himself before transforming? It seemed unlikely, but she prepared a cancellation spell before hastily dismissing the thought. Without clear eye contact with her target, it was quite possible that she would accidentally disarm her wards instead. She rose to her feet and crossed the gap to the edge of the wards.

Warm breath touched her face. She stumbled backwards, breathing in the stench of rotting meat. The giant dogs she'd played with, back when she was looking for a familiar, smelled nicer. And she'd hated them.

"A Night Walker," Lady Barb's voice said.

Emily jumped. She hadn't realized that the older woman had awakened. Grimly, she turned away from the wards and looked at Lady Barb. Her face looked paler than ever due to the night-sight, a thin sheen of sweat covered her face—and her hand was trembling slightly.

Emily felt a cold shiver running down her spine. Before now, she would never have imagined that Lady Barb could *tremble*.

"He can't get through the wards," Lady Barb added. "But he wouldn't hesitate to attack if he could."

Emily sighed. "What do I do with him?"

"Nothing," Lady Barb said. "Just sit still and wait for him to lose interest."

The sound of breathing grew louder as the wards shimmered. Emily watched the interplay of magic around the creature, shuddering inwardly. If the creature was completely invisible—and none of her spells showed her anything but its footsteps—it would be deadly dangerous, even to a sorcerer. She suspected she wouldn't sleep a wink all night—and would be terrified when she walked through the forest, the following day. How would she know there *wasn't* a creature after her?

"They sleep during the day," Lady Barb said, when she asked. "I think it's part of their magic."

Emily scowled. Another Faerie-created monster, then, just like almost every other magical creature. She could imagine what use they'd had for an invisible creature. If nothing else, it would be a very effective terror weapon. Maybe it was meant to discourage people from visiting the Faerie ruins in the mountains. But hardly anyone would go visit unless they were compelled.

She settled back on the ground, resting her hands in her lap, and felt the wards shimmer as the creature paced the edge of the field. Time and time again, it brushed up against the wards, then retreated, apparently balked. Lady Barb closed her eyes and returned to sleep, but Emily couldn't force herself to relax. Just knowing the creature was there...she kept trying to see it, even though it was definitely futile. All she could see were the signs of its passage.

Maybe there was a captured Night Walker at Whitehall and I just couldn't see it, she thought, with morbid amusement. *Mistress Kirdáne would love a new pet.*

Sergeant Miles had taught his students that invisibility was only as good as the sorcerer who cast the spell. It was easy to turn invisible, harder to hide the tracks of one's passage. Emily had watched him point out how they still disturbed the world around them—and how a simple spell could reveal their location, even if it didn't break the invisibility spell itself. And besides, there was no such thing as a perfect invisibility cloak. A properly constructed set of wards could rip it to shreds.

Her fingers itched, ready to cast a spell that would create a mist or something else that would show the creature's rough location and form, but she held the impulse under control. Instead, she toyed with the bracelet around her wrist. She could release the Death Viper, send it out after the creature, and then...she shuddered, unable to contemplate the prospect of seeing the lethal snake crushed under the creature's feet. The bond had tightened around her mind, as the books had warned. But she hadn't paid close enough attention at the time.

She looked over at Lady Barb, sleeping peacefully, then returned her gaze to the creature, trying to gauge its size and shape. Her first impression had been correct, she decided; it definitely walked on four legs. Other than that...it was hard to estimate anything else about the creature. The way it walked suggested it was large, but was it really as big as she'd thought? Or was it just playing games with her mind?

A shiver ran down her spine as the wards shimmered again, right in front of her. She peered into the darkness, unable to escape the feeling that the creature was looking right back at her, but saw nothing. High overhead, she heard something hooting and glanced up, just in time to see an enormous Snowy Owl fly through the darkness. A wriggling shape was caught in its talons, desperately trying to escape. When she looked back down, the creature was gone.

Or was it? Emily slowly rose to her feet and paced over to stand at the edge of the wards. As long as the creature stayed still, it wouldn't reveal anything to show where it was hiding. It could be crouched right in front of her and she would never see it. She listened, carefully, but all she heard was the faint sounds of rustling from the undergrowth and owls hooting in the distance. A faint glow flickered in the forest, then faded into nothingness.

Emily peered into the darkness for a long chilling moment, then turned and walked back to her blanket. If the creature was lurking outside the wards, it could wait until doomsday. She had no intention of crossing the wards until the sun rose and she had to find water and perhaps another rabbit. A motion caught her eye, at the edge of the clearing, and she looked over sharply, just in time to see...*something* moving through the air. For a long second, her mind refused to process what she was seeing. It looked like a blanket hanging in the air, yet the way it flapped told her it was a living creature. She wasn't even sure how it *flew*.

They used to prove that bumblebees couldn't fly, she reminded herself. She'd ridden on a dragon and she had no idea how it managed to fly, save by magic. But then, Alassa hadn't believed Emily when she'd tried to explain about jumbo jets. It sounded absurd, completely impossible, to someone raised in Zangaria. And yet she could turn someone into a frog with a wave of her hand.

The newcomer seemed to hesitate, then flapped its way into the clearing. Emily stared, fascinated, as several others joined it, spinning through the air like dishcloths as they moved. She'd never seen anything like them on Earth, or in classes at Whitehall. Had they even been discovered officially? They didn't look dangerous, merely absurd.

A low growl echoed through the air. Emily started, realizing that she'd been right and the first creature *had* been hiding near the wards, hoping she'd be stupid enough to step outside and be eaten. The dishcloths—as she couldn't help thinking of them— stopped their flapping and advanced towards where the first creature had to be. There was a rustle of motion, but it was already too late. Powerful jaws savaged the first dishcloth, but its companions fell on the creature and attacked it. Emily saw hints of giant teeth—she had no idea where they'd been hiding—before the brief bloody battle came to an end. Victorious, the dishcloths retreated, carrying their prey with them. She couldn't help noticing that, enfolded by the dishcloths, the invisible creature was actually *larger* than a lion.

Shaken, unable to sleep, Emily watched as the nightlife flowed through the forest. Some wildlife was mundane enough to have come from Earth, others were strange and wonderful creatures, including several others she hadn't seen at Whitehall. Foxes sniffed at the edge of the wards, then ran off; tiny spiders scuttled along the edge of the clearing, moving in large groups. Emily remembered the warped spiders near the Dark City and shivered, feeling sorry for whatever creature the spiders overwhelmed. Individually, the spiders were largely harmless, their poison insufficient to kill a grown human. Collectively, they were absolutely lethal. And, unlike spiders on Earth, they preferred to move in groups.

She looked up, just in time to see something large flying high overhead, blotting out the stars as it moved. The magic field seemed to shift around her as she realized she was staring up at a dragon, the first she'd seen since her passage to Whitehall. Dragons weren't exactly *rare*, but the ones old enough to be intelligent stayed away from humanity. She still had no idea what Void had done to earn a favor from a dragon, let alone one that had been expended so casually. Void could easily have teleported her to Whitehall if he hadn't wanted to use his favor. But she had to admit that being flown by a dragon had allowed her to make one hell of an entrance.

Golden eyes glinted, peering down at her. Emily stared back, wondering if it was the dragon she'd met, years ago. But the dragon made no move towards the clearing. It merely flapped its wings and flew away, into the darkness. She was sure it had noticed her...

Feeling an odd sense of loss, Emily lay down on the blanket and stared up at the night sky. The moon was rising now, casting rays of silver light over the ground. Magic seemed to dance in response, now they were well away from human settlement. She remembered all the tales about people warped and twisted by wild magic and, suddenly, believed them all. There was something eerie about being outside in the forest, with the moon calling to the magic in her blood. If she'd been a werewolf, she realized, she would have transformed by now.

The lunar magic gives them a boost, she thought, as she tried to relax. *Their curse is charged up by the moon, allowing them to transform. Like most transfigured people, they lose themselves in the transformation—and, even when the spell snaps, they still carry the mental scars.*

She must have dozed off, despite the danger, for the next thing she knew was warm sunlight playing across her body. Her eyes opened and she hastily scanned the clearing for danger, but saw nothing, apart from a handful of splashes of blood and scales where the Night Walker had been killed. She stood up, brushing down her shirt, and walked over to the edge of the wards, looking for any hints that they were being watched. But there was nothing there, as far as she could tell.

Carefully, she checked the cauldron and discovered that there was enough water left to make two mugs of Kava. The fire had dimmed low, but it was still alight. She pushed pieces of wood into the fire, built up a blaze and then started to boil the water. Lady Barb moaned slightly, then opened her eyes. Emily shivered, deeply worried. Every day, Lady Barb had awoken first and left Emily to sleep. But now...

"I'm making Kava," she said, as she poured the water into the first mug and added the ground powder. It reminded her of instant coffee, save for the taste. She'd grown used to it, but she doubted she would ever like the flavor. "Are you...are you all right?"

"I've been better," Lady Barb grated. She managed to sit upright, crossing her legs. "You may have to entertain yourself today."

Emily looked at her, stung. She might be inexperienced–perhaps even naive–compared to the older sorceress, but she didn't know she was being babysat. Or perhaps she was. There were dangers in the countryside she wouldn't even have noticed, if Lady Barb hadn't pointed them out to her.

She finished making the cup of Kava and passed it to Lady Barb, who took it and drank carefully. Every movement she made looked precisely calculated, rather like Professor Lombardi; it took Emily a moment to realize that Lady Barb was carefully controlling herself, trying not to lose control of her body. She had to be dangerously ill.

"I need to know," she said, quietly. "What is happening to you?"

"I told you," Lady Barb snapped. She took a breath, then continued in a quieter tone. "I spent a great deal of magic to repair the damage Lord Gorham suffered, under the influence of the runes. In doing so, I weakened my life force and became vulnerable to backlash shock."

She finished her mug and passed it back to Emily. "This is manifesting as a disease," she added, darkly. "Don't worry. You can't catch it from me."

Emily winced. She hadn't even *considered* the possibility. But she should have, considering this world didn't have vaccines or even a proper theory of medicine. Or at least not a non-magical one. Emily knew she was unprepared for diseases that had been wiped out on Earth decades ago, diseases that would eat her up as soon as they infected her body if she hadn't had access to magic or magical healing. What might she catch, simply by not having the immunities that were conferred by being born in the Allied Lands, if she hadn't had magic herself?

"I was hoping that it would fade today, but no such luck," Lady Barb added. "That means it has yet to reach its peak. When it does...just keep giving me water, when I ask for it. Don't try any magic, whatever happens."

Emily frowned. "Why?"

"Because my magic will regard yours as an intrusion," Lady Barb explained. She sighed and lay back on the blanket. "This isn't a normal disease or a broken bone, just my magic responding to my abuse. Give it time to recover and I'll be fine."

"What if you're not fine?" Emily asked. "What should I do?"

Lady Barb gave her a long considering look. "If I die...you should have a contingency plan," she said. She chuckled, rather harshly. "You seem to move between complete dependence or complete independence, depending on how far you trust your companion. Go back to the town, use the money in my pouch and catch a ride with the postal coach. He can take you down to the nearest city, where you can get a portal to Dragon's Den. Make sure you take everything useful from my body before leaving it."

Emily swallowed. The matter-of-fact instructions were more worrying than shouts and screams. She wanted to retort that Lady Barb's death would be more than a minor inconvenience, but she didn't quite dare. "What should I do with your body?"

"Burn it to ash," Lady Barb said. "Don't worry about prayers. You don't know the ones my family uses, so..."

She shook her head. "Just leave me to sleep, now," she added. "Make yourself breakfast, then do some practicing...but nothing with the staff. Leave the staff alone."

"I will," Emily promised. Lady Barb had told her not to experiment without supervision, but she hadn't expected to get unwell. "Can I practice with pocket dimensions?"

"Carefully," Lady Barb said. "Very carefully."

She closed her eyes. Emily watched her for a long moment, then turned and stepped past the wards, one hand raised in a defensive posture. Nothing moved to attack her, nothing moved at all, apart from a rabbit at the edge of the clearing. Emily shot a stunning spell at the creature and knocked it out before it could escape. The sergeants would have reproved her for wasting magic, but she didn't have time to set traps. She certainly didn't want to leave Lady Barb alone for longer than strictly necessary.

Gritting her teeth, she picked up the creature, snapped its neck and started to cut it apart for food.

Chapter Twenty-Seven

L ADY BARB REMAINED ASLEEP, EVEN WHEN EMILY COOKED SEVERAL PIECES OF RABBIT IN THE fire and ate them with Kava. Emily watched her, concerned, then placed several more pieces of meat under stasis spells, so they would be ready when Lady Barb was awake. Reaching into her bag, she found one of her notebooks and started to brainstorm, working out how best to create a pocket dimension that could serve as an emergency shelter. When she ran out of ideas for that, she jotted down everything she could remember about the very first aircraft to leave the ground on Earth. Maybe, just maybe, a craftsman in Zangaria could produce his own version of the *Kitty Hawk*.

She looked back at her earlier pages and sketched out an idea for a slide rule that might be useful for craftsmen. But she couldn't remember enough about the concept without memory spells to write down everything. She made a silent promise to herself to explore the concept more thoroughly when she returned to Whitehall, then opened a new page and jotted down more ideas for her bank. One branch would be opened in Cockatrice, but another would be opened in a nearby independent city-state. She had the feeling that it would be better to keep the bank as separate as possible from her other innovations. And sticky-fingered aristocrats.

It would be a headache to make it work properly, even with magical versions of ideas from Earth. She would need to find someone to manage it full time, someone she could trust, but who could do that in Zangaria? Bryon was busy with Cockatrice, Imaiqah's father had his own business...and besides, neither of them could stand up to King Randor. And yet, political interference would doom her bank as surely as anything else. She might be better starting the whole project somewhere well away from Zangaria.

"I wonder if Aloha would like the job," she mused, out loud. Aloha had worked out a word processor-like device, using the concept Emily had taught her, even if it would be years before they came up with a working computer. But it was possible to devise a spell processor...Emily had sketched out notes, although she wasn't sure how to make them practical. Or, if that happened, what it would do to society if it worked.

She went back to her patient and touched Lady Barb's forehead, wincing at the heat. The older woman seemed to be burning up from the inside. Emily placed a mug of water next to her, then stood up and walked out of the wards, carrying the bag with her. Once she was outside, she started to practice with the pocket dimensions again, carefully. She managed to put together two stable dimensions in a row using the square before placing it behind her and concentrating on creating one in thin air. But it took several tries before she managed to make it work properly.

"The wood must be a crutch, too," she muttered, as she sat down just outside the wards, exhausted. She didn't see how the square prevented the pocket dimension from expanding outwards, but perhaps it was just a matter of perception. She saw nothing, so there seemed to be no barrier to prevent expansion. Concentrating, she tried to visualize it in her mind, but she lost it every time she opened her eyes and saw nothing. "Or maybe I'm not doing it properly."

She glanced over at Lady Barb before getting one of the books she'd brought along and starting to read. It wasn't as interesting as she'd hoped, but it did help to pass several hours while she recovered from using so much magic. The writer knew what he was talking about, yet he wrote in such a boring manner that Emily found herself yawning halfway through the first chapter. It was odd—Alchemy was exciting, sometimes terrifyingly so—but this style of boring readers to death seemed to be typical of half of her textbooks. But then, maybe the writer was trying to *discourage* experimentation.

Emily sighed as she reached the end of the third chapter. Part of her just wanted to whine that Alchemy would never be one of her skills, while the other part of her knew that she needed a basic grounding in the subject even if she never sought mastery. Potions and concoctions brewed by oneself worked better, she'd been told, than anything brewed by anyone else. But her rational mind refused to grasp why this was so. Maybe it was just the simple fact that she'd never been very good at cooking... or maybe it was her inability to understand things that the locals took for granted.

She found herself worrying about the future, distracting herself from the present. Would she pass her exams in Fourth Year? Like Alassa, she could skip the exams without threatening her future...but she didn't want to skip or fail them, not when she'd worked so hard. Exams on Earth were largely useless, in her opinion; exams in Whitehall were terrifyingly important, at least to students without an aristocratic background. And she didn't want to disappoint her supervisors by refusing to take the exams or flunking them. And yet...

Maybe I can hire a tutor, she thought. Professor Thande was a genius, but he didn't have enough time to give one-on-one coaching to his pupils. Whitehall's teaching staff were overworked and underpaid, yet they weren't the only masters of their subjects. Emily made a private resolution to hire a tutor at the end of Third Year, if she didn't improve by then, and study intensely over the summer.

She looked over at Lady Barb, then stood up and started to cast spell after spell, cycling through every pattern she remembered. Her magic seemed to sparkle as it danced around her, then faded back into nothingness as she finally relaxed, gasping for breath. Her tutors had told her to practice often, but they probably hadn't expected her to practice so furiously—or to be alone, without supervision. Not for the first time, she realized just how lucky the students were to have Whitehall. Their spells could be carefully monitored, even without a tutor in the room, and emergency measures could be taken if necessary.

Tiredly, she sat back down and tried to relax. But the book was boring rather than relaxing, and she was too worried about Lady Barb to do any more brainstorming. Instead, she pulled the bracelet off her wrist and placed it on the ground, then undid the spell keeping the snake as a bracelet. Her mind twisted uncomfortably as the snake returned to its natural shape, then relaxed. It seemed unbothered by the experience of being held in stasis.

Emily reached down to pet it before catching herself. The snake might not be poisonous to her, but the only way to test the snake's skin was to touch it—and if it still threatened her, she risked losing a hand. She got an odd sense of reassurance from the snake, yet she still didn't dare touch it. Instead, the snake slithered over towards the bloodstains on the ground and sniffed at them. Emily had a mental impression of a reptilian-like creature stalking the countryside in pitch darkness. It didn't seem to worry the Death Viper.

"But it wouldn't bother you," Emily said, addressing the snake. "Would it?"

The snake didn't seem to understand. Emily was almost disappointed. Some familiars she'd seen at Whitehall seemed almost intelligent—but then, they'd spent long enough with their owners to bond with them completely. They'd picked up a little of human intelligence, if she recalled the books correctly, although they would never be autonomous entities. The Death Viper, on the other hand, hadn't been with her for more than a day—at least, it hadn't been awake.

"Not fair, is it?" She said. The snake seemed to bob its head in agreement. "I have to wear you as a bracelet, so the bond can never really deepen."

On impulse, she picked up a twig and tossed it towards the edge of the clearing. The snake gave her an unreadable look—she felt a sense of puzzled amusement coming from its mind—then gave chase. It picked up the twig in its mouth, then carried it back and dropped it in front of Emily. Emily smiled and looked down at the twig. It was marred slightly where the snake had bit it. She didn't dare touch it with her bare hand.

The snake's amusement seemed to grow stronger. It was laughing at her!

"I should have gone for a dog," Emily said, reprovingly. "What do you think of that?"

The snake seemed to twitch, as if it knew the humans didn't really get to choose what animal they bonded with. Dogs were among the best, because they were faithful and loyal; cats seemed more inclined to take advantage of the bond, as if the human was their slave. Snakes...she knew nothing about how snakes reacted to the bond, if only because there were no other snake familiars in Whitehall. Maybe they were just as faithful as any other familiar, they just showed it differently.

Emily sighed and reworked the spell. The snake shrank down into a bracelet, which she picked up and put back on her wrist. It wasn't intelligent enough to know that it was losing time by being transfigured. She felt a moment of guilt—being an inanimate object was bad enough, but she thought it would be worse if she wasn't even aware of time passing—which she ruthlessly pushed aside. The snake was simply too dangerous to treat as a normal pet.

She heard a gasp and spun around. Lady Barb shuddered violently, then started to choke on her own tongue. Emily had thought that was impossible.

She jumped through the wards and lifted the older woman into a sitting position, grimacing at the sweat that now stained Lady Barb's clothes. There were spells to help someone who was having difficulty breathing, yet she didn't dare use any of them. She tried frantically to remember how to give CPR, but apart from a few snide jokes she couldn't recall a thing. It was a skill that should be taught in school. Desperately, she took a breath and then pressed her mouth against Lady Barb's lips, blowing into her chest, time and time again. There was a hiccupping sound, then Lady Barb started to breathe again. Emily almost collapsed in relief.

This must be the peak, she told herself, as she held the older woman tightly. Lady Barb was shaking, magic sparkling around her body. Emily tightened her grip, shivering herself as the temperature started to drop. She couldn't tell if it was a side-effect of the magic or something else, something darker. Could Lady Barb's coldness be seeping into her? Or was she just imagining it?

The older woman let out a strangled cry, then subsided. Emily took her pulse—at least she knew how to do that, thanks to lectures at Whitehall—and realized, to her relief, that it was growing stronger. She didn't let go until Lady Barb sagged, then fell into a more comfortable sleep. Emily lowered her back onto the blanket, then stood up and walked back to the spring to pick up some more water. When she got back, Lady Barb was still, but clearly breathing normally. Emily mopped her forehead, settling down to wait.

Magic can't solve everything, she thought, bitterly. It would have been so much easier if she could just click her fingers and put everything to rights. But she couldn't. Magic had caused the problem in the first place—and, unlike some of the nastier hexes and curses she'd seen, it wasn't something magic could fix. *What if it had been worse?*

She reached for her book and tried to read another two chapters, but her mind refused to concentrate, leaving her with no memory of the words she'd read. Frustrated, she stood up and started to pace the edge of the wards. It was early afternoon and it didn't look like they would be moving anytime soon. She damned herself for her selfishness a moment later. Lady Barb had been on the verge of a very serious illness, perhaps even death, yet she'd been thinking more of her own convenience rather than her mentor.

A rustling sound behind her made her snap around, just in time to see Lady Barb sit upright. "That was unpleasant," she said, tartly. She still sounded weak, but she was definitely getting better. "Water?"

Emily filled a mug from the cauldron, then used a spell to cool the liquid before passing it to Lady Barb.

"Thank you," Lady Barb said, between sips. She finished the water; Emily hastily filled the second mug, then refilled the first. "You're a good nurse."

Emily flushed, wondering just how much Lady Barb remembered.

"We'll stay here for the night," Lady Barb said, looking up at the sky. "We should be able to start walking again tomorrow."

"Good," Emily said, doubtfully. She looked the older woman up and down, noting just how badly her clothes were soaked with sweat. "Will you be all right to walk by then?"

"Probably," Lady Barb said. "Once the peak is over, magic tends to replenish itself fairly quickly. A few more hours of sleep probably won't hurt."

She pulled herself to her feet, then staggered through the wards and over into the bushes to answer nature's call. Emily returned to the cauldron and brewed up another mug of Kava, although she knew she'd have problems sleeping. She didn't have any way to calculate just how much caffeine was in the drink, but a mug or two had kept her awake over long nights when she'd been trying to finish an essay at the last moment. There was probably more caffeine in Kava than the average cup of coffee.

Lady Barb returned, stumbling slightly as she walked. "Thank you for taking care of me," she said, as she sat down on the blanket. "I don't know if I would have made it without you."

Emily gave her a long look. "Did you know that would happen?"

"I knew it was a possibility," Lady Barb said, mildly. "But it had to be done."

"You shouldn't have risked your life," Emily protested. "I...you could have *died.*"

Lady Barb coughed, rudely. "Remind me," she said. "Just who was it who stormed King Randor's castle, *alone*, to save her friend?"

"That's different," Emily said.

"Oh," Lady Barb said. "How so?"

Emily found herself struggling for words. The truth, she suspected, was that she didn't want to lose the older woman. They might have started with a prickly relationship, but they'd become friends—or as close to friends as they could, given their relative positions. And there were times when she thought of Lady Barb as a mother...

"I don't know," she said, finally. She wasn't sure she wanted to confess the truth. "I just...I don't want to lose you."

Lady Barb reached out and touched her hand. "I am a Mediator of the Allied Lands," she said, softly. "Putting my life in danger is part of the job. In this case, we have a rogue magician—perhaps a necromancer—running around, doing something that is almost certainly dangerous. It is my duty to take whatever risks are necessary to stop him before it gets too far out of hand."

Emily scowled. As soon as a necromancer went to work, she suspected, it was already out of hand.

"And in this case, I needed to snap Lord Gorham back to normal as soon as possible," Lady Barb added. "Whatever the necromancer wanted, Emily, those runes were a big part of it."

"But what did he want?" Emily asked, mournfully. "It makes no sense!"

"That generally means that we're missing part of the puzzle," Lady Barb reassured her. "But the sooner we get on to Easter, the better. I have a feeling we'll find our answers there."

She looked over at the preserved rabbit. Emily took the hint, canceled the spells and then passed the warm meat to Lady Barb.

"We will take a slight detour to a village on the route," Lady Barb said, as she ate. "I'd prefer not to have to forage for food any more than strictly necessary."

Emily nodded, remembering foraging expeditions with Sergeant Miles. He'd assigned push-ups for every poisonous mushroom they'd picked by accident, then lectured them on the dangers of eating the wrong thing. She'd privately resolved never to forage for food again if she had any alternative. Even something that was technically safe to eat could make her very unwell.

"I saw a dragon last night," she said, changing the subject. "Is that a good sign?"

"It's a good sign as long as it didn't try to eat you," Lady Barb said. "The mountainfolk tend to leave dragons and their eggs alone, but there's no shortage of idiots who come up to the mountains in hopes of catching and bleeding a young dragon. Or trying to take an egg before it's hatched."

Emily scowled. Dragon's Blood was one of the most terrifyingly magical substances in the world—and pricy too, even for a baroness. And dragons didn't like being hunted, though it often took them some time to notice. She'd read stories of villages being attacked years after the hunters had been and gone. But then, everyone agreed that dragons were truly alien. As far as she knew, only she and Void had talked to a dragon in recent years.

She asked Lady Barb about the dishcloth-creatures, but Lady Barb couldn't identify them from her description and suggested she wrote down the details for Mistress Kirdáne. Emily found her notebook and wrote down everything she remembered, then replaced the security spells and returned it to her bag. It was temping to think that the creatures would be named after her...assuming, of course, they hadn't already been discovered. There were more things in the woods than held in Whitehall's zoo.

"Make sure you get some sleep," Lady Barb ordered, as she lay back down on her blanket. "We'll have to walk fast tomorrow—and find a place for some practice. And a swim."

"If you're up to it," Emily said, firmly. "We can stay here for another day or two if necessary."

"I'd prefer to avoid it," Lady Barb said. "And I think you'd get bored."

Emily blushed, embarrassed. Was she really that easy to read?

Chapter Twenty-Eight

DESPITE EMILY'S CONCERNS, THEY LEFT THE CAMPSITE THE FOLLOWING MORNING, WALKING up a long rocky pathway that eventually led them to a gorgeous, spring-fed lake nestled within a rich, green valley. There was no sign of any other humans, apart from an abandoned hut that seemed to have been deserted for years. She couldn't help wondering if there was a danger here they couldn't see, like the Night Walker. But nothing suggested itself as she perched on a rock and watched as Lady Barb undressed and plunged into the cold water.

"Come on in," she called, as her head broke the surface. "The water's fine."

Emily shook her head. Even if the water hadn't been freezing cold–she'd dipped her fingers into the lake, once she'd checked for unpleasant surprises–she wouldn't have felt comfortable undressing and skinny-dipping. Some of the boys did it on camping trips with the sergeants, but Emily had never felt the urge to join them. Some of their invitations had been downright rude and unwelcome.

She took some water and boiled it as Lady Barb swam effortlessly from one side of the lake to the other. It was impossible to tell that she'd been ill, not considering the speed she was moving; Emily couldn't help feeling a little admiration. She'd learned how to swim at Whitehall, between Alassa and Sergeant Miles, but she wasn't a very strong swimmer. Lady Barb, on the other hand, tore her way through the water like a rocket.

By the time she emerged from the water–Emily couldn't help thinking of the very first James Bond movie–there was boiling water ready to make Kava.

Emily looked away as Lady Barb dried and dressed, then washed half of her clothing in the lake. It wasn't ideal, Emily suspected, but they couldn't do anything else until they reached the next town, where they could hire someone to wash their clothes. The last time she'd washed something herself, it had shrunk so badly she'd had to use magic to fix it.

"You can take a dip now, if you like," Lady Barb urged. She tied her hair back in a bun, then took the mug Emily offered her. "The water isn't *that* bad."

Emily shook her head, firmly.

Lady Barb smiled, then drank her Kava. "I understand," she said. "What did you do while I was...unwell?"

"Pocket dimensions," Emily said. She outlined her practice, confessing that the dimension never lasted very long without the square. "I just can't get it to work right."

"You need practice," Lady Barb said, shortly. "But I was thinking we would practice something else today."

Emily looked up, interested. She loved learning new types of magic and mental disciplines, even though the more she learned, the more she had to work to keep them all straight in her mind. She'd been told that the different schools of magic were linked together, but she'd also been warned not to think about it until Fifth Year.

"You know how to evade someone, of course," Lady Barb said. "I want you to evade me."

Emily hesitated. Lady Barb had almost choked to death the previous night. Even if she didn't remember, *Emily* did. Asking might get her head bitten off—or worse—but she couldn't just follow orders, not now.

"Are you really well enough to chase me?"

"Yes," Lady Barb said. Her eyes were flinty hard, but her tone was even. "You don't always get to be at your best when you have to fight. Now...do as I tell you."

Emily swallowed. She'd never been *that* good at evading her fellow students, particularly the ones who had grown up in the countryside. Sergeant Miles was an absolute devil at tracking down his students, to the point where some whispered he'd cheated. And then he'd proved he'd used no magic at all.

"All right," she said, after a moment. "How long should I try and stay ahead of you?"

"At least thirty minutes," Lady Barb said, after a moment's thought. "Same rules as Martial Magic. If I catch you before time runs out, you will do a push-up for each minute left."

"Incentive," Emily said, mimicking Sergeant Miles. He'd done the same, only less mercifully. On the other hand, it was great for building up upper body strength. "Is that the only thing we will be practicing?"

"No," Lady Barb said. She glanced up at the sun, then smiled at Emily. "But the next thing can wait until I catch you."

She put out the fire, then packed up the bags and swung them both over her shoulder. Emily smiled, although she knew that the older woman wasn't really hampering herself too much. It wouldn't give Emily much of an advantage. She stood, then turned and ran down the path into the woods. Once hidden by the trees, she slowed and moved off the path, watching where she put her feet. There were fewer rocks under the trees, forcing her to walk carefully, but at least she wouldn't be leaving footprints behind her. Bracing herself, she kept moving, wondering how long she had to hide. Outrunning Lady Barb probably wasn't an option.

Finding a large tree, she scrambled up it into the branches, marvelling at just how many skills she'd picked up over the previous two years. She'd certainly never climbed a tree before in her life. But there was no time to reflect. She heard the sound of someone crashing through the forest and held herself as still as possible. It wasn't good enough.

"Five minutes to track you down," Lady Barb called from below. "That was pathetic."

Emily held herself very still. It was just possible that Lady Barb was bluffing...

The tree shook violently and she yelped, then scrambled off the branch as quickly as possible. Lady Barb smirked as Emily dropped down to the ground.

Emily scowled at the older woman. She couldn't have caught her so fast unless...a quick check revealed that Lady Barb had sneaked a tracking hex onto her clothes, before she ran into the forest. If she'd thought to look, she could have removed it before hiding.

"Cheat," she said, with some feeling.

"If you're not cheating, you're not trying," Lady Barb said. Her smirk grew wider. "I believe that's twenty-five push-ups."

Emily groaned, but dropped to the ground and started to count them off, one by one. At least she was better at it now, thankfully. The first time Sergeant Harkin had made her do them, she'd had aching arms for hours afterwards, until Jade had helped her find a potion that made her feel better. Lady Barb watched until she had finished, then helped Emily to her feet.

"You should have looked for the hex," Lady Barb said. Emily glowered at her. "Ready to try again?"

"Yes," Emily said. She paused, wondering if she dared push her luck. "Will you do push-ups if you don't catch me?"

"Depends," Lady Barb said. She turned around, looking back towards the lake. "We'll see how well you do."

Emily turned and fled into the trees, changing her path as soon as she removed the tracking hex. After a moment, she stuck another one on a tree, half-hoping that it would distract the older woman long enough for Emily to put some distance between them. She didn't know how long Lady Barb would wait before she started to come after her, after all. This time, she crouched low behind a tree and hid herself behind a glamor. Without magic, Lady Barb would have to look very carefully for her if she wanted to succeed.

She jumped as a hand fell on her shoulder. "You did too well," Lady Barb said, mischievously. "Your glamor was too good. It just looked *unreal* when I saw it."

Emily glanced at her watch. Lady Barb had taken twenty-two minutes to find her. Sighing, she dropped to the ground and counted out eight more push-ups, then stood up.

Lady Barb shrugged, waggling her fingers at Emily. Taken by surprise, Emily froze. It took her several minutes to break the spell and escape.

"Work faster, next time," Lady Barb said, as she turned to lead Emily back to the path. "You could be easily killed while you are helpless."

"I know," Emily confessed. She needed to move her hands to work magic, mostly. It was harder, somehow, to cast spells without moving. She'd worked hard, with Mistress Sun and Sergeant Miles, to master the art, but she was still only a beginner. "But it doesn't always work properly."

Lady Barb made a rude sound as they reached the path and started onwards. "Just you wait until you find a proper apprenticeship," she said, darkly. "Your mistress or master won't be so kind."

Emily remembered some of Jade's stories and nodded in agreement. Master Grey, whatever his faults, pushed his apprentice really hard. Jade could cope, Emily suspected, but he hadn't had the benefit of a second year of Martial Magic. Master Grey was pushing him right to the limits, as well as teaching him to be a duelist. The thought reminded her of something she wanted to ask.

"Why didn't you take part in the dueling contest?"

Lady Barb seemed surprised by the question. "I did, when I was younger," she said. "And then I lost my ranking and decided I could bow out gracefully. I preferred to fight, rather than duel."

She smiled. "It wasn't something I really wanted to keep," she added. "Dueling isn't something that should be done casually."

"I see," Emily said.

"Master Grey holds the topmost ranking at present," Lady Barb said. "This *is* who you were talking about, isn't it?"

Emily nodded.

"Clasp your hands behind your back," Lady Barb ordered. Emily opened her mouth to ask why, but Lady Barb went on before she could say a word. "To answer the question most girls ask, he can't decline challenges without forfeiting his ranking. So he insists that all challenges be to the death, just to keep them down."

"Men," Emily said.

"Indeed," Lady Barb agreed. She smiled, rather dryly. "Unclasp your hands."

Emily tried...and discovered that her hands were stuck, bound by a spell. "You have twenty minutes to break the spell," Lady Barb said as she walked away. "And don't even *think* about standing still."

"Cruel," Emily muttered, as she followed her mentor. She struggled, but her hands refused to unlock. "Why...?"

"Because you need the practice," Lady Barb said, in a surprisingly reasonable tone. "And believe me, you have to learn how to defeat these spells before it's too late."

There was something in her tone that bothered Emily, a suggestion she might need to learn fast—or faster. She cast the canceling charm, but wasn't too surprised to discover that the charm failed. Lady Barb wouldn't have trapped her hands with something simple and easy to break. Gritting her teeth, she tried a more complex charm, then another. Neither one worked.

She trailed along behind Lady Barb, struggling with the hex. It was odd; the touch was so light that she couldn't sense the magic, merely the effects. She should have been able to sense something, certainly after two years of advanced study with Mistress Sun and Sergeant Miles. But there was nothing...

It clicked and she glared at the older woman's back. There *was* nothing, at least nothing on her hands. The spell had affected her mind, forcing her to keep her hands locked no matter what she tried. Once she knew what it was, it was easy to counter. Emily freed her hands, rubbing them frantically. She'd gripped them so tightly that her skin, already pale, had gone white.

"You took far too long to realize how the trick was done," Lady Barb told her, without turning around. "That may be a problem, later."

Emily nodded, sullenly. There were spells she disliked intensely and almost all of them related to ways of rendering someone helpless—and open to outside commands or influence. Quite a few of the traps in Blackhall manipulated the target's mind, either inserting commands or merely messing around with their perceptions. Emily's standard tactic was to avoid them where possible. They were just too tricky to overpower.

Lady Barb kept tossing tests at her as they walked, each one slightly more complex and twisted than the last. Emily fought down her outrage and concentrated, but most of the tests required careful thought to defeat, though they were designed to make thinking difficult. It was worse than trying to study while someone was playing music, she decided, remembering days at school when she'd studied there, rather than go home and risk meeting her stepfather. Her mind was all she had and it could be twisted so easily...

"Set up the wards," Lady Barb ordered. "And make sure you get plenty of sleep."

Emily eyed her suspiciously. "Are you...are you going to do anything tonight?"

"Sleep," Lady Barb said, innocently. "Or should I be setting you punishment exercises?"

"No," Emily said, quickly. "But..."

Lady Barb's expression softened. "It wasn't very easy for me either," she admitted. "But you have far better cause than I to learn how to resist mental attacks."

Emily shivered, remembering Lin–and how the bodies had almost been wiped from her mind.

Lady Barb went back into the forest and returned, carrying a pair of rabbits and a handful of vegetables. Emily watched in some amusement as she dropped water into the cauldron, then boiled the meat and half of the vegetables until she'd made a tasty stew. The sergeants had done the same, she recalled, only with larger animals. But then, they'd had more mouths to feed.

"Your training has been enhanced, but you have a long way to go," Lady Barb said. "Still..."

Her voice trailed off. Emily looked at her, sharply. The older woman almost seemed to be *hinting* at something. But what? She braced herself and asked.

"I can't tell you, not now," Lady Barb said. "But it is *important* that you concentrate on all of your defenses, not just the physical ones. You will need them."

Emily ate her stew, then fell asleep almost at once. Nothing troubled the wards–or at least nothing woke her in the middle of the night. When she awoke, it was morning and Lady Barb was already awake. Emily felt a tight knot undoing itself in her stomach, one she hadn't realized was there. Lady Barb was back to normal.

"I didn't see anything last night," Lady Barb said. "We might have slept in the wrong place."

Emily shrugged as she washed her face, then drank the Kava. For once, Lady Barb had prepared breakfast, such as it was. The reheated stew tasted a little gamy, but she gulped it down anyway. Lady Barb packed up, passing Emily her bag. Emily sighed and took it.

"We're going to pause overnight in a town on the edge of Easter," Lady Barb informed her, once she'd pulled the bag over her shoulders. "We should have some time to get information out of the locals before we go visit Lady Easter."

Emily nodded. The Sergeants had taught her the value of intelligence, although they'd also added that most people didn't know anything outside their own limited experiences. It was rare to find a lower-class tourist in the Allied Lands, apart from magicians and traders. Even the upper classes didn't travel very far from their homelands. Of course, that might change once the steam railways were finally in place.

Lady Barb kept testing her as they made their way along the path, heading down towards the nearest town. Emily sighed and concentrated on breaking the spells, one after another. Several of them caught her so firmly she couldn't escape, forcing Lady Barb to free her, before teaching her how to escape and then casting the spell again. The second time that happened, Emily discovered that even the smallest change in the spell made it harder for her to escape. Her head was pounding uncomfortably when Lady Barb finally called a halt.

"You will need to keep practicing," Lady Barb warned. "But the true danger lies in subtle magic. We may need to carve a rune into your flesh."

Emily glowered at her, rubbing her forehead. Carving runes into one's flesh could be dangerous, even if it worked perfectly. There was no way someone else could do it and expect it to work; she'd have to carve the rune herself, without benefit of anaesthetic. And she wasn't even sure *why*.

"Unfortunately, it probably wouldn't be missed," Lady Barb added.

"Missed," Emily repeated. "Missed by whom?"

Lady Barb said nothing. Emily was about to ask again, demanding answers, when the pathway suddenly widened and revealed a tiny village hidden within the trees. It looked alarmingly like the first village, save that it was organized differently and large carved stones had been placed in front of each of the shacks. A handful of people were moving from house to house, but something was missing. It took her a moment to realize that there were no children in sight.

Someone sounded an alarm and the women scurried into the nearest house, while the men produced a handful of makeshift weapons. Emily tensed, preparing a spell, as two men started towards them, their expressions frozen somewhere between grim determination and fear. But then, she wouldn't have cared to face a sorceress either, not if she didn't have any magic of her own.

"Greetings," Lady Barb said, with studied casualness. "May we enter the village for the night?"

The two men exchanged glances. "Are you magicians?"

"Yes," Lady Barb said, flatly.

Emily blinked in surprise. They were two women, travelling alone. What else could they be? And why had they been greeted with weapons?

"The headman told us that a magician would be coming," the guard said. "He needs your help."

"Then we will assist him," Lady Barb said, regally. "Take us to your leader."

"Prove it," the second guard said. "We need..."

Lady Barb snapped her fingers. A frog looked up at her from where the second guard had been, quivering slightly.

"It'll wear off," she said, then looked at the first guard. "Convinced?"

The guard gulped. "Yes, Lady Sorceress," he said. "If you will please come with me?"

Lady Barb followed him, holding her head up high. Emily followed her, glancing around with some interest. The village looked deserted, but she could tell that they were being watched.

"Stay alert," Lady Barb muttered to her. "Something bad happened here."

Emily nodded. She couldn't disagree.

Chapter Twenty-Nine

EMILY COULDN'T HELP THINKING OF ONE OF THE HERBALISTS AT WHITEHALL WHEN SHE first set eyes on the headman. He was tall and almost painfully thin, with a long white beard that drifted to his knees. Beside him, there were four other bearded men, each staring at the two magicians with expressions that ranged from relief to outrage. Somehow, Emily doubted that they'd called the magicians for anything minor.

Lady Barb nodded at them politely, then lifted an eyebrow.

"We have a problem," the headman said. His companions nodded in agreement. "We need you to interrogate a prisoner."

Rudolf, Emily thought, in sudden horror. *Did they capture Rudolf?*

But they hadn't. The whole story came tumbling out, slowly. Clearly, *this* headman did not have unlimited power. His companions inserted their own comments, argued and bickered with each other, pushing forward their own views as the headman spoke. Emily found it hard to follow the explanation, even though the headman generally waited for his companions to finish and then went on. By the time she had a fairly complete idea of what was going on, the sun was setting.

"Let me see if I've got this straight," Lady Barb said. "Two children vanished from your village."

The headman and his companions nodded in agreement.

"The only stranger who came to the village was a postal worker," Lady Barb continued, calmly. "Your people decided that he was responsible for their disappearance and threatened to lynch him. You managed to lock him up instead."

Emily winced as she realized the dilemma facing the headman. If the postal worker was killed without proof of guilt, there *would* be eventual retaliation from the outside. Even if all they did was cut the village out of the postal route, it would have dangerous effects. The village didn't import much, but it wouldn't be allowed to import *anything* if strangers weren't allowed to come and go safely.

But if the mob *wasn't* allowed to kill the person it blamed for the disappearances—the deaths, if the kidnapped children were the dead she'd seen after meeting Rudolf—it might easily turn on the headman. There was a degree of consensus in this village that was missing from Hodge's village, an understanding that there were limits to the headman's authority. He was caught between two fires, either one of which might kill him.

Fortunately for him, he'd been lucky enough to have a pair of traveling magicians walk into his village.

"That is correct," the headman said. "If he is guilty, particularly if you verify it, we can kill him. But if he isn't—"

"I understand," Lady Barb said, cutting him off. "We will hold a morning trial, I think. But I will have to see the suspect first."

"Of course," the headman said. He sounded relieved. "And I would be honored if you would join me as my guests for the night."

Lady Barb nodded. "We would be honored," she said. Emily knew her well enough to detect a faint hint of irritation in her tone. "Please take us to the prisoner."

Emily was mildly surprised that the tiny village had a prison in the first place. Peasant customs of law and order were usually very limited. There was simply very little to steal and, for all the hardness of their lives, very few thieves. Those that *did* appear were normally beaten, sometimes to death, or were thrown out of the village. But then, there were very few things the peasants considered crimes. Beating one's wife—or husband, for that matter—was certainly nothing unusual.

Once they rounded the houses, she saw the prison—nothing more than a wooden cage. Inside, a young man sat in the stocks, his hands and feet firmly trapped. Emily shuddered when she saw the extent of his bruises, as if the villagers had beaten him on the way to the cage. There were no guards about, so the villagers could come by to hurl stones any time they liked. She was surprised that he was still alive, under the circumstances.

"Leave us," Lady Barb ordered.

The headman bowed and retreated. Emily watched as Lady Barb healed a handful of injuries, then spoke briefly to the prisoner. She couldn't hear the mumbled responses. After a few days of such treatment—and probably no food or drink—the prisoner might be on the verge of death. Emily had never been in the stocks herself, but it looked thoroughly uncomfortable. And escape would be impossible without magic.

"He's delusional," Lady Barb said, as she stepped backwards. "He was confessing to stealing money from the temple and defacing the statue of the god."

Emily lifted an eyebrow, surprised.

"It's not uncommon when one is being tortured to death," Lady Barb said. "They tend to confess to just about anything, in hopes of getting a quick end. But he didn't confess to kidnapping anyone."

"Which saved his life," Emily guessed. It was unlikely that anyone in the village would care about stealing money from a temple. They certainly didn't have a temple in their village. "If he'd confessed to the right crime..."

She shook her head, then pressed on. "*Is* he guilty?"

"I don't know," Lady Barb said. She frowned at the prisoner before giving Emily a long, hard look. "I need to have a few words with the headman. You stay here and keep an eye on him. If someone tries to hurt him"—she nodded towards a handful of stones on the ground near the stocks—"stop them. But *don't* talk to him."

Emily nodded. Lady Barb turned and strode back towards the headman's hut, moving with a confidence Emily wished she could master. She found herself praying that Lady Barb hadn't weakened herself again, then pushed the thought aside. Instead, she shook her head as she looked at the prisoner.

Even with some of his wounds healed, the prisoner still looked to be on the verge of death. Failing to treat non-fatal injuries could easily make them lethal if the wounds were allowed to fester. She looked closely, wondering which of the cuts and bruises were already infected. Chances were, the prisoner would need weeks of recovery, even with magic repairing the damage.

She was still mulling it over when Lady Barb returned, two younger men in tow. Their eyes passed over Emily without ever quite seeming to register her presence, something that puzzled her until she realized that they were afraid. The guard Lady Barb had turned into a frog was probably back to normal by now, filling their ears with tales of the all-powerful magicians. His fellows wouldn't want to show any interest in *Emily*...

"Clean him up, bind his wounds and then stand guard," Lady Barb ordered, addressing the two men. Neither of them looked very pleased at the orders, but they hastened to obey. "I do not want him *touched* in any way until we hold the trial. Do you understand me?"

"Yes, Lady Sorceress," the guards stammered in unison.

Emily followed Lady Barb back to the headman's hut, wondering if they were doing the right thing. What if the prisoner *was* guilty? It seemed unlikely–the bodies she'd seen had been used in a necromantic rite and a necromancer could have burnt down the entire village without raising a sweat–but he might be working for the necromancer. If that was the case...she remembered Alassa executing her treacherous aunt and shuddered. The headman would have to execute the prisoner at once. Nothing else would suffice.

"I trust you remember how to cast a truth spell," Lady Barb said. "You'll be casting it tomorrow."

"Only the first three levels," Emily said. The first one was light, easy to brush off if the victim knew what was happening. "What if he's strong enough to resist?"

"I use a heavier spell," Lady Barb said. "But I don't think he has any incentive to resist."

Emily swallowed, remembering an old problem from Earth. If someone didn't have anything to hide, the reasoning ran, why would they object to having their bags searched and their computers monitored? But the reasoning didn't take into account a person's natural outrage at not being trusted, let alone an equally natural desire for privacy. The prisoner might resist, even without meaning to, a spell intended to force him to tell the truth. And if that happened, the mob would conclude that he had something to hide.

"What...?" She swallowed and started again. "What if he is guilty?"

"Then we deal with him," Lady Barb said. "But I don't think he is." She shrugged. "But you may have to cast the spell on someone else, just to prove it works, or perhaps over a general area. In that case, we will work out the questions in advance. The spell won't last very long, no matter how much magic you pump into it."

Emily nodded. One area-effect spell made everyone within its sphere of influence tell the truth–and nothing but the truth. It didn't compel them to answer, it just prevented them from lying outright. But she'd had enough lessons with Master Tor to know that a poor choice of questions could present misleading responses. They would have to do a great deal of research in a very short space of time, just to make sure that there was no room for evasion.

The headman's wife welcomed them as they stepped back into the house, offering them the master bedroom, such as it was. Emily was embarrassed to even *think* of kicking the older couple out of bed and Lady Barb clearly agreed, because after some haggling she managed to talk the woman into letting them sleep on blankets in front of the fire instead. There was no real privacy—she reminded herself to set up wards to ensure some privacy, once they were lying down—but there was no alternative. It would have been rude to ask to sleep outside the house.

"Tell me what happened," Lady Barb ordered, as dinner was served. "Who did you lose and why?"

"A boy and a girl," the headman said. He seemed to be attaching more importance to the girl than the boy, which was unusual. "One was the oldest son of his parents, the other was the middle daughter of my son."

Emily kept her face expressionless. *That* explained it.

Lady Barb's lips pressed into a thin line. "How old are they?"

"Both are eleven," the headman said.

Emily shivered. Old enough to have magic within their blood, young enough not to be able to access and use it deliberately. A necromancer would consider them prime targets—if, of course, they *did* have magic. There was no way a peasant village could test for it. Or would if they could.

"Might they have run off on their own?" Lady Barb asked. "They were certainly old enough to fancy themselves in love."

Emily gave her a sharp look. *Now* who was forgetting the bodies? But then, they didn't have any proof that the bodies and the missing children were one and the same. Lord Gorham's castle was two days walk from the village. While it wouldn't be a problem for a magician to do something like that, why go to all the effort of transporting the children when there were plenty of prospective victims closer to the castle? Unless the necromancer had feared that missing children would break the power of the runes...

Lord Gorham didn't need us to break free, she thought. *All he needed was a good reason to start questioning why he acted in a way he shouldn't--*

She contemplated it, piece by piece. The serving girls had been quite open about working for Lord Gorham. He'd been a good master, certainly by local standards. They earned money, they saved enough to ensure they had some independence even after marriage...and they weren't beaten, harassed or molested. Compared to Emily's predecessor in Cockatrice, he was a paragon of humanity. And his son, too, had kept his hands to himself. Given how vulnerable the girls were—they literally could not say no—it was odd...and it spoke well of the two aristocrats.

Emily shook her head, annoyed. She was going native. Since when had merely *not* molesting the girls become the mark of a good man?

She returned to the original train of thought. Lord Gorham *cared*—and if children had gone missing from his lands, he might well have investigated. And that, in turn, might have ripped apart the haze of magic created by the runes. If he realized that the dead bodies were slipping in and out of his mind, he might have broken free...

The headman snorted, breaking into her train of thought. "I do not believe that either of them had developed to the point where they noticed the other sex," he said, rudely. "And the girl was not mature."

Emily hastily replayed the conversation in her mind. It had taken her some time to realize that, while a girl was considered marriageable once she started her periods, most girls outside the aristocracy started their periods much later than girls on Earth. They simply didn't eat enough to allow their bodies to develop earlier. Visions of child brides had faded, slightly, when she'd realized that periods might start at sixteen or even later. But that didn't stop children from being betrothed and told they had to marry once they were mature.

"In any case," the headman's wife offered, "they knew better than to run off."

Emily had to smile at her. She clearly wasn't interested in being her husband's subordinate, let alone his punching bag. The woman had enough muscles to pass for a sumo wrestler and a hard, but surprisingly pleasant face. If her husband—who looked tiny compared to his wife—tried something, Emily suspected it would be the last thing he ever did.

She turned her attention back to the food as Lady Barb kept asking questions. The stew tasted vaguely spicy, with potatoes, cabbage and a handful of tiny pieces of meat. But meat was rare—or at least expensive—for peasants in such a small village. They couldn't slaughter all their animals or they would have no way to replace them. Even sheep and goats native to the mountains weren't numerous. But alcohol wasn't; she made sure to protect herself against drunkenness before taking a swig of the beer. It tasted foul.

They're either showing off their wealth or blowing a month's wages to feed us, she thought, with a pang of guilt. *Can they afford to keep us here for long, even if we pay? Where would they spend the money?*

"I was surprised you didn't send the prisoner to the castle," Lady Barb said. "Would that not have solved your problem?"

The headman shook his head, his expression oddly torn between irritation and surprise. "We wished to handle it ourselves," he said. "Our Lady is much too busy to be bothered with small matters."

Emily puzzled over that until she worked it out. Lady Easter might or might not be under the same influence as Lord Gorham, but she would be more concerned about the politics of the situation than the dead children. Releasing the postal worker, even if he was guilty as sin, would repair links between her tiny kingdom and the rest of the Allied Lands. The peasants knew that handing their prisoner over to the aristocracy was effectively the same as letting him go.

At Lady Barb's muttered suggestion, Emily helped the headman's wife wash the dishes, which also allowed her a chance to inspect the kitchen. The headman's wife seemed astonished, but allowed her to help without argument. Emily had to admit she was privately impressed, although it was simplistic compared to Whitehall's giant kitchens. It was certainly more efficient than the kitchens in the guesthouses. Once she had finished washing and drying the dishes, she went back into the main room. Lady Barb was alone.

"Think about what questions we should ask, tomorrow," Lady Barb ordered. "We will need to ask multiple versions of the same questions."

Emily nodded. The prisoner might not know the names of the children, even if he *had* taken them from the village. Asking him if he'd taken the children by name might produce a negative response. They would have to ask vague questions, then narrow it down—and hope that the villagers were prepared to be patient. What would happen, she asked herself, if the mob tried to lynch the prisoner anyway?

She watched as Lady Barb sorted out the blankets, then lay in front of the fire and stared at the wooden ceiling. Emily hesitated, then came over to join her, casting a handful of wards as she sat down. Lady Barb gave her an odd look before nodding in understanding.

"This could get problematic," Lady Barb said, once the privacy ward was in place. "If the prisoner really is working for a necromancer..."

Emily shuddered. Shadye had been defeated through luck. The next necromancer she encountered might be outside Whitehall, away from the nexus. And if they were dealing with a necromancer now...but if they were, it was a very odd necromancer.

"The more I think about all of this, the less I like it," Lady Barb admitted. "Any necromancer should be completely insane by now, which would make him very noticeable."

"Unless he was disciplined enough to keep himself under control," Emily said. But she remembered the runes and knew that wouldn't be enough, not indefinitely. The necromancer's perceptions of the world around him would be warped, along with his mind. "How long can a necromancer seem reasonably sane before he cracks completely?"

"There's no hard and fast rule," Lady Barb admitted. "Merely...the reports of experiments carried out by people with more magic than common sense. If there was only ever one victim, the necromancer might seem reasonably sane for *years*. But the power is addictive and the necromancer would need new victims, sooner or later."

Emily nodded.

"Get some sleep," Lady Barb added. "Tomorrow is going to be very bad."

Chapter Thirty

IT FELT LIKE SHE'D BARELY CLOSED HER EYES BEFORE SHE FELT SOMEONE JAB HER RIBS. SHE snapped awake. Outside, a faint light glimmered through the cracks in the walls—no windows in such a poor house - suggesting that the sun was on the verge of rising above the mountains. Emily looked to see Lady Barb sitting next to her, her face twisted into an odd grimace. Outside the wards, the headman's wife was already laying out bowls of oatmeal on the table.

"Time to get up," Lady Barb said, mildly. "There's no shortage of work."

Emily sat up, running her hands down her shirt and trousers. They felt grimy, but she hadn't wanted to undress, even behind the privacy ward. Lady Barb stood and walked through the wards, then sat down at the table and started to eat. There was an assumption of superiority about her action that bothered Emily more than she cared to think about, an assumption that was little different from King Randor's. Sighing, Emily climbed to her feet and joined her. The oatmeal tasted almost flavorless.

"Everyone will be at work in the early hours," Lady Barb said, as the headman and his wife walked out the door, leaving the two magicians alone. "We won't hold the trial until at least ten bells."

Emily glanced at her watch, then nodded. They had three hours, more or less, to prepare.

"Get into your golden robes," Lady Barb added. "We need to make an impression."

"I could use a glamor," Emily suggested. The robes had been buried at the bottom of her bag ever since they'd left Lady Barb's house. "They'd never know..."

"Put on your robes," Lady Barb ordered, tartly. "The less deceit we use, the better."

Emily kept her opinion of that to herself as she washed her face, then found her robes and pulled them over her head. As always, they were scratchy and uncomfortable—and felt very much out of place. Lady Barb's own robes looked spectacular—the black robe of a combat sorceress set off her blonde hair nicely—and Emily felt a moment of envy, before pushing it aside. She worked her hair into a long ponytail, considering the idea—again—of cutting it short. But somehow she found herself unable to do it.

"I thought they would have children," she said, as she looked around the hut. Most peasant families lived together, multiple generations sharing the same house. "Or have they kicked them out for us?"

"The headman doesn't get many benefits from his position," Lady Barb said. "Having a house that he shares with his wife and no one else is about the best of them."

Emily nodded, remembering how cramped Imaiqah's house in Alexis had been. The children were constantly supervised by older members of the family, which didn't allow them to get into much mischief...while the married sons would be expected to bring their wives to join the extended family. There would be absolutely no privacy for the newcomer—or anyone else, for that matter.

The thought made her sick. She couldn't have endured such an existence for very long.

"I'm glad I don't live here," she said, finally.

"Most people would be," Lady Barb agreed, dryly. "But just remember that your loyal subjects are largely living in similar conditions."

Emily nodded.

Now they had prepared the questions, there was almost nothing to do until the trial, so Emily read her way through another book, then talked Lady Barb into a lecture on advanced uses for healing. Lady Barb might be short-tempered teacher, but she did know what she was talking about, something that put her ahead of many of Emily's teachers on Earth. She listened with rapt fascination and was almost disappointed when the headman finally stuck his head into the house and told them that the trial was ready to begin.

Emily followed Lady Barb out of the house...and then had to fight down the urge to run as the villagers turned to stare. The golden robes shone brightly in the sunlight, drawing their attention like a moth to a flame. Emily gritted her teeth and kept walking, keeping her eyes firmly fixed on Lady Barb's back. She hadn't realized how many people there were in the village. It looked as though there were over a hundred men, women and children.

The stage had been set up in the center of the village, with the prisoner—still in the stocks—perched at one edge of the stage. Emily forced herself to follow Lady Barb up onto the stage, wishing she'd taken up the suggestion that she join the dramatics club in Whitehall. It might have made it easier. Even Master Tor's lessons in public speaking hadn't made much headway.

"We are gathered here to investigate the accusations made against this prisoner," Lady Barb said. Her voice was quiet, but she must have used a spell because no one seemed to have any trouble in hearing her. "My apprentice will perform a truth spell, after which we will interrogate the prisoner. Once we have answers, we will know how to treat him."

A dull rumble passed through the crowd. Most of them must have believed the prisoner was guilty, and hadn't really thought about what might happen if he were proven innocent. It might cost the village dear if they lost all contact with the outside world. Perhaps the whole affair would be smoothed over, once some compensation was paid. But what did the villagers have that could compensate for attempted murder?

Lady Barb looked up at Emily. "Do it," she ordered.

Emily swallowed nervously and worked the spell. It took her two tries to get it right. The sheer weight of so many people staring at her was distracting—and terrifying. Magic crackled around her fingertips as she stepped backwards, spell in place. Lady Barb checked her work, nodded and then cast a spell to amplify the man's voice. Everyone would hear what he had to say, good or bad.

"Tell us," Lady Barb said. "What is your name?"

For a long moment, the prisoner didn't answer. Emily wondered, helplessly, if he'd managed to shrug off the spell...or if he was so badly wounded that he wasn't aware of what was actually going on or he couldn't talk. Lady Barb touched his forehead, then pulled a bottle of potion out of her robes and pressed it to his lips. The crowd muttered angrily as the prisoner drank the potion, then started to splutter as it worked its magic.

"Healing potion," Lady Barb said. She looked back at the prisoner. "What is your name?"

"Reginald," the man croaked. His eyes were sudden alive with life–and terror. He'd been almost completely out of it until he'd drunk the potion. "My name is Reginald."

"Good," Lady Barb said. "Why did you come to this village?"

"I had to deliver a letter to one of the peasants here," Reginald said, between coughs. "He was meant to reply, so I waited for his reply."

Lady Barb and Emily shared a glance. Who in the village would be receiving letters from *anyone?* The postal system serviced aristocrats and magicians, not commoners. But it wasn't a question they could ask, not legally. They could only ask about Reginald's involvement with the missing children.

"Two children are missing from this village," Lady Barb said. "Did you take them?"

"No," Reginald said.

"He's lying," a female voice shouted. "He took my son!"

Lady Barb glared her into silence, then returned to Reginald. "Did you take any children from this village?"

"No," Reginald said.

"Good," Lady Barb said. "What did you do in the village while waiting for your reply?"

"I courted a girl," Reginald said. For the first time, he seemed shocked at his own words. "I spent time with her."

Emily had to bit her lip to keep from giggling. On Earth, it would be funny; here, the consequences could be disastrous. The peasants might overlook a little affair like premarital sex if the non-virgin was a boy, but it was different for girls. *They* didn't have access to spells that could determine parentage, not like the aristocracy, nor did they have any form of workable contraception. It was quite possible that Reginald had impregnated his lover.

She'd need three or four months before they were sure she wasn't pregnant, Emily thought, and shivered. *Poor girl.*

Lady Barb bounced other questions off him, one by one. No, Reginald had no sexual interest in children. No, Reginald had no interest in young boys or young girls. Sometimes, she rephrased the question in the hopes of closing any loopholes. A handful of catcalls from the crowd suggested that the listeners weren't too happy with the result. Emily braced herself, silently preparing to cast protective spells. The village had good reason to be worried about the results, now.

"The spells have proven that Reginald was not responsible for the abduction of the children," Lady Barb said. She looked over at the grieving parents. "I believe that others should be interrogated now."

The crowd broke down into small clumps, arguing frantically. Some villagers wanted the parents to be interrogated, some thought that was too much and just wanted to bury the whole thing.

Emily felt sick at heart. If she was wrong and the bodies they'd discovered earlier had nothing to do with the missing children, where had the children gone? Their parents might easily have murdered them and then framed Reginald. Or maybe they'd just vanished in the forest.

Lady Barb released Reginald from the stocks, motioning for Emily to heal the rest of the damage the peasants had inflicted. Emily nodded, keeping a wary eye on the arguing crowd as she bent over Reginald and went to work. The damage was worse than she'd guessed; they'd broken several of his ribs when they'd arrested him. One of his arms was badly damaged, perhaps dislocated...she winced in sympathy as she healed it. Lady Barb would need to take a look at him later, she decided. There was so much damage that Emily wasn't sure she'd managed to repair it all.

"Thank you," Reginald muttered. His voice was so low that Emily had to strain to hear it. Lady Barb had clearly removed her spell. "I thought...I thought I was dead."

"Not yet," Emily said. She recalled, all too clearly, the days she'd been suspected of destroying the Warden. "You'll be able to ride soon enough."

The headman's voice suddenly boomed over the crowd. "We arrested the wrong person," he said. "We should now consider other possibilities."

Emily winced, inwardly. Most of the people in the village were related, which meant they had to consider that they might be related to a murderer. Lady Barb motioned and a middle-aged woman, tears streaking down her face, stepped up onto the stage. Emily sensed Lady Barb casting a complex truth spell, then questioning the woman. The mother of the missing boy, it seemed, was completely innocent of his disappearance. So were the other three parents.

"We could question everyone," Lady Barb muttered to the headman.

He shook his head. Emily wondered, briefly, if *he* was responsible for the missing children, then realized that it was unlikely. The headman wouldn't risk his position by abducting children.

"It's a trick," an older man shouted. "They cast no spell on that...*person*."

He waved a hand at Reginald. "He did it and they covered for him. They're working together."

Lady Barb gave him a long look. "I could have taken Reginald out of the stocks at any moment," she said, tartly. Emily would not have dared to argue with that tone of voice. "If he had been guilty, you could have killed him and I would have done nothing to stop you. But he is innocent. I will not allow you to kill an innocent man while the real murderer runs and hides."

Her voice softened, carrying magic. "Calm down," she ordered. The compulsion hung on the air, utterly undetectable to anyone without magic of their own. "And go home."

The crowd seethed, but started to slowly disperse. Emily let out a long breath as the danger receded, then concentrated on helping Reginald to his feet. Lady Barb spoke briefly to the headman, who nodded and headed back to his house with his council.

"His horse is in the field," Lady Barb said. "I'll have it brought around."

"Thank you," Reginald said. "They would have killed me."

"Yes, they would," Lady Barb said. "You might want to consider taking your girl-friend with you. She won't be safe here."

Reginald swallowed. Emily read reluctance in his eyes. From his point of view, the girl had been nothing more than a diversion; from hers, perhaps he'd been the man who would take her away from the village. Emily could understand her desire to escape; if she stayed, she'd marry someone she knew all her life and move into his house along with his parents, trading one form of imprisonment for another. And if she didn't have magic, she wouldn't be able to escape to Whitehall or another magical school.

"Just make sure you don't drop her somewhere," Emily added. "If you take her, take care of her."

Lady Barb nodded. "Who in this village received a letter?"

Emily winced. It wasn't something she could legally ask, while Reginald had been under the influence of her spell, but now here was no guarantee of receiving a honest answer.

"One of the older villagers used to be a soldier," Reginald said. "He worked for Lord Easter before he died. I was charged with taking him a letter, then taking back a reply. But then..."

He shrugged, expressively.

"I'll write you a letter," Lady Barb said. "Once you've delivered the reply, take it down to the nearest carriage house and get it on its way."

"Of course," Reginald said. "Anything for my saviors."

Lady Barb dismissed him, then led the way back to the headman's house. "Unless the village is housing a child-killer, we have to assume it was the work of the nec-romancer," she said, casting a privacy ward around them. "But if the dead bodies we found didn't come from here..."

"Then other children have gone missing," Emily finished, remembering the rumors. "Could...?"

She hesitated. There were possibilities she didn't want to think about, but there was no choice. "Could there be another use for the children?"

Lady Barb looked at her. "Like what?"

"Shadye wanted to sacrifice me," Emily reminded her. Shadye could have killed her at once if all he'd wanted was another victim to feed his lust for power. "Could the necromancer have decided to sacrifice the children instead?"

Another idea occurred to her. "Or...were they drained of life energy instead of magic?"

"No way to tell," Lady Barb said. She sounded disturbed by the prospect. "A sacrifice should have left traces of demonic magic, but there were so many obfuscating charms around the bodies that I couldn't detect anything specific. Life energy..."

Emily frowned. "What would the bodies look like if they were drained of life energy?"

"Dead," Lady Barb said, flatly. The prospect clearly disturbed her. "I'd keep those questions to yourself, if I were you. There are people who would take strong exception to you asking them in the wrong places."

She shrugged. "There was no sign of rapid aging, but the ritual might have worked quickly enough to prevent it," she added. "Still, it's a worrying thought."

They paused outside the headman's house. "You did well," she said. "They might not be satisfied, but at least an innocent man has been spared death by torture."

Emily nodded. "What are we going to do now?"

"The headman invited us to a dance tomorrow," Lady Barb said. Emily winced. "Yes, I thought that would be your reaction. Besides, I want to head on to Easter as soon as possible."

She looked up at the sun, poised high in the sky. "It will take two days to reach Easter in any case," she added. "We might as well start walking now. And besides, you still need more practice."

Emily groaned. She'd barely recovered from the last set of practice exercises—and, while she knew that Lady Barb was right about them being important, she still didn't know *why*.

The headman didn't seem offended when Lady Barb told him they had to leave after they'd changed back into more practical clothes. In fact, he seemed almost relieved.

Emily puzzled over the reaction, then realized that the headman was hoping to quiet everything down. It would be easier if Lady Barb, Emily and Reginald were elsewhere. Lady Barb seemed to agree; she wrote her letter while Emily packed up the bags, took the food the headman's wife offered her and then led Emily back out the door.

Reginald was waiting for them, sitting on a bored-looking horse. "Make sure the letter gets into the system," Lady Barb ordered. "And *don't* leave it lying around."

"Hexed, is it?" Reginald said. He took the letter, placed it into his saddlebag and then smiled at them both. "Thank you, once again."

He dug in his heels and cantered out of the village.

"He didn't have the girl with him," Emily said, quietly.

"No," Lady Barb agreed. "He didn't."

She shook her head sadly, then led the way towards the next path. Emily was mildly surprised that they weren't taking the road, but she suspected that Lady Barb wanted to remain unseen. Instead, they started to climb almost as soon as they passed into the trees.

"Tell me," Lady Barb said. "Did you notice how many children were missing?"

"Two," Emily said. She'd hardly been able to miss that detail. The headman had repeated it more than Master Tor had repeated his tedious legal facts about the Allied Lands. "Why...?"

She saw it, suddenly. There had been more than two bodies hidden behind the obfuscating charms. "Where did the other bodies come from?"

"That is indeed the question," Lady Barb said. "Which other villages have also lost people to the mystery magician? And just what is he trying to do?"

Chapter Thirty-One

Easter Castle came into view long before they saw Easter Town. Like Lord Gorham's castle, it was a brooding monstrosity perched on top of a mountain, but there was something about it that looked more welcoming than the previous castle. Lady Barb spent several minutes staring at it before leading the way down into the town, a troubled expression on her face. Emily followed her, feeling her body aching from tiredness. She just wanted to get some sleep before she did anything else.

It wasn't yet sunset, but the town seemed as quiet and fearful as the previous village. Emily saw the faces at many of the windows peek out at them, before vanishing behind curtains. She looked around, half-expecting to see guards, yet no one showed themselves. By the time they reached the guesthouse and started to dismantle the locks, Emily felt thoroughly spooked.

"Someone tried to break in again," Lady Barb observed, as she opened the door. "But this time they didn't succeed."

Emily frowned. "The same person as before?"

"Unknown," Lady Barb said. She sounded rather perturbed. "I didn't recognize the traces of magic, but that proves nothing."

Inside, the guesthouse was clean. Emily checked the potions cabinets and discovered, to her relief, that all of the ingredients were still in place. She put her bag down in the room, then stepped into the kitchen. As Lady Barb lit a fire, Emily unpacked the remaining food and laid it on the table. Welcome warmth slowly spread through the guesthouse.

"This town is as scared as the last village," Lady Barb said, once she'd made them both some warm soup. Emily took her bowl and sipped it, gratefully. "The fear is almost tangible."

"They might have lost children too," Emily said. She finished her soup and moved on to the bread. "How are we going to proceed?"

"I'm going to pay a silent visit to the castle tomorrow," Lady Barb said. "You're going to remain here and take care of our patients."

Emily swallowed. "What if something happens I can't handle?"

"I'll be very disappointed in you," Lady Barb said, lightly. "But if you really can't deal with it, place the patient in stasis and wait for me to return."

She finished her bread and stood up. "I'm going to talk to the headman," she added. "Set up the beds, then plan what you're going to brew tomorrow."

Emily groaned—*more* potions—but nodded. If nothing else, she was certainly gaining in confidence while doing something useful. Professor Thande would be pleased, even though she was only creating First Year potions. Maybe she could apply for extra ingredients for Third Year and do some private alchemical work, perhaps with Imaiqah's help.

"We should teach them how to make their own," she said, softly. "Would it be so difficult?"

Lady Barb smiled. "Would you like to encourage mundanes to experiment with alchemy?"

Emily shook her head, embarrassed. Away from Thande's protective wards, alchemical explosions could be even worse. Whole houses might be wiped out by disasters a magician could have avoided, if only by disintegrating the cauldron before it exploded. Besides, she had a feeling that magicians would object to sharing the more complex recipes. Who knew what would happen to them?

She watched Lady Barb leave, then walked into the potions lab and inspected the ingredients one by one. There were enough, she decided, to make everything the townspeople could want—and bottles to store it—if she had the time to do it. She suspected that, normally, an alchemist would have nothing to do with actual patients, which was probably a good thing. Even someone as...innocent as Professor Thande would be unable to resist the urge to experiment on his patients. There were enough horror stories about alchemists to convince her to keep them well away from mundanes.

Once she'd sorted out the ingredients, she walked back into the main room and into the bedroom. It was smaller than she'd expected, with one large king-sized bed rather than several smaller ones. The room was cold enough for people to want to huddle together, but magic would take care of that, suggesting that the designer had had other things in mind. Irked, Emily placed her blanket on the floor and silently promised Lady Barb the bed. The older woman had been ill, after all.

It was nearly an hour before Lady Barb returned, by which time the sun had vanished completely, throwing the entire town into darkness. Emily used the night vision spell as she peered out of the window, but saw hardly anyone on the streets.

Lady Barb was right. This town was definitely gripped by fear.

"The headman was too nervous to talk to me," Lady Barb said. "But I managed to get some answers out of his wife. They've lost at least a dozen children and young men."

Emily blinked as she boiled the water for a hot drink. "Young men?"

"Conscripted," Lady Barb said, shortly. "Lady Easter seems to be preparing for war. She's taken over half of the unmarried men from the town, men the townspeople desperately need to prepare for the coming winter. They went into the castle and haven't been seen since."

She ran her hands through her long hair. "And the children have definitely vanished," she added. "They started to lock them up after three children went picking mushrooms and never came home. It didn't make any difference. The children kept vanishing at night."

Emily shivered. "How?"

"Good question," Lady Barb said. "Most supernatural creatures won't come into a town, unless summoned. But if it is a necromancer, he should be completely mad by now."

She took her drink, drank it and then headed towards the bedroom. "We need to be up early tomorrow morning," she added, as she walked. "Make sure you are ready to brew in the morning.

"Shouldn't I come with you?" Emily asked. "If it is a necromancer..."

Lady Barb turned and met her eyes. "Could you defeat one through the power of love?"

Emily blushed bright red. One of the ballads bards sang about her claimed that she had defeated Shadye with the power of love. It said a great deal about some of the others that it wasn't the worst of the bunch. What kind of enemy could be defeated by *love?* Shadye had probably never known the meaning of the word.

"Or," Lady Barb pressed, "do you have the power to beat one now?"

"I don't know," Emily said, thinking of the nuke-spell. But it would be completely devastating—and almost certainly suicidal. "Maybe..."

"I've sneaked around necromancers before," Lady Barb reminded her, gently. "If I don't come back, you can do as you see fit, but until then you must do as I tell you. Obedience is one of the rules of apprenticeship, is it not?"

Emily nodded. She *was* Lady Barb's apprentice, at least for the summer, even if she hadn't taken the usual oaths. Obedience, loyalty and servitude were the terms, in exchange for training and practice. She could argue, she could ask for explanations or clarification, but she couldn't disobey. Or at least a normal apprentice couldn't disobey. She felt a moment of pity for Jade, combined with a grim awareness that she might have to take on an apprenticeship after leaving Whitehall. What would happen if she ended up apprenticed to someone less reasonable than Lady Barb?

She followed Lady Barb into the bedroom, then rolled her eyes as she realized the older woman had taken the blankets, rather than the bed. Emily hesitated, then tactfully pointed out that she'd meant to give the bed to Lady Barb.

"I'm not that old," Lady Barb said, with a smile. "Besides, I cannot get too used to comfort."

Emily lifted an eyebrow. "Did you sleep on nails at Whitehall?" she asked, remembering that she hadn't seen Lady Barb's private chambers. Students were rarely allowed entry to any of the teaching staff's quarters. "Or did they just give you a hard bed?"

"Go to sleep," Lady Barb ordered, shortly. "It takes years to build up a tolerance for moving from place to place, but only days to lose it."

The thought nagged at Emily as she lay in the giant bed, feeling an odd twinge of guilt. It had been fun to camp with the sergeants, but she'd always felt relieved when she finally returned to Whitehall. And yet she'd adapted well to the changes on their walk, sleeping under the stars one night and in an insect-infected hovel the next. But would she have coped so well if she hadn't had camping experience? Or, for that matter, the magic to make it easier to handle? No wonder so few new magicians went home.

She drifted off to sleep, but her sleep was broken by nightmares that eventually sent her back into wakefulness, two hours before sunrise. Lady Barb snored quietly, her heavy breathing almost hypnotic; Emily sat upright and tried to concentrate, calming her heartbeat until she could sleep again. But she tossed and turned for nearly an hour before giving up, climbing out of bed and slipping into the main room, where she cast a light spell and read until the sun started to rise in the sky. The book wasn't boring enough to send her back to sleep.

A hand fell on her shoulder and she jumped. "You scared me," Lady Barb said. "You never wake up before me."

Emily blushed. At Whitehall, students normally woke up at eight bells, in time to get some breakfast before running to their first classes. The peasants, on the other hand, rose with the sun and went to bed with the moon. Despite living with them, Emily knew her sleeping habits hadn't improved from Whitehall.

"I couldn't sleep," she confessed. It felt oddly warming to know that Lady Barb had been worried. "And I didn't want to wake you."

"I normally play Kingmaker or read when I want to sleep," Lady Barb said. She wandered over to the window and peered outside into the semi-darkness. "And several of the staff have started playing poker."

Emily couldn't help snickering. She'd designed playing cards easily enough, although charming them to prevent cheating had required Aloha's help. But then she'd run into the problem of simply not knowing the rules. Her stepfather had gambled heavily, but he'd never invited Emily to play, let alone taught her the rules. Aloha had listened to what little Emily could recall, then worked out her own set of rules. Emily had no idea how close they were to Earth's rules, but it hardly mattered. "Poker" had spread through Whitehall like a wildfire. She was probably lucky that most people blamed it on Aloha. Students being students, it hadn't taken long for them to start gambling for more than matchsticks.

"Yes, I *thought* that was your fault," Lady Barb added. She smiled as Emily's flush deepened. "Who *else* would invent a whole new game because she was bored?"

Emily shrugged. She hadn't really *invented* chess, of course, but it was the story almost everyone chose to believe. It had been Aloha who had invented "poker." Somehow, it had sparked off a quiet competition among the students to invent new games that held together reasonably well. Emily hadn't entered, knowing that it wasn't fair. But she hadn't been able to resist planning out a Risk-like game for the Allied Lands.

"Make us some breakfast, then go start your brewing," Lady Barb ordered. In the distance, the sun started to glimmer at the horizon. "I need to make sure that no children vanished overnight."

Emily wanted to insist on coming with her, but bit her tongue and walked over to the kitchen, where oats and milk had been stored in preservation cabinets. She made oatmeal, then waited until Lady Barb returned to eat.

"Eat at once, next time," Lady Barb said. Her voice was stern, but her eyes looked distracted, preoccupied by a greater thought. "There's no point in waiting for me."

"It's rude to eat without you," Emily said. The older woman seemed caught between two different priorities. "What's wrong?"

"A baby was taken from his mother last night," Lady Barb said, once she finished eating. "There were strange traces of magic around the house."

Emily sucked in her breath. "Can you follow them?"

"I think so," Lady Barb said. "Stay here. Do your brewing, then see patients. Can you handle it?"

"Yes," Emily said, stung. "I'll wait for you."

She left Lady Barb to put the dishes in the sink, then walked into the potions lab and started to brew, one after the other. Her irritation caused two potions to spoil before she managed to calm herself enough to brew properly. If nothing else, she told herself, the remaining potions could be bottled and handed over to the headman for later distribution. There would be no need to waste anything. She had worked her way through five potions when there was a sharp knock at the door.

Shaking her head, Emily walked over—readying a spell in her mind, just in case—and opened the door. A young man was standing there, resting on a cane. Emily listened to a story of accidentally damaging his leg while climbing a tree, then motioned for him to sit down while she worked on the wound. It had been treated by a mundane doctor, she realized, who had bound up the wound, but done nothing else.

"This may hurt a little," she said. "Do you want something to dampen the pain?"

The man shook his head. Emily rolled her eyes—some of the male students in classes were just the same, showing off how much pain they could endure—and cast the spell without any further hesitation. There was a faint crunching sound as the bones were knit back together; the man let out a strangled gasp, then went very pale. Emily concealed her amusement as she concentrated on completing the job. Thankfully, he managed to remain still long enough for her to do it without complications.

"Take it easy for a few days," she said, knowing that it wouldn't be easy for him. The town was bigger than any of the villages, but it wouldn't have much room for freeloaders. "If you put too much weight on that leg, it will probably break again."

She rolled her eyes again as the young man stood up, clearly resting his weight on the repaired leg. "You're much nicer than Mother Holly," he said. "And you did a better job."

"Thank you," Emily said, puzzled. "Who's Mother Holly?"

"A witch," the man said. "She lives some distance from town. If someone is badly injured, they will go to see her. Sometimes she helps."

A shadow crossed his face. "They also say she's the one stealing the children."

Emily frowned. A hedge witch? She didn't know much about them, save for the fact that most magicians looked down on them as untrained amateurs. They were sometimes related to the Travellers, sometimes completely isolated from the magical mainstream. But she was the first magician Emily had heard of since beginning her time with Lady Barb.

"Tell me," she said. "Why didn't *you* go there?"

"She can be very unpleasant if she doesn't think you're worth her time," the young man said. "Or so I have been told."

Resolving to discuss the matter with Lady Barb, Emily chased the young man out just in time to see a child with a problematic tooth. Her mother and father insisted on staying with her at all times, watching Emily as if they expected her to snatch the child and run. Emily tried not to keep one eye on the scythe the man was carrying as she gave the child some healing potion, then inspected the rotting tooth. She wasn't an expert dentist, insofar as the Allied Lands *had* dentists. The only thing she could do was pluck the tooth out of the child's mouth and reassure the parents that a new tooth would grow in time.

She watched them go, then started working her way through the other patients. It amazed her just how quiet and orderly the waiting townspeople were, not even chattering amongst themselves as they waited in a meek little line outside the building. The handful of times she'd been to a clinic on Earth, the waiting room had been noisy and the doctor's staff had been driven almost to distraction. But here...she could turn them away, if they annoyed her. Lady Barb would understand.

One girl was having problems with cramps. Emily gave her a bottle of potion—the same she used at Whitehall—and told her to take one sip the day her cycle began. An older man worried over a nasty cough, which Emily handled, telling him to stop smoking home-grown tobacco. She had no way to be sure, but she suspected that it was stronger than anything she'd seen on Earth. The man didn't seem too happy with her suggestion. Tobacco, like alcohol, helped relieve boredom and calm the nerves.

Emily sighed, then went on to the next patient. A red-faced boy confessed to having problems with his penis, which Emily noted down before telling him to come back and see Lady Barb later. She wouldn't be happy about that, Emily knew, but she couldn't force herself to be clinical. It had been hard enough practicing on the training homunculus. By the time she had worked her way through the entire line, it was early afternoon and she was exhausted.

There was a knock on the door. Cursing under her breath, Emily stood and opened the door to reveal another young man who seemed oddly familiar. It still took her a moment to place him. He'd changed his clothes—he looked like a merchant now, rather than a peasant—but his hands were still dead giveaways.

"Rudolf?"

"The same," Rudolf said. He gave her an oddly hopeful smile. "Can I come in?"

Chapter Thirty-Two

RUDOLF LOOKED FAINTLY...ODD TO EMILY AS HE STEPPED PAST HER AND TOOK A SEAT AT THE table. It was impossible to place her finger on it, even though he carried himself like an aristocrat while wearing clothes belonging to one of the lower orders. She wondered, suddenly, if Rudolf could be the mystery magician, but there was no scent of magic around him. Unless he was masking very well, he didn't have the potential for magic, let alone actual access to his powers. He was just a mundane.

She closed the door, cursing herself for forgetting Sergeant Harkin so quickly. *He'd* been a mundane, and yet he'd taught at a school for magicians. Rudolf might have no magic, but she shouldn't dismiss him out of hand. He might still be very dangerous, even though his servants all agreed that he was a good person, for an aristocrat.

She mentally prepared a spell before sitting down at the table, facing him. This time, she didn't want to let him get away.

"Your father was under outside control," she said, placing her hands on the table. "He wasn't in his right mind."

Rudolf looked relieved. "I knew he must have been under *someone's* influence," he said, once Emily had finished explaining. "But I thought it was Lady Easter."

Emily quirked an eyebrow, so he hastened to explain.

"She needs to marry off her daughters as soon as possible," Rudolf told her. "To someone who could protect them when the old lady finally died. I would be one of the few acceptable sons-in-law for her."

"Oh," Emily said. She knew how snobbish aristocrats could be when it came to marriage, but there were strong reasons why Rudolf *wouldn't* make a good match for Lady Easter's daughter, starting with the simple fact that he would take power from his wife's mother. "Why you?"

"Lady Easter cannot rule forever," Rudolf pointed out. "Sooner or later, she is going to need a successor."

Emily had to admit he had a point. Aristocrats might cling greedily to their power, but they knew that they had to make provision for the succession. King Randor had had good reason to worry about handing power to Alassa—or at least the royal brat she'd been prior to Whitehall—yet he was now training her in proper governance, intending to share his power as soon as Alassa left school. Barring accidents or war, Alassa would outlive her father and then have a son of her own to take her place. Still, there were always problems when one generation took over from the next.

"You'd think they'd accept a woman could rule," Emily said, curious to see how Rudolf would react. "Lady Easter seems to do it well enough."

"She's also old," Rudolf pointed out. "She isn't distracted by female issues."

Emily rolled her eyes. *That* was a common excuse for denying women power and place, although men could be just as emotional as women with far less cause. But then, people often came up with the prejudice first and then invented reasons to justify it later. And it wasn't as if Lady Easter couldn't or wouldn't have children. She had three daughters.

"Tell me something," she said. "Why don't you want to marry her daughter?"

"She's ugly," Rudolf said, at once. "I couldn't abide the thought of touching her."

Emily felt a hot flash of anger. How *dare* someone just dismiss his prospective bride like that? She'd been mocked enough to know just how badly it would sting the girl, if she ever heard Rudolf say it. And besides, Rudolf could spend time with a mistress, if he liked, once he'd impregnated his wife. He had a freedom his wife would probably lack.

But then she took a closer look, controlling her anger. Rudolf didn't seem to quite believe his own words. Like Alassa, he had been raised to know that his marriage would be arranged for matters of state—and to accept it, as the price for being the aristocrat he was. He shouldn't have any problem marrying the girl, even if she was a one-legged hunchback who kept her face hidden under a bag. And...

And he should have just accepted it, Emily thought, puzzled. *The runes would have seen to that, wouldn't they?*

Rudolf hadn't known the runes were there or he would have alerted his father—and no amount of subtle magic could hide something, once people were actually *looking*. In that case, the runes should have affected him. Even powerful magicians could be affected, without ever knowing that they were being influenced. So why had Rudolf turned so sharply against the idea of marrying the poor girl?

"I have never observed men having problems with touching girls," Emily observed, tartly. "What other reasons did you have?"

Rudolf eyed her, sharply. "Why do you care?"

"Because your planned marriage was organized by a magician who might well be a necromancer," Emily said, bluntly. "And you're changing the subject. What reasons do you have to resist the marriage?"

"A necromancer?" Rudolf repeated. "But why...?"

"A very good question," Emily agreed. Shadye hadn't given a damn about the politics of the Allied Lands, as far as she could tell. "And you're *still* changing the subject."

"I should have known not to argue with a woman," Rudolf said, giving her a sly grin. "They always notice the unanswered questions."

"It's a gift," Emily said. She was tempted to point out that being snide in front of a magician wasn't a good idea, but kept it to herself. "And you have yet to answer my question."

Rudolf sat upright. "I am the heir to Gorham," he snapped. "I do not have to answer you."

Emily gave him a long look as the pieces fell into place. A young man who hadn't tried to lure any of the serving girls into his bed, let alone molest them. It wasn't as if he wouldn't have found a willing girl, either. A young man who had been so vigorously against marriage that he'd fled his father's castle, rather than try to reason his way out of it. And a young man who had been so intensely defensive that he'd been prepared to snap at a magician, even knowing that it could get him turned into a toad.

And he hadn't shown any real awareness of *her* femininity either.

"You're not interested in women," she said. "Are you?"

Rudolf turned bright red and looked down at the table, answering her question without saying a word. Emily felt a wave of pity for him, understanding just how he must feel. The Cairngorms were not kind to homosexuals, even when the homosexual didn't have a duty to provide his tiny kingdom with an heir. Given Rudolf's position, the secret could have undone his father's lands. Hell, given how homosexuality was often equated with weakness in the mountains, he'd be challenged by almost everyone as soon as he took his father's place.

"I understand that there are oaths healers take," Rudolf said, when he could speak again. He kept his eyes firmly fixed on the table. "You cannot talk about this to anyone, can you?"

Emily hesitated. It was true that healers swore such oaths—but she'd never taken the oaths herself. Lady Barb had just told her never to discuss anyone's condition with anyone else unless there was no alternative. Parents had a right to know what was wrong with their young children, she knew, but no one else had any right to know. A careless word on her part, she'd been warned, could cause years of gossip for the villagers.

"I won't talk about it with anyone, apart from my mistress," Emily said. Lady Barb *had* sworn such oaths. "Is that acceptable?"

"Yes," he said.

She hated asking blunt questions, but it needed to be asked. "When did you realize you didn't like girls?"

"I didn't notice any difference between me and other boys, at first," Rudolf said. He still didn't look up at her. "But father...father used to say that a young man should be experienced with women. He picked the prettiest chambermaids for me, even dressed them in revealing clothes. But I felt nothing for them, even when"—his face grew even redder—"he explained the mechanics to me."

Emily felt her own face heat. No one had ever explained the mechanics to her—she'd had to learn the facts of life from books and the Internet—but she could appreciate just how agonizingly embarrassing the talk must have been for Rudolf. Men didn't mature at a specific age any more than women. There would have been times when Rudolf was still trapped in the mindset of a child...and afterwards, when he did mature, he would still have been horrified at talking over such matters with his father.

She couldn't help wondering just how far Lord Gorham had gone to ensure his son had *experience*. Had he paid the maids extra to put out for him?

"I still felt nothing," Rudolf said. "But I started to notice men instead. My father's huntsman, some of the soldiers...I couldn't help thinking and dreaming about them. And then..."

"You did it with someone," Emily guessed.

She'd known one boy at school who'd come out of the closet—and that had been in a fairly liberal society. He'd still been teased and tormented mercilessly by his peers.

In hindsight, it was easy enough to see that most of them had been worried that it was catching, but it hadn't been easy for him.

But it would be far worse in a society where everyone expected him to get to work and produce an heir. Whoever had...done it with him would be in a position to blackmail Rudolf for the rest of his life. Or, for that matter, someone who caught them together.

"I did," Rudolf said. He smiled, suddenly. "It took a while to learn how, but we did. And..."

Emily hastily held up her hand. She'd overheard enough boys bragging about their sexual conquests—real and imaginary—to know that she didn't want to hear the gory details. If there was one thing the magicians of Whitehall had in common with their counterparts from Earth, it was bragging endlessly about sex. And magicians enjoyed a far greater sexual freedom than anyone else.

"So you were so fixated on men that the runes couldn't get a grip on your mind," Emily said. She wondered, absently, what would have happened if Lady Easter had a son. Would Rudolf have wanted to marry *him*? "And you fled, rather than tell your father the truth."

Rudolf looked up at her. "Wouldn't you?"

Emily winced, inwardly. That hit far too close to home.

"He'd want to take me to a healer," Rudolf said. "Someone who could make me... normal."

He met her eyes. "Is that even possible?"

"I don't know," Emily hedged. Subtle magic obviously hadn't worked. More direct compulsion spells and charms might work, but they came with a cost. "It would be much simpler for you to marry someone, then transfer sperm without sex. You could then let her have freedom to do whatever she wants."

Rudolf's face reddened again. "You do realize that my wife couldn't take a lover?"

Emily met his eyes. "Why not? Isn't that what you want for yourself?"

Rudolf started to splutter. "It would suggest that I couldn't control my wife," he mumbled, embarrassed. "And if I couldn't control her, it would suggest I couldn't control my kingdom."

"Oh," Emily said, sardonically. "It's all about *control*."

It was, she knew. The obsession with legitimate heirs was bad enough, but few people in the mountains would be able to comprehend someone *letting* his wife look for love and romance elsewhere. He was right; they *would* take it as a sign of weakness. And the villagers weren't much different—or were they? She'd seen battered wives and wives who were quite prepared to keep their husbands in line through force.

"Yes," Rudolf confirmed. "It is." He paused. "My parents grew to love one another," he added. "Is it wrong to want such a relationship for myself?"

Emily winced in sympathy.

Rudolf looked back down at the table. "Can you make me normal?"

Emily gave him a sharp look. She had no idea if homosexuals were produced by nature or nurture, but given how far Lord Gorham had gone she suspected the former. In that case, Rudolf's nature would be clashing with a culture that told him that homosexuality was disgusting, as well as a despised sign of weakness. If homosexuals on Earth could get twisted between two contradictory points, why not homosexuals from a far more restrained culture?

"I think it would break your mind to try," she said, gently. Maybe he could be charmed into preferring women, but the charm would be pushing against his nature. "Do you feel nothing for women at all?"

"Nothing," Rudolf confirmed.

On Earth, there were people who would advise a homosexual—and provide assistance, if necessary. They would even help talk to parents who were less than accepting of their son's homosexuality. But there was no one here...and Lord Gorham had more important problems than homophobia. If his son was unable to produce a grandchild, he would have to cast around for some other solution, just to keep the succession intact.

"Then my honest advice, again, would be to marry someone who won't mind bearing a child and then being ignored," Emily said. Ideally, he should marry a lesbian. Oddly—or perhaps it wasn't so odd—the guidebooks had mentioned nothing about lesbians. "And you would have to be honest with her from the start."

Rudolf blinked. "Honest?"

"Women are told that men are sex-mad fiends," Emily said, remembering drunken remarks by her mother. "If you don't *act* like you're interested, she'll *know* you're not interested and start wondering why. And then she would be in a position to embarrass you."

Or, she thought silently, *would you lock her up to keep her from talking?*

Could a wife be kept as a prisoner? The culture of the mountains insisted that a bride moved from her father's house to her husband's, who assumed complete responsibility for her. There were few aristocratic fathers who would challenge a lord over the treatment of his daughter. Why not? Daughters existed to forge ties of blood, not wield power...

"You could marry me," Rudolf said. "As a magician, you would be a social equal."

Emily gaped at him, then shook her head. "Millie" could marry him—a common-born apprentice could hardly hope to do better, if she wanted to marry into the local aristocracy—but Baroness Emily had more lands and money than Lord Gorham. At the very least, it would cause all sorts of problems; King Randor would probably have to approve the match, which he wouldn't unless he benefited in some way. And it was hard to see how he could.

"I think you want someone who already knows," she said. "But it wouldn't be a very satisfying relationship for me."

It had its advantages, she had to admit...but she shoved the thought back into the back of her mind. Maybe, if she'd been so totally repulsed by men, she would have considered it. But she had been friends with Jade...

"I did," Rudolf said, shamefaced. "Do you know any magician who would be interested?"

Emily remembered Hodge's claim that magicians—female magicians—had no restraints on their activities. She wondered, briefly, if she *did* know any lesbians. Statistically, there was a good chance that there were more than a handful at Whitehall. But she didn't know who they were...and even if she did, would they be interested in spending the rest of their lives in a cold castle in the middle of nowhere?

"I don't think so," she said. "What are you going to do now?"

"I think I need to speak with your mistress, then go home," Rudolf said. "Can I stay here?"

Emily nodded, relieved. It was easier for him to stay willingly than doing something to keep him prisoner. Besides, they could chat about something else.

"Tell me," she said. "Why did you come here?"

"I had the idea that I could talk Lady Easter out of accepting me as a husband for her daughter," Rudolf said. "But then I realized just how hard it would be to get into the castle and decided to wait for an opportunity."

"Your father knows better now," Emily reassured him. "But you really should talk to him more openly, before he arranges a match with someone less...provocative."

Rudolf nodded and changed the subject. He was smarter and more knowledgeable than the princes who'd tried to court Alassa, Emily decided, although there were some curious gaps in his knowledge. Rudolf could recite family relationships for every aristocrat within the mountains, but knew almost nothing about the other aristocracies in the Allied Lands, even though they were prospective marriage partners. But somehow Emily doubted that a king's younger son—assuming he had one—would be interested in marrying into the mountain families.

"Father always said that reading too much was bad," Rudolf said, at one point. "Is that actually true?"

"Depends what you read," Emily grunted. Her stepfather had said the same thing, which had only spurred her determination to read every book she could find. "You have to keep an open mind—but not too open. Or bad ideas might come crawling in."

Rudolf laughed. "But how do you tell a bad idea?"

Emily shrugged. *Anything* could be made to sound convincing with a little effort, particularly if the reader didn't know enough to notice the omissions. Politicians on Earth had specialized in making two plus two equal five, with a little careful dancing.

She found herself enjoying the discussion more than she'd expected, but a nagging worry slowly grew stronger in her breast. Where *was* Lady Barb? Emily stood and made dinner for both of them, silently thanking God that Lady Barb had brought enough food for several days, then left some of it on the stove. When Lady Barb returned, she'd want food...

But, by nightfall, Lady Barb had not returned.

Chapter Thirty-Three

Emily HALF-EXPECTED TO SEE LADY BARB WHEN SHE OPENED HER EYES THE FOLLOWING morning, as soon as a rooster outside began to welcome the sun. But the blankets by the side of the bed were untouched, as were the wards she'd erected to protect the bedroom. Pulling herself to her feet, she stumbled through the wards and peered towards the fire. Perhaps Lady Barb was there...

But the only person in the room was Rudolf, snoring so loudly that Emily was surprised he hadn't kept her awake.

She checked the outside wards and discovered that no one had passed through them since Rudolf, yesterday afternoon. Lady Barb hadn't returned, then; she might have left Emily's wards alone, but not chosen to stay outside the house all night. Emily put the cauldron over the kitchen fire and started to boil water, thinking hard. Lady Barb hadn't returned and that meant...what?

There's a necromancer—a suspected necromancer—out there, Emily thought.

Yes, Lady Barb was good at hiding, but if she got caught she would have to fight a necromancer at knife-range, making it almost impossible to escape. What if she'd been killed—or captured? An adult combat sorceress would be a tempting source of magic for any necromancer, while no one else would take the risk of keeping Lady Barb alive.

I should have taken the full master-apprentice link, she thought, bitterly. She would have been able to find Lady Barb with ease—or know she was dead—if she'd taken the bond. But she hadn't been planning to stay an apprentice for longer than two months, instead of the full two-year period. And dissolving the bond ahead of time tended to cause unforeseen repercussions.

She finished boiling the water, then prepared two mugs of Kava out of habit. Rudolf snorted, then sat upright, looking around as if he wasn't quite sure where he was. Emily winked at him, then used a spell to levitate the first mug over towards where he was sitting. Rudolf's eyes went wide, then he took the drink and sipped it. She had to smile at his expression. It was rare for anyone to drink Kava in the mountains, according to Lady Barb.

"Thank you," Rudolf said, doubtfully. "Didn't she come back?"

Emily shook her head, more worried than she cared to admit. If Lady Barb had been killed...what should she do? What *could* she do? Part of her wanted to head out of the mountains and summon help, but the other part of her wanted to go after the older woman and avenge her death. If she were dead, that is...it was possible to hold a magician helpless, if you knew how to do it. Emily had been stripped of her magic once and found it disconcerting, even though she'd spent her first sixteen years without magic.

"Eat the rest of the stew," she said, feeling a twinge of guilt. There was no way she could abandon Lady Barb, at least as long as she didn't *know* the older woman was dead. "Then we need to go talk to the headman."

The air was cold as they stepped out of the guesthouse and started to walk towards the center of town. Emily couldn't help noticing that there were only a handful of people on the streets, glancing around as though they expected something nasty to be following them. They gave Emily and Rudolf a wide berth, making signs to ward off evil when they thought Emily wasn't looking.

Do they think, she asked herself, *that Lady Barb is responsible for stealing their children? Or are they just fearful of magicians?*

She gritted her teeth as she walked past the guards and into the headman's hut. *This* headman looked alarmingly like Imaiqah's father, complete with the pleasant expression that masked a very sharp mind. His wife looked bigger, with a gleam in her eye that suggested she was just as cool and calculating as some of Zangaria's noblewomen. An equal, Emily realized, feeling oddly relieved. This woman wouldn't hesitate to tell her husband when he was making a mistake.

"Lady Sorceress," the headman said. His gaze shifted to Rudolf. "And...?"

"A wandering minstrel, I," Rudolf said, with practiced ease. "And sometimes a guide."

Emily fought to keep her face expressionless. Minstrels were common in Zangaria—some of them were very good, some of them were so appallingly bad that she'd wanted to turn them into birds—but rather less common in the mountains. But they also wandered from place to place, bringing news and rumors. As covers went, she had to admit that it wasn't a bad one. Like most noblemen, Rudolf had been taught how to sing.

The headman didn't seem too pleased—and his wife looked worried. Emily remembered how Reginald had seduced a girl in the last village and realized that they thought that Rudolf would do the same. The thought made her smile. Rudolf wouldn't be interested in any of the girls in the village, but would any of them think to chaperone him with the men?

"My mistress has not returned," Emily said shortly, pushing the thought aside. There was no time for politeness. "Do you know where she went?"

"I took her to examine Tam's house," the headman said. His face showed nothing of his thoughts. "She found traces of magic and followed them into the forest. I didn't go with her."

Maybe that was a good thing, Emily told herself. If there was a necromancer, all the headman could have done was provide him with another power source. Anything Lady Barb couldn't handle would be far too much for a mundane human. But she couldn't help wishing that the headman had gone instead of her mentor.

"Right," she said. "Do you know where she intended to go?"

"I believe she was following the magic," the headman said. "I could sense nothing, myself."

Emily scowled. He was mocking her, very politely. There would be no way to know where Lady Barb had been going...or if she hadn't been lured into a trap. What sort of magician would leave a trail for someone to follow? It was unusually subtle for a necromancer, but it would bring a prospective power source right to him.

"I see," she said. She'd have to retrace Lady Barb's path, assuming that she could find it after a day and night for the tracks to be lost. "You can take me to the house in a moment."

She scowled down at her hands. "Who is Mother Holly?"

The headman jerked in surprise. "Who told you about her?"

"Never you mind," Emily said, trying to channel Lady Barb. "Who is she?"

It was the headman's wife who answered. "She's an old witch who lives in the next valley," she said. "She likes her own company; sometimes, she will help someone who asks, or sometimes she will just banish him from her sight. No one goes there unless they are desperate."

That matched with what Emily had been told earlier, she knew. "Do you think she might be behind the stolen children?"

The headman hesitated, noticeably. "It would be unlike her," he admitted. "She never comes to town."

Emily felt a moment of pity for the old witch. Powerful enough to use magic, but not strong enough to go to Whitehall...or perhaps she'd simply fallen through the cracks. There was a bounty on magic-using children, Lady Barb had told her, paid by whichever magical school collected the child. But Mother Holly had clearly been missed. Instead, she'd had to learn on her own—or from her predecessor—and live away from her former friends and family.

But they were looking for a magician...people from Whitehall tended to think and react one way, but would a hedge witch think differently? Maybe she didn't know the limits, so she accidentally broke them...and, living alone for so long, she might be on the verge of madness in any case. And yet...if it was that simple to make necromancy work, it would have happened by now.

She shook her head. There was no proof, one way or the other.

"Take us to the house," she ordered. She paused as a thought struck her. "Were any children taken last night?"

The headman and his wife exchanged glances before shaking their heads in unison.

Emily was torn between relief and fear; relief that no more children had vanished, fear that it meant the mystery necromancer had spent his time draining Lady Barb instead. Or *her* time, if it was Mother Holly.

She looked up at the headman, then at his wife. "What does Mother Holly *do* for people who visit her?"

The wife hesitated, then looked directly at Emily. "Some healing, some potions— she gave a girl in the village something to help her get pregnant—and not much else," she said. "Most people won't go into her valley unless they have no other options."

Emily sighed and asked several more questions, but received nothing apart from vague and useless responses. No one knew much about Mother Holly, which suggested...what? Had someone done something to make them forget? Or were they simply unconcerned with an old and vulnerable woman? They didn't know who in the town was related to her, just how old she was, or anything else that might be useful. Emily couldn't help wondering if they really cared about their people. But then, a hedge witch might be too terrifying to face.

The headman led them to Tam's house on the outskirts of town, a small house barely large enough for five people. Tam's wife was pale and thin, Tam himself looked deeply worried and his parents looked fearful. The only person who showed no overt reaction was his younger sister, who might well have resented Tam's wife for coming into their home.

Emily eyed her suspiciously for a long moment, then closed her eyes and concentrated on sensing magic. Apart from her own, thrumming around her like a living thing, there was a strange sense of darker magic in the house.

"Someone opened the door using magic," she said without opening her eyes. Few homes had locks in the countryside—and even if they had, magic could open them with ease. She felt out the next traces, feeling them growing stronger as she looked for them. "They cast a spell first, one to keep everyone asleep. Then they entered the house and took the child."

Tam's wife let out a gasp and fainted. Her husband caught her.

Emily opened her eyes and looked at them, seeing their fate written all over their faces. Life was cheap in the mountains and not all children lived to reach their first birthday, but they would never recover from losing their child to a necromancer. If it *was* a necromancer. There was something oddly *dark* about the traces of magic.

Emily closed her eyes again. "They went outside and headed into the forest," she added, softly. "The trail leads there."

"So we go after them," Rudolf said. "Let's go."

Emily's eyes snapped open. "You..."

She shook her head. "I'll write out a letter for you," she said, addressing the headman. There would be time to argue with Rudolf when there was no one else around. "If we don't come back, send the letter on and others will come to help."

She led the way back to the guesthouse, Rudolf shadowing her like a lost puppy. Once inside, Emily found a sheet of paper and scribbled out an update—and an explanation of what she intended to do. If she were killed too, at least the Allied Lands would know what had happened. They'd be able to send Void or another Lone Power to deal with the mystery necromancer.

"You shouldn't come with me," she said, once the letter was finished. "If you die, your father will be left without a successor."

"The person who took the child might well be the same person who ensorcelled my father," Rudolf pointed out. "I have a right to seek revenge."

Emily sighed. The odds were he was right. Rudolf's father had been pushed into marrying Rudolf to Lady Easter's daughter—and children had gone missing from both lands. There was definitely a connection there. But she didn't want Rudolf to risk his life.

"You could end up dead," she pointed out, carefully. "Or ensorcelled yourself."

Rudolf took a breath. "As heir, it was my duty to serve as justice," he said. It took Emily a moment to realize that he'd effectively been the chief of police for his father's lands. Alassa, in theory, had been the same in Zangaria, someone with enough power and position to hold firm against anyone. "This...*person* has been stealing children and butchering them, then casting spells on my father and his people."

"This isn't on your lands," Emily said.

"I still have a duty," Rudolf said, stubbornly. "And I will not leave you alone."

Emily sighed, wondering if Rudolf was deliberately courting death. His life wouldn't be easy, particularly not if he told his father the truth. Death due to a necromancer wouldn't be suicide, at least not precisely, but it would end his problems. She sighed again, wondering just which god Rudolf worshipped. Some of them considered suicide a noble and rational act, if done in the service of the greater good.

"Fine," she said, finally. "But you will do exactly what I say."

Rudolf looked rebellious for a long moment, before nodding reluctantly.

Emily sealed up the letter, stamped it with a sigil that would keep it safe until it reached the Grandmaster, and hesitated. A thought occurred to her.

Bracing herself, she walked over to Lady Barb's bag and cast the detection spell. Magicians almost always protected their possessions...and it would be the height of irony to be accidentally immobilized by Lady Barb's defenses. But she found nothing, allowing her to probe through the bag. Rudolf watched in puzzlement as she dug through the various components until she found her pencil-sized staff. It tingled oddly as she picked it up and stuffed it into her pocket.

Lady Barb wouldn't be pleased that she'd taken it, Emily knew. She'd have to explain afterwards—and try to avoid using it, if at all possible. But it might prove an advantage if she *did* encounter someone she had to fight. She briefly considered giving it to Rudolf to carry, but dismissed the thought. If she needed it, she'd need it very quickly.

Rudolf leaned forward. "What's that?"

"Something," Emily said, evasively. She stuffed Lady Barb's clothes back into the bag, then closed it up. "Let's go."

She wrote out another note—for Lady Barb, just in case she returned—and then led Rudolf back out of the guesthouse. The headman was chatting with a pair of older men, but they retreated the moment they saw Emily. Emily sighed, then passed the headman the letter. He took it and wished them luck.

Emily walked back to Tam's house and did her best to track the traces of magic. They led into the forest, a trail that almost any magician could follow. Emily felt a chill run down her spine as she led the way into the forest, wondering if it could be any more of an obvious trap. But the magic traces faded into nothingness the further they walked into the forest...

"Odd," she muttered. "The trail just came to an end."

She looked around. They were in the midst of the forest, with no trace of any hiding place, let alone a building. She looked up, half-expecting to see a treehouse, but saw nothing.

It puzzled her. Had the magician finally realized that he or she was leaving a trail and stopped bleeding magic? But how had they survived for so long without realizing what they were doing wrong? Bleeding magic could be very dangerous.

Rudolf looked around, his hand on his belt dagger, but otherwise stayed very still.

Emily cast a detection spell, but found nothing. There was no magic here, save for the constant hum of background magic, stronger—as always—away from civilization. But there wasn't enough to hide anything. She tried to spot a trail she could follow, yet Lady Barb hadn't left any footprints for her.

They'd come to a dead end.

"It rained last night," Rudolf said. "Any tracks will have been thoroughly buried."

"Maybe," Emily said. She hesitated. Another idea occurred to her, but she couldn't help wondering just how *Rudolf* would react to it. And yet...there was no choice. "Can you promise me something?"

Rudolf gave her a puzzled look. "It depends," he said. "What do you want me to promise?"

Emily cursed under her breath. Honor, no matter how twisted, wasn't a joke to the aristocracy. Most of them would keep their word, although that wouldn't stop them searching for loopholes.

"I need to show you something," she said. What good was a secret weapon if *everyone* knew about it? "I just need your word you won't tell anyone."

Rudolf still looked puzzled—she wondered what was going through his mind—but nodded.

Emily pulled the bracelet from her arm, placed it on the ground and released the spell. Rudolf let out a yelp and jumped back as the Death Viper reappeared. Emily had a sudden series of jarring impressions, starting with the sense of Rudolf being good enough to eat, that had to come from the snake. But, moments later, she managed to push the snake into sensing Lady Barb's scent. It had smelled her back when Lady Barb had suggested turning it into a bracelet.

"Just like a hunting dog," she said, reassuringly.

The snake slithered off, then paused, waiting for them to follow.

Emily started to walk down the path, motioning Rudolf on with a wave of her hand. His face was very pale. But then, only an idiot *wouldn't* be scared of a Death Viper. "Come on."

Chapter Thirty-Four

RUDOLF STAYED WELL BACK OF THE SNAKE AS IT LED THEM FIRST THROUGH THE FOREST, then up a winding path that led out of the valley. Emily couldn't really blame him for wanting to keep his distance from the Death Viper, knowing just how fast the tiny snake could move. As a child, she'd been deathly scared of cockroaches, even though they were mostly harmless. A Death Viper was very far from harmless, even to a strong young man.

She glanced over at the castle, then looked down into the next valley...and stopped dead. For a long moment, it was hard to comprehend what she was actually *seeing*. There was a humanoid skeleton lying on the ground, half buried in the mud, but it was many times the size of a normal human. Emily wasn't good at estimating distances, yet she was sure that it was over fifty feet long

"The White Giant," Rudolf said. He kept a wary eye on the snake as he paused beside her. "Legend has it that he turned on his own people in defense of human villagers, all for the love of a girl. But no one knows the truth."

Emily had her doubts. The giant was colossal—and she found it hard to imagine how such an interracial romance could ever be practical. But she had to admit it was a nice story. The giants might have been created by the Faerie as yet another terror weapon, then released to seek food and drink in the mountains. Given their size, she suspected that they had needed enormous amounts of food just to live from day to day.

But they weren't that intimidating. Sergeant Miles had told his class that giants were very rare, yet magic or determination could take one down very quickly. They had the same vulnerabilities as a human, only magnified. Breaking their kneecaps was even more effective than doing it to a normal-sized human, if only because gravity dragged them to the ground hard enough to make the damage worse.

On the other hand, Emily thought, *would someone seeing a giant have time to realize how to take one down?*

Unlike the previous valley, there were only a handful of massive trees looming over the remains of the long-dead giant. Instead, there were smaller bushes and plants that seemed to be laid out in a complex pattern. It reminded Emily of some of the plantations near Dragon's Den, where alchemical ingredients were produced for Whitehall and the local alchemists. Someone had clearly created a plantation of her own...whatever else she was, Mother Holly was clearly a capable brewer. But how much training did she actually have?

Emily stared at the skeleton for a long moment before following the snake down the rocky path. She heard a stream in the distance, but she couldn't see the water, no matter how hard she looked. The snake projected impressions of wariness at her as the scent from the plants grew stronger, making her head swim. Emily gritted her teeth, cursed her oversight and cast a spell intended to filter out the scent. The dancing poppies ahead of her, blowing in the wind, were a prime ingredient in sleeping potions. Breathing in too much would be enough to send them into a coma.

"Try not to breathe too deeply," she advised, as they pressed further into the maze. "This place could be dangerous."

"They said that people went to see her when they were desperate," Rudolf said. "How did they escape the plants?"

Emily shrugged. A damp cloth would be enough, if the victim reacted quickly. Or perhaps they just fell asleep, then Mother Holly pulled them out of the plantation and helped them to recover. It wouldn't take long for the effects to wear off, once they were out of the aroma. She couldn't sense any wards, but some herbalists had a sixth sense for the condition of their gardens. Mother Holly might have the inclination, even if she didn't have the training.

She knelt down beside the suffering snake and picked it up, absently. Rudolf let out a strangled sound, staring at her in absolute horror. Emily blinked in surprise, then remembered the rotting touch. But the snake felt harmless in her palm...she stared down at it, feeling no pain at all. The familiar bond, she realized as she shook in relief, protected her from its poison.

The snake licked her finger, then gave her a heavy-lidded look and a series of impressions that suggested tiredness. Emily worked the spell that transfigured it back into a bracelet, then returned it to her arm.

Rudolf's mouth worked frantically, but no words came out. From his point of view, she'd just picked up the most dangerous snake in the world and held it, without losing a hand.

"I have a link with it," she said. She honestly hadn't realized the danger...because the link had ensured that there was *no* danger. "Don't try to pick it up yourself."

She hid her amusement as they picked their way down the path. Rudolf had asked her to marry him...but he was probably having second thoughts, after seeing her pet. And the connection she had with it. No one would question a death by Death Viper. Everyone knew the snakes couldn't be tamed.

Unless, of course, one forged a mental link out of desperation.

The sound of running water grew louder as they stepped into a clearing with a series of carefully-organized ponds. Emily glanced at one and saw...*things*...swimming through the water. Fish, she knew, were often chopped up and used as potions ingredients. Another held tiny crabs, the mere sight of them sending a chill down her spine. Smashing them up for alchemical research wasn't her favorite activity. Professor Thande assigned the preparation of various disgusting ingredients instead of using the cane whenever he wanted to punish someone. Emily had a feeling that most of his students would have preferred to be caned.

"This place is a tiny farm," she said, as they walked past the ponds and into another clump of plants. "Some of these are magical, some serve as the neutral baseline for specific potions."

Rudolf looked around, carefully. "How many hedge witches are there?"

Emily had no idea, and said so. Hedge witches were usually solitary creatures, unwilling or unable even to talk with their fellows. It seemed odd that one person could have done all this, but Mother Holly was supposed to be ancient...and she'd presumably had a mentor. Maybe the hidden valley was far older than it looked, or maybe Mother Holly had friends and allies. There was no way to know.

They passed through a final set of plants and stopped, staring at the house at the center of the valley. It looked, on the surface, like any of the other hovels she'd seen in the villages, but it seemed to have drawn trees and bushes into the wooden walls. Emily took a step forward, reaching out with her senses...

She recoiled at the dark magic she sensed surrounding the hovel, powerful and threatening. She held up a hand to stop Rudolf, then got her staff out of her pocket and enlarged it. Rudolf nodded in understanding as Emily advanced forward, trying to feel the shape of the wards. They were tainted with dark magic, but not as complex as some of the tricks she'd encountered in Blackhall.

She looked around, carefully. There hadn't been any warning ward, as far as she'd been able to tell, but Mother Holly might well have sensed their presence. If, of course, she was inside the building. Even if she wasn't...she might have sensed something. How closely were the wards tied to her?

"I need to break the wards," she said, to Rudolf. "Keep an eye out for trouble."

Rudolf snorted. "You mean something more dangerous than what we've found already?"

"Mother Holly herself," Emily said. If the hedge witch was innocent, which was starting to look rather unlikely, she would be understandably upset at discovering two youngsters trying to break into her home. She could legally do whatever she wanted to them—she could do *anything* to them, if she had the power to do it. "Let me know the moment anything changes."

She stepped forward and tapped her magic against the wards. Sergeant Miles had taught her that it was a way of ringing the doorbell, if there was a ward in place to alert the owner that she had visitors. Emily waited for several moments, but nothing happened. Carefully, balancing the staff on its tip, she walked forward and started to untangle the wards.

They snapped and spat at her as she worked. Most of them were basic, barely enough to repel a mundane visitor, but some of the more complex ones were *nasty*, tapping into very dark magic indeed. Two of them were even outside her experience and she had to work frantically to counter a series of hexes that would have caused her permanent injury if she failed to block them in time. The wards were wasteful and ill-designed, but she had to admit that they were craftier than they seemed.

Still, a trained magician like Lady Barb should have had no difficulty breaking in. *But*, she asked herself, *was the real problem breaking out?*

There was a final flash of multicolored balefire—Rudolf gasped in shock—then the wards snapped out of existence.

Emily paused to catch her breath. If Mother Holly was innocent, they would be in some trouble. Rudolf stepped forward as she picked up her staff and leaned on it, reaching out for the door. Emily hissed at him to stop just before he touched it.

"Let me test everything first," she ordered. If there was one thing she had learned from Blackhall, it was that the big showy threat might mask something more dangerous. "You could touch something one moment and find yourself a frog the next."

But there was no charm on the door, at least as far as she could tell. She used her staff to nudge it open, then peered inside, half-expecting something to jump out at her.

But there was nothing inside, apart from darkness...and a stench that made her recoil. There were no windows, nothing to provide any illumination at all. Bracing herself, fearful of any reaction from undiscovered defenses, Emily crafted a globe of light and sent it bobbing into the room.

"Interesting," Rudolf said, one eye on the ball of light. "What else can you do?"

Emily ignored the question as the light illuminated the interior of the hovel. It was messy, as if Mother Holly had stopped caring about housekeeping. A large fireplace sat in one corner, a black cauldron positioned over it, while the tables were covered with herbs and half-dissected animals. Several bottles were placed on top of the table, their lids removed and protective spells destroyed. She guessed they were the bottles stolen from Lord Gorham's town.

She created a second light globe and sent it bobbing over towards the pile of blankets at the far edge of the room. Had Mother Holly slept there? She felt another stab of sympathy, which she angrily repressed. Unless she was dreadfully mistaken, Mother Holly was responsible for the death of at least twenty children, as well as trying to enchant Rudolf and his father. What sort of pity did she deserve?

None, she told herself. The only pity Emily could or would offer Mother Holly was a quick death. She'd become too dangerous to leave alive. It didn't escape her that some people in the Allied Lands believed the same of Emily herself. After all, there were dark rumors that Emily was a necromancer herself.

She pushed the thought aside as she saw something concealed under the blankets. Bracing herself, she reached down and pushed the blankets aside, keeping a wary eye out for traps. The blankets stank, but there were no other defenses, allowing her to uncover the skull. It sparked a memory in her mind; Yodel had told her, back when they'd first met, that some magicians stored their memories, even their personalities, in skulls, waiting for someone to find them and put them to work. There were even stories, cautionary tales, of magicians who primed their skulls to decant their personalities into the first idiot who touched them. It provided a kind of life after death.

Careful not to touch the skull with either her bare hand or magic, she used the blankets to pick up the skull and deposit it on the table. Up close, there were a handful of runes carved into the skull, only two of which she recognized. One of them would keep the skull intact, no matter what happened, the other would feed a faint trickle of magic into the skull, holding the enchanted personality firmly in place. Bracing herself, expecting a backlash of some kind, she used a simple detection spell and found...nothing.

"No magic," she said, puzzled.

Rudolf came over to stand behind her. "Is that a bad thing?"

"I don't know," Emily confessed. "The skull was once home to a magician's personality, but it doesn't seem to have endured."

She looked down at the skull, contemplatively. Was it a fake? Or something Mother Holly had been trying to make work? Or had the personality sunk into Mother Holly, leaving the skull empty? It was possible, wasn't it? But all the cautionary tales she'd read had suggested that the skull would remain dangerous indefinitely.

Rudolf swore. Emily turned and followed his gaze, staring into another corner. A body lay on the ground, one too small to be anything other than a baby. Sickened, Emily crept closer, directing the light globe to hover over the child's body. The most obvious wound was a stab to the heart, but there were several others, all of which might prove fatal to a baby. Dark magic surrounded the corpse, clinging to the dead body like a living thing.

"I thought we could save the child," Rudolf said. He sounded stunned, as if he didn't quite believe what he was seeing. His voice was almost plaintive. "But why did she need a *child*?"

Emily swallowed. The answer was obvious; Mother Holly hadn't been looking for magical power, but life force. A trained magician would be the most promising source of the former, yet a newborn baby would be the best source of the latter. After all, a baby had his or her entire life to enjoy. She shook her head, unwilling to discuss the possibility. Lady Barb had been right, again. In the long run, transferring life force might be even more dangerous to the Allied Lands than necromancy.

"I don't know," Emily lied. The skull's face seemed to mock her as she looked at it. Had it decanted something—or someone—into Mother Holly's head...or was it just a repository of information?

"So," Rudolf said, as she returned the skull to its hiding place. "What else can we do? Where else can we *go*?"

Emily hesitated. There was no trace of Mother Holly—or Lady Barb. She briefly considered releasing the snake again, then realized that she already knew where to look next.

"The castle," she said, softly.

Throwing caution to the winds, she stood in the middle of the hovel and cast a powerful magic detection charm. The skull showed no reaction, while some of the potions ingredients glowed faintly—and a bright glow could be seen from a hidden drawer. Emily opened it carefully, disarming a nasty protective hex as she moved, and swore aloud as she produced the book. Like some of the grimoires preserved in Whitehall's library, it was made from human skin and written in blood. The magician who'd written it, she suspected, might even have used his *own* blood. Once he was dead, the book would be bonded to his family line...

No, that couldn't be right, she told herself. Mother Holly wasn't related to a magician, was she? But there was no way to know.

She picked up the book, carefully, and opened it. There was no table of contents, forcing her to inspect each spell one by one. Some of them were surprisingly common, used at Whitehall; others were deadly dangerous. One of them was a compulsion spell so powerful that the victim wouldn't have a hope of resisting, once the magician had obtained a sample of his blood. It reminded her of the spell Shadye had used on her, years ago. Others told her how to blind a disobedient child or turn him into a toad; make a woman permanently barren or nothing more than a slave; cripple a man or give him permanent bad luck...the writer, she realized, had been filled with hatred and malice towards the world. The evil the book could have caused was terrifying. And most of the people in the mountains would be absolutely defenseless.

And, when the writer had finally died, he'd meant his malice to live on.

The final spell was alarmingly familiar. It was the basic necromantic rite.

"We have to take this with us," Emily said, placing the book under her arm. "And we have to go to the castle."

Rudolf gave her a sharp look. "Are you sure?"

"I don't know where else to go," Emily said, simply. Had Lady Barb gone to the castle after searching the hovel? There was no sign of a fight. But somehow Emily doubted that Lady Barb would have missed the grimoire. "If we can't find her there..."

She refused to consider the possibility as she led the way outside, into the slowly darkening sky. Clouds were gathering overhead, threatening to pour rain on their heads. Emily cast a protective charm over the book, wondering if she should destroy it. But she couldn't bring herself to destroy any book, no matter how evil. Instead, she kept it under her arm, despite her fears. The book was surrounded by magic that might seek to do her harm.

Rudolf followed her outside. "And what if we can't get into the castle?"

"You go back to your father and alert him," Emily said, nettled. She didn't want to consider the possibility of failure. "I go down to the Allied Lands and call for help."

Moments later, the first raindrops started to fall.

Chapter Thirty-Five

EMILY HAD INTENDED NOT TO RISK USING MAGIC TO SHIELD THEM FROM THE RAIN, BUT within moments she realized that she had no choice. The downpour grew so rapidly that their clothes were drenched within minutes, while visibility fell so badly she could barely see more than a foot or two ahead of her and thunder crackled in the sky overhead. If she hadn't been so determined to reach the castle, she would have found a place for them to hole up and wait for the storm to end.

She cast another protective charm on the grimoire, then looked over at Rudolf. He looked like a drowned rat–she knew she probably didn't look much better–but was grimly determined to follow her to the castle. Emily briefly considered suggesting that he took the book back to the guesthouse, then reminded herself that Rudolf wouldn't be able to get through the wards and into the building. Bringing him with her was risky, but she suspected he wouldn't go quietly if she asked him to go back to the village.

The rain grew stronger, beating against her wards and washing against her feet. Any tracks that might have been left would be obliterated, she realized numbly. There was no proof that Lady Barb had actually reached the castle. Coming to think of it, she thought sourly, there was no proof Lady Barb had ever entered the hovel. She might have been waylaid somewhere just outside the building.

"She could have rebuilt the wards," Rudolf pointed out. "And *then* gone to the castle."

Emily had her doubts. Lady Barb was far more skillful with magic than Emily, but rebuilding Mother Holly's complex series of wards would be very difficult–and besides, she'd left the grimoire in place. And there had been no trace of her magic in the wards. No, Emily decided, Lady Barb had *not* gone into the hovel. So where had she gone?

She paused in thought. There had been no sign of a battle outside the shack. Lady Barb wouldn't have gone quietly, certainly not to a hedge witch, so what had happened to her?

Emily briefly considered releasing the Death Viper and inspecting the rest of the plantation, but it would probably be useless. The ground would be sodden by now, all tracks and scents utterly destroyed. It was a marvel that the plants had lasted long enough under the bombardment of rain to supply generations of hedge witches.

"I don't think so," she said. Lady Barb was still bound by her oaths. If she encountered a grimoire, she was required to confiscate it at once. Instead, she'd just left it in the hovel–if, of course, she had seen it at all. Emily suspected she hadn't seen the cursed book. "I think something happened to her along the way."

She jumped as a row of small animals ran across the path and into the undergrowth. Rudolf didn't seem too surprised; Emily guessed he was used to it. As an aristocrat, he could spend time hunting while peasants worked; he'd probably spent weeks out in the countryside, merely enjoying himself. But Rudolf was an only son.

Like many of the older noble children of Zangaria, surely he would be expected to spend time learning to rule.

"Father always said that all he needed was an awareness of the realities," Rudolf said. "He never wanted me to learn to read."

Emily shuddered. It still surprised her that so many people had been unable to read, even in the script the Allied Lands had used before she'd introduced English letters. Magicians could generally read—Whitehall offered classes for students—but the other segments of society were largely illiterate. No wonder the Scribes Guild had got away with so much for so long.

"You should learn," she said, although she suspected the words would fall on deaf ears. On Earth, reading might be a gateway to countless other worlds, but the books simply didn't exist in the Allied Lands. Not yet. "It can be quite helpful."

Rudolf snorted and changed the subject. "Shouldn't we get help to storm the castle?"

Emily looked at him. "From whom?"

"My father..."

His voice trailed off. It would take at least two days to get his father's troops to Easter...and that would be too long. Emily wondered, absently, if he'd ever considered arming the peasants and sending *them* against the castle, but it was the sort of tactic that only worked in bad vampire movies. In the real world, any magician could deal with an angry mob and—if the magician happened to be a necromancer—use them as a power source. They'd just be giving the enemy more targets.

And Lord Gorham is still too ill to lead his troops, in any case, Emily thought.

"If you want to go back to your father and ask," she said, "you can. But it won't make much difference."

Rudolf scowled at her. It took Emily a moment to realize she'd effectively accused him of being a coward, a sure-fire invitation to a duel in the Allied Lands. For Rudolf, given his leanings, the suggestion had to sting. Emily mentally rolled her eyes. There was nothing wrong with being scared of a necromancer, not when even the most powerful magician would think twice before challenging one. She was scared herself.

"Come on," Rudolf said, stalking past her. "We need to get there before the rain stops."

Emily concealed her amusement as she followed him up the rocky path. The castle was a dark brooding shape in the distance, larger than Lord Gorham's castle but much more vulnerable. Thankfully, the designer hadn't seen the merits of placing it on top of a needle of rock, with only one way to reach the entrance. Even so, it was still a forbidding shape.

"Stop there," she called, as they reached the edge of the path. "Let me check for surprises first."

Rudolf looked impatient, but paused.

Emily gritted her teeth as she sensed the first ward surrounding the castle. It wasn't anchored properly, nothing like the wards surrounding Lady Barb's home, and there was something about it that puzzled her. She probed it, carefully, and realized that it didn't seem to be attached to any warning system. It could just be taken down...and no one would notice.

Emily shook her head in disbelief before probing further. A second ward was nestled behind the first, monitoring its existence. If she crossed or took down the first ward, it was the second that would sound the alarm.

"Clever," she muttered. She'd seen something comparable in Blackhall—and had been caught, every second time she'd attempted to sneak through. "And we don't have any blood this time."

Rudolf gave her a sharp look. "Blood?"

"You can trick a ward if you have blood from someone keyed into their structure," Emily said, absently. She'd done it herself in Zangaria, but those wards hadn't been linked into a magician's mind. They certainly hadn't been smart enough to notice that one person was in two separate places at the same time. "But we don't have any, so it doesn't matter."

She probed further, satisfied herself that there wasn't a third ward monitoring the first two, then looked up at Rudolf. "When I start moving," she ordered, "follow me as closely as possible."

Rudolf nodded. Emily took a breath, then reached out with her magic and touched the first ward. Breaking it would have been simple—it was a very basic design—but that would have alerted the second ward. Instead, she twisted the ward, praying silently that the second ward was incapable of noticing anything less dramatic than the first ward snapping out of existence. But then, it would be tricky to program for *every* contingency without a nexus for power.

She took a step forward, then another and another, bending and twisting the ward around them. Rudolf followed her, his breath touching the back of her neck, unaware of the complex interplay of magic surrounding him. Emily let out a breath as the first ward snapped back into place, seemingly unaware of being warped out of shape. The second ward did nothing in response. As far as Emily could tell, they'd made it through without being detected.

"The gates are locked," Rudolf observed, as Emily caught her breath. She was sweating, despite the cold. The effort had taken more out of her than she'd expected. "But we could climb the walls."

Emily looked up at the smooth stone and shivered. Sergeant Miles had taught her how to climb—she'd been up and down structures she would have sworn were impossible to climb before his training—but the walls of the castle seemed too dangerous to risk. One gust of wind and they would be sent falling to their deaths. But there was no way through the gates either, she realized, grimly. The guards would know they'd broken through the wards and alert their superiors.

She took the bracelet off and placed it on the ground. Rudolf gave it a wary look, clearly expecting her to send the snake through the portcullis to kill the guards. Emily doubted it would work. The guards might well be innocent...and, in any case, the wards would probably monitor their condition. She dared not make any assumptions about what the wards would or would not consider alarming. Mother Holly wasn't a properly-trained magician.

The best swordsman in the world doesn't fear the second best, Sergeant Miles had said. *He fears the worst, because he doesn't know what the idiot will do.*

Emily looked up at the battlements. It was hard to be sure, but there didn't look to be any guards up there. But then, in this weather they were probably hiding in the guardhouse. She shaped a plan in her mind, then looked at Rudolf. Some magicians would have pushed ahead without asking, but she knew how badly it would hurt him if she did. She wasn't one of those magicians.

"I can turn you into something small, then turn myself into a bird and carry us both up there," she said. She would have to carry the snake-bracelet in any case. Transfiguring something into one form and then into another could have dangerous side effects. They'd been taught never to do it, unless there was no other choice. "Unless you really think you can climb up there?"

Rudolf looked torn. Emily left him to think about it while she buried the grimoire, then left a couple of protective and concealment spells to ensure that it remained unharmed—and undiscovered. Like most people, Rudolf probably dreaded the thought of being transfigured, particularly as he had no way to reverse the spell himself. But climbing up the walls might prove impossible. If Mother Holly had established wards, she might have worked a few nasty surprises into the walls, too. Whitehall certainly had a few tricks to deter students from climbing the walls.

"Do it," he said.

Emily felt a surge of respect and admiration as she cast the spell. Rudolf shank and became a small statue of himself. Emily gritted her teeth, then sat down and cast the second spell. Her vision warped and twisted; she closed her eyes too late to stop her seeing feathers growing out of her hands. When she opened them again, she was staring through the eyes of a hawk.

She picked up the bracelet in her beak, then the statue in one claw and took off, feeling the winds gusting around her. The hawk's mind seemed to love the thunderstorm, even though Emily's human awareness was tempted to panic. She'd never flown before coming to Whitehall, but being on a dragon's back was far superior to flying under her own power. Maybe it would have been different if she'd been able to fly on a broom.

The hawk's mind screamed at her as she dropped towards the battlements, sweeping the stonework with eyes that were so sharp she could see tiny marks on the stone. It didn't like trying to land, but Emily forced it down. She didn't dare let go of herself, not now. It wasn't possible to protect her mind from a spell she'd cast on herself. If she fell into the hawk's mind, no one would ever see her again.

There were no guards on the battlements, she realized, as she finally forced the hawk to land and released the spell. She slipped, almost at once, and barely managed to catch herself before either dropping her cargo or falling over the edge. The hawk's eyes had seen the battlements as more than large enough to protect her, but in truth they were barely larger than something from a model village. Desperately, Emily crawled forward until she was lying on flat stone. The designer of the castle, she realized, hadn't really given any thought to protecting the soldiers on the roof. They might be blown off by a gust of wind if they got careless.

Carefully, she returned the bracelet to her wrist and released the spell on Rudolf, using a minor sticking hex to hold him in place until he had gathered himself, his eyes wide and staring. Emily felt a shiver of guilt, which she ruthlessly suppressed. Rudolf wasn't unaware that he lived in a world where magicians could turn men into swine with a wave of their hands, but he'd never experienced anything like this until now. How could he take it in stride? But there had been no alternative...

"The guardhouse," Rudolf said. He pointed towards a small stone hut; Emily couldn't help thinking of a penthouse perched on top of a skyscraper. "The stairs will be hidden inside."

Slipping and sliding, they made their way to the door. Rudolf opened it—and came face to face with a guard. He cocked his fist as Emily readied a spell, then hesitated. The guard was standing still, as if he was utterly unaware of their presence. He didn't even show any reaction as Rudolf waved a hand in front of his face.

"He's under a spell," Emily said, softly. "I don't think he can see us."

Rudolf gave her a sharp look. "Are you sure of that?"

"...No," Emily admitted.

She studied the guard's blank expression thoughtfully. There were upper-level obedience and loyalty spells that were so powerful that they damaged their victim's mind, leaving them little more than robots, even if they had been forced to accept the spells. Could Mother Holly have enchanted the whole castle? It would be simple enough, Emily decided, assuming that the hedge witch had long lost any moral objections she might have had to taking someone's free will. Lady Easter could just have called her guards in, one by one, to be enchanted.

But is she doing it of her own free will, Emily wondered, *or is she merely the first victim?*

"Leave him," she said. She braced herself, then squeezed past the guard, uncomfortably aware of his body pressing against hers. He showed no reaction at all. "Hurry."

Rudolf followed her as she found the stairwell leading down into the castle. It looked almost painfully cramped, just like some of the stairwells in Zangaria. An attacking force that happened to get over the walls would still have to advance one by one into the castle itself. And they probably couldn't swing their swords properly inside the stairwell.

"Let me take the lead," Rudolf said. "You're probably more capable of helping me than I am of helping you."

Emily watched as he stepped into the stairwell, then followed, feeling claustrophobic as the stairs led down and down. There was almost no lighting, leaving her feeling her way forward. If she'd worn a dress, she might well have tripped and fallen down the stairs.

By the time they reached the bottom, she was on the verge of creating another light globe and to hell with stealth. Rudolf sucked in his breath sharply as he stepped out into another guardroom. There were more guards waiting for them. But they didn't move.

"They're under a spell, too," Rudolf said.

Emily nodded as she followed him out into the guardroom. There were five men, wearing light suits of armor, standing in the room. They showed no reaction to the intruders, not even when Emily walked over to the other door and opened it. Outside, she saw a servant marching through the corridor, eyes as blank and unseeing as the guards. She couldn't help thinking of the Borg from *Star Trek*. They'd ignored intruders on their starships until the intruders had posed a threat.

"I could smuggle an entire army past them," Rudolf muttered, as he joined her in the corridor. "What's the point of keeping them all under control like this?"

Emily shrugged. "A magician wouldn't need an army," she said, although she knew it wasn't strictly accurate. Shadye had produced an army of monsters to attack Whitehall. "But if these guards are loyal to Lady Easter, they might react badly if they knew she was under outside control."

The interior of the castle wasn't as bare as Lord Gorham's castle. Tapestries hung everywhere, each one showing an achievement of Lady Easter and her three daughters. Emily would have thought they were propaganda if it hadn't been for the fact that no one outside the castle staff would see them. Or maybe the guards and soldiers were expected to admire them and understand that while Lady Easter had the body of a weak and feeble woman, she had the skill and determination to do well by her tiny kingdom.

Would that have been enough, Emily asked herself, *if Rudolf had married one of her daughters? Or would the guards have switched their loyalty to him at once?*

They stopped when they reached a large chamber. A throne, painted gold, sat at one end, while a large stone table was placed in the center of the room. Emily froze as she heard singing, then dragged Rudolf to one side, hastily casting concealment spells over them both. As long as they were quiet, she muttered, they should remain undetected.

It was only just in time.

Chapter Thirty-Six

THREE GIRLS LED THE WAY, WEARING LONG WHITE DRESSES THAT WERE TIED AROUND THEIR waists with rune-sewn cloths. All three of them were singing softly, chanting words that Emily didn't recognize, their faces blank and almost motionless. There was something about their appearance that reminded Emily of Alassa, save for the birthmarks all three of them had on their faces, just below their left eyes. Lady Easter's daughters, Emily guessed.

Rudolf tensed beside her. His father had tried to force him into marriage with a brainwashed girl.

He'd described the oldest girl as ugly. Emily didn't see it; the oldest girl looked plain, but very far from ugly. Her face was pale, as if she hadn't seen the sun since the day she was born, while long dark hair cascaded down her back. The white dress, almost translucent, revealed that her breasts were high and firm, bigger than both of her sisters. Emily suspected, rather cynically, that if Rudolf hadn't been homosexual he would have found far fewer complaints about the marriage.

The two younger girls weren't really prettier, she decided. One of them had dark hair too, while the other had red hair that hung down to her shoulders. Unlike her sisters, she didn't seem to want to go in for the long hair that was traditional for aristocrats, probably deciding that it was a pain to wash. Emily privately suspected that the fashion was just another way to control women; they were forced to spend hours washing and dressing or they wouldn't look fashionable. Thankfully, magic made personal grooming a great deal easier.

She watched as the three girls, still singing, came to a halt beside the stone table. Moments later, an older woman entered, her back as straight and stiff as a board. Emily glanced into her eyes, very briefly, and saw a furious struggle taking place inside the older woman's mind. Lady Easter wasn't a willing participant in what was going on, she realized numbly. Mother Holly had laid compulsion spell after compulsion spell on her until it was a miracle she could still resist, even if only mentally. Her body did as it was commanded by the hedge witch.

Lady Easter sat on her throne, eyes locked on the stone table. Emily studied her for a long moment, wondering if she dared try to cancel the spells, then turned her attention back to the entrance, just in time to see a young girl enter. She looked to be about twelve, young enough to be innocent, old enough to be poised on the edge of womanhood. Like the others, she wore a long white dress, her face scrubbed clean, then carefully made up by experts. There was a vacant expression on her face that suggested she was drugged rather than under any form of magical compulsion. Emily gritted her teeth as the girl inched towards the stone table, then was helped to climb onto the stone by the three daughters.

The magic field rippled suddenly as Mother Holly entered the room. Emily had never seen her before, but she couldn't be anyone else. She walked like an old woman, she had the face of an old woman, yet her body seemed to be middle-aged at most.

Rudolf trembled beside Emily, either in fear or in anger, and she caught his arm before he could do something stupid.

She focused her attention on Mother Holly. Why did she look so *old*? Emily puzzled over it for a long moment before deciding the rituals that stripped children of their life force had been misapplied. Or maybe Mother Holly just wasn't vain enough to try to rejuvenate her face as well as her body. There were sorceresses who didn't care about their appearance, just as there were sorceresses who wasted hours rejuvenating themselves or applying careful glamors.

But there was something deeply wrong with the old woman, she realized. Her face twisted constantly, moving from a faintly regretful expression to an expression that delighted in the pain and fear she was inflicting. The woman's hands twitched constantly, as if she was on the verge of casting a spell, while her long white hair moved in odd patterns. Emily couldn't help thinking of gorgons, except there were no snakes in place of hair. There was nothing, as far as she knew, that could account for such an effect. Maybe she was having a reaction to all the magic she was using.

Mother Holly walked up to the throne, passing close enough to the hidden couple to touch, then turned and faced the table. Two guards appeared, both wearing black robes, carrying Lady Barb between them. Emily had to cover her mouth to stifle a horrified gasp. Lady Barb had been beaten bloody, then chained so heavily that she could barely stand upright -- hands cuffed behind her back, chains encircling her ankles. And a nasty, but familiar, scent wafted over the room...

Emily cursed mentally as she realized what must have happened. There was a potion that damped a person's magic, at least for a few hours, rendering them helpless. Emily had been forced to drink it, two years ago.

They forced her to drink it, she thought, fighting to keep from springing out to help her mentor. *They wouldn't have been able to batter her halfway to death if they hadn't stolen her magic...*

She shuddered. And now Lady Barb had no magic, not as long as they kept forcing her to drink the potion...

She switched her attention to the guards, resisting the urge to leap out and attack the old witch. One of them looked as blank as the other guards, obeying orders robotically, while the other seemed to be practically shaking with horror. Emily looked into his eyes and realized that the guard had seen terrible things. She wondered if they could count on him as a possible ally, but dismissed the thought. The guard was too terrified to do anything but watch helplessly, no matter what happened.

The horrible spell book had talked about spells to terrify people into servitude. Perhaps Mother Holly had tested one on the guard, only to discover that it rendered him largely useless. And then she'd just left him that way...

Emily heard a loud thump as the door slammed closed. The chamber was sealed.

"Well," Mother Holly said. Her gaze was fixed firmly on Lady Barb. "You came to restore the old order."

Lady Barb showed no reaction. Emily cringed, mentally. Just how badly had the older woman been hurt? She didn't look to have any broken bones, but someone could be beaten into submission without breaking any bones. The bruises suggested that she'd been worked over by experts, using everything from their bare hands to the flat of their blades. Blood had dried on her bare flesh.

"But you have failed," Mother Holly said, when Lady Barb showed no reaction. "The old order has failed."

Lady Barb coughed, then spat. Emily couldn't avoid noticing she'd spat blood.

"You are messing with powers you don't understand," Lady Barb said. Her voice was strong enough to hold attention, despite the beating. "You have to stop this."

Mother Holly stepped forward until she was standing in front of the table, looking down at the young girl. "I have seen too many aristocrats"—the word was a curse—"abuse the common folk," she snapped. "Why should I not wage war on them?"

"You're killing more commoners than the aristocrats ever did," Lady Barb pointed out. "I know you've taken at least twenty children—and I'd bet you took more. How can you justify *that* to yourself?"

For a moment, Emily thought the question had started to unravel Mother Holly's determination to proceed. Her face shifted rapidly, as if there were two personalities struggling for control. She must have done *something* to the skull, draining it of the personality its creator had left in place.

What if the personality had tried to overwhelm Mother Holly, only to come to a draw? Or perhaps they were still fighting.

"I have watched peasants starve because they are not allowed to keep enough food for winter," Mother Holly said. "I have watched girls taken into the high castles because they are pretty. I have watched boys beaten for daring to go too close to the castle and older men crippled for trying to hunt for food. I will do whatever it takes to prevent the aristocrats from abusing their subjects."

Emily puzzled over it. If that was the case, why hadn't she killed Lord Gorham and Rudolf, rather than trying to control them? And why try to have Rudolf marry Lady Easter's daughter? Unless...perhaps the objective was to give the mountains a single royal family once again? There would be fewer people trying to claim tax, for one thing, and it would be far easier for Mother Holly to control them.

"I will break your mind if you refuse to pledge your servitude to me," Mother Holly hissed as she produced a knife from her belt. A wave of dark magic washed across the room. Emily didn't need to see the knife directly to know that it was made from grey stone. "And what is left of you will never be found."

"Go to the devils," Lady Barb said. She managed to stand up straighter, despite the chains, looking Mother Holly right in the eye. "You're already halfway there."

Mother Holly snarled and raised the knife, ready to plunge it into the girl's chest. Rudolf moved before Emily could stop him, throwing himself at Mother Holly's back. She turned, surprised, as the concealment spells snapped. They couldn't hide someone who drew attention to himself. Rudolf barely made it halfway to her before his entire body froze and he fell to the ground.

Emily cursed and hastily returned her staff to normal size. Mother Holly stared at her, lifting her hand. Emily threw herself to one side as a fireball rocketed past her and struck the far wall, setting fire to one of the tapestries.

She channeled her power through the staff despite the risks, trying to use a basic freeze spell on Mother Holly. A wave of raw magic deflected her spell, followed by another that yanked the staff out of her hand and sent it flying across the room. Emily shaped another spell in her mind, but it was too late. A third wave of magic caught her, picking her up and holding her upside down, hanging helplessly in front of Mother Holly.

"Well," Mother Holly said. Up close, her breath stank—and there were faint hints of red light in her eyes. Emily remembered Shadye and shuddered. "Who might you be?"

She cast a spell that made magic crackle around Emily, but nothing happened. Mother Holly repeated the question; Emily braced herself to resist a compulsion… yet there was nothing.

It took her a moment to realize that the spell Void had given her, the spell that made it impossible for her to be forced to share her secrets with the world, was still protecting her.

Mother Holly frowned, motioning with her hand. Emily found herself slammed to the ground, then trapped flat against the floor. Leaving Emily there, Mother Holly picked up Rudolf, cast a spell on him, then started to ask questions. Rudolf answered them, helplessly.

"Your apprentice," Mother Holly said to Lady Barb. "Wouldn't *she* make an excellent sacrifice?"

She turned back to the table and nodded to the three daughters. The spell holding Emily to the floor snapped, but she couldn't really move very much. She gritted her teeth as the daughters pulled her up into a sitting position, then started to pull at Emily's clothes. One of them removed the bracelet, then Emily's shirt and carried them both away from the table.

Emily felt an odd moment of hope. If she took the bracelet too far from Emily…

There was a piercing shriek as the Death Viper returned to its normal form. The girl had been holding it, and the mere touch had burned her badly.

Mother Holly jumped as Emily felt one of Holly's compulsion spells snap. The girl was in so much pain that the spell had lost its grip on her completely. Her sisters seemed equally shocked.

Emily gathered all the strength she could, then thrust it against the spell keeping her down and weak. It snapped, too. She broke free, then slapped Rudolf hard on the head. The shock should help him recover from the charms Mother Holly had used on him—and besides, it was his fault they were in this mess.

She heard a yelp behind her. As she turned her head, one of the guards doubled over as Lady Barb pulled her hands free. Emily gaped at her, then turned just in time to dodge another fireball from Mother Holly. Her vision seemed to split in two for a second as the Death Viper sensed that she was in danger and went after Mother Holly, almost causing Emily to black out.

Mother Holly screamed with rage, then clutched her knife and brought it down on the helpless child. Emily didn't hesitate; she cast a spell and yanked the girl towards her, dropping her on the far edge of the chamber. Drugged as she was, the girl didn't even cry out as she hit the floor.

Got her out, Emily thought. *And now...*

Mother Holly twisted, then threw a whirling mess of a spell right into Emily's face. The sheer force of the impact picked her up and slammed her into the wall. Emily grunted in pain as she fell down and landed on her bottom, then picked herself up as another fireball flashed towards her. Heat scorched her hair as it passed over her and struck the wall.

Rudolf threw himself at Mother Holly—this time, the madwoman had no time to react before he struck her. But she recovered within seconds, casting a spell that turned him into a slug. Emily gasped in horror as Mother Holly lifted her boot, intending to squash him, then threw a fireball of her own. The madwoman stumbled backwards as it hit her wards.

Emily followed up with a twisting hex that required several moments of uninterrupted concentration to break. Mother Holly jumped to one side, throwing another blast of raw magic at Emily. The sheer level of power—Emily hadn't sensed anything like it since Shadye had died—slashed past her and smashed right *through* the walls.

The entire castle shook as stone crumbled into dust. Emily saw corridors ripped apart, followed by the main wall itself. In the distance, she heard the sound of falling masonry.

Outside, it was still dark. The wind blew rain right into the chamber. For a long moment, everything was still, as if no one could quite believe what had happened.

And then Lady Barb threw a piece of rock right at Mother Holly's head.

It should have killed her. Or at least knocked her out. But instead, all it seemed to have done was resolve the inner conflict in the madwoman's mind. The constant changes in expression were gone, leaving only one face, one personality, staring at them.

Another low rumble ran through the castle. It had been designed to weather the very worst storms, to stand tall and proud when gales whistled through the mountains and valleys, but it wasn't designed to stand up to magic. Emily heard the sound of something else crashing in the distance and wondered if the entire castle was about to fall down around their ears.

The madwoman stared at them, cold rage written all over her face. She lifted her hands, as if she intended to cast a spell, then there was another surge of magic. Emily ducked, bracing herself to evade, but the magic didn't leap out at her or anyone else. Instead, the madwoman floated into the air and flew right through the gap in the castle's walls. She cackled out loud as she made her escape, vanishing into the distance.

Emily threw a cancellation spell after her, hoping to send her plummeting to her death, but the spell either missed or didn't work.

She turned to look at Lady Barb. "Are you...are you all right?"

"You'll need to purge my system," Lady Barb said. "Don't worry about any of the bruises, just purge my body."

Emily nodded as Lady Barb sat down, still wearing the shackles around her ankles. She cast another cancellation charm at Rudolf, breaking the spell keeping him as a slug, then concentrated on Lady Barb. The purging spell was only meant to be used if someone had swallowed poison or a poorly-prepared potion, and she'd never liked using it.

The spell worked. Lady Barb shuddered, then vomited violently. Emily looked away as the older woman kept throwing up until she was dry-heaving. The stench made Emily want to be sick, too.

"We have to get after her," Lady Barb said, staggering to her feet. "She drained some of her power now, but she can repower herself..."

"She took the knife," Emily told her.

She looked around the room. The drugged girl looked to have fallen asleep, thankfully. One of the guards looked to have lost his mind completely—he was sitting on the ground, humming—while the other was groaning in pain. Rudolf looked badly shaken at just how easily he'd been defeated and almost killed. Lady Easter looked angry, somehow, while two of her daughters were desperately trying to tend to the third who'd been burned by Emily's familiar. And the Death Viper...

Emily looked around and discovered that it was lying next to her, waiting for attention. She turned it back into the bracelet and placed it on her wrist before anyone could start demanding that it be turned into potions' ingredients.

"The knife doesn't matter that much," Lady Barb reminded her. She waved her hand over her shirt, but it took several tries before the vomit fell to the ground, leaving her relatively clean. "We need to keep her away from prospective victims. Even one person would provide enough power to make her immensely dangerous."

She looked over at Lady Easter. "Send a guard to find my staff," she added. "We cannot give her time to escape."

Emily winced. Now that the personality conflict had been resolved, Mother Holly would be twice as dangerous...and she was already mad. Given time, a necromancer could rip the mountains apart.

And there was no one else who had even a hope in hell of stopping her.

Chapter Thirty-Seven

Emily talked rapidly as Lady Easter took control of her guards—most of whom seemed to have either snapped back to normal or collapsed—and directed them to bring Lady Barb her staff, some food and a change of clothes, perhaps not in that order. Lady Barb listened as she outlined what they'd found at Mother Holly's hovel, then swore as Emily described the skull.

"She must have tried to use it wrongly," Lady Barb said. "That's why she has a split personality."

Emily nodded. Mother Holly had claimed to be fighting for the common folk, but had stolen their children and used them as a power source. She would hardly be the first person to believe that the ends justified the means, or that there was nothing wrong with exploiting their own people because the cause was righteous, but it was still disappointing. Part of her was clearly more idealistic than she'd thought.

She looked over at Rudolf and wondered, absently, if he would make a good lord.

"Go see what you can do for the poor girl," Lady Barb ordered, as a guard returned with a change of clothing. "She'll lose that arm if she isn't very lucky."

Emily swallowed hard before walking over to the wounded girl. She was cradling her arm and sobbing quietly. The pain seemed to have faded, which wasn't necessarily a good thing. Death Viper venom spread so rapidly that it might well have destroyed the nerves that carried pain sensations to the brain. Emily knelt down beside the girl and winced as she saw the arm up close. It looked bruised and broken.

"Stay still," she advised, as she focused her mind. The venom remained dangerous to others, which was one of the reasons it was so deadly, but it shouldn't be dangerous to her. Or would that stay true if she wasn't actually touching the snake? It should— she hadn't wiped her hands after picking it up—yet she wasn't sure she wanted to test it. "Let me work on it."

She cursed as she used a spell to probe the extent of the damage. Thankfully, the girl had dropped the snake quickly enough to prevent the poison spreading all the way up her arm, but there was a good chance that she was going to lose it completely. Emily concentrated, carefully removed the poison, then winced as she realized there was no way to repair all the damage. Even magic couldn't rebuild an arm from scratch. The Allied Lands did have peg-legs and hooks, but she'd never seen a prosthetic arm.

Rudolf looked down at her, nervously. "Is there anything you can do?"

"I think I need a second opinion," Emily confessed. She waved frantically to Lady Barb, who was pulling a new shirt over her head. "Maybe Lady Barb can do something."

Lady Barb shook her head as soon as she saw the damage. "You could purge the body of poison, but not repair the wounds," she said. She looked up into the frightened girl's face. "We'll have to take the arm, completely."

Emily closed her eyes in pity. The girl—it struck her suddenly that she didn't even know the girl's *name*—would be permanently crippled, in a world that wasn't kind to the injured and disabled. And it was her fault for bringing the Death Viper into the castle. The girl hadn't asked to be mind-controlled into servitude, or used as a servant by a madwoman. She'd never had a choice at all.

Lady Barb poked her arm. "*Not* your fault," she said. "And don't you forget it."

Emily said nothing as Lady Barb carefully severed the arm from the rest of her body, then broke it down into dust. The girl started to cry again, helplessly. Rudolf eyed Lady Barb for a long moment, then sat down and took the girl in his arms. Somehow, the girl found it more comforting than Lady Barb's looming presence.

The castle shook again, very gently, as the wind battered against the damaged walls. "This place will have to be evacuated," Lady Barb said, standing up. "Take your people and get them down to the town."

Lady Easter nodded and started to issue orders to her guards. A long line of guards, servants and conscripted soldiers filed through the room, heading out. Emily rolled her eyes as several of the maids arrived, carrying a stretcher, which they used to help carry the injured girl out of the castle. She prayed silently that the wind wouldn't send them falling like ninepins before they reached safety, if there was any safety to be had in the town. The storm was only getting stronger.

Could it be Mother Holly's work? Weather manipulation was possible, but the books at Whitehall hadn't gone into detail about how it was actually done. Emily had a feeling that large-scale manipulation would require more than one magician, perhaps using a ritual like Lady Barb had shown her, yet there was no way to be sure. Necromancers might not work together, but they had enough raw power not to need to work in groups.

She took a piece of bread and cold meat from one of the servants and chewed it quickly, realizing—for the first time—just how ravenous she'd become. Lady Barb didn't press for them to move as they ate, suggesting that she was building up her strength, too. Once they finished eating, Lady Barb spoke briefly to Lady Easter, then motioned for Emily to follow her out of the castle. Rudolf started after them, but a sharp look from Lady Barb froze him in his tracks.

Outside, the wind was howling through the mountains, blowing rain into their faces. Both of the protective wards surrounding the castle had vanished, along with Mother Holly. Emily guessed that her burst of magic had shattered more than just the walls protecting the castle.

She cast a night vision spell, then found where she'd hidden the book and dug it up for Lady Barb. The older woman inspected it carefully, then swore for several minutes. Emily listened, silently committing several of the words to memory. Lady Barb had an impressive vocabulary.

"This shouldn't even be here," Lady Barb muttered, when she had finished swearing. "How did a hedge witch get her hands on *this*?"

Emily looked at her, silently casting protective wards to keep the rain from touching the book—or themselves. "Do you recognize it?"

Lady Barb hesitated, then made a visible decision to talk. "It doesn't have a name," she said, finally. "Most students of grimoires call it nothing more than *Malice*. The book doesn't just list hundreds of very unpleasant spells, it affects the mind of whoever tries to use the more complex hexes and curses. There are only five copies, as far as I know, and all five are under tight security. No one knew there was a sixth."

Emily swallowed as another possibility occurred to her. One could be missing and no one knew it. "What are you going to do with this copy?"

"I should be asking you," Lady Barb said. She passed the book back to Emily, who took it in surprise. "You captured the book."

"Oh," Emily said. "But I stole it."

Lady Barb shrugged. "I don't think the magician who crafted the book gave a hoot about stealing," she said. "All that matters is that you took possession of it. The magic woven into the book probably sees you as its owner now. If I tried to take it, the results might be unpleasant."

Emily frowned. "But I took it," she pointed out. "Why didn't it object to me taking it?"

"No way to know," Lady Barb said. "It depends what magic was woven into the book."

Magic, Emily thought. Every time she though she understood it, something happened to remind her that there were entire fields of magic beyond her understanding. Although, if the book had been written in the writer's blood, it was quite possible that it had absorbed more magic than a more normal book from Whitehall. Besides, the magician who had crafted the textbook might want it to move from weak magicians to more powerful ones.

"Besides, tradition says it belongs to you, too," Lady Barb added. "Just make sure you don't lose it."

Emily nodded and followed Lady Barb as she made her way down the slippery path. Water splashed around her ankles, washing down into the darkness. Emily shivered despite the protective wards. They were being thoroughly soaked.

"She won't have gone back home, will she?" Emily asked. "We know where she lives."

"Her place of power," Lady Barb answered, bluntly. She turned and gave Emily a grin, illuminated by a flash of lightning from high overhead. "If you ever feel the urge to fight the Grandmaster, *don't* do it in Whitehall. He's practically unbeatable as long as the wards protect him."

Emily nodded, remembering Sergeant Miles talking about how dangerous a magician's home could be. There could be so much magic flowing through the walls that the slightest mistake could have disastrous consequences. And magicians could legally do whatever they liked to anyone who tried to break through their wards.

Mother Holly, knowing that they would come after her, might well try to choose the battleground. A place where she had woven spells for years would give her a definite advantage.

"Maybe we should face her somewhere else," Emily said. She stopped as she realized the flaw in that plan. "But how do we get her elsewhere?"

Lady Barb smirked. "You don't," she said. "If she has any sense at all, she'll stay in her valley and build up her power."

"I didn't see anyone else there," Emily said. But she hadn't seen *all* of the valley—and Mother Holly could have transfigured her captives and then hidden them elsewhere for later sacrifice. She'd certainly had the power and knowledge to make such spells work. "Do you think she's completely lost it?"

"If she was under the influence, possibly," Lady Barb said, shortly. She stopped, then took hold of Emily's arm. When she spoke, her voice was deadly serious. "We cannot afford to hold back, Emily. If you get a clear shot at her, take it."

Emily felt the blood drain out of her face. She'd killed before, directly or indirectly, yet it always pained her—and she hoped it would *always* pain her. But Lady Barb was right. By now, Mother Holly had to be completely insane, utterly beyond reason. And, once she built up enough power, she might well become unstoppable. The only hope was to get to her before she could slaughter an entire village of innocent victims and use them for power.

She looked up at Lady Barb as the older woman let go of her. "Do you believe her? When she said she was trying to help people?"

Lady Barb hesitated, then made a face. "I believe that she might have believed, once upon a time, that she could improve the lot of the people around her," she said. "But necromancy"—she nodded to the book in Emily's hand—"and certain other kinds of magic have always made it harder to maintain a moral center. You should know that by now."

Emily nodded, doubtfully. She wasn't so sure. Most of the people in the village hadn't spoken highly of Mother Holly; they'd clearly been more than a little scared of her, not without reason. Something that had been a minor prank at Whitehall could be disastrous if used in the countryside, away from magicians who could repair the damage if necessary. Mother Holly had been shunned and excluded, merely for being what she was. Emily wouldn't have been too surprised if the madwoman saw preying on the town children as a form of revenge, even if she was reluctant to admit it to herself. Maybe she'd already been half-mad and that had given her some protections from the ravages of necromancy.

"But it doesn't matter," Lady Barb said, unaware of Emily's inner thoughts. "Whatever she was, whatever reason she used to start her rampage, she's become a monster—a deadly dangerous wild animal that needs to be put down. We have to stop her."

"I understand," Emily said, bracing herself. She clutched her staff in one hand, inserting spells. Lady Barb hadn't reacted to its presence at all, beyond a simple raised eyebrow. But, unlike some teachers at Whitehall, she wasn't the type to make a fuss when there was a valid reason for breaking the rules or disobeying orders. Emily knew she could expect a long talk about it in the future, but probably not any form of punishment. "Do you have a plan of attack?"

"Wear her down, force her to expend power and *keep moving*," Lady Barb said. "By now, she might be too far gone to form proper spells, but don't take that for granted.

Try and send your little friend to poison her, if possible. She might have passed beyond the stage where she can be poisoned."

Emily shuddered, remembering Shadye's obsession with the nexus under Whitehall. As far gone as he'd been, he needed a constant source of power just to stay alive, let alone complete his transformation into an eldritch abomination. The nexus would have provided such a source of power, she knew, or overloaded him so badly that the explosion would have devastated the country for hundreds of miles in all directions. But Shadye had been a necromancer for over a decade, as far as she knew. Maybe Mother Holly had only become a necromancer recently...

"We should call for help," she said. "Couldn't more magicians be teleported here?"

"Not easily," Lady Barb admitted. She shook her head as lightning flashed high overhead, illuminating the rocks surrounding them. "It would take far too long to organize a group of magicians to help."

Emily wished, bitterly, that she had some way of calling Void. Or the Grandmaster. Or even Master Grey, as unpleasant as he'd seemed. They *needed* help, but there was no one close enough to get to the mountains in time. And they'd wear themselves out teleporting into the valley...she shook her head, running her fingers through her damp hair. No, they were on their own. She looked over at Lady Barb and smiled.

"I meant to ask," she said, as another flash of lightning blasted through the sky. Each flash seemed to make it harder for night vision spells to work. "What happened to you?"

Lady Barb stiffened. "There was a trap for magicians near the hovel," she said. She sounded privately furious with herself. "I...I walked right into it."

Emily gaped at her. "*You* walked into a trap?"

"Don't rub it in," Lady Barb said, crossly. "Sergeant Miles definitely will."

She shook her head, sourly. "There was no magic in the trap at all," she added. "I didn't have anything to sense, so...it escaped my notice. If I'd thought through the implications of facing a hedge witch, with the limited power that implied, I would have been more careful."

Emily nodded, wishing she dared say something sympathetic. Some of the traps in Blackhall consisted of trapdoors or falling pieces of masonry...or even contact poisons on doorknobs and other items an unwary visitor might be expected to touch. It was why they'd been taught to take extreme care...and why relaxing after dismantling a particularly complex set of wards could be disastrous. She'd lost count of the number of times a simple trick had caught her or one of the other students.

"He'll probably force you to run through Blackhall again," she said, instead.

Lady Barb gave her an odd look, but said nothing.

"The transfiguration spell keeps defeating me," Emily said. "No matter what I do, I wind up a cat or another small animal."

Lady Barb snorted. "There's no way out of the trap," she said. "The trick is to avoid the spell altogether."

"But there's no way to avoid the spell," Emily protested. "Or...what did I miss?"

"The spell is keyed to affect a human," Lady Barb pointed out, dryly. "Turn yourself into something else first, then open the door. Or you can try going through the pipes anyway, but that would make life difficult for you..."

Emily nodded. The pipes had been bad enough when she'd been a cat. As a human, they would be impossibly claustrophobic—and the snake is a deadly threat. She touched the one at her wrist thoughtfully, wondering if that was still true. The Death Viper could certainly clear the way.

"Thank you," she said, irked. The trick, in hindsight, was simple. Most of the tricks at Blackhall generally were, she had to admit, but they fooled most of the students. "Will the sergeant be annoyed with you for telling me?"

"Probably," Lady Barb said. There was an oddly fond note in her voice. "But he will probably want to give you a more personalized curriculum for next year, then you can retake the second year of Martial Magic in Fourth Year."

Emily looked at her. There was something in her tone...she had a sudden flash of insight and blinked in surprise. Did Lady Barb *fancy* the sergeant?

The thought left her feeling oddly conflicted. If Lady Barb developed a relationship with someone else, where would that leave *Emily*? She'd come to think of Lady Barb as a mother...but when her biological mother had remarried it had destroyed Emily's life.

She damned herself for her own selfishness a moment later. Lady Barb deserved a chance to be happy. And Sergeant Miles was a good and decent man.

She pushed the thought aside as the rain stopped, so abruptly that Emily couldn't help wondering if someone had turned off a tap. High overhead, the clouds were thinning out, allowing the moon to shine through and cast rays of light over the darkened landscape. Emily looked up at the bright object, wondering briefly if magic could take her to *this* moon, then back down into the valley. Ahead of her, she saw the first plants of the garden...

And then there was a pulse of magic, dead ahead.

Lady Barb swore. They were too late.

Chapter Thirty-Eight

EMILY CAUGHT HER BREATH AS WAVES OF MAGIC CRACKLED OUT, SETTING FIRE TO THE plants surrounding Mother Holly's home. The flames grew brighter as the magic grew stronger, wiping out decades of work in mere seconds. She spared a thought for the creatures Mother Holly had kept as potions ingredients, then braced herself as the necromancer appeared, walking through the flames towards them. Her eyes were brilliant red.

Just like Shadye, Emily thought.

Lady Barb nodded to her, stepping to the side. It was a bad idea to stand close together. The necromancer would surely start throwing blasts of raw magic at them. Emily held up her staff, preparing to channel magic through it, as the necromancer came to a halt. Her eyes, no longer remotely human, stared at them with cold malice. Behind her, illuminated by the fires, Emily saw three bodies.

All children. All dead.

She shuddered. Just how many children had died to fuel Mother Holly's dreams of power?

Mother Holly let out a screech before throwing a fireball towards Lady Barb. The combat sorceress ducked, then threw back a fireball of her own. Mother Holly didn't do anything to block it, but when it struck her body it did *nothing*.

Emily shuddered as the implications sank into her mind. Mother Holly had already started the transformation into something inhuman—and, if she escaped, she would be able to find enough victims to keep her alive.

Lady Barb kept moving, ducking and dodging as Mother Holly threw fireball after fireball at her. Emily noted, as she started to throw fireballs of her own, that Mother Holly still seemed to recall some of the habits of a hedge witch. She wasn't used to having such vast power at her disposal; even now, her spells were conserving power. Normally, Emily would have been impressed, but now it was deadly dangerous. She thought wistfully of the drain a spell like *Berserker* could have caused, then jumped aside as another fireball slashed past her and struck the far side of the valley. A dull explosion told her just how much power Mother Holly was feeding into her attacks. One hit would be lethal.

Emily threw a set of lightning bolts, then tossed a transfiguration spell at her target. Mother Holly didn't show any reaction to either, as if she was no longer human enough for the transfiguration spell to work. The hedge witch made a gesture, and a wave of flames blasted towards Emily, then vanished once Emily hastily summoned water and threw it at the blaze. Mother Holly inched forward, then stopped as Lady Barb struck her back with a rock. The necromancer turned angrily, forgetting Emily as she reached out with her magic towards Lady Barb...and found nothing.

Mother Holly screamed in rage, blasting out a wave of raw magic. Emily hesitated, then cast another series of spells of her own, directing them at the ground below Mother Holly's feet. It turned to mud, then quicksand; the necromancer started to sink, her feet caught in the mire.

Mother Holly kicked angrily—she didn't seem to realize where the attack had come from—and then struck again with her magic. The shockwave shook the ground, sending Emily to her knees, but it also blasted Mother Holly free.

Emily cursed and pulled herself to her feet, just as a knife struck Mother Holly's back. Lady Barb had hidden herself, then attacked from the rear.

For a moment, seeing the magic crackling around the blade, Emily thought they'd won. But then the blade shattered, tossing pieces of red-hot metal everywhere.

Mother Holly turned, moving with inhuman speed, and caught hold of Lady Barb's shirt before she could retreat. There was a flash of light and a rat jumped out, scurrying across the ground before Lady Barb snapped back to normal.

Emily took advantage of the necromancer's confusion to blast her with a lethal spell, one that should have killed her instantly. It didn't work.

She felt the snake-bracelet around her wrist, but dismissed the thought of trying to use it against the necromancer. If killing spells didn't work, poison was unlikely to do any better—and besides, there was so much energy crackling around that the snake might be vaporized instantly. She darted to one side as yet another fireball narrowly missed her, then twisted in midair and came after her. Emily barely had a second to block it before it struck, the explosion picking her up and tossing her through the air. Somehow, she managed to keep hold of her staff. She landed badly, almost breaking her leg. Gritting her teeth, she applied a quick-heal spell even though she knew she would pay for it later. There was no time to have Lady Barb heal her.

Lady Barb tossed an odd spell at Mother Holly. Emily frowned in puzzlement; the spell didn't look even *remotely* dangerous.

But Mother Holly howled in outrage and started lashing out, blindly.

She *was* blind, Emily realized. The spell was one of the pranks they were forbidden to use at Whitehall, a spell considered too cruel even for magicians who regularly turned their rivals into animals or inanimate objects. Emily could understand their logic, although she thought it was long overdue. She pulled herself back to her feet as the necromancer stopped, as if she were listening. But if she was blind, she couldn't see them coming.

Seeing a large rock, Emily cast a levitation spell on it and launched the rock towards Mother Holly's head at colossal speed. She must have sensed something, because she started to move just before the rock hit her, but it was too late. There was a colossal explosion as the rock disintegrated, revealing a battered human form blazing with energy. For a moment, Emily thought that Mother Holly's body—more energy than living flesh—was about to explode and braced herself, before the energy faded back into nothingness. Moments later, Mother Holly pointed a finger at Emily and she had to jump aside, a moment before a supercharged spell blazed through where she had been standing. The blindness spell had been broken.

"Do it again," she called to Lady Barb. She'd never learnt how to cast the spell herself, even in Martial Magic. "Hurry!"

Mother Holly howled and struck the ground. An earthquake rocked the valley, forcing Emily to lean on her staff to remain upright. In the distance, she heard the sounds of trees falling and rocks crashing down the edge of the valley...just how far had the earthquake reached? She glanced towards the castle, only to see nothing but darkness. What if the castle, already damaged, had been ruined by the earthquake? Or the town they'd stayed in the previous day...?

Emily lifted her staff as the shaking subsided and cast a series of spells, one after the other, feeling her magic flow through the staff. A prank spell turned the ground under Mother Holly's feet to ice, sending her falling to the ground. Another triggered a blaze of fire under the necromancer's body, a spell she'd been taught to reserve for zombies and other forms of undead life. Mother Holly howled, but showed no sign of harm as she climbed back to her feet. A spell from Lady Barb sent her back down again. The ground shivered, as if it was repulsed by Mother Holly's touch, sending chills down Emily's spine.

And then the necromancer turned to look at her.

Red eyes, blazing with inhuman power and madness, met Emily's gaze. She froze, like a deer staring into headlights, remembering Shadye and just how close he had come to killing her and taking Whitehall for his own. She'd cheated then, drawing on the power of the nexus and Earth's concepts of science to wipe him from existence, but there was no nexus here. All they could do was hope they could exhaust the necromancer, a necromancer born from a woman who knew how to conserve her power. It struck Emily as she stood, helpless, that they might not win this battle.

Mother Holly gestured with one clawed hand, and an invisible force yanked the staff out of Emily's hand. Emily screamed, feeling as if part of her had been ripped away as the staff flew through the air and into Mother Holly's grasp.

She stared down at the staff, as if she wasn't quite sure how it worked, then focused her magic on it until the staff disintegrated into sawdust.

Emily stared in horror, feeling her magic flickering helplessly without the staff. Mother Holly looked up, triumph somehow readable on her maddened face, and flicked a finger at her. Emily found herself tossed through the air and slammed against a rock, held in place by an irresistible force.

She felt panic bubbling at the corner of her mind as Mother Holly started to advance towards her, one hand clutching the stone knife. Shadye had wanted to sacrifice her, too...but she'd been alone then.

The knife flew out of Mother Holly's hand, then slammed into a fireball Lady Barb had created and tossed into the air. It shattered into pieces of stone. The force holding Emily in place vanished.

Mother Holly turned to face Lady Barb, curling her hands into fists and then uncurling them to reveal inhuman claws. Magic flashed around her as she prepared yet another strike.

Lady Barb acted first.

For a moment, Emily thought that Lady Barb had summoned Basilisks or another set of giant snakes to help. They seemed to come out of nowhere, crashing into Mother Holly and grinding her into the ground. It took her a moment to realize that Lady Barb had animated them from rocks, a feat Emily knew she couldn't hope to match for years. Magic flared around the snake that was trying to kill the necroman-cer, then it glowed with light and disintegrated.

Emily barely managed to raise a ward before pieces of stone flew everywhere, sev-eral bouncing off her protections. Lady Barb started to throw more spells as Mother Holly rose back to her feet...then floated upwards into the air.

Emily hesitated. Part of her wanted Mother Holly to run, but she knew the nec-romancer would just find more victims and devastate the countryside. She gritted her teeth and cast a spell intended to cancel the witch's flying spell, but nothing happened.

Horror flared through her mind as she realized she'd become far too dependent on the staff. She closed her eyes, recalled her very first lessons in magic, then recast the spell. Magic flashed around her and she almost collapsed in relief, then opened her eyes as Mother Holly hit the ground. The witch looked absolutely furious.

Cold ice ran down Emily's spine as Mother Holly stood up. Emily was tired—and Lady Barb, despite having more reserves, couldn't be in a much better condition. If they exhausted themselves, rather than the necromancer, they were both dead.

Then Emily remembered what she'd done to Shadye and cast an illusion spell, cre-ating copies of herself that advanced towards Mother Holly with threatening intent, while she ducked and hid.

Mother Holly didn't seem to care about which Emily was actually real; she threw blasts of magic at each in quick succession. The blasts passed through the illusions and slammed into the far edge of the valley, exploding in light and fire.

Emily shuddered—if one of those blasts hit her, she would be vaporized—and then created more illusions. Mother Holly kept blasting them, one after the other. There was so much magic flaring through the air that Emily couldn't help wondering what it would do to the local environment.

Lady Barb added her own illusions, creating copies of herself and several other magicians. Emily saw a Master Grey blown apart by a blast of magic, then a Grandmaster smirking as he lifted his staff. But the illusions weren't actually danger-ous...Mother Holly must have come to the same conclusion, as she stopped throwing magic at them.

Emily braced herself and shaped a very deadly spell in her mind, then stood up and cast it. For a long moment, nothing happened...

And then, Mother Holly started to choke. The spell transmuted the oxygen in the air around her to something else. Sergeant Miles hadn't known just what it did, merely that the spell made it impossible for the target to breathe.

And since Mother Holly *did* need to breathe, Emily wondered if she dared unleash the snake. Maybe poison would work after all.

But then the madwoman stopped choking...

Emily cursed under her breath, searching her mind for ideas. Prank spells pre-vented panic—she'd never quite realized that she wasn't breathing when she was turned into something inanimate—but other spells didn't have safety features built into their structure. Mother Holly must have believed that she needed to breathe, even if she'd passed beyond such human weakness. But once it had been put to the test, she'd discovered the truth.

Emily stood, catching her breath. Everything seemed very still; she was vaguely aware of Lady Barb, standing behind the necromancer. Even Mother Holly didn't seem inclined to keep fighting. But she knew it was just a matter of time. Emily was sweaty, exhausted and pushed to the edge of her endurance. Unless Mother Holly ran out of energy in the next few minutes, they were going to lose.

An idea occurred to her, an idea that might at least allow them to take Mother Holly down even as they fell themselves. She hesitated, then started to work her way around Mother Holly, heading towards Lady Barb. The necromancer eyed her through brilliant red eyes, but did nothing to stop her.

Lady Barb held up a hand, warningly. They didn't dare get too close together or Mother Holly might try to kill them both at once.

"You're being consumed by your own madness," Lady Barb said, addressing Mother Holly in tones one might use to address a dangerous animal. She sounded calm, reasonable and, above all, understanding. "But you can still stop this."

Emily gaped at her. Was she trying to talk Mother Holly out of embracing necromancy? Surely it was already too late. Mother Holly had passed beyond humanity into a twilight stage between human and something else, a stage that would need a constant influx of power to maintain. She would die if she couldn't find more victims to sacrifice. Or did Lady Barb believe that Mother Holly could be useful? The thought was horrifying, but easily dismissed. Even if the Allied Lands had been prepared to tolerate someone taking innocent children and using them for power, her madness would make her an unreliable weapon.

No, Emily realized. Lady Barb needed to regenerate her powers, just as much as Emily herself. *She's trying to buy time.*

Mother Holly turned to face her, but said nothing. Emily wondered if she was still *capable* of speech–Shadye had been able to talk, right up until the end–then decided that it didn't matter. She might have plunged further into madness than Shadye–or any other necromancer who had learned to live with his new existence. Emily felt a stab of pity–all Mother Holly had wanted to do was make things better–then carefully shaped the spell in her mind. A single mistake might prove disastrous.

She held up her hands, signaling to Lady Barb. Sign language was nowhere near as developed in the Allied Lands as it had been on Earth, but she'd been taught the basic signs in Martial Magic, as well as how to use them in combat situations. Lady Barb lifted her eyebrows as she saw the instructions–*knock her away from us*–but nodded and cast a spell on the ground below the necromancer's feet. Before Mother Holly could react, she was lifted up and flung across the valley. Magic flared around her as she hit the ground, mocking Lady Barb. Even being slammed into a rocky wall wasn't enough to kill her. Emily could only hope that her secret weapon *was*.

It would change the world, she knew, if it worked. Every magician with ambition would be trying to duplicate it. And it might kill all three of them...and devastate the valley...and cause hardship to the local population. But there was no choice. Mother Holly had to be stopped.

Emily cast the nuke-spell, praying desperately that it would work. There had been no way to test it, even if she'd dared find somewhere uninhabited. She felt the magic shivering into existence, brewing in power. It would detonate within seconds, she hoped, although she wasn't entirely sure. There were too many variables within the spell, not to mention fixed limitations she'd engineered in when the full implications struck her. Her nightmares had suggested that it was entirely possible that using magic to split atoms would result in cracking the entire planet in half.

She ran over towards Lady Barb as the spell started to work. It felt evil...or perhaps it was just her imagination. "Teleport us out," she snapped, grabbing hold of the older woman. "Now!"

Lady Barb stared at her. "I can't," she snapped back. Her face was torn between horror and puzzlement. The nuke-spell was coming to life, a faintly shimmering hex that was both beautiful and deadly...and it was completely outside of her experience. "I don't have the power left!"

Emily looked over at the magic—and, beyond it, Mother Holly rising to her feet. The hedge witch was staring at the spell as if hypnotized. Emily hesitated, wondering if all three of them were about to die, then hastily closed her eyes and concentrated on creating a pocket dimension. All the variables she'd designed when Lady Barb was ill sprang into her mind, then into her spellwork. There was no time to test it, no time to ensure that it was actually *safe*; she opened her eyes, then yanked the dimension forward, surrounding them. Mother Holly's angry face vanished into a grey haze...

...And then there was an odd sense of timelessness, as if the stasis spell hadn't worked quite right...

...And then they were in the midst of hell.

"Emily," Lady Barb said. She sounded badly shaken—and drained. "Emily, what the hell have you *done?*"

Chapter Thirty-Nine

E MILY HAD NO ANSWER.

It was broad daylight, almost noon, judging by the position of the sun. But the valley had been completely devastated, burned to a crisp. Some parts of it were still burning, as if the spell had set the very stones themselves on fire. The hovel and all that remained of the garden were gone, replaced by a blackened crater that seemed to shimmer ominously. She looked up, towards the castle, and saw a ruin. The blast might have been directed up and outward by the shape of the valley, but the castle had been slapped hard enough to complete its destruction.

Lady Barb caught her arm. "Emily," she snapped. "What did you do?"

Emily swallowed. "I can't tell you," she said. She wasn't sure she wanted to discuss *anything* relating to splitting atoms with Lady Barb, no matter what oaths she'd sworn. "It's not something to talk about, really."

"Really," Lady Barb repeated. She looked around the remains of the valley. "Did you kill her?"

Emily hoped so. The blast would have shattered Mother Holly's body and broken down the energy holding it together. But there was no way to be sure. She looked around, wondering if she would see Mother Holly slowly reassembling herself, but saw nothing. The necromancer was dead, she told herself. Any other outcome was unthinkable.

Lady Barb had another question. "How long were we in the pocket dimension?"

"It should have been a few hours," Emily said. It had been near midnight when they'd fought Mother Holly, which suggested they'd stayed in the bubble for over ten hours. "But I don't know."

She hesitated, then swore inwardly. There was one danger from a nuclear blast–or something akin to it–that was utterly beyond this world's comprehension. Radiation. They were standing at ground zero. Radiation might be a very real threat. She cast the ward she had designed, back when she'd first contemplated the possibility, but they'd already been dosed. If, of course, there was a danger in the first place.

"We have to get out of here," she said. The ward was showing no reaction, but that proved nothing. "And we need to seal this valley off completely."

Lady Barb didn't argue, merely led her back towards the edge of the valley and a treacherous climb up and outwards. Fire had scorched the rocks, blackening them and sweeping away all traces of plants, bushes and soil. The ground below their feet had been turned to glass. Emily remembered, as her thoughts searched for hope, a story about a girl who had lived in a valley after a nuclear war and shuddered, then dismissed the thought. No one in the Allied Lands knew anything about splitting atoms, apart from her. It would remain that way, she hoped, for a very long time.

But the Blighted Lands are dead, she recalled. *They don't need nukes to destroy whole countries.*

Outside the valley, the devastation had been channeled by the mouth of the valley. Countless trees were burning brightly, or had been knocked down by the force of the blast and left lying on the ground. Emily hastily cast a spell to protect them from smoke and fumes, then led Lady Barb onwards, back towards the town.

She let out a long breath when they finally reached the outskirts and saw hundreds of people fighting the fires, hastily erecting firebreaks to prevent the flames from reaching the town. They included soldiers from two different kingdoms. Rudolf's father had come to find his son.

"He must have worked out where Rudolf was going," Lady Barb said, when Emily commented on it. "I need to speak with him and Lady Easter."

Emily shook her head. "Wash first," she said. Even if the radiation had faded away in the hours between the nuclear blast and the pocket dimension unlocking itself, there was still a risk of fallout. She shuddered, wondering just how much damage she'd done to the mountainfolk. There had been birth defects and other problems at Hiroshima for years after the city had been destroyed. "We need to be *clean*."

Lady Barb gave her a sidelong look, which only got worse as they entered the guesthouse and Emily forgot her usual reluctance to undress in front of anyone. Her eyes followed Emily, concerned, as Emily stripped naked and washed herself with warm water, then used magic to compress the clothes she'd worn down to a small block, which could be buried somewhere safe. After Emily was finished, Lady Barb washed herself and reluctantly destroyed her own clothes. The look in her eyes bothered Emily more than she cared to admit.

She wracked her brains for some way to test for radiation and came up blank. There was a way to do it without modern technology or magic, she was sure, but she had no idea how the trick was actually done. She'd read about it in a book set in a post-atomic war hellhole, yet the author had concentrated more on the horrors of the aftermath than any useful details. The best she could think of, eventually, was to have Lady Barb scan her body for anything that might be caused by radiation. If there was damage, perhaps magic could heal it.

Or perhaps there wasn't any radiation at all, Emily thought, grimly.

It was possible, she conceded, but it sounded like wishful thinking. They didn't dare take it for granted. She looked down at the snake-bracelet and shivered, again. Had she poisoned the snake as well as herself? Her lips twitched in bitter amusement. She was perhaps the only person in the Allied Lands who would regard that as a bad outcome.

A knock on the door brought her out of her thoughts. She glanced over to make sure that Lady Barb was decent, then pulled one of her robes over her head and then opened the door. Rudolf was standing there, looking tired but happy. Behind him, there were a handful of soldiers, wearing the colors of both families. She couldn't tell if they were his bodyguards or his escorts.

"Come in," she said, feeling genuinely pleased to see him. "What happened last night?"

Rudolf gave her an odd look as he stepped inside and closed the door, leaving the soldiers on the other side. "I was going to ask you the same question," he said. His voice was awestruck. "There were flashes of light and the sound of thunder, then there was a light as bright as the sun and a roaring sound that shook the ground. And there was a fiery cloud shaped like a mushroom...some of the peasants even say they saw a god in the flames."

Emily was uncomfortably aware of Lady Barb's gaze boring into her back.

Rudolf shook his head. "And then the castle came tumbling down," he added. "If we hadn't been here, we would have died."

Emily shuddered. The castle had been built of heavy stone. Her blast might easily have sent pieces flying through the air and slamming down into the town like bombs from high overhead. How many people had died, directly or indirectly, because of the spell she'd unleashed? She suspected that she would never know.

"I'm sorry," Emily said. It seemed so inadequate. "Was anyone hurt?"

"Several people who looked at the flash went blind for a few hours," Rudolf said. "Others were scorched fighting the flames. What *happened?*"

"We battled Mother Holly," Emily said, shortly. "We killed her."

"And that's all we can say," Lady Barb said. "I think we need to talk to your father."

Rudolf nodded, rather shamefaced. "I did talk to my father," he said. "And...well, let's just say he had the same problem."

Emily laughed. Talking to his father about his sexuality had to have taken considerable courage, more than Emily had ever shown when talking to her relatives. Lady Barb gave her an odd look, then shrugged, clearly deciding it wasn't important.

"We'll be on our way," she said. "You go tell them that we're coming."

The atmosphere of fear seemed to have faded away, Emily decided, as they made their way through the town to the temple. Lady Easter and her daughters had moved in, billeting their soldiers and servants in a number of smaller houses, but everything seemed to be remarkably peaceful. Perhaps she'd realized that losing the castle made her vulnerable, Emily wondered, or perhaps everyone was just relieved that the threat was over. Maybe it wouldn't last...

Lord Gorham seemed stronger than Emily remembered, sitting next to Lady Easter and sharing a joke with her. He rose to his feet as Lady Barb entered the temple, then bowed sweepingly to both magicians. Emily dropped back and curtseyed as Lady Barb nodded. She didn't really want their attention, no matter the situation. It was better they just thought of her as "Millie."

"Mother Holly was a necromancer," Lady Barb said, without bothering with the formalities. "She lost control of her powers and released her stolen magic, causing a massive explosion."

Emily blinked in surprise, then understood. There had to be *some* kind of cover story, even if it wasn't entirely believable. But anyone who might recognize the holes in the tale wouldn't believe what they heard, at least unless they walked into the mountains and inspected the blast site for themselves. For the locals, people largely ignorant of magic, there was no reason to doubt Lady Barb's explanation.

"That is understandable," Lady Easter said. "She was always known to be unstable."

You weren't that brave when she was a real threat, Emily thought, vindictively. *You were under her control from start to finish.*

She scowled. In her own twisted way, Mother Holly had been an idealist—not too different from Emily herself. Like Emily, she'd discovered the tools to change things... and put them to use, without any of the scruples Emily liked to think she would show. But the real world didn't respond well to idealism, let alone attempts to force it to go in a specific direction. If Emily tried to force things forward too fast...

The thought chilled her. She'd seen, in Zangaria and elsewhere, the effects of comparatively minor innovations she'd introduced. And she'd seen how far the old order was prepared to go to resist change. What would happen, she asked herself, when old and new clashed openly again? And how much of that would be her fault? Maybe King Randor was right in trying to co-opt those who had benefited from the changes, but he was riding a tiger. What would happen when he fell off?

Mother Holly only knew the bad, she thought, remembering what she'd been told. No one had visited the hedge witch unless they were desperate. Mother Holly had never had any balance, let alone a detached view...but then, it was hard to have a detached view when one was directly involved. And then there had been her simplistic attempt to steer the course of the mountains...

"We will gladly forbid anyone from entering the valley," Lady Easter said. "And we thank you for your assistance."

Emily frantically dragged her attention back to the here and now, silently relieved that Lady Barb hadn't been looking at her. Not paying attention in her classes could be unfortunate.

"You're welcome," Lady Barb said, dryly. "But you might want to consider how much blame *you* bear for this disaster."

Lord Gorham gaped in surprise. "Blame *we* bear?"

Emily was equally surprised. She looked at Lady Barb's back, wondering just what she was thinking—and why? It wasn't like Lady Barb to bend the rules on limiting interference with local politics...although, with a necromancer involved, the rules had probably gone out of the window long ago.

"Your families—you aristocrats—have been exploiting your people since you killed your former monarch," Lady Barb said, sharply. "Even without Mother Holly, the resentment and rage was staggeringly powerful. I would have expected an explosion, sooner or later, even without a necromancer becoming involved. And now you have been proven to be vulnerable."

Lord Gorham didn't understand, Emily saw, and Lady Easter didn't seem to agree with Lady Barb. But Rudolf was nodding his head in quiet understanding, while Lady Easter's daughters seemed to be mulling it over. A few months of being slaves in all but name had taught them a few lessons. They'd just have to see if they remembered the lessons now they were free.

She felt a moment of hope. The next generation of aristocracy would have a chance to reshape their country without a violent revolution. But only time would tell.

"But...they are *ours*," Lord Gorham said, finally. He didn't understand at all. Emily remembered that he'd lined up extra-pretty maids for his son, expecting Rudolf to make love to them, and shuddered. "We are their masters."

"*They* don't see it that way," Lady Barb said. She sighed. "Not that I really expected you to understand."

She stood straighter, then bowed to the aristocrats. "My apprentice and I will return to Whitehall," she added. "I would request that you prepare reports of your own for the White Council. They will want an explanation of what took place here."

"It will be done," Lord Gorham said.

Lady Barb turned and strode out of the temple. Emily followed her, unwilling to spend any more time looking at the aristocrats. Rudolf followed her, then called out as he left the temple. Emily hesitated, then turned back to speak with him.

"I wanted to thank you," he said. "You saved more than just my life and..."

Emily understood. Rudolf had at least a *chance* at a happy life, which was more than he'd had before Mother Holly started playing games. She doubted it would be easy, but it would be possible to make it work.

"You're welcome," she said, toying with the bracelet at her wrist. "And thank you for coming with me. I might not have made it without you."

Rudolf beamed. Emily remembered Imaiqah's advice for talking to young men—praise them endlessly—and smiled, inwardly. Imaiqah had definitely had a point. Maybe, just maybe, Emily would risk a date with someone at Whitehall. Or maybe it would take longer to overcome her fears.

"The offer...well...the offer has to be closed," Rudolf said. He looked as though he expected her to blast him on the spot—or turn him back into a slug and stamp on him. "I'm sorry."

It took Emily a moment to realize what he was talking about—and then she started to giggle helplessly. Rudolf had asked her to marry him, partly in jest...and even though she'd declined, the offer was technically still open. But he'd had second thoughts when he'd seen just how much she could do, just like Jade. She shook her head, feeling amusement rather than rejection. It helped that she'd never seriously considered his offer.

"I hope you find someone suitable," she said. The thought of her giving relationship advice to *anyone* was ludicrous, yet there was no one else who could say what had to be said. His father certainly wouldn't. "But remember what I said and be *honest* with her."

"I will do my best," Rudolf said. He reached out and gave her a short, brotherly hug. "Goodbye, Millie."

Oddly, Emily didn't feel worried or disturbed by his touch. She wondered, briefly, what he would say if she told him the truth. If society pages had reached this far from their kingdoms, he had to have heard of the Necromancer's Bane. But she knew she didn't want the attention, so she said nothing. Instead, she curtseyed to him and turned back towards the guesthouse. Lady Barb was waiting for her at the end of the street.

"You did very well," Lady Barb said, as they started to walk. "I'm sorry about your staff."

"I don't mind losing it," Emily assured her. The brief moment of panic when she'd feared that she'd lost the ability to cast spells without a staff for good had been terrifying. "If I hadn't taken it..."

"You might well be dead," Lady Barb told her, bluntly. "Young Lady..."

Emily looked up at her, puzzled and alarmed. "You are in training to be a combat sorceress, not an obedient servant," Lady Barb said. "Yes, I set rules for you, and yes, I am quite prepared to punish you when you make the wrong choice—but you need to develop a sense for when those rules can be put aside. Taking the staff was the right thing to do at the right time. It saved your life, and mine, too."

She patted Emily on the back, then sighed. "We're going to have to cut our trip short," she added. Her voice suggested that she wasn't too pleased. She'd enjoyed the walking from settlement to settlement, helping the people who needed help. "The Grandmaster will need to see us both, I think."

"I'm sorry," Emily said.

Lady Barb poked her arm, none-too-gently. "And how much of what happened here was actually your fault?"

Emily flushed. It wasn't, not really. Mother Holly hadn't been driven to necromancy by anything Emily had done; hell, she'd been on the slippery slope a long time before Emily had entered the Allied Lands. Madness would have overwhelmed her, sooner or later, and then the mountains would have been drenched in blood. And, once she'd killed everyone in the mountains to feed her power, she would have descended into the surrounding countryside.

"None of it," she said, finally.

"Right answer," Lady Barb said. She sounded pleased. "But here's something else you can think about, if you like."

She pushed open the door to the guesthouse, then closed it once Emily had stepped inside and set a privacy ward. "Skulls of Memories are not entirely *common*," she said, once the ward was in place. "And that book was pretty close to unique."

Emily nodded. The book might still be buried—or it might have been destroyed by the blast, leaving one fewer copy in the Allied Lands. She would have to go and check before they left the town. If it was still intact, it was *hers*. She wouldn't use the spells, but she wouldn't give it up either. It was a *book*. The thought of destroying it herself was unthinkable.

"Someone *gave* them to her," Lady Barb added. There was a grim note in her voice, a promise of trouble for the future. "But who? And why?"

"Maybe she stole them," Emily suggested. "Void told me that a necromancer was killed on the other side of the mountains. Mother Holly was *good* at misdirection..."

"Hardly enough to kill a necromancer, certainly not one who had been a necromancer for years," Lady Barb interrupted. "So who gave her the tools?"

Emily had no answer.

"And just what," Lady Barb concluded, "did they have in mind?"

Chapter Forty

"IT WOULD SEEM CONGRATULATIONS ARE IN ORDER," THE GRANDMASTER SAID, HEAVILY. HIS sightless eyes sought out Emily. "Congratulations, Necromancer's Bane."

Emily flushed and squirmed in her chair. It had taken three days to ride back to a place where they could step through a portal to Whitehall, but word had somehow spread ahead of them. Somehow, the Allied Lands *knew* that it had been her who'd killed a second necromancer, although they didn't seem to know precisely *how*. Thankfully, the cover story about the explosion had held up to scrutiny.

"Thank you," she said, finally. The last thing she wanted was more fame, followed by increasingly absurd rumors about just what she'd done to Mother Holly. But, in this case, absurd rumors would probably be better than the truth. "Who told the world?"

"I wish I knew," the Grandmaster said. He looked down at his hands. It struck Emily, suddenly, that for all his power he was a very old man. "No one I have spoken to has been able to answer that question."

He shook his head. "But we are grateful for your work," he added. "You saved thousands of lives."

Emily nodded, although she had her doubts. Neither she nor Lady Barb had been able to find anything suggesting radiation damage, which meant...what? Had there been no radiation, or was the damage just beyond their ability to detect? She played with a strand of her hair miserably, wondering if the first sign of real trouble would be her hair falling out. There was no way to know.

But if there *was* radiation, she knew, it would have been swept up into the ecosystem and then deposited on the ground by rainfall. God alone knew what the long-term effects would be.

"We would like to know what happened," Lady Barb said, from behind Emily. "The explosion was more devastating than any recorded necromancer death."

"It shouldn't be talked about," Emily said, carefully. "There are too many dangers in revealing *anything*."

She hesitated, then added three words. "It was *small*."

The nuke-spell wasn't *that* complicated, she knew. All it would take to cast it was a single magician with bad intentions and enough power to make the spell work. If deployed properly, it could end the necromantic threat overnight...and then rip the Allied Lands apart in the aftermath. It normally took a ritual to perform a Working of Mass Destruction, as Emily had come to think of them. But with the nuke-spell, a single magician could take out an entire city.

"Then we shall tell them that it is a specialist skill of yours, should anyone ask," the Grandmaster said. He gave her a long considering look, his hidden eyes twitching. "Did you enjoy your trip otherwise?"

Emily had to fight to hide a giggle. She'd broken up with Jade—if what they'd had could be considered a real relationship. She'd helped a girl to go to Whitehall or another school of magic. She'd seen mundane horrors she couldn't prevent, she'd almost been raped by a village lout, she'd nursed Lady Barb when she'd fallen ill...

But there had been parts of the trip that had been almost enjoyable. Seeing the countryside, learning new magic with Lady Barb...generally, the parts of the trip that hadn't involved other people.

"It had its moments," she said, finally.

"You've grown up a little," the Grandmaster added. He smiled at her. "That's always good to see."

Metaphorically in his case, Emily assumed. Although, when magic was involved, it was hard to be sure. She had no idea why the Grandmaster tolerated his own blindness when he could have had his eyes rebuilt. Perhaps losing his sight was the price of his power.

"Thank you," she said. She looked down at her hands, clasped in her lap. "If you don't mind, I'd like to go back to my room and sleep."

"Understandable, but unnecessary," the Grandmaster said. "I have taken the liberty of moving you into a private room, at least for the summer. You won't be supervised—well, not any closer than students are normally supervised. I suggest you behave yourself."

"And restrict your experiments," Lady Barb added. "We can discuss a program of further study tomorrow."

Emily sighed, but nodded. There had never been a time in her life when she hadn't had to work, either at school or looking after herself. She'd always envied the children who talked about lazing around all summer. They didn't know how lucky they were.

But then, most of Whitehall's students weren't that lucky. Alassa had to learn how to rule, Imaiqah had to assist her family, and the Gorgon...she shook her head, thoughtfully. Just what did the Gorgon do over the summer?

"It wouldn't be legal to take the book from you," the Grandmaster added. "But I would advise you to make sure it is secure."

"I've put it in my trunk," Emily assured him. "I'll add additional wards to Cockatrice before moving it there."

"And don't read it here," Lady Barb said, firmly. "People could get the wrong impression."

"I understand," Emily said, as she rose to her feet. "And thank you for everything."

"Mistress Irene will show you to your room," the Grandmaster said. "And one other thing?"

Emily tensed, suspiciously.

"I suggest—very strongly—that you don't tell anyone about your new pet," the Grandmaster said. "It would only upset people."

Emily looked down at the bracelet wrapped around her wrist. She *could* hide it, she knew; it wasn't as if Third Year students were expected to waste time trying to find familiars. Either they found one in Second Year or they assumed that they weren't likely to find an animal that clicked with them. But it felt wrong to be keeping something from her friends.

And yet, she knew the grandmaster had a point. There were students who had bonded with wolves or even tigers, but familiars were generally smart enough not to hurt anyone unintentionally. The Death Viper, on the other hand, would be lethal to anyone apart from Emily herself. There was no way she could risk letting it curl up on her pillow to sleep next to her.

"I won't," she promised. It made one hell of a secret weapon, she had to admit. "No one will hear about it from me."

Lady Barb gave her a sharp look, then nodded.

Emily nodded back and left the room. Outside, she sagged, feeling sweat trickling down her back. The world had changed and, once again, she'd made it happen.

Mother Holly could have been you, a voice whispered at the back of her head. *If things had been a little different...*

"Welcome back, Emily," Mistress Irene said. Emily hastily pulled herself back upright and tried to look attentive. In or outside classes, Mistress Irene was a stickler for good appearance and behavior. "I'll show you to your room. Dinner will be at seventeen bells precisely."

"Thank you," Emily said.

The room turned out to be bigger than she'd expected, slightly more colorful than the barren rooms she'd shared with her roommates. She placed her bag on a hard wooden desk, then sat down on the bed and stared down at her hands. Her emotions churned through her head, mocking her. She'd done well, she knew she'd done well, but she didn't really know where it would all end.

There were a handful of letters placed on her pillow, sealed with simple charms that would destroy them if the wrong person tried to tear them open. She opened the first one with her fingernail, then pulled out the sheet of paper—they'd improved the quality, she noted—and read it quickly. Imaiqah's letter was bright and chatty, but said almost nothing of substance. There was just a note that she would tell Emily everything when they met in person. Emily wondered what had happened to her, then dismissed the thought. She'd find out soon enough.

The next letter was from Bryon. Emily skimmed it without paying much attention; it merely noted that he'd spoken to both the Faire Master and Paren, Imaiqah's father, about the planning for the Faire next year. Emily nodded to herself, deciding that she could leave the matter in his capable hands, then moved on to the third letter. The Gorgon talked briefly about living in the village, then to a discussion of magical theory that would be better shared with Aloha. Emily read it anyway, making a handful of notes for later research in the library. At least there wouldn't be any other students trying to compete with her for scarce books.

It was odd to see that most of the letters had been written before the nuclear blast had vaporized Mother Holly and changed the world. They were almost a snapshot into a more innocent past...she shook her head, dismissing the absurd thought, then reached for the final letter. Jade had written to her a day ago, according to the postmarks. He'd just been lucky enough to be in a city connected to the portal network.

Master Grey, he'd written, was upset about the explosion, although he didn't say why. Emily read it twice, unable to avoid a sense that Master Grey was complaining for the sake of complaining, then mentally started to compose an angry reply before she thought better of it. Maybe he'd worked out that the explosion had been too powerful to have been the work of a necromancer, even one who had lost control completely, or...

She scowled, then put the letters back on the table and lay back on the bed. There would be time to reply later, she told herself, once everything had settled. Maybe then she would know what to tell her friends. Placing the snake-bracelet beside her head, she closed her eyes and fell asleep.

Her dreams, thankfully, were peaceful.

Epilogue

THE GRANDMASTER SAID NOTHING ELSE UNTIL SERGEANT MILES HAD JOINED THEM AND complex, almost impenetrable privacy wards were erected around his office. Lady Barb nodded politely to the sergeant, then turned to look back at the Grandmaster. The older man looked borne down by the weight he was carrying. It was hard to play mentor to an entire community of magicians, certainly when combined with his other responsibilities.

"Well," the Grandmaster said, finally. "What do *you* think she did?"

Lady Barb gave him a cold look. She'd sworn not to reveal any of Emily's secrets, but Emily hadn't told her anything about the spell that had caused the blast.

"I don't know," she said. "It's possible that Emily somehow caused Mother Holly to lose control of her magic, but the blast was far greater than it should have been."

The Grandmaster looked unconvinced. "And she's more notorious than ever," he added. "Is she ready for Mountaintop?"

"No," Lady Barb said, bluntly. "She is nowhere near ready."

"I must concur," Sergeant Miles agreed. "She has mastered more than I expected, given how...early she was forced to join my class, but she is still young and inexperienced."

"She didn't freeze this time," Lady Barb said. She briefly related the whole encounter with Hodge. "Still, she isn't ready."

"We have few options," the Grandmaster said. "Do either of you have a better one?"

Lady Barb and Sergeant Miles exchanged glances. Neither of them spoke.

"For better or worse, Child of Destiny or not, Emily has tipped our world upside down," the Grandmaster said, quietly. "People have started to notice. Lin's infiltration of Whitehall was merely the most blatant intelligence-gathering attempt...and it succeeded beyond their wildest dreams. We need to counterattack as quickly as possible."

"And you plan to use her to gather intelligence," Lady Barb sneered. "Emily is good at many things, Grandmaster, but she isn't ready for this."

"Yes, I *thought* you liked her," Sergeant Miles said. He shook his head, bitterly. "But the Grandmaster is right. There isn't anyone else who can do this for us."

Lady Barb sighed. "Then I suggest you give her a few days to recuperate before you broach the topic with her," she said, tiredly. "And then we will plan out a crash-course in mastering all the skills she needs to complete your mission."

"Understood," the Grandmaster said. "I have faith that you will prepare her to the best of your ability."

"No matter how prepared she is," Lady Barb said, "she may well fail."

She glared at the Grandmaster. "You are not to guilt her into this," she added. "She is not to feel that she has no choice, or that the whole mess is her fault. If she chooses to undertake your mission, she is to do it of her own free will. I will not stand for anything less."

Beside her, Sergeant Miles nodded in agreement.

"I will speak to her in a week," the Grandmaster said. "And I give you my word that she can make up her own mind. But we are truly out of other options."

"Then may the gods help us all," Lady Barb said.

The End

The saga will continue in

The School of Hard Knocks

About the author

Christopher G. Nuttall is thirty-two years old and has been reading science fiction since he was five when someone introduced him to children's SF. Born in Scotland, Chris attended schools in Edinburgh, Fife and University in Manchester before moving to Malaysia to live with his wife Aisha.

Chris has been involved in the online Alternate History community since 1998; in particular, he was the original founder of Changing The Times, an online alternate history website that brought in submissions from all over the community. Later, Chris took up writing and eventually became a full-time writer.

Current and forthcoming titles published by Twilight Times Books:

Schooled in Magic YA fantasy series
    Schooled in Magic—book 1
    Lessons in Etiquette —book 2
    A Study in Slaughter —book 3
    Work Experience —book 4
    The School of Hard Knocks —book 5

The Decline and Fall of the Galactic Empire military SF series
    Barbarians at the Gates—book 1
    The Shadow of Cincinnatus —book 2
    The Barbarian Bride—book 3

Chris has also produced *The Empire's Corps* series, the *Outside Context Problem* series and many others. He is also responsible for two fan-made Posleen novels, both set in John Ringo's famous Posleen universe. They can both be downloaded from his site.

Website: http://www.chrishanger.net/
Blog: http://chrishanger.wordpress.com
Facebook: https://www.facebook.com/ChristoperGNuttall

If you enjoyed this book, please post a review
at your favorite online bookstore.

Twilight Times Books
P O Box 3340
Kingsport, TN 37664
www.twilighttimesbooks.com/

The Girl
in a Coma

Books by John Moss

The Girl in a Coma

The Girl
in a Coma

John Moss

The Poisoned Pencil

An imprint of Poisoned Pen Press

The Poisoned Pencil
An imprint of Poisoned Pen Press
6962 E. First Ave., Ste. 103
Scottsdale, AZ 85251
www.thepoisonedpencil.com
info@thepoisonedpencil.com

Printed in the United States of America

For Beverley because I love her.

Acknowledgments

Book One:
Murder My Love

One

Allison

Imagine you can't move. You can feel yourself being touched but you can't tell where. You think you are lying down but you can't be sure. You can see nothing, taste nothing, smell nothing, but you remember what it was like to do these things. It is not as if you have been this way forever. It's like being dead but you're not dead.

My name is Allison Briscoe.

They say I'm in a coma.

They think I'm a vegetable, for glory's sake—they call it a *persistent vegetative state.*

They don't know I'm listening when they discuss my case.

I lie here as still as a corpse. They don't know I can think. My heart beats, I can feel it inside my skull, but no matter how hard I concentrate I can't make the blood rush any faster. I can't slow it down. If I could, maybe I could signal I'm in here, I'm alive, this is me. But I can't.

When they took me off life support I didn't die. Now they don't know what to do with me.

My brother, David, calls me *Potato*.

When he first called me that, my mother was horrified. He knew I would think it was funny. He's two years older than me. He's kind of gawky, while I'm more on the pretty side. Or was. Still am. He lives at home. I live in a hospital, if you can call it living.

Well, yes you can, and I do. I may be as still as death, but I'm alive. And I'm going to stay that way—for a lifetime, at least.

I can identify most of my doctors and nurses and orderlies by their voices and by their different touches. Touch is like a signature, even though I can't tell what part of me they're touching.

My only visitors these days are David and my mother. I don't have a dad, to speak of. When my mother comes in, she tries to wrap me in sadness. "Allison, Allison." She chants my name over and over. "Allison, Allison, Allison." She doesn't know how to mourn for a daughter who seems to be dead but refuses to die. She cries a lot. But you can't cry forever. Me, I'd rather be locked in my head than be nowhere at all. I mean, they haven't buried me yet!

So no tears, that's my motto.

No tears.

Imagine being music that no one can hear. That's what it's like. Except when I sleep. I call it sleep but I don't know whether anyone else can tell the difference. I mean, I'm just lying here, eyes closed, same as always. I dream a lot.

Lately I've been dreaming about this one girl over and over, and I remember the dreams. They're not like regular dreams that fall apart when you wake up. These dreams tell me a story, they seem to be trying to give me a person to be when I can't be myself, someone who can walk and talk and run and laugh.

The girl I'm dreaming about, she's dead, I guess. She must be, because she lived a long time ago. But she's as real as anyone ever was.

When I'm dreaming, it's as if I'm inside her life. I'm still fifteen when I'm her but I wear dull colors, shapeless dresses with long sleeves and no collar. I wear coarse black stockings and a black pinafore done up with pins. There are no zippers, no buttons, no hooks and eyes. My hair is parted in the middle and held back with a piece of twine.

Personally, I like bright colors with neat names: chartreuse, magenta, vermillion, azure, topaz, indigo, emerald.

The girl in my dreams sees colors like that all around her but she doesn't have names for them. They're part of God's grandeur, she thinks.

Myself, I've never had much time for God. Long before I was shot in the head I stopped going to church. In my dreams I believe in God, I believe in religion. To make religion work, you have to believe that it works. In my dreams I am a Mennonite. We sometimes call ourselves the Plain People. We like things to be plain and simple.

We live in a time warp. We live in the past: it's how we imagine the past must have been. But nothing is really that simple when the rest of the world moves ahead.

I don't actually know whether Mennonites *like* to live in the past but that's where they live. And not just any past. They live in the times when their religion was invented, about five hundred years ago. That's when their ancestors rebelled from the established church so they could live plain and simple lives closer to God. That's what they believe. When I'm asleep, I believe it too.

When I'm awake I'm in Peterborough, Ontario, Canada, North America, planet Earth. When I'm asleep, I'm in

5

Pennsylvania. That's in the United States but in my dreams the United States doesn't exist yet.

When I'm awake, it's now.

I'm here.

I must be in a hospital room: I imagine there's a window and then in my mind I see a window. There has to be a door, so there's a big door. There's probably a table or a dresser but no television. I mean, what's the point?

My days are uneventful. It's not like when I'm working at Tim Horton's. Every day at Timmy's is different, and yet each is sort of the same. I was planning on going to work there full time as soon as I turned sixteen. I'm thinking now maybe I'll stay in school. I like it at Timmy's but I don't want to serve coffee and doughnuts for the rest of my life.

David will graduate next year. He wasn't impressed when I told him I was going to drop out. My mom doesn't care but to him it's a big deal. He's very smart. I don't know whether he's smart because he stayed in school or if he stayed in school because he's smart. Maybe it's all the same.

If you want to know how smart I am, just ask Jaimie Retzinger.

No, don't bother.

Come on, Allison, think about something else. That's me, talking to myself—

Sometimes I used to try really hard not to think of anything at all.

Thinking can make you unhappy.

I think a lot now. There's nothing else to do.

Sometimes I think about taking a bullet in the head.

I don't dwell on it, but it's hard to ignore.

I worked late at Tim's one night last winter. I helped to close up. On my way home, there was a gunshot, there was screaming. I was screaming. And then there was nothing. Now I'm in a hospital, in a room with a window and a big door.

In the mornings the doctors arrive with their assistants. They discuss my case. I don't change much. They say I'm not getting better, but I don't think I'm getting worse. And I'll tell you, I'm not ready to die. So I persist. Remember: *persistent vegetative state*. I persist.

They say it was a random bullet but it wasn't. I can't figure out why anyone would shoot me but I know whoever it was, he did it on purpose. Someone wanted me dead.

It was a male, I'm pretty sure of that. I wonder if he's satisfied now? Or does he need to finish me off? It hardly seems worth the effort. There might have been someone else in the car, sitting in the shadows. I'm not sure.

I don't know how long I've been like this. There were times when I wasn't aware of time passing. I was in a deep coma. Then I came out of it but nobody noticed.

Right now, I'm aware of every second of every minute of every hour, except when I'm dreaming. When I'm in a dream, I live inside time like an ordinary person. When I'm awake, it's more like I'm on the edge of time, looking in from outside.

Each night, when this place quiets down, I drift off to sleep and enter my dream. And that's when I'm real.

Rebecca

The girl in the black pinafore looked at herself in the window. It was a dull day and she could see her reflection floating in the glass. She wondered if she were pretty. She felt guilty for wondering. She had never seen herself in a mirror. She blushed and lowered her eyes.

Rebecca Haun was sure Jacob Shantz thought she was pretty. He would never say or admit such a thing. Rather, he might confess to being a little put off by her slight frame and high spirits.

Jacob was almost sixteen. He had finished his studies last summer and now worked alongside his father and brothers on their farm.

A boy and a girl never shared a desk at school, but for the last three years Rebecca and Jacob had shared an aisle, so that she was almost as close to him as to Sharon Ebie. Sharon had been her seatmate since the first grade, or what they called *the first book*.

Rebecca always sat close to the edge of her seat to be closer to Jacob. She was sure Jacob did the same thing, although if anyone ever noticed he would have become angry and denied it.

When he got angry his cheeks turned bright red. When he

laughed, they turned bright red. Actually, whenever he allowed himself feelings, his cheeks turned bright red.

Usually he kept his feelings to himself. He never told anyone about his father but everyone in the school knew he beat him. Even the teacher. Sometimes Jacob came to school with swollen eyes and it wasn't from crying. He had bruises on his arms, one on top of another. New ones appeared before the old ones had healed.

After Jacob left school, Rebecca saw him mostly on Sundays. He would drive his smaller brothers and sisters to church in a farm wagon and nod in her direction when their buggy came close. He was now old enough that he wore a broad-brimmed black hat like his father. When he nodded, his cheeks were bright red.

Rebecca worried. She thought his high color was from seeing her, and that pleased her, but she also knew he was feeling overwhelmed. He believed in God and the wrath of his father and in George Washington. That was a dangerous combination. Almost everyone else in Warwick, Pennsylvania, believed in God and King George.

It was almost impossible among Mennonites to separate the King from the Lord who appointed him. Their loyalty was not to the British crown but to God.

The Revolution loomed ominously over their lives. Men in Warwick talked openly about what Washington's rag-tag army was fighting for. Women talked quietly among themselves. The women spoke about the horrors of war. The men talked about the evils of war. They all accepted their holy obligation to stay out of it. The world beyond their Mennonite community in Lancaster County was their concern.

That morning in early April, Rebecca helped her brothers and sisters get ready for church. They always wore clean clothes on Sunday and their outfits were always the same. During the long service she kept the young ones in order with a scowl, but she was restless herself. After church, Jacob looked her directly in the eye as the families around them were clambering into black buggies and battered wagons or standing in the shade to exchange small talk and chat about last year's crops and next year's weather.

Jacob and Rebecca were still too young to be courting. In a year or two, he would be able to visit on the occasional Sunday afternoon for an hour, and a year later they might take buggy rides through the countryside. She wondered if that was when she would be overwhelmed by love. She liked Jacob, he was her secret special friend, but she didn't love him yet. She hoped it would happen before they were wed.

Jacob indicated he wanted to talk to her privately.

Rebecca would never disobey her father so she did not ask for permission to slip away, she just did. She knew it was wrong and this upset her, but she felt she had no choice.

She and Jacob met in the shadows on the far side of the church, and for the first time in their lives they talked directly to each other. Jacob's cheeks were bright red and Rebecca's heart was beating so fast she could hardly breathe. Perhaps this was the beginning of love. She hoped so, it would make everything easier.

"Rebecca, I will be leaving tonight," he said very formally. "I am going to join up with General Washington."

"You should not tell me!" she exclaimed. His confession seemed an unbearable secret. Then she recovered herself and addressed him with a formality equal to his own.

"I am sorry to know that, Jacob. You will never come back

"I might."

"We are Plain People, not soldiers. The war is not our concern."

He shuffled his boots in the spring dirt. He was not searching for words, he was simply waiting for her to realize there was no argument that would change his mind.

She found his commitment exciting, though she had no words, either, to describe the unfamiliar feelings running through her.

"You will be killed, Jacob," she at last declared with conviction.

"Perhaps not." His eyes glowed.

"You will not be allowed to come home. The elders will never permit it. And your father...aren't you afraid of your father?"

He smiled his rare private smile. Rebecca offered him a smile in return, but hers was neither rare nor mysterious. She was often admonished by her teachers and parents for smiling too easily. This world was not such a happy place as she seemed to imagine.

They stood facing each other, close but not touching. She had no right to tell him what he could do. But she felt her future was being reshaped as she looked into his eyes, trying in vain to see her reflection.

Suddenly they kissed. It was a sweet kiss, their lips were pursed, their arms remained at their sides. Rebecca realized that Jacob didn't kiss her, they kissed each other.

Then Jacob stood back. He was beet red. He lowered his eyes, wheeled out into the April sun, around the side of the church and out of sight. Rebecca remained in the shadow of the church, trembling.

Two

Allison

When I wake up, I remember everything I dreamed about Rebecca. It's hard to believe Rebecca doesn't remember me. But then Rebecca was alive two hundred years before I was born. I am a vegetable in a hospital room in Peterborough, Ontario, and Rebecca was a kid on a farm in Pennsylvania.

Maybe I'm just making her up out of stories I heard from my Grandmother Friesen.

Nana can't get here to see me. She lives in an old house in Niagara-on-the-Lake. She uses a walker and gets around town but it's difficult for her to travel. And there's not much here for her to see.

Nana is a Sunday Christian but she used to talk about our Mennonite ancestors who came up to Canada during the American Revolution. They were called United Empire Loyalists because they were loyal to King George and the British Empire. Americans thought they were traitors and were happy to see them leave. Loyalists and traitors: it's funny how you can be opposite things at the same time.

12

It's like me, being alive and dead, when really I'm neither.

Anyway, in the evening, David and my mother visit together. When they leave, I lie very still, waiting to hear the heavy door close, marking the end of my day. The door closes, the lights must be out. I want to sleep now and enter Rebecca's world again. But I can hear breathing and it isn't my own.

I wait for something to happen.

Nothing happens.

I can *hear* myself being watched.

Is it him? Is he thinking about how he shot me?

Time passes. It's torture when you're waiting and don't know what for. Then I hear the door swing open again. I can feel the difference in the air. He's gone.

So what was that all about?

How can you be scared when you're a vegetable? What's left to be afraid of? Being sliced and diced, chopped and shredded? I dunno, but I am. The little life I have left is all that I have; it is precious. When I drift off to sleep, it's a tremendous relief.

Nighttime for me will be another day for Rebecca Haun.

Rebecca

There was a commotion outside the window of the upstairs front bedroom Rebecca shared with her sisters in the weathered farmhouse. She could hear men's voices; they were speaking urgently. The boys were still asleep in the next room. Her mother and father had been doing chores for an hour, well before the sun had broken over the horizon.

She scrambled from bed and looked down. Johannes Haun, her father, was staring up at her window. Rebecca was one of four sisters and four brothers, but she knew that the men were talking about her. Her father saw her through the glass and waved for her to come down.

She dressed quickly ran down the narrow stairs, splashed icy water on her face from the basin in the sink, and slipped on her boots. She grabbed a shawl from behind the door and walked out into the yard.

"Rebecca," her father said in his sternest voice, "what do you know about Jacob Shantz?"

"I know him."

"He has disappeared. What do you know about that?"

She couldn't lie, especially to her father. But she didn't know

14

what he wanted to hear. The two men beside him were British soldiers. One thing she did know was that Jacob was in trouble.

"I haven't any idea where he is," she answered honestly. She knew he was on his way to Valley Forge, but she didn't know how far along the road he had made his way.

"Did he go off to find George Washington?" one of the men asked.

Rebecca said nothing. She knew what Jacob had planned to do. But you never know what someone actually does until they do it.

Her father put his hand on her shoulder. It might as well have been the hand of God. Her eyes filled with tears but she refused to cry.

"What happens to Jacob is not our concern," her father answered. His tone declared the death of a romance that had never really been born. Rebecca shuddered. Her father would never make her marry someone against her wishes. He was a kind man at heart. But he could prevent her from marrying someone if he chose. He was a righteous man, sure of God's will. "These men would like to talk to him," her father said.

One of the soldiers offered Rebecca a smile and the other looked angry. The smiling man had a scar running down his right cheek and a handsome mustache. His scarlet uniform was quite clean. The other man had not shaved in a week. His filthy uniform was mended in several places with coarse black thread.

The smiling man introduced himself. "I am Corporal Jonas," he said. "This here is Private Panabaker. We're looking for your young man, Miss Haun. It is very important"

Rebecca's cheeks flushed with color. Her eyes flashed. Jacob was not *her young man*. Not now, and maybe never.

Her father's hand tightened on shoulder.

"He killed a man," said Johannes Haun. "He killed his own father. They found the body in their barn early this morning. Noah Shantz died from a blow to the head. One of his horses is missing and so is Jacob."

Allison

I wake up suddenly. I'm surrounded by quietness. Not silence, because I can hear hospital sounds, the whirring of machines keeping other patients alive, muffled voices through the door drifting down from the nursing station. It's the quietness you get in the dead of the night.

But I'm not scared anymore. I'm focused. Whoever this heavy breather was, since he didn't try to kill me, why should I bother thinking about him at all? My dreams are more interesting.

I concentrate on Rebecca's world.

What I was hoping for was a romance. I wanted Rebecca and Jacob to discover how much they were in love. I wanted them to get married and leave Pennsylvania and travel north by covered wagon. I wanted them to settle in Canada and raise a family. I wanted them to be my ancestors.

But it doesn't look like it's going to work out that way. Not if Jacob has killed his father and stolen a horse. Mind you, Rebecca doesn't believe it. Maybe she's right.

As for me, I have a sort of boyfriend myself. Put that in the past tense. I *had* a sort of boyfriend.

I fell in love with his family's golden retriever. Jaimie Retzinger happened to be on the other end of the leash.

He wanted to get married.

I'm fifteen, for glory's sake.

He wanted me to change my name! I swore if I ever got married, I wouldn't be a Retzinger. He didn't like that I'm very fond of the name Allison Briscoe. Briscoe is the one good thing my mom ever got from my father, unless you count David and me.

Jaimie Retzinger entered my life early last fall. We hung out together in a kind of witless oblivion but ended up getting on each other's nerves. He's not much for thinking or doing things, he's not much for anything, really. It seemed a nice change at the time. He just lives in the moment, he doesn't talk very much, or listen. Mostly he rides around on his secondhand Harley, which he bought when he was working for awhile and hasn't paid off. He's three years older than me but he still lives at home.

My relationship with Jaimie Retzinger is complicated. We went to a school dance once. That was our only dress-up date. Somebody took our picture and it ended up in the yearbook. He didn't like me being in school, he didn't like being in the yearbook, he didn't like when I passed my exams. He was happy when I decided to drop out. That would put us on a more equal footing and he liked that. You fill in the blanks: we split.

More or less.

He'd still come by occasionally after the snow forced him to stop riding his "chopper." That's what he calls his motorcycle, even though there is nothing custom about it. It's just like he bought it, dints, dirt, and everything. He'd drop in to Tim Horton's, order a double-double to go, then hang around, drinking it out of the cardboard cup at a table, taking up space.

My good glory, if falling for Jaimie Retzinger was the dumbest thing I ever did, getting rid of him, more or less, was the smartest.

I mean, talk about no future in a relationship, with Jaimie Retzinger there was hardly a present. Whatever we had was all in the past.

Thinking about him makes me want to swear. I used to swear a lot. I don't any more. *Glory* is about it. It's what my Nana says. We've been using that word in our family for hundreds of years.

As I drift back into Pennsylvania, the last image in my mind is of Jaimie Retzinger. He's smiling that scary smile of his, like he doesn't know what he's smiling about.

Three

Rebecca

Rebecca squinted against the rising sun and gazed directly at the two British soldiers. This seemed to make them uncomfortable. They were not used to Mennonite women making eye contact. Even among the Mennonite men, some would confront them face-to-face, as if daring the soldiers to challenge God's authority, but others looked away, being shy, or fearful, or less certain of their faith.

Johannes Haun stared Corporal Jonas straight in the eye.

He hardly bothered to acknowledge Private Panabaker's squalid existence.

"It is not likely, so, that the boy would kill his own papa, or steal a horse," said Rebecca's father. He spoke English with a heavy German accent, echoing what was commonly called Pennsylvania Deutsch. This was the language his people had brought with them when they fled Europe in search of religious freedom.

While the men talked, Rebecca's mind burst with images of Jacob Shantz in the shadow of the church. Could he possibly have murdered his father? When they had kissed, did he know he was going to do it? Was that why he wasn't afraid about what his father might think? No, she answered herself. Satisfied with her conclusion, she let the images fade.

Jacob's father was not a popular man. If Mennonites had been allowed to dislike someone, they would have disliked Noah Shantz. But that didn't justify murder. Therefore, Rebecca thought whoever murdered Jacob's father, it could not have been Jacob. It had to be someone from outside their community. Her mind was made up.

"It wasn't Old Bess, was it?" she asked.

"Who?" said the corporal with the scar on his face.

"The horse. She was his, you know. Jacob's father wanted to use her for meat because she was old. Jacob promised to work twice as hard if she would be spared." She knew his argument had cost him a terrible beating but his father had given Bess another year.

"Maybe she's his and maybe she isn't," said the soldier who looked like he hadn't washed in weeks. "The old mare still belonged legally to the boy's daddy and the boy took her away."

Jacob might have borrowed Old Bess. He didn't steal her. Jacob was not a horse-thief.

The corporal smiled at her. She glowered back and he blushed. Although his face was in shadow, she could see he had good teeth and he was clean. Why should she care how he looked? She was annoyed with herself. She backed up so that her father stood between them.

The filthy soldier called Panabaker asked her again, practically shouting, if Jacob was on his way to join Washington.

"Why should I know where Jacob Shantz has gone?" she shot back.

"*Sei Still!*" her father scolded. His sharp tone declared she must be polite. He took it for granted she was being truthful.

And she was. She had avoided the soldier's question with one of her own. She had not answered falsely, which she knew was a sin. She had not answered at all.

It would be better if they did not know Jacob was on his way to Valley Forge. If they knew, they would judge him guilty of treason as well as murder. If he were caught, he would be shot for one crime or hanged for the other. Either way, he would die in disgrace and Rebecca would be a tragic figure for the rest of her life.

Behind her, she could hear the familiar sounds of morning activities as her brothers and sisters did their chores and got ready for breakfast. She was hungry. It was almost time to set out for the long walk to school.

"You go ahead now, Rebecca," her father said. "You help your mother. The soldiers are finished with you."

It struck her as odd that he spoke in English. He was declaring to the soldiers their business with her was done. He was being protective.

For a fleeting moment, she wondered what her father would do if they tried to arrest her for being Jacob's friend. Could they do that? Would Johannes Haun resist? Was her stern and gentle father capable of violence? To protect his children, perhaps? To protect the people he loved?

Rebecca felt she should say something else on Jacob's behalf. She thought perhaps she should lie. She could say he was on his way to Upper Canada on the far side of Lake Ontario to join the British troops. But that would dishonor him, and anyway, why not join right here in Warwick? And of course, it would be wicked to lie.

"Rebecca, *Gehen Sei jetzt!*" Her father was ordering her to leave. She knew he was uncomfortable with her being in the presence of such worldly men. It was his duty to shield her from exposure to the larger world.

They were part of a small group of soldiers garrisoned at the edge of town. They had been there since October. The Mennonites sold them food from their meager supplies but they never got used to them. Soldiers in uniforms carrying guns were an ugly reminder of the war they wanted to ignore.

And the soldiers were a temptation.

Some of the Mennonite boys secretly played at being in the army. Some of the girls secretly admired the handsome red uniforms, especially of officers on horseback who carried swords and wore dangerously attractive hats. And at least one of the older boys, who thought of himself as a man, had seen them as agents of a foreign King. That was Jacob Shantz, and whether for adventure or his unruly beliefs, Jacob Shantz had gone off to join the Revolution.

Rebecca turned her back to the three men and walked away. She calculated that the soldiers could never catch up to Jacob. Not even if they knew where he was going. It would take him two days to get to the winter camp of the Continental Army at Valley Forge. Even less, if he were riding old Bess.

But something worried her.

As she stepped back into the warmth of her own home, she wondered what would happen to Jacob if Washington's Revolutionaries found out he was suspected of horse-theft and murder. Would they be obliged to arrest him? To turn him over to the British? To execute him themselves?

Allison

When I wake up this morning, I seem to be in the middle of a thought. It's not a pleasant one. I'm thinking about Jaimie Retzinger. He's a little strange. He's only a little of anything. He just doesn't measure up as a human being. He gets a job and forgets to go to work and gets fired. He forgets to go home. He forgets my name.

But if that sounds like he's stupid, he's not. That's what makes it so bad. I could live with stupid. He just doesn't care about anything, even himself.

Me, I care. I like people, I like working at Tim's. I like the people who work there, and I like the people who come in. The regulars and the tourists. I'm planning on doing a cooking course at Sir Sanford Fleming College after university. I want to be an educated chef, maybe with my own restaurant someday. I want to travel.

The only traveling I can do right now is inside my head.

It's a small world in here.

That's a joke.

Maybe it isn't. In some ways, a mind is bigger than the entire world, the universe, infinity, eternity, everything. Because we can imagine these things. We can reduce them to thoughts.

One of my problems, according to Jaimie Retzinger. I think too much. I always explain my jokes and I think too much.

It's funny, I feel safe in my hospital room right now because I know it is daytime. During the day, nurses and doctors come and go. The cleaning staff comes in. The lights must be on and the curtains are pulled back. At night, the door is closed and the curtains are drawn. I can tell by the muffled sounds, by the stillness of the air. I'm pretty much on my own in the dark.

Except for my visitor. He's in the dark, too. So, is he just listening? That's creepy. It really is. I wonder if he'll be back again? They haven't removed the bandages. I'd know if they had. I wonder if he's waiting to kill me. If so, why wait?

Unless he knows I'm aware, in here. Unless he's taunting and torturing me on purpose.

That's pretty funny, if the only person who knows I'm alive is waiting to kill me.

My world is a very limited place. But I have Rebecca Haun in my dreams, even if she's terrified herself right now, because the soldiers want Jacob for murder.

At least she has a life.

Four

Rebecca

After her sisters said their prayers and they all crawled into the big bed, Rebecca lay awake, staring at the ceiling. If she pulled the blue quilt down a little, she could tilt her head and see out the window. There was no moon and the sky was alive with a billion points of starlight.

Where would Jacob be by now? If he had traveled all night and then all day, he might have reached Valley Forge.

She tried to understand a world where soldiers were trained to kill people. People just like themselves. But if someone were suspected of being a killer, he could be hanged. She preferred the Mennonite ways, where death was a decision left up to God.

She tried to fall asleep but she couldn't stop worrying about Jacob. She decided something had to be done. He was wanted for murder.

Rebecca dressed very quietly so as not to awaken her sisters. She walked down the stairs one step at a time to prevent them from creaking. She poured a little water from the jug directly into one hand and dabbed at her eyes. She combed her long brown hair and braided it, then wrapped it around her head and secured it with the wooden comb her oldest brother, Christian, had carved for her when she turned thirteen.

She took two apples from a basket on the table and tore off a piece of dark brown bread from a loaf in the breadbox. She wrapped the apples and bread in a small bundle. She did not want to take more than her share.

She pulled on her boots and put on her black bonnet with the white trim. She lifted her heavy gray shawl from the back of the door and slipped out into the night. She bent to lace up her boots, then wrapped the shawl around her shoulders and began walking.

Her parents would be horrified.

Johannes and Margaret Haun would not worry about her safety. She was a very resourceful girl. She was smart and she was independent, a quality not admired by Mennonites but one that would give them comfort. No, they would be horrified by how she was going against the law, God's law and man's law.

Their God would be angry at disobedience. Running away, even for a good reason, was disobedient. Running away for the sake of a man, or a boy, who might have broken the Lord's Commandment against murder, that was an unforgiveable sin.

Her father would have no choice but to forbid her return. The moment she stepped out the door into the starlit night, she knew there would be no turning back. But the same God, whose wrath she invited, knew she was moving into the darkness for love. If not for love, for justice and mercy.

Surely their Lord knew Jacob was innocent. The least she could do was to warn him that his father was dead. And that he was wanted for stealing Old Bess.

The unspoken vows between them demanded that much, even if those vows were in ruins.

It was cold but the moon cast its light across the fields, making the frost glimmer like a fairyland. The road was a ribbon stretched tightly across the landscape in front of her. She huddled into her shawl for warmth and walked briskly.

When the sun came up and her brothers and sisters were out of bed, they would discover she was gone. Daniel, Luke, and Matthias, Sarah, Rachel, and Ruth would all scurry around looking for her. Christian, who was the oldest, was away in Massachusetts, studying the Bible at a college in Concord near Boston.

Rebecca knew her mother and father would be frantic with worry. They would know where she was going. But they would not come after her.

She had made her decision.

The rest was out of their hands.

Allison

I'm awake now. Reluctantly. It must be morning but I want to stay with my dream. I've got to figure this out. Who killed Noah Shantz? If her father won't follow Rebecca to bring her back home, she had better find Jacob or she'll be completely alone in the world. Except for me.

And, yes, last night my watcher was back. If he was the guy who put a bullet in my brain, he is a sadist like Hannibal Lector and he's getting his kicks seeing me suffer.

Am I suffering? That is an interesting question. I don't feel any pain. That's a good thing. I don't feel anything at all.

And yet I have feelings. Just because I can't cry doesn't mean I don't want to. When David tells me a joke, I wish I could laugh. I'd love to tell my mom it isn't her fault. She thinks it is, because she's my mom. I feel sorry for her.

I feel like I'm walking through the starlit night into the dawn but the sun won't ever come up.

My days can seem long. I take imaginary trips to entertain myself. Today I tried to imagine I was in the fashion section of a department store. A really expensive one. Women were coming and going, trying on clothes that I've seen in magazines like *Vogue*. I'm more into *People* and *Seventeen*. Not *Cosmo*, I find it depressing. They're obsessed with sex. I'm not.

It's time I work out who shot me.

I realize I probably saw him do it. Have I blacked him out because of the horror? It was no fun being shot in the head. Is it amnesia? Is it temporary? Or did I black out because I knew him and don't want to think about it?

That night, I worked until midnight. It was still winter. I've been in the hospital for a few months. I haven't bothered counting the days because I was in a complete coma for awhile. Maybe I should. I know it must be April by now. I could hear nurses talking about Easter.

So, anyway, that night I worked late. Some Tim Horton's stay open all night but ours in East City, on Hunter Street, closes earlier. There's not enough traffic passing through. We cleaned up. I was the last to leave except for the night manager—that means I wasn't actually the last to leave, I suppose.

Peterborough is a very safe town. Especially the East City area. And I can generally look after myself. I'm quite independent.

After we broke up, Jaimie Retzinger would still walk me home sometimes. He'd ride over from his place and give me a ride. Mostly we'd walk and he'd leave the Harley in the parking lot. When the snow came, he stashed his Harley.

Sometimes he'd show up and sometimes he wouldn't.

It was the kind of logic you can't argue with.

I was tired after a long shift and trudged along Hunter Street and turned right. A car came along. It was a dark blue Chevy. It parked ahead of me. No one got out. I crossed over to the sidewalk on the other side.

I wasn't afraid, but you might as well avoid trouble. If you can't, then you fight. I mean, even David knows enough to stay out of my way if I get really focused on something. When we were little we used to wrestle. He'd pin me down and that would make me furious. But I wouldn't cry. Then when I got to be about eleven, one time I pushed him off and before he knew what hit him, I was straddling him like a donkey and twisting both ears as hard as I could. His eyes filled with tears and his nose started to run. He whispered, "I give, I give," which was like crying "Uncle." He never tried to pin me down again.

Still, he looks after me because he's my older brother. But that night he wasn't there. Jaimie Retzinger wasn't there. I was alone. It was cold and dark.

A guy got out of the car. The interior lights flashed on for a moment. That's when I saw someone in the passenger seat. A bald-headed man.

The guy who got out had his head down, away from the streetlight. I couldn't see his face. Was it covered? I don't think so. I can't remember.

I heard a shout, or was it the bald guy banging on the glass? Or was it the car door slamming shut? Or the crack of a bullet exploding.

My hand in my coat pocket clutched at a can of bear spray. Every year or two you hear about someone being attacked by bears. I've read that ten times as many people die from dog attacks. I bought the spray at Wild Rock, where they sell camping gear. There are no bears in Peterborough. We're probably too far south. But just the same, bear spray has other uses.

The guy didn't cross over to my side of the street. My hand relaxed on the bear spray. Then I saw him raise what looked like a big stick. Only he wasn't lifting it up like a club. He was aiming it at me. It was a rifle. Turns out it was only a .22, but even a .22 can kill if the bullet hits the right place. Like your brain.

Next thing I knew, I was here in my hospital room. And more alive in Pennsylvania in the spring of 1778 than I am in Peterborough today. I know what year it was back then because I was good in history. Before I left school, we studied about the United States and the American Revolution and the winter encampment at Valley Forge.

I learned most of my own family's history from what my Nana Friesen used to tell me. She wouldn't want to see me like this.

Five

Rebecca

On the evening of her third long day of walking, Rebecca approached the outskirts of George Washington's Continental Army camp. Except for the two apples and the brown bread she had packed, she had not eaten since she left home. She did not want to beg for food, in case the British soldiers were following her. She didn't want anyone to know she had been there.

She had slept by the roadside, huddled in her thick woolen shawl, with leaves piled up like a nest all around her.

In the mornings, she combed and braided her hair. She used the cloth from her bundle to scrub her face in the streams she crossed along the way.

When the road came out alongside the Schuykill River, she could see where the bush above Valley Creek opened up into fields. She could see the small hills whimsically called Mount Joy and Mount Misery and she knew she was almost there. She grinned from ear to ear and forgot about how hungry and tired she was.

But her heart sank when she came into the open and saw a city of over one thousand identical log cabins. Each had a log chimney lined with mud and stones, a small door, and no windows. Each was the home of a dozen soldiers. Most of the soldiers were outside in the brisk spring weather, having a smoke by an open fire.

The air was thick with the smell of tobacco and burning wood and twelve thousand men who needed soap and a bath. She was surprised at how many women and children were among them.

"I am looking for Jacob Shantz," she said to the first soldiers who paid her any attention.

A pleasant looking young man, wearing a uniform covered in soot and mud, got up from the log he was sitting on and held out his hand to take hers.

Her own clothes were muddy after the long walk, but her face was gleaming clean, while the soldier's face was smeared with grime.

"Here," he said in a soft voice. "Won't you join us for a bit of late supper?"

No one had ever treated her like a lady before.

"No, thank you," she said shyly, drawing her hand away. "My name is Rebecca Haun. I am looking for my friend, Jacob Shantz, if you please."

"It would please me, of course." He smiled. "My name is Edward de Vere. I would be happy to assist. But first, before our search begins, you must eat."

Since it would be bad manners to refuse twice, she sat down and ate a plate of Boston baked beans. She chewed on a small square of cake. They called it fire cake and, true to its name, it tasted like a piece of burnt wood. She drank a pint of ale from a clay pitcher and some water from a wooden bucket. She had never tasted alcohol before, except for her mother's medicine, but she liked the ale. The beans were sweetened with maple syrup and flavored with small bits of salted pork and almost as good as her mother's.

The men were not much older than her. They were boys, really, dressed in tattered uniforms. Some wore several layers, one over the other. Their jackets were blue and their pants were light brown where the mud allowed the color to show through. Some wore boots without laces and some wore farm boots and a few had only rags wrapped around their feet.

They were surprisingly cheerful. And they were surprisingly polite.

"Now," said Edward de Vere, when she had finished eating, "it will be dark very soon, Rebecca Haun. We will get you settled in for the night and I'll help you search for your friend in the morning."

"He is a Mennonite," she declared, looking around her. "He should not be difficult to find."

"He isn't a Mennonite, no more," said a boy with curly red hair.

"Well, he has not killed anyone," she argued.

"Not yet," said one of the men and they all laughed.

Edward de Vere looked annoyed.

"Sorry, Captain," said the boy with red hair. "Sorry Miss."

"You will please come with me to the women's cabins," Captain Edward de Vere said to her. "I'll see that you're comfortable. They will help you clean up and bed down. Tomorrow, I will find your lucky young man who has killed no one."

He smiled gently and in the firelight she thought he was the handsomest man she had ever seen in her life. She had not actually seen many men. He was the handsomest man she could imagine ever seeing.

Allison

In the fall of Grade 10 we took *Romeo and Juliet* by William Shakespeare. I tried to transfer into the Applied Stream. I really liked the teacher, Mrs. Muratori. And I'm not saying Shakespeare is a bad writer. People still read his work and he's been dead since God-knows-when. But Juliet was only thirteen, for glory's sake.

And it turns out they take the same play in Applied, and anyway Mrs. Muratori convinced me I should stay in the Academic Stream. Then I met Jaimie and got sidetracked. That was what you might call a temporary aberration.

Rebecca is my age. Jacob is nearly sixteen, which means he's really fifteen, too. Rebecca thinks if she finds Jacob she'll discover whether or not they're in love. But it doesn't work like that. I mean Romeo and Juliet hardly knew each other and they fell for each other instantly. With me and Jaimie Retzinger, it was more like Rebecca's situation. We decided we were in love and then waited to see if we were. And it turns out we weren't.

At fifteen there's no way I would have walked three days for a guy who might have murdered his father. Even if I was sure that he didn't.

Or maybe I would have. My own father walked out when I was seven. I haven't seen him since I was eight. He moved to

Vancouver and has another family. I don't actually want him dead, though. I just don't care one way or another. Rebecca believes Jacob is innocent. Since I figure she's family, it's up to me to prove that she's right, or, if she's wrong, it's up to me to expose him.

Potato detective. That's me. Fearless, feisty, intrepid potato detective. And who am I going to prove anything to? No one, except myself. But if we're related, then that's important, too. Like, for me to know. We're part of the same story.

I've got to laugh at myself. No one else does. Except David, and it's not because he's cruel. He believes I'm in here. He believes I can hear him. He's a good guy and I love him to pieces.

I haven't said that in a long time. *Love you to pieces.* I don't know what it means. I don't think it means anything. But I used to tell Jaimie Retzinger, "I like you to pieces." That was before the pieces fell apart.

He didn't make me feel good about myself. Whatever else love is, if it doesn't do that it's not the real thing.

That much I know.

Love has to make you feel good about yourself.

I wonder if someday I'll get out from inside my head and be somebody again.

Stop! No tears.

No crying.

The story of Jaimie Retzinger and Allison Briscoe is this:

I was in a bad relationship.

A guy whose name I will never say to myself decided we were in love. I had turned fifteen. He had a car. He was good looking, with a cartoon tattoo on the side of his neck. He wore a gold earring. He had eyes like Johnny Depp. Then one day he hit me. Not too hard, just enough to scare me without leaving marks.

Only he didn't scare me. He made me angry.

He swore a lot. I used to swear a lot. After him, I stopped swearing. What's the point? I mean, I'm not perfect. I fall off the wagon when I get really mad. But I try not to get really mad. What's the point?

Anyway, over near the old Quaker Oats factory one night, this guy decided I needed a lesson. I had mouthed off, I guess. So we got out of the car and he slapped me hard.

I got up from the ground. I didn't back away. He was a lot bigger than me. I stood right in his face. He sneered. I punched him between the eyes. I could hear his nose crack.

Oh, glory, my fingers hurt.

Blood sprayed, he staggered, I punched him again. This time, in the gut.

He doubled over and went down. I jumped on top of him. The hell with getting blood on my clothes. He was the one who needed a lesson.

He started crying. Can you believe it?

And Jaimie Retzinger, who was walking his family's golden retriever along the Hunter Street Bridge, he saw us. He rushed over to where the action was.

"Okay, girl. You've done enough damage," he said, dropping his dog's leash.

I stopped punching the guy. I refuse to say his name.

"Aren't you a tiger," Jaimie Retzinger said.

My skirt was around my waist, my T-shirt was splattered with blood. I could hardly breathe and I was trembling. When Jaimie Retzinger hauled me off the guy, I didn't know if it was to protect me or to save the creep before I killed him. It didn't matter, it was turning out to be one of the best days in my life.

"I promise," Jaimie Retzinger whispered, "I will never get you angry."

"And I promise," I told him, "I will never beat you up."

We actually helped the creep to get into his car. He wasn't hurt very badly, except for his nose, but he was confused. When he drove away, he didn't squeal his tires. He drove very carefully. He must have had enough excitement for one night.

Jaimie Retzinger walked me home. I told him the only person I had ever hit before was my brother. He didn't believe me. He waited while my mom cleaned me up. Then we went out for a couple of cherry Cokes and some really greasy *poutine*.

Six

Rebecca

The very handsome Edward de Vere called on Rebecca in the morning at Cabin 27. He had washed up and brushed so much dirt off his uniform it looked almost clean. Rebecca had already eaten a breakfast of bread and beans. She was sitting with some women and a few kids by the fire outside, watching the tea water boil and chatting.

"You've settled right in," he said when she stood up to greet him.

She smiled shyly as he walked over to one of the older women and leaned down to kiss her on the cheek. She was the same woman he had left her with the previous night. Her name was Madge. She had helped Rebecca get cleaned up.

"What do you think?" the young man asked Rebecca. He spread his arms slowly in front of him to take in the whole camp. It was a city of sticks and mud. He was proud of it.

"There are more than twelve thousand of us," he said. "Nearly a thousand women. You look surprised. They are known as the Camp Follower Brigade."

He winked at Madge.

Rebecca blushed.

"Yes," he said, responding to Rebecca's embarrassment. "Some of the women are prostitutes."

Rebecca was not very worldly. She wasn't exactly sure what *prostitutes* were, but she thought they must be like whores in the Bible.

"And there are scavengers," he continued. "Women who crawl out into the battlefield and bring back valuable weapons from the dead."

She couldn't imagine a more terrible job.

"There are cooks and the women who mend clothes. There are sisters and wives and daughters. There are mothers."

Edward de Vere stopped talking and walked back over to Madge, a handsome woman dressed in clothes that had been worn and washed so often they were little more than rags. He put his hand on her shoulder and said proudly:

"Madge de Vere is my mother."

Rebecca was stunned. Madge looked poorer than a beggar woman. But she had a broad smile, good teeth, and her eyes flashed when she talked.

"Now then," said Edward, "here comes my boss. I'll have to be going to do drills and practice fighting but I'll come back early this evening. We'll walk about the camp and find your lost young fellow."

A man of medium build wearing a strange gray uniform came over to them and bowed formally.

After Edward de Vere presented Rebecca, the man bowed again.

"I am Baron Friedrich Wilhelm von Steuben, acting inspector general of the Continental Army. I am German, like you, *Fräulein* Rebecca Haun, and it is much my honor your acquaintance to make."

Rebecca had not ever thought of herself as German. She had been born in Lancaster County. She was British and she was Mennonite. She was what they called "Pennsylvania Dutch."

The man in the unusual uniform bowed to her a third time and turned away.

"Come, Edward, we must to work, to work. Good day to you, *Fräulein* Haun, good day, *Frau* de Vere." He gave Madge an informal salute.

When Edward and Baron Friedrich Wilhelm von Steuben disappeared among the rows of cabins, Rebecca turned to Madge.

"And just who is he, when he's not being a very fine gentleman?"

"Oh, a gentleman, he is, *Fräulein* Haun. He is the second most powerful man among us and a good friend of Frederick the Great, the King of Prussia. He's here to make soldiers of farm boys and storekeepers. He doesn't mind getting down in the mud, unlike some other officers I could name."

"Really?" Rebecca had never met a baron who knew a king. She had never talked to an officer before meeting Edward, not even a British officer at the garrison near Warwick. Only the private and corporal who came looking for Jacob.

"Even though he doesn't speak English so well, he is very smart," Madge continued. "And they say in battle, he is a bloodthirsty villain. You want him on your side, for sure."

"And what about Edward, is he a bloodthirsty villain?"

"Edward is a terrifying soldier in battle, I'm told. Her real name is Edwina. She is my only daughter."

Rebecca's mouth hung open like a flytrap.

What kind of a world had she come to?

Allison

Last night I woke up and he was standing so close I could feel the air move from his breathing. It's like he's haunting me, only he's real and I'm the ghost.

He watches me while I lie here, imitating a vegetable.

If I batted an eyelid, I bet he'd freak. I know I would.

I heard a clicking sound just after he arrived, like he was flipping open a smart phone or something. I wonder if he's taking my picture.

Now that's a scary thought.

Really. It is.

Sometimes, I think I can feel my eyelids. I can't focus on any other part of my body. It's like I'm a blob of jelly in the shape of a girl. A woman. A pretty woman. I wonder if I'm still pretty, with a hole in my head? With tubes going in and out?

There must be tubes. I don't eat or drink and I don't poop or pee, so there must be tubes.

I think I can tell where my eyelids are. I can't make them move or anything. But at least I'm making progress. Yeah, well, potatoes have eyes.

That's another joke.

David always laughs at my jokes. He did.

Life with our mother wasn't the most cheerful thing in the world. She tends to feel sorry for herself a lot. Like, all the time. She works as a receptionist for a plumbing contractor called Dripless. She watches television. She gave up having friends after my dad went away.

Me, I'm sociable, I used to have friends. But let's face it, what's the point of coming in to visit a vegetable? So they don't.

Anyway, I wanted to fall asleep again but it seemed impossible, knowing the creep was still watching me. I wonder if he can tell when I'm asleep and when I'm awake?

I wonder if anyone can tell the difference?

Back to Rebecca: If I thought she was going to give up on Jacob and fall in love with the handsome soldier, Edward de Vere, I was on the wrong track. I mean, no one was more surprised than me to find out Edward was Edwina, for glory's sake.

Somebody once told me about women soldiers in the olden days disguising themselves as men. Maybe it was Mrs. Muratori in history class. She taught me both English and history, but in different grades.

Lots of soldiers and sailors back then were in their mid-teens. They seldom bathed or changed their clothes. If their voices were soft, it was because they were young, not because they were secretly growing boobs under their shirts.

And women can fight. We can be fierce. Just ask the former boyfriend whose name I will never say again in my entire life. He's got a crooked nose to prove that it is not nice to hit women. They might hit you back.

Rebecca

It wasn't that difficult to track down a young Mennonite recruit. Before nightfall, Edward de Vere and Rebecca strolled along an avenue of mud to an intersection with signs. One sign pointed to the east: New York. One pointed to the South: Richmond. pointed to the west: Ohio. One pointed to the north. It said New France but that was stroked out and someone had scrawled North Pole.

"That's so we know where we are in the world," said Edward de Vere, laughing. As usual, his face was smeared with dirt. Now Rebecca understood why. As long as it was smudged, no one would know that the young officer never needed to shave.

Rebecca still thought of him by his man's name, not as Edwina. Rebecca wondered if the other soldiers knew. They probably did, but it didn't matter. Edwina was a soldier and she was fierce. They would fight side by side with her to the death.

At the intersection, Rebecca and Edwina turned south and walked along to the third cabin. Several men were sitting out front, smoking and staring into the flames of a roaring fire.

Jacob Shantz was among them. He saw them coming and stood up. His blue uniform was still clean. His cheeks flared bright red. He smiled at Rebecca and grasped her hand.

The only time they had ever touched before was when they kissed goodbye.

He was pleased to see her but confused. The Mennonite world he had left behind must have seemed very distant.

"How are you, Becky?" he asked.

He had never before called her Becky. Only girls at school and her sisters called her that. To boys and men and grown-up women, she was Rebecca, as God had intended.

"How are you, Jacob?"

"Quite well, thank you."

They were very formal.

Edward, or Edwina, backed away.

"Well," said Jacob Shantz, "it is good you have decided to join the Revolution. I see you have found a young gentleman to look after you."

Rebecca was confused.

"No, this is my friend."

She introduced Edward de Vere, who stepped forward to return Jacob's salute.

"Captain de Vere, I am honored, very much," said Jacob, flustered at being in conversation with an officer.

Rebecca had no idea what being a captain meant, although she assumed that Edward de Vere was important.

"Where's Bess?" she asked Jacob. She could think of nothing else to say.

"I don't know any Bess."

"Your big gray mare."

"Old Bess? She's still in the barn, I imagine. Or out in the fields, doing spring plowing with Noah behind her, flicking his whip."

"Jacob, you don't know?"

"What don't I know? A lot I suppose. But I'm willing to learn."

"Your father?"

"Damn my father," he said with a snarl.

She had never heard Jacob swear. She had never heard anyone swear. She cringed a little, fearing God might strike them both dead.

But God struck neither of them.

Before she could warn Jacob that he was wanted for murder, she realized it made no difference. No one would find him here. He was a soldier, now, swept up in historical events. She decided not to tell him his father was dead. It would only confuse him. She decided not to tell him about Old Bess. It would make him unhappy.

"It is good to see you, Jacob."

"It is also good to see you, Rebecca."

Edward de Vere spoke up to relieve the awkwardness. "Perhaps we had better go," he said. "It will be dark soon, we should be getting back."

"Goodbye, Jacob," Rebecca said.

She was surprised they had nothing more to say. The past slipped away as she searched his eyes and found no connection. The boy she had gone to school with, the man she had intended to marry, he no longer existed. The boy had been displaced by a young soldier with a florid face who showed not the slightest curiosity or imagination about why she was really there.

For a brief moment she was confused, then she smiled. She leaned forward and kissed Jacob on the cheek. He turned brilliant red. She turned to her escort and nodded to say she was ready to leave.

As they walked back to the women's cabin that she shared with Madge de Vere, Rebecca took Edward's arm to keep from slipping in the mud.

She gazed straight ahead.

She refused to cry.

Seven

Allison

When I rise up and walk out of this hospital, I will become a vegan. I identify with vegetables. I will eat *only* vegetables. Or fruits and grains and nuts. When I open my restaurant, no meat. Nothing with a face. Nothing with a mother. Nothing dead.

The truth is, lying here like a slab on a platter turns me off meat.

So what! Surely you've got better things to think about, Allison Briscoe.

You're getting stupid. If you let your mind wander, you'll wander in circles, off the cliff, into the deep end, over the edge, whatever.

I've got to get my mind working. Logically, rationally.

I'm in charge of how I think. I'm in charge of what I feel.

Just thinking that, I feel better.

Today David told me about something mysterious they'd learned in history class. There's nothing like a good mystery to get the mind thinking.

They got their teacher talking about buried treasure.

It's on Oak Island in Nova Scotia, just over from Maine. No one has been able to reach it. There's a pulley on a tree at the top of a deep shaft with layers of stones and logs going down over a hundred feet. Six men have drowned or suffocated when the hole caved in or flooded while they were digging. No one has reached the bottom. Drills have dug up bits of gold and Spanish doubloons. It's pirate treasure, they say. It was buried by Blackbeard. Or maybe it belonged to the French government when they still controlled the area. Some say it belonged to a secret club called the Freemasons. Some have suggested it was part of the American treasury.

I like the Blackbeard version best. He was the most famous pirate in the world before Jack Sparrow.

It's hard to beat a mystery about buried treasure that people die trying to reach. When I get out of here, maybe I'll go down to Nova Scotia and see Oak Island. It's just offshore, there's a bridge. David's teacher has been there. He says the island is cursed and it's haunted. He's a teacher—he shouldn't be talking like that. Unless he believes it. Unless it's true.

David's story grabbed my attention but I have a mystery or two much closer at hand. I have murder to deal with.

There's Noah Shantz. He may have been an unholy terror but he didn't deserve to be clubbed to death. A good beating would have been enough. I need to stay close to Rebecca to find out who killed him.

And there's another attempted murder, even more pressing. My own. Let's start with me.

I've been thinking a lot, but I've been on the wrong track. I've been wondering *who*, instead of *why*. Why would anyone hate me so much that he'd want me dead?

I don't know. I've come up against a brick wall. *Why* would someone want me dead? Why me? Why dead?

There must be a motive that connects me with the shooter.

In fifteen years I've done some bad stuff, I suppose. Like pounding *what's-his-face* until he cried. But it wasn't him who shot me. I'd recognize him with my eyes closed.

Is that a joke? I mean, they won't open.

Anyway, he left town. Peterborough wasn't big enough for the two of us. He moved to Lakefield or Toronto.

Don't know, don't care.

What else have I done that's really bad? Bad enough to be killed for? Well, why do people murder people?

Out of anger. I don't go around making people mad at me.

For jealousy. Come on, who'd be jealous of me and Jaimie Retzinger?

For money, then. Yeah, the big insurance payoff. Jackpot!

What about mistaken identity? I repeat, what about mistaken identity?

But no, he drove his blue Chevy close beside me before pulling ahead and stopping. I guess the cops don't know it was a blue Chevy. I mean, they couldn't find out from me, could they? There was fresh snow on the ground. It was bright. I was standing under a streetlight. He knew exactly whose head he was shooting at. I heard a shout before he fired. Was the guy in the car trying to stop him? I remember grabbing the bear spray. With the other hand I clutched the silver medallion hanging on a chain around my neck. It's what they call a talisman, a good-luck charm and family heirloom. It has been in my family for generations. But for good luck! Good glory, I was shot in the head.

And yet, like…wait, good luck for sure: I'm not dead. And I'm dreaming of ancestors as if they were real. Well, they were, of course. My wounded brain is awash in remembering blood.

What about revenge?

Good. We're back to square one. What did I do to deserve to be shot?

Maybe I'll do better thinking about Rebecca and Noah Shantz.

She's convinced Jacob didn't take Old Bess. But Old Bess went missing. So where did she go? Jacob doesn't understand that Rebecca came to warn him about being wanted for murder. But it turns out he's well hidden in plain sight. He doesn't even know his father is dead.

She's just someone from home who joined the Revolution. Since he turned his back on his Mennonite brethren, it doesn't surprise him that she could do the same. It seems he's not the sharpest knife in the box. More like a spoon.

I feel myself drifting into sleep. I know my midnight stalker is watching. What's he looking for? Does he know what I did to get myself shot? Does he know *why* he did it—if it was him? Who else? There could be a conspiracy, a horde of villains determined to eliminate Allison Briscoe. I doubt it, but who knows? Glory, glory, I'm safer asleep. Good night, Allison. Sleep tight.

Rebecca

Rebecca lay on her straw mattress, staring up into the rafters. It was still dark outside, but bright enough with the new moon that a few chinks of light shone through the boards in the gables, between the logs and the sloped roof. She refused to sob but she couldn't hold the tears back. She could feel them burning her cheeks and soaking her pillow.

Now she understood the kiss, the one beside the church. Jacob was saying goodbye to the world he had grown up in. She had been the best thing in that world, just like his father was the worst thing. It was not because she was extra special. It was because she was pretty and kind and smiled at him whenever their eyes met.

It was not about romance. Coming to school must have been a relief for Jacob from the horrors of home. Sitting across the aisle from her had been the best part of his day.

It made her happy to know this, in spite of being sad.

She felt very old and very young at the same time. She knew that whatever love between a man and a woman was, Jacob had not been in love. Neither had she. They might have got married and had children and lived long lives, but they would never have been in love.

A warm hand came to rest on her forehead. It was Madge de Vere, Edward's mother. Rebecca felt a calmness sweep over her. She fell asleep, almost happy.

In the morning, Madge took her around and introduced her to a woman who put her to work sewing. Her job was to stitch up the blue jackets and the brown pants of the soldiers. Sometimes, the men wrapped themselves in blankets and waited while she sewed. Some of the men flirted with her.

She was always cheerful but she didn't have any idea how to flirt. She just smiled her sweet smile and lowered her eyes and dozens of young men fell in love with her.

Not Jacob Shantz.

She never saw him again in her life.

She was told he died of typhoid fever. The first week, a bloody nose; the second week, delirium; the third week, intense pains in his gut. Before he had been at Valley Forge for a month, he was dead.

He had just turned sixteen.

Captain de Vere came to tell her. It was the morning of May 6, 1778.

Together, they visited his fresh grave. It was one among many. The cemetery was close to a stand of tall maple trees with bright green leaves just beginning to unfurl. The old soldiers who cared for the graves were tapping some of the trees to make syrup. The real maple syrup season was over but there was still a bit of a flow. She could smell the sweet smoke from the fires where they were boiling down the sap.

"He didn't have immunity," de Vere explained.

She didn't know what that meant.

"His system was weak."

"No, he was very strong."

"But his body wasn't used to being sick."

"There is not much sickness among the Plain People."

"And perhaps that was his problem. Our insides build up immunity. It's like scar tissue. Each time we're sick and recover, we're a little bit tougher."

"But I didn't get the fevers and I grew up just like him."

"Then you're very lucky, Rebecca."

Captain de Vere stood back while Rebecca kneeled down beside Jacob's grave and prayed to her God to love and forgive him.

Theirs was a stern God but she thought Jacob deserved His love.

When she stood up, she removed her black bonnet with the white trim. She set it on top of his grave. She was not angry at God but she knew she was no longer a Mennonite.

She wasn't sure about anything else.

Captain de Vere returned her to the sewing room in one of the cabins. Rebecca still thought of him as a handsome young man, even though she knew he was a girl only a few years older than herself. If the Continental Army of George Washington accepted Edwina as a gentleman officer, then that's what she was!

"Don't forget to come down to The Grand Parade," he said before leaving her.

"I don't feel very much like a party, Captain."

"It might be just what you need, *Fräulein*."

"Will I see you out there on the field, marching and saluting?"

"You will, and ten thousand more just like me. The French have joined our cause and Baron von Steuben has declared a military holiday."

"A military holiday? What's that?"

"We fire our cannons and our muskets in a *feu de joie*. That's French for 'fire of joy.' It will be spectacular, I promise."

"I don't like guns."

"Then you're in a funny place, aren't you?" Edward de Vere grinned.

Rebecca smiled shyly.

"And," said de Vere, "you'll get to meet my older brother, William."

Edwina de Vere was full of surprises.

She wondered what Christian would think of her now!

"William has been in hospital in Virginia. He was wounded but he's recovered nicely. Come along with Madge to the celebrations. She'll make sure you meet him. He's a handsome devil."

"I won't meet the Devil, Captain de Vere, handsome or otherwise," she snapped back, suddenly not at all shy.

But after a morning's work she was excited. She looked forward to joining Madge on the big field known as The Grand Parade.

Eight

Rebecca

Madge de Vere had a small satchel which she kept tucked between her straw mattress and the log wall. She opened it. To Rebecca's surprise she took out a carefully folded blue silk dress and some cotton petticoats.

All the women in their cabin crowded around, standing on the mattresses spread over the floor. Everyone except Rebecca knew by the way she talked so properly that Madge was a fine lady from Boston. Rebecca thought everyone at the camp spoke English with an accent, but it was Rebecca who had the accent. The Mennonites of Lancaster County spoke German, which they called Deutsch or Pennsylvania Dutch. She had spoken English at school.

Madge held the gown up against Rebecca. All the girls and women clapped. Rebecca blushed. She had never seen a fancy dress in all her life. She could not imagine anyone wearing it. She had never worn anything but plain, drab colors. But since God made the world full of color, she could not think why He would object to a shimmering blue dress.

And the Mennonite elders were not there to tell her different.

"Yes, I think that will do," said Madge. "Let's get to work, ladies."

No one asked Rebecca if she would like to wear the dress. They sent her down to the stream to clean up. When she got back, with her cheeks glowing from the cold water, they were already busy with needle and thread, taking the dress in to be a good fit.

No one asked her when they drew the petticoats up around her waist or laced up the bodice. She was aghast when they dropped the dress over her head and settled it around her slender body. She could not believe this was happening to her.

When they had finished with her hair and pinched her cheeks, she was led out into the sunlight.

The rest of the women were in tattered clothes, some no more than rags. And they were so proud of her, some had tears running down their cheeks.

"Now then, every one of us is a lady," Madge announced. "But you are the champion of Cabin 27."

Cheers rang out all around them. A crowd had gathered. She was the champion of the entire women's camp, George Washington's Regimental Camp Followers. In all the excitement, Rebecca had entirely forgotten what the elders might think back in Warwick. She was a long way from home.

Allison

When I woke up, I knew something was wrong. Usually, I wake up fast and Rebecca's world is very clear in my mind. But this time I became aware of the world very slowly. I had vague memories of a blue silk gown.

I listened. I tried to sort out the voices. They sounded excited.

"She's coming back," someone said.

"We almost lost her," said another.

"Her heart and her lungs are working again. We can take her off life-support. She can breathe on her own."

Well, apparently I've had a setback and given everyone a good scare. I wonder why they didn't let me die? Someone out there must believe I will someday jump up from my bed and get on with my life. Me, too. I've got to believe that.

I don't believe in God, at least not very much. I've got to believe in myself.

I don't really know what time of day it is. It must be afternoon because David is here. Unless it's the weekend.

My good glory, it gets confusing. If you let it, if you panic.

Now everything's quiet. It's evening. David's still here. He is telling me about his history class. The teacher assigned the students a project: They're to imagine a way to get the treasure out of the Money Pit on Oak Island and write their plans as an essay. They'll be marked for originality. And for grammar, of course.

David's gone. My mother came and cried for a while and went home. The midnight stalker is back. He never talks to anyone. No one talks to him. He just sits there. Or stands. *Whatever.*

Wait!

There was this one guy!

Why didn't I think of him? I guess because he doesn't live in Peterborough. So, why does my killer have to live in Peterborough? Good question.

Four of us from Tim's went to Toronto to celebrate last New Year's Eve. The others were older than me. We rented a hotel room right down town, just off Yonge Street. Party central.

I knew I was in over my head, so I was wary.

We went out for a light dinner. Sushi. Apparently, you always eat light before clubbing. Then we went back to our room for a few drinks. I don't drink, but no one noticed. Then we went out.

No trouble getting into Club Bizarro. I look older than I am if I want to. I danced mostly with my friend Helen. We laughed a lot. Helen drank a vile blue concoction. One was enough. Otherwise, we nursed Shirley Temples. With irony: kids pretending to be grown-ups pretending to be kids.

A guy cut me out on the dance floor like a sports car swerving to cut off a bus. Not that I look like a bus. I was looking good.

He said his name was Basset. Said he went to *universe-itty*. The way he said it, I knew he was lying. Said he was single. I knew he was lying about that, too. He was trying too hard to have fun.

I dumped him. So he shifted his attention to Helen. Okay by me, except I had no one to dance with for a while.

Helen went to the restroom. Basset followed her. I followed Basset. He was trying to make out with her but that's not what Helen wanted. By the time I got through the door, she was crying.

I grabbed Basset's hand and twisted his arm around his back so hard I could hear his shoulder pop. He collapsed. Helen and I returned to the dance floor, but we figured it was time to leave.

We didn't pay any attention when Basset came out of the washroom. He was talking to a bouncer when we got to the front door. The bouncer was a big guy, of course. He stood in front of us. We weren't going anywhere.

Basset wanted to lay assault charges against both of us. We had to wait until the cops came.

The cops knew exactly what had happened. They weren't born yesterday. So, they had all of us give them our names and home addresses right there. Basset got scared, of course. He wanted to punish us, but he didn't want his wife to find out that he had been in the ladies restroom in Club Bizarro.

He dropped the complaint or whatever it was. But not before he wrote down our information. He said "for insurance purposes." The cops gave him a ride to the hospital. I guess I hurt his shoulder pretty bad.

About two weeks later, I got a letter by snail-mail. It had a note inside one word: Cow!

I was kind of proud of that note, although the message was pathetic. I mean, *cow*. I suppose, when everyone swears, a non-swearing insult is meant to really sting. It didn't. I carried it around for a couple of weeks as a trophy. Then, when I was housecleaning my purse, I threw it in the garbage.

But it wasn't Basset who shot me. If he did, he would have come after Helen, too. And he didn't.

Then why bother thinking about him? Because the whole episode was an exciting action-packed adventure. That's why.

Helen came in to see me when I was in the first coma and still on life support. She hasn't been back, but David would have told me if anything had happened to her. Like, if she'd been shot.

Anyway, I'd know.

I have a sixth sense for things like that.

Nine

Rebecca

A little girl of seven or eight disappeared under the folds of Rebecca's petticoats, carrying her boots. With another girl holding her hand for balance, Rebecca stepped into one boot, then the other. The little girl laced them up. They were farm boots, but no one would see them.

The girl emerged from under the dress and looked up. "When I get big, Miss Rebecca, I'm going to be beautiful just like you."

Rebecca blushed. Someone stepped in front of her with a fragment of mirror. She had never looked at herself in a mirror before. She was astonished. And a little embarrassed. She wished Jacob Shantz could have seen her now.

She shuddered at the thought of poor Jacob.

Madge de Vere reached under the thick braid of hair that hung down the back of her own neck. She undid a clasp and drew a thin silver necklace away from her shoulders, exposing a medallion of polished silver with a smooth piece of golden amber at the center. The silver was still warm from its nest between her breasts when she placed the chain around Rebecca's neck and the medallion rested against her bosom. No one in the camp had seen it before, except Edwina.

Together, the women of Cabin 27 walked over to The Grand Parade where thousands of soldiers were assembling in formations for the *feu de joie*. The women crowded around the edges of the vast field. They watched officers riding on horseback. They watched canons being pulled into position. Then they watched in awe as George Washington rode on his huge brown horse right around the parade field.

The soldiers cheered him, the women and children of the Camp Followers Brigade cheered him. When he was opposite Rebecca and her friends, he pulled up his horse. She was a vision in blue, even for the Commander of the Continental Army.

General Washington touched his large black hat, which seemed to Rebecca to be on sideways. He bowed his head. His sad eyes caught hers for a moment and the great man smiled. He took his hat off and bowed again. The breeze caught his white hair and made it glimmer. Then he sat up abruptly and trotted away.

Rebecca was confused.

"Ah, my dear Becky," Madge whispered in her ear. "You remind the general of all that we are fighting for. *We*, Becky. *You and me and the girls of Cabin 27 and the rest of us.* God bless you, Rebecca Haun."

Allison

My silver medallion! I'm sure it's the same one Mr. Washington must have seen on Rebecca at The Grand Parade. It's nice to think it connects me with him. It's at home, now. David told me the ambulance woman gave it to him when they brought me here. I hope he'll bring it in. My Nana Friesen gave it to me. The silver is old and worn but the amber is like new. It shines as if there was a light inside.

Amber is very old pine gum, like millions of years old, after it has turned into stone. And silver, well it's silver from a silver mine.

I've never been into jewelry. I got my ears pierced, of course. I think I was thirteen. I once had a stud in my belly button. Not in it, beside it. But I took it out. No reason, I just got bored with it.

The adventure was having it done.

Helen Fielder and I had belly buttons done at the same time. I think she's still got hers. It became infected but she kept it. That's a different Helen from Tim's Helen at the Bizarro.

When I get out of here, I'm going to get a tattoo. Maybe. But not a cartoon, no way.

Or maybe I won't. A sweater I like today I might hate tomorrow. Imagine a tattoo, a lifetime from now.

Meanwhile, who tried to shoot me?

I've still got a thinking mind. So, think.

The guy got out of his car. He had a gun behind the seat. It was a rifle. He held it up to his shoulder and stared down the sights. It was a .22. There was a shout, Stop! He pulled the trigger. It was cold that night. He must have taken off his gloves. He knew what he was doing. He was an experienced shooter.

It was a rifle, for sure, not a handgun. But it was a .22. If he had been a hunter, it would have been a bigger gun. Nobody hunts with a .22.

So, who keeps a .22 rifle around? A farmer, not a hunter. Nobody from the city. A farmer needs it to shoot rodents. Groundhogs and rats and things.

It wouldn't be for target shooting. Anyone in the city who shoots at targets would use a pistol. Or a cowboy revolver.

So, we're back to the farmer.

I was shot by a farm boy.

About my own age. You can always tell the age of a guy by the way he stands. Most of the time. Sometimes you'll be wrong.

Now we're getting somewhere.

Rebecca

The *feu de joie* was terrifying. If there were British spies, they would have been shaking in their boots. The American Revolution might not be over for several more years and many thousands would likely die, but Rebecca believed the outcome was determined right there, on The Grand Parade at Valley Forge!

Cannons blasted down a long line, one after the other, in a furious wave of sound and fury. Then the muskets were fired in wave after wave of explosions, one after another, up and down the lines.

General Washington might have worried about wasting ammunition. He had been a British officer himself, before the Revolution. He worried about running out of gunpowder. But Baron Friedrich Wilhelm von Steuben, the friend of Frederick the Great, the King of Prussia, insisted. It was necessary to impress their new friends, the French. It was necessary to frighten the British. And it was necessary to make the soldiers of the new nation proud.

And proud they were.

Near the end of the military display, officers rode right around The Grand Parade at a full gallop, with their swords drawn.

When Captain Edward de Vere rode by, Rebecca was astonished. She was used to seeing him in tattered uniform, covered with mud. But standing in his stirrups, raging with his sword cutting through the air, he was dazzling. And splendid. And frightening.

After the riders had charged around the edge of the field, two horsemen approached Rebecca and Madge and the other women from Cabin 27. The men walked, leading their horses behind them. The horses were in a lather and looked fierce. Nothing at all like Old Bess or the workhorses of Warwick.

One of the officers was Captain Edward de Vere. Rebecca knew in an instant that the other must be his brother, Captain William de Vere. Edward was smiling. William looked stern, but there was fire in his eyes. They were like amber in sunlight.

Rebecca fell instantly in love.

Ten

Allison

I've been thinking about why I deserved to be shot. I keep wondering if it was my fault. I know it's ridiculous, but that's what I keep thinking.

It's not always about you, Allison.

That's what Mrs. Muratori said when I told her history was boring. *Maybe history isn't boring, maybe it's you.* I objected. *It isn't always about you, Allison.* She said that.

And I swore I'd never be bored, ever again in my life.

Well, maybe this case *isn't* about me. Maybe it's about him, the guy who did the crime.

Maybe I *didn't* deserve it.

So far, I've figured he probably lives on a farm. He's a good shot. He got me right in the head and that's what he was aiming for.

Now, the problem is, I've never been on a farm in my life. I don't know any farmers. I've talked to a few at the Saturday Market down by the hockey arena. But who would try to kill me because I didn't buy their green beans?

Some of my customers at Tim Horton's might have been farmers. East City is an older section of Peterborough and there's not a lot of through traffic. Farmers would more likely go to Saint Tim's out on Ashburnham or up north on Chemong.

So, let's move backwards.

High school? Lots of boys. Lots of farm kids but no one I really knew.

Public school? I remember a few kids would come in by bus from the country. I don't think I talked to a single one of them in over eight years. I didn't avoid them. They just weren't my friends.

I still remember the name of every kid in my room from back then. The name Russell Miller springs into my mind. Why do I remember him? He wasn't in my grade. But he had a little sister, Sharon. They were farm kids. She was in my room in Grade Three then she died. She was killed in a car accident. No, she was drowned. Or in a house fire.

Anyway, it was a horrible death and everyone in the school was upset.

Russell Miller was in Grade Five. His sister's funeral was on a weekend. He came to school on Monday, as usual.

No one talked to him. We were all scared. We didn't know what to say. The teachers treated him special. His sister had just been killed; he should have been at home with his parents. We all knew that.

On Tuesday, he didn't come to school.

On Wednesday, a policeman came and asked if we had seen Russell.

He told us to keep our eyes open.

Well, we did. I found him in a shed beside the school where the janitors kept snow shovels and stuff. I don't know why I looked there. It just seemed like a place where I'd hide from the world if my sister had died.

He was crouched in the shadows at the back and I went in without saying anything and we sat together in the gloomy light of that shed for an hour. Then I found a teacher who was out in the yard, looking for me.

I don't think Russell and I talked but we might have. He held my hand. I clearly remember that he held my hand.

I don't remember much about Russell Miller after that. He was two years older. Sometimes, he would just stare at me. I don't think I was cruel but I ignored him.

What if he saw me as his only friend in the world?

Oh, for glory's sake!

He went to Thomas A. Stewart Secondary School, same as me. He came in by bus. Half way through Grade Nine I began to notice him. There were a lot more kids there than in my public school. By then he was only one year ahead of me.

What if I was still his only friend? And I didn't pay any attention. He had sad brown eyes. He had light brown hair. It was always matted, like a clump of dried grass. I don't know about his teeth. He never smiled.

When I was in Grade Ten, he was still around. He had dropped out of school but there he'd be, by my locker, in the parking lot, across the cafeteria, near the water fountain. Just hanging around. We never talked. Our only real memory in common was too upsetting to talk about. For him, I mean. Not really for me. His sister and I were never friends. Like I say, I can't remember how she died.

Maybe he was stalking me.

But why would be want to kill me?

Because he was in love with me.

Allison Briscoe!

The only way Russell Miller could live without me—was if I were dead.

Some people are unbalanced that way. They confuse love with hate, and life with death. They fall in love with a movie star and murder them. It's a sickness. I'm not a star but maybe Russell Miller thought I was.

Why wait until I was fifteen?

Because David or *what's-his-name* and then Jaimie Retzinger were always around.

Then I split up with Jaimie Retzinger.

And then one night, I was walking alone through the snow.

And the rest, as Mrs. Muratori would say, is history.

She was wrong about one thing, though.

I'm not boring, I refuse to be boring. Only bored people are boring and I'm never bored.

Not ever.

Rebecca

The two Captains de Vere looked very much alike. William was a larger version of Edward. William was quiet. He was older and he had been wounded at the Battle of Québec in December of 1775.

While very young, he had joined the Sons of Liberty and fought against unfair taxes and no representation in government. This led to a serious quarrel with his father, also named William, who was torn between passionate commitment to his rebellious compatriots and deep gratitude to King George. The de Veres, like the more famous Reveres, who had changed their name from Revoire, had fled France after thousands of Protestants had been slaughtered in the streets of Paris for their religious beliefs, until the River Seine ran crimson with blood. The British provided them refuge, the Boston colonies offered prosperity.

One day the elder William, Madge's husband, was shot dead by a drunken British soldier. The de Veres were very traditional. But after nothing was done to punish the soldier, the whole family decided to follow William's example. They wanted no more of British rule.

When Edwina joined Washington's army at Valley Forge, after nursing her brother in the hospital in Virginia, their mother followed. Madge de Vere closed up their house, packed up their household goods, and sold what she could to raise money for the Revolution. She joined her daughter early in 1778 as a member of the Regimental Camp Followers, with special skills in organizing workers. In Boston, she used to have six servants indoors and two for the garden. None was a slave. One, who worked for them briefly, was a black patriot called Crispus Attuks. He was killed in the Boston Massacre of 1770, while William was still in his teens.

Rebecca admired how the de Vere family got along. William treated Edward like a fellow officer, not a kid sister. Madge treated them both like soldiers. And all three of them adopted as one of their own the foundling Mennonite girl who had stumbled into their lives.

While the de Vere brother and sister looked alike, they were very different. Edward was usually filthy. William, who preferred to live among the general staff, was spotless. His uniform was like new, his long blue coat had buttons that shone in the sunlight. Edward's uniform, in spite of the sewing and washing his mother did, was in rags. Edward preferred to stay close to his men. There was not one of them who would not have taken a bullet for their slight young leader.

Whether they knew she was a woman or not, she was among the most revered officers at Valley Forge.

Baron von Steuben kept his officers working but, after they met, William quite often took time to call on Cabin 27 to visit Rebecca. If all the signs of war and of want had not been so much in evidence, they might have been courting.

On the evening of June 18th, the young couple strolled around the edge of The Grand Parade. She sometimes took his arm as they skirted puddles. But then she would let go, determined to walk on her own. Still, they walked closely enough. Their relationship was apparent to all.

There was more activity than usual, given the hour. Soldiers were packing up. Some were already on the move toward Philadelphia. The women had been getting ready for several days and were doing last-minute things. The next morning, the small city of Valley Forge would be no more.

"What about you, Becky?" William asked. "Where will you go?"

"I will stay with Madge. I can't go back to Lancaster County. I disobeyed my father. Well, not exactly, but I left his house. In his eyes and God's, I broke his trust. I would be shunned."

"Shunned? What's that?"

"No one will talk to me. If I walk among them, even my own mother must treat me like I'm not there. To my family and my church, I am dead."

"What a terrible church."

"Don't say that, William. They are good people but they believe in a stern God. I left by choice. I needed to warn my friend, Jacob Shantz, that he was wanted for murder."

"So I've been told. For killing his father. And did he?"

"No, of course not."

And as if to prove she were right, almost by an act of the Almighty, Himself, Rebecca glanced over among the cabins and looked straight into the familiar face of a soldier from home.

"William, stop," she exclaimed.

But the soldier was already walking toward them.

He seemed as surprised as she was. Here was a Mennonite girl dressed in colorful rags, walking with a handsome young officer in a fresh, clean uniform.

It was Corporal Jonas, the Redcoat soldier with the scar down the side of his face who had come looking for Jacob.

He still had his big mustache but now he was dressed in tattered blue.

"Sir," he said, first addressing Captain William de Vere. Then he turned to Rebecca. She remembered his warm smile. "Miss Rebecca Haun. I met you at your father's farm three months ago. I am Peter Jonas. I was on the other side back then. A lot can happen in three months. We had given you up for dead, Miss Rebecca. Did you ever find Jacob Shantz?"

"I am very much alive," she explained. "Jacob is deceased."

"I'm sorry to hear of it."

"He died from the fever. He did *not* kill his father."

"I know that, Miss. But how do you prove it? He has gone to the grave with the mark of murderer on him forever."

"Do you know who did it?" she demanded.

"I have my suspicions, Miss Rebecca."

"Well, speak up, man," said Captain de Vere.

"No sir, I cannot. I have no proof. But the whole affair upset me enough that I have joined our Continental Army."

"Well, that's one good thing to come out of Noah Shantz's death," said Rebecca. She held out her hand. "Perhaps we'll have a chance to talk again."

"Are you following us to Philadelphia, Miss?" Peter Jonas inquired.

"Yes, but I have something to do, first."

She smiled at the soldier and took William's arm, leading him away.

"I intend to leave right now. There will be a full moon tonight and I enjoy walking in the dark. I promise I will be safe and I will catch up with you later. Will you take me back to Cabin 27? No, do not, I wish to go by myself. I will pack what little I have and get on the road. If I miss your mother, please tell her and tell Edward, thank you for everything. But I owe it to Jacob and his righteous God to clear his name."

"Be careful," said William.

"Thank you for not asking me to explain myself," she said. She took his hand and laid it against her cheek, then turned away so neither he nor the renegade soldier could see her tears.

As she walked off, all by herself, she heard Corporal Jonas call after her:

"Follow the horse, Miss Rebecca. Follow the horse."

Eleven

Allison

I have dark brown hair and hazel eyes. I wear a size four. My shoe size is 8, my bra size is 34B. My preference is for bright clothes with solid colors. Sometimes I dress a little skanky, but when I do, I know I'm doing it. I'm about three feet tall, including the bed.

Okay, that last bit was a joke.

If I could stand up, I would be about average height.

Why am I telling you my data? Just to establish I'm me.

I wonder if it gives my midnight stalker satisfaction, seeing me like this? I mean, I'm not even a zombie. They have no mind but they can move. I have a mind, and can't.

Yeah, well, I'm alive! Maybe not kicking, but I'm alive! As that woman in the States used to say, the one from Alaska who ran for President or whatever: *You betcha*!

I couldn't have voted for her, anyway. Only Americans can vote for the President. Which doesn't seem fair, since their President is pretty much the boss of the world.

If my Pennsylvania Dutch ancestors did not come up during the Revolution, or soon after, I would have been an American. But they did, they crossed over at Fort Erie near Niagara Falls. My family became Canadians before Canada existed. Nana Friesen used to tell me about them. She could remember things that happened before she was born. Maybe you don't need a bullet in the head for the blood to remember. Sometimes, the past is just there, within us.

My ancestors were known as United Empire Loyalists. They packed as many of their belongings as they could into what they called Conestoga wagons. They hitched up plow horses and oxen to pull them. And they came north. Some of them had been in Pennsylvania since 1683, so it wasn't easy to leave. They had been there for over a hundred years. They had buried grandparents and parents and children in the cemeteries of Lancaster County.

But the British had promised them they would never have to fight in a war. The British King had the power to enforce God's laws. But King George was losing the battle. So my family came north to Upper Canada because the King was still in charge up here and everyone was free—slavery was against the law here, over seventy years before it was illegal in the United States.

Upper Canada became the Province of Ontario in the Dominion of Canada. And I became a vegetable in a hospital in Peterborough, with a bullet hole in my brain.

I don't think Russell Miller wanted to hurt me. I've decided it must have been Russell Miller. He just wanted me dead.

In his screwed up mind, then I would be his.

But he would have had to kill *himself* to join me. I wonder if he thought of that?

Good question, Allison. When I get better, I'll have to ask a shrink. Meanwhile, he watches over me. Russell does. It must be him. I don't know what he's told the night nurses. They must know he's here.

They probably think he's my long lost lover, on a deathwatch.

Rebecca and her people had their God. I have Russell Miller.

But what about the witness, the other guy in the car, the guy who yelled "Stop?" Where'd he get to? Maybe I just made him up, maybe I want to imagine Russell has a conscience, so in my memory I've created the other guy to try and save me. He's what they call a *figment* of my imagination. I thought of fig newton cookies when Mrs. Muratori first told us about making up things on purpose. She could have just said, "intentional hallucination." Sometimes words have no meaning, sometimes they mean too much.

I'm thinking in circles, like a figure skater going faster and faster as the circles get tighter, the closer I get to the truth.

I'm drifting off to sleep. Where is he? It must be evening. Yeah, David was here a couple of hours ago. My mom didn't come in.

The door into the hall opens and closes. I can feel the air in the room moving. I can hear him breathe.

His breathing is getting louder.

Is this it, Allison? Is this the end?

The breathing is slowing down. He must be sitting in a chair. I listen and listen. Good grief, he's snoring.

My night stalker is asleep.

He snores again.

Oh, my good glory! I'd recognize that snore in a hailstorm.

It's Jaimie Retzinger.

Rebecca

By the time Washington's army reached Philadelphia in pursuit of the British, Rebecca was trudging through familiar landscape. She had found Madge to say goodbye but missed Edward. Madge had put together a respectable outfit for her from borrowed clothes and packed up some brown bread and fillets of smoked fish caught in the Schuykill River. She had hugged her when they parted, like Rebecca was her own daughter.

As Rebecca entered familiar country, she thought about her mission. She knew enough of the world by now to realize it would do no good to announce Jacob's innocence, simply because he didn't know his father was dead. Peter Jonas had told her to follow the horse. Somehow, Old Bess could prove that Jacob had committed no crime—apart from leaving his community, defying their God, and joining the forces of a great revolution.

Rebecca stopped at the end of the long lane into her family's farm. She was wearing a blue muslin skirt and a blouse of light green cotton. She had the gray woolen shawl, the one she had taken with her when she left home, draped over her shoulder.

The fields were lying fallow. They hadn't been plowed or planted. The barn doors were open. In the distance, she could see her brothers and sisters. Daniel, Luke, and Matthias. Sarah, Rachel, and Ruth. Christian would still be away in Massachusetts, studying at Bible College in Concord outside Boston.

They were busy loading up two Conestoga wagons. Her mother came out of the house and gazed in her direction. Her mother waved.

It was a friendly wave to a stranger. Rebecca knew it would not have crossed her mother's mind that her own daughter was standing at their gate, wearing bright blue and green, with flowing brown hair and no bonnet.

Rebecca waved back. She took the shawl and laid it over the fence post. Her mother would be able to use it in Canada. Then she turned and walked toward the community that had grown up around the white painted Mennonite church—the church where she and Jacob Shantz had shared her first and only kiss. The kiss on his cheek when they parted at Valley Forge wasn't really a kiss.

Warwick had three churches and a hostelry called The Warwick Hotel. Rebecca went to the hotel, which had been bought a few years earlier by a man who owned two slaves—a man and a woman. The Mennonite elders had told him he could not run his business there if he had slaves. So he sold them.

Rebecca paid for a room for one night with some of the money Madge de Vere had given her. After cleaning up, as a treat she went to Nixon's Dry Goods store and bought some clothes. She returned to the hotel to leave her parcel of clothes and then walked down the main street in the direction of the British garrison.

She passed many Mennonites as she walked, people she had known all her life. The men and boys looked straight through her. The women cast their eyes to the side. Girls her own age or younger blushed and pretended not to see her.

Rebecca walked with her head down. She nearly bumped into a woman dressed in black. She moved to the side. The woman moved the same way.

"Excuse me," Rebecca said.

The woman, who was carrying a gray shawl over her arm, stood her ground.

"Look at me, girl. Won't you look at your mother? Did you not know I could recognize my own child? Hold your head up, Rebecca."

Her mother was defiant.

"Let those who are without sin be our judges. Only them." She seemed to sigh. We are going to Canada, Rebecca. I am sorry you cannot come. Your father would forbid it. We will be among our brethren, just across the river near the great Falls. But when this war is over, you will come to visit. I will see that your father allows it."

"*Danke, Mutter.*"

Suddenly, Rebecca realized her mother had been speaking to her in English. Standing on Main Street. Looking her straight in the eye. Without shame.

"Thank you, Mother," she repeated in English.

"And do you know who killed Noah Shantz, Rebecca? That is why you are here, yes?"

"That is why I am here."

An idea was beginning to form, but she couldn't be certain.

"I will go with you," her mother announced.

Together, they marched down the street to the outskirts of town. They found the commanding officer of the garrison. He was busy. The British had fled from Philadelphia when

George Washington arrived. The commandant was packing up to join his fellow Redcoats in retreat.

He seemed surprised to see a Mennonite woman accompanied by a girl who was obviously not Mennonite.

"Captain, I am here about Jacob Shantz," Rebecca announced.

"He did not murder his father," her mother declared.

"And how do you know that?" the officer demanded, speaking to Rebecca.

"*How do you know that?*" her mother asked Rebecca in German.

Suddenly, it all became clear. If Jacob did not take Old Bess, like everyone thought, then someone else did. The soldier with the scar had been trying to tell her, the person who took Bess murdered Noah Shantz when he tried to stop him.

"There were two soldiers who came looking for Jacob," said Rebecca. "But, earlier that morning, did someone sell a horse to the British Army? Do you keep records?"

"I don't have to look at the records. The answer is 'yes.' Private Panabaker sold us a horse. We had not eaten meat for three weeks. It was a life saver and very tasty."

"Old Bess!" Rebecca exclaimed. "Poor Old Bess." She took a deep breath. "Your soldier stole him."

"Well, I'm sorry for that. But I'm not surprised."

"And he killed Noah Shantz."

The officer looked shocked. Then he offered a grim smile.

"Well, he won't be hanged," said the officer.

"And why not?" Rebecca's mother seemed almost afraid to ask. She did not approve of hanging, but she believed in stern justice.

"Private Panabaker tried to leave us. It was the day after the soldier with the scar on his face got away. Corporal Jonas."

"And what happened to Private Panabaker?" Rebecca demanded.

Her mother had never heard a woman, never mind a girl, talk to a man as his equal. She gazed at her daughter with proud concern.

"Private Panabaker cannot be hanged because he was shot for desertion," said the captain.

"Oh," said Rebecca.

"I will tell the elders that Jacob is innocent," said her mother.

"It is war. Mistakes are made. People die," said the British officer. "I am sorry. If I live to see the end of it, I will join you in Canada."

"You are a Mennonite?" Rebecca couldn't believe it.

"No, I am a Loyalist from Connecticut. My family is already in Halifax. But I am a soldier first. I know my duty."

Rebecca and her mother exchanged looks of puzzlement. They excused themselves and walked close beside each other down Main Street and out of town. Jacob Shantz was redeemed.

"I will tell his family," said her mother. "Perhaps now that his father is gone, he will come back."

"*Mutter.* Jacob Shantz is dead."

"*Ja,*" she exclaimed. "*Es ist so.*"

When they reached the gate of the Johannes Haun farm, Rebecca and her mother briefly touched hands. As Rebecca leaned forward, her mother looked down at the silver medallion on her bosom, with the amber gleaming at the center. Her eyes widened but she said nothing. She reached out and touched the medallion with her fingertips. She smiled shyly, then turned and walked slowly down the lane to help load the Conestoga wagons. She stopped suddenly and turned back.

"Rebecca!"

"*Mutter?*"

They approached each other. They touched hands but did not embrace.

Her mother whispered: "I am not permitted to talk about Christian. You must look out for him."

"I don't understand."

"He left Bible College last year. He is a soldier, an officer."

"For the British?"

"No, *meine liebchen*, my little sweetheart. He is a Captain in Mr. Washington's Army. He fought in the very first Battle at Concord. We do not talk of Christian, now. It breaks my heart."

Suddenly, her mother hugged her. She wrapped the gray shawl around Rebecca's shoulders. Then she turned and walked briskly down the lane.

Rebecca returned to the hotel.

The next morning she set out for Philadelphia.

Twelve

Allison

It is an exciting world for an intrepid potato! Certainly not boring. It's exciting for a girl of sixteen walking back into a war. Rebecca has cleared the name of her friend, Jacob Shantz. She will find her Captain William de Vere.

And I am still alive!

Wait. You're going to want to hear this.

Jaimie Retzinger is sitting beside me, yapping away. He hardly used to say anything at all. Now he won't stop talking. At first I want to go to sleep and finish the walk to Philadelphia with Rebecca. We've been through a lot together. And if she's going to be my great great great, great great grandmother, I'd like to be there when she falls into her lover's arms.

But Jaimie Retzinger has a pretty good story about me and I nearly missed finding how it turned out. He saved my life.

Here's what happened, as far as I can tell.

He has been visiting me almost every night since I was shot. He comes late because he's going to night school. He wants to get his High School Equivalency. The smartphone

I'd sometimes hear was a laptop. He was studying, and this is the quietest place he knows. Sometimes he'd just doze off. He wants to be a chef. Like me! He works in the daytime at Home Depot. He knows a little about everything. He moves around from section to section when the regular staff go on holidays. It's all pretty exhausting, especially for Jaimie Retzinger.

So, I guess it was him all along. My night stalker.

Last night, Jaimie Retzinger was sitting here, reading his computer. Who knew Jaimie Retzinger could read? And he fell asleep, but he woke up real quick because in walks Russell Miller.

Now Jaimie didn't know Russell Miller from Adam, but he didn't look like a doctor. Jaimie was on the other side of my bed-light, so he was hidden by the glare.

I guess Russell Miller stood there, staring at me. He leaned over and kissed me on the lips. I might have stirred but I can't tell a kiss from a bag of jellybeans. I think he must have cried. I felt his tears, I think I did. I'm sure I did. Then he took out a Swiss Army knife.

Jaimie Retzinger, my ex-boyfriend, watched. He couldn't believe what he saw. And before he could do anything, Russell Miller used the knife to cut some of the tubes going in and out of my body. He then held the knife to his own throat. He was going to slit it and bleed to death, right there.

That's when Jaimie Retzinger, my ex-boyfriend, finally sprang up from his chair and dived right over my bed and knocked Russell Miller to the floor. I guess he knocked me out of bed, too. Russell didn't fight. He just lay there. But Jaimie Retzinger held him down, anyway.

There was a lot of noise. Nurses came running. Orderlies came running.

Doctors were called.

They got me back into bed and hooked me up again. I was still alive, not that they could see much difference from me being dead.

My tumble from bed might have sent me back into a full coma. Jaimie Retzinger might have killed me. He saved my life. And he saved Russell Miller from slitting his own throat.

He told me this, himself, even if he didn't think I could hear.

Rebecca

By the time Rebecca caught up with George Washington's army near Philadelphia, the Battle of Monmouth was over. The British soldiers had been pushed back. Both Captains de Vere had fought with great courage.

France and Germany were now officially part of the Revolution. The war had become international. With George Washington's organization and Baron von Steuben's training methods, the Continental Army was a powerful force. The conflict had become a war of professional soldiers fighting on both sides.

So the Regimental Camp Followers were disbanded, although many stayed around to do what they could. Madge de Vere made the decision to return home to Boston. From there, she could do good work by raising money. She could organize women to knit and to sew and to make bandages and to nurse the wounded. Her days in the battlefield were done.

Madge insisted that Rebecca go with her to Boston. It was understood that Rebecca would one day be the bride of Captain William de Vere, if the war ever ended. And if he survived. Rebecca would sometimes sit for hours on the window seat at the front of the house, rubbing her fingers over the silver medallion. Madge had insisted she keep it. It reminded Rebecca of William's bright amber eyes.

"It was given to me by a very dear friend, Mr. Paul Revere," Madge explained. "He is a silversmith and, after my husband was murdered, Paul made this medallion as a token of my love for the man I had lost. I had my portrait painted, a widow dressed in black with the medallion hanging proudly at my neck. It is in my bedroom. Paul made a silver bowl at the same time to honor the Sons of Liberty who continued to resist British tyranny over the colonial people—who are also British, I should remind you. Or *were*. We'll see how this war turns out. Paul knew my husband was not a revolutionary but they were both Freemasons. That was very important, perhaps more important than politics or religion."

Rebecca was startled to think there might be something more important than religion. Even here, in Boston, her Mennonite God was a presence not to be taken lightly. Madge explained the Freemasons were an ancient secret society and George Washington belonged, as did Paul Revere and his obstreperous friend, Mr. Samuel Adams.

After explaining that *obstreperous* meant "loud and unmanageable," Madge smiled when Rebecca suggested she might better have said just that, rather than use such a bewildering word. Madge pointed out a small mark stamped on the back of the medallion which contained the word REVERE inside a rectangle etched into the silver.

"It is a treasure," she repeated. "I want you to keep it forever."

Soon after they had settled in, not long after discussing the origins and destiny of the medallion, Captain Edward de Vere turned up for a visit. His face was as smudged and his uniform was as grubby as ever. Edward, or Edwina, had another young officer with her.

"*Oh, mein Gott,*" Rebecca declared when she saw who it was. She was not sure if she were swearing. "Christian, *mein Gott, bis du es?* Is it you?"

The last time she had seen her oldest brother, he had been wearing a coarse black woolen suit. His hair was cut like a skinned badger. He had a scowl etched into his face. That was three years ago.

Now, he looked dashing and handsome. There was a war on, and he was a soldier. He looked absurdly happy!

He gave his sister a big hug. They had never touched before, not since they were very small.

And then he did the most unusual thing.

He took Captain Edward de Vere's hand and held it. He leaned over and kissed Edwina's cheek, even though it was dirty. Then Christian turned to Madge and to Rebecca.

"When this war is over, Edwina and I shall be married. With your permission, Mrs. de Vere. And, Miss Rebecca Haun, you are my only family now. We would like your blessing, as well."

The two officers stood side by side. One in a clean blue uniform with light brown pants and polished boots, and the other in a tattered uniform covered with mud and dust.

"Until the fighting is done," Christian announced, "we will be fellow officers and the best of friends."

Rebecca smiled. She longed to see her own Captain de Vere. It seems the de Veres and the Hauns were going to join together, one way or another.

Madge de Vere smiled. She had lost her husband. A war was raging that would change the world. But she, too, seemed content.

Allison

And that is how Madge de Vere became my great great great, great great great grandmother. Six greats, one grand.

David is here. Last night was disturbing but I'm feeling fine. Well, I don't feel anything exactly. Not so I can pin it down. But there's feeling and there's feelings. There *are* feelings! I am feeling wonderful.

We've solved the murder of Noah Shantz. We've given Jacob back his good name. Sort of. He left Warwick and his Mennonite community so he's still an outlaw. But he died a renegade hero in the service of a great Revolution.

When I say *we* solved the murder, I mean Rebecca and me. I think I'll leave her to live out her life, I think my dreams will move on.

And we solved who shot me.

When I say *we*, I mean the cops who explained things to David and my mom. I'd mostly figured it out for myself.

I feel sorry for Russell. The police determined he only visited me that last time and that was to put me out of my misery. That's why he was crying. I knew it, I knew I felt tears. David tells me they've sent him to a special hospital for treatment. I hope something can be done to help him. He sort of confessed to the shooting. At first, he raved about a sinister man who made him do it, a stranger who wanted something mysterious from me. Russell didn't understand what it was. A key of some sort. And he talked about Sharon. No one seems to know that Sharon was his little sister, the one who died in Grade Three. Then he got all quiet, and now he says nothing.

As for the mystery man, no one has turned up. Echoes of yelling, of banging on the car window, resound in my head, as if the bald man in the car was trying to prevent Russell from shooting. But if there was a witness, whether he tried to save me or rob me or wanted me dead, he has disappeared.

If he ever existed.

Russell is in a hospital cell. He's locked inside a tiny world as much as I am. Since his mind has collapsed, his is even smaller.

And *we*, meaning me, we've saved Jaimie Retzinger from a wasted life. *Maybe.*

He told my brother that when he saw me in the hospital he fell for me all over again. He can't say "love." He never could. But, get serious, Jaimie Retzinger, what kind of person falls for *a potato!*

That's what he said, though. And it changed him forever— he promised.

David is not his biggest fan.

Before I drifted off to sleep last night, I tried to remember what Nana Friesen told me about where I came from. I never used to pay much attention. I'd listen because it made Nana feel good. But the past before I was born, well it didn't interest me very much. That was before I got shot in the head, before I ended up here, before I remembered the life of Rebecca Haun.

Nana was my mom's mom. She once told me the family brains skipped a generation, then she apologized for telling me that and said my mom was just one of those people in life who is always *distracted.* I'm not sure what that means but that's Mom, for sure. She's never completely in the moment; she's distracted.

Nana is proud to be Pennsylvania Dutch. And to be from Boston, back when it was British, more than two centuries ago.

She used to talk about our Mennonite ancestors from Lancaster County. But Rebecca Haun wasn't a Mennonite anymore, and William de Vere was a Boston Protestant, so, I'm confused. My good glory!

Of course.

My direct Haun ancestor was Christian, it wasn't Rebecca.

I have to stop for a moment, I need to think. I have a horrible feeling that her beloved William died in the war. I'll have to check when I get out of here. But there are some things you just know.

I wonder if she ever married.

I don't think so.

I don't think she had children of her own. If she did, the silver medallion would have gone to them.

Rebecca was Christian's sister and my ancestral aunt but I am *actually* the great great great, great great granddaughter of Christian Haun and Edwina de Vere. Five greats and a grand.

Rebecca and I are like blood sisters.

Just when I'm getting really upset, thinking about Rebecca and William, David leans close. Then I feel something cool. I can't tell where. I feel a weight. I know what it is. David is talking to me, he's whispering.

"I thought you'd like this, I brought it from home," he says. "As potatoes go, you're the best." And he fastens the silver medallion around my neck. I know he does. It's a gift from my Great Aunt Rebecca, from Becky. It's a gift from Nana Friesen. It's a gift from my brother.

Well, angels couldn't ask for more. That's what Nana says. I never knew what it meant until now. It means, it doesn't get any better than this!

Jaimie Retzinger has come in while David's here. That's unusual. He's always tried to avoid my family. He's leaning right over my face. I can feel his breath. I can feel the medallion. Last night I could feel Russell Miller's breath, I know I could.

What's Jaimie Retzinger doing? Is he showing affection? No, just curiosity.

Still, I've got to start thinking of him as Jaimie. Not Jaimie Retzinger. I mean, we're not a couple but it's kind of nice, having him here. Even if it's just because my room is a good place to study and snooze. Peace and quiet, that's the best I can offer.

But, oh glory, His voice is trembling. He's saying something important.

Listen!

"Her eyelid moved! She opened an eye." He takes a deep breath. "Only one eye but she's in there! I knew it!"

Me, too, Jaimie Retzinger. I knew it all along.

I can see the light.

Book Two: Execution

Thirteen

Allison

It's not an ideal situation, my relationship with Jaimie. I mean, the walking dead don't know they're dead. And that's what I am, even though I'm not walking. I know how he thinks. He likes me better undead than alive. It's not an ideal situation, my relationship with Jaimie Retzinger. He used to be my boyfriend. We broke up before I was shot. We get along better now.

And like it or not, I'm still here! Even though things have changed.

They've moved me into a home for the hopeless. They call it Shady Nook Hospice, which is meant to be comforting. Sounds more like a cemetery. They think the only way I'm going to leave is feet-first, flat on my back, very dead. But they are wrong. For the last few months they thought I was only a vegetable, a corpse with a pulse. Then I shocked them. I opened my eyes. I'll shock them again, just give me time.

Okay, I opened *one* eye. My left. Not exactly like I'm running the Boston Marathon. Still, I'm making progress.

My eye opens and closes very slowly when it wants to. I can't control it. It droops and gets moist and opens again. I can see out of it, straight ahead. Everything is kind of fuzzy, but I'm learning to focus a little. Right now, I only see where the wall meets the ceiling on the far side of the room. It's not exactly like watching *The Wizard of Oz*.

Sometimes a nurse or an orderly will lean close but they never stay still long enough to be more than a blur. Jaimie Retzinger avoids getting in front of me. My brother, David, is the only one who looks me straight in the eye.

Even my mother avoids what David calls my "glassy gaze" as she ducks in to kiss me hello and goodbye and to drop a few tears. David picked up that phrase, glassy gaze, in school. We didn't read much at home. The only writers I remember at all are Stephen King and William Shakespeare, and the Twilight writer and whoever wrote *The Hunger Games* and, of course, the Harry Potter writer. I can't recall all their names.

Jaimie Retzinger used to say I have a wicked tongue and an evil temper. If he was right, then how come he still hangs around? Last week, out of the blue, he told me I'm beautiful. I mean, get serious. Anyway, it was only once. He could have been talking about the orchid on the table beside my bed. I imagine there's an orchid with swooping white petals. There are probably no flowers in my room. I mean, what's the point?

It doesn't matter. The orchid is real in my mind.

Life hasn't changed much since they moved me to Shady Nook. Mostly I lie here and think. At night, when it's quiet, I lie here and dream. Until a few days ago, when I woke up, my dreams would fall apart, just like they did before Rebecca came into my life. She's been so real she's a part of me, the way your memories are from when you were a kid. I was inside her world. Like two hundred years ago. But I'm not anymore. If there's such a thing as remembering blood—that's what I call the memories we inherit—when they no longer shape who we are, we leave them behind and move on.

Of course, I'm not moving much! But maybe that's how it works, you have to take a bullet in the skull to make the past present. And then it becomes the past again. And then? Well, I don't know, not yet.

So.

I'm in a stupidly named hospice. Jaimie is still around, I'm still alive, and Rebecca is gone.

When I'm awake, I listen. That's the only thing I can do. Listen. Or panic. And I refuse to panic.

Jaimie Retzinger talks to me. But it's like he's talking to his television set.

Before he saved my life, he was silent as the grave. Now he rattles on. For a while there, after I opened my eye, he thought I was going to rise up and do the polka. I didn't, of course. I don't know how to polka.

Seeing me hovering near death has changed Jaimie Retzinger. He doesn't study in my room anymore, like he did at the hospital. He says I'm a distraction. But he still comes in now and then to tell me what he's been up to. Like, I'm a diary? Or maybe a sponge?

I have mixed feelings about Jaimie Retzinger.

My brother, David, is the only one who *knows* I can hear. Don't ask me how. He just knows.

He finished Grade Twelve this week.

I was gearing up to drop out of school before I got shot. Now I'm kind of hanging in limbo. I was slinging double-doubles and doughnuts but I want to go back and finish school, go to university, then take a chef's course at Sanford

Fleming College. *Sir* Sanford, I think it is. He was a knight who invented time zones.

I'd like to run a business of my own. I'll call it "Allison's Restaurant."

My mother doesn't visit as much since I've come to Shady Nook. I understand that. A person has to get on with her life.

She doesn't believe I can hear. Same with the nurses. And my open eye doesn't excite them. It doesn't even blink when I try.

The problem is, I can't figure out how to let them know I'm in here and I really need to. Especially now.

Listen!

I've been in Shady Nook for a couple of months. Long enough to realize there's too much death around here. I mean, yes, people die. It's that kind of place. But there's something going on that no one has noticed.

Somebody is murdering patients.

Someone is killing people like me.

We aren't actually *patients*. We're called *guests*. Most of us are stuck in bed. At intervals, one of us dies. Nobody is surprised. I hear the nurses talking. If you listen, you can figure out what's going on around here. And they talk about this guest and that guest dropping dead. There's nothing suspicious about really sick people dying.

But here's the strange thing: one of us dies every seventeen days.

There are other deaths of course, but for sure there's one every seventeen days.

And, glory, no one seems to have noticed but me.

On the night after I arrived at Shady Nook, a cranky old lady died. Seventeen days later, a kid who stole a car and crashed it, he died. Everyone thought he was getting better.

Seventeen days after that, a girl died. She was in a coma but stable, and then she stopped breathing, just like that. Last week a man with brain damage died. He couldn't remember his own name but he was happy and he made people smile.

It might be my turn next.

Unless I can figure out who is killing us. And then figure out how to stop him. Or her. It might be a nurse. Most of my nurses are women.

It would not be hard to murder me.

I'm breathing on my own but I've got tubes going in and tubes coming out, and wires and monitors for everything. Cut them all off in the night and I'd probably be dead by morning. That's what Russell Miller tried to do. He was never going to slit my throat, only his own. Or maybe you could smother me with a pillow. No one expects me to live, anyway.

The killer couldn't do it during the daytime. Nurses are wandering around. The door is left open. I have a roommate. They have to look after both of us. Anyway, they keep our curtains open and our lights on during the day in case visitors come. It would be too depressing if we were lying here in the dark.

My roommate is Doris Blonski. She's a year older than me. She's in a coma. Just like everyone thinks I am.

It would be funny if she's lying there with a working mind, listening. Like, the two of us, side by side, both locked in bodies that don't work. And we can't even talk to each other to share our experiences. Not funny-funny. Funny-weird.

When Jaimie Retzinger drops in, he chatters. He argues with himself. I try not to listen. He's the only person in the world who can argue with himself and lose. Since he's studying to be a chef, he's got books to read. With lots of pictures. Jaimie Retzinger has never read a chapter book in his life.

I'd break up with him all over again, but he wouldn't notice, so why bother?

Anyway, I know there won't be another murder for ten days. So, for the time being, I sleep well.

And during the night, I dream. Recently my dreams have been gathering into memories again. Last night, it was all very real. I dreamed of Lizzie Erb. Her world is as vivid to me as Rebecca's. She has to live her life so I can live mine. Her story is terrifying and exciting and romantic and maybe a little bit strange.

It's 1812 and she's a year older than me—sixteen, maybe seventeen. And she has just witnessed a murder.

Now the killers want her dead.

Lizzie

Lizzie Erb was hiding from the Redcoats. She was covered in hay. She had climbed high into the haymow inside her uncle's huge barn. She had trudged for three days from her home in the Grand River Valley to find General Brock and instead she was being hunted by his own soldiers. If she peered out she could see three men, two stories below. She burrowed deeper into the hay but she could hear them talking.

"Are you really saying we should kill her, Captain?"

Lizzie couldn't hear what the officer answered, but it was clear what he wanted.

"Yes sir, Captain Blaine. And then we'll burn this place to the ground," said the other soldier.

Again, a muffled response

"What about the house?"

The officer's voice rose and he snarled, "Don't burn the house, you damned fool. We just moved in."

"Only the officers did, sir," said the first soldier.

"Do you have a problem with that, Mr. Cameron?"

The voices faded. For a few minutes, Lizzie could hear nothing but the October wind seeping through the walls. She climbed up so she could see better. Narrow bands of moonlight shone between the boards. She could see across the huge space where her uncle, Matthias Haun, had stored enough hay to feed his animals until spring.

Two voices became clear again. The Redcoat soldiers were standing by the ladder just below Lizzie. The officer was no longer with them. She wriggled back into the hay but kept her head clear so that she could hear.

"I don't think we should kill a woman," said one. "She's just a wee lass."

"Me neither," the other agreed. "But killing is killing, that's what we do."

"Being soldiers, you mean. Well, there's killing and there's killing."

"There you go, Mr. Cameron, playing with words."

"I'm just saying we need to think about this."

"She walked here over the fields, she saw Captain Blaine shoot the farmworker in cold blood. He weren't doing nothing, that farmer, but now he's dead. So I guess she had better die, too. It isn't complicated. We gotta find the young witch."

"There's a full moon tonight. She's sailed off on her broom. Come on, Beazley, I think we should go."

"The captain told us before we goes anywhere, we kill the woman who seen us."

"You're very conscientious."

"I am not!" The man seemed indignant, as if he didn't know what the word meant but assumed it was an insult. "I'm not conscience at all," he muttered.

"It wasn't us, Mr. Beazley. We would have stopped him killing the man if we could."

"You would have, maybe. I'm not sure about me."

Lizzie saw sparks from a flint and then a flare as one of

the soldiers lit his pipe. After a minute of quiet, she saw more flickering light, followed by voices:

"Here! Damn you Beazley, what've you done?"

"It were quite accidental, I assure you."

Flames leapt upward, catching the dry hay.

"Damn it, man. The animals are still in the stable below."

Lizzie peered over from her loft and watched as the men scrambled to extinguish the fire. Sweat on the shorter man's chubby cheeks glistened as he swiped at the flames with his jacket. The tall lean man had set his own jacket aside and was using a pitchfork to beat the flames down. After a flurry of activity, the two men recognized the futility of their efforts.

"Come on, Beazley," the tall man shouted. "We'd better get the animals out."

"Captain Blaine didn't say to set the animals free."

"He thought we were smart enough to figure it out for ourselves."

The flames were licking higher. Clouds of smoke rose up under the roof beams and choked Lizzie Erb.

"Too late for the critters," yelled the one called Beazley. "We'd best save ourselves."

"Damn it," Cameron exclaimed.

"We're in for it now. I think we'd better get a long ways away, Mr. Cameron. Let's go upriver. We'll join the Americans."

The two men were yelling to be heard above the roaring flames.

"Damnation, Beazley. Let's go then, we'll make a run for it."

Lizzie listened as the roar of the fire smothered their voices. She slid down the haymow, shielding herself from the soaring flames. She landed with a thump on the wooden floor over the stable. It was right where the soldiers had been standing, but they had run off to join the American invaders. Or liberators. Depending on how you saw things.

Lizzie pulled open a trap door and slid down a ladder into the stable below. Smoke filled the stone-walled room. Wisps of flame scurried across the ceiling. She ran from stall to stall, untying the horses and the oxen. She jumped over a barrier made of cedar rails into the cattle pen and pushed open a large door to the outside. Madly waving her arms, she chased the cattle out into the barnyard.

Then she ran back and removed the cedar rails so the horses and oxen could get through. The boards in the ceiling were on fire. Chunks of burning wood dropped all around her. She edged past the horses, who were frantic with fear and kicking wildly. She slipped around the oxen, who were standing stupidly, waiting to die. When she got behind them, Lizzie Erb let out a blood-curdling series of screams. The horses and oxen stampeded out through the cattle pen into the open air.

Captain Blaine and some of the Redcoats who hade taken over her uncle's farm were herding the animals to safety. Lizzie Erb stood in the burning doorway. Ahead were soldiers who wanted to kill her. Behind was a roaring wall of flames and certain death.

Timbers crashed onto the stable floor, sending out waves of sparks. She could smell the fire singeing her hair. Her clothes were about to burst into flames.

A man yelled at her, almost a scream. Someone she had never seen before. He was standing off to the side, close to the burning barn. Lizzie glanced over at him. He had a huge blond mustache and deep-set eyes. He was wearing a buckskin coat with fringes and beadwork. The stranger was holding a heavy workhorse tight by its halter. She recognized it as a gelding called Fleetfire which her uncle had invited her to name when it was a foal and she was a little girl. The man tied a blue scarf around the horse's eyes. Lizzie could have sworn the man smiled. He slapped the horse hard on the rump. The horse reared. It plunged straight toward the flaming inferno. Right into Lizzie's grasp.

She seized the halter, tucked her long skirts up, and swung herself around and onto the big gelding's back. She reached forward and whipped off the scarf from his eyes. Terrified, the horse reared again. Lizzie clutched her fingers into its mane. Then she dug her right knee hard into its side. The big horse bucked and took off, wheeling around and heading straight toward the Redcoat captain who wanted her dead.

Captain Blaine dodged out of the way as Fleetfire sped by at a frenzied gallop. Lizzie was carried away from the burning barn, and from the soldiers who wanted to kill her because she had witnessed a murder.

She rode into the moonlight along the Portage Trail, guiding Fleetfire by tugging his mane since he had no bit in his mouth and she had no reins. When she approached the top of Niagara Falls, she tied the blue scarf around her face to keep off the terrible chill. The Falls flowed like liquid thunder. And even though it was only mid-October, a cover of freezing mist had settled over the landscape.

Turning up off the main road past Wilson's Hotel, she pulled the huge gelding up to the gate in front of her intended destination. Leaning forward, she rubbed Fleetfire between the ears, then slid awkwardly down to the ground and took a deep breath. She needn't tie him; he wouldn't wander away. She stepped onto the porch of the solid frame house and saw welcoming candles ablaze in the ground-floor windows.

Lizzie Erb had been nearly burned to a crisp and was almost frozen to death. She hesitated, then she knocked.

Too late, she saw a Redcoat uniform approach from the side, coming around the corner of the house.

She pressed against the thick pine door and battered it with her fists, urging whoever was inside to hurry, to save her from death impaled on a soldier's bayonet.

Fourteen

Allison

I immediately recognized the woman who opened the door, though she has been dead for two hundred years. Rebecca Haun, framed by flickering candlelight fluttering on the walls as she moved. She was not exactly a ghost, but she had aged since I saw her last in the Beacon Hill area of Boston.

When I woke up, I recalled every detail through Lizzie's eyes. It was like when I was back in Rebecca's world. Now Rebecca is older; she's someone I observe as a witness. Strangely, it doesn't confuse or frighten me, this new adventure, although I'm scared for Lizzie as the Redcoat approaches. I can hardly wait to sleep. I need to get back into her life and find out what happens.

Meanwhile, I don't think my roommate, Doris, is doing very well.

She gurgles and, unless you're a river, gurgling isn't a good thing. I've listened to her all day. It's funny, because I really feel badly for her, but the noise is annoying. I hope I don't ever gurgle.

David comes in but since school is over he doesn't have any more jokes for me. I can tell something is bugging him. He calls me Allison instead of Potato. Whatever is on his mind, it must be serious. He leans into my field of vision. I try to bring him into focus but he moves away. Still, I did see him, or a shadowy version. When he leaves, I can hear him talking to a girl. I listen carefully. I know the voice. Who is it? I know who it is!

Maddie O'Rourke.

The two of them are speaking quietly. As if they'll wake us up, for glory's sake. It's like in a funeral home—young people speak quietly there. Older people use ordinary voices. They've seen more of death. They're not so impressed by it.

David leaves and then I hear Maddie talking to Doris in a low soothing voice. I try not to listen. I don't want to be nosy. I try hard to think about Lizzie Erb, but Maddie O'Rourke's words are warm and friendly. I don't have many friends these days. It's funny. Her warmth makes me lonely.

Then she comes over to me. She touches me. I can't tell where, but it's a gentle touch. Then she says, just as if we were having a conversation:

"I love your medallion, Allison. I've always liked amber better than diamonds and pearls."

She laughs and says:

"My only real jewels are on the models in *Vogue*."

I know she reads *Vogue*. She lives a *Vogue* life in a strange and lovely way.

Maddie O'Rourke was two years ahead of me in high school. She works at a cosmetics counter in the People's Drug Mart on Chemong. She is small, only four feet tall, and has a twisted back. But she stands as straight as she can and she is fiercely proud. No one has ever teased her. Even when she was a kid, she could burn a hole in your heart with her eyes. In her teens, Maddie discovered *Vogue*. She came from a poor family but she was smart. She had flare. She sewed and made beautiful clothes. The rest of us learned about fashion from watching her. And her hair! Good glory, no one in Peterborough has hair like Maddie O'Rourke. Jet black, tumbling in waves around her face, wild and tame, all at the same time. Perfect complexion! Pale like a china doll, flawless, and not much makeup, except lip-gloss and lots around her eyes. Her eyes! Dark blue like huge blueberries, as big as Angelina Jolie's. Better lips, though. She doesn't look like she's blowing bubbles all the time.

So, Maddie O'Rourke, the most beautiful girl in Peterborough, is my new friend.

Am I impressed? Of course. "You're looking a little tired. Tomorrow I'm going to make up your eyes. Keep track of my buddy Doris for me. Night, night, Allie."

Allie! I drift off to sleep, almost forgetting about murder.

Lizzie

Lizzie took a step back as the woman flung open the door. She still had the blue scarf wrapped around her face. She did not want to startle her Aunt Rebecca, but Rebecca did not seem startled.

Lizzie glanced back at the Redcoat who was leading Fleetfire away by the halter.

"Well Lizzie Erb, since you've arrived on a horse in a lather and it's your uncle's gelding, at that, you must be on an important mission."

Her aunt's gentle mockery made her feel surprisingly secure.

"Everything's important in times like these," said Rebecca. "Come along, there's a gentleman here you'll be wanting to meet."

Rebecca led her like a military commander down the long hallway and into the kitchen.

There were nearly a dozen men sitting around the large room that had an open fireplace across the back, with a fire blazing and crackling. The low beams and the plaster ceiling glinted in the firelight. Some of the men were eating stew and bread. Others were smoking pipes and talking quietly among themselves. They were dressed in a variety of heavy cloth coats. Several Redcoats mingled among them.

Sitting hunched over a table with his back to Lizzie was a Redcoat officer in full military dress. She realized there had been a meeting that was now over. The British military wanted the support of the local people. Rebecca had provided dinner for them all.

The officer did not rise when Lizzie and her aunt approached him. He must think himself very important, Lizzie thought. The man turned his head to acknowledge her, then gazed back into the candle flame in front of him.

At least he was not Captain Blaine from the burning barn. If he had been, she would be as good as dead.

Another Redcoat came into the kitchen through the side door.

"I've put the young lady's horse in the stable," he explained. "She's been riding it hard."

"Thank you Mr. Breckenridge," said the officer. There were two other men at the table. Sitting beside the speaker was another officer, in dress uniform. Peering more closely through the candle's flickering light, Lizzie recognized the other as her uncle, Matthias Haun. It seemed she was related to almost everyone in this part of Upper Canada. She nodded to Matthias.

"Lizzie. You are keeping well. Your father is healthy?"

"Uncle," she said, her voice charged with emotion. "I have just come from your farm. These Redcoats are set to destroy you."

"You see, Macdonell," said the first officer. "Even this wild young woman hates us. But if we are very lucky, she will fear the Americans more. Sit, sit, young woman. Do you have a name? What have we done?"

"I have no desire to sit with you, sir. My name is Lizzie Erb and I will speak with the commander of the British Forces and no one less."

The officer rose to his feet, although he had to stoop to avoid bumping his head on the low ceiling. He bowed in Lizzie's direction and then looked to her Aunt Rebecca to make introductions.

"Lizzie Erb," said her grandmother, "this is Major-General Sir Isaac Brock, Commander of the Defense of Upper Canada and a guest in my kitchen. You will treat him with respect."

"I will treat him with what he deserves," she snapped.

General Brock spoke firmly: "June eighteenth, eighteen hundred and twelve, Lizzie Erb. That is the day the United States of America declared war on these backwoods farms and country lanes—since that day, you will respect me, for I am all there is between chaos and order. You will respect the Crown. And I am the Crown. Sit down."

Lizzie sat down beside her uncle, across the table from Isaac Brock. She had never seen a general before and this one was famous. He was in his early forties, exceptionally tall and very handsome, with a wildness to his dark brown eyes that matched her own, and a fierce intelligence in his solemn face that seemed to forbid the presence of a smile. He was clean-shaven and his golden hair was perfectly groomed. His high forehead and noble features picked up the firelight and gleamed with a peculiar intensity. Here was a man born for great things, a man stuck in the backwoods who understood the importance of a few acres of snow in the defense of the mightiest empire in the world.

"Now, then, Lizzie," continued the General, "you have come from the Grand River. Good. Your father was Christian Haun. Your stepfather is also named Christian, Christian Erb. Your mother was Edwina de Vere, the sister-in-law of my good friend, Matthias, who was your late father's younger brother." He nodded at Lizzie's uncle. "Matthias, of course is the brother of my friend, Miss Rebecca Haun." He acknowledged Lizzie's aunt with a warm smile. "Don't let it confuse you, Miss Erb. Families are complicated things."

"I am not confused," she said, "but I'm surprised that you know all this."

"I am a general," he said. "Generals must know many things. Now, then, I understand you have brought me some much needed assistance."

"You seem to know more about me than I do about you, sir."

"It is my business to know who is carrying a large purse for our efforts."

"If I do have money, sir, it is to be given at my discretion."

"At your *discretion*? I see. And do you have this money with you?"

Lizzie smiled wickedly. She had trekked for days from her family farm in the Grand River Valley, across the Beverly Swamp and through vast tracks of forest, carrying a leather saddlebag over her shoulder. It was stuffed with bank notes and gold coins. When she came to a clearing that overlooked the Niagara valley, she had hidden her treasure in a hollowed out section of a stone wall. It was less than half a day's ride away but secure until she decided what was to be done with it. "I am not a courier," she declared. "I am here in my own good judgment, on behalf of my father and his friends."

"Your own good judgment?"

"To decide whether we will support your cause."

"What you call *my* cause is also *yours*. Without us, you would become American subjects."

"Citizens, sir. They are subject to no one."

"You admire the invaders, do you?"

"I do not fear them. But my people chose to remain British during their Revolution and we choose to remain British now."

"Although your father and his friends *choose* not to fight," he observed.

"We will not. But we are prepared to invest in our common cause."

"Invest, indeed. Many of your neighbors have joined the militia."

"And many who are not inclined to make war will give you funds to support them. If we think it a sound investment."

"Good God, this is not a business transaction. Will you not give freely to your king, to his general, to fight the evils of Manifest Destiny? Do you know what *Manifest Destiny* is, girl?"

"Lizzie Erb," Lizzie said.

"I beg your pardon."

"My name is Miss Erb, sir. And yes. Manifest Destiny is the American belief that it is their lot to rule the entire continent."

"Which is nonsense, of course," said Sir Isaac Brock.

"No more nonsense, sir," Lizzie answered, "than your own belief that the British should rule the world."

She glowered at Major-General Sir Isaac Brock. A hint of a smile passed across his stern face.

"Here now!" exclaimed Macdonell. "You mind your manners, girl. Who do you think you are?"

"You mind yours, sir! I think I am Lizzie Erb. I was not addressing you."

No one questioned the young woman's importance. She was from the rich Mennonite communities around Berlin. And she was carrying a lot of money to help finance the British defense of Canada—unless she felt it was a lost cause or morally corrupt. It was her decision. She was seventeen years old, but she was a powerful woman. And Brock was the most powerful man in the colony.

"It is not an accident of fate that I have found you here, General Brock. To be sure, there is a Redcoat captain wanting to kill me, but I'm here of my own free will."

"You have a price on your head? Well, Colonel Macdonell," General Brock seemed suddenly jovial as he turned to his friend, "we had better do something about this murderous Redcoat."

"You may laugh, sir, but it is not amusing," said Lizzie. "I saw your Captain Blaine murder my uncle's hired man." She turned to Matthias Haun. "It was Whittington, Uncle. The captain and two ruffians were stealing a cow."

"Hush, now, Lizzie Erb. One dead cow in the whole scheme of a war is not significant."

"But Whittington, sir, Captain Blaine shot him dead."

Her uncle said nothing. Lizzie realized he was intimidated by the Redcoat commander.

"And they burned your new barn to the ground," she added.

The color drained from Matthias Haun's face. The loss of a hired man was one thing, the loss of his barn another.

"What about the house?" he asked. "Did they burn that, too?"

"The house is standing proud, sir."

He had hardly finished building his new stone house by Lake Erie when the British officers moved in. General Brock himself sometimes occupied the master bedroom. The modest ballroom was set up as a command center with maps everywhere. The kitchen at ground level had been turned over to cooks to feed the officers camped with a battalion of soldiers between the house and the water.

Matthias had not yet lived in his new house. His family, including his ancient parents, Johannes and Margaret, were still living in the log cabins they had first built when they fled the Revolution.

His large Pennsylvania-style barn had been completed the previous year. It had been filled to the rafters with hay and grain to get his animals through the winter. If there was no food for his livestock, he would have to slaughter the animals rather than let them starve to death. There would be terrible wastage.

In an even voice, Matthias spoke to General Brock: "The Third Amendment to the American Constitution protects landowners from being ravaged by their own military."

"Ah, Matthias, are you quoting the enemy's Constitution to a British General? You are fortunate we are friends or I would have you shot for treason."

"You would do no such thing," declared Lizzie, with a vehemence that surprised even her.

"And you might be shot as well, Miss Lizzie Erb, for boldness unbecoming in a young lady."

"I doubt that," she said.

"Which part?" Brock responded with a devilish smile. "That you are excessively bold or that you are a *lady* or, indeed, that I could have you shot? I could, you know."

He turned to address her uncle. "Now, Matthias, I assure you, we are equally as civilized as our belligerent foe. I have already agreed to pay for the use of your house. If my men have burned down your barn, we will pay to have it rebuilt. Perhaps with some of the treasure your niece has brought us." Before Lizzie could protest, he asked her, "What about the animals? Were they burnt as well?"

"I saved them."

"Of course you did." He grinned as if nothing would surprise him about this intrepid young woman. Again, he turned back to her uncle. "So, Matthias, you have my word. We'll give you whatever your barn is worth."

Lizzie wondered if General Brock had any idea what he was talking about. You cannot pay money to build a barn.

The Matthias Haun barn had been built by a hundred volunteers. There was a large stable and above that was a threshing floor entered from the back on a ramp made from built up earth. It was a vast structure, built with cooperative effort by neighbors and friends. Did Brock think it could be replaced by money? Did he understand this strange world he found himself in, halfway around the globe from where he had been born, a world where people labored together to build a barn? This was not a land of castles and palaces, but of barns and dairies and mills. There were no lords and serfs in this place, no subjects, only freemen and workers.

Matthias turned in his chair to look at Lizzie.

She was pretty with her long brown hair coiled at the back of her head. Her deep-brown eyes betrayed stern compassion with a hint of playfulness at the edges.

Lizzie knew Matthias was proud of her. His own family had divided loyalties. Many in Upper Canada who sympathized with the American cause would welcome the invaders. Many had relatives still living in the States.

Lizzie's own grandparents, Johannes and Margaret Haun, had come north during the Revolution and settled on the Canadian side of the Niagara River near Fort Erie, not far from where their son Matthias had built his stone house and huge barn. Not very far from the great Falls where Lizzie was right now, sitting across her aunt's kitchen table from Isaac Brock, himself.

After the Revolution was over, Lizzie's parents, Christian and Edwina, had moved into the de Vere house in Boston with Edwina's mother. Madge's only son, William, had been killed in the siege at Yorktown, Virginia, which many believed decided the war in Washington's favor. William's betrothed, Lizzie's Aunt Rebecca, lived in the house on Beacon Hill as well. Like her brother, Christian, she had left the Mennonites, though not without a sorrow that almost matched her grief for the loss of her beloved William.

Lizzie was born in the house on Beacon Hill. She was very close to her grandmother, Madge de Vere. But when she was five, her parents decided to leave the new nation. Even though they had fought for its independence, Christian and Edwina were more comfortable with the orderliness of British rule. With their children, they joined the Erb family and other Mennonites from Pennsylvania and trekked north by Conestoga wagon to the Province of Upper Canada. They stopped in to visit the Hauns near Fort Erie, then journeyed onwards to the Grand River Purchase near the town of Berlin.

They cleared land bought from the Six Nations Iroquois people, where the Speed River meets the Grand. The land was rich beyond anything they had left in Pennsylvania, and they prospered. They opened a mill and soon a village sprang up around them.

At six, Lizzie was keen to go to school and learn how to read and write, so she could exchange letters with her grandmother back in Boston. For the next decade, they wrote weekly letters. At first Lizzie's were printed and included crude drawings of her memories of Beacon Hill. But she developed beautiful penmanship and her sketches became elegant pictures of life in Upper Canada. The bond between them grew stronger over the years as the girl matured and embraced the world while Madge grew ancient and retired to a darkened room. Their letters became a mirror for the serene old woman to see her own youth and for the girl to see the best of what was within her. Madge shared their correspondence with Rebecca.

Lizzie kept hers to herself, the one thing of her very own in a tumultuous household.

Lizzie was a British Loyalist and Madge was an unwavering American Patriot, but they had much in common that was more important than politics. In peacetime, boundaries and borders seemed unimportant. What counted was the bond they felt between them. Each recognized in the other something of herself.

When Lizzie was thirteen, her father died. Re-reading her letters from her grandmother Madge de Vere gave her the strength to endure.

Soon afterwards, news came that Madge herself had passed away. Lizzie felt strangely as if the bond between them had strengthened. She was sad, but she did not mourn. Madge had lived a full and generous life.

Lizzie's mother Edwina married again, a Mennonite also called Christian with seven children of his own. By then, Edwina had six. Christian Erb was a good man and the children of her first marriage, including Lizzie, took the name Erb. As the oldest girl of thirteen children, a great deal of their care fell on Lizzie's shoulders. She had to drop out of school. She grew strong and fiercely self-reliant, qualities admired by her neighbors in a man, yet she was lithe and pretty. This confused them; it confused her own family. It sometimes confused Lizzie.

The house on Beacon Hill was sold and Rebecca moved to Niagara on the Canadian side of the river to be closer to her family. But not too close. Her father had accepted her back, as he had his oldest son, Christian, but neither Rebecca nor Christian became Mennonite again. They had seen too much war, too much of the world.

Madge had left Rebecca enough money to live comfortably by herself in her frame house near the great Falls. Rebecca never married. It was said that General Brock was a frequent visitor to her home, although she was several years his senior. But she had given her heart to William de Vere. It was not in her nature to marry a man who could only be second-best, even if he was a knight and a general and exceptionally handsome.

Rebecca sometimes journeyed from Niagara to the Grand River valley to help Edwina with her thirteen children. Several died very young, most survived. Rebecca and Lizzie had grown very close over the last few years, although they never talked about the Revolutionary War or about her lost fiancé. And they certainly never talked about General Brock, except as Rebecca's very dear friend.

Lizzie gazed at them both.

She wondered about their conflicting loyalties.

Was Aunt Rebecca still an American at heart, in spite of living on the British side of the River? In spite of her fondness for the most powerful man in Upper Canada?

What about Uncle Matthias? Did he really have a choice when his house was occupied by Redcoats? Was he loyal to the British or simply trying to survive.

And what about Lizzie herself, what was she?

Canadian, she supposed, though she was uncertain what the term meant.

Fifteen

Allison

Before I turned into a turnip, my dreams never made sense. Usually, they'd fall to bits and pieces when I woke up. Like a slow explosion.

I wonder if it's possible to have a slow explosion. Probably not. But that's what my dreams were like.

Then along came Rebecca Haun. And now I have Lizzie. Lizzie is as real as I am. In a way, she's more real than I am. She's living her life.

Well, so am I! I'm living her life and mine as well. I'm in here. Get used to it, Allison.

But not *too* used to it.

I'm not going to be here forever.

Well, none of us are.

Through the last couple of days, I've been thinking a lot about Maddie O'Rourke, the most beautiful girl in Peterborough. Just wondering what it would be like to be her. She must wonder what it would be like to be me. I mean, she talks to me like I'm a person. So does David.

So, damn it, I must be in here!

Don't swear.

I, Allison Briscoe, swore not to swear. Before Jaimie Retzinger, there was that stupid dumb creep who tried to slap me around. I beat him up—I refuse to remember his name—but *that* guy, he swore a lot. A lot. So I don't swear. It's an absolute rule for being Allison Briscoe. Except I occasionally do. Swear. A little.

I'm being cranky. But who else is going to bawl me out, if it isn't me?

I'm not thinking anything in particular about Maddie O'Rourke. It just makes me feel good, knowing she's out there. I hope she comes in again soon to see Doris. Poor Doris, she's getting worse. She gurgles and wheezes. I hope she's in a real coma, not just lying there listening to herself.

As a detective, I'm a bust. A potato detective. The nursing staff talks openly in front of me like I'm not even here. I keep up with the Shady Nook news. And so far, no one has seen the pattern. Every seventeen days.

They worry there are more deaths than usual. But they talk like it's a problem in arithmetic. You know, one plus one, plus one, plus one. Death is just a part of the job around here. Oops, there goes another one.

It has to be an insider. This place is locked up at night like the Kingston Pen. I know, because Jaimie Retzinger stayed past eleven two nights ago. He practically went nuts before they agreed to turn off the alarm to let him out.

Myself, I would have just walked out. If the alarm went off, so what? It's not like he robbed a bank. He just wanted to escape.

Me too!

I guess Shady Nook is my real home, now.

Last night, David and my mom came in. It was a bit distressing.

"Hi Potato," he said.

I like *potato*, although now I usually think of myself as a turnip.

"Mom's here," he explained, as if she couldn't talk by herself. He mumbled a bit and then he said: "We just wanted you to know we've moved your stuff out of your room. It's mostly in the basement."

David must have leaned closer because his voice softened to a whisper: "I'll help you set up again once you get out of here."

So that's why he was upset the last time he visited. He knew this was coming. I was being moved out of my home. They weren't asking permission. Like, how could they? They just went ahead and did it. I was now officially a permanent resident of Shady Nook.

My mom hugged me and cried. You've got to feel sorry for her. David tapped the back of my hand. That's what I figure he's doing when he touches me. I can't actually tell where I'm being touched. But I'm learning. If it feels like tapping, it must be my hand.

After Mom left, I was sad. David stayed. I saw him as he moved around to sit on the side of my bed. Then I could only see the hair on the top of his head. It's dark brown, the same as mine, only his is what they call *unkempt*. He combs it carefully to make it look like he doesn't. He's got hazel eyes, too, the same as me. I tried to bring his hair into focus until I got caught up in his story.

He wanted to tell me the latest news about Russell Miller. It seems Russell told the shrink at his hospital that the Devil was trying to control him. He said he was fighting back. The Devil told him to rob me after my shift at Timmy's. He wouldn't say what he was supposed to steal. Russell decided to kill me, instead. To protect me. Then he was going to kill himself and shoot the Devil as well. David laughed. Neither of us believes in Satan, the Devil, or hell with a capital H. Then Russell tried to put me out of my misery in the hospital. He meant to be kind. That's when Jaimie Retzinger rescued me. David says Jaimie tells people around town he wants to be called Zinger, now. David says no one does it, even though he's had *Zinger* painted on the side of his Harley. Who gives themselves their own nickname? But then, who brags that his girlfriend is in a *comma*. He says "comma," like I've been punctuated. Not c-oh-ma. And I'm not his girlfriend, whether he saved me or not.

David heard all this because the cops are snooping around, asking if anyone has seen the Devil. Well, you know, the guy who told Russell to rob me. They're having trouble since Russell only told them he was, like, very *ordinary*.

David stopped talking. Or I stopped listening. I lay here thinking about a stranger who came into Timmy's a week or so before I was shot. He said he admired my silver medallion. I thought he was looking down my blouse. Just another creep. Then he offered to buy it, the medallion. I didn't even bother to answer him. Some things aren't for sale. But one thing about him I can't forget: He was extremely ordinary. Like, not handsome not homely, not young not old, not rich-looking not poor, not tall not short. Just exceptionally *ordinary*. Partly bald. Very pale.

He came in a couple of evenings later. He stared at me but we didn't talk.

Someone religious once told me the Devil looks like everyone else, that's what makes him so scary. Since I don't believe in such things, I'm not ascared—afraid, I'm supposed to say. There's no such word as "ascared."

Well, there is, I just used it, didn't I?

So, trying to picture the *ordinary man* in my mind, I fell asleep. I didn't hear David go out.

Lizzie

After General Brock and Colonel McDonnell left, the other men talked among themselves. No one asked Lizzie for her opinion, yet when she offered it, they listened. She liked that, even if it was only because she had money.

"We're caught between Peter and Paul," she finally said. Several of the older men nodded in solemn agreement, but the younger men were nervous she might be talking about religion.

Whatever was happening, it was politics. Religion had nothing to do with it. Nor language. The settlers spoke English the same as the British Redcoats, the same as the Americans.

At her father's table, the men often discussed how the British wanted control of the routes to the west for trading furs. The Americans wanted their dream of a continent. They wanted to see Napoleon in far-Europe defeat the British, and if they could, they would help. No one, she suspected, cared much about what really happened to the farmers and tradesmen of Upper Canada except the Upper Canadians themselves.

"We are a far off corner of the Empire," she said. "But we are important strategically to Britain."

"About as important as Gibraltar," chimed in a man with a thick grey beard. "*Strategically*, speaking." He liked using such an unfamiliar word.

"Perhaps more so," Lizzie shot back. She knew where Gibraltar was. She wondered if the graybeard did. "If we join the Americans, we will be swallowed up and forgotten. So we must remain British."

The men were listening but they were restless.

"But," she declared, "ee must be free."

Rebecca Haun's kitchen parlor turned quiet. To speak of such things was scandalous. The Americans believed in *freedom* and kept thousands of black people in slavery and bondage. The French had tried *freedom* in their own revolution but ended up chopping off peoples' heads willy-nilly. They preferred to be ruled by Napoleon who made himself an emperor. And as for the British, *freedom* was subversive. King George III might consider it treason.

"Some day…" Lizzie said, but she let her thoughts die out in the embarrassing silence.

In the end, the men all agreed that they would throw their support behind Brock. They were British now and would remain British forever.

Nothing lasts *forever*, Lizzie thought. But she said nothing. She agreed that, at least in her lifetime, being British was the best protection against the vast wilderness at the edge of their fields.

In the morning, she would walk back to retrieve her treasure. She would deliver it to General Brock to support his Canadian militia. They were either at Queenston Heights on the Lake Ontario side of Niagara, or Fort George at Niagara-on-the-Lake. It wouldn't be hard to find them. Then she would return home to her father's household.

Her mother Edwina wasn't well, and more and more, Lizzie ran the home. She also helped with the various Erb businesses, including the mill and a foundry. She looked after the accounts. Christian Erb depended on her. So important had she become to the family's prosperity, it seemed unlikely she would ever find time to secure a husband. After the men left, she kissed her Aunt Rebecca good night and settled into the cot beside the fire. She watched as the flames flickered and died into embers and the embers slowly faded to ash. When the fire grew cold she fell asleep.

Lizzie woke up with the rising sun. While she was pouring icy water into the basin for a good wash, Rebecca appeared, still dressed in her nightclothes.

"You've made up your mind, child. You're going to put your Papa's money into our side, aren't you?"

"It's not just my father's money, Aunt Becky. It's from most of the farmers in the Grand River valley. And, yes, if by 'our side' you mean the British, that's what I'm going to do."

"We're all British here, Lizzie. We don't have a choice."

Was that true? Lizzie wondered, as she ate a breakfast of bread and strawberry jam. Is choice an illusion?

She could hear the falls. They seemed to be rumbling inside her head. She found Fleetfire in the stable and an old leather bridle with reins and a large steel bit hanging from the stall door. She held the bit out to him and he took it in his mouth with no hesitation. There was no saddle but she was an excellent rider. She positioned the horse near a fence and then clambered up onto his back. With a last look to see Rebecca Haun waving through the window, she struck out for the road that would take her onto the escarpment where her treasure was hidden.

As she guided her horse up a narrow lane to the main road past Wilson's Hotel, she couldn't help wondering whatever happened to the handsome young frontiersman with the blue eyes and bushy mustache. He had helped her escape the fire.

Did he know she was also trying to escape from the murderous Captain Blaine?

In the neighboring village of Chippewa, Lizzie noticed a pair of young ruffians skulking around Macklem's Tavern. It looked like they had slept outdoors all night in their clothes and were nearly frozen to death. They appeared to be waiting for the bar to open so they could get a drink to warm up.

Lizzie drew her horse to a stop beside the two men.

"Gentlemen," she said, "no wonder you're cold, you seem to have lost your red coats."

"We threw 'em away, ma'am," said the short stout one. "We isn't soldiers no more. Better cold than dead, we was thinking."

"Oh, you're going to get caught, Mr. Beazley," she said. "You'll hang or they'll shoot you."

"Who're you?" he asked nervously. "And how do you know me damned name?"

"Damned you are, I am sure," she said. Then she turned to the taller man. "You speak a little better, sir, and with a fine Scottish brogue. You must be Mr. Cameron."

"From Lochiel, yes," said Cameron. "You observed us last night when the fire got started. That's how you know who we are. And you saved the animals. I'd glad you escaped."

"My God," said Beazley, "you're that woman we was supposed to murder."

"But there's no point, now," said Lizzie. "You're on the run, same as me."

"Only it's just Captain Blaine that wants you dead," said Beazley. "And it's the whole bloody British army what's after us. Maybe if we killed you right here, we could go back.

Lizzie smiled. "Do you want to?" she asked.

"Kill you? I don't much care. Go back? Of course. I ain't no American. I'm a poor Yorkshireman who has lost his way."

"We could take you prisoner," said Cameron.

"If you turn me over to Captain Blaine, that's fine. I'm sure he will give you a very good welcome. And after he does, he will have you shot as deserters."

"A convincing argument," Cameron observed.

"Or you will be hanged for murder," she said.

"It were the captain hisself. It weren't us who killed that farmer," said Beazley.

"He was my uncle's hired man," said Lizzie.

"Well, it were the captain that shot him dead."

"I'm sorry we accidentally burned down your uncle's barn," said Cameron. His Scottish cadence was easier to grasp than Beazley's heavy Yorkshire accent.

"We was supposed to do the fire on purpose," said Beazley.

"But we didn't," said Cameron. "It was an accident, ma'am."

"I'm Miss, not Ma'am."

"Forget about her," said Beazley to his friend. "She's only a girl. We'd better get out of here. We can still join up with the Americans, they'll think we're heroes."

"Or fools," said Lizzie. "The Americans are practical. You burned a perfectly good barn to the ground."

They stared at her as if surprised at her matter-of-fact language.

"I'll tell you what," she continued. "I'll place you under arrest. Then I will take you directly to my friend General Brock. And we can tell him about your Captain Blaine murdering Mr. Whittington. General Brock will thank you and execute your captain. And you'll be home by Christmas."

"I'm not sure I want to go home," said Cameron. "I think when the fighting is over, I might settle right here."

"If you're alive," said Beazley, laughing. Looking at Lizzie, he added: "She'll be long married by then."

"If you mean me, sir. I think you are presumptuous."

"Yes, ma'am, I am for sure."

"You say you will arrest us," said Cameron. "How're you going to do that?" He seemed oddly amused by the whole situation.

"It is simple. I am a subject of King George the Third and by the king's authority I place you under a citizen's arrest."

"There isn't no such thing," said Beazley.

"There should be," she said. "It might save your miserable lives if I am your witness."

"Actually," said Cameron, "it is her obligation by English common law to arrest wrongdoers, malefactors, and scoundrels."

"You can speak for yourself, Mr. Cameron," said Beazley. "I ain't none of those things."

Cameron looked at Beazley, Beazley looked at Cameron. They both looked at Lizzie.

"You think General Brock would give us a reward?" Beazley asked her.

"He might," said Lizzie. "Or he might just decide not to have you shot."

"Well, then," said Cameron, suppressing a smile, "we are under your arrest and protection. You may take us to General Brock."

Lizzie Erb sat forward on her huge horse and nuzzled him between the ears. He had the warm smell of the stables that made her homesick. And here she was, the custodian of two foolish men, a girl who would bring Mr. Whittington's killer to justice.

"First I have business," she said.

She reached into a small leather purse tied around her waist and drew out two coins. "You go into the tavern when it opens, you get cleaned up, you have some refreshments. I'll be back for you by late afternoon. Then we'll go and see King George's good friend and mine, Major-General Sir Isaac Brock."

She still had to get the money she'd hidden. Brock had indicated he would need it as soon as possible. He needed it to pay the settlers who had joined in their own defense.

Beazley bowed to her in an awkward salute and stretched a hand up to take the coins. Cameron, who had a longer reach, took them instead.

Lizzie was sure the two of them would still be there when she returned with her treasure.

Sixteen

Allison

This evening, when David comes in, I know right away there's more bad news.

"Hi, Allison," he says.

He tries to tell me a joke. Normally I listen almost desperately. When the only thing you can do is hear, you're usually all ears. But I can tell he's anxious. I wait until he goes quiet, then I know the joke must be over. He doesn't laugh.

"Potato," he says.

I'm *Potato* again. Thank you, God.

Actually, I'm not sure about God, but that doesn't mean I can't be thankful.

I was kicked out of Sunday School when I was nine. I think it was because I asked too many questions. They didn't actually kick me out. They asked me to be seen and not heard. So I left.

"Allison," David says, "there was a plane crash in Chicago this morning."

I don't know anyone in Chicago.

"Nana Friesen was on the plane."

Oh, my God. Why on Earth was she going to Chicago?

"She's okay."

I know that. I would have known if she wasn't. David would have come in crying.

Nana lives near Niagara Falls at Niagara-on-the-Lake, which calls itself "the loveliest town in Canada." They haven't seen Peterborough! Nana is my mother's mother. My mom used to dump us on Nana for six weeks every summer. That was before Nana had to use the walker. My dad lives in Vancouver with his new family. He wouldn't know us if we sat on his chest and scooped out his brains with a spoon.

We loved hanging out with Nana Friesen. Gray hair, glasses, and a beautiful smile. What happened, David? Tell me?

"She was on her way to Philadelphia to visit Auntie Vi."

Aunt Violet is her younger sister.

"It was an indirect flight. Nana was flying from Buffalo to make a connection. It's awkward for her to travel but I guess they put her in a wheelchair to move around the airport. They look after her. Anyhow, one hundred and forty-two people survived. One guy was killed. A barber from Toronto. He was sixty-five."

Did that make it better, that he was sixty-five?

"People are saying it was a miracle."

You've got to be kidding.

"People are saying God saved one hundred and forty-two passengers and crew—isn't that amazing?"

Did God kill the sixty-five-year-old barber on purpose? I don't think he does things by accident. Wonder what the guy did to anger the Almighty?

If you're going to take the credit, you've got to take the blame. Even if you're God.

That's an Allison rule. Of course, God might have rules of His own.

Nana Friesen took us to church a few times, but it was mostly for something to do. I don't know if Nana believes in God, but she's a good person, a good Sunday Christian.

God is a puzzle I haven't figured out yet. I'm working on it. When you're in a vegetable state but you can think, you're bound to think about God sooner or later.

Anyway, David and I aren't churchgoers, but you wouldn't say we're anti-God. We just like to argue. Usually, we take different sides. It makes a better argument if you don't agree.

"Nana Friesen is okay. She's gone on to Philadelphia." He pauses, like he is thinking of something else he wants to say. Then he announces: "Okay, I've got to go. See you soon."

I feel little taps on the back of my hand. I'm guessing it's my left hand, the one closest to the door. I know where the door is because when it's open I can hear people in the hall. I sometimes think I can feel the air moving when they walk past. Maybe it's only the shifting light patterns as they go by.

I'm happy my Nana is alive but I'm also sad. Nana hasn't visited me since I took a bullet in the head. It's hard for her to get around. Harder to get here than to Philadelphia. Unless there's a crash. And I understand, she doesn't want to see me this way. But when David leaves, I feel so lonely I just wish I could sleep.

Maddie O'Rourke arrives.

She walks right past my bed, straight to Doris. Doris is gurgling and wheezing. Maddie stays with her until after the eleven o'clock closing.

A few other people come in.

At about midnight, Doris gives one last gurgle and dies. It hasn't been seventeen days. It was a natural death, if you can think of death as natural. I can't. Inevitable, yes. But not natural. Not unless you're really old. Which I'm not. And neither was Doris.

Lizzie

Lizzie guided Fleetfire away from Portage Trail and along Chippewa Creek, known locally as The Crick, until they reached a pathway too narrow for wagons or carts. They climbed a narrow ravine through the rocky Niagara Escarpment to reach an overgrown road surrounded by primeval forest. The road dwindled to a rugged trail as they moved farther away from settled farmland.

By the time they approached a scattering of scrub poplars and alders, it was mid-afternoon. Lizzie looked down at the remains of a stone wall someone had built when they tried to clear a farmstead. They must have abandoned it. Just too many rocks, not enough soil. The heartbreak of their failed labors touched her deeply. Along the Grand River, fences were made from upended tree stumps marked. Here, stones piled into walls revealed land too poor to yield crops or raise animals.

The battlefront along the Niagara River seemed far behind her. The burning buildings and the bloodshed belonged to another world. Through a clearing, she could see beyond the river to the green rolling fields of the American States. She had been born there, in Boston. She was American by birth, yet George was her king. She felt restless inside, like she had swallowed butterflies. She wanted to go home.

She followed along the wall, approaching the place where she had tucked away the saddlebags filled with bank notes and coins.

Fleetfire had saved her life, now she was determined to save his. If she returned him to Matthias, he would be butchered. There was no shelter and not enough hay to get him through until spring. Her cousin would have no choice but to sell him to the Redcoats for food. Otherwise, if the Americans came through, they would butcher him themselves. One way or another, Fleetfire would be slaughtered unless she protected him. She would fulfill her duty to Brock and his Redcoats and take him home to their Grand River farm. When the fighting was over, she would give him back to her Uncle Matthias.

Perhaps she should just pick up the money and return home. There was nothing noble about war. It was ugly. She longed for the safety of her family.

I'm being silly, she thought. There's business to do.

She lifted one leg over the horse's neck, trying not to get her long skirts tangled in his mane, and swung free, dropping to the ground by his side.

After all, she had walked all the way over in the first place. It had taken her three days. Each night she had called in on a farmstead along the way and stayed with the family members, who were glad for the company. No one had asked about the leather saddlebag she carried over her shoulder and guarded so carefully. They figured it was none of their business.

Leading Fleetfire by his reins, Lizzie trudged along beside the stone wall, looking for the hollowed-out niche in the rocks where she had hidden her treasure. Rounding a corner she almost jumped out of her skin. There was a man sitting on a pile of boulders not fifty feet from where her treasure was hidden. He smiled.

Seventeen

Lizzie

Lizzie was startled. She was not terrified. Nothing scared Lizzie Erb for very long. Once she recognized the man on the rock pile, her alarm changed to confusion.

There was no mistaking him, with his bushy blond mustache and his buckskin jacket covered in beadwork and tassels. How could she forget his enormous smile?

And his eyes were as dark as night, with lines at the edges from squinting into the sun. It was her frontiersman from the burning barn who had saved her from the murderous Captain Blaine.

"I was expecting you sooner," he said, rising from the rock pile to take hold of Fleetfire's bridle.

Lizzie took a step back. She removed the blue scarf from around her neck and handed it to him.

"No, you keep it," he said. "It's a gift."

She wrapped the scarf around her neck again.

"I was delayed," she said. "I had to arrest a couple of your soldiers who had lost their way."

"They're not mine."

"Well, I arrested them anyway."

"You can't just arrest people."

"I did."

"They must be very dull-witted."

She wanted to say, only one of them was, but instead she observed: "You were with the British Redcoats when they burned down Matthias Haun's barn."

"I was. That doesn't make me a soldier. You don't see me in uniform. I'm a born and bred Canadian, same as you. I'm a free man."

His declaration thrilled her.

"But how could you be expecting me?" she demanded.

He nodded in the direction of his own little horse, tethered beyond the rock pile.

"I ran into some friends," he explained. "I'm a scout. I grew up at the trading post down near Detroit on the Canadian side. My family has been in business there with the Indians for over a hundred years. When the Americans crossed over, I had to choose sides."

"And which did you choose?"

He smiled.

"I'm here to choose sides, myself," she said. "I'm from the Grand River Purchase and you haven't told me how you knew I'd be here."

"I had an encounter with General Brock and Colonel Macdonell early this morning."

"You know some important people," she snapped, then added: "But who doesn't?"

"It's a very small world," he said.

"Really? I thought it was rather large."

"Well," he said, "they told me you had money for them, but you'd hidden it away somewhere. They told me you'd come from up near Berlin. It didn't take much to guess you would have passed through the Beverly Swamp and along this trail. It didn't take a genius to figure you would stash your treasure about here, before descending into the war zone. So I've been waiting for you."

"Really?" said Lizzie with as much sarcasm as she could muster. "You're quite brilliant, aren't you? But why wait, if you know where it's hidden? Of course, you don't really know, do you?""

"Not exactly. But I'm here to see it gets where it's supposed to go."

His teeth gleamed white and the stars deep in his eyes sparkled from the sunlight. He seemed to find her confusion amusing.

"Well, I'm not going to show you. If it is *here* at all. Maybe it isn't."

"Oh, I'm sure it is." He rubbed his mustache in satisfaction. He tilted his head back as if he would laugh, then he tilted his head forward and smiled. "After all, it's yours."

"Yes it is."

"Well, you get it then and we'll be on our way."

Lizzie pondered her dilemma. She could leave her money hidden but then it would do nobody any good. She could dig it out from the stone wall, but then this man might take it for himself.

She didn't trust anyone so handsome.

But she could see no other option.

She handed him Fleetfire's reins and scrambled along the wall until she came to the niche where she had left her saddlebag.

For a moment she thought it was gone.

She reached into the shadows and felt around.

It was there.

Lizzie walked back to the man with their horses, carrying the leather saddlebag over her shoulder.

"Here," he said, "I'll take that."

He reached out and took it before she had a chance to fight him off. She grabbed for it.

"By the Lord's sake, girl. I'm only going to strap it onto my saddle. You've riding bareback, you have nothing to tie it to."

"I hope you are not a thief," she said.

"If I was, I'd probably have to kill you before I ran off with your money."

"You wouldn't!"

"I don't think so. Not yet."

"What's your name, sir?"

"Will Richardson. What's yours?"

"None of your damn business."

Lizzie had never sworn before in her life. It was a word she had picked up from Beazley. It made her feel strange. She smiled. Her handsome escort blushed as he boosted her onto Fleetfire's broad back and prepared to mount up himself.

It wouldn't hurt to have a handsome escort.

Allison

Today is the seventeenth day. Someone will be murdered tonight. That is a stark and terrifying fact. And I can do nothing to stop it from happening. Even if the victim is me.

Doris died a few days ago so she doesn't count in the killer's pattern. They haven't put a new *guest* in her bed yet. I wonder if Maddie O'Rourke will come back?

Jaimie Retzinger came in earlier in the day. He just sat like he usually does but he didn't say anything. It was a nice change from the mindless chattering, although I missed the distraction. After a while, he left. Just like that. Maybe we're breaking up. Again.

With a bullet in my brain, I'm still a handful, I guess. I'm awfully quiet. You'd think he'd like me better this way. But now the bloom has gone off the romance and he's getting restless. I wouldn't be surprised if he moves on. One day, he'll forget to come in. Then the next day he won't come in again. And so on and so on.

I'll miss Jaimie Retzinger. He has a sweet streak. That's why I fell for him. But he has a mean streak. That's what kept me interested. I was sort of in love with him but I never really liked him that much. It would be better if he finds someone else. Someone he can handle, a woman who isn't such a handful and likes Harleys.

My brother just came in.

"Allison," he says. "I've got to go tree-planting."

What!

"I've been accepted at Victoria College in the fall."

My brother! He's going to university!

"I've got to make some money so I'm heading north for the summer. A good tree planter can make thousands."

If the black flies don't tear the flesh from your bones.

"The season's almost half over, but I can still make enough to get me through with student loans."

Maybe the black fly season has passed.

I'm so happy for him, it makes the pain of losing him worth it.

David makes small talk for a while. He tells me about what he wants to study. I cling to every word, every sound, but I don't really hear him. It's like he's already gone.

He doesn't say goodbye when he leaves. He doesn't lean into my field of vision. He just slips out. I'm lost in mixed up feelings for the next couple of hours. Who will call me *Potato*?

Then Maddie O'Rourke comes in. Oh, glory.

Maybe there is a God and I just haven't figured Him out. Or Her.

"Hey, Allison," she says. "Sorry I haven't been in. I don't know if you know but Doris died. Yeah, I expect you've figured it out. You were always smart."

I feel a weight pressing against me somewhere. It must be Maddie's makeup case. She's set it on my chest. I don't think I'm wearing a bra so there's kind of a platform.

Maddie chats like we're old friends.

"I remember you walking through the halls of Thomas A. Stewart Secondary School, Allison. Like, you really knew who you were. You were nice, but you wouldn't take nonsense from anybody. I guess maybe not *always* nice—but strong. And here you are now. Still strong."

As Maddie works away on my eyes, she looms into view. Sometimes I can make out her features, her beautiful face surrounded by gleaming folds of black hair, the flash of her blueberry eyes. I think I can feel her breath. It must be blowing across my face. For a while, I'm happy. Not worried about killers, not lonely, just happy.

She gently closes my eye with her fingertip.

"I want to get them the same," she says.

After awhile, she appears again.

"Now it looks like you're winking. When they're both closed, you look like a sleeping princess. It must be a drag but at least you're not dead." She took a deep breath. "I just did Doris, you know. Working on cold flesh just isn't the same."

I don't want to hear this.

"So, I don't like open coffins," Maddie continues. "But Doris' sister from Miami asked me to do her makeup. You know, at the funeral home. I've never worked on a dead person before. I just kept thinking, it's Doris. It's okay, it's just Doris. Well, Doris was never beautiful but she turned out looking the best she could. Everybody was really pleased, especially her sister from Miami."

Maddie talks like we've always been friends.

"That eye of yours seems to have a mind of its own. But there we go, you're finished. You're lovely. We'll just take your silver medallion from the drawer and I'll put the chain around your neck."

The funny thing is, I thought I was wearing it. I imagine David put it away for safekeeping.

"That's perfect," Maddie says. "It highlights your eye."

The amber glimmers like golden honey in the summer sunshine. I can see it. She must be holding it up to the light.

"And what about this!" she says. "I can see right through; there are lines cut into the silver behind the amber. It looks like two capital V's. One of them is upside down. There's some smaller print, too. I can't make out what it says. There's a word stamped into the silver on the back. It looks like it says REVERE. The letters are inside a box of lines."

I love my medallion because it's old, not for whatever it says. And I love it because it's been in my family for a very long time. And for the clear color of the amber and for the silver that's smoothed with the fingerprints of my ancestors.

"I should go now," Maddie says. She leans close to say goodbye, slides down off my high hospital bed, and leaves.

I listen. That's what I do best. The warning buzzer goes off, then the eleven o'clock bell tolls. I can hear two nurses talking in the corridor. A man and a woman. Then someone closes my door.

I wait. I lose track of time. I wait some more. Maybe two hours go by. I'm wondering about my medallion. Is that what *the ordinary man* was after?

My door opens and closes. I think I can feel the air shifting around me. Maybe I imagine it.

Shuffling sounds. I think it's a woman, she smells like soap. I can hear her breathing through her nose. She's very close.

Suddenly a narrow light beam glares in my face, right through my eyelids. Both of my eyelids. In the midst of terror, a revelation! Both my eyes with their beautiful makeup can see, even if only one eye can open.

More shuffling. I'm being touched. I feel the weight of
a hand, of two hands, of fingers pressing. She's stealing my
silver medallion!

My left eye flashes open.

The light beam flails through the air. She's dropped the
penlight. I hear scrambling, then the light beam shines across
the ceiling and down in the direction of the door.

The room goes dark. I hear the door open. I feel the rush
of air, the door closes.

My heart is racing, I'm alive.

My left eye must have scared her to death. Or my lucky
medallion did.

I'm freaked out by the intruder, but I'm excited because I
can see light with both eyes. I've got to work on getting both
of them to open. My mind is racing. Gradually it slows down.

I drift into a comfortable sleep.

Eighteen

Lizzie

Guiding their horses past occasional clearings through the forest, Lizzie and her escort didn't talk. It was late in the day when they descended the rocky cleft in the escarpment. Soon they were on mud roads packed down through the long summer months by wagons and carts. As they approached Chippewa, they passed fences made from the stumps of big trees that had been hauled out of the fields by oxen. Then the fences became cedar rails laid out in a zigzag fashion. A few cows wandered about, nibbling on the dried grass.

They crossed The Crick and pulled up their horses in front of Macklem's Tavern, where Lizzie had left Cameron and Beazley.

"You wait where you are," said Will Richardson as he dismounted. "It's too hard to get you back up on that beast again."

Lizzie was appalled. Her escort had managed to insult her, suggesting she was heavy, and to insult her horse, calling him a beast. Just because Will Richardson was young and handsome and very dashing by anyone's judgment, that didn't give him the right to be rude.

But she stayed on Fleetfire's back, leaning forward to rub his ears, and said nothing. Will disappeared through the doors into the tavern.

Soon, Lizzie could hear the rough sounds of men laughing. She waited. There was more laughter. She waited a little longer. It was going to be dark before long.

Finally, in exasperation she swung her long skirts up over Fleetfire's head and slid down from his back. She marched across the sidewalk made of wooden planks. She knew women were not allowed in the saloon. She pushed open the doors and strode inside like she owned the place.

There were only three customers at the bar. There was Beazley, looking fat and quite drunk. There was Cameron, standing at ease and pretending to be sober. And there was Will Richardson, tipping a large glass of whiskey back so vigorously that some of it missed his mouth and dribbled down his cheeks.

The laughter died. All three men stared at Lizzie in amazement. The bartender was astonished. There had never been a woman in his establishment since the day it was built.

Lizzie was dressed in coarse drab clothes but there was no mistaking that she was a woman. None of the men had seen anything so unnatural ever before.

Even Will Richardson appeared shocked.

He moved away from the bar, hitched up his trousers, and took a couple of steps toward her.

"Well, I'll be damned," he exclaimed.

"I'm sure you will be," she responded.

He grinned.

"Just what are you doing?" Lizzie demanded. "These men are under arrest for desertion and for arson and you're to escort me to General Brock. Did you forget your responsibilities when you walked through that door, Will Richardson?"

"No, ma'am," he said, still grinning. "I was just getting fueled up for the rest of the journey."

"Drunk," she said. "You were getting drunk."

"Yes, ma'am. A little drunk. Now you wait with the horses and I'll bring these two rascals out and we'll be on our way. Better go quick, before someone places you under arrest, yourself."

She went out and crossed the road. She purchased a handful of oats for the price of a smile and fed it to Fleetfire. She saved a little for Will's horse. A half hour later, the three men walked into the late afternoon sunlight. The two soldiers were staggering, but Will Richardson held himself upright and sober. Despite the frontier clothes and an untrimmed mustache, he looked quite dashing.

Allison

The first thing on my mind when I wake up is that Maddie O'Rourke's eye shadow saved my life. I'm positive I was about to die but my killer suddenly fled. My eyes all made up like that, then one eye opening. I scared her. Or him.

Could it have been *the ordinary man*, trying to steal my medallion? Not trying to kill me at all, just rob me, like stealing from a corpse. But no, I'm pretty sure it was a woman. And it was the seventeenth night.

In spite of a close encounter with death, I feel better than I have for a long time.

I can hear voices outside my door. It's three nurses and they sound very excited. One of them has a harsh voice, like there is something broken inside her throat.

I don't know whether they're real nurses, like in the hospital. They call them *nurses* at Shady Nook, whatever they do. It must be hard, looking after people like me. They can call themselves astronauts, if that's what they want.

Some of them must be real nurses, though. They do medical stuff.

Anyway, they're all excited.

They move into my room to talk, so no one can hear them.

"She was a stranger in town."

"Crossing the footbridge over the Otonabee River."

"Killed right on the bridge."

"They've got her body downstairs. I've seen her."

"Me, too. She was whacked on the head."

"Strangled."

"Strangled after she was whacked on the head."

"Bare hands?"

"Wearing surgical gloves."

"A woman killed her."

"You don't know that."

"Small hands. You can tell from the bruises."

"It's horrible, she was only in her forties."

"Thirties."

"Really? I thought she looked a lot older."

"She's dead."

"Speak well of the departed."

"What? I liked her."

"You didn't know her."

"I was joking."

"Not funny, and we shouldn't be joking," said the nurse with the rasping voice.

"How else do you deal with murder?"

"It's no joke. It's scary. I'm not working after dark ever again."

"You will."

"Yeah, probably."

"What about this one?" That was the nurse with the unusual voice.

"Her? Allison Briscoe. She's as good as dead, already."

Hey, that's me! I'm not dead. Get the hell out of here, go! And they leave.

Maybe swearing does help, even if they can't actually hear me.

So, the pattern continues. There has been another death on the seventeenth night. It wasn't me. Not this time. Thank you. But I made the killer mad enough that she went out and killed somebody else. Not even one of the *guests*.

I feel badly about that.

Lizzie

Standing on tiptoes, Lizzie reached up and grasped her horse's mane with her fingers. Will Richardson cupped his hands under her raised left foot and hoisted her onto Fleetfire's back. She pulled herself straight. He handed her the reins. It had been a long day; she ached all over.

She towered high over her escort after he mounted up. Fleetfire was a huge draft animal, normally used for pulling a plow. She marveled, remembering that she had been able to swing herself onto him when she had escaped the fire.

I must have been lifted by angels, she thought. Risen on the wings of terror, more likely.

This strange company of travelers made their way along the Portage Trail that ran parallel to the mighty river. Fort Erie was being rebuilt and many of the Redcoat soldiers were camped near Matthias Haun's new home, but Lizzie was certain General Brock and the militia were to the north, near Queenston Heights.

As they passed Wilson's Hotel in the village of Niagara, Lizzie gazed out over the falls. She loved to see the mist rising. The road swooped above some houses and she caught sight of a broad column of smoke above the rooftops twisting into the evening sky.

"Someone's on fire," she exclaimed. The smoke was coming from the direction of Rebecca Haun's frame house.

"There's always a lot of fires this time of year," said Will Richardson. "People start up a roaring blaze after they've been cooking outside all summer. Their chimneys catch fire. We've got to keep moving."

He urged his horse forward, forcing Lizzie on her big gelding to go the same way.

"No," she declared and pulled on the reins to turn Fleetfire back. She was determined to check on her aunt. Cameron and Beazley stood aside to watch as her big horse forced Will to turn around.

"It's nothing," snapped Will Richardson in annoyance.

"I've got to make sure. Anyway, we need a place to stay for the night. We can't reach Queenston before dark. You three can sleep in the stable and I've got a nice warm cot by the hearth."

She turned her horse down the cobblestone lane she had passed through early that morning. The others followed. When they reached the river road, Lizzie's worst fears were confirmed. All that was left of Rebecca Haun's house and stable were burned-out stone foundations and some smoldering beams amidst piles of charred debris.

A man she had seen the night before in Rebecca's kitchen was standing by the ruins. He had a shovel and a rake. He was making sure the fire didn't spread to other buildings close by.

"Underhill," said Will Richardson, nodding to the man.

"Richardson," the man acknowledged Lizzie's companion perched on his little horse. He ignored the two ragged soldiers on foot.

"Mr. Underhill." Lizzie spoke the man's name as an anxious greeting.

"Miss Erb," he offered, followed by a nervous cough.

"Where is my aunt, Mr. Underhill?"

"It's a very sad business, Miss Erb."

"Is she dead?"

"She must have tipped over a lamp."

"There were no lamps burning when I left her this morning."

"Well, she must have anyway."

"Mr. Underhill, is she dead?" said Lizzie.

"We didn't find no remains, if that's what you mean. It were an accident."

No, it had not been an accident. Lizzie felt horror deep in her bones but she had no urge to cry. Cold fury stifled her grief. Her three companions waited to see what she would do.

After gazing deeply into the ashes and collecting her thoughts, she wheeled Fleetfire around with ferocious determination. "We will stay at Wilson's," she announced and cantered ahead of her band of ruffians toward the hotel perched on a precipice near the brink of the falls.

"Here," called Frank Underhill, running after her. She slowed in when she heard him and he handed her something wrapped in a swatch of smoky cotton. "We found this among the ruins."

Lizzie pulled Fleetfire to a full stop and unfolded the cloth. Inside, wiped clean from rubbing in Mr. Underhill's pocket, was a silver medallion with a gem of clear amber at the center.

She had never seen it before but she knew what it was. Her mother had told her that Aunt Rebecca wore a piece of jewelry within the folds of her clothes. Rebecca was no longer a Mennonite; she chose to wear this keepsake from her beloved William's family hidden from sight. Like her love, itself, it was not secret, but it was private.

Lizzie was amazed at how the evening sunlight turned golden as it passed through the nugget of amber. Her eyes welled up but again she refused to cry.

She lifted her hair at the back and settled the thin silver chain around her neck so the medallion glistened on her breast.

As she did this, she declared to herself with conviction: though we live among Mennonites, I will wear this medallion with pride. I am an Erb and a Haun but I am also a de Vere of the Boston de Veres. My Aunt Rebecca's story is safe in the past. I have my own story to live. Aunt Becky would have wanted it so.

Lizzie's eyes burned.

She dug her heels into Fleetfire's sides and trotted on.

Nineteen

Allison

All day long, I've been picking up the scent of smoke. I guess it's a residual memory from Lizzie's world. Unless it's the killer? I can't tell for sure but I don't think she stole my medallion before I scared her off. It's been a long day. I feel more alone than usual. I still don't have a roommate. And there's a lot of traffic in the hall. Having people around can make you feel lonely. Especially if they're talking about murder.

My door has been open and I can hear them. Two police officers interviewed nurses just outside my room. I can tell they're police because their voices are loud and clear. They learn to speak that way at police school. It gives them authority. One of the officers is a woman. Her voice is loudest and yet it's soothing.

The police have no idea that the murderer works here at Shady Nook—or that this is just the latest in a series of murders. They're trying to figure out if the victim knew her killer. You can't sneak up on a stranger, on a footbridge, with a club in your hands.

With a club? I've been listening, trying to figure out what weapon was used to bash in her head.

Then it turns out she was only strangled. I don't mean *only*. But there was a lot of blood because she hit her head when the killer let her drop backwards onto the steel walkway. The killer was looking into her eyes when she died. You would have to hate someone in order to watch her die like that.

Or be in a terrible rage.

And damn it all to hell, I was the cause of the rage.

The killer saw I was alive in here, not just a vegetable. She knows! And then she changed her pattern. She still had to kill.

If only I could figure out who works on what shift, I could connect the killer to the dates of each death.

I can pretty well tell the time in here by listening to voices. When shifts change, the voices change.

Some of the nurses work twelve-hour shifts, from eight to eight. But some work a shift and a half. From eight in the morning until two at night, or from two in the morning until eight the next night. It's confusing trying to follow their schedule just by listening.

What I do know, for sure, is the killer was going home after doing a shift and a half at two in the morning.

That would narrow the suspects down, you would think.

I want to tell the cops.

I need to tell the cops.

The killer knows I'm in here. She's scared of me, and not just for the eye shadow and the staring eyeball. She's already broken her pattern. And she's afraid I know too much.

She needs me dead.

The question is, will she wait another seventeen days?

Maddie comes in. I wish I could get her to explain about the nurse. I sometimes forget she can't tell what's inside my mind.

So, right away she says: "I looked up REVERE from the back of your medallion. I think the guy who made it is the same Paul Revere we studied in school. He was a silversmith as well as a Revolutionary hero in a famous poem. Do you remember?

"Listen my children and you shall hear
"Of the midnight ride of Paul Revere.

"That was by Henry Wadsworth Longfellow. You took English from Mrs. Muratori. A different grade from me but she must have done the same things. Remember:

"Once upon a midnight dreary, while I pondered, weak and weary...

"Quoth the Raven, 'Nevermore.'

"That was a poem by a sad-looking horror writer called Edgar Allan Poe."

The only poems I remember are song lyrics.

"Anyway," Maddie continues. "I looked up the symbol with two V's that you can see on the other side of the amber. Turns out one is a compass, not the direction kind, the kind for making circles. The other is called a square, like a ruler with a right angle. One over the other, they form a symbol used by the Freemasons. That's like the Shriners, the guys who wear funny hats and do silly things in parades and raise money. Except the Masons are a solemn and secret society—not all that secret, since we know Paul Revere was one of them. So was George Washington and Ben Franklin. I couldn't make out the small letters, you can hardly see them but they look foreign."

Maddie holds up the medallion so I can see the amber glistening.

Paul Revere gave it to Madge de Vere. Her husband was a Freemason.

It's a big, big world but, at the same time, it is very small.

Lizzie

When Lizzie demanded that Will Richardson give her the leather saddlebag with her treasure inside, he hesitated. They were standing outside the hotel stable where the horses and three men would spend the night. She intended to sleep in a hotel bed.

"I'll just keep it safe for you, Miss Erb."

"I didn't tell you my name," she snapped.

"No, your friend Mr. Underhill did. But I already knew it, of course."

"Of course. General Brock told you. I'll take my property, if you please."

Cameron and Beazley watched with interest. They were both almost sober after their walk from the saloon. Will undid the cinch and lifted the saddle down. Lizzie stepped forward and placed her hand on her bag.

"I wouldn't do that, Miss." Will Richardson spoke severely.

"It is mine," she insisted. She glowered. Her fury at Rebecca Haun's fate showed through. She was in the middle of a war and almost on the front lines. No one was going to order her about, not even the handsome frontiersman, Will Richardson.

Cameron stepped forward between them.

"If it belongs to the lady," he said to Will, "then you had better let her have it."

The two men stared at each others. Lizzie was amazed. She was used to seeing the soldier slouching and disinterested. Right now he stood as straight and tall as his adversary. He had scavenged a jacket to replace the one he discarded. It had a bullet hole in the breast and was stained with dried blood. He was ragged and filthy, while the buckskin jacket on Will Richardson looked impressively clean. But despite his tawdry appearance, Cameron presented himself with surprising dignity.

Will backed off. Cameron untied the bag from the saddle and held it out to Lizzie.

"It must be important, whatever is in there," he said.

She took the bag and turned to enter the main door of Wilson's Hotel. She didn't thank Cameron. He was, after all, her prisoner. She wasn't sure of the legality of their relationship but they definitely were not friends. She did not like being indebted to a man she had placed under arrest.

Lizzie slept uneasily. She had nightmare visions of Rebecca Haun being murdered but her killer always stayed in the shadows. Even with flames licking the air all around him, he somehow remained concealed. When Lizzie awoke at dawn, she reached for the medallion on the bedside table and clutched it until her fingers hurt.

Twenty

Allison

Lizzie is smart and Lizzie is tough. But she doesn't know much about the world beyond the Grand River Purchase. Except what she'd learned in her letters from Madge de Vere. She doesn't know much about men. And she certainly doesn't know much about warfare and murder.

Not that I do, either.

There haven't been many men in my life. I mean, my dad lives in Vancouver. I just called him my *dad*. I usually think of him as *father*, not *dad*. And then there's Jaimie Retzinger. I'm not even sure I would call him a man. He's a boy who somehow got older.

And all I know about our famous war with the Americans is this: We didn't defeat them but we weren't conquered. That was a victory of sorts. And I know General Brock was killed at Queenston Heights in the autumn of 1812. There's a big monument just up the river from my Nana's place at Niagara-on-the-Lake, and his dead body is inside it. So is the body of Colonel John Macdonell, as far as I know. The two soldiers died on the same day before our troops chased the Americans back across the river to their own fort on the other side.

Nana took me to Brock's monument several times. She told me about the War of 1812. I used to think she remembered it from her own childhood.

It's funny how history and memories become confused. General Brock and Colonel Macdonell are history to me, but they are recent acquaintances of Lizzie Erb.

On the morning when Lizzie woke up at Wilson's Hotel, the general and the colonel were still alive. She knew they were at Fort George. That's where she needed to go, to deliver the saddlebag she had kept with her under the covers the whole night long.

All day today I've been worrying about Lizzie. I should be worried about me!

My executioner is close. She may not wait another seventeen days.

That's how she must see herself, as an executioner.

I wonder if it's because she's insane. Or is she seeking revenge for some terrible thing that happened to her? Actually, I don't think it matters. She wants me dead.

Why she wants me dead isn't important. If I'm dead, knowing *why* won't make me feel better. I'll be dead.

But let's consider the pattern.

If she is angry at the whole world, why not go out and kick a rock?

If she's nuts, then how come she's so organized? Every seventeen days! And why kill really sick people—until last night when she broke the pattern?

Does this mean she'll begin killing whenever she *wants* to? Not when she *has* to?

I'm betting my life that she'll wait for another seventeen days. Her fear and frustration last night got the better of her. She went out and killed someone who wasn't sick. She might even regret doing it. I doubt if she regrets killing people like me, though.

Killing vegetables.

I mean, vegetables don't really die, do they?

They get sliced and diced, cut, crimped, chopped, puréed, and julienned. Roasted, braised, boiled, broiled, stewed, and baked, fried, or eaten raw.

If I could eat French fries right now, would that make me a cannibal?

What about turnips? I don't even like turnips.

I wonder where Jaimie Retzinger is? I need him to save my life again.

I confess: I miss Jaimie Retzinger. Even after we broke up, he was always around. And when I got shot, he spent hours in the hospital every night, ignoring me. But at least he was there.

He used to say he never got in a word edgewise. Whatever that means. So chattering away while I'm lying in a *comma*, that works for him.

For me, too. I'm not actually in a *coma*, but I hardly listen—I think that's what they call *irony*. I'm desperate for diversion, but Jaimie drones on like a confused swarm of bees. I'd rather have silence.

So what's wrong with this relationship!

That wasn't a question.

David just came in. He taps the back of my hand. He must have kissed me because I felt gentle warm pressure somewhere. That must be where my left cheek is. I open my eye, but he has already moved out of my field of vision.

"Look after yourself, Potato. I'll see you." He is at the door, now, I guess he's looking back in.

I try to understand. I mean, a person has to get on with his life.

"Look after yourself," he repeats. He doesn't mean this to be as stupid as it sounds. David is not stupid, he just isn't thinking. He's off to plant trees in Northern Ontario. Near Kapuskasing, way up there.

See you, David. Take care. Look after yourself. Watch out for the bears.

Lizzie

When Lizzie finished breakfast, she took some bread and jam out to the men. Will Richardson greeted her with a smile but Cameron and Beazley were gone.

"I sent them packing," he said. "There's a big fight brewing at Queenston Heights. The Americans have crossed over from Fort Niagara. Brock is heading that way and he will need every man he can get. Even them."

"Why aren't you there, then? Why didn't you go, too?"

"It's not safe," he laughed.

"Of course."

"I have to look after you, Miss Erb."

"And my treasure."

"Indeed, and your treasure. We'll head south and then west."

"No, Mr. Richardson. We must join General Brock."

"He is about to be overtaken by the Americans. We would do better to go the other way."

Will had already led Lizzie's horse out of the stable and his own was saddled up and ready to go. He hoisted her onto Fleetfire's back before she had time to protest. It was like he was tossing a bag of grain around and not a young woman in skirts.

She still had her saddlebag clutched in her grip. He reached out and took it. She didn't protest. He tied it to the back of his saddle and mounted.

Lizzie hardly knew what had happened before he slapped Fleetfire on the rump and suddenly they were trotting down the road side by side. They must have been quite a spectacle, if anyone had bothered to notice. She was small and awkwardly elegant on her giant steed and he was large and powerful on his little one.

There was no question, Will Richardson had taken charge.

They passed through Chippewa and were halfway along the Portage Trail to Fort Erie before they drew their horses in and proceeded at a walking pace. Fort Erie was still in the hands of the British. Will Richardson made a point of saying it that way: Fort Erie was not in the hands of the Canadians but of the British.

"We are all British, here," she proclaimed, "even Colonel Macdonell, who was born in Scotland. I've been told he's now the attorney general of Upper Canada."

"But he's only second-in-command to Sir Isaac Brock."

"Who is a great man, wherever he was born. The people of Elizabethtown renamed their community in his honor."

"Brockville! It's a village of transplanted Americans."

"He was made a knight for capturing Fort Detroit for Upper Canada."

"By a fool."

"I beg your pardon, sir. King George is no fool. You are speaking treason."

"Hardly."

"Then you are speaking like an American."

"Perhaps."

She wheeled around on Fleetfire's broad back to look down at her handsome escort. His cheeks were smooth. He had obviously shaved that morning. His mustache was grand, his blue eyes were flashing. But he was not smiling. His lips were pursed in grim determination.

"Are you an American, then?" The quavering in Lizzie's voice suggested anger and apprehension. "Are you a spy?"

"If I am, Lizzie Erb, you are my prisoner."

"Am I?"

"Yes."

"Damn you," she said, swearing for the second time in her life.

She drew her horse to a halt. Will Richardson rapidly dismounted and seized her reins. She slid off Fleetfire's back and stood directly in front of her captor.

"Be an American if you want," she said, glowering up at him. "You can give me my money and I will be off. We'll say no more about it."

"Your money is for General Van Rensselaer and his American militia at Lewiston."

"No, sir!"

"It is."

"You've been planning to steal it all along!"

"I have."

"You are an evil man and a rogue."

"As I told you, Lizzie Erb. We have to choose sides. I chose long ago to be a Canadian."

"An American!"

"A Canadian."

"But you spoke to General Brock yesterday. He told you about my treasure. He trusted you."

"You are mistaken, Miss Erb. I have never met General Brock."

"Then how did you know about me?"

"Rebecca Haun told me."

"My God," said Lizzie. She wasn't swearing. "It was you who killed her."

Will Richardson embraced Lizzie with his eyes, showing unexpected warmth. It was as if he wanted to protect her. He remained silent. But Lizzie was determined to resolve her aunt's fate.

"Is she dead?" Lizzie demanded.

"No," said Will Richardson at last. "She is alive and on her way to Boston."

Lizzie was confused, angry, and relieved. She waited for an explanation.

"Some foolish American sympathizers set her place on fire," said Will Richardson. "It was still early morning when I arrived on the scene, although you were already on the road to retrieve your treasure. They were a drunken rabble; they didn't know she was inside. She was in her nightclothes and she was furious at me when I saved her. At least when I rescued you from the flames, you wanted to be rescued."

"She would not have wanted to die. She's a fighter."

"Well, she kept yelling about her medallion from Paul Revere. Damn it, I told her, your life's more important. She didn't seem to think so. She wanted to go back in. I wouldn't let her. I'm glad to see it turned up."

He gazed at the silver medallion on Lizzie's breast. She glanced down at the medallion and, in spite of herself, she smiled.

"I don't understand about the fire," she said. "Was it because of the meeting last night Were they angry?"

"With General Brock, not your aunt. Some of them were, and some of them just wanted to raise hell. They had been drinking all night."

"Did you force her to tell you where I had gone?"

"I didn't torture her, Lizzie, if that's what you mean. I got her some clothes from a neighbor. She said she had relatives in Boston. I gave her some money and sent her along to cross over to the American States."

"She couldn't, we're at war."

"Oh, there's places she could. And she did."

"But she's a friend of General Brock."

"That's the point. Where better to hide than in the midst of the enemy?"

Lizzie was annoyed that his logic made sense. But did he mean, she hid among the British, here, or among the Americans, there? Which were the enemy? As Lizzie had noted before, loyalties could be very confusing.

"So, then what?" she said.

"Then I galloped full speed to meet you."

"She told you about the money?"

"She was worried for you, Lizzie. She thought you'd be safe with me. Since I rescued her from the drunken louts, she assumed I was a loyalist."

"But you're not," Lizzie declared.

"Depends what you mean by loyalist. I'm a Canadian patriot, through and through."

Lizzie bit her tongue while she tried to think.

She was this man's prisoner, but he was her guardian. She was under the care and protection of a thief and a traitor.

She decided she would see him hanged before she'd say another civil word to him.

She sat down on a stump at the side of the road.

He sat down on a boulder beside her.

He was smiling.

Twenty-one

Allison

Something wakes me! I've been dozing. I didn't hear anyone come in. Suddenly I can hear breathing. I hope it's Maddie O'Rourke. It must be late but the lights are still on. Anyway, if it was Maddie she'd talk to me. Maybe it's a visitor for my new roommate. I don't even know her name. They wheeled her in, plopped her in bed, and left her before the shift change at eight p.m. She must be in a vegetative state. Like me, they figure. Two peas in a pod.

No, the heavy breather is leaning over me. I can make out a fuzzy image. She's in shadow. She moves away. The lights go out. The door closes and there are no more shadows. But she didn't leave. It's pitch dark. I see a small penlight beam. I wait for something to happen.

She is just standing there, staring, breathing through her mouth like she can't get enough air.

I can feel her breath on my cheeks. Oh, good glory, I can feel where my cheeks are. What a time to make a discovery like this! I don't know what I felt, really. Dear God, woman, go away—I need to think.

But she doesn't go away. My left eye closes. I have to concentrate to make it open again. It's not like I can wink and blink but if I focus all my energy I can make it open.

It opens. The room is still black but her penlight flashes in my face.

My open eye startles her. I can hear her gasp. She whispers and her voice is like razor blades. Sharp and smooth, all at the same time.

"You're in there, Allison, aren't you?"

There's a long pause. I'm trying to sort out her voice. There's something strange about it. It's like a ghost speaking through a shroud.

"I'll be coming for you very soon, dear Allison."

Her words hang in the air. They're a threat. She won't kill me tonight. But she will before long. She's making a promise. Like, she won't let me down, she'll return. I get it! To put me out of my misery.

Listen, listen! No misery, I'm not miserable. I'm Allison Briscoe. I am a human being. I want to live.

Shadows fill the room as the door opens. Then she's gone and it's dark again.

My eye closes. Time passes. I nearly fall asleep. Then, suddenly it's light. I can see through my eyelids.

"Come on, now, Allie. Open your eye. That's my girl."

It's Maddie O'Rourke.

"Somebody left you in the dark," she says.

I guess it isn't as late as I thought. It must be only mid-evening.

Maddie chats as she cleans off yesterday's makeup. She dabs a cleanser on my face. I think I can feel it. I can feel pressure.

The pressure is on my face. That means I can feel my face. It's not like normal but it's a beginning. It *is* a beginning.

My mind is swirling. I think I can feel where my face is. I'm discovering my body from the inside. And my killer has vowed to return. She'll drop in to see me from time to time, but in sixteen days I'll be dead.

Well, not if I can help it.

"Easy, girl. You're going to pop a blood vessel. Have you had a bad day?"

I can see Maddie as a blur, her black hair shimmers like a dark halo around her pale face. I can't see her eyes or mouth because the light is behind her. She bends over me; I can feel the pressure of her weight. I can't tell where the weight is, but it must be against my left side.

Of course, sometimes I forget Maddie O'Rourke is very short and her back is twisted. She must hoist herself up onto the side of the bed. She—

Hold it! What does she mean, I'm going to pop a blood vessel? She can tell I'm upset?

Allison Briscoe! Think bad thoughts; think mixed up swirling awful terrible thoughts. Think about murder, whatever. Bad stuff. Make your blood pop.

"You're doing it again, Allison. The veins in your forehead are pulsing like crazy. Sorry, sweet thing. Do you want me to stop? I'll come back tomorrow?"

No, I'm pleading. No, please please stay. Watch my temples, watch my pulse. See, I'm thinking good thoughts. No popping veins. Maddie, Maddie, Maddie, please stay.

She leaves. After the lights go out and the door closes, I lie here listening to my blood run through my body.

Maddie comes back the next night and the next and the next. She makes up my eyes, she cleans the makeup off and makes them up again. She talks to me. She tells me my new roommate is an elderly woman called Kate. She'll be gone by Christmas, they say.

Each day, I work at thinking miserable thoughts, then happy thoughts. Each evening Maddie comes in and I try to make the veins in my temples become bigger and smaller.

She notices. At first she worries that she's upsetting me. I can't shift my moods fast enough. She can't see a pattern.

Then one day, just like that, I open my other eye.

It just opens.

Both eyes are open.

When Maddie comes in, she sees my eyes. She calls a nurse but the nurse doesn't care. I'm just staring ahead. I'm a turnip. A potato with eyes. They think I can't see. But I can. Maddie knows that. She already knows I can hear.

She leans into my field of vision and looks into my eyes as she applies eyeliner, and she talks to me.

"You're happy tonight," she says.

I am, but how does she know?

She's looking into my eyes—oh, glory, I've got it!

I think about cherry chocolate cheesecake.

My pupils get big, I know they do.

My irises are golden-hazel. My pupils are very black so you can see them clearly.

Maddie gazes into my eyes. She's stopped applying eyeliner. I relax.

The pupils get smaller.

"Allison?"

I think good thoughts. The pupils get bigger.

"Allison, you're here!"

I am, I am.

I think terrible thoughts. The black of my pupils contracts.

I relax. My pupils get bigger.

"Allison, the buzzer just went. I've got to go. Tomorrow we're going to have a talk, you and me."

Maddie O'Rourke leans down and kisses my cheek, I can feel the warmth.

"Night, night," she says. Then she slides off the bed, turns out the light and closes the door. She leaves me alone in the dark. I close my eyes. I am crying on the inside. Crying with joy.

Twenty-two

Lizzie

As Lizzie sat on the stump with Will on the boulder beside her, it occurred to her they made a handsome couple. But they were outlaws. He was a dangerous renegade. Until she figured out a way to turn him in, she could be considered an American sympathizer.

The treasure he had stolen had been entrusted to her by the people of the Grand River Purchase. Unless she figured out a way to get it back, she was almost as guilty of treason as he was. Treason was punishable by death.

Will Richardson rose to his feet.

"It's time to get moving, Miss Erb."

"Don't Miss Erb me, you scoundrel."

"Right then, Lizzie. Let's get a move on. I want to cross over the river before dark."

"I'm not moving."

"Suit yourself."

That surprised her.

"I thought you promised my Aunt Rebecca you'd protect me."

"I'm only a man, Lizzie. A humble Canadian. I can't make a fierce and determined woman do anything against her will."

"Indeed, you cannot."

"Of course, I'm Will, and where there's a will there's a way." She wondered whether she should be amused by his wit. She decided not to give him the pleasure.

She thought, Will Richardson, you're a *will-o-the wisp*, one of those ghostly clouds of light seen hanging over the Beverly Swamp that some people believe illuminate demons at play. She was sure they were glowing bubbles of gas with no substance at all. Just like her companion. Both of them looked up at the hullabaloo down the road where they had come from. Lizzie's heart soared, then sank a bit when she saw only two men emerge through the dust and the din. Still, she would ask for their help to overpower her captor. She recognized Cameron and Beazley.

They looked like they had been drinking, although it was only midday. And they certainly weren't going in the direction of the British forces at Queenston Heights.

"Well, well," exclaimed Beazley, "what a welcome surprise."

"Isn't it?" Will Richardson responded. His voice made it clear their arrival was perhaps a surprise, but not at all welcome.

"And Miss Erb," said Cameron, bowing slightly in her direction, "it's a good thing you're here. There is much fighting in the other direction."

"Which you're managing to avoid," she observed.

"There is no point joining a lost cause," said Cameron, blushing. "We're on our way to Fort Erie, like you, I expect." She caught a strange look in his eyes but she couldn't make out whether it was shame or regret.

"I guess we're all heading the same way," said Beazley. "We'll walk along with you. We want to join up with our friends, like we told you, Miss. We're going to turn in Captain Blaine. We're still counting on you to say we was innocent of killing Mr. Whittington and only guilty of setting a fire by the mistake of our own stupidity."

That was the most she had ever heard Beazley say. With his thick Yorkshire accent she had to guess at his meaning.

"No!" declared Will Richardson.

"No what?" asked Cameron.

"No, we will not travel with you. We prefer to go on our own. We have things to do on the way."

"Is that the story, Miss?" Cameron stared deep into her eyes. There was no mistaking a genuine sympathy. He wished her to know he cared what happened to her.

Lizzie was concerned for the two soldiers. They would be no match for the big frontiersman. She was concerned for herself. Will Richardson was a brute, he wanted her money, he didn't care what promises he'd made to Rebecca Haun. She tugged at her blue scarf. She clutched the silver medallion against the coarse material of her dress. Then, in spite of her determination to wear it publicly, she tucked it down inside her dress for safekeeping. She could feel the coolness of the silver press against her beating heart.

She rose from her stump and directed the two soldiers to proceed to Fort Erie. She would follow them soon and speak on their behalf. They nodded politely and moved on down the road.

"Good girl," said her captor.

"Don't call me a girl, you blackguard."

"That is a mean term, Miss Erb. I may be a villain by your lights, but I'm not a *blackguard.*"

Since she had no idea what the word meant, Lizzie mumbled an apology.

"Now here's the situation," he said. "You may trot on and catch up with your soldier friends. They will escort you to the fort, which the British still hold. You may come with me while I deliver the money to General Van Rensselaer. But then you'll be stuck for the rest of the war on the American side of the river. I suppose you could travel south to Boston to stay with your Aunt Rebecca. Or you can turn around and go home. You came through the Beverly Swamp on your own, you may surely return with no problem."

"Except for the treasure being lost."

"Exactly. You may say it was stolen by a handsome rogue."

She wanted to box the man's ears for his arrogance, but he was too big and too strong.

She glanced down and saw a good-sized rock by their feet. She could use it as a weapon. She did not feel bound by her Mennonite heritage to avoid violence altogether.

Will Richardson gazed down the road. Someone was coming from the direction of Fort Erie. She picked up the rock. As her captor turned back to face her, she swung the rock against his head. He collapsed at her feet.

Suddenly, Cameron was at her side.

"Well done, Miss. Now give me that strap from his saddle and we'll bind him up before he knows what hit him."

Lizzie did as Cameron said. He hadn't ordered her, merely offered advice.

Once Will Richardson was secured, with only a little blood on his buckskin jacket, she turned to the Scot.

"Thank you," she said. She brushed the dust off her dress. "The man is a traitor and a thief."

"You are most welcome, Miss Erb."

"You are not surprised?"

"Well, I was never quite sure which side this fellow was on. By the look on your face when we passed just now, I realized it wasn't ours."

"Do my feelings show so clearly, then?"

"For those who can read them, I suppose they do."

Cameron stood straight and tall. In spite of his shabby clothes and unkempt appearance, there was something noble about the man.

She gazed at him quizzically. She didn't know how to ask but she wanted to know more about him.

"There's nothing to tell," he replied to her unspoken inquiry. "I'm a soldier from Lochiel, plain and simple. Now let's get this rascal to Fort Erie so I can get back to the battlefront before the war is over."

This dark stranger was no longer a ruffian deserter. But who he actually was—that was still a mystery.

Allison

I've spent the day opening and closing my eyes. It's like working out at the gym, only for eyeballs.

When Maddie O'Rourke comes in, I open my eyes really wide.

I can tell she's excited. She doesn't say anything. She perches on the edge of my bed and cleans off yesterday's mascara and eye shadow and liner. She's shifted around so I can make out her face. She is so beautiful it hurts.

"Now then, Allie. Prove I'm not crazy. Are you ready?"

I think furiously about good and bad things. I decided today, good stuff would be a sausage breakfast sandwich from Tim Horton's. Then I worried I'd gain weight so I switched to sunflowers in Nana Friesen's garden. Choosing a very bad thing was easy. I would think about the flash of the gun when I was shot in the head.

I focus on sunflowers, then the gunshot, mixing them up.

"Allison, your pupils are shifting, I can't figure out what you're saying."

I think only about the sunflowers.

"Your pupils dilated! You can hear me!"

Dilated? I'm not a nurse, girl. Dilated, that means getting big.

"I did a web-search on pupils," Maddie explains. "They're nothing but holes that swallow the light, and they get big when they want more light, so they dilate, and they get small when they want to cut the light down, they contract or constrict."

She pauses to let her lesson sink in. I signal, sunflowers, no change, then gunflash, let's get moving, here.

"Now they're small, they're constricted."

Okay, the sunflowers and big black pupils is *Yes*. Gunflash and small black pupils is *No*. But I've got to pay attention. When I'm happy, it's a Yes. Big eyes are Yes. When I'm upset it's a No.

Maddie explains our code the other way around. Big means No. Small means Yes.

I don't like that. When I'm relaxed I want to be sending Yes as a message.

I think Yes, with sunflowers. Relaxing my thoughts.

"No?" she asks.

I think Yes thoughts again.

"Two No's. A double negative. So Yes is No, and No is Yes. Are you playing games with me, Allison?"

I give her my version of Yes.

"I love you right now, Allie Briscoe. Don't take that in the wrong way. But I love you, I really do."

I can see Maddie's blueberry eyes shining as she leans over. They are filled with tears. And I love you, Maddie O'Rourke.

"Okay," says Maddie, "we've got an hour. I didn't get off work until nine. So let's get busy."

I try to relax.

"Are you Allison Briscoe?"

Sunflowers, Yes.

"Am I the Easter Rabbit?"

Gunflash, No.

"Am I Madeleine O'Rourke?"

Sunflowers.

"Am I absolutely beautiful?"

Yes.

Maddie goes all quiet. I can hear her take deep breaths.

"Should we keep doing Yes or No questions?"

Gunflash, No.

"Alphabet?"

Sunflowers, Yes.

"You need to explain something?"

Yes.

"Is it urgent?"

Yes.

"Okay. When I reach the right letter, you say Yes. You got it?"

Yes.

Maddie begins to recite the alphabet very slowly. When she gets to M, I signal Yes.

"Okay, it starts with M."

Yes.

"Let's go again."

Maddie works her way so far through the alphabet she seems worried, until I signal U.

"M, U. Mud, mum, mut, mugwump? No? Okay, continue."

Maddie goes through the alphabet again, and twice more.

"M,U,R,D,E. That's French for poop. No, they spell it *merde*. So, what's up Allie? We're running out of time. The buzzer went five minutes ago. I've got to get out of here."

I can tell Maddie has slipped off the bed.

"I'll be back tomorrow. I haven't finished your eyes. You go to sleep now. You're real, you know. As real as anybody in the whole world. Night, night."

At the door she switches out the light and calls back into the darkness. "Good-night, Allie, and good-night Kate."

I had forgotten all about my roommate.

The door closes and I stare into the darkness. Suddenly the door bursts open again.

"MURDER! That's the word isn't it, Allie? Allison Briscoe, I hear you."

As the door swings closed again, I listen to the final bell tolling. I close my eyes, feeling strangely uneasy. The killer is working night shifts. She will come in soon. I will be waiting.

What else can I do?

Twenty-three

Lizzie

Working together, Lizzie and Cameron lifted Will Richardson's unconscious body and draped it over Fleetfire's back. Their burden groaned as they tied him in place.

"Good," said Lizzie. "He's not dead yet."

"Well, I suppose we all die eventually," Cameron responded in a surprisingly cheerful tone. "But he's a good fellow, really. We don't want to hurry him along to his Maker, not before his time."

"When they hang him—or do they shoot traitors?—will that be what you call *his time?*"

"It's a pity if they have to execute him, Ma'am. He's a good man at heart. He is confused about whether he is an American, a Canadian, or a Brit. I can understand that. He didn't hurt you, did he?"

"No, but he wanted to steal my treasure." Too late, Lizzie realized she had said too much. She waited for the inevitable query.

"Ah," he said, "you're carrying a treasure, are you?"

She had no reason to trust a polite young Scotsman who passed himself off as a ruffian. She had no reason not to.

"It belongs to Major-General Sir Isaac Brock."

"Well does it, now. Then what are you doing with it?"

"I've brought it from the good people of the Grand River Purchase. It's our way of supporting the cause. We're mostly Mennonites. The British and their Canadian militia are fighting for our right *not* to make war. That includes you, if you ever find your way back to the batttlefront."

"Fighting for your freedom to be British?"

"To be Canadian."

"You're as confused as your friend, here. As far as I can see, they're exactly the same thing, Miss Erb. To be Upper Canadian is to be British and you can be Mennonite, too."

"I am, more or less." She wondered if it was possible to be less Mennonite, rather than more. Her father had given up Mennonite teachings and fought in a war; her stepfather had turned from counting his blessings to running businesses which included a distillery. Like her father and her stepfather and many of their friends, she embraced the present, if not the future. She did not want to live in the strict, austere and limiting past.

"He was going to turn the money over to the Americans," she said. "To fight us."

"Us! So you admit you are British, lass."

They were talking in circles. It was time to move.

Cameron helped Lizzie onto the smaller horse, then he took Fleetfire's reins in hand and began walking. After a while, he paused to fill his pipe and light up. Then he kept walking, with Lizzie following behind.

They caught up with Beazley, who was leaning against the upended stump in a fence. He was smoking his pipe and seemed in no hurry to move. Beazley said nothing about Fleetfire's burden. It was apparently the most natural thing in the world to be transporting an unconscious Canadian dressed in a buckskin jacket over a country road.

About half a mile from Fort Erie, when they could see the palisade rising in the clearing ahead, Cameron stopped. He turned and boosted Will Richardson into an upright position, straddling the horse. Lizzie wondered how long their prisoner had been conscious. His face was flushed from riding slung over the Fleetfire's back. There was a small trickle of dried blood on his forehead.

"I think now is the time, Miss Erb." There was something awkwardly formal in Cameron's voice. He wasn't asking her a question, he was giving her a command. Politely, but firmly.

"For what?" she asked. But she knew.

Cameron helped Will Richardson down from Fleetfire. Lizzie watched as he untied the prisoner's hands. The two men embraced briefly. Will turned to Lizzie.

"I truly did not try to murder your Aunt Rebecca," he declared. "She is on her way to Boston."

Before Lizzie could say anything, Will Richardson slipped into the thick trees by the side of the road and disappeared down toward the river. Instinctively, she reached behind her to feel that the saddlebag full of treasure was still there.

She looked at Cameron. He wasn't smiling. She could turn him in for letting a traitor escape. He could be courtmartialed and executed. He took a firm hold of Fleetfire's reins. He began walking slowly toward the fort, staying close to the old horse's side. Beazley trudged behind him.

Lizzie sat quietly for a few minutes, until her little horse became restless. She urged it forward and caught up with her two soldiers. Together they passed through the gates in the thick stone wall of the fort. It was late in the day.

The Union Jack was flying at half-mast.

Bad news.

Allison

After Maddie left, three nights ago, the word *murder* hung in the air. I waited. It didn't take long. My night visitor came in. She turned the light on, then turned if off quickly. She would rather talk to me in the dark. She is afraid of my eyes.

She whispered in her strange rasping voice. She knows I know she's there. She wanted me to understand, she needs more time. She has death on a schedule. She will release me from suffering but the time must be right.

She said, "Sometimes you have to be cruel to be kind."

Spare me your kindness.

She's nuts.

But she can't be completely insane because no one knows what she's doing. She seems normal. I've heard the craziest people often seem normal, just ordinary like everyone else.

Glory, good God, I hate this. I don't want to die. I'd refuse if I could. But I can't. Not if she has her way. The agony, the horror, I know when it's coming.

Imagine a twist in time so you knew you had only a week to live. Then only three days, then it's tomorrow, this evening, in an hour, a few minutes, ten seconds, nine, eight, seven, six, five, four, three, two…you take a deep breath. You never exhale. Not ever. Everything stops. You never reach zero.

I could hear her voice after she'd gone. I can hear her inside my head right now.

Two nights ago, Maddie brought nurses in to show that she could read my eyes. A male nurse and a female nurse. They watched. They left.

Maddie O'Rourke is, as you know, outrageously beautiful and very short, with a twisted back, but as far as they were concerned, she is not a doctor.

So much for that.

Last night Maddie didn't come in. My night caller did.

I was miserable but I survived.

It's evening again.

Maddie returns with Jaimie Retzinger tagging along.

She hoists herself up onto my bed and kisses me on the cheek.

"Sorry about last night. I'm really sorry. They kept me at work until after eleven." She's talking about the People's Drug Mart on Chemong. They have a great cosmetics section.

"Jaimie's here," she says. "He's going to help us."

Jaimie? Help us? Oh really.

Maddie asks, "Are you ready?"

Sunflowers in Nana's garden. Yes.

"You said *murder*."

I try not to think bad thoughts.

"Is that a No?

Sunflowers, sunflowers.

"Yes! Okay, who? You, Jaimie Retzinger, pay attention. Write this down."

"It's not exactly like the words are pouring out of her," he says.

Creep.

"Who, Allie? Who is being murdered?"

Two runs through the alphabet and I spell out U and then S.

"The United States? No, oh, *us*? Patients? Sorry, *clients*?"

Yes. It's hard to do Yes when I feel No.

"Clients are being murdered?"

"Oh, come on," says Jaimie. "She's staring at the ceiling."

I take the time to spell out J, R, K.

"It's her," says Jaimie. "You're a *jerk*, too, Allison Briscoe"

I ignore him. I spell out B, D, G and a long pause, then N, S, E.

"She's a lousy speller," says Jaimie. "She's spelling out *nose* and bidge, *bitch*, bitch, now that's a surprise.

He's never heard me say *that* word, not ever.

"She's saying *bridge* and then *nurse*." Maddie says. She is excited. "The woman killed last week walking over the Otonabee foot-bridge. I wonder if a nurse did it? What else, Allie?"

"M, E.

"You! You're next?"

It's hard to think sunflowers when you're talking about being murdered. I focus hard on Nana's garden.

"Yes!" I can hear Maddie catch her breath. "Oh my God, Allison. When? How do you know? Who is the nurse? Oh, my God, I'm sorry. One question at a time. When, Allie? Tomorrow?"

Gunflash, No.

"The next day?"

Gunflash.

"No."

I'm thinking this could go on for a while. How many days are left? I've lost count. Now that's a stupid thing to do. I just don't want to know my life has a deadline. Dead line.

Oh, good glory, I'm explaining my jokes to myself.

"Tonight, Allie? Are you in danger tonight?"

"You just asked her that," says Jaimie.

"No, I asked her 'tomorrow.' You talk directly to her if you want. She can hear you, you know."

I can tell Jaimie is upset. Knowing I really am in here, his ex-girlfriend inside a living corpse. Listening, thinking. I'm a zombie, undead. It scares him.

I want to tell Maddie, Yes, maybe tonight. But I don't think so, my killer won't strike yet. She's teasing with terror in small doses, even if she means to be kind.

I signal No.

"No what, Allie? No, you're all right tonight. Good. The buzzer will go off any minute. We'll come back tomorrow. Jaimie will come, too. Whether he wants to or not."

I manage to communicate the number "seventeen," which doesn't mean anything to her, of course. They leave.

I wait with the lights off until my night visitor slips into the darkness. Let's get this over with so I can go to sleep. I'm exhausted. Her harsh voice creeps me out. Is she talking to Kate in the next bed? No, she's talking to me. She's whispering. Her voice rumbles and squeaks.

"Your friend with the beautiful hair told us she speaks to you, Allison. I believe her. That makes my work more important. I want you to understand."

She pauses. She needs to pull herself together.

"Seventeen, Allison. It took my baby seventeen days to die. I burned my little girl, I set her on fire. In the garage, Allison. My baby walked into spilled gasoline. She came up behind me. I was startled. I dropped my cigarette. We burst into flames. I tried to save her. She screamed *Daddy! Daddy!* She screamed over and over. We were on fire, Allison. It took seventeen days of agony before they let her die. She was six years old. Do you understand, Allison? They made her suffer, they kept her alive. I don't want you to suffer like my little girl. I love you, Allison. I don't want you to suffer."

I do understand. My killer nurse is a man. A small man. His voice is pitched high and muffled from burns. From scars around his mouth. In his throat. He tried to save his six-year-old daughter. She took seventeen days to die. The accident was his fault.

As he goes out, my visitor whispers: "Not tonight, Allison. But I'll be back soon."

Twenty-four

Lizzie

After Lizzie and her two companions passed through the gates, they were surrounded by a hysterical throng of soldiers and natives. Everyone was talking about the tragic news from Queenston Heights. The Americans had crossed over the river and General Brock had been slain in the midst of a fierce battle. His valiant aide, Colonel Macdonell, was also dead. The British forces were re-grouping, reinforced by Iroquois warriors under the command of John Norton and John Brant from the Grand River valley.

Lizzie felt grief-stricken for the beloved General Brock. It was hard to believe that the man she had spoken to so vigorously only the day before was now dead. It was hard to believe Macdonell was dead and her Aunt Rebecca was gone.

Lizzie was distressed to hear the Iroquois from the Six Nations country surrounding the Grand River Purchase were in the thick of the fighting. She knew the native leader, John Brant, very well. He had often been a guest in her stepfather's house. Christian Erb, like Christian Haun and the other Mennonite settlers, had bought their land from a man who owed a great deal of money to Brant's father and the Iroquois people. She had never met Norton but he was a revered leader as well and a fearsome fighter. Like the Brants, he was Mohawk, one of the Iroquois Six Nations to have fled northern New York after the American Revolution so they could remain under British rule.

The Iroquois were ferocious supporters of the Crown and still feared the Americans as much as when they had fought against Washington. To be ruled by King George was an unpleasant restriction. The prospect of having their lands taken away by President Madison was far more ominous. Manifest Destiny would consume them.

Only a week before, the native commander, Tecumseh, had been killed by an American sharpshooter after the fall of Detroit. His Shawnee Confederacy, gathered from tribes in the Ohio and Mississippi valleys, was in disarray after a shameful British retreat.

Lizzie worried about her Six Nations friends.

The war was personal now. The fighting was still a long way from the Grand River Purchase but the presence of Grand River natives at the battlefront made the conflict loom close on the horizon. It was sorrow, not fear, that made the horrors so real.

She was not frightened. She was angry. War seemed an abomination. How could people be that savage? It was an offence against God.

She said as much to Cameron as she dismounted.

"Well, God is apparently on many sides, Miss Erb. Your God is offended. The Mennonite God wants peace. The British God wants the king to rule. The Americans believe God wants their country to grow large and be prosperous."

"And what about your God, Mr. Cameron?"

"He wants to be left out of the quarrels."

"Then you are a Mennonite at heart."

"No, Ma'am, I am not."

There was much scurrying around them, not only soldiers and natives but women and children. The fort was preparing for the worst. If Queenston fell, then the Americans would advance south on Fort Erie.

Draft horses were being harnessed to farm wagons. The wagons were being loaded with cannons and ammunition. After delivering their deadly load at Queenston, they would be used to carry the wounded away from the battles downriver.

"Come," said Lizzie. "We must find the officer in charge."

"To have us arrested?" asked Beazley. "I believe we should forget about that."

Before she could respond, the villainous Captain Blaine stepped out through a door in the thick stone walls and into the open. He saw her; he saw Beazley and Cameron.

"My God, man," he said to Beazley "I told you what to do with her, didn't I?"

Beazley looked to Cameron.

The captain appeared as if he were about to strike Beasley across the face. Cameron stepped forward and grasped the captain's upraised arm. Captain Blaine looked stunned.

"I'll have you court-martialed for this," the captain exclaimed.

"Not before you answer for the murder of John Whittington," said Lizzie, stepping up and standing face to face with the man who had instructed his soldiers to kill her.

"Who in damnation do you think you are?"

"*Your* damnation, Captain Blaine. I intend to see you hanged."

"Or shot," said Beazley, emboldened by Lizzie's fervor.

A small crowd had gathered, amazed that a young woman

was challenging one of their officers. They were also astonished to see the officer being restrained by a common foot soldier.

No one came to Captain Blaine's assistance. He was a cruel and unpopular man.

Cameron pushed his captive through to the Commanding Officer's offices and forced him into a chair.

"We're rather busy fighting a war," said the officer in charge. "I assume there's an explanation for this."

"There is," Lizzie said. She stepped forward and laid her bulging saddlebag on his desk. "This is from the people of the Grand River Purchase. There is a lot of money here. It is to support the war effort, to pay for the militia. I promised it to General Brock, but I'm told he is recently dead."

"He died a hero, Miss. I'll sign for your treasure, and thank you. I will see it gets to the right places. And what about my captain, Mr. Blaine? You seem to have placed him under arrest."

"So I have. He murdered a farmhand, Mr. John Wittington. He did so in cold blood. As I told General Brock, I witnessed the crime."

"And what did General Brock say?"

"He told me Captain Blaine would be tried for murder and executed."

"If found guilty," said the officer.

"Oh, he's guilty, all right," said Cameron. "Mr. Beazley and myself were there."

"It were a disgrace to the uniform," said Beazley, poking Captain Blaine on the arm.

Blaine said nothing. Like so many bullies, once his power was lost, he was meek.

"We will find our way out," Lizzie announced.

She and her companions exited into the open. It was getting dark.

"I will stay with Matthias Haun and his family in their log cabin by the river," she said. "The Redcoats are living in their new stone house and their barn was burnt to the ground. They will still offer me good Canadian hospitality, I'm sure. "

"And us," said Beazley. "If we ain't being arrested, Miss, we'd best be getting back to our company. With General Brock dead and gone, they'll be needing us."

Lizzie turned to Cameron.

"You, too, Mr. Cameron? Are you going back to fight at the front?"

"For sure, I am."

"On which side?"

"I am a true Scot and as British as you are, Ma'am."

"That's not saying much. You were going to desert."

"No, Ma'am, we were trying to stay out of Captain Blaine's reach. We'd burned down a barn by mistake and failed to kill you."

"I'm glad you did."

"And I am, as well. You've a lot of life left in you yet."

Was he being cheeky or offering a compliment?

"What's your name?" she asked.

"Hugh, Ma'am. Hugh Cameron."

"Well, Hugh Cameron, I hope we meet again after the war is over."

"I promise you, Lizzie Erb, we will. I intend coming to the Grand River country, finding you, and courting you, if you'll let me. We will quite possibly marry and we'll settle down and I'll open a blacksmith shop and we'll be happy forever."

Lizzie choked, and then gathering herself together, she reached behind her neck and undid the chain that held the silver medallion hidden from view. Withdrawing her medallion from the folds of her dress, she handed it to Hugh Cameron.

"Forever is a long time, sir. Return this to me when you return."

She walked off, smiling broadly to herself and disappeared into the excited crowd, listening to news from the front.

The tide had turned; the battle of Queenston Heights was won. The Americans had been outflanked and retreated to their own side of the river. It was a costly victory and the war was far from over. But Lizzie felt her part was done.

As she sidled away, the stout figure of Beazley appeared at her side. He leaned close to Lizzie and whispered.

"He's a gentleman, you know. He may be a common soldier like me, but he comes from good stock. His family fell on hard times, I believe, but he learned himself the smithy trade and he's an honorable man."

"Mr. Beazley, are you pleading his case?"

"No Ma'am, Mr. Cameron can plead for hisself. I'm just saying, you know—"

"Go, Mr. Beazley. Here, take this." She untied her blue scarf and gave it to him. "Go and fight your war. And never fear, I fully intend to marry Mr. Hugh Cameron, should he survive."

"Oh, he will, Ma'am, I'll see that he does. God bless."

"Yes," Lizzie responded as she walked into the single women's quarters. "Yes, sometimes He does."

Allison

I slept terribly last night. Lizzie Erb has her life in order and that's a relief. Hugh Cameron must have survived the war and returned her medallion. He must have courted her; they must have been married. They must have had children. I know this because the medallion was passed on to me. So, she is my grandmother, with some greats thrown in. And Hugh Cameron is family as well.

As far as I know, the medallion is on a silver chain around my neck. Maddie showed it to me and the nurse who is going to kill me isn't interested. As for *the ordinary man*, he may want it desperately, but Shady Nook seems to have scared him away. He's patient, he'll wait. As long as it takes. I don't believe he's above robbing a corpse.

Now it's almost time for Maddie. I don't know if Jaimie Retzinger will come with her. It doesn't matter. I'm just curious.

But Maddie doesn't come. Neither does Jaimie. They're not worried about me. I told them I wasn't in danger, not last night nor tonight. That was before my late night caller said, "Soon!"

Maddie must be working late again.

Finally the buzzer sounds, then the bell tolls. Someone turns out my light.

They leave lights on for Kate and me until it's time for visitors to leave. Even though Kate's never had a visitor, and I don't have any except Maddie O'Rourke. I can't really count on Jaimie turning up anymore. David's gone and my mom, well, she's living her life.

Sure enough, around midnight, my door opens and closes.

A voice whispers. I can't make out the words.

The beam from a flashlight shines in my face. It turns and shines on the face looming in front of my eyes. Then another face appears in the light.

It's Maddie O'Rourke and Jaimie Retzinger is with her.

Maddie whispers, "Don't worry, Allie, we're here."

I hear them shuffling around. Then the flashlight goes off and there is deathly silence.

After about half an hour, my door opens again and someone slips in. The killer nurse comes close to my bed. Not a word is spoken. I feel pressure. It must be my throat. I can't breathe. I'm choking to death. Where are Maddie and Jaimie? I'm screaming inside. Screaming into the wind.

Suddenly a flashlight flares in my killer's face.

The room lights go on. Jaimie yells. The pressure stops. I can breathe again. There is a lot of shouting. Jaimie is swearing. He knows I hate when he swears.

And then it's all over.

Just like that.

After a while police come into the room.

There is a lot of talk.

I can hear Maddie explain that I told her about a serial killer in Shady Nook and gave her the number "seventeen." She figured it must be important. She came in today and checked the records with the nurse in charge. It was Maddie who discovered there was a death every seventeen days exactly.

She asked questions. She discovered a male nurse had been in a fire that killed his daughter. He was terribly scarred. He usually worked the night shift and he was present for each of the deaths. Maddie wanted to call the police right then but the nurse in charge thought she was nuts and asked her to leave. Maddie got hold of Jaimie Retzinger. They snuck into Shady Nook after the buzzer and bell went off. It doesn't surprise me that Jaimie knows how to pick a lock.

Maddie had climbed up on the edge of my bed while she was talking.

"Did you follow all that?" she asks me.

Sunflowers in Nana's garden. Yes.

"So," says Jaimie Retzinger. "I saved you again."

He comes into my line of vision, then he withdraws. I make him nervous.

"Well," he says, "I'm going."

He is talking to Maddie, not me.

Soon everyone leaves except Maddie O'Rourke. Then Maddie slides down onto her feet.

"Night, night, Allie. I'm not working tomorrow. I'll come in after lunch. We'll play with our makeup. I've got a new eyeliner you'll love."

It's very late and I'm tired.

When I wake up, I'm not thinking about Lizzie or remembering her life in 1812. I'm staring at the ceiling. My sight is improving.

Around two in the afternoon, I hear Maddie O'Rourke.

She is talking to someone as she comes through the door.

"Wait just a few minutes," she says. Then, to me, she says, "So Allison, we caught the killer, you and I." She doesn't mention Jaimie Retzinger. I know what she thinks; she thinks I can do better than him. She climbs up on my bed, sets her makeup case on my chest and carefully does my eyes.

"There, you look beautiful, Allie. Now, are you ready, I've got a big surprise."

She leaves for a minute, comes in again, climbs up, leans close, and her huge blueberry eyes are wide. Her amazing waves of black hair sweep across my field of vision. She kisses me on the cheek. I'm getting better at knowing where the pressure is when I'm touched. Then she moves away and another figure leans over me. Gray hair. Glasses.

"Hello, Darling."

It's Nana Friesen! Oh, good glory. Angels couldn't ask for more.

"Madeleine tells me we can have a real chat," she says. "I see you're wearing our silver medallion. She's polished it up for you. And glory, glory, you're as pretty as ever."

Sunflowers! Oh sunflowers!

"I've brought you a gift, Allison." Nana presses something into my hand and curls my fingers around it. "It's a very old coin, a gold Spanish doubloon. It's a gift from the past. Your friend Maddie O'Rourke will look after it until you're up on your feet."

Sunflowers! Sunflowers! Sunflowers!

Nana Friesen kisses me.

I can feel my lips glowing where Nana's lips brush against mine. I close my eyes and open them again. Just like that!

It's the first time I've blinked.

Book Three:
Killing Time

Twenty-five

Allison

I've moved on. Not really moved, but you know what I mean. Lizzie has her life, Rebecca has hers. I have mine. I've sixteen and I'm at Harvard University. That would surprise anyone who knew me before I got shot in the head.

Mrs. Muratori told me if I worked hard I'd get to college. Well, I didn't work hard but I'm here. They tell me Harvard is a pretty good school.

Only I'm not a student.

And I'm certainly not a genius professor. I'm not like Sheldon. I'm not even Leonard or Raj. I am what they call a study *subject* in the Department of Neurobiology. I lie here in bed like a corpse on display and doctors come in and look at me. They poke around and talk to each other.

They don't talk to me. Allison Briscoe.

I say my name over and over to myself.

If I say it often enough, I can almost believe I'm a real person. I'm not sure the doctors believe it. I'll get better someday. I'm sure of it. So I don't panic. What good would it do to panic?

Besides, I can move my eyelids now. I can see pretty well. I'm improving.

Harvard's in Boston. I'm in the medical school. It's not far from where Madge de Vere lived on Beacon Hill. She was my great great great great great great grandmother. I'm not far from where Paul Revere made his silver things.

My brother, David, moved to Toronto before I left Canada. He's going to Victoria College. My Nana calls him "our family scholar." Well, I'm at Harvard, which is just as good. But I'm not jealous. He deserves the attention. He studies. All I did was take a bullet in the brain. As for my mom, well, who knows what she's up to? She's in Peterborough. She's never traveled to the States or anywhere else.

I've been here since early summer. It's September now. My friend Maddie O'Rourke came down from Peterborough with me. She's the only person I can truly communicate with.

I can't speak, of course, but Maddie can read my eyes.

Sometimes she guesses what I'm trying to spell out by making my pupils get bigger or smaller before I get halfway through the word. She's usually right. She knows my mind.

That's why she's here.

Harvard has a lot of money. Some doctors in this place heard about me after I helped catch a serial killer in the Shady Nook Hospice. That's where I was living, if you can call it living. Well, yes, I'm alive, so it's living. Which is better than being dead.

Jaimie Retzinger isn't part of my life anymore. That's sad but it's a good thing. Something can be sad and good at the same time. Just like something can make you happy and still be bad. That's Jaimie.

After the fuss died down at Shady Nook, I asked him to stay away. I asked Maddie to tell him. She said he seemed relieved. It creeps him out, knowing I'm in here, thinking. The undead are easier to deal with.

He still drifts into my mind, of course. I know he'll be riding around town on his dented Harley with *Zinger* painted on the side. He'll be stopping in at Tim Horton's in East City. East *Village* is more like it. He'll be drinking double-doubles, trying to get them free. Not leaving a tip. He'll be soaking up sympathy as he explains how he saved me again. He'll explain how I've been shipped off to the States, and he'll soak up more sympathy. He's a sponge. If you squeezed him out, there'd be nothing left but empty holes.

So, anyway, here I am. These doctors at Harvard want to learn more about how I can seem like I'm nearly in a coma, and yet I can hear and see a little bit and, mostly, how I can think. I can dream, too, and sometimes my dreams are important, but I don't tell anyone about my dreams, not even Maddie O'Rourke. I'm sure not going to tell these guys. The researchers are both sexes, but I use *guys* to mean either.

After Lizzie Erb got her life sorted out and decided on the man she would marry, my dreams began falling apart again, just like dreams usually do. Sometimes I dream of *the ordinary man* and in my dreams he looks like the Devil. When I wake up, I can't picture him anymore, and I have no idea what the Devil looks like. I mean, I don't even think he's real.

And speaking of "real," some of these doctors are real doctors and some of them are professors with PhDs. A PhD means you're smarter than anyone else about a few things but don't know a lot about anything else. They call themselves *doctor*, too. Just like my dentist and the chiropractor I nearly went to, but didn't. That was when I hurt my back lifting stuff at Timmy's. My back got better by itself. My teeth are okay. I don't eat many doughnuts.

So, these doctors want to study me. I've heard about studying rats and monkeys, but I'm a human being. I thought I'd say so, in case there were doubts. Then I told them no. They explained to Maddie that they would cover all of my medical expenses. I said, hey, this is Canada, I don't have medical expenses. Didn't you ever hear of OHIP? Maddie explained OHIP was like taxes and made our medicine free in Ontario.

Oh. Well, then.

Next they said they would pay for Maddie to come down to Boston with me. Now you're talking, I thought.

I asked Maddie if she would like to live in Boston for awhile.

Maddie O'Rourke is a free spirit. She said yes. She would take a few months off from the People's Drug Mart where she works in cosmetics.

So, I had a brain wave. When the Harvard doctors came to see me at Shady Nook, I told them: "You have to fix Maddie's back. If you're as good as you say you are, you can do that. That's the deal, or I won't be your potato."

Well, Maddie translated this by reading my eyes. Then she asked the Harvard doctors to leave the room.

She had already climbed up onto the side of my high bed the way she usually does so she can do my eye makeup. Or so she can see into my eyes to read what I'm saying. But this time, she leaned close so I could see *into* her eyes.

"Allison!" She was angry. "I am who I am. If that's a problem, you're not the girl I think you are." Maddie O'Rourke took a deep breath. "Do you imagine they can make me taller? Do you imagine they can make me straighter, or a better person? Do you imagine then you would like me more?" She took another deep breath. "I spent the first five years of my life in hospitals, Allie. I like who I am. I am as perfect as I ever need to be. I'm perfect for me."

She paused. Deep breath. "It's you we want to work on."

I could hear a smile break into Maddie's voice.

If I could cry, I would have.

I blinked and I blinked. I'm sorry! Forgive me?

Yes.

And that was that. Maddie O'Rourke is here at Harvard. They laid me out on a stretcher and flew us down in a private plane. They found Maddie a part-time job working in a lab where they do research on flowers. She loves it.

As for me, during the day I am an interesting *subject* for the doctors to study. And last night, finally, my dreams began coming together again. I was somewhere else, living another life. Not Rebecca's or Lizzie's, but it was just as real.

I've just met Mary Cameron but I feel like I've known her all my life, only longer. She is almost nineteen. She is dressed in strange clothes, they're in tatters and her feet are wrapped in rags. There's a calendar on her wall. The wall is stone. And every day of the year 1842 is stroked off, up to June 11th.

Mary

Mary was wild and Mary was free—but only in spirit. Mary was in prison. Her plea of innocence was overruled in court. But Mary had killed no one. The man who died was her friend, Amos Durfee. Because his body was never recovered and because Mary was a Canadian Rebel, she was convicted of treason, not murder.

Treason! She thought of herself as a patriot, the same way George Washington was a patriot in the United States when her great grandmother Madge de Veer was alive. Mary didn't hate the British who ruled her world but she wanted to be independent like the Americans were.

For a single month, a little place called Navy Island in the middle of the river above Niagara Falls had been declared The Republic of Canada. Over Christmas and into the new year of 1838, Queen Victoria and her ministers were no longer in charge, not on Navy Island. And Mary Cameron had been there.

Now, Mary was in prison, but they could not keep her locked up forever. And when she was released or escaped, she would find the man who killed Amos Durfee. She believed Amos was murdered because he was a black man and because he was an American. Or because he was Mary's friend.

She would find his killer. And she would kill him. She would have her revenge. Then they could lock her up again and throw away the key. They could hang her. She didn't give a damn what they did.

Twenty-six

Mary

Mary Cameron sat at a table, sewing as badly as she could. She took no pride in her work. None of the prisoners did. They were repairing fine gowns for the ladies in town.

Mary shared her cell with three other women. They sewed during the daylight hours. They didn't get much done. They weren't being paid. Work was supposed to make them better people. That's what the warden told them.

Mary looked at her cellmates. Agnes: early twenties, no teeth, a streetwalker. Lily: late thirties, looked seventy, a sickly beggar, a heavy drinker. Apple: sixteen or seventeen, she wasn't sure, a failed thief. Apple was roughly the same age as Mary Cameron when Mary first arrived at the prison for women.

And Mary, herself: a political prisoner. She had rebelled against Queen Victoria. She had never met Queen Victoria. The queen lived in England. Her ministers lived in the great stone houses of Kingston. And Mary lived in the largest stone house of all, the Kingston Penitentiary.

A calendar pinned to a crack in the stone wall said it was June 11. There was excitement in the air. They were going to have an important visitor. They often had visitors at the prison, especially in the Women's Department. People came to gawk at them. The same way they would go to public hangings—to be entertained.

Mary usually ignored the visitors but sometimes she'd stare right back at them.

She had bright hazel eyes and light brown hair. She was pretty. That upset the gawkers.

They wanted prisoners to be ugly and stupid. That made them feel better about themselves.

Today, the visitor was going to be a famous writer from England, Mr. Charles Dickens. He had an interest in prison conditions and in helping convicts, especially women.

Mary was the only prisoner who knew about Charles Dickens. While she was on Navy Island during the Rebellion, she had read the first installments of his novel, *Oliver Twist*, in a magazine called *Bentley's Miscellany*. It was the story of an orphan boy who worked like a slave and joined up with some thieves. She was arrested before the final parts came out. She didn't know how it ended.

Mr. Charles Dickens came and went. He was clean-shaven and had sad eyes and a large nose. His hair was long and wind-blown, even though the air in the prison was gloomy and still. He talked to Mary like they had met before. She asked him how the story of Oliver Twist story turned out, and did Oliver have a good life. Mr. Dickens smiled.

"You don't belong here," he said to Mary.

"Because I'm pretty?" said Mary.

The great author blushed.

"I've been here nearly three years, sir. Good glory, it's hard to keep pretty for three years in a hole like this. But I'm not staying."

"When will you get out?"

"When I want to, sir. I can escape—they might let me go if I plead guilty, but I'm not going to do that. I didn't murder anyone, not Amos Durfee or anyone else I can think of. I'm in here because I'm a Canadian Rebel. I am a political prisoner, a prisoner of conscience."

"Are you, now? Well, the Rebellion is over. But good luck to you and your conscience, young lady."

"My name is Mary Cameron."

Charles Dickens smiled. He turned his back to the warden. He dug into his pocket and pulled out some large coins. He took Mary's hand through the bars and wrapped her fingers around the coins.

Then he whispered: "Here's a little help, Mary Cameron, for when you escape."

As he walked away, she heard the great writer say to the warden: "I'd like to know about that girl. There's a devil lurking in those beautiful eyes. It will take more than prison bars to keep Mary Cameron under control."

Well, of course there was a devil in Mary's eyes. And in her heart. A few years behind bars weren't going to change her nature.

But the fire in her eyes was not kindled by politics. It was from her need for revenge. She had been accused of murder and of that she was innocent.

Her eyes flashed brown and green and golden. She watched Charles Dickens walk away. She looked down at the four heavy coins in her hand. They were gold.

Thank you, Mr. Dickens!

She looked around at her cellmates. Agnes, Lily, and the girl who called herself Apple, because she loved eating apples—if they didn't have worms. A toothless prostitute, a sickly rum-soaked derelict, and a slow-witted thief. Until Charles Dickens came along, these were her best friends in the world. They were her only friends. But life would be different now.

She watched as the iron door swung closed, nearly catching the great writer's coattails. She smiled and her eyes caught the light of the sun coming through the bars in the window. They glistened.

She had murder in her heart and revenge on her mind.

The Rebellion of Canada was over. Victoria ruled. But Mary Cameron's rebellion was a long way from being finished.

Allison

When I woke up this morning, I was unhappy. The problem is Mary. I like her. But her vow that she'll kill someone is upsetting. Even if it's to avenge the death of her friend. If they catch her she'll be hanged. She may not care if she's executed, but I do. Who wants a hanging in the family tree?

So I'm lying here, thinking about Mary in prison. I've got to figure out how to stop her from becoming a killer, but I'm in a prison of my own. I don't know how much I can do.

It's my dream, but it's her life.

It's not pleasant having too much time to think.

I can feel my silver medallion pressing against me. Maybe I just imagine the weight but I know it's still on a chain around my neck. It connects me with who I am. I'm sure it will connect me with Mary Cameron. She was a rebel just like Paul Revere. Just like me.

The medallion is one of my greatest treasures. Why on earth does *the ordinary man* want it so much? If he does. Does *the ordinary man* even exist? Maybe Russell Miller made him up and called him the Devil. Maybe I made him up out of the dark shadows at Shady Nook. Maybe he still wants my medallion; maybe he wants me dead so he can get it. It doesn't make any sense. It's only a piece of silver, and amber is not really rare. It's precious to me for personal reasons.

Maybe he has personal reasons, too.

When the Harvard researchers tried to remove the medallion for safekeeping, Maddie O'Rourke told them, "No way! If this university is rich enough to bring us here, they can sure as the devil protect our valuables."

Maddie is someone you want to have on your side in a quarrel.

She looks after my other prize possession. It's a golden Spanish doubloon, a very old coin my grandmother Friesen gave to me last summer.

Even though she has to use a walker, Nana visited me at Shady Nook just after we caught the killer nurse. She even managed to lean over the bed so I could see her.

Sunflowers! Sunflowers!

She said, "If I can go to Philadelphia and survive a plane crash, then good glory, I can get myself to Peterborough to see my Allison."

Maddie made sure she knew I knew she was there. But the way she talked to me, she had no doubts.

Sometimes the researchers forget I'm in here. Most of them only talk to me if Maddie is present, even though they know I can hear. Since she's the person who can read my eyes very well, they talk to her as if she's me. Like, as if I'm a ventriloquist's dummy.

For glory's sake!

Damn it, at times, swearing isn't the sign of a limited mind, it's just because you're really disturbed, disconcerted, discombobulated. D, D, and D. I'm nobody's dummy. When I get back to planet Earth, I'll prove it.

I'll finish school. Like, all the way. Probably I'll go to Trent; that's the university in Peterborough. It's not Oxford and it's not Harvard, but I hear it's pretty good. Then I'll do the chef's diploma at Fleming College, because after you get educated you need to learn a trade. I'll open Allison's Restaurant. I just need to figure out where to get the money. It's not like I can sue Russell Miller.

I won't be hiring Jaimie Retzinger to cook for me. He dropped out of the course. Like, before he got there. He'd be lousy, anyway. He couldn't boil water in hell.

From what Maddie has told me about the food around here, Harvard could do with a few pointers in the cooking department.

Myself, I'm on tubes, so it makes no difference. I don't eat and I don't drink. Not yet. But I will. I can remember what things taste like. When I think about Dutch apple pie, I can feel my mouth watering.

So, I'm here, I'm Allison Briscoe, I'm real, not a dummy, I need to take charge.

How do I do that? Well, what do I do best? I think. Thinking is about all I can do right now. So, Allison Briscoe, if you're ever going to escape this narrow prison of your own body, there is only one way. You think your way out.

Twenty-seven

Allison

This morning, Maddie comes prancing in and asks me: "Guess what happened?"

I signal to her: "Someone got murdered."

She usually writes down whatever I tell her on a blackboard, so she writes: "Someone got murdered."

"Maddie!" I can hear a guy called Gordon exclaim. "She's reading your mind!"

Gordon is a graduate student. Maddie says he's tall and skinny. He works as a research assistant. I can't see him clearly; he doesn't come that close. He watches the machines recording my brain waves when no one else is around. "You were going to tell her about the murder last night, the Harvard strangler, weren't you? But she already knows. How does she do it, Maddie?"

"Magic!" Maddie exclaims. "She's a Canadian wizard and I'm a sorceress and that's why we're down here in the U.S. of A. Now go get us a couple of coffees. Please."

Maddie is very good at working out who is in charge.

Once Gordon has left, Maddie scoots up onto my high bed. This one isn't hospital white. It's a pale shade of green. Chartreuse, Maddie calls it. Color-words make my world more exciting. So, she leans over into my field of vision. She knows I can't follow movement with my eyes, but if she stays still for a minute I can see her almost as clearly as normal.

I wasn't mind reading. I can read Maddie's tone of voice. Nothing gets either of us quite as excited as a new murder.

Before Gordon returns, Maddie explains that an elderly woman, a retired professor, had been walking across Harvard Yard last night. She was strangled. Maddie explains that Harvard looks like a university is supposed to look, with red brick buildings and huge trees, spreading lawns, stone benches, winding paths. A *sanctuary*, she calls it. A sanctuary in the middle of a city. Although, really, it's next door to Boston, not downtown.

Sanctuary means a safe place. Not a place to be killed, not a place to be strangled.

I don't even know Gordon has returned with the coffee until he chimes in. "They say she was smiling," he says.

I can smell the coffee.

A woman was murdered. Gordon thinks she was happy.

Sometimes, I just want to close down my mind.

Mary

Mary was building a dress for herself, one scrap at a time. *Building* was the right word. It was like putting together a piece of furniture from old boards and stuff other people had thrown out. Actually, she was stealing. She was cutting out panels of cotton from petticoats and crinolines that came into the prison with the fine dresses she and her cellmates were supposed to repair.

Mary, Agnes, Apple, and Lily wore the clothes they had come into prison with, which were now mostly rags. But Mary was making a white muslin dress.

She figured it would take her about a week.

The ladies who owned the fine dresses would never notice the missing panels. She was careful to unstitch a panel of muslin along its seams and then sew the petticoat back together so the missing bit wouldn't be noticed. Mary could sew very well when she wanted to. The ladies would just think they were getting fat. They wouldn't complain.

Mary tried to collect the material and do her criminal sewing without the guards noticing. Of course, she didn't really care if she got caught. What could they do to her? Throw her in jail!

But she figured they would take her new dress away and she would have to start all over again.

Her cellmates knew what she was doing. It didn't make any sense. Where can you go with a new summer dress in prison?

Still, Agnes and Apple wanted to get involved. Mary's dressmaking was a plot, a conspiracy. It brought some excitement into their lives, which were otherwise very dull. There wasn't much to do when you were locked in a room with stone walls—apart from waiting for time to pass.

Doing time, the convicts call it.

No, *swallowing* time was more like it. *Eating* time.

Lily wasn't interested in the dress or anything else. Lily was wilting like a plucked flower. She was sick and lay propped up in her bed. She watched the other three work but her eyes seemed empty. Mary wasn't sure if she saw anything at all.

In spite of Lily being sick, Mary and Agnes and Apple were almost happy. The secret dress had become the center of their small and dismal world.

Without being asked, Agnes had set to work as soon as she realized what Mary was doing. She made Mary some drawers. These were two tubes of cotton, one for each leg, which tied with a drawstring at the waist. She sewed the tubes together and called them bloomers. She explained that she sometimes received gifts from her boyfriends. Bloomers were underpants worn next to the skin. They were becoming the fashion among women in her line of work in the States.

When she offered the finished bloomers to Mary with a big toothless grin, Mary hugged her and Agnes cried. So Mary stopped hugging her. Agnes had never been hugged in friendship before in her life. She cried quietly for almost an hour.

Not to be outdone, Apple ripped pieces from a fine silk dress and made Mary a camisole. Apple was simple and sweet and excited by her project. But the lady's silk dress was ruined. There was no way to repair it.

That night, Mary held what was left of the ruined dress close to the lantern and set it on fire. By the time a guard arrived with a bucket of water, the dress was ashes. They all took the blame, knowing they would get only oatmeal and potatoes for a week as punishment.

When Mary tried on the camisole, she was surprised. It was loose fitting but had cups for her breasts. The cups were lopsided. And Mary wasn't. Without letting Apple see her, Mary cut and stitched the silk to make a better fit. She modeled the silk camisole, along with her cotton bloomers. Agnes and Apple cheered. Then she put on the dress, which was almost finished, and they cried.

Mary looked over at Lily. She thought Lily smiled.

The night guard came to the bars but couldn't see what they were giggling and weeping about. By the time he went back for his lantern and returned, the three conspirators were sitting at the table, wearing their threadbare prison dresses, with their backs to the bars.

"Lights out!" he shouted and walked away.

Mary called after him, demanding that a doctor be called for Lily. Lily was changing from ghastly white to a shiny pale green. The guard stopped for a minute. He was caught in the moonlight that streamed through the bars of a window. It made him look like a ghost. Then he turned again and left, clanging the big steel door behind him.

No doctor came.

On the evening of the eighth day after Mary began making her dress, Lily died.

Twenty-eight

Allison

Sometimes, making a dress is an act of defiance. I feel terrible about poor Lily but I'm proud of Mary. She's a fighter. It's going to be a long day, today until tonight, to find out what she's up to.

I mean, there are no shortcuts: naps don't count. Little snatches of this and that; they leave nothing to remember. But when I fall into a deep sleep at night, I know Mary as well as I know myself. Better, perhaps, because I'm inside her life, but I'm observing from the outside as well. That's sometimes how being Allison Briscoe seems—on the outside, watching, but in here, being. Being me.

I feel bad about the retired professor who was murdered. The funny thing today was that when my Harvard colleagues came in, no one mentioned the strangled woman who died with a smile. It was like she had never existed. That's sad, isn't it?

I call the researchers my *colleagues* because that's what they call each other. They're very polite and quite formal. I figure I'm one of them. After all, they wouldn't be here without me.

Well, they would, but they'd be gathered around a rat running in a wheel or a monkey with wires sticking out of its brains or a human cadaver on a dissecting table.

Gordon isn't a *colleague* yet, he's an assistant. No one is polite or formal with Gordon. He's only a graduate student.

I listened to him yesterday when he was trying to explain his status to Maddie. He already has two college degrees, so he's a graduate. Most people would think that's enough. But he's working on a PhD, which stands for Philosophy Doctor. A doctor for philosophers. Ha, that's a joke!

From what I've heard, I wouldn't call Gordon much of a thinker. When he has a PhD, then he'll be able to talk down to graduate students, which apparently is the point of higher education, in Gordon's mind. When he talks about status, Maddie laughs at him.

This infuriates Gordon. She is already more important than he is around here. She's a researcher. He's a research assistant. She's with me and I'm important.

Even if I don't feel like it, I am.

I'm not a rat or a monkey or a corpse.

I'm Allison Briscoe.

Mary

A doctor arrived at the prison around midnight. Mary was in a rage because he didn't come sooner. She said nothing but she knew he might have saved Lily's life. The doctor and the warden talked. They decided Lily had died from pneumonia. It didn't matter, she was dead.

Apple and Agnes were even more afraid of Lily than they were of the doctor. The dead body wasn't Lily anymore, it was Death.

When the guards threw a brown canvas sheet on the floor and ordered the women to wrap Lily in it and sew the bag up, they were terrified. Mary did most of the work.

She had met Death before, face-to-face on Navy Island in the Republic of Canada. If you weren't dead yourself, it was just something to deal with. If you actually were dead, it didn't matter. You were dead.

When Lily was sewn into the canvas bag, they were ordered to lift it onto the work table. Early in the morning, a burial crew would take her away. Two guards offered to help, but the warden made them stand back.

"No sir," said Mary, staring the warden straight in the eye. The doctor looked away. "We will not leave Lily on the table. She will spend her last night in her own bed."

The warden turned red, like he might explode, but the doctor was there as a witness. And the doctor frightened the warden almost as much as he frightened Agnes and Apple. It was because he knew so much about things no one else understood.

Mary motioned to the other two women. They hoisted the brown canvas bag up and laid it on Lily's bed. Mary pulled the gray blanket around Lily's body, as if she were tucking her in.

Agnes and Apple retreated to their own beds. The warden, the doctor, and the guards took their lantern and left the women in darkness. Mary was still sitting on the side of Lily's narrow bed, as if she were praying.

She wasn't praying.

Mary was waiting.

After a while, she scurried around in the moonlight that shone through the bars in their window. Agnes and Apple sat up to watch.

They were horrified when Mary took her sewing scissors and began cutting open the brown canvas bag. The scissors were blunt so they couldn't be used as a weapon. Still, Mary had to be careful not to cut into Lily's body.

It was all her cellmates could do not to scream. Apple jumped into Agnes' bed and they clutched each other in holy terror.

"Here then," Mary commanded, once she had opened the side of the bag. "I need your help."

Neither of them moved from the bed. They huddled closer to each other.

"Damn it, Agnes, Apple, for glory's sake, it's only Lily. She's just dead, she won't bite."

They stayed where they were.

Mary struggled by herself to pull the canvas bag down and away from the corpse. Lily's body glistened in the moonlight.

The warden had made them strip Lily naked so her clothes, ragged though they were, could be washed and re-used.

When Mary finally got Lily free from the canvas, she went over to her own bed and opened up the end of her pillowcase. She had been hiding the white muslin dress, bloomers, and silk camisole inside. She laid her clothes out on the foot of Lily's' bed.

Then Mary lifted Lily in her arms. Lily had been sick for so long, she was not much more than a sack of bones. Mary carried Lily over to her own bed. She tucked Lily under the blanket, lying her on her side.

It could have been Mary, asleep. Except for the hair. Mary's hair was light brown, and seemed like spun gold in the moonlight. Lily did not have much hair left but what little there was, was gray and black. Mary arranged the blanket to hide it. You couldn't see that it was Lily's corpse in Mary's bed. It might have been Mary.

Allison

I wonder if Mary knew Lily was going to die? Did she start making the dress as part of a plan? I'd say she has seen enough in her life to know there must always be a plan. But I'm sure she's not so rigid that she can't change her plans when a new opportunity arises.

How can I explain Mary? To whom?

When Maddie comes in after work, I want to talk to her about my dreams. But I don't want her to think I'm a nut.

Maddie would like Mary. Actually, Mary would like Maddie. But the only way they could meet is inside my head. And they won't be saying much to each other in there.

Mary and Lizzie and Becky are the only private world I have. I lie here exposed to doctors and scientists, nurses and graduate students and research assistants. I don't even know whether I'm as naked as Lily's corpse or if I'm covered up.

I'd like to share with Maddie but I wouldn't if I could.

There have got to be secrets, even from your best friend.

Sometimes I think what makes me a person are the things I don't share. Not the things I do and say, but the things I dream and keep to myself.

I've been homesick today.

At Shady Nook Hospice in Peterborough, I could tell by the light that my bed was parallel to the window and I guessed that the window opened onto a view of the Otonabee River at the bottom of the hill. I grew up in Peterborough. It was easy to fill in the whole town in my mind. Not like a map but from memories. I knew where I was.

In Boston, it's different. I've never been here before.

Neither has Maddie but she's been exploring. Gordon took her on a tour of the Boston Museum of Fine Arts. It was sort of a date. When she told me about it, she was very excited. She described a silver bowl made by Paul Revere, the guy who made my medallion. It has the same mark stamped on the bottom: the word REVERE inside a rectangle. It's called the Sons of Liberty Bowl and it is inscribed with the names of fifteen local patriots who refused certain orders from King George III. There's a sketch of the Magna Carta on one side of the bowl, only Revere spelled it "Charta." He makes an ancient bill of rights sound like a map. And there's also a sketch of a paper torn into pieces. Maddie rattled on. She was excited. I suspected the excitement was really about Gordon, not Paul Revere's silver bowl.

I didn't tell her that Paul Revere gave Madge de Vere my medallion. I haven't told her anything about Madge or the others.

Maddie is here when the *colleagues* come in. She slides off the bed. They talklike they're in a hurry. One of them is quite young with a scruffy beard; he's mostly bald. He says, "We're just checking in." He is very polite, addressing Maddie. And at the same time he is very rude: He is not addressing me. Surely he knows I can hear. Maddie tells me he's the one who arranged to have me brought down here to be studied. He's originally from Canada. That's why he doesn't have an accent. He sounds ordinary, just like Maddie and me.

When I first heard this guy's voice, he sounded familiar. Now I'm used to it, but he still gives me the creeps.

Twenty-nine

Mary

Mary stripped off her prison dress. They weren't allowed undergarments. She stood naked in the moonlight. Agnes and Apple sat up straight. Mary was like a goddess.

They shifted over and sat on the edge of Agnes' bed. Then, shyly, they got up and helped Mary put on her new clothes.

They still didn't know what Mary was going to do. But she was a goddess in a beautiful gown, surrounded by moonlight. She could do whatever she wanted.

Mary reached under her bed and pulled out her square-toed black slippers. For three years she had been wearing rags bound around her feet. Winter and summer. She had been saving her slippers. She wore them the day Charles Dickens visited. She was ready to wear them again.

She picked up her sewing bag from the bench beside the table and walked over to Lily's bed. The other two women watched with their eyes wide and their mouths gaping. They were in awe but so scared of what she might do, they were shaking.

Mary wriggled into the brown canvas bag. She was careful not to crush her dress any more than she had to. She checked that her gold coins from Charles Dickens were sewn into the little pocket she had made in the top of her bloomers. She checked to see that her silver medallion with the polished amber at the center was safe on its silver chain around her neck—it had been in her family for a long time. It was her only possession in the world.

Then she handed her sewing bag to Agnes.

"Now, my darlings," she declared. "You must sew me up."

"Inside there," Apple squealed. "You're not even dead."

"Not yet," said Agnes.

Agnes couldn't help herself, she was grinning from the excitement. Without any teeth, her face in the moonlight looked like a death's head and yet prettier than she had looked in years.

"You're crazy, you know," said Agnes. "You are out of your bloody skull."

But Agnes and Apple started sewing, taking turns. When there were only a few inches left, Mary puckered and blew them each a kiss. Mary asked for her sewing bag and Agnes slipped it through the narrow slit still left in the canvas.

"I'll finish up from in here," said Mary.

"Have you got your scissors?" Agnes asked her.

"Glory, yes. I'll need to cut my way out of here, won't I? Of course I've got my scissors, unless Apple has stolen them."

"Glory, no," said Apple, horrified. She was embarrassed to be in prison only for being a thief.

"Glory is the bloody right word," said Agnes. "Miss Mary, they're going to bury you alive. What'll you do then, with a mouthful of dirt?"

"I'll be dead, I guess," said Mary.

The room was quiet. Mary finished sewing the bag closed from the inside.

"I love you both," she said in a muffled voice.

She could hardly hear Agnes say, "We love you, too, Mary Cameron."

And then Mary felt the air squeezed out of her as Apple gave the brown canvas bag with Mary inside a huge bear hug.

"Go to sleep, girls," she wheezed.

"All right, Mary. Night, night," Agnes whispered through the canvas.

"Good-bye Mary Cameron, don't get yourself dead," said the girl who called herself Apple.

Allison

The Harvard geniuses didn't come in today. It must be the weekend. Science keeps regular hours. If you're a *colleague*. Gordon was here but he ignored me. I'm sure he doesn't see it that way. He's reading a bunch of instruments that let them know I'm alive.

He's always here. It really seems like he is. Or maybe it's just, when he's gone, I don't notice. I suppose he goes home to sleep, he goes out to eat. But I seem to be the center of his life.

Well, Maddie and me.

When Maddie comes in, she clambers up on my bed and begins doing my eyes. But this evening she talks to Gordon. At first they talk about nothing. I ignore them. I have better things to do with my time.

Then they start talking about the murdered woman.

Suddenly, I'm listening.

They talk about the old woman's smile.

It turns out there was another murder about a month go. At night, in Harvard Yard. A beautiful young woman. She was so beautiful, Gordon explained, that she had no friends. But she was smiling when they found her. Her corpse was smiling.

"So, what's this yard?" asks Maddie.

"It's not a yard," Gordon explains.

"Then why call it a yard?" Maddie is very straightforward. You can't get much past her. If it's called a *yard*, it's a yard. If it's something else, call it whatever it is.

"It's a park, sort of, with lots of trees and buildings and statues." Gordon says this with a certain amount of pride.

"That's what we call a campus," says Maddie.

"Well, good for you."

They chatter on like this and I try to tune them out. But when they're talking right over top of you, it's hard to ignore. When they get back to the murder, I listen again.

"It's a serial killer," says Maddie in her matter-of-fact way.

"Only two so far. It's a tragic coincidence."

"They both died smiling in Harvard's Yard."

"Harvard Yard."

"Gordon, you mustn't let words get in the way of thinking."

"Do you want to go for a coffee?"

Just like that, Maddie climbs down, they turn out the lights and leave.

I feel as if I've been socked in the gut.

I watch as the door swings shut. I feel abandoned. She didn't even say goodbye. I stare at the door.

Slowly, it dawns on me. I'm staring at the door.

My eyes have moved in their sockets. My anger disappears, swallowed up in wonder. Until now, I've only been able to stare straight ahead.

Slowly, I bring my eyes back to the center, so I'm staring straight ahead. Then I shut them.

I open them again and concentrate. I make them shift the other way. I expect to see a window but there's only a blank wall. It's green, like Granny Smith apples before you cut them up for a Dutch apple pie.

Good glory, when I thought about pie yesterday, or was it the day before, my mouth got all watery.

My eyes move, I can make spit!

I'm lying here, amazed at my astonishing progress, when Maddie and Gordon return. I can smell coffee in the air. That's the second time I've smelled coffee. I can smell things. Thing. Coffee. But that's good, it's progress!

They turn on the lights.

"Hi, Allie," Maddie says, climbing up on the bed. "You were asleep, so we went for a coffee. How're you doing, sweetheart?"

"It's still asleep," Gordon mutters.

Maddie swivels around violently and slides off the bed. Her voice is trembling.

"Don't you ever call her that again, you ignorant lowlife good-for-nothing ice-for-brains jerk."

"What. I just said, *it's still*—"

She punches him. I can tell by the thud. It isn't a smack or a slap, it is a punch to the jaw. She would have blackened his eye but she couldn't reach that high.

I can hear something crash as he staggers backwards. He must have fallen into a chair because the pitch of her voice shifts direction.

"Allison Briscoe is my friend," she declares in a low and powerful voice. "She is a human being. Get that through your skull. She is a human being. Look at me, Gordon. Look, I am a human being. You—a human being? I'm not so sure about you."

"But—"

"Get the hell out of here, Gordon. Your shift is over. I'll close up and tuck her in for the night."

"But I. It was just one word."

"Yes. *It.*"

"Sorry."

"Go! Get, disappear. Now.'

"I, I—"

"You are nothing! Tomorrow, you nothing jerk, you will apologize to Allison. Now get the hell out of our sight."

She looks over at me. I've moved my eyes and have been watching the whole blurry scene.

If she recognizes anything astonishing, she doesn't let on.

Gordon putters around and then leaves. Maddie turns down the lights and climbs back up beside me.

"I know," she whispers.

She dabs at my eyes with a tissue. Good glory, I've been crying. Not in anger or humiliation. I've been crying for joy.

I can cry!

Maddie stretches her bent body out beside me. I can feel her settle in. I'd swear I can feel her settle in.

Maybe she didn't notice that my eyes moved. She saw my tears.

She's staying for the night!

I'm bone-tired. I'm determined not to sleep.

My eyes close.

Thirty

Mary

Mary stayed awake all night. She could hear through her canvas shroud but the moonlight was extinguished. The canvas against her face was rough and smelled. She had a sickening feeling that it had been used for other dead bodies before. That didn't make sense. It was a burial shroud. But it smelled of death.

The air in the bag was thick. She was choking. She could hardly breathe. She desperately wanted to cut the bag open. But Mary was determined. She had a plan. Come hell or high water, she would follow it through.

Agnes and Apple stayed awake, too. Mary could hear them whispering. They were both in the same bed, but Mary couldn't tell which bed. Probably Apple's. It was farthest away from the bed where Lily's corpse was resting under Mary's blanket.

They wouldn't dare speak to Mary. Not now that she had taken the place of a dead woman.

"Arhrrrrrrr," Mary growled.

Agnes and Apple screamed.

Mary giggled and decided she had better be still. But the night guard didn't bother to check about the screaming. There was a dead body in the cell. Screaming would not surprise him.

Mary began to doze off but roused herself when the darkness began to fade. The cell door clattered as it were being unlocked. The burial crew had arrived.

She tried to stiffen up as much as she could.

Two men, one on each end, picked the body bag up roughly and dropped Mary onto a flat wheelbarrow.

"Oomph!" Mary groaned when the air was knocked out of her. She rolled a little to the side.

"A noisy one," said the man at her feet.

"Sometimes they moan and groan," said the man at her head. "They fart and belch. You never know what the dead ones are going to do. I never yet heard of one sneezing, though."

Mary could hear Agnes and Apple whimpering. Then Apple sneezed. Mary nearly choked, trying not to laugh in spite of her bruised ribs.

"That'd be funny," said the man doing the pushing. "Farting and sneezing."

They maneuvered the barrow out through the door, both of them grunting and complaining.

"This here's a heavy one."

"She looked like nothing but a sack of bones, did you see?"

"Well, she's still got a good bit of meat on her," said the man trying to pull from the front. He gave Mary a slap across her thigh.

It was all Mary could do not to yell through the canvas, *keep your fat hands to yourself.* She stiffened and prepared for more blows, but the other man exclaimed:

"Here Joe, you mustn't be hitting a dead one. She won't like it none and her ghost will come back in your dreams."

"You think so? Do you really?" They pushed and pulled through the long hallway.

"No, you idiot. But we'd best treat her with due respect."

"*Due respect* means she got what was coming to her."

"She's dead. It's comin' to us all."

"That don't bear thinking about, so just keep pushing."

Neither man spoke another word as they wheeled Mary into the early morning light.

She nearly slid off the barrow as they turned sharply and headed down a steep hill. The steel wheel clattered on the cobblestone path and the barrow wobbled. The burial crew struggled to stop it from tipping over and Mary was thrown around. It was all she could do not to protest. Or at least moan and groan. But she was supposed to be dead. Dead people don't complain.

At the bottom of the hill, they came to a stop. The air was bright and Mary could see shapes through the canvas. It was her two-man burial crew moving around as they tilted the barrow on its side and dumped her on the rough ground.

She lay still. She could hear water lapping against wood. There were no other voices. She heard a shovel ring out as it struck gravel. This must be the cemetery, just outside the prison wall. They were down by the wharf where supplies were dropped off for the prison. It was an abysmally isolated spot. That was good.

A shovel clanged against gravel again.

"Damn," said the one. "This is hard going. You got any ideas, Mike?"

"You're thinking what I'm thinking?"

"Yeah, probably."

Mary clutched her scissors in her left hand. She was counting on a shallow burial. Later in the day, if she were lucky, a priest or a minister would come and say a few words over an *empty* grave. If she didn't suffocate, if she could cut the canvas, if she could claw to the surface, if she could crawl out of the earth with no one seeing her.

If the grave wasn't empty—then Mary would be in it. She would be dead.

She wanted her burial to speed up. She was afraid the guards would discover Lily's body in her bed. She hoped Agnes would tell them it was Mary under the blankets and she was sick. Maybe sick with whatever killed Lily. They had better let her sleep.

Mary had not asked Agnes to say that. But Agnes had been around. She'd try to give Mary as much time as possible.

Still, Mary was almost relieved when she heard the shovels again, scraping away at the coarse ground.

Then they stopped.

"Okay, that looks like a burial mound."

"For sure, for sure."

"Grab an end."

Each man took hold on an end of the canvas bag. They hoisted Mary into the air and then dumped her hard on the wooden wharf.

"Tie her up good."

"Got her, don't worry."

Mary felt a rope bind her ankles. It dug in through the canvas.

They were tying a weight to her feet. It sounded like a big piece of scrap iron.

"Okay, Mike, up and over. It's easier than digging. And it looks like she's buried."

"They'll be saying prayers over an empty grave."

"And this one won't know no difference."

Mary felt herself swinging through the air. For a moment she was soaring. Then the weight on her ankles lurched her around. She hit the water.

And sank, feet first. Cold water rose up around her. She could make out the sun through the canvas. It looked like a big wheel on the horizon. She took one last breath before water seeped through the canvas around her face. Then the light dimmed as she went under completely.

She stifled a scream as the brown canvas bag settled against the rocky bottom Water pressed all around and the sun disappeared.

Allison

If I could take a pill now and go back to sleep so I could help her, I would. But I can't. I can't even control my own breathing. I just breathe. I can't breathe for Mary. But my pulse is racing, my heart is pounding. What have I got her into?

I'm awake. Does that mean she has until I go back to sleep to save herself? No, it's not up to me. It's her life. I can't change anything.

I feel helpless. I'm not the one drowning with my feet tied to a weight. Inside a canvas bag. I'm just here, I'm worried sick.

If I hadn't started dreaming about Mary, maybe she'd still be—where? In prison? Not Mary, not when she had a chance to escape. She's her own person. I respect that.

If you're going to take the risk, you've got to take the consequences. Mary never whined, she never complained. She takes risks because she's Mary. She'll survive. I know she will. I'm wearing the silver medallion she was wearing. That's proof she'll be okay. Unless they took it from her drowned body and gave it back to her family.

I'm feeling D, D, and thoroughly D.

And who walks in but Gordon. I realize, it's morning. Maddie has left. She must have got up and gone to work. It's not like she would have pinned a note on my pillow.

I open my eyes and stare straight ahead. Gordon leans over. He looms, he's very tall.

"Knock, knock," he says.

Who's there?

"It's Gordon."

Gordon who?

"*Gor'd on-ly* knows what a jerk I've been. *God only knows*— d'you get it?"

He paused. He seems embarrassed by his own awkwardness. Then he continues:

"Allison, I'm really really sorry. I've been up all night. Thinking."

Did it hurt?

"Thinking about you and what it must be like if you're really in there."

If! But, okay, I'm listening.

"In my line of work, we use our brains but sometimes we don't think."

I've noticed.

"Intellectuals aren't always smart, Allison."

Do you actually call yourselves *intellectuals?* You and the *colleagues!*

The poor guy is distressed. I wonder if it's about me, or if he's upset about Maddie. He likes her. He knows she's bright. Maybe she's not an *intellectual*, but she's fearsomely smart. And she's awesomely beautiful. And interesting, intriguing, amazing.

Gordon is standing there, staring. He's a blur.

I concentrate.

My eyes bring him into focus.

I bring him into focus.

He backs away a little.

My head is totally still but my eyes follow him.
I follow him with my eyes. Really!
He gasps.
"Holy good Lord," he says. "Good God Almighty."
I've made Gordon's day.

Thirty-one

Mary

Two thoughts filled Mary's mind as the water-soaked canvas pressed against her. *Survival*—she would not drown without a fight. *Revenge*—she would kill the killer of Amos Durfee.

Mary had expected to be buried in a shallow grave in dry earth! Instead, she was twisting underwater, tied to a iron weight.

How long could she hold her breath?

Water flooded into her nose. She pushed her tongue against the roof of her mouth. She squeezed her lips shut. She wanted to cough, to gasp. She let a few bubbles flow through her lips.

She had maybe a minute before she would drown.

The canvas pushed at her face. She squirmed until her arms were free. She struggled to hold the canvas away. It was thick and heavy. She stabbed at the canvas with her scissors. The blunt ends slid away. She pushed hard at the canvas to get her hands up in front of her face. One finger caught at the thread where she had sewn the bag from the inside. She pulled at the thread, got a scissor blade under it. She squeezed and the thread broke.

Her lungs ached like she was going to explode. She felt invisible fingers around her throat. They were strangling her.

The canvas bag opened a few inches.

She could see a sliver of murky sunlight. She pulled and cut at the thread until there was a hole big enough to crawl through. But her ankles were tied to the weight.

She pushed the canvas away, peeling it down so she could get her hands on the rope. The knot was big but clumsy. Her fingers were numb, she saw clouds of black in her head, her lungs felt like she had swallowed hot steel. The knot came loose.

She kicked frantically at the canvas shroud. With a powerful sweep of her arms, she rose upwards, blowing out air as she went.

Just as the clouds in her head were turning to darkest night, she broke into the air.

Dazzled by the light, she heaved until her lungs were filled, again and again. For a moment she forgot to swim and went under. She got a mouthful and came up coughing. She tried to stifle the cough. But there was no one around to hear her. The burial crew was far up the hill, trudging back to the gate in the wall.

Her white muslin dress was pulling her down. She slipped out of the dress. Treading water, she folded it and tucked it under the drawstring at the top of her drawers. Her bloomers, as Agnes called them.

She checked that her sewing bag with her thimbles, her thread, and her comb was still tied around her wrist. She slid the scissors into the bag. The water was cold. She was grateful for the camisole, although it only kept her warm in her mind. She began swimming.

Mary swam close to the stone prison wall which rose up from the shore. Once she got past the prison, she realized there was no place to get out. The village of Cataraqui edged close to the prison wall. She turned around and wearily swam back toward Kingston.

Not far past the prison, the shoreline was made of limestone slabs. Here and there, they had been pushed up by ice over many winters till they lay on top of each other. Mary found slabs that formed a cave big enough for her to crawl into. When the prison guards came looking for her, she would need to hide.

There were no houses nearby. She had shelter. The sun was shining and she soon stopped shivering.

She squeezed water from her dress and laid it on a rock to dry. She took out her comb and combed her long hair until it fell into light brown waves across her bare shoulders.

By the time the bells clanged and the sirens wailed to announce her escape, it was late afternoon. Mary was dizzy from hunger but she had all the water she could drink. It was lapping up almost to her cave.

The guards must have left Lily's body undisturbed all day in Mary's bed. They thought it was Mary, asleep with a mysterious sickness. Once they found the body, they would blame Agnes and Apple. But Agnes and Apple would swear on the Bible that they thought it was Mary in her bed and that Lily had gone to her grave.

Mary's cellmates would say they were as surprised as the guards.

Then who was in Lily's grave?

Well, if it wasn't Lily, it had to be Mary. But the grave was empty! The warden would realize what the burial detail had done. Mary had tried to escape and was drowned.

Then they would discover the brown canvas bag in ten feet of water with an iron weight tied around one end. The warden would know for sure that Mary had escaped.

Meanwhile, Lily would have to be buried all over again. By a different burial crew, since Mike and his buddy would be behind bars themselves.

Mary could see it all happening in her mind. She got dressed and settled into her cave.

A search party walked right over her. The men stumbled on the limestone, as it was growing too dark to see. They were carrying torches made of dry reeds but the rocks were at all angles. The men swore a lot.

A boat went by with a lantern, looking for Mary's body along the shore.

Later, Mary sat on the slab of rock above her cave and gazed out over Lake Ontario. In the bright moonlight, she could see Wolfe Island against the southern sky. It was named after General Wolfe, who fell in the Battle for Quebec. She had seen a copy of the painting by an American artist, Benjamin West, that showed his heroic death.

Mary smiled. She had escaped death, herself. She was content.

Allison

For reasons known only to Gordon, he says nothing about my eye movement to the *colleagues* when they come in. It might have something to do with power. Maybe he wants to see if they'll notice. Then Maddie comes in. They've brought her away from her work with flowers to help them. She clambers up on my bed. She leans over and smiles her warm open smile. She is not keeping secrets, she doesn't know about my progress.

She saw my eyes last night through the glistening tears. She didn't see them move. Crying didn't seem a breakthrough. It confirmed I was me.

"Today," says a man with an important voice. "We will test for intelligence, yes. So, Dr. Alstein, please proceed."

Dr. Alstein tells Maddie that he will ask questions and Maddie should pass them on to me. I wonder if he's a medical doctor or a PhD.

"She can hear them, herself," explains Maddie with irritation. "Her hearing is excellent."

I decide not to show them my eyes can move when I want. Knowledge is power for Gordon. Keeping secrets is power for me.

"I'm sorry," says the man with an important voice, "Speak up, what did she say?"

Oh, for Glory's sake, boys. Get it together.

"Now, then," says Dr. Alstein. "Who is the President, what is his name?"

Maddie observes my eyes and gives my response:

"The president of what?"

"I see," says Dr. Alstein. "She has difficulty with abstract concepts. Ask her what year it is."

"You just did," snaps Maddie. Then after a few moments, Maddie says, speaking my words in quotation marks, "'What year is *when?*'"

"Uh, now. Never mind. Ask her who delivered the Gettysburg Address."

I give the first answer that comes to mind: "Fed-Ex."

I know it was Abe Lincoln, of course.

"Ask her where Elvis came from."

That one I know: "Mississippi."

"No, no, no. He was from Tennessee, from Memphis."

I argue: "Born in."

"That's in Mississippi," Maddie clarifies.

"Ask her: 6 times 8?"

"What about them?" I ask right back.

"Ask again."

Maddie smiles, then gives my response: "5 times 10 minus 2."

"Enough," says the man with the important voice. "She is not so smart, I think."

I can't see him but I'm sure he has a beard. He sounds like a regular at Tim Horton's who had a greay beard and used to order a double-double every Saturday with a honey cruller and a plastic knife. He would cut the cruller precisely in half and leave half on the plate, but he'd drain his coffee to the bottom.

Dr. Alstein says: "She was maybe not so smart before the accident."

Accident! If I could speak, I'd give him a piece of my mind. Wrong expression. I wouldn't give him squat.

After the researchers leave, Gordon explains: "Those were psychologists, except for the boss, he's Dr. Arthur Ellis, a neurobiologist. They deal with minds, not brains."

"What's the difference?" asks Maddie.

"Good question. If I had a mind to, I'd answer you. And if I had a brain, I would have been nicer to Allison last night."

"Not just last night, you imbecile."

"Okay. But listen, Maddie, just watch. Allison and I need to show you something. Look over here."

Maddie looks.

"No, Maddie no! I'm speaking to Allison."

Long tall Gordon stands by the side of my bed. I slowly shift my eyes and draw him into focus. Then I look back at Maddie. She's beaming like the light is coming from inside her head.

I tell Maddie I can smell coffee, I can make my mouth all watery by thinking of Dutch apple pie. I show her. She tells me I'm drooling.

Hot damn! I can drool.

My lips move, I smile. I actually smile.

Thirty-two

Mary

Mary woke up stiff and chilled from sleeping on the limestone slabs. She was happy. She was free. But her escape wasn't over until she got far away from Kingston.

The sun was already high above Wolfe Island and ships were moving with the wind out into the open lake. Mostly they were under sail but there were several steamboats among them. That's what she needed, a steamboat to take her home.

Suddenly, Mary wanted to cry. She had not thought of home as anywhere but the Kingston Pen for the last three years. She had refused to think of her family back in Niagara-on-the-Lake.

She had not lived at her actual home since the Rebellion, when she was fifteen. She was no longer welcome in her father's house after the Rebellion was over.

For one month, while the Republic of Canada existed, Mary was proud of being a citizen. Her father, Hugh Cameron, was outraged. Victoria was Queen. Canada was British. Period. He had been born in Scotland. Mary couldn't understand why he liked the Queen, if he was a Scot.

And he couldn't understand her. His beloved Mary was nearly an American! Under General Brock and his successors, he had fought against the Americans. His lovely daughter with golden-brown hair and hazel eyes, rode horses like a boy and smiled like an angel—she was a traitor.

It broke his heart. He disowned her. And that broke Mary's heart.

Mary was the youngest of three children. She had two brothers who left home when she was still a baby. Her mother, Lizzie, had died when she was born. Mary's middle name was in honor of her mother's family. She was Mary Erb Cameron. Her father mourned Lizzie for the rest of his life. He kept on working as a blacksmith but he never took another wife. He raised Mary with love as if she were an only child.

Mary knew, no matter how much he hated her politics, her father would never have believed she was a killer. But when her trial for treason was held in Fort Erie, he did not attend.

She wrote him one letter from jail. He did not answer.

Mary removed two of the four gold coins from the pocket she had sewn into the top of her bloomers. She smoothed out her white dress and brushed off her slippers with some dried seaweed. She pushed back her hair and pulled her silver medallion up from between her breasts and let it hang down in the open. The amber at the center glistened in the sun.

Then she climbed up over the limestone slabs and walked through the woods until she reached the main road into town. She stepped out boldly onto the road and walked with her head held high, like she owned the whole world.

It would never have occurred to anyone that she was a convict. Not this beautiful young woman in a beautiful white dress wearing a beautiful medallion and black slippers, almost like new. She must be a lady.

And like a lady she walked past great stone houses on King Street, right into the steamship office near the capital building, and demanded passage on the next boat bound for Niagara-on-the-Lake. In a private cabin. The agent looked at her oddly. A young woman traveling alone was unusual.

Mary plunked down a gold coin on his desk.

"Yes, Ma'am. Of course. The *Frontenac* leaves at noon."

"Thank you," said Mary.

"And you'll be paying with this Spanish doubloon, Ma'am?"

"Is that what they are?"

"I beg your pardon."

"Yes, of course. But I'd like my change in English money. Or American. It doesn't matter."

"That's the full fare, Ma'am. One Spanish doubloon."

"Then give me proper change in real money for this one." Mary dropped a second gold coin on the desk.

"Yes, Ma'am, of course."

"It's Miss," Mary corrected him.

"Yes, Miss. One moment."

Mary smiled to herself. The great Charles Dickens had given her four very fancy coins. *Spanish doubloons*, indeed!

She gave the agent her name as Agnes Apple.

The agent smiled up at Mary like she was a royal princess or a pirate queen.

"Thank you, Miss Apple."

Mary smiled back. She was a citizen of the Republic of Canada. A convict on the run, perhaps, but not a pirate and not a princess, not even a subject of the Empress, Victoria.

For Mary, the Rebellion was not over, not until she had cleared her name and avenged her friend, Amos Durfee.

And she knew just where she would find his killer.

Allison

Being underwater with Mary was awesome. Like, being shot in the head all over again, only without passing out. I can still feel my pulse as the blood races through my veins.

But Mary, Mary. I've been hoping, now that she's free, she will forget about killing. I think she's confusing her outrage at being accused of murder with sadness over her father's anger. She thinks the only way she can make things right is through murder.

Well, no. That will simply mean her father can never forgive her all over again. It means she will be hanged by the neck until dead. Even if the killer of her friend Amos deserves to die, he has the right to a trial. You can't just go around executing people.

And what about me? I'm confused. It's confusing. When I woke up this morning, I realized I can feel my blood in my veins. I can create spit on demand, I can smile a little and I'm getting control of my eyes. It's great, wonderful, thrilling. And I'm depressed.

When Maddie and Gordon left last night, I was relieved they had gone. After I did my tricks a few times and they had exclaimed their delight, then we all needed time to absorb what was happening.

So, I lay there in the dark, feeling low. I guess, when it seems I might be improving, it makes me realize how bad things have been. Like, being a potato is okay when there is no alternative. A potato who can think, who can dream. That's better than being dead.

But the possibility of returning to normal is overwhelming. Being normal is like a place that's too far to reach.

Imagine swimming in the ocean and you can't see the shore. You look up. There's a bird carrying a twig. There must be land somewhere ahead. It's almost enough to make you stop swimming. It's heartbreaking. You realize how far you are from solid earth.

Enough, already! Hope isn't defeating, you ridiculous person. It's exhilarating. You are Allison Briscoe. And let's not forget it.

Suddenly the lights go on. It isn't Maddie and Gordon but someone approaches. He speaks. It is the *colleague* with no accent.

"Hello, Allison," he says.

So the guy who arranged to get me to Harvard knows I am actually a person. He moves close to my bed. It is hard to see him against the light but he looks vaguely familiar.

"I'm just going to peek at your silver locket," he says.

It's a medallion! A locket would have something precious inside. It's a pendant. It's not a locket.

He leans down—he doesn't undo the chain. I can see him holding my treasure up to the light, I can see the glimmer of amber, the gleam of polished silver.

"I will have to get a closer look. There is something written behind the gemstone." By the way he casts shadows over me, I can tell he is trying to open the clasp. But it is his voice I really notice. Good glory, his voice!

He's the guy who talked to me at Timmy's. He asked about the medallion. Bald head, small beard. He is *the ordinary man.* He is the Devil, himself.

I don't believe in the Devil, but he's here!

I think if I could I would faint.

Or kick him square in the teeth.

I don't believe in violence but the Devil does.

Thirty-three

Mary

Mary took the money from the second Spanish doubloon and bought a Macintosh apple and a biscuit, which she ate as she walked. Fortified, she went into a store on Brock Street and purchased a sturdy leather valise. She walked into a women's clothing store like she owned it and bought a skirt, two blouses, and some undergarments.

In another store, on Rideau Street beside a handsome stone building with a plaque announcing it was the office and residence of John A. Macdonald, a rising young lawyer, she bought a light canvas greatcoat to shield her from wind and rain. She walked into a men's clothing store further along Rideau where the clerk looked at her strangely. Women did not usually shop there. The store smelled of cigars. She asked for a pair of men's pants suitable for riding horses. Brown cotton twill, in her own size. Much to the clerk's embarrassment, she insisted on trying them on.

She stopped in at a men's hat shop back on Brock Street

and bought a sailor's watch cap, what the Lower Canadians called a *tuque*. It was made of finely knitted navy blue wool.

On the market square, she picked up some bread and a small crock of honey. At a different stall, she bought three more apples.

She had paid enough for her ticket so that she would be given meals on the *Frontenac* as long as the weather was good. If a storm blew up, nobody could cook. And if it were stormy, most passengers wouldn't be hungry, anyway. She wanted some food to take with her, just in case. She knew she wouldn't get seasick.

Mary walked down to the harbor and sat on a bench by the water. She tore off chunks of bread which she dipped into the honey crock. After she finished eating, she wrapped the leftover bread in newspaper and put it in her valise. She pushed the cork firmly into the top of the honey crock and put it in as well. She left the apples in the valise for later.

While she was staring at the great stone walls of Fort Henry across the river, two women sat down on the bench beside her.

"She's a murderess," one woman said. "They should have hanged her. I don't care how young she was when she did it."

"I hope she's drowned or she'll kill us all in our beds."

"Slit our throats, most likely."

"Or maybe she'll chop off your heads," said Mary. She rose to her feet as the two women gasped. "You'd better keep your lamps burning all night," she called to them over her shoulder. "Or even better, don't sleep at all."

She waved with a grin as she walked.

The two women waved back but neither one smiled.

It was time to board the steamboat.

The voyage would take two days to Rochester. Then another two days to York, which the government was now calling Toronto after its original Iroquois name, *Tkoranto*. They would stay in York a day and a half, then take another full night to reach Niagara-on-the Lake. Almost a week, altogether.

It was not faster than traveling by coach or horse but it was far more comfortable.

Her friend, Amos Durfee, had grown up in Rochester.

Mary found her small cabin. She cleaned herself and had a good nap. She was asleep when the *Frontenac* pulled out of Kingston and headed into the great expanse of Lake Ontario.

When she woke up, she washed the clothes she had been wearing and put on a new skirt and blouse, with a fresh petticoat. She strolled around the deck. She was amazed at how large the boat was, and yet how small it felt, out there with no land in sight.

As wide as two canoes laid end to end. As long as ten canoes in a row. With huge paddle wheels, each as high as a house. There was a great roaring engine in the middle, belching black smoke. A pair of sturdy masts with filthy gray sails set to the wind. The decks were covered with a layer of soot. The *Frontenac* had been on Lake Ontario for over twenty years. For a freshwater boat, that was a very long time. She was an old lady now.

Mary Cameron liked life at sea. She strolled around for a while, then went back to her cabin to read a book she borrowed from the ship's salon. She might have been a sailor, she thought, if she had not become a Canadian Rebel.

Allison

When Maddie and Gordon come in, I try to tell them about *the ordinary man.* Maddie assures me the medallion is safe on the silver chain around my neck. She says I must have been dreaming.

Perhaps that's all it was, just an *ordinary* dream.

They want to talk about my smile. I try to focus on the Harvard Yard murders. I mean, an old lady had been strangled and before her, a beautiful young woman. Both died with smiles on their faces. And here we are, treating my little smile like the biggest event in the world.

Well, in my little world, I suppose it is. When the topic changes, I'm disappointed.

They chatter about a time capsule someone discovered under a cornerstone of the Massachusetts State House. It had some folded newspapers in it and old coins including a half-cent, a penny, a dime, and a half-dime and, guess what, it was buried there by Samuel Adams and his good friend, the silversmith Paul Revere. More than two hundred years ago. Another connection! Good glory, everything connects.

But let's keep things in perspective, detective.

That's what David used to say from the time we were small. "Allison, let's keep things in perspective." Neither of us knew what it meant, exactly. I guess some things are more important than others, even when it doesn't seem that way.

I miss my brother. I wish he could see me smile. My lips haven't moved in eight months. I'd like him to know I'm practically back to my old self.

I am making progress. I'm trying to solve crimes. The intrepid potato detective is eager to work. I'm not a defective detective, I'm the real thing.

And this morning, I'm thinking about murder.

So, think, Allison, think.

What do the victims have in common?

They're both women. Check.

They're both connected to Harvard. Check.

They both died in what they call Harvard Yard. Check.

They were both strangled. Check.

Gently, it seems. They both died smiling. Check.

Is the smile like a baby's burp, an involuntary response to gas or something?

Well, no. Or people wouldn't be commenting about it.

So, they died happily. How could you be happy, being strangled? Drugged, perhaps? But there was nothing reported about drugs.

I have an idea.

I ask Maddie to do some research for me. I know there were only two murders here, at Harvard. But I want her to check for similar murders on other university campuses.

Oh, my glory, here they come, the *colleagues.*

And now they're gone!

What they did was insulting. They flashed brilliant lights in my eyes, forcing my eyelids to stay open. They played musical scales in my ear. At top volume. They rubbed down my arms and my legs. Vigorously. To get the blood flowing, they said. They forced air into my lungs in a rhythmic pattern.

"If anything will get her going, this will," announced the man with an important voice. "Sensory stimulation. We'll do it again 'tomorrow and tomorrow and tomorrow' and measure the progress."

No one notices he's speaking Shakespeare. They're scientists. I recognize the words. They're from Mrs. Muratori's favorite passage from *Macbeth*, a horror story I've never actually read. *Out, out, brief candle!* I remember that. *Life is a tale Told by an Idiot, full of sound and fury Signifying nothing.* Very depressing, was her friend, Will Shakespeare.

But what I'm thinking about "sensory stimulation" on a daily basis is, *the hell with that.*

Actually, it's hard to refuse when you're a potato. Veggies are pretty passive. But I'm not just any potato.

Amidst their chatter, I picked out the voice of the Devil. He just blended in.

When they left, I asked Maddie to explain *sensory stimulation*. She has her doubts. She says it's all about tickling my senses, getting my mind to work. She and I know my mind's working as well as it ever did, maybe better. She'll speak to the man with the important voice.

"Did you hear him quoting Mrs. Muratori?" she asks.

I signal, Yes.

She writes *Macbeth* on the board.

I signal Yes.

Gordon looks bewildered.

Maddie thinks massaging might be a good thing.

"We need to get your body ready for when it connects with your brain."

She and Gordon work on me together. I can't feel anything they're doing, but I wink and I blink and I smile. I smile.

Before they leave, I again ask Maddie to do the research about campus murders. The next one will be soon, unless we can stop it from happening.

Thirty-four

Mary

The *Frontenac* stopped at Rochester, stayed over in muddy York, and was two hours out of Toronto when a storm cracked open the sky. Mary was sewing in her cabin, working in the evening light that came through her window. She had slit her canvas greatcoat up the back, almost to the waist. She finished stitching across the top of the cut so it wouldn't rip.

Then she stepped out onto the deck. The wind was raging. Her coat flaps beat on her legs. Thunder hammered against the black sky. Bolts of lightning shattered the darkness. Black water spit plumes of white spray high into the air.

Mary loved it.

She made her way to the bow of the boat, which was rising and plunging into the waves with a fury.

A man with long, tangled hair faced away from her into the storm. He was holding onto a rope hanging from a furled sail. Mary grabbed the same rope to keep from being thrown onto the deck.

The man whirled around. Lightning flashed across his face. He was scruffy but surprisingly young.

"Behold," he screamed. "The end is at hand."

Beneath his wet beard, his lips were twisted in a horrible grin. He glared into Mary's eyes and vehemently declaimed, "Doom. We are drowned! And the sea shall give up its dead. Their flesh shall be torn from their bones. They shall burn in the fires of Hell. Praise the Lord Almighty, we are doomed, we are saved. Eh, girl! It's an almighty God-given storm."

Mary yelled back to make herself heard over the wind.

"Which is it?" she demanded. "Are we doomed or are we saved? Do we drown or do we burn?"

"It is the same, all the same," he screamed into the wind. And then he leaned down and in a very calm voice he spoke into her ear. "It is how God does things, my dear. And it's a lovely beautiful night for raging with the rain in my teeth, the storm in my hair. Ah, but it is good to be a mad man and still be alive."

"You do realize how silly you sound?"

"Of course, of course. I'm Joshua Friesen at your service. I love to pretend to be mad. Tonight I'm a preacher, tomorrow I might be a clown or a judge."

"Or locked in a madhouse."

He turned again to address the storm, and he bellowed: "My damnation slumbereth not. Behold God's wrath and his fury are upon us."

"Good night," Mary shouted at him.

She walked back to her cabin to get some sleep before they landed at Niagara-on-the-Lake.

The *Frontenac* tied up at the government wharf early in the morning. The storm had disappeared. Mary slept for another couple of hours. A small breakfast was brought to her cabin door. She ate and washed up and then dressed.

The young man who stepped out of Mary's cabin at ten in the morning was dressed in cotton twill riding pants, a white shirt, with his hair tucked up under a navy blue *tuque*. He had on a brown canvas greatcoat with a slit up the back, suitable for riding a horse, and a silver medallion around his neck. It was polished but worn and the amber inset glistened. He carried a sturdy leather valise filled with Mary's dresses and a few other items of female apparel.

The young man walked to the gangplank and descended onto the wharf. Leaning against a post at the bottom was Joshua Friesen.

His hair was still mussed up from the wind and the rain. His beard was still scruffy. But he was wearing clean clothes. That meant he had traveled in a cabin of his own on the steamboat. He didn't sleep in the open, below deck, like most of the passengers.

"Good morning," he said, tipping his hand to his head as if he were wearing a hat.

"Good morning," said the person with the navy blue *tuque*.

"May I walk with you?"

After a few minutes, he spoke again. "You're quite the young gentleman, Miss Agnes Apple. Not many men would dare to wear slippers like yours."

She turned on him.

"How do you know my name?" Mary demanded.

"I followed you back to your cabin last night. I asked the purser. For a shilling, he told me. Probably would have for sixpence, but I was feeling generous. And who are you now?"

Mary glowered at Joshua Friesen. She hated him intensely.

"My name is William Chambers," she said. Mary had a cousin in the States called William Chambers. Then she said proudly, "I am Mary Cameron. And if you reveal my disguise I will slit your throat."

"Ah." Joshua Friesen grinned as they walked past Saint Mark's Church with its high stone tower. "Really?" he said, as they passed red brick houses with well-kept gardens. "Then you will need a knife."

"Pardon?" said Mary.

"To slit my throat. You will need a knife, William Chambers. Or Agnes Apple. Or Mary Cameron."

"Oh, for glory's sake, call me Mary. But quietly, please."

They walked past the stone walls of Fort George and past some shops. Mary tried to match her pace and her stride to Joshua Friesen's. The young man's hair and beard were a mess but he was quite handsome.

Mary had grown up in Niagara-on-the-Lake on Brock Street. Every town had a Brock Street. She knew her way around. She knew where she was going.

"Why are you following me?" she demanded.

"I have nothing better to do."

"You must be a lawyer," she said.

He laughed.

"A lawyer without much business," she continued. "You have an income, free time, and no other interests but me."

He looked startled. She went on. "You have no wife or you'd be better groomed. And you've left muddy York to set up a law office here. And if you are man enough, one day you might become a judge."

"And you, Mary Cameron, are an escaped convict, a famous patriot, and a Canadian Rebel."

Allison

He knows exactly who she is!

Mary and I have different reactions.

She feels a chill because he knows she's a criminal. But I think it's exciting. Mary and Joshua Friesen will fall in love. They will be married and have children. And Nana Friesen will marry one of their descendants. And she'll have my mother. My mother will have David and me. And I'll end up in a Harvard research lab, and endure *sensory stimulation* as my contribution to medical science.

I doubt my *colleagues* are accomplishing much with their flashing lights and blaring noises, but Maddie's massage is working, for sure. Last night I could actually tell they were kneading my muscles, rubbing my skin. Around my arms and shoulders especially. It's not like these were exact feelings. It was more like tingling sensations.

But if you had no more feeling than a block of cheese and then you knew you were being touched—well, imagine! It was like the sounds of mouth-watering apples being crunched underfoot. It was like rainbows and moonlight shimmering inside me.

My body was becoming familiar again.

Tingle by tingle.

Maddie comes in. She ignores Gordon and does my makeup. She talks to me, "Allie, I found other examples of women and girls being strangled with smiles, and there's a university connection. But there's no pattern."

I signal for more information.

"Three died at York University in Toronto. That was two years ago. And there was one at a college in Illinois a few years before that. But each victim was different from the others. One was sickly, one was impoverished, one was broken by love, and one was emotionally disturbed. And of the two here, one was outrageously beautiful, one was sad. See what I mean? No pattern."

I sigh. Maybe it was an interior sigh.

They massage me for a while and leave together, my beautiful Maddie and long lanky Gordon.

I lie here and think.

Time passes.

The *colleagues* arrive. It's getting late. Sometimes they work long hours. *The ordinary man* removes my medallion. Right there in front of everyone. He explains he will give it to Maddie. He'd better, or else!

The *colleagues* leave, including him. When Maddie and Gordon return, they don't notice the medallion is gone. I don't say anything. We'll see what the Devil does with it. I'm curious.

I mean, everyone knows he has it, so he has to return it.

M and G just dropped in to say goodnight.

That was nice but I like being alone.

I'm feeling more and more myself.

I can feel my body from the inside.

I'm here, I'm real.

It's not a theory.

You know how butterflies are like mummies wrapped in a cocoon and then they push their way out and fly free? Well, damn it, good glory, I am going to be a butterfly. I'm going to be free

I am. I am.

I am.

Thirty-five

Mary

Mary Cameron, trying to look like William Chambers, sat with Joshua Friesen in a dark booth in the Royal Tavern. They were eating rabbit stew, each with a big mug of beer. Women by law were not allowed in the tavern—either to protect them from drunks, or from getting drunk. No one suspected William Chambers was a woman.

"But they will, you know. Your disguise won't work close up."

"Well, no one is getting close up, Joshua Friesen."

"Your walk is good. You're on the small size. Take longer steps and strut like a rooster. Your voice is pleasant, enough. A little high. Keep your shirt buttoned up. You've no Adam's apple. But here, let me make an adjustment."

He lifted the glass chimney off their lantern—it was lit at noon because the room was dingy—and he rubbed a finger on the soot inside. Then he reached across the table and dabbed a bit of soot on her jawline and chin.

"You rub that in and you'd fool a barber. Good, you're

looking less pretty all the time. Now, what are you doing here, Mary? It's a dangerous place to be—for an escaped convict."

"You're a sympathizer, aren't you? Or you would have turned me in to the police."

"I'm a patriot." He lowered his voice. "The Rebellion was over three years ago, Mary. I was never a Rebel, but, yes, I suppose I am a sympathizer."

"Then you'll help me kill the man who killed Amos Durfee?"

"Amos Durfee? The black man on Navy Island?"

"You know about him? He was my friend. I was there when he died on the *Caroline*. He was tied up below deck when the British soldiers set the boat on fire. They floated it over Horseshoe Falls on the Canadian side. Some people think I killed him."

"But, Mary. Sorry, William. Or is it Agnes Apple? What a lovely name. Mary, the *Caroline* didn't go over the falls. She got hung up on the rocks."

"Aren't you listening, Joshua Friesen? I was there. And that's where I'm going after we finish eating our stew."

"Where? I'd like to tag along."

"You want to come with me and you don't even know where I'm going. You are a strange man."

"Not as strange a man as you are, Mary Cameron."

Mary used one of the two Spanish doubloons she had left to rent a horse with a saddle and to buy a few things. On the north side of the stable was a shoemaker, where she bought riding boots. On the other side was Hugh Cameron's Blacksmith and Forge.

She could see her father through the open door. He was hammering red-hot steel. He glanced up and looked Mary straight in the eye. He had no idea who the handsome young man was, with light brown hair peeking out from under a sailor's watch cap. But he smiled. She looked quickly away.

She refused to cry.

Mary rode like a man, with her coat open at the back and the flaps down each side of the saddle. She had left her valise with her slippers and most of her clothes at the Royal Tavern where they rented rooms. She had picked up a small saddlebag at the shoemaker and a wicked-looking knife at a hardware store.

"It's to cut throats," explained Joshua Friesen, when the clerk in the store asked why his companion wanted the knife. "Give my young friend a blade with a sharp edge. Dull blades are painful and much too messy."

Mary and Joshua rode upriver all afternoon, along the rising banks of the Niagara River on the Portage Trail, up past Queenston and the memorial tower for General Brock, up past the falls. By evening they were opposite Navy Island. A little farther on, they stopped at a fine stone farmhouse close to the lake belonging to one Matthias Haun. A handsome old man of Mennonite background. He was a distant relative of Mary's.

They stayed there as guests for the night, no questions asked.

In the morning, they left their horses with the Hauns and hired a boat to take them downstream to Navy Island.

"This was the Republic of Canada," Mary declared when they stepped ashore.

"For only one month, my dear," Joshua paused, then added, "William."

The boatman looked at the two young gentlemen. One was scruffy around the edges, the smaller one was very clean-shaven. Why on earth would they want to be dropped on Navy Island? And not at the main wharf.

"Should I come back for you?" the boatman asked.

"No," said William. "We'll hire another boat. I don't know how long we'll be." Then William, or Mary, turned to Joshua and asked, "Do you want to go back with the boatman, Josh?"

"Not on your life," he declared. "You couldn't get by without me."

"Oh, I have, I certainly can, and I will if I want to."

"No, William Chambers, you need me in your life."

They walked together through the village. At first, Mary slouched as if she were hiding in plain sight. Then, as they passed by a shop window, she saw their reflection and she stood proud and walked boldly.

Nothing had changed on Navy Island since Mary had been there over three years earlier. When she left, accused of murder, she wore steel chains around her wrists and her ankles. Now she was free.

Mary explained to Joshua that she had no doubt who killed Amos Durfee. She was going to kill the man with her sharp new knife. Joshua shuddered but said nothing.

They stood at the wharf where the *Caroline* had been tied up. It was a small American vessel with a complement of twelve sailors. And this was where the British soldiers had set the *Caroline* ablaze with Amos Durfee tied up in the hold.

Mary turned and walked straight to a frame cottage with a bright blue door. Every other door in the village was a dull red from paint made with ox blood. The cottage itself had a nameplate over the door, like many of the homes on the island. This one was called "Crispus Attuks," after a black patriot who was killed by British soldiers in the Boston Massacre of 1770. But Mary knew the house belonged to Felix LaRoque.

With Joshua standing behind her, she used the handle of her knife to bang on the door. When the door opened, she planned to stab Felix LaRoque through his miserable heart.

He was the spy who betrayed the Rebellion. He had come on board the *Caroline* with the British soldiers. And when the soldiers found Mary and her friend hiding below deck, LaRoque tied up Amos Durfee. Eleven white American sailors were released, but the black man was sentenced to death on the spot.

The soldiers took Mary ashore, then lit the boat on fire and pushed it out into the river. They claimed Amos Durfee was dead when they found him. They claimed Mary had killed him. LaRoque bowed to Mary, then he turned and went home.

There was no human being in the world Mary hated so much as Felix LaRoque.

The bright blue door slowly swung open.

Joshua Friesen moved closer. Mary suspected he would try to stop her from murder; he would try to save her from being hanged. She leaned closer to him, in spite of herself, but her fingers tightened on the handle of the knife. She raised her arm.

The door opened wide and Mary stared into the smiling face of Amos Durfee.

Allison

Gordon is shy with me, now. I suppose I should be flattered. It proves he thinks I'm a real person. It proves he's in love with Maddie O'Rourke. As for me, just before he came in this morning, I had an itch. I tried to scratch it.

Did you get that? Are you paying attention?

Dead people and potatoes don't itch. And I tried to scratch.

I moved my arm, my fingers, not much, but I moved them. Potatoes don't have fingers, they have eyes but no fingers.

I don't let on to Gordon. I don't let on to the *colleagues*.

When Maddie arrives, she's bubbling with news. I want to hear what she has to say. I can wait awhile to tell her about me—my life has changed utterly, but her news is important and I'm not going anywhere. Not yet.

"Allie," she exclaims while she's clambering onto my bed. "Allie, I did what you asked, I checked around Harvard, looking for a new professor who had come from Illinois after a few years in Toronto. Dead end. Then I checked on graduate students. There's a guy doing his PhD in psychology. He fits the bill. He began his studies at Bradley College. That's in Peoria, Illinois. Then he did his master's degree at York in T.O. Now he's here, doing a doctorate."

Sunflowers! Sunflowers! Wide-eyed, I smile.

"He could be our killer," says Gordon.

I'm thinking: Catch up with us, Gordon.

"Psych students are usually psycho," he says.

"Don't be ignorant, Gordon," Maddie whispers softly.

"Sorry."

"But, but," I signal, "this one might be."

I begin to explain and Maddie speaks my words out loud: "I'll bet he's one of those creeps who encourages people who are lost in life to kill themselves. That makes him a killer."

"Yes," says Gordon. "But these women were strangled, not talked to death."

"Don't be so sure," says Maddie. She knows where I'm going with this.

Each of the victims was vulnerable. The elderly woman was a retired professor. She had not bothered to make a life for herself. She had nothing to live for. She was overwhelmingly sad. So were the rest of them, bitterly sad. The beautiful girl was too attractive. Other students treated her like a bimbo no matter how brilliant she was and they shunned her. I've had the same problems myself—just kidding. But, I can see myself in all of these women. The sickly one, of course, the impoverished one, the heart-broken one, and the emotionally damaged one. They were all horribly sad and lost.

Now, what if this guy worked hard at becoming their friend? What if he was clever and warm and treated each like she was totally special? Like he could feel what she felt. Like he could see into her soul. And then he convinced her that life was not worth living.

He convinced each of them that it would be better to die. He offered to help them.

He understood enough about anatomy to promise them a quick release. I've read about this in a mystery novel. All he had to do was press on something called the carotid artery sinus. Death in seconds. Painless. Merciful. He made it look like strangulation. He was their savior.

I can understand the appeal.

As I explain all this to Maddie and Gordon, tears well up in my eyes.

The psycho offered them love that would last forever.

"*Forever,*" I say out loud. My voice echoes inside my head.

There is an overwhelming silence.

That was my first word in nine months!

I reach up with my hand and cover my mouth and I giggle.

Thirty-six

Mary

Amos Durfee was talking: "I knew you would come, Mary Cameron. We heard you had escaped from the Kingston Pen. Felix and I were sure you'd turn up. I've seen you dressed as a boy before. But now you're a man. I love your outfit. Except for the cap—navy blue is a no-no with eyes like yours. And who is your handsome young friend in need of a shave?"

Mary stared with her mouth gaping open.

There was no doubt that the black man with the carefully trimmed beard was her old friend, Amos Durfee.

When Felix LaRoque moved out of the shadows and peered over Amos' shoulder, Mary took a step backwards and dropped her knife. Joshua steadied her. He bent down and picked up the knife and stuck it under his belt.

"Come in, come in," said Felix LaRoque.

"I'm Joshua Friesen," said Joshua, shaking the hand of Amos Durfee and then the hand of the smaller man, Felix LaRoque. "I'm a lawyer about to set up an office in Niagara-on-the-Lake." He seemed to be presenting himself to the two men for their approval. "My family is from muddy York. Toronto, now. I intend to marry Miss Mary Cameron, if ever she will emerge from her disguise as William Chambers and stop pretending she's Agnes Apple."

Mary sat down on the stone stoop.

She looked up.

"I have never said I would marry you, Joshua Friesen. I hardly know you. You are a madman and you scream at the wind."

"Oh, lovely," said Felix LaRoque. "So do we. But with love, not because we're mad. Who could be mad at the wind?"

"You should try shouting into the falls," said Amos Durfee. "It swallows your voice in its roar."

Joshua looked down at his companion. "I'm asking you now. Since it turns out you're not a murderer, I think we would make a very fine couple."

"I'm not a murderer, yet!"

He helped her to her feet. She turned her back on him and took Amos Durfee's hand in her own and then she hugged him. When she stood back, her eyes were filled with tears.

"I am not crying," she announced. "But I am very happy to see you, Amos Durfee. As for you, Felix LaRoque, I will not hug you until I hear your story. We will come in." She paused. She reached back to grasp Joshua's hand. "Both of us."

Felix and Amos were not Canadian Rebels. Amos was American and Felix was French from Lower Canada. They kept their politics private.

When the British soldiers forced Felix to go on board the *Caroline*, he was horrified. He knew his friend Amos was hiding out with the girl who rode horses like a boy. He was trying to protect her. She was a spy of fifteen who delivered messages, sometimes in dresses with her hair down and sometimes dressed like a young gentleman. She would often pass through the enemy lines to let the Rebel Canadians know what the British were doing. The Americans liked her, although it was not their battle.

After Mary and Amos were discovered, some of the soldiers led Mary up onto the deck. They ordered Felix to tie Amos up. Felix was terrified. But it did not occur to the soldiers that this man from Navy Island was a friend of the black man, even if Amos was a free man and not an American slave.

Felix tied a very loose knot.

As soon as the *Caroline* burst into flames and was pushed out into the river, Amos Durfee cast his bonds aside and rose up through the fire and dived into the water. He swam powerfully against the current but was nearly swept down over Niagara Falls. Just in time, he grabbed a log sticking out from the shore. He had nearly burned to death and he almost drowned, but he managed to pull himself to safety on the New York side of the river.

As it turned out, the *Caroline* got hung up on the rocks above the falls. The charred wreck was still there, slowly falling to pieces.

Within a year, the Rebellion was all but forgotten. Amos Durfee came back to Navy Island and moved in with Felix LaRoque. If the villagers thought Amos was the servant and Felix was the master, the two men didn't care. They were together.

They had promised each other, if Mary Cameron were convicted of murder, they would come forward. They would be hanged in her place. But they could not save her from being jailed for treason. Mary was an unrepentant Rebel.

Allison

This morning the *colleagues* arrive early. They poke and prod a bit. Then they leave. But not before *the ordinary man* with the Canadian accent makes a show of returning my silver medallion.

"It will probably be safer right here than with her little friend," he said. He meant Maddie. He's certainly ignorant enough to be the Devil.

Maddie says Gordon told her he was an assistant professor. After all the education it takes to work at Harvard, you'd think he could be a real one. Maddie says with his scruffy little beard he looks like an armpit with eyes.

He waited until the others had gone out the door, then he came closer and leaned down to whisper: "Your silver trinket is no use to me, girl. Or to anyone else. You might get a few bucks for it at an auction. A very small fortune. I'd prefer a much larger one. As for the Sons of Liberty bowl," he said, then stopped. He seemed confused. "There's no damned connection at all, except they were both made by Paul Revere."

What on earth made him think they connected? Besides the name, they were silver, they were old, that's about it. But he sounded desperately disappointed.

"My associates and I have spent half a lifetime searching for the secret of the Freemasons' treasure. Your little piece of silver tells me nothing. It's worth no more than a few dollars for the name REVERE stamped into its back. And you should get the amber re-set. I had to pry it out. I put it back, but it may be loose."

I moved my eyes. I smiled.

What a very sad man, haunted by a treasure he can't retrieve from the past. He's pathetic. Not sinister. Not the Devil. Just an *ordinary man* obsessed with greed.

He didn't even mention the Freemasons' symbol behind the amber. Or the mystery words scrawled into the silver. But he's got me wondering. How could the medallion be a key to lost treasure? How does the silver bowl fit in? Is the bowl a puzzle with a secret locked into its design? Is it somehow a map that needs a key to be read? Does Madge de Vere's medallion contain something he didn't see? I think of it as hers, not Paul Revere's.

What am I missing?

Not long after he slipped out, Maddie arrives. I tell her what happened. I tell her about Madge. Not about my dreams. I just explain Madge was my ancestor and she received the medallion as a gift from Paul Revere. Maddie is excited by that.

She leaves and after a couple of hours comes back. She is good at research, she follows questions as far as they go. She tells me she went over to the Museum of Fine Arts.

"Why?" I signal. I think I know.

"There's a painting of Madge de Vere over there. I wanted to see it. Seeing how she looked makes her real."

She's real to me, as real as I am. But, of course, to Maddie, she's only a name.

"She is wearing your medallion, Allie, on a silver chain."

Or I'm wearing hers!

"After I saw her portrait, I walked right past the Sons of Liberty bowl. And that made me think about the time capsule buried by Samuel Adams and Paul Revere. I mean, Paul Revere is the link."

"We're the link," I say.

"So I took a look at the contents of the capsule. They're on display. An old copy of *The Boston Bee* newspaper had been folded inside. The museum people have it laid out in a glass case. It's open to show an advertisement which credits the Revere silversmith shop as the makers of the Sons of Liberty bowl and such sundry valuables as a silver locket owned by Mrs. William de Vere.

This is exciting! I figure *the ordinary man* saw the same notice.

"When was the capsule buried?" I ask.

"In 1795."

"And when was the silver bowl made?"

"In 1768."

"And?"

"Good grief, Allie. There was a twenty-seven-year delay before Revere took credit for the bowl in his own advertisement."

Could that notice be a message meant for the future? I'm sure *the ordinary man* thought it was meant for *him*. Look to the bowl, it said. Look for the key.

He had been searching for Freemasons treasure for years. The Sons of Liberty was a secret society, closely related to the Freemasons. The maker of the bowl was a Freemason. Madge's husband was a noted Freemason leader. The message led *the ordinary man* to check out the de Veres. He saw Madge's portrait in the Museum gallery. He saw the silver medallion. The parts of the story came together.

"Do you remember when the portrait was painted?" I ask Maddie.

"No, but Mrs. de Vere isn't, like, terribly old."

Of course not. She gave the medallion to Rebecca Haun only a few years after Paul Revere made it for her in 1768, the same year he made the silver bowl.

"There must be a connection," I signal.

"Between you and Paul Revere?"

"Between the bowl and my medallion."

"Yes," says Maddie. "Like I said, between you and Paul Revere."

The ordinary man figured out the same connection. He thought my medallion could be the key to the Freemasons' wealth. He traced it through our family on Google and ended up with me. He saw my yearbook picture with Jaimie Retzinger at a school dance. You can find just about anything online if you look. I was wearing the medallion. He came north. He talked to me in Timmy's. He saw Russell Miller hanging around. He intimidated Russell, he pushed Russell to get the medallion for him. Russell had a pathetic obsession. He was easy to manipulate. So it seemed.

When the ordinary man realized Russell was going to shoot me, the poor devil panicked. He called for Russell to stop. He banged on the car window. By then it was too late. I think he expected Russell to steal the medallion, not shoot me in the head.

By the time Russell confessed to the shooting, the ordinary man was long gone. And Russell wasn't even sure he'd been there.

Maddie can see I'm pleased but she's confused when I ask her to show me the bowl.

"It's in the museum, Allie. But Gordon can bring it up on his laptop."

Of course he can. If my yearbook picture is there, the bowl must be, too. When he finds the best image, I look at it very carefully.

I can see the torn page etched into the surface. It's called a general warrant, whatever that means. It doesn't matter. It looks like a map. It really looks like a closeup chart. And there's the word *charta* above it. Magna *Charta*.

But the map could be showing us anywhere.

Suddenly I have an idea!

I ask Maddie to remove the piece of amber from my medallion. She gets Gordon to do it. It makes him feel useful.

Now then, there's the Freemasons symbol. And there are the words we couldn't make out before: *INSULA QUERCU.*

Maddie exclaims, "*Insula* is Latin for island."

"And what about *quercu?*" says Gordon.

"Look it up, genius. I only took Latin for a year."

"Oak," he says, "*quercu* means oak."

Oak Island? I know about the treasure on Oak Island.

Good glory! The square ruler and compass symbol tells us the treasure was buried by Freemasons.

David told me some people thought it was Blackbeard's hoard. But others thought that the Freemasons hid it away for the French government after the fall of New France. Since the French supported the American Revolution, the Freemasons might have been planning on giving it to Washington. Or they might have planned to keep it for themselves. The loyalties get very confused.

Okay, but there is a major problem. This tells us who put the treasure there, but not how to get it out. At least six men have died trying.

I fill M and G in, as much as I can. Gordon doesn't seem concerned that one of the *colleagues* could be the Devil. "People are strange," he says. I wait to hear something more but he has no more to say on the subject.

After we think for awhile, he says: "If the Devil believed your medallion is a key, maybe it is. He's a brilliant scientist but that doesn't mean he's good at puzzles and locks and maps and things."

I don't know about *things*, but Gordon is good at puzzles. He's actually very clever. I'm good at puzzles, too.

We look at the image of the bowl on Gordon's laptop.

Then I make signs for Gordon to do a search for maps of Oak Island. I look at the engraving on the bowl and at the torn general warrant that looks like a map. It's beginning to make sense. It's not a map of the island, it's a map of the shore. Of course!

I ask Gordon to do a Web-search for how the rocks fit together along the Nova Scotia shoreline. He looks at me strangely, then he looks up *geology* maps for the area. It seems there are underground caves and tunnels in the limestone across from the island. Our map shows how to enter those caves. The treasure was never meant to be reached from the island, itself. The pulley over the hole and the wood platforms and stone layers were a decoy and a deadly trap. The treasure can only be reached from the shore.

Gordon sighs. "The *ordinary man* couldn't read the words. He didn't even know what language they were."

"He never studied Latin," says Maddie. "Or critical thinking. It never occurred to him they were anything but a silversmith's scrawl."

Mary

After spending two nights in the house with the bright blue door, Mary and Joshua picked up their horses at the Haun house and dropped them off back at the stables in Niagara-on-the-Lake. It was not yet dark. They walked over to the Royal Tavern for a pint of beer and a bowl of rabbit stew.

"It's a funny place to be," said Mary. "The Royal Tavern should be for royalists who love the Queen."

"And the Pig and Whistle is for pigs who can whistle."

She reached across the table and placed her small hand over his hand. He pulled quickly away. She laughed. She was still dressed as William Chambers.

"You know," Joshua told her, "Upper Canada is now Canada West. We're getting there, Mary."

"But we're not a Republic yet. We still have the Queen."

"It could be worse, Mary. It could be worse."

After dining, they took a walk in the evening air. Without even planning it, they ended up in front of a white frame house on Brock Street, one block over from Hugh Cameron's blacksmith shop. It was the house where Mary grew up. Where her mother, Lizzie, had died. Where her father, Hugh, lived alone.

There was a candle in the window of the front room. Two more candles flickered on the table Mary had broken by climbing over it when she was little. She had fixed the leg herself with rope and glue. She wondered if the rope was still wrapped around the leg, the way her father had left it.

"Mary, you must," said Joshua urgently. "If he turns you in, I'll help you escape. But you must, for his sake and for yours."

"I must! What *must* I do?"

"You know, Mary Cameron. Just knock on the door."

Mary had never knocked on this door in her life. You don't knock on your own door. Mary had spent three brutal years in prison. She had nearly drowned in her escape. She was not afraid of anything. Except knocking on her father's door.

Joshua reached around her and knocked. There was a long wait, then the door opened. A man with a worn and friendly face looked out into the night.

"Yes?" he said. He offered a smile as he peered past the glare of his candle. He could not see who the two gentlemen were.

"Father?" said Mary.

"Oh glory, Mary, is it you?"

"It is."

"I was hoping, I was hoping."

"You were!"

Joshua pushed her a step forward.

"I would hardly recognize you, daughter. You had better come all the way in before someone sees you dressed like that."

Mary and Joshua moved into the light and Hugh Cameron closed the door behind them. He had a bushy mustache, gray hair, and wore glasses. He set the candle down on a table and picked up a letter with a big red seal on the back.

He smiled almost shyly as he handed Mary the letter.

It was addressed to her but the wax seal was broken.

"It's from Governor Sydenham's office. Someone called John Clitherow."

"You have read my letter! Father, how could you?"

He smiled his shy smile. His thick mustache twitched.

"Mary, Mary, you haven't changed. I didn't know where you were, not since you went a-wandering from Kingston. But I knew if you had a letter from Lord Sydenham's office, it had to be important. I thought I might have to chase after you."

Suddenly, father and daughter fell into each other's arms.

"Mary, you're home, you're home at last."

Joshua Friesen leaned forward and spoke over Mary's head. "I am Joshua Friesen from York, Mr. Cameron, which they now call Toronto, and I'm newly arrived in Niagara-on-the-Lake. Sir, your daughter thinks I will someday be a judge. And sometimes, sometimes I shout into the wind, but I would like to ask you for her hand in marriage."

Mary and her father broke apart.

"You will not ask any such thing," Mary exclaimed.

"No, young man, you had better ask Mary, herself," said her father. "It will not be up to me, though you look a good strong lad. Have you ever tried working a forge?"

"Look at his nails," said Mary. "They're almost clean. He hasn't worked an honest day's work in his life. He's a lawyer."

Joshua Friesen and Hugh Cameron shook hands.

"Now read your letter then, Mary," said her father.

Mary started to read. She stopped. She looked at her father, she looked at Joshua Friesen.

"Yes," she said. "Now I'll marry you."

Her eyes filled with tears and they rolled down her face. She removed her watch cap and shook her hair free.

Joshua looked at Hugh Cameron. He was bewildered.

Mary's father explained: Lord Sydenham had received an urgent plea from the famous writer, Mr. Charles Dickens. It was written on Mary's behalf. The Governor of Canada West, in the name of Queen Victoria, was pleased to overrule the courts. Governor Sydenham declared Mary Cameron a free woman with no criminal record.

Joshua Friesen and Hugh Cameron beamed with pleasure. "I will cry if I want to," Mary declared. "Now, Joshua, we must kiss. We have never kissed and we're going to be married. And tomorrow we'll send parcels of food and some clothes to my very good friends, Agnes and Apple."

Allison

I think Mary is on her own now. My dreams will go back to the kind that break up when you're awake. She still had a golden doubloon when I left her. I'll bet it's the same one Nana Friesen gave me. It must be. You don't find many doubloons kicking round.

Maddie told the police my theory about the graduate student and the murders of the unhappy women. They checked him out and arrested him. Everyone who knows the guy says he's really nice. A little strange, maybe, but you can't always tell. Sometimes things aren't how they look.

At noon, Maddie and Gordon come in to announce they are in love. Maddie agrees that it was time for me to go home to Peterborough. If the research *colleagues* knew about my dreams, they'd want me to stay. I'd be special. But now I'm just a girl in a coma who isn't, not anymore. They find it disappointing that I'm improving. I think *the ordinary man* has convinced them I'm no longer useful. To them. To him.

Maddie asks me how I knew so much about Madge de Vere. She looks like a very fine lady in her portrait. I shrug. A small shrug but she gets the message. She'll ask me again, for sure, but she lets it go for now. She says she'll travel with me to Peterborough. She's got to get back to her job. She says she'll miss Harvard, she'll miss her flowers. Gordon will come up to visit at Christmas. He says he'll apply for a job as an assistant professor at Victoria College as soon as he finishes his PhD. He hopes it will be done by spring.

"You're lucky spring comes late in Toronto," Maddie tells him and giggles. I have never heard her giggle before.

While Maddie talked to Gordon about home and stuff, an image of Jaimie Retzinger drifted through my mind. I might have sighed. I'm not sure.

And it's almost uncanny. Maddie knows what I was thinking about.

"Your time will come" she says. "Real love is worth waiting for, Allie. It can find you in the most unlikely places. I mean, it found me in Boston. You made the right decision."

And then Gordon says the most unexpected thing: "Never settle for less than you deserve."

This time, I know I sighed.

They leave to make plans. I'm happy for them. Maddie is a lovely person. She really is. And Gordon's okay. Actually, he's pretty great. Good luck to the both of them. Yeah, and I'm fine. Maybe we'll all go treasure hunting next summer. Or maybe we'll leave the Freemasons gold where it is. For a while, at least.

When *the colleagues* come in, I speak a few words. Very short ones. There is a bit of a problem, though. They can't understand me. I can hear the words in my head. I can see them in my mind. But when they come out, they're a blur. Even to me.

I'll have to work on that. Maddie and I, together. Meanwhile, she can translate for me, since she usually knows what I mean.

They're here to say goodbye. When they leave, *the ordinary man* leans close and whispers. He sounds bitter and very sad.

He sounds like he's on stage or in a bad movie. "Don't waste your life on buried treasure, sweet Allison. It's never where you think it's going to be." He takes a deep breath. "I hope Russell Miller learns to live with himself. I hope you do too."

And I hope you do, as well.

My thought echoes as he trundles off to join the others.

I don't think for a minute I've heard the last of that man. He's as obsessed with treasure as Russell is obsessed with me. Obsessions aren't just habits you kick when you want to. They're *obsessions*. They can lead to twisted reasoning and twisted behavior. And there is a fortune in buried treasure waiting to be dug up. He or his so-called associates might realize he was wrong about the medallion. It really is the key! Then what?

For now, he's a sad man and he thinks I'm sweet.

Sweet! Can you imagine that? He called me *sweet*. I'm not. I'm tough, I'm difficult, I wouldn't take death lying down. I'm a fighter, damn it. And I'm lucky. I know everyone who gets shot in the head doesn't have dreams they remember, dreams of their past, and I know everyone who is a potato doesn't recover, solve murders, find treasure. I'm lucky, I'm plucky, intrepid, feisty, fearless, and I'm very grateful.

I'm entering an awkward stage. Awkward, but not impossible. I'll need therapy when I get home. Physical therapy, speech therapy, something they call occupational therapy—which sounds like job training but it just means how to get on with your life.

I look around. For a few minutes, I'm alone in my room.

I grope for my silver medallion. It takes a lot of effort but I hold it toward the light. The amber glistens, it feels warm in my hand.

I'll need to go down to Niagara-on-the-Lake and spend some time with Nana Friesen. Maybe my mom will take a break from Dripless Plumbing and visit me there, because when I get back to Peterborough I'm going to move in with Maddie.

For a while. Until I can take care of myself. When I'm up to it, I'll work part-time at Timmy's. I'll finish school. If Mrs. Muratori is still around, I need to thank her. For what? Whatever. She's been important in my life and I want to let her know.

Maybe I'll tell Nana about Mary Cameron and about Lizzie Erb and about Rebecca Haun. I'm not sure. Maybe not.

A few days later one of the colleagues comes back.

It's Dr. Ellis, the man with the important voice. He leans over me. He has a beard, I knew it. He kisses me on both cheeks. Like I'm a person.

He says, "I have been told you and your friend solved our murders, yes. A young man killed some very sad women."

Some of them, yes.

"Out of kindness, they say."

Like Russell tried to kill me.

"I think you are not so stupid, yes."

I smile.

Before he leaves, he tells me, as if it nearly slipped his mind, that his young colleague was killed in a hit-and-run accident. I look quizzical. He explains, an assistant professor, young-old, had a scruffy beard, nearly bald. Very unfortunate.

Then he goes on to tell me gently, that they can't promise I'll ever get back to normal. I may be in a wheelchair for the rest of my life. Who knows?

Good glory, what's normal?

I'm here, I'm alive!

I'm Allison Briscoe.

And angels couldn't ask for anything more.

To receive a free catalog of Poisoned Pen Press titles, please provide your name, address, and email address in one of the following ways:

Phone: 1-800-421-3976
Facsimile: 1-480-949-1707
Email: info@poisonedpenpress.com
Website: www.poisonedpenpress.com

Poisoned Pen Press
6962 E. First Ave. Ste 103
Scottsdale, AZ 85251

CPSIA information can be obtained at www.ICGtesting.com
Printed in the USA
BVOW08s0907060716

454620BV00002B/72/P